SONG OF THE SPIRITS

SONG

of the

SPIRITS

SARAH LARK

TRANSLATED BY D. W. LOVETT

amazon crossing

Text copyright © 2008 by Verlagsgruppe Lübbe GmbH & Co. KG, Bergisch Gladbach
English translation copyright © 2013 by D. W. Lovett

Song of the Spirits was first published in 2008 by Verlagsgruppe Lübbe GmbH & Co. KG as *Das Lied der Maori*. Translated from German by Dustin W. Lovett. Published in English by AmazonCrossing in 2013.

Published by AmazonCrossing
P.O. Box 400818
Las Vegas, NV 89140

ISBN-13: 9781477807675
ISBN-10: 1477807675
LCCN: 2013905869

Contents

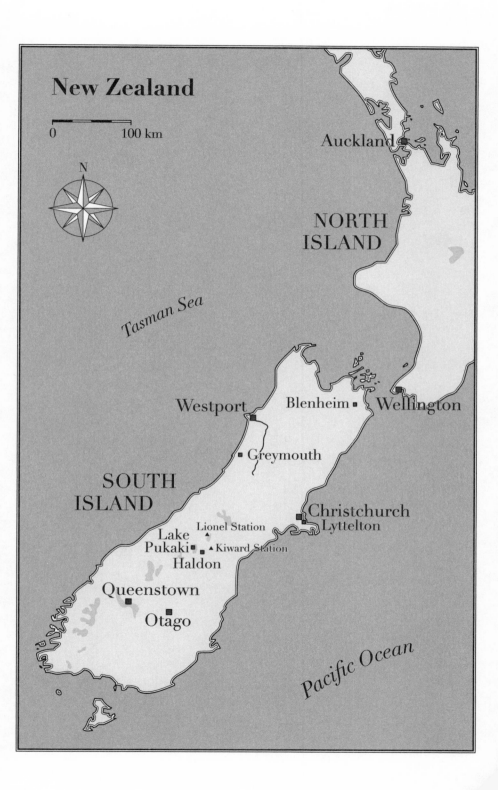

The Heiress

QUEENSTOWN AND CANTERBURY PLAINS

1893

1

"Are you Mrs. O'Keefe?"

Puzzled, William Martyn looked at the petite redhead who greeted him at the reception desk. The men in the gold-mining camps had described Helen O'Keefe to him as an older woman, or rather as a sort of dragoness who spits more fire as she ages. Strict propriety was said to reign in Mrs. O'Keefe's hotel. Smoking was forbidden, as was alcohol, not to mention guests of the opposite sex without a marriage certificate. The gold miners' stories had him expecting a prison rather than an inn. However, in Mrs. O'Keefe's establishment, he knew he could expect a bathhouse rather than fleas and bedbugs.

It was this last point that had convinced William to ignore all of his new friends' warnings. After three days on an old sheep farm that the gold miners used for shelter, he was prepared to do anything to escape the vermin. He was even willing to put up with this "dragon," Helen O'Keefe.

But it was no dragon that greeted him—rather, this exceptionally lovely green-eyed creature, whose face was framed by an indomitable mass of red-gold curls. Without a doubt the most gratifying sight since William had left his ship in Dunedin, New Zealand. His spirits, having reached new lows over the past few weeks, rose markedly.

The girl laughed.

"No, I'm Elaine O'Keefe. Helen is my grandmother."

William smiled. He knew his smile made a good impression, as an attentive look had always crept onto the faces of the girls in Ireland when they had seen the sparkle in his eye.

"That almost makes me sorry. Here I'd thought I had an idea for a new business: 'Water from Queenstown—discover the Fountain of Youth!'"

Elaine giggled. She had a narrow face and a small, maybe slightly too pointy nose dotted with countless freckles.

"You should meet my father. He's always making up slogans like that: 'Life's good as long as your shovel's good! Get your mining gear at the O'Kay Warehouse!'"

"I'll take that to heart," William promised and did actually take note of the name. "So how about it? Can I get a room?"

The girl hesitated. "Are you a gold miner? Then . . . well, there are rooms available, but they're rather expensive. Most of the miners can't afford the lodging here . . ."

"Do I look so hard up?" William asked with feigned sternness, wrinkling the brow beneath his ample head of hair.

Elaine looked him over shamelessly. At first glance, there was little to differentiate him from the countless other gold miners she saw every day. He had a somewhat dirty and tattered appearance and wore a waxed jacket, blue jeans, and sturdy boots. Upon closer inspection, however, Elaine—the daughter of a merchant—recognized the quality of his accessories: an expensive leather jacket was visible beneath his open coat; he wore leather chaps; his boots looked as though they'd been made of costly material; and the hatband on his broad-brimmed Stetson had been woven from horsehair. That alone would have cost a small fortune. Even his saddlebags—which he had initially slung casually over his right shoulder but had since deposited on the floor between his legs—appeared expensive and well made.

None of which was typical of the adventurers who came to Queenstown to search for gold in the rivers and hills—since hardly a soul ever became rich from his efforts. Sooner or later, the vast majority left town as poor and ragged as when they'd arrived. This was largely because the men, as a rule, squandered their gains in Queenstown right away instead of saving them. Only the immigrants who had settled there and founded a business of some kind had ever made any money—businesses including Elaine's parents' warehouse, her grandmother's inn, Stuart Peters's smithy and stables, Ethan's post and telegraph office, and, first and foremost, the ill-reputed but generally beloved pub on Main Street that housed Daphne's Hotel, the brothel, upstairs.

William repaid Elaine's probing gaze with a patient if somewhat mocking smile. Elaine noted that dimples appeared in his youthful cheeks when he smirked. And he was clean-shaven. That was unusual too. Most of the gold miners only reached for their razors when there was dancing at Daphne's on the weekends, if even then.

Elaine decided to tease the newcomer a bit in an effort to draw him out of his shell. "You don't smell as strongly as the others at least."

William smiled. "Up to now the sea's been offering an opportunity to bathe for free. But not for much longer, I've been told, and it's getting cold. Though I understand gold seems to like body odor. He who bathes the least takes the most nuggets from the river."

Elaine had to laugh. "You shouldn't take your cues from that or there will be trouble with my grandmother. Here, now if you'd fill this out." She handed him a check-in form, attempting not to peek *too* curiously across the counter. As furtively as possible, she read along as he energetically filled in the blanks. That, too, was unusual; few gold miners could write so fluently.

William Martyn . . . Elaine's heart beat louder as she read his name. A nice name.

"What should I fill in here?" William asked, indicating the blank asking for his home address. "I've just arrived. This will be my first address in New Zealand."

Elaine could no longer contain her interest. "Really? So where are you from? No, let me guess. My grandmother always does that with new customers. You can tell by the accent where a person is from."

With most of the settlers, it was simple. Of course, she occasionally got it wrong. The Swedes, the Dutch, and the Germans, for instance, all sounded the same to Elaine. But she could usually tell the Irish and Scots apart without difficulty, and Londoners were especially easy to recognize. Experts could even identify the neighborhood where a person had been raised. William, however, was hard to place. He sounded English, but he spoke more softly, drawing the vowels out a bit more than the English typically did.

Elaine ventured a guess. "You're from Wales." Her grandmother on her mother's side, Gwyneira McKenzie (formerly Warden), was Welsh, and though Gwyneira did not speak any distinct dialect, William's inflection reminded Elaine a little of her. She was the daughter of a landed noble, and her tutors had always made a point of teaching her accent-free English.

William shook his head but didn't smile as Elaine had hoped he would. "Where did you get that idea?" he asked. "I'm Irish, from Connemara."

Elaine's cheeks flushed. Though there were many Irish working the mines, she never would have guessed he was one of them. Most of those men spoke in a rather heavy dialect. William, however, expressed himself more elegantly.

As if to emphasize his heritage, he now filled in his most recent address in large letters in the blank space: Martyn Manor, Connemara.

That did not sound like a family farm; that sounded more like a lord's estate.

"I'll show you your room now," Elaine said. She was not really supposed to accompany the guests upstairs herself, especially not the men. Her grandmother Helen had drilled into her to always call the superintendent or one of the twins for this task. But Elaine was delighted to make an exception for this man. She stepped out from behind the reception desk, holding herself erect and ladylike, as her grandmother had taught her to do: head raised with a natural grace, shoulders back. And absolutely no lapsing into that alluring, swaying step that Daphne's girls liked to put on for show.

Elaine hoped that her barely half-formed bust and her very thin, newly corseted waist would count for something. She hated wearing a corset. But if she caught this man's eye because of it . . .

William followed her, happy that she could not see him as he did so. Indeed, he could hardly restrain himself from staring pruriently at her figure, petite but already gently rounded in all the right places. All told—including the time in prison, then the eight weeks to get here, followed by the ride from Dunedin to Queenstown's gold fields—it had been about four months since he had even come close to a woman.

An unimaginable length of time, really. It was high time he set things right. The boys in the gold mines had gone on and on about Daphne's girls, of course; they were supposed to be rather pretty and the rooms clean. But the thought of courting this sweet little redhead pleased William considerably more than the prospect of seeking instant gratification in a prostitute's arms.

Even the room Elaine now opened for him delighted him. It was tidy and furnished simply but lovingly with furniture made of light-colored wood. There were pictures on the wall, and a pitcher with water for washing up stood ready.

"You can use the bathhouse as well," Elaine explained, reddening a bit. "But you have to sign up ahead of time. Ask my grandmother. Or Mary or Laurie."

With those words, she was about to turn away, but William held her back gently.

"And you? I can't ask you?" he inquired softly, looking at her attentively.

Elaine smiled, flattered. "No, I'm not usually here. I'm only standing in for Grandmum today. But I . . . well, normally I help out at the O'Kay Warehouse. It's my father's business."

William nodded. So she was not just pretty then but also from a good family. He liked the girl more and more. And he needed several items for gold mining anyway.

"I'll stop by sometime soon," William said.

Elaine positively floated down the stairs. She felt as though her heart had turned into a hot air balloon that was lifting her in a lively updraft above earthly concerns. Her feet hardly touched the ground, and her hair seemed to blow in the wind, though naturally no breeze stirred inside the house. Elaine was beaming; she had the sensation that she was standing at the beginning of an adventure, as beautiful and invincible as the heroines in the novels she secretly read in Ethan's general store.

With that same expression still on her face, she did a little dance in the garden of the large town house that contained Helen O'Keefe's hotel. Elaine knew it well; she had been born in this house. Her parents had built it for their growing family when their business first began turning a profit. However, it had eventually become too loud and busy for them in the middle of Queenstown. Elaine's mother, Fleurette, hailed from one of the great sheep farms in the Canterbury Plains, and she in particular missed the open country. Elaine's parents had therefore resettled on a bucolic piece of land on the river, which was missing only one thing: gold deposits. Elaine's father, Ruben O'Keefe, had originally marked it off as a claim, but despite his many talents, he had been a hopeless case when it came to discovering gold. Fortunately, Fleurette had quickly realized that, and had invested her dowry in merchandise delivery—primarily shovels and gold pans, which the miners practically snatched out of their hands—rather than in the futile "gold mine" enterprise. The O'Kay Warehouse had grown out of those early sales.

Fleurette had called the new house on the river "Gold Nugget Manor" as a joke, but the name had eventually taken root. Elaine and her brothers had grown up happily there among the horses and pigs, even a few sheep, just like where Fleurette had been raised. Ruben complained when he had to shear the sheep every year, and his sons, Stephen and George, likewise cared little for farmwork—in stark contrast to Elaine. The little country house she'd grown up in was nothing like Kiward Station, the large sheep farm her grandmother Gwyneira managed in the Canterbury Plains. She would have loved to live and work there and was a little envious of her cousin, who was set to inherit the farm one day.

Elaine, however, was not one to brood for any length of time. She found it almost as interesting to help out in the store and manage things in the hotel for her grandmother. She had little desire to go to college like her older brother, Stephen. He was studying law in Dunedin, thus fulfilling his father's dream, as he too had once wanted to be a lawyer. Ruben O'Keefe had been a justice of the peace in Queenstown for almost twenty years, and there was nothing he liked better than chatting about legal matters with Stephen. Though Elaine's younger brother, George, was still in school, it looked like he would be the businessman of the family someday. He was already zealous about helping out in the shop and had thousands of ideas for improvements.

Helen O'Keefe—still unaware of her granddaughter's high spirits and their origins in the form of newcomer William Martyn—was gracefully pouring tea into the cup of her guest, Daphne O'Rourke.

This tea party in public view gave both ladies a certain mischievous delight. They knew that half of Queenstown whispered about the friendship between the two "hotel owners." Helen, however, felt no compunction about it. Some forty years earlier, a thirteen-year-old Daphne had been sent to New Zealand under her tutelage. An orphanage in London had wanted to get rid of a few of its charges, and people were looking for maids in New Zealand. Helen had been about to leave England for an uncertain future with a fiancé she had never met, and the Church of England had paid for her crossing as the girls' chaperone.

Helen, who had served as a governess in London until then, made use of the three-month journey to polish the girls' social skills, skills that Daphne still employed to this day. Her position as a housemaid, however, had been a fiasco—as had Helen's marriage. Though both women had found themselves in insufferable conditions, they had each made the best of it.

They looked up when they heard Elaine's footsteps on the rear terrace. Helen raised her narrow, deeply wrinkled face, whose pointed nose betrayed her kinship with Elaine. Her hair, once dark brown with a chestnut-colored shine, was now streaked with gray but remained long and healthy. Helen wore it in a bun at the nape of her neck most of the time. Her gray eyes glowed with life experience and curiosity—especially just then, as she'd noticed the radiant expression on Elaine's face.

"Well now, child! You look like you just got a Christmas present. Do you have some news?"

Daphne, whose feline features looked a little hard even when she smiled, appraised Elaine's expression a little less innocently. She had read it in the faces of dozens of easy women who thought they had found Prince Charming among their customers. And every time, Daphne spent long hours comforting the girl when her dreamy prince ultimately proved himself a frog, or worse, some disgusting toad. Daphne's face therefore reflected a certain wariness as Elaine approached them cheerfully.

"We have a new guest," she exclaimed enthusiastically. "A gold miner from Ireland."

Helen frowned. Daphne laughed, and her glowing green eyes flashed derisively.

"Are you sure he wasn't lost, Lainie? Irish gold miners usually end up with my girls."

Elaine shook her head emphatically. "He is not one of those . . . Forgive me, Miss O'Rourke, I mean . . ." she spluttered. "He's a gentleman . . . I think."

The wrinkles in Helen's brow deepened. She had some experience with "gentlemen."

Daphne laughed. "Dearie, there's no such thing as an Irish gentleman. Anyone who is considered a noble over there is originally from England, since the island has been an English possession for ages—a fact that still has the Irish howling like wolves after a few pints. Most of the Irish clan leaders were deposed and run out by English nobility. And they haven't done anything since but get rich off the backs of the Irish. Now they're letting their tenants starve by the thousands. Some gentlemen! But your miner could hardly be among them. They cling to their dirt."

"How do you know so much about Ireland?" Elaine asked, intrigued. The brothel's proprietress fascinated her, but she rarely had the opportunity to speak at length with her.

Daphne smiled. "Sweetheart, I am Irish. On paper at least. And when the immigrants get mopey around me, that is a great comfort to them. I've even been practicing my accent." Daphne lapsed into an Irish drawl, and even Helen laughed. In reality, Daphne had been born somewhere near the docks in London, but she went by the name of an Irish immigrant. A certain Birdie O'Rourke had not survived the passage to New Zealand, and her passport had fallen into Daphne's hands by way of an English sailor.

"Come, Paddy, you can call me Birdie."

Elaine giggled. "That's not how he talks though . . . William, our new guest."

"William?" Helen asked indignantly. "The young man has you calling him by his first name?"

Elaine shook her head quickly to deter her grandmother from forming any resentment toward the new resident.

"Of course not. I simply read it on his forms. His name is Martyn. William Martyn."

"Not exactly an Irish name," Daphne remarked. "No Irish name, no Irish accent . . . assuming everything is aboveboard. If I were you, Mrs. O'Keefe, I would sound the boy out first thing!"

Elaine fixed her with a rancorous look. "He's an upstanding man, I know it! He even wants to buy his mining equipment from our shop."

The thought comforted her. When William came to the store, she would see him again, regardless what her grandmother thought about him.

"That, of course, makes him a man of honor," Daphne teased. "But come, Mrs. O'Keefe, let's talk about something else. I've heard you'll soon be receiving a visitor from Kiward Station. Is it Mrs. McKenzie?"

Elaine listened to the conversation a little longer, but then went on her way. After all, her other grandmother and her cousin's visit had already been discussed extensively in recent days. Not that Gwyneira's fly-by-night visits were so sensational. She visited her children and grandchildren often and was, moreover, close friends with Helen O'Keefe. Whenever she stayed at Helen's hotel, the women often

11

talked all night long. The only thing that was unusual about this visit was that Gwyneira was to be accompanied by Elaine's cousin Kura. That had never happened before, and it did seem . . . well, scandalous. Fleurette and Helen usually lowered their voices when discussing this subject, and they had not allowed the children to read Gwyneira's letter. Kura did not seem to think much of traveling, at least not to visit her relatives in Queenstown.

Though Elaine was only a year older than Kura, Elaine hardly knew her. The girls had never had much to say to each other during Elaine's rare visits to Kiward Station. They were simply too different. When Elaine was there, she thought of nothing except riding and sheepherding. She was fascinated by the endless expanse of grassland and the hundreds upon hundreds of wool providers grazing on it. In addition to that, her mother, Fleurette, blossomed on the farm. She loved racing with Elaine toward the snowcapped mountains, which never seemed to get any closer even when they were going at a breakneck gallop.

Kura, on the other hand, preferred to remain in the house or garden and only had eyes for her new piano, which had been sent from England to Christchurch with a goods shipment for the O'Keefes. Elaine thought her a complete idiot because of that, but then again, she had only been twelve years old the last time she visited. And envy had no doubt also played a role. Kura was the heiress of Kiward Station. All the horses, sheep, and dogs would someday belong to her—and she didn't appreciate any of it!

Elaine was now sixteen and Kura fifteen. The girls were sure to have more in common than before, and this time Elaine would be able to show her cousin her own world. Surely she would like Queenstown, the lively town on Lake Wakatipu, which was so much closer to the mountains than the Canterbury Plains and much more exciting, with its countless gold seekers from every corner of the globe and a pioneer spirit not confined to mere survival. Queenstown had a flourishing amateur theater group directed by the pastor, there were square-dancing associations, and a few Irishmen had formed a band and played Irish folk music at the pub and the community center.

Elaine reflected that she should absolutely tell William about that as well—maybe he would even want to go dancing with her! Now that she had left the skeptical ladies in the garden, the wistful glow returned to Elaine's face. Full of hope, she positioned herself once more behind the reception desk. William might come by again, after all.

Helen got there first, however. She thanked Elaine graciously for watching the desk and in doing so let her know that her presence was no longer necessary. Darkness had nearly fallen—undoubtedly one of the reasons Helen and Daphne had cut their time together short. The pub opened in the evening, and Daphne had to be there to keep an eye on things. Helen felt obliged to glance at the registration card of the new guest who had made such a lasting impression on her granddaughter.

Daphne, already on her way out, looked over her shoulder as she did so. "He's from Martyn Manor . . . Sounds noble," she mused. "A gentleman after all?"

"I will look into it straightaway," Helen declared resolutely.

Daphne nodded and smiled to herself. That young man had an inquisition waiting for him. Helen had little grasp of romantic relationships.

"And keep an eye on the little one," Daphne remarked as she headed out the door. "She's already fallen for that Irish golden boy, and that could have consequences. Especially when it comes to gentlemen."

To Helen's surprise, however, her appraisal of the new guest did not prove negative in the least. On the contrary, when the young man first presented himself to her, he was scrubbed clean, shaven, and nicely dressed, and Helen, too, recognized that his suit was made of the best cloth. He politely inquired where he might dine that evening, and Helen offered him the board service she had at the ready for her hotel guests. In theory, one was supposed to sign up for it in advance, but her eager cooks, Mary and Laurie, would manage to whip up an extra meal. As a result, William found himself in a tastefully furnished dining room at a finely set table alongside two bank employees and a stiff young lady who worked at the newly opened school. The service confused him at first: Mary and Laurie, two happy, buxom blondes, revealed themselves to be twins, and William could not tell them apart no matter how closely he looked. The other guests assured him with a laugh that this was quite normal, that only Helen O'Keefe could tell them apart at a glance. Helen smiled at that. She knew that Daphne could as well.

The communal meal naturally presented the ideal framework for sounding out William Martyn. Helen did not even need to question him herself. The other guests, curious about him, took care of that.

Yes, he was in fact Irish, William assured them several times, and a little gruffly, after both bankers had mentioned his lack of accent. His father had a sheep farm in the Connemara region. This information confirmed the assumption Helen had formed when she had first heard William speak: the young man had been brought up in the best circles and had never been allowed to pick up the Irish dialect.

"But you are of English origins, are you not?" inquired one of the bankers. He was from London and seemed to know a little about the Irish question.

"My father's family came from England two hundred years ago," a heated William explained. "If you still want to think of us as immigrating . . ."

The banker raised his hands in a gesture of appeasement. "No, no, my friend. The way I see it, you're a patriot. So what brings you here from the Emerald Isle? Frustration with the Home Rule Bill affair? It was to be expected that the lords would shoot it down. But if you yourself are—"

"I'm no great estate owner," William remarked icily. "Let alone an earl. My father may sympathize with the House of Lords in certain respects, but . . ." He bit his lip. "Forgive me. Now is neither the time nor the place."

Helen decided to change the subject before this hothead reacted any more impetuously. Judging from his temperament, there was no doubt he was Irish. Moreover, he'd had a falling out with his father. It was possible that this was the reason he had emigrated.

"And now you would like to look for gold, Mr. Martyn?" she asked casually. "Have you already staked a claim?"

William shrugged, suddenly appearing unsure.

"Not exactly," he replied with some restraint. "I was advised about a few places that look promising, but I cannot decide."

"You should look for a partner," the older of the two bankers advised. "Your best bet would be an experienced man. There are certainly plenty of veterans in the gold fields who already participated in the Australian gold rush."

William pursed his lips. "What do I want with a partner who's been panning for ten years and still hasn't found anything? I'll pass on that sort of experience." His light-blue eyes flashed contemptuously.

The banker laughed. Helen, on the other hand, found William's superior attitude rather unbefitting.

"It would be hard to fault you," the older banker said at last. "But hardly anyone makes their fortune here. If you want a serious piece of advice, young man, forget this gold-mining business. Stick to something you know. New Zealand is a paradise for founders. Practically every calling promises a bigger income than gold mining."

The real question was whether this young man had ever learned a practical calling, Helen thought. So far, he struck her as the well-brought-up but rather spoiled scion of a wealthy house. It would be interesting to see how he reacted to the first blisters on his fingers when he went out mining for gold.

2

"Now what do you boys think you're doing?"

James McKenzie let his already foul mood loose on his son, Jack, and the boy's two friends, Hone and Maaka. The three of them had tied a basket to one of the cabbage trees that gave the approach to the manor of Kiward Station an exotic flair and were practicing throwing balls into it. Or they were until Jack's father appeared, his irritated countenance giving the boys pause.

They did not understand why he had gotten so angry. Sure, the gardener might not be thrilled about the transformation of the front yard into a playground. After all, it required a great deal of effort to rake the pale gravel evenly and care for the flower beds. And Jack's mother considered it important to maintain a suitable appearance for the front of the manor—she might not be pleased to discover a basketball hoop and trampled grass there. Jack's father, however, did not tend to care much about such superficialities. Indeed, the boys had rather expected him to pick up the ball that had landed at his feet and take a shot himself.

"Shouldn't you boys be in school right now?"

Ah, so that was what this was about. Relieved, Jack beamed at his father.

"Actually, yes, but Miss Witherspoon released us early. She still has to pack and get ready . . . for the trip. I didn't even know that she was going."

The boys' expressions—both on the Maori boys' wide brown faces and Jack's freckled one—revealed their delight at the prospect of more free days ahead.

James, however, was ready to explode. Heather Witherspoon, their young governess, offered a far more attractive target for his rage than the three basketball players.

"That's news to me too!" grumbled James. "I wouldn't get my hopes up if I were you. I'll rid the lady of her travel plans soon enough."

He picked up the ball, threw it at the basket and, much to his own surprise, made a perfect shot.

Monday, his dog, who followed close at his heels wherever he went, chased after the ball excitedly. Jack had to work to beat her to it. He could not even bear to imagine her tearing the basketball to pieces, the real one that he had dreamed of for weeks before it was finally delivered from America. Christchurch, the largest settlement close to Kiward Station, was inching its way slowly toward being a proper city, but there was still no basketball team.

James grinned at his son as Monday gazed at the ball with her lovely three-colored collie eyes, as hurt as they were greedy.

Jack called the dog to him, stroked her, and returned James's smile, visibly relieved. Clearly all was well again. Father and son rarely fought; Jack was not just a chip off the old block physically—Gwyneira having passed on only the red hue of her hair and her propensity toward freckles to her son—but also with regard to his character. Even as a toddler, Jack had followed his father through the stalls and shearing sheds like James's sheepdog's pups followed her. He'd sat in front of his father in the saddle, the horse never able to go fast enough for him, and tussled with the dogs in the straw. Since then, the thirteen-year-old boy had become a real help on the farm. He had been allowed to ride along the last time they herded the sheep down from their summer pastures and was undeniably proud to have "held his own." As were James and Gwyneira McKenzie, both of whom were delighted every single day by the wonder of this late-born child. Neither of them had even thought children were a possibility when, after many years of luckless love, separation, misunderstandings, and contrary circumstances, they had finally exchanged vows. Gwyneira had by then already passed her fortieth birthday and no one had counted on another pregnancy. Little Jack, however, had not been bothered by that, being in rather too much of a hurry: he came into the world seven months after their wedding, after an uneventful pregnancy and relatively easy birth.

In spite of the piqued temper that had him taking the approach to the house in long, purposeful strides, James smiled tenderly just thinking of Jack. Everything about that child was easy: Jack was uncomplicated, bright, and a great help with the farmwork. And he would be a good student as well, if Miss Witherspoon would just exert herself a little!

James frowned. Just the thought of the young teacher Gwyneira had brought into the house, primarily for her granddaughter Kura, caused his anger to flare up again. He did not blame his wife in the least: Kura-maro-tini, the daughter of her son from her first marriage, and his Maori wife, had desperately needed a foreign tutor. The girl had long since become too much for Gwyneira—let alone for her own mother, Marama. Nor was Gwyneira exactly the most patient teacher. Though she had endless reserves of patience when it came to horses and dogs, she lost her nerve in a flash when she was helping someone who could only clumsily write. Marama was calmer in that respect but had remarried two years before and thus had other preoc-cupations. Besides, she had only attended Helen's improvised school in the "wilderness"—and Gwyneira wished for a more comprehensive education for the heiress of Kiward Station.

Heather Witherspoon had appeared to be the ideal choice—even though James suspected that Gwyneira had chosen her first and fore-most because "Heather" sounded a bit like "Helen." James would have trusted Gwyneira to assemble an entire sheepshearing team any day of the week. But when it came to judging governesses' qualifications, she lacked the knowledge and interest. So the decision had been made in a rush—and now they were stuck with Miss Witherspoon, who was undoubtedly well educated but still only half-grown herself, no less spoiled than her pupil. James would have preferred to send her back ages ago; a passage to New Zealand did not have to be a once-in-a-lifetime journey these days. Since steamships were now employed, the crossing had become both briefer and safer. Within eight weeks, Miss Witherspoon could have been peddling her talents in England again. But that would have gone against the express wishes of Kura-maro-tini, who had immediately befriended her new governess. And neither Gwyneira nor Marama had wanted to risk one of the child's tantrums.

James ground his teeth in anger as he took off his jacket in the house's entryway. Originally, it had been the vestibule for the resplendent parlor, complete with a little silver tray for receiving calling cards. Gwyneira had long done away with the tray though. Both she and the Maori maids had thought it superfluous to constantly be cleaning it. A flower vase now stood in its place, filled with branches of the native rata bush, which made the room feel more inviting.

However, the sight could not soothe James that day; he continued to nurse his resentment against the young instructor. For over two years now, the McKenzies had looked on as Miss Witherspoon carelessly neglected her duties toward Jack and the other children, despite her contract explicitly stating that she was to see to the elementary education of the Maori village's children as well as Kura's private studies. She was supposed to hold classes in the village daily. Jack would not have minded and it certainly would not have hurt Kura any to take part in these lessons. Yet Heather Witherspoon put it off whenever she could. The adult natives scared her, she said, and she could not stand the children.

When she did, nevertheless, condescend to hold class, she designed the content of the lesson entirely around Kura—which demanded too much of the village children and therefore bored them. She read, for example, exclusively books for English girls, preferring those in which a young princess suffered through the fate of a Cinderella until she was finally rewarded for all her good deeds. Such a tale did not resonate with the Maori girls, as it was completely foreign to their reality, and Heather Witherspoon made no effort to help them understand it. The Maori boys were nearly driven mad by the stories, as patient princesses did not interest them in the least. They would much rather have listened to tales of pirates, knights, and other adventurers.

James cast a quick glance at the onetime parlor that now served as Gwyneira's office. His wife was not present, so he crossed through to the salon furnished with expensive English furniture, still muttering to himself. Would it kill Heather Witherspoon to read *Treasure Island* to her class just once—or the stories of Robin Hood or Sir Lancelot that had so delighted Fleurette and Ruben in their childhood?

Piano music poured into the salon from what had once been the study—now transformed into a sort of school and music room. James stuck his head in briefly, since it was theoretically possible that his prey was giving Kura a lesson at that moment. But the girl sat alone in front of those damn ivories, playing Beethoven without a care in the world. James had not expected otherwise. It was typical of Kura to leave all the preparations for a trip to her grandmother and governess while she saw to her own amusement. Later she would complain that they had not packed the right clothes.

James allowed the door to close without saying a word to the thin, black-haired girl. He did not have eyes for Kura's obvious beauty, which everyone else praised the first time they laid eyes on her. Particularly since Kura had ripened into a woman, observers often found themselves breathless. James McKenzie saw her only as a child—a spoiled child whose moods often drove her family and the servants to distraction.

James was climbing up the broad staircase that connected the social and work rooms of the lower level to the upper story when he heard angry voices coming from Kura's room. Gwyneira, and Heather Witherspoon. James smirked. It seemed that his wife had beaten him to it.

"No, Miss Witherspoon, Kura will have no need of you. She will have no trouble making it through a few weeks without singing lessons—besides, I do not recall hiring you on as a singing instructor. You lament constantly as it is that you can hardly teach Kura anything more where we are. And as for piano lessons and the rest of her instruction . . . if Kura will truly, as you say, dry up like a petal in the desert, my friend Helen will intercede. Helen has taught more children their ABCs in her lifetime than you can imagine, and she has played the organ in church for years."

James smiled to himself. Gwyneira really knew how to take someone to task. He had often been on the wrong end of her temper himself—and was always torn between anger and admiration. Even by the way she seemed to rear up during an argument! She was small and very slim but unusually energetic. When she was in a rage, her red hair seemed charged with electricity and her excited azure-blue eyes appeared to shoot sparks. It was as impossible as ever to guess her age. Though she had begun putting her hair up in a bun, instead of simply tying it at her nape as she had previously done, a few strands always managed to free themselves. Naturally, the years had carved a few wrinkles into her face. Gwyneira had never had a high regard for parasols, and umbrellas were no better—and her skin had been exposed the caprices of the Canterbury Plains a great deal over the years. Yet James would not have wanted to erase a single one of her laugh lines, nor the deep crease that formed between her eyes when she was angry, as she was now.

"No 'buts' about it!"

Heather Witherspoon must have made some reply that James had not heard.

"You are needed right here more than anywhere else, Miss Witherspoon. Several Maori children can still neither read nor write. And my son could stand to be challenged at his own age level. So unpack your bags and return to your actual work. The children should be in school. Instead they are outside playing with a ball."

So Gwyneira had not missed that either. James applauded her as she swept out of the room.

Running into James startled Gwyneira, but then she smiled at him.

"And just what are you doing here? Were you also on the warpath? Our Miss Witherspoon's high-handedness is really too much."

James nodded. As always, his mood improved when Gwyneira was with him. For the last sixteen years they had hardly been apart for even a day, and yet the sight of her still made him happy. Which made it all the worse that he would not have her around, maybe for several weeks.

Gwyneira recognized immediately that he was upset.

"What's wrong? You've been running around all day with a long face. Are you against our going?"

Gwyneira had been about to follow her husband down the stairs, but then she heard Kura playing the piano. They both turned into their private apartments as though at an invisible signal. The walls of the salon might have ears.

"Whether I'm 'against' it is hardly the point," James said moodily. "I just don't know whether traveling is the answer . . ."

"To bring Kura 'under control'?" Gwyneira asked. "Don't deny it. I heard you talking to Andy McAran about it in the stables—not exactly discreet, if you ask me."

Gwyneira removed a few items from her wardrobe and put them in a suitcase, thereby signaling that her trip was set in stone. James's uneasiness flared into full-blown anger.

"It was Andy's expression. If you really want to know, he said: 'You have to see that you bring that girl under control. Otherwise, Tonga's going to marry her off to the next Maori rascal who'll act like his slave.' How was I supposed to respond to that? Let Andy go? For doing nothing but telling the truth?"

Andy McAran was among the oldest workers on Kiward Station. Like James, Andy had been there even before Gwyneira was sent to New Zealand as a bride for the farm's heir, Lucas Warden. Indeed, there were no secrets between Andy, James, and Gwyneira.

Gwyneira did not keep up her agitated tone. Instead, she lowered herself listlessly onto a corner of the bed. Monday rubbed herself against Gwyneira's leg, hoping to be petted.

"What should we do then?" she asked, stroking the dog. "'Bring her under control' sounds easy enough, but Kura is not a dog or a horse. I can't just order her around."

"Gwyn, your dogs and horses have always been happy to listen to you, even without the use of force. Because you raised them properly from the beginning. Lovingly, but firmly. You let Kura get away with everything. And Marama didn't help." James wanted to take his wife into his arms to take the edge off his words, but then he changed his mind. It was time to talk seriously about the situation.

23

Gwyneira bit her lip. She couldn't deny it. No one had ever set boundaries for Kura-maro-tini, the heiress of Kiward Station and symbol of hope for the local Maori tribe and the farm's white founders. Neither the Maori—who never raised their children strictly, instead confidently leaving their discipline to the land in which they would have to survive—nor Gwyneira, who really should have known better. She had loosened the reins too much on her son Paul, Kura's father, also. But that had been different. Paul was borne of a rape, and Gwyneira had simply never really been able to love him. As a result, he had been a difficult child who'd grown into an angry, belligerent young man, and his feud with the Maori chieftain Tonga had ultimately led to his death. Tonga, who was both intelligent and cultivated, had triumphed in the end by way of a governor's decree: the purchase of the land for Kiward Station had not been entirely in accordance with the law. If Gwyneira wanted to keep the farm, she would have to reimburse the natives. But Tonga's demands had been unacceptable. Marama had been the one to effect a peace agreement. Her child, of both *pakeha* and Maori blood, would inherit Kiward Station, and thus the land would belong to everyone. On the one hand, no one would question the Maori's right to reside there, and on the other, Tonga would make no claims to the farm's heartland.

Gwyneira and most of the members of the Maori tribe were more than happy with this arrangement—it was only in the young chief's breast that anger for the *pakeha*, the hated white settlers, continued to swell. Paul Warden had been his rival while he was alive, not only with regard to possession of the land but also when it came to Marama. No doubt Tonga had hoped that after Paul's death and an appropriate mourning period, the beautiful young woman would come to him. But Marama did not seek a new spouse at all at first, instead moving into the manor with her child. And later, she had not chosen Tonga or any other man from his tribe but had fallen head over heels in love with a sheepshearer who had come to Kiward Station with his company one spring. The young man, Rihari, had felt the same way about her, and they too were soon joined in matrimony. Rihari was Maori but belonged to a different tribe. He was approachable and friendly, and he understood Marama's situation at once: they could not take Kura away from Kiward Station, nor could Marama follow him alone to join his tribe in Otago. So he asked to be taken in by her people, to which Tonga, gritting his teeth, had agreed. The couple now lived in the Maori village; Kura remained in the manor by her own request.

Yet she took the path to the village by the lake with ever greater frequency these days. Though visiting her mother was the reason she gave for her appearances there, the truth was that Kura had discovered love. The youth, Tiare, was courting her—and not as innocently as would have been expected among *pakeha* adolescents of her age.

Gwyneira, who had once calmly tolerated the love between Ruben O'Keefe and her daughter, Fleur, was now alarmed. After all, she knew about the Maori's loose sexual morals. Men and women were allowed to sleep together as they wished. A marriage was only considered sealed when the two shared a bed in the tribe's meeting hall. The tribe did not care what happened before that, and children were always welcome. Kura seemed to want to take her cues from these customs—and Marama had made no move to interfere.

Gwyneira, James, and anyone else with any imagination on Kiward Station were afraid of Tonga exerting his influence. Gwyneira hoped that Kura would marry a white man of her social standing—something Kura had no desire to hear about at the moment. The fifteen-year-old had gotten it in her head that she wanted to be a singer, and her exceptionally beautiful voice and pronounced musical talent certainly indicated that she had the potential for that. But an opera career in a new land like this, let alone one so thoroughly puritanical? In Christchurch, they were only just now building a cathedral, and railroads had only just begun to crisscross the rest of the country . . . Nobody was thinking about a theater for Kura Warden. Heather Witherspoon had naturally put ideas of conservatories in Europe in Kura's head, telling her of opera houses in London, Paris, and Milan that were only waiting for a singer of her caliber. But even if Gwyneira—and Tonga—were to approve, Kura was half-Maori, an exotic beauty who everyone admired, but would anyone take her seriously? Would they see her as a singer or as a curiosity? Where would that spoiled child end up if Gwyneira sent her to Europe?

Tonga seemed to want to solve the problem in his own way. Andy McAran was not the only one who suspected him of pulling strings when it came to Kura's young love. Tiare was Tonga's cousin; an alliance with him would have considerably strengthened the Maori's position on Kiward Station. The boy had just turned sixteen, and, in Gwyneira's estimation, was not the brightest lad. If Tiare—indifferent to all farm-related matters except the piano-tickling Kura—were to become master of Kiward Station, it would no doubt be the high point of Tonga's life. But it was unthinkable for Gwyneira.

"It won't help to pack Kura off to Queenstown for a few weeks," James said. "On the contrary. She'll just have dozens of gold miners down on bended knee. Everyone will find her ravishing, she'll bask in their compliments—she'll only end up with a bigger head than ever. And when she comes back, Tiare will still be there. Even if you find some way to get him out of the picture, Tonga will find someone else. It won't do any good, Gwyn."

"Still, she'll grow older and wiser," Gwyneira said.

James rolled his eyes. "Do you have any evidence of that? Up until now, she's only grown crazier. And this Miss Witherspoon isn't helping. I'd send her back to England first, whether the little princess likes it or not."

"But if Kura digs in her heels, we don't win either. We'll just be driving her into the Maori's arms."

James had sat down next to Gwyneira on the bed, and she leaned into him in search of consolation.

"Why does everything have to be so difficult?" she sighed finally. "I wish Jack were the heir. Then we wouldn't have anything to worry about."

James shrugged. "We wouldn't need to worry if Fleurette were the heiress either. But no, Gerald Warden simply had to have a male heir, even through force. Still, I feel a certain satisfaction that he must be turning over in his grave right now. His Kiward Station not only in the hands of a half Maori, but moreover a girl!"

Gwyneira had to smile. In matters of inheritance, the Maori were decidedly wiser. It had not been a problem when Marama gave birth to a girl, as men and women had the same rights of inheritance. It was only a shame that Kura had inherited nothing from the energetic, if less musical, Gwyneira other than her azure eyes.

"First things first, I'm taking her along to Queenstown," Gwyneira said firmly. "Maybe Helen can put her head aright. Sometimes an outsider can find a way. Helen plays the piano, after all. Kura will take her seriously."

"And I'll have to get by without you." James pouted. "The livestock . . ."

Gwyneira laughed and put her arms around his neck. "The livestock should keep you busy enough. Jack's already excited about it. And you could take Miss Witherspoon along—in the catering wagon. Maybe she'll even volunteer to come with you."

It was March, and the sheep that had been living half-wild in the hills needed to be herded together and brought back to the farm before the coming winter. It was a job that took several days every year and required all the hands on the farm.

"Be careful what you suggest." James stroked her hair and kissed her tenderly. Her embrace had aroused him. And what objection could there be to a little love before noon? "I've fallen in love with a woman who rode along on the catering wagon before."

Gwyneira laughed. Her breath was growing quicker too. She patiently held still as James undid the hooks and eyelets of her light summer dress.

"But not with a cook," she asserted. "I still remember how you sent me out right on the first day to herd back the sheep that had broken off from the herd."

James kissed her shoulder, then her still-firm breasts.

"That was to save the men's lives," he remarked with a smile. "After we tasted the coffee you made, I had to get you out of the way."

While Gwyneira and James enjoyed a few peaceful hours, Heather Witherspoon repaired to Kura's room. She found the girl at the piano—and now had to tell her of her grandmother's decision about the trip to Queenstown. Kura took the news with surprising composure.

"Oh, we won't be gone long anyway," she remarked. "What are we supposed to do out in the backwoods? It would be one thing if we were going to Dunedin. But that hick mining town? Besides, I'm hardly related to those people. Fleurette is something like a half aunt, and Stephen, Elaine, and George must be fourth cousins, I think. What do they have to do with me?"

Kura turned her pretty face back to her music. Fortunately, there was a piano in Queenstown; she had made sure of that. And maybe this Mrs. O'Keefe really did know something about music, perhaps even more than Miss Witherspoon. Either way, she would not miss Tiare. Naturally, it was nice to let him worship, kiss, and caress her, but she had no intention of risking becoming pregnant. Her grandmother might think she was stupid, and Miss Witherspoon reddened whenever the subject turned to anything "sexual." But Kura's mother, Marama, was not such a prude, so the girl was well aware of where babies came from. And she was quite sure of one thing: she did not want one of Tiare's. In truth, she only clung to the relationship to irritate her grandmother.

If she really thought about it, Kura did not want children at all. She could not have cared less about the inheritance of Kiward Station. She was ready to leave everyone and everything behind if, in so doing, it meant coming closer to her goal. Kura wanted to make music, to sing. And no matter how many times Gwyneira said the word "impossible," Kura-maro-tini would hold onto her dream.

3

William Martyn had until that moment thought of panning for gold as a quiet, even contemplative act. You held a sieve in a stream, shook it a bit—and gold nuggets would get caught in it. Maybe not right away or every time but often enough that he would become a millionaire in the long run. Now that he was in Queenstown, the reality looked quite different. To be precise, William had not discovered any gold at all before joining Joey Teaser—even after selecting the most expensive tools in the O'Kay Warehouse, where he'd had the pleasure of chatting once again with Elaine O'Keefe. She had hardly been able to contain her excitement at the sight of him, and as his first day of gold prospecting wore on, William found himself wondering whether the true vein of gold did not rest in knowing this girl. That is, whenever he managed to wonder anything. Joey, an experienced gold prospector of fifty—who looked sixty, however, and who had already tried his luck in Australia and on New Zealand's West Coast—took one good look at William's freshly staked claim, declared it full of potential, and went straight to work chopping wood to build a sluice box. William had looked on a little confused at all this, at which point Joey shoved a saw in his hand and gave him the order to cut the logs into boards.

"Can't we . . . can't we just buy the boards?" William asked glumly after he had failed miserably at his first attempt. If they were really going to build the twenty-yard-long sluice that Joey seemed to have in mind, it would take at least two weeks before they struck their first bits of gold.

Joey rolled his eyes. "You can buy anything, boy, when you've got money. But do we have any? I don't, in any case. And you should hold onto yours. You're already living like a lord in your hotel and all that junk you bought."

In addition to purchasing all the essential gold-mining tools, William had also invested in a proper camping set and a few hunting rifles. After all, he might need to spend the night at the claim—definitely when there was gold to be guarded. And William did not want to sleep without something over his head when that time came.

"We have trees, an ax, and a saw here anyway. So we might as well build the sluice box ourselves. Grab that ax. You can't mess up chopping down a tree. I'll take the saw and do the skilled work."

After that, William felled trees, if not particularly quickly. He had managed to bring down two middle-sized southern beech trees, but it was sweaty work. Though the men had shivered that morning as they paddled out to their claim, they were already, at ten o'clock, toiling with their shirts off. William could hardly believe that the day was not even half-over.

"It would be better to try something that really suits you." The banker's remark bounced around inside William's head. At first, he had waved it away as the phrasemongering of a risk-averse office lackey, but the life of a gold miner no longer seemed so appealing. Of course, he was out in the fresh air—and the landscape around Queenstown was fantastic. After William had gotten over his initial ill humor, he could not help but recognize that. The majestic mountains surrounding Lake Wakatipu that seemed to embrace the countryside were alone a sight to behold, as was the play of colors that now, particularly in autumn, blended the lush vegetation into a kaleidoscope of red, purple, and brown. Some of the plants seemed exotic, like the cabbage trees that looked like palms, and some strangely alien, like the violet lupines that gave the area around Queenstown its distinctive look. The air was clear as crystal, as were the streams. But after a few more days of working with Joey, he would undoubtedly begin to hate the trees and waterfalls.

Over the course of the day, Joey proved himself to be a real slave driver. First, William was too slow for his taste, then he was taking too many breaks, and finally, he called William away from chopping down trees to help with the sawing. In addition, he cursed in the foulest way whenever something went wrong—which unfortunately happened most often when William took the saw.

"But you'll get it yet, boy," the old man finally said encouragingly after calming himself down. "I guess you didn't do much with your hands back home."

At first, William wanted to contradict him, but then he realized that the old man was not entirely wrong. True, he had worked in the fields with the tenant farmers in the last few years, after the blatant injustice with which his father administered his lands had gotten to him. Frederic Martyn gave little and demanded much—the farmers could hardly make their rent, and though it was bad enough that they had barely anything left over to live off in good years, they could expect no help if the harvest was bad. The families were still recovering from the great famine of the sixties, and practically all of them had victims to lament. In addition, nearly a whole generation was absent, as hardly a single farmer's child of William's age had survived the years of the potato blight. So the work in the fields now lay primarily in the hands of the very young and very old; nearly everyone was overexerted, and there was no hope of relief in sight.

None of that touched Frederic Martyn—and William's mother, too, although Irish herself, made no move to advocate for the people. So William had begun helping the tenants with the work in the fields. Later he had joined the Irish Land League, which was striving to help the farmers achieve fair rents.

At first, Frederic Martyn had found his younger son's attitude more entertaining than disconcerting. William would never have much say about the lands anyway, and his older son, Frederic Jr., displayed no humanitarian leanings. However, after the Land League cited its first successes, his joking and teasing about William's involvement with the league grew increasingly cruel, driving the young man ever deeper toward the opposition.

When William ended up supporting—if not inciting—a revolt among the tenants, the old man couldn't forgive him. William was sent to Dublin. He was to study a little, law if nothing else, so that he could one day stand up for his beloved tenants in word and deed. In that respect, the elder Martyn had been generous. The main thing was to avoid keeping the boy around to instigate his farmers any further.

At first, William had launched himself into his work with enthusiasm, but it was not long before struggling through the finer points of English law began to bore him, especially when an Irish constitution was to be proposed soon anyway. He attentively followed the debates over the Home Rule Bill, which promised to give the Irish considerably more say in the issues that affected their island. But then when the upper house rejected it again . . .

William did not want to mull all that over again. The affair had been too mortifying and the consequences fatal. He could have come to a much worse end than living in peaceful Queenstown's lovely environs.

"What did you do for a living anyway, over in Ireland?" Joey now asked. They had finally finished their work for the day and were tiredly paddling homeward. The bathhouse and a catered evening meal at Mrs. O'Keefe's hotel awaited William—while Joey had a whiskey-heavy evening at the fire of Skipper's gold-mining camp ahead of him.

William shrugged. "Worked on a sheep farm."

That was mostly true. The Martyns' extensive land holdings included first-class meadowland. Frederic Martyn had hardly suffered any loss from the potato blight for that reason. It had affected only his tenants and farmhands, who grew their own food on small patches of land.

"Wouldn't you rather be in the Canterbury Plains then?" Joey asked jovially. "There's millions o' sheep there."

William had heard that too. But his role in the farmwork had consisted more of managerial duties than actual labor. Though he knew theoretically how to shear a sheep, he had yet to actually do it—and certainly couldn't have done it in record time like the men who worked for the Canterbury Plains shearing companies. The best were supposed to be able to divest eight hundred sheep of their wool in a single day. That was not much less than the Martyns' entire herd.

On the other hand, some farmers in the east might have need of an able manager or foreman—a job William thought himself to be well suited for. But a man could hardly get rich that way—and William did not intend to make permanent reductions in his quality of life.

"Maybe I'll buy myself a farm when we've found enough gold here," William mused. "In one or two years."

Joey laughed. "At least you've got fighting spirit! All right, you can get out here." He steered the boat toward the shore. The river wound to the east past Queenstown before flowing into the lake south of the city below the gold-miners' camp. "I'll pick you up here again tomorrow at six in the morning, bright and early."

Joey waved to his new partner happily as William made his way wearily back to town. After resting in the boat, all of his bones hurt. He did not dare think about another day of chopping wood.

Nevertheless, something pleasant crossed his path on Main Street. Elaine O'Keefe stepped out of the Chinese laundry with a basket of clothes. She was headed toward Mrs. O'Keefe's hotel.

William smiled at her. "Miss O'Keefe! A prettier sight than a nugget of gold. Can I take that for you?"

Despite his sore muscles, ever the gentleman, he reached for the basket. Elaine did not play coy. She handed her load over to him happily and strolled along beside him with lightened step—to the limited degree that one could move both lightly and in a ladylike manner at the same time. It would hardly have been possible with the heavy basket on her arm. How had the heretical Miss O'Rourke once put it? "To be a lady, you need all your resources."

"Have you already found many nuggets today, then?" Elaine inquired. William considered whether she was simply naïve or if she meant that ironically. He decided to take it as flirting. Elaine had spent her whole life in Queenstown. She had to know that you did not become rich that quickly by mining.

"The gold in your hair is the first today," he admitted, combining the admission with a bit of flattery. "But, alas, that already has an owner. You are rich, Miss O'Keefe!"

"And you should introduce yourself to the Maori. They'd declare you *tohunga* straightaway. A master of *whaikorero*." Elaine giggled.

"Of *what?*" William asked. He had hardly met any Maori, the natives of New Zealand, up to that point. There were tribes at Wakatipu, as there were throughout the Otago region, but the fast-growing gold-mining town of Queenstown was too hectic for the Maori. Though a few Maori men had joined the gold miners' ranks, others only rarely ventured into the city. Most of them had not chosen to leave their villages and families. They were lost or had gone astray—like the majority of the white men seeking their fortune there. As a result, their behavior hardly differed from that of the whites, and none of them used such strange words.

"*Whaikorero.* It's the art of beautiful speech. And *tohunga* means 'master' or 'expert.' My father is one, according to the Maori. They love his court opinions." Elaine opened the hotel door for William. He declined, however, to go in before her and skillfully held the door open for Elaine with his foot. The girl beamed.

William remembered that her father was the justice of the peace and that her brother Stephen was studying law. Maybe he should mention his own efforts in that field sometime.

"I never got that far with my legal studies," he commented, as though in passing. "And do you speak Maori, Miss O'Keefe?"

Elaine shrugged. But her eyes had brightened as expected at the mention of his legal studies.

"Not as well as I should. We've always lived rather far from the nearest tribe. But my mother and father speak it well; back in the plains, they went to school with Maori children. I only really see any Maori when there's a conflict between them and the *pakeha* here and my father has to arbitrate. And that's thankfully rare. Did you really study law?"

William described his three semesters in Dublin in vague terms. But the two had to go their separate ways at that point anyway. When they'd entered the hotel, the draft had set a melodious wind chime ringing. Mary and Laurie appeared at once, happily twittering at William and Elaine. One twin took the laundry from William and could hardly restrain her excitement at his aid, while the other explained to him that his bath was ready. He had to hurry, however, because dinner would soon be served; the other diners were already there and would undoubtedly not want to wait.

William politely took his leave of Elaine, whose disappointment was clearly visible. He had to make another move soon.

"What does one do in Queenstown when one would like to invite a young lady to partake in respectable amusement?" he inquired of the younger of the two bankers just before dinner a short time later.

He would have preferred that Mrs. O'Keefe not overhear, but the old lady had sharp ears. She seemed to focus her attention inconspicuously but still noticeably on the two men's conversation.

"That depends on how respectable," the banker sighed. "And on the lady in question. There are ladies for whom no amusement is virtuous enough." The man knew what he was talking about. He had been trying for weeks to court their housemate, the young teacher. "You can accompany those girls to church on Sunday at most . . . which is not necessarily amusement. But you can invite normal young ladies to the community picnic if there's one taking place. Or maybe even to a square dance when the housewives' association puts one on. Daphne's has one every Saturday, of course, but that is not exactly respectable."

"Just let little Miss O'Keefe show you the town," remarked the older banker. "She would no doubt be happy to do that. She grew up here, after all. And a walk is an innocent undertaking."

"As long as it does not lead into the woods," Mrs. O'Keefe interjected drily. "And if the young lady in question really does happen to be my granddaughter, and therefore a very special young lady, you might want to obtain her father's permission first."

"What exactly do you know about this young man?"

Although it was a different dinner, the subject was the same. In this case, Ruben O'Keefe was questioning his daughter. Because although William had yet to dare to issue an invitation, Elaine had run into him again the very next day. Once more purely "by chance" of course, this time in front of the entrance to the undertaker's. A poorly chosen meeting place, but Elaine could not think of any other place that would do the trick on short notice. Not only was Frank Baker, the undertaker, an old friend of her father's, but his wife was a chatterbox. As a result, the whole town knew about Elaine O'Keefe's relationship with William Martyn—"A fellow from the gold-miners' camp," as Mrs. Baker would no doubt have put it.

"He's a gentleman, Daddy. Really. His father has an estate in Ireland. And he even studied law," Elaine declared, the last bit not without pride. That was her ace in the hole.

"Aha. And then he emigrated to look for gold? There are too many lawyers in Ireland, is that it?" Ruben asked.

"You wanted to look for gold once too!" his daughter reminded him.

Ruben smiled. Elaine would not have been a bad attorney herself. He found it difficult to be strict with her because, as much as he loved his sons, he worshipped his daughter. Elaine was, after all, simply too much like his beloved Fleurette. Aside from the color of her eyes and her mischievous little nose, she took entirely after her mother and grandmother. The red shade of her hair differed a bit from that of her female relatives, Elaine's hair being darker and perhaps even finer and curlier than Fleurette's or Gwyneira's. Ruben had passed on his placid gray eyes and his brown hair to his sons alone. Stephen in particular was "just like his father." His youngest, Georgie, was the adventurous one. By and large they fit together wonderfully: Stephen would follow in Ruben's footsteps with regards to jurisprudence, while Georgie dreamed of opening branch offices of the O'Kay Warehouse. Ruben was a lucky man.

"There was a scandal involving William Martyn," Fleurette remarked casually as she set a casserole on the table. They were having the same thing for dinner as the guests at Helen's hotel, since Fleurette had asked Mary and Laurie to make her a dinner to take home.

"Where did you hear that?" Ruben asked as Elaine almost dropped her fork in surprise.

"What do you mean by 'scandal'?" she mumbled.

A glow passed over Fleurette's still-elfish face. She had always been a talented spy. Ruben could still recall all too well how she had once revealed to him the secret of the O'Keefe and Kiward Stations.

"Well, I visited the Brewsters this afternoon," she said offhandedly. Ruben and Fleurette had known Peter and Tepora Brewster since they were children. Peter was an import-export merchant who had once built up the wool trade in the Canterbury Plains. But then his wife, Tepora, a Maori, had inherited land in Otago, and the couple had moved there. They now lived near Tepora's tribe, ten miles west of Queenstown, and Peter directed the resale of all the gold extracted there across the globe. "They are entertaining visitors from Ireland at the moment. The Chesfields."

"And you thought this William Martyn would be well-known throughout all Ireland?" Ruben inquired. "Where did you get that idea?"

"Well, I was right, wasn't I?" Fleurette replied mischievously. "All joking aside, of course there was no way for me to know that. But Lord and Lady Chesfield belong unmistakably to the nobility of English origin. And based on what Helen had already found out, the young man comes from similar circles. It's not as though Ireland is all that big."

"And what has Lainie's sweetheart been up to?" Georgie asked inquisitively, grinning impishly at his sister.

Elaine exploded. "He's not my sweetheart!" She swallowed any further remarks though. After all, she, too, wanted to know what scandal clung to William Martyn.

"Well, I don't know the specifics," Fleurette said. "The Chesfields only dropped a few hints on the subject. In any event, Frederic Martyn is quite a powerful landlord. Lainie was right about that. William, however, does not stand to inherit anything. He's the younger son. And the black sheep of the family besides. He sympathized with the Irish Land League—"

"That speaks rather well for the boy," Ruben interjected. "What the English are doing over there in Ireland is a crime. How can you let half the population starve while sitting on full grain stores yourself? The tenant farmers work for starvation wages, and the landlords grow fat. It's wonderful if the young man is advocating for the farmers!"

Elaine beamed.

Her mother, however, looked concerned. "Not when that advocacy degenerates into terrorist activities," she remarked. "And Lady Chesfield hinted at something along those lines. William Martyn is supposed to have taken part in an assassination attempt."

Ruben frowned. "When was this? As far as I know, the last major uprisings took place in Dublin in 1867. And there has been nothing in the *Times* recently about individual actions by Fenians or similar groups." Ruben received English newspapers, though mostly with a delay of a few weeks, and he read them attentively.

Fleurette shrugged. "It was probably thwarted in time. Or it was only planned, what do I know. This William fellow isn't sitting in prison, after all. No, he's publicly courting our daughter using his real name. Oh yes, there was another name mentioned in connection with the matter. Something about a John Morley."

Ruben smiled. "Then it's surely nonsense. John Morley of Blackburn is the chief secretary for Ireland. He resides in Dublin, and he supports home rule. That means he's on the side of the Irish. It would certainly not be in the interests of the Land League to kill him."

Fleurette began to fill the plates. "Like I said, the Chesfields did not express themselves very clearly on the subject," she said. "It could very well be that there's nothing to the story. Only one thing is clear: William Martyn is now here and not in his beloved Ireland, which is strange for a patriot. When they emigrate of their own volition, it's usually to America, where they meet like-minded people. An Irish activist in the gold mines of Queenstown strikes me as rather strange."

"But not sinister," Elaine declared fervently. "Maybe he wants to find gold to buy the land from his father and—"

"Very likely," Georgie said. "Why doesn't he just buy all of Ireland from the Queen?"

"We should, in any event, see the young man for ourselves," Ruben said, bringing the subject to a close. "If he's really to go walking with you"—he winked at Elaine, whose breath nearly caught at the prospect—"and that's an intention he's voiced, a little bird told me, you might invite him to dinner. There, and now on to you, Georgie. What did I hear this morning from Miss Carpenter about your math work?"

Her brother turned to find out what exactly he had heard from Miss Carpenter. Meanwhile, Elaine was so excited that she could hardly eat anything. William Martyn was interested in her! He wanted to go on a walk with her! Maybe even go dancing. Or even to church. Oh, this was marvelous. Everyone would see that she, Elaine O'Keefe, was a sought-after young lady who had managed to catch the eye of the only British gentleman to ever wander into Queenstown. The other girls would burst with envy. And her cousin most of all. This Kura-maro-tini whose beauty everyone spoke of endlessly. And whose visit to Queenstown hid some dark secret that definitely had something to do with a man. What others sorts of dark secrets were there, after all?

Elaine could hardly wait for William to ask her to go walking. And she wondered where he would take her.

Elaine finally did go for a walk with William—after he had artfully asked her if she would not mind showing him around town once. Elaine knew he didn't need to be shown around. After all, Queenstown still consisted only of Main Street; and the barbershop, the smithy, the post office, and the general store did not really require further explanation. Daphne's Hotel presented some excitement, but Elaine and William would naturally make a wide detour around that establishment. In the end, Elaine decided to extend the term "town" a bit and lead her romantic interest down the riverside promenade to the lake.

"Though it may not seem all that big because of the surrounding mountains, Lake Wakatipu is gigantic. It covers one hundred and fifty square miles, and it is continually in motion. The water is constantly rising and falling. The Maori say it's the heartbeat of a giant who sleeps at the bottom of the lake. But obviously, that's just a myth. The Maori have a lot of fairy tales like that, you see."

William smiled. "My country also has a wealth of stories. About fairies and sea lions that take human form at the full moon."

Elaine nodded excitedly. "Yes, I know. I have a book of Irish fairy tales. And I named my horse after a fey: Banshee. Would you like to meet Banshee sometime? She's a cob. My other grandmother brought Banshee's ancestors over from Wales."

Though William pretended to listen to her intently, he was not especially interested in horses. Banshee would not have mattered any more to him if Gwyneira McKenzie had imported the horse's ancestors from Connemara. He found it much more important that that evening, after this walk, he was to meet Elaine's parents, Ruben and Fleurette O'Keefe. Of course, he had already seen and spoken briefly with them. After all, he had made all of his purchases in their store. But now he had been invited to dinner, and would therefore be socializing with them more intimately. He was in desperate need of that. That morning, Joey had dissolved their partnership. While the old gold miner had initially been patient with him, William's "lack of drive," as he called it, had gotten on his nerves after just a week. William, however, had found it completely normal to slow down after the first hard few days. The pain in his muscles needed to abate, after all. And there was time. William was in no hurry. Joey, on the other hand, had made it clear to William that, for him, every day without a gold find was a day lost. He was not dreaming of whisper-worthy sized nuggets, just a bit of gold dust to buy his whiskey and secure his daily portion of stew or mutton at the campfire.

"Nothing'll ever come out of workin' with a spoiled boy like you!" he yelled. Apparently, another partner had turned up who had at least as promising a claim and was prepared to share it with Joey.

Joey's own claim had long since been exhausted; he'd had little luck with his allotment.

William would now have to carry on alone or seek alternative employment. He decided on the latter. Already the early mornings and late evenings offered a foretaste of winter in the mountains. Queenstown was supposed to be completely covered in snow in July and August—which was no doubt very lovely—but panning for gold in icy rivers? William could think of pleasanter things. Perhaps Ruben O'Keefe would have an idea or two.

William had already seen the O'Keefes' property from the river. Compared to Martyn Manor, it was not very impressive, consisting only of a homey wooden house with a garden and some stables. But here in this new land, one had to make allowances when it came to the stateliness of residences. And aside from its primitive architecture, Gold Nugget Manor did indeed have several things in common with the homes of the English landed nobility, including the dogs that leaped at you as soon as you stepped onto the property. William's mother had owned corgis. Here they employed some sort of collie— sheepdogs—which, as Elaine excitedly explained, were imports from Wales. Elaine's mother, Fleurette, had brought the bitch, Gracie, from the Canterbury Plains, and Gracie had proliferated with enthusiasm. Why they had brought the dogs to New Zealand was a mystery to William, but to Elaine and her family, nothing could have been more natural.

Ruben O'Keefe had not yet arrived home, so William let himself be taken on a tour through the stables to meet Elaine's wonderful Banshee.

"She's something special since she's white. That's rare among cobs. My grandmother has only had bays and black horses otherwise. But Banshee descends from a Welsh mountain pony that mother received when she was a child. She lived to be incredibly old. I even rode her myself."

Elaine prattled on unceasingly, but that did not especially bother William. He found the girl charming, and her effervescent temperament raised his spirits. Elaine seemed unable to keep still. Her red locks bounced in rhythm with her every movement. Moreover, she had made herself pretty for him today. She wore a grass-green dress set off with brown bobbin lace. She had attempted to tie her hair into a sort of ponytail with silk ribbons, but it was hopeless; even before Elaine had ended her tour of the town, her hairstyle had become disheveled. William began to contemplate what it would be like to kiss this tomboy. He'd had experience with many girls in Dublin who were more or less up for sale, as well as with the daughters of his Irish tenants; some of the girls had been very obliging when a few perquisites for their families came in exchange, while others had put on exceedingly virtuous airs. Elaine, however, awakened his protective instincts. William saw her, at least for the moment, more as an endearing child than as a woman. Surely a fascinating experience—but what if the girl took it seriously? There was no doubt in his mind that Elaine was head over heels in love. The feelings she nourished for William were impossible for him to miss.

Nor did they escape Fleurette O'Keefe. She was more than a little concerned when she greeted the two young people on her veranda.

"Welcome to Nugget Manor, Mr. Martyn," she said, smiling and holding her hand out to William. "Come in, and enjoy an aperitif with us. My husband will be joining us presently. He only has to change his clothes."

To William's surprise, the O'Keefes' house bar was well stocked. Fleurette and Ruben seemed to be wine drinkers. Elaine's father uncorked a bottle of Bordeaux first thing in order to let the wine breathe before dinner, but there was also first-class Irish whiskey. William swirled it in his glass until Ruben toasted to him.

"To your new life in a new land! I'm sure you miss Ireland, but this country has a future. If you let yourself, it's not hard to love."

William clinked glasses with him. "To your beautiful daughter, who has made my move to town so marvelous!" he replied. "Thank you very much for the tour, Elaine. From now on I shall only see this land through your eyes."

Elaine beamed and sipped some wine.

Georgie rolled his eyes. His sister couldn't possibly deny that she was in love!

"Were you really with the Fenians, Mr. Martyn?" the boy asked curiously. He had heard of the Irish independence movement and was hungry for adventure stories.

William suddenly looked alarmed. "With the Fenians? I don't understand."

What did this family know about his past life?

The situation was visibly uncomfortable for Ruben. The young man was not supposed to learn about Fleurette's spying within the first five minutes of their acquaintance. "Georgie, what are you talking about? Of course Mr. Martyn wasn't a Fenian. That movement has all but disappeared in Ireland. Mr. Martyn must still have been in diapers when the last uprisings took place. Excuse him, Mr. . . . ."

"Call me William!"

"William. My son has simply heard rumors . . . for the boys around here, every Irishman is a hero of independence."

William smiled. "Unfortunately, not everyone is, Georgie," he said, turning to Elaine's brother. "Otherwise, the isle would long since have been free . . . but let's move on. You have a beautiful estate here."

Ruben and Fleurette explained a bit about how Nugget Manor came to be, during which time Ruben wittily recounted the story of his fruitless gold-mining efforts. That encouraged William. If Elaine's father had failed at mining himself, he would undoubtedly appreciate William's troubles. For the moment, however, he did not mention them, and instead allowed the O'Keefes to determine the topics of conversation throughout dinner. As he'd expected, they listened closely to what he had to say, but that was not a problem. He artfully delivered extensive and relevant information about his origins and education. The latter was the norm for his social class: a tutor in his early years, followed by an elite English boarding school, and finally university. William had not graduated from the last one, but he left out that detail. After giving only a vague account of his work on his father's farm, he went on to embellish his legal studies in Dublin. He knew that Ruben O'Keefe would be interested in that, and when Ruben then brought the conversation around to the Home Rule Bill, William could more than keep pace. By the end of the dinner, he was rather convinced that he had made a good impression. Ruben O'Keefe appeared relaxed and friendly.

"And how is the gold mining going?" he finally asked. "Have you come any closer to riches?"

This was his opportunity. William assumed a distressed mien. "I'm afraid that was a mistake," he remarked. "Which is not to say that others did not warn me. Even your charming daughter brought it to my attention at our first meeting that panning for gold was really more for dreamers than for serious settlers." He smiled at Elaine.

Ruben looked astonished. "Last week you couldn't have sounded more different! Didn't you just buy all that equipment, including that camping tent?"

William made an apologetic gesture. "One's follies can grow costly," he said regretfully. "But a few days on my claim sobered me up quickly. The rewards simply don't measure up to the work."

"That depends," Georgie interjected excitedly. "My friends and I were gold panning last week, and Eddie—the blacksmith's son—pulled out a piece of gold that he got thirty-eight dollars for!"

"And you panned all day and didn't even make a dollar," Elaine reminded him.

Georgie shrugged. "That was just bad luck."

Ruben nodded. "That would sum up the problem of the gold rush. It's a game of chance, and only rarely does a real prize come along. Generally, it goes up and down. The men manage to hold their heads above water with the yields from their claims, but everyone's hoping for a lucky break."

"I believe my luck is waiting somewhere else," William explained as he glanced quickly over at Elaine. The girl's face brightened—all of her senses were concentrated on the young man next to her, after all. But their eye contact did not remain concealed from Ruben and Fleurette either.

Fleurette did not know exactly what bothered her, but she had an uncomfortable feeling. Ruben, however, did not seem to share it. He smiled.

"And what do you have planned instead, young man?" he asked in a friendly tone.

"Well . . ." William trailed off meaningfully, as though he had hardly asked himself this question before. "The evening I arrived, one of the local bankers told me I should concentrate on the things I can really do. Well, those things naturally have most to do with running a sheep farm."

"So you want to leave here?" Elaine sounded scared and disappointed, though she tried to act disinterested.

William shrugged. "Unwillingly, Miss O'Keefe, most unwillingly. But the center of the sheep breeding business is naturally in the Canterbury Plains."

Fleurette smiled at him. She felt strangely relieved.

"Perhaps I could give you a recommendation. My parents have a large farm near Haldon and excellent contacts."

"But it's so far away." Elaine attempted to control her voice, but William's announcement had struck her like a knife in the heart. If he was to go away now, probably never to see her again . . . Elaine felt the blood leaving her face. Did it have to be now? Did it have to be him?

Ruben O'Keefe registered his wife's relief as well as his daughter's disappointment. Fleurette wanted to shoo this young man from Elaine's side sooner rather than later, though the reason for that was not clear to him. Up until that moment, William Martyn had been making a good impression. Giving him an opportunity in Queenstown did not mean an engagement, after all.

"Well . . . perhaps Mr. Martyn's abilities are not limited to counting sheep," he said. "How are you with bookkeeping, William? I could use someone in the store to take all that exasperating scribbling off my hands. But of course if you're looking to start in a management position . . ."

Ruben's expression made clear that he considered that to be illusory. Neither Gwyneira McKenzie nor any of the other sheep barons in the east were waiting for an inexperienced young upstart from Ireland to tell them how to run their farms. Ruben himself was not terribly interested in sheep, but he had grown up in the business. He knew that animal breeding and husbandry in New Zealand had little to do with agriculture in Britain and Ireland—Gwyneira, his mother-in-law, had always alluded to that. In Wales, Gwyneira's father had not even had a thousand sheep and was considered one of the largest breeders in the region. But here, even his father's farm, with three thousand sheep, had been too small to make a profit. Moreover, Ruben hardly believed that William would be able to control the roughnecks who worked as shepherds and for the shearing companies.

William smiled incredulously. "Are you offering me a job, Mr. O'Keefe?"

Ruben nodded. "If you're interested. You won't get as rich as my bookkeeper, but you'll gain experience all the same. And if my son really makes good on his plans for branch offices in other towns"—he nodded at Georgie—"there will be room for advancement."

William had no intention of making a career as the manager of a branch office in some little town. He had in mind a chain of stores of his own or a marriage into this one, if things should continue developing so happily. Still, Ruben's offer was a start.

He gave Elaine another radiant look, this one a fraction of a second longer than the last, which she returned as one blessed, turning alternately red and pale. Then William stood up and offered Ruben O'Keefe his hand.

"I'm your man!" he declared with assurance.

Ruben clasped his hand. "To a good partnership. We should pour another whiskey to that. This time something local. Since you plan to set yourself up in this country for a while after all."

Elaine walked William outside when he finally made a move to leave. The area around Queenstown was showing its best side that night. The immense mountains were illuminated by the moonlight, and myriad stars sparkled in the sky. The river looked like flowing silver, and the forest was filled with the calls of nocturnal birds.

"It's strange that they sing in the moonlight," William mused. "As if we were in an enchanted forest."

"Well, I wouldn't exactly call that noise singing." Elaine had a limited understanding of romance, but she was doing her best. She nudged herself up next to him inconspicuously.

"To their females, that noise must be the loveliest of songs," William remarked. "The question isn't how well someone does something, but for whom."

Elaine's heart overflowed. Of course, he had done it for her! It was for her that he had ignored a well-paid job managing a sheep farm in order to help out her father. She turned to him.

"You would have . . . I mean, you didn't have to do that," she said vaguely.

William looked into her open, moonlit face, which held an expression between innocence and expectation.

"Sometimes you don't have a choice," he whispered. Then he kissed her.

For Elaine, the night exploded in that kiss.

Fleurette observed her daughter from the window.

"They're kissing!" she remarked and sloshed the rest of the wine into her glass, as though wishing she could empty the memory of what she had just seen along with the bottle.

Ruben laughed. "What else did you expect? They're young and in love."

Fleurette bit her lip and emptied her glass in one gulp. "I just hope we don't regret this," she murmured.

4

Along with Kura, Gwyneira McKenzie intended to accompany a goods transport for Ruben O'Keefe and to travel to Queenstown in its protection. She would be able to load their baggage on the freight wagon and they themselves could travel in a light chaise. Gwyneira thought that would be the most comfortable way to travel; her granddaughter did not express herself on the point. Kura faced the trip to Queenstown as ever with an almost unsettling apathy.

The ship with Ruben's delivery was taking its time, however, so their departure kept being pushed back. Apparently, the first autumn storms were making the crossing difficult. So the sheep had already been herded down from the mountains before Gwyneira could finally depart—which actually calmed, rather than annoyed, the concerned sheep breeder.

"At least I have my sheep somewhere dry," she joked as her husband and son shut the last gate behind the herds. Jack had once again proved himself. The workers praised him as "a man's man," and the boy raved about camping in the mountains and the bright nights during which he had slipped out of his sleeping bag to observe birds and other nocturnal creatures. There were many of them on New Zealand's South Island. Even the kiwi—that strange, plump bird chosen as the symbol of the settlers—was nocturnal.

James McKenzie was likewise cheered to see Gwyneira when he returned from the sheepherding. The two amply celebrated seeing each other again, during which time Gwyneira put her concerns about Kura into words.

"She still prances about brazenly with those Maori boys, even though Miss Witherspoon keeps reprimanding her for it. When it comes to behaving appropriately, her head is somewhere else entirely! And Tonga wanders around the farm from time to time as though it will soon belong to him. I should not let him see that it drives me mad, but I'm afraid he can tell."

James sighed. "The way it looks, you're going to have to marry that girl off soon. It doesn't matter to whom. She's always going to cause trouble. She has this . . . I don't know. But she's a sensual one."

Gwyneira gave him an indignant look. "You find her sensual?" she asked mistrustfully.

James rolled his eyes. "I find her to be spoiled and insufferable. But I don't have trouble recognizing what other men see in her. And that would be a goddess."

"James, she's fifteen!"

"But she's developed remarkably fast. Even in the few days we were out herding, she's filled out. She's always been a beauty, but now she's turning into a beauty that drives men crazy. And she knows it. Although I wouldn't spare a thought for this Tiare. One of the Maori shepherds did some eavesdropping on them the day before yesterday, and apparently she was treating him like an untrained puppy. No chance of her sharing a bed with him. The boy is the object of jealousy, but he also never hears the end of it from Kura and the other men. He'll be happy when he's rid of the girl." James drew Gwyneira back into his arms.

"And you think she'll find another one right away?" Gwyneira asked, unsure.

"One? Don't joke! If she so much as wiggles her pinky, there'll be a line all the way to Christchurch!"

Gwyneira sighed and snuggled into his arms.

"Tell me, James, was I really . . . um . . . sensual too?"

The freight wagons finally arrived in Christchurch, and Ruben's drivers reached Kiward Station driving two gorgeous teams of cart horses pulling heavy covered wagons.

"There's space to sleep in there too," one of the drivers explained. "If we don't find any lodging on the way, the men can sleep in one wagon, and we'll let you have the second, madam. If that's to your satisfaction."

Gwyneira was satisfied. She had slept in less comfortable places in her life and was looking forward to the adventure. She was in high spirits when the chaise, pulled by a brown cob stallion, took its place behind the covered wagon.

"Owen can cover a few mares up there," she said, explaining her decision to harness the stallion. "So that Fleurette's pure-blood cobs don't die out."

Kura, to whom she had directed these words, nodded apathetically. She had probably not even noticed which horse her grandmother had chosen. Kura cast much more interested glances at the young freight-wagon drivers—glances that were returned with no less enthusiasm. The two young men immediately set about courting Kura—or better yet, worshipping her. Yet neither dared flirt openly with the little beauty.

Gwyneira's enthusiasm for the trip grew still more when they finally left Haldon, the nearest town, behind them and headed toward the mountains. The snow-covered summits and the endless grassland of the Canterbury Plains that stretched out like a sea had fascinated her ever since her arrival in her new homeland. She could still clearly remember the day she had come over the Bridle Path between the harbor town of Lyttelton and the city of Christchurch—on a horse instead of a mule, which the other London ladies she had come with on the *Dublin* were riding. She still remembered how that had vexed her father-in-law. Yet her cob mare, Igraine, had brought her safely through the landscape, which had seemed so cold, rocky, and inhospitable that one wanderer had compared it to the "hills of hell." But then they had reached the highest point, and in the flatland before them lay Christchurch and the Canterbury Plains. The land where she belonged.

Gwyneira held the reins loosely as she told her granddaughter about her first encounter with this country. Kura let the words bounce off her with no comment whatsoever. Only the mention of the "hills of hell" seemed to register. It reminded her of the ballad "The Daemon Lover," and she even began to hum the song.

As Gwyneira listened, she wondered which branch of the family Kura had inherited her extraordinary musical talent from. Certainly not from the Silkhams, Gwyneira's family. Though Gwyneira's sisters had played the piano with more enthusiasm than she had, they had not done so with any greater skill. Her first husband had possessed considerably more talent. Lucas Warden had been an aesthete who played the piano beautifully. But he had surely gotten that from his mother, and Kura was not related to her by blood.

Gwyneira preferred not to think any more about the convoluted relations within the Warden family. It was probably Marama alone, the Maori singer, who had passed on her talent to Kura. It was Gwyneira's own fault for having bought the girl that confounded piano after having given away Lucas's instrument years before. Otherwise, Kura might have limited herself to the traditional instruments and music of the Maori.

The trip to Queenstown lasted several days, and the travelers almost always managed to find nightly lodging at one farm or another. Gwyneira knew just about every sheep breeder in the area, but even strangers were generally taken in hospitably. Many farms lay in seclusion on rarely traveled paths, and the owners were excited about every visitor who brought news or carried mail—which the O'Kay Warehouse's drivers, who had taken this route for years, did.

The travelers had almost reached Otago when, in the open country, they had no other choice but to make camp in the covered wagons. Gwyneira tried to make an adventure out of it in an attempt to draw Kura out; up to that point, she had mostly sat glumly next to Gwyneira, seeming to hear nothing except the melodies in her head.

"James and I often lay awake during nights like this and listen to the birds. Listen, that's a kea. You only hear those here in the mountains as they don't come as far as Kiward Station."

"In Europe there are supposed to be birds that can really sing," Kura remarked in her melodic voice, which was reminiscent of her mother's. But where Marama's voice sounded light and sweet, Kura's was full and velvety. "Real melodies, Miss Witherspoon says."

Gwyneira nodded. "Yes, I remember them. Nightingales and larks . . . they sound lovely, really. We could buy a record with bird sounds. You could play it on your gramophone." The gramophone had been Gwyneira's present to Kura the Christmas before.

"I'd rather hear them out in nature," Kura sighed. "And I would rather travel to England to learn to sing than to Queenstown. I really don't know what I'm supposed to do there."

Gwyneira took the girl in her arms. In truth, Kura had not liked that for years, but here, in the grand lonesomeness beneath the stars, even she was more approachable.

"Kura, I've already explained it to you a thousand times. You have a responsibility. Kiward Station is your inheritance. You have to take it over or pass it on to the next generation if it really doesn't interest you. Perhaps you'll have a son or daughter someday for whom it will be important."

"I don't want children. I want to sing!" Kura exclaimed.

Gwyneira brushed the hair out of her granddaughter's face. "We don't always get what we want, sweetheart. At least not right away and certainly not now. You must move on, Kura. A conservatory in England is out of the question. You'll have to find something else that makes you happy."

Gwyneira was thrilled when Lake Wakatipu finally appeared before them and Queenstown came into view. The journey with a sullen Kura by her side had seemed to grow increasingly long over the last few days, and by the end, she had entirely run out of topics of conversation.

But the sight of the prim little town, the mountain backdrop, and the massive lake immediately revived her optimism. Perhaps Kura only needed some company her own age. She would certainly find common ground with her cousin Elaine, who had always struck Gwyneira as quite sensible. Maybe she would be able to set Kura's head on straight. Her spirits buoyed, Gwyneira pulled ahead of the freight wagons and steered the elegant Owen onto Main Street. She received quite a bit of attention, and many settlers who knew her from previous stays called out greetings.

When she saw Helen's former charge standing outside talking with a girl, Gwyneira finally brought the stallion to a halt in front of Daphne's Hotel. She, too, had known Daphne for over forty years and had no reservations about interacting with her. Daphne's appearance unsettled her a bit, however, as she seemed to have aged since Gwyneira's last visit. Too many nights in a smoke-filled bar, too much whiskey, and too many men—in Daphne's line of work, one aged quickly. The girl next to her, however, was a beauty, with long black hair and snow-white skin. It was a shame that she wore too much makeup and that her dress was so overloaded with flounces and frills that her natural beauty was not so much supported as submerged. Gwyneira asked herself how this girl had ended up in an establishment like Daphne's.

"Daphne!" she called. "One has to grant you: you have an eye for pretty girls. Where do you get all of them?"

Gwyneira stepped out and gave Daphne her hand.

"They find *me*, Mrs. McKenzie." Daphne smiled, returning her greeting. "Word gets around when the working conditions are right and the rooms are clean. Believe me, it makes the job much easier when only the boys sting you and not the fleas too. But even my Mona here is nothing compared to the girl with you! Is that your granddaughter Kura? Well, man alive!"

Daphne had only meant to cast a quick glance into Gwyneira's chaise, but then her eyes had stuck on Kura, which was usually only the case with men. Kura didn't respond, however; she stared straight ahead. Daphne was without a doubt one those women Miss Witherspoon had warned her about.

After her initial excitement, though, a look of concern crept across Daphne's feline face.

"No wonder you have trouble with this girl," she remarked quietly before Gwyneira climbed back into her carriage. "You should marry her off as quick as you can!"

Gwyneira gave a somewhat forced laugh and signaled her horse to trot onward. She was a little vexed. Daphne was unquestionably discreet, but just who might Helen and Fleurette have told that Gwyneira and Marama felt hopelessly outmatched?

Her anger dissipated, however, as she approached the facade of the O'Kay Warehouse and saw Ruben and Fleurette speaking with the freight wagon drivers. They both turned to her when they heard Owen's powerful hoofbeats, and a moment later, Gwyneira was embracing her daughter.

"Fleur! You haven't changed at all! I still always have the feeling that I've traveled back in time and looked in a mirror when I look you in the face."

Fleurette laughed. "You don't look as old as that yet, Mother. I'm just not used to seeing you not riding a horse. Since when do you travel by carriage?"

Whenever James and Gwyneira visited their daughter together, they liked to just saddle two horses, as they both still enjoyed nights together under a tent of stars. They preferred to travel during the summer, though, after the shearing and herding of the sheep up into mountain pastures, when the weather was considerably more consistent.

Gwyneira made a face. Fleurette's observation had reminded her of her rather unpleasant journey.

"Kura doesn't ride," she said, trying not to sound disappointed. "So, where are George and Elaine?"

Elaine and William's relationship had solidified in recent weeks. Which was hardly a surprise since they saw each other practically every day. Elaine also helped out in the O'Kay Warehouse, of course.

And after work or during their lunch break, there was always one excuse or another to be together. Elaine surprised her mother by suddenly throwing herself into an array of domestic activities. There was always a pie that needed baking so that she could casually offer William something for lunch, or she would invite him to a picnic after Sunday service and spend the entire day before preparing various treats. William now kissed her more often, which did not, however, lessen the kisses' appeal. Elaine still felt faint with happiness whenever he took her in his arms, and she simply melted into them whenever she felt his tongue in her mouth.

Ruben and Fleurette tolerated the romance between their new bookkeeper and daughter with mixed feelings. While Ruben viewed the matter with a certain goodwill, Fleurette remained concerned. William had settled seamlessly into his new job. He was intelligent, he knew how to manage accounts and keep books, and he quickly learned the difference between managing a farm and a store. Beyond that, he won customers over with his fine manners. The women in particular were happy to have him wait on them. Ruben would not have had anything against a son-in-law like that—had he appeared a few years later. For the moment, however, Ruben O'Keefe was forced to agree with his wife. Elaine was too young for a more intimate relationship. He had no intention of allowing her to marry yet. As a result, it came down to the young man's willingness to wait. If William could summon a few years' patience, all would be well; if not, Elaine would be bitterly disappointed. While this was precisely what Fleurette feared, Ruben saw things more equanimously. With whom exactly was William going to run off? The other respectable girls in town were even younger than Elaine. And any of the new settlers' daughters from the outlying farms were out of the question: Ruben did not think William the type to fall head over heels for a girl without means, with whom he would have to start from scratch. After all, the young man harbored few illusions about the ways of the world, a faculty to which he owed his position in the O'Kay Warehouse.

For that reason Ruben loosened the reins—and Fleurette acquiesced with gritted teeth. They both knew from their own experience that young love could hardly be controlled. Their own story had been far more complicated than Elaine and William's dalliance, and their father and grandfather's resistance had been far greater than Fleurette's displeasure. In spite of all that, they had come together. This country was large and societal control minimal.

Early in the morning on the day of Gwyneira's arrival in Queenstown, Elaine and William had set off on a long errand together. William had offered to take a shipment of goods to a distant farm, and Elaine was accompanying him with a collection of clothing and petty wares from the store's ladies' department. The farmer's wife would then be able to look at and try on the goods at her leisure—and ask Elaine's opinion. It was a service that Fleurette had offered since the earliest days of the business—and one that the farm women had enthusiastically taken up. It offered isolated women not only the opportunity to shop but also a chance to catch up on the gossip and news from town, which always sounded different when it came from another woman's mouth rather than from the wagon drivers.

Naturally, Elaine had organized a picnic for William, for which she had brought along a light Australian wine out of her father's stock. The two of them feasted like royalty on an idyllic cliff by the lake while listening to the giant's heartbeat that caused the water to rise and fall. Afterward, Elaine even allowed William to open her dress a little bit to caress the small buds of her breasts and cover them with little kisses. She was so fulfilled by this new experience that she could have joyfully embraced the whole world. She hardly took her hands off William, who—equally satisfied with the day's course of events—serenely managed the team's reins. That is, until the two mares raised their heads and whinnied at a dark-brown horse in front of the store. Elaine recognized the stallion right away.

"That's Owen! My grandmother's stud! Oh, William, it's wonderful that she brought him. Banshee can have a foal now! And look, Caitlin and Ceredwen want to flirt. Isn't that marvelous?"

Caitlin and Ceredwen were the cob mares pulling the light goods wagon, which could now only be kept in line with some effort. The four-legged ladies knew exactly what they wanted. William pursed his lips indignantly. Elaine was unquestionably well-bred but sometimes she behaved like a common farmer's daughter! How could she speak about breeding so brazenly and in public? He considered whether he should chide her, but Elaine had already sprung from the wagon and was hurrying over to the handsomely dressed older lady, easy to recognize as her grandmother. While Fleurette revealed what Elaine would look like at forty, Gwyneira now gave a view of her at sixty.

William vacillated between a smile and a sigh. This was the only drop of wormwood in his courtship with Elaine: if he decided to marry her, life would hold no more surprises for him. His work and private life would move forward like a train on the tracks.

He stopped the team behind one of the heavier wagons and was careful to secure the draft horses well. He took measured steps on his way to be introduced to Elaine's grandmother, and her cousin. Probably another version of a redhead with hourglass form.

Meanwhile, Elaine was greeting her grandmother, who had just let go of Fleurette. From the look of it, she had just arrived.

Gwyneira kissed Elaine, pressed her tight to her, and then held her out for a moment to get a look at her.

"It's definitely you, Lainie! And you've gotten so pretty, a real woman! You look just like your mother did at that age. And I hope you're just as much of a tomboy too. If not, I've brought the wrong present . . . Where is it anyway? Kura, do you have the dog basket? What are you still doing in the carriage anyway? Come out and say hello to your cousin!" Gwyneira suddenly sounded a bit irritated. Kura did not have to make it so plain to all just how very little she cared about this visit to Queenstown.

But the girl had only been waiting for an invitation. Serenely and with lithesome, graceful movements, Kura-maro-tini Warden alighted from the carriage to take possession of Queenstown. And she noticed with satisfaction that her entrance did not lack for effect. Even on the faces of her aunt and cousin she detected a look of amazement that bordered on awe.

Elaine had only just begun to think of herself as pretty. Her love for William had done her good. She radiated from inside out; her skin was clean and rosy, her hair gleamed, and her eyes were more alert and expressive than before. Yet as soon as she found herself beside her cousin, she felt as if she had shriveled into an ugly duckling—as would any girl on whom nature had not lavished so many advantages as on Paul Warden's daughter. Elaine was looking at a girl who towered over her by half a head, which was not merely because she held herself naturally erect and moved with feline grace.

Kura's skin was the color of coffee generously mixed with thick, white cream. Her skin had a light-golden sheen that was warm and inviting. Kura's straight, deep-black, waist-length hair shimmered in such a way that it looked like a curtain of onyx had fallen down over her shoulders. Her eyelashes and her gently curved black eyebrows made her eyes—big and azure-blue like her grandmother Gwyneira's—all the more remarkable. Kura's eyes, however, did not twinkle in the teasing or willful way that Gwyneira's did, but instead looked calm and wistful, almost bored, which endowed her rare beauty with an aura of mystery. Her heavy eyelids further underscored the impression that she was dreaming and only waiting to be awoken.

Kura's full lips were dark red and shimmered moistly. Her teeth were small, perfectly straight, and white as snow, making her mouth irresistible. Her face was narrow, her neck long and beautifully curved. She wore a simple burgundy traveling dress, but her body would have stood out even beneath the plainest frock. Her breasts were taut and full and her hips wide. They swayed lasciviously with every step; however, her movements didn't seem practiced, as with Daphne's girls. It looked as though Kura had been born with an innate sensuality.

A black panther. William had once seen one in the London Zoo. This girl's lithe movements and hot-blooded beauty awakened memories of it in him right away. William could not help smiling at Kura, and it took his breath away when she returned the smile. Only briefly, naturally, for what did this goddess care about a young man standing by the side of the road?

"You . . . er . . . are Kura?" Fleurette got ahold of herself first and gave the girl a slightly forced smile. "I have to admit that I almost didn't recognize you. Which just goes to show that we haven't been to Kiward Station in an awfully long time. Do you remember Elaine? And Georgie?"

School had just gotten out, and George had been walking up to the store when Kura made her grand entrance, which he had followed with as the same dumbly gaping face as the rest of the male bystanders. Now, however, he made use of his luck to push his way up to his mother and his gorgeous cousin. If he only knew what to say to her.

"*Kia ora*," he finally wrung out of himself, thinking he sounded markedly cosmopolitan. After all, Kura was Maori; he supposed she'd like to be greeted in her language.

Kura smiled. "Hello, George."

A voice like a song. George remembered reading this description somewhere and finding it unbelievably absurd. But that was before he had heard Kura-maro-tini say hello.

Elaine made an effort to shake off her exasperation. Granted, Kura was pretty, but more importantly she was Elaine's cousin. And therefore, a completely normal person, and, moreover, younger than she was. There was absolutely no reason to gawk at her. Elaine smiled and tried to greet Kura nonchalantly—but her "Hello, Kura" sounded a little forced.

Kura was about to respond, but a whimpering and howling from the carriage suddenly drew everyone's attention. In the dog basket, which Kura had of course not brought out with her, a puppy was fighting heroically for his freedom.

"Now what's that?" Elaine asked, sounding natural again. She neared the carriage in a state of excitement, having nearly forgotten Kura.

Gwyneira followed her and opened the basket. "I thought I'd do something to carry on the tradition. With your permission—Kiward Callista. A great-great-granddaughter of my first border collie, the one who came with me from Wales."

"For . . . me?" Elaine stammered, gazing into the face of a tiny three-colored dog with large, alert eyes that seemed quite prepared to adore her liberator.

"As if we didn't already have enough dogs!" Fleurette cried. But she too found the new pup more interesting than the icy Kura.

For Ruben, George, and, above all, William, that was not the case. George was still struggling to come up with a clever remark, when his father pulled himself together to formally welcome Kura to Queenstown.

"We're very happy to have a chance to get to know you better," Ruben said. "Gwyneira says you have an interest in music and art. You might like it better here in town than out in the plains."

"Even if our town's cultural offerings do still leave something to be desired." William had finally regained his composure and, with it, his talent for *whaikorero*. "Though I'm sure they'll rise to the occasion when you, miss, are sitting in the audience. Unless you take their breath away. We have to account for that, naturally." He smiled.

Kura did not react as promptly as most girls. Instead of giving him a spontaneous smile, her mien remained serious. Yet he could detect a flicker of interest in her eyes.

William tried another approach. "You make music yourself, miss, isn't that so? Elaine told me that you are a talented pianist. Tell me, do you prefer classical or folk music?"

That was clearly the correct strategy. Kura's eyes brightened.

"Opera is my first love. I'd like to become a singer. But I see no reason not to combine classical and folk elements. I know that is considered daring, but it can be done. I have tried to underlay some old Maori songs with a conventional piano accompaniment, and the result has been very lovely."

Elaine did not observe the exchange between Kura and William. She only had eyes for the little dog. Fleurette's and Gwyneira's eyes met, however.

"Who is the boy?" Gwyneira inquired. "Good God, I've been sitting next to her for a week trying to start a conversation, but she didn't say three sentences the whole trip. Suddenly now . . ."

Fleurette frowned. "Well, our William Martyn just knows the right questions to ask. He has been working for Ruben for a few weeks. A clever one with clear designs for the future. He's been courting Elaine quite attentively."

"Elaine? But she's still only a child . . ." Gwyneira broke off. Elaine was a year older than Kura. And everyone was thinking about a speedy marriage for her.

"We think she's too young too. Otherwise, it would be suitable. A landed Irish gentleman."

Gwyneira nodded with a mildly bewildered expression. "What is he doing here then instead of tending to his soil in Ireland? Or did his tenants kick him off his land?" Even in Haldon, the occasional English newspaper had begun to appear.

"A long story," Fleurette said. "But allow me to intervene here first. If Kura starts off by making Lainie jealous first thing, I see little chance of a happy family gathering."

William had introduced himself by this time and made a few clever comments on the body of old Irish songs that seemed on the verge of conquering the world.

"There's a version of 'The Maids of Mourne Shore' to lyrics by William Butler Yeats. We Irish don't actually care for it when old Gaelic songs are given new English lyrics, but in this case . . ."

"I know that song. Isn't it called 'Down by the Salley Gardens'? My tutor taught it to me."

Kura was obviously having a grand time, which Ruben too had begun to notice.

"Mr. Martyn, would you see to the store?" he asked in a friendly but firm tone. "My family and I will be riding home presently, but Mrs. O'Keefe would surely be happy to send one of the twins over to help. I need you to carry in the new shipment of supplies . . . There will no doubt be other opportunities for you to discuss music with my niece."

William took the hint, said his good-byes, and felt more than flattered when Kura appeared to be disappointed. He had completely forgotten Elaine, but then, as he was about to turn away, she drew attention to herself.

"Look what I have!" Radiant, she held a panting ball of fuzz in front of William's nose. "This is Callie. Say hello, Callie!" She took one of the dog's paws and waved it. The puppy gave a quiet but high-pitched bark, and Elaine laughed. A few hours earlier, William would have found her laugh irresistible, but now, next to Kura, Elaine suddenly seemed childish.

"A sweet little dog, Miss O'Keefe," he said, though it came out a little forced. "But I have to go now. Your father wants to be on his way, and there's a great deal to do." He indicated the shipment that had to be unloaded and registered.

Elaine nodded. "Yes, and I have to see to Kura. She's certainly attractive, but otherwise strikes me as rather dull," Elaine added under her breath.

Georgie came to the same conclusion after trying to lure Kura into conversation the entire way to Nugget Manor. The girl had grown up on a sheep farm, so he brought up sheep husbandry first.

"How many sheep do you have on Kiward Station these days?"

Kura did not so much as glance at him.

"Around ten thousand, Georgie," Gwyneira answered instead. "But the number fluctuates. We're focusing more and more on cattle, since these new refrigerated ships now make meat exports possible."

Kura registered no response. But she was Maori. Surely she would want to talk about her people.

"Say, did I pronounce *kia ora* correctly?" he asked. "You speak fluent Maori, right, Kura?"

"Yes," she replied.

George wracked his brain. Kura was beautiful, and beautiful people undoubtedly liked talking about themselves.

"Kura-maro-tini is quite an unusual name," the boy said. "Does it have any special meaning?"

"No."

George gave up. It was the first time he had ever been interested in a girl, but this appeared to be a hopeless case. If he was ever to marry, he thought, then let it be to a woman who at least spoke to him, regardless of what she looked like.

Fleurette served tea shortly thereafter and was not much more successful in drawing the girl out of her shell. Kura had entered the house, studied the relatively simple furnishings with an indefinable but decidedly ungracious gaze—the O'Keefes had entrusted themselves to local carpenters rather than having furniture sent from England— and not said a word since. Now and again, she eyed the piano in one of the salon's corners covetously, but she had been too well raised to simply walk over to it. Instead, she nibbled morosely on tea cake.

"Do you like it?" Fleurette inquired. "Elaine baked it herself, granted, not for us but for her friend." She winked at her daughter, whose attention was still entirely focused on her puppy.

Gwyneira sighed. Her gift had undeniably been a success, but with regard to the aim of bringing the two cousins closer together, the puppy was proving to be more of an obstacle than a help.

"Yes, thank you," Kura said.

"Would you like some more tea?" Fleurette asked. "You must be thirsty after your journey. If I know your grandmother, there was only black coffee and water to drink on the way. At least that's how it always was during herding." She smiled.

"Yes, please," Kura said.

"So, what is your first impression of Queenstown?" Fleurette had desperately attempted to formulate a question that could not be answered with *yes* or *no*, *thank you* or *yes, please.*

Kura shrugged.

Helen, who arrived together with Ruben, had a little more luck a short while later. He had brought her as soon as she could get away from the hotel.

She was conversing fluidly with Kura about her musical studies, the pieces she was currently practicing on the piano, and her preference for various composers. The girl's outward appearance did not make the least impression on Helen, and she behaved entirely normally toward her. Kura seemed to find that alien at first, but then warmed to it. Unfortunately, no one else could contribute to the conversation. Kura had once again succeeded in bringing the discussion to its knees. Aside from Elaine, who was busy with her puppy, everyone else in the room was bored to death.

"Maybe you'd like to sing something for us," Helen finally prompted. She felt that tension was building, especially in Gwyneira and Fleurette. Georgie had already fled to his room, and Ruben seemed to be musing over some legal documents. "Elaine could accompany you."

Elaine played the piano reasonably well. She was considerably more gifted musically than Gwyneira, whose musical education in Wales had been a form of torture. Helen had been teaching Elaine for years and was proud of her progress. Surely that was the reason she had suggested it. Kura was not to think that all other New Zealanders were philistines.

Elaine stood up willingly. Kura, for her part, looked skeptical and appeared downright horrified when Elaine played the first few bars and Callie joined in, howling at the highest notes. The rest of the group found the whelp's song hilarious. Elaine laughed until she cried but then shut the dog away as instructed. Of course, then Callie howled heartbreakingly from the next room, disturbing her young mistress's concentration. That was most likely the reason Elaine missed notes several times. Kura rolled her eyes.

"If you don't mind, I'd rather accompany myself," she said. Elaine had the same shriveling feeling she'd had when Kura had stepped out of the chaise. But then she threw her head back defiantly. Let her cousin have the piano! She could get back to caring for Callie.

The music that wafted in through the closed door made Elaine feel even smaller. The piano never sounded so beautiful when she played it herself—and not even when her grandmother Helen played. Perhaps it was in the way Kura threw herself into the music, putting her soul into it; Elaine couldn't put her finger on it. Whatever it was, she only sensed that she would never be able to play like that, even if she practiced her whole life.

"Come. We're going outside," she whispered to her dog. "Before she starts singing. I've had enough perfection and spotless beauty for today."

She tried to think of William and his kisses back at the lake's cove. As always that raised her spirits. He loved her, he loved her . . . Elaine's racing heart sang with Kura's voice.

"What do you think of her?"

Gwyneira's patience had been tested for quite a long time before she finally had Helen to herself. Not only tea but the little family dinner was over, and they had sent the children off to bed. Elaine and Georgie had gone willingly, and Kura, too, seemed happy to retire. She explained that she still had a letter to write—Gwyneira could all too well imagine what she would report to Miss Witherspoon about her family.

Helen took a sip of wine. She loved the Bordeaux that Ruben regularly had sent from France. She'd had to endure too many years without those kinds of luxuries.

"What would you like to hear? About how beautiful Kura is? You already know that. How musical? You know that too. The problem is that she also knows it—all too well."

Gwyneira smiled. "You've come straight to the point. She's horribly conceited. But what about her voice, for example? Is that really enough for the opera?"

Helen shrugged. "I have not attended an opera performance for forty-five years. So what can I possibly say? What does her teacher think? She should know about that sort of thing."

Gwyneira rolled her eyes. "Miss Witherspoon was not engaged as a music teacher. In truth, she's supposed to be giving all the children on Kiward Station a proper education. But it looks like I've made an awful mistake. She comes from a very good house, you see. First-class education, boarding school in Switzerland. On paper she looked grand. But then her father overreached on some deal, lost all his money, and threw himself out a window. Suddenly little Heather had to make her own way in the world. Unfortunately, it's been difficult for her to move past that. And she'd hardly unpacked before Kura started filling Miss Witherspoon's head with all the things that had always filled her own."

Helen laughed. "But she must have studied music. Kura plays exceptionally, and her voice. I mean, you can recognize that she's had some training."

"Miss Witherspoon had voice and piano instruction in Switzerland," Gwyneira informed her. "For how long, I didn't ask. I only know that she complains it was far too little, and that she can hardly teach Kura anything else. But Kura soaks up everything that has to do with music like a sponge. Even Marama says she can't teach the girl anything more, and as you know, she's considered a *tohunga*."

"Well, then her voice should be enough for the opera. A conservatory could only do Kura good. If she were there, she would finally just be one among many and would no longer be worshipped by everyone she came into contact with."

Gwyneira dissented. "I don't worship her!"

Helen smiled. "No, you're afraid of her, which is worse! You live in fear that this child might get into some mischief that would lead to the loss of Kiward Station."

Gwyneira sighed. "But I can't send her to London."

"Better that than into the arms of some Maori boy serving as Tonga's marionette. Look at it this way, Gwyn: Even if Kura goes to London and marries in London, she remains the heiress. And even if Kiward Station is of no interest to her, she won't sell it—at least not as long as she doesn't need money. And you are not lacking for money, are you?"

Gwyneira shook her head. "We could furnish her with a generous stipend."

Helen nodded. "Then do it! If she marries overseas, the cards will be reshuffled, of course, but that wouldn't necessarily be a bad thing.

As long as she doesn't fall into the hands of a philanderer or a gambler or a criminal, her husband won't lay a hand on a farm in New Zealand that pays out money every month. The same goes for her children. If one of them feels a calling to become a farmer, then that child can come here. Though they might prefer to take the money and make a nice life with it."

Gwyneira chewed on her lip. "We would only have to ensure a steady flow of money—and later, Jack, when he takes over the farm. We couldn't afford bad times anymore."

"But based on what you've told me, Jack seems to be growing into quite an able farmer," Helen observed. "How is his relationship with Kura? Would she have anything against his taking over the farm?"

Gwyneira shook her head. "She doesn't care about Jack. Just as she doesn't care about anything that can't be transcribed in music notes."

"Well, all right! Then I wouldn't brood too long over what could, would, or should happen if the farming doesn't go well at some point in the distant future. You can't always assume the worst. There's not even any guarantee that Kura will remain dependent on an allowance from you. She could very well work her way up to being an internationally renowned opera star and find herself swimming in money. Or she might make something of her looks and marry a prince. I can't imagine that this girl will burden your pockets her whole life. She's too pretty and too self-assured for that."

Gwyneira lay awake for a long time that night mulling over Helen's suggestion. Perhaps her categorical refusal to consider Kura's plans up to that point had been wrong. In the cold light of day, there was nothing to keep Kura on Kiward Station—if Tonga was unsuccessful with his plans, she could sell the farm as soon as she was an adult. Though Gwyneira had never seriously considered it as a viable option, Helen had cast things in a drastically different light for her. Her guardianship of Kura would end soon, and then Kiward Station would be delivered up to the young woman for weal or woe.

By the time the gray dawn had begun to edge out the darkness, Gwyneira had almost reached a decision. She still had to speak to

James about it, but when she laid out Helen's arguments to him, she was certain that he would come to the same conclusion.

Kura-maro-tini Warden had never been closer to the fulfillment of her wishes than on that radiantly beautiful fall day—on which William Martyn came to dinner at Nugget Manor.

5

Ruben O'Keefe had been thoroughly bored that first evening
with Gwyneira and Kura—and he did not intend to repeat
that anytime soon. The two of them would not be staying at Nugget
Manor much longer; the house was too isolated for long-term guests,
especially for someone who had never sat on a horse. Helen had rooms
in her hotel ready for her friend and her friend's granddaughter, and
Gwyneira wanted to move there soon.

The first few days of her visits, however, were always dedicated to
her shared interests with Elaine and Fleurette. Gwyneira and Fleurette
discussed the inner workings of Kiward Station and Haldon down
to the very last detail. Elaine was dying to show the progress she
had made in riding, and to have her grandmother ride Banshee so
she could hear what Gwyneira thought of her beloved horse. Elaine
talked practically nonstop of riding the stallion that her grandmother
had brought—that is, when she was not talking about her new dog.

While Kura rarely uttered a word, Elaine tended to prattle, and
Ruben was already dreading another dinner with the two teenagers.
But then he came upon William in the store, hard at work registering the new shipment, and he concocted a brilliant plan to avoid a
repetition of the previous evening.

His young bookkeeper and would-be son-in-law had conversed
quite enthusiastically with Kura the day before. Moreover, he could be
depended on to keep Elaine from chattering on endlessly about dogs
and horses, as William did not care for either. In William's presence,
Elaine expressed herself only on subjects that were of interest to him.
This drove Fleurette crazy, but Ruben found it rather practical. So
practical that he issued the invitation as soon as William had completed

the gargantuan task of registering all the new merchandise and stacking it on the shelves masterfully with hardly any help.

"William, I hope you'll join us for dinner tonight. Elaine would be delighted, and you seemed to get along quite well with my niece yesterday."

William Martyn appeared both surprised and happy. Of course he would come. Naturally, he had no other plans—he needed only to notify Helen and the twins that he would not be present for dinner. During his lunch break, William walked over to the hotel, where he found Elaine at the piano, with her puppy, Callie, at her side. The dog accompanied her piano performance with piercing howls, causing the twins to fall over laughing. The house servant and one of the bankers heartily enjoyed the show, and even the ever-strict Miss Carpenter managed a smile.

"I think she sings much better than my cousin," Elaine was joking. "But fortunately, she hasn't decided on pursuing opera yet."

William did not know why this quip, harmless in and of itself, annoyed him, but he had already experienced a wave of mild anger when Ruben O'Keefe had casually described his niece's behavior. How could Kura Warden be "morose"? However, he had quickly forgiven his boss, to whom he felt greatly indebted for such a wondrous invitation. Since seeing Kura the previous day, he had thought about nothing but when he would run into her again and what he would say to her then. She was without a doubt a very bright girl. Naturally, she would not have any inclination to discuss such petty things as . . .

At that moment, Elaine spied her beau, and her eyes brightened. She had been counting on seeing William in town and had made herself pretty for that reason. A green circlet held her hair out of her face, and she was wearing a green-and-brown checkered batiste dress, for which it was already almost a little too cold outside.

"Come and play something with me Mr. Martyn!" she called out in a high-pitched voice. "Or are you busy? I promise to keep Callie quiet while we play."

Mary—or Laurie—took the hint right away, picking up the dog and disappearing with it into the kitchen. Meanwhile, Laurie—or Mary—pushed a second piano stool up next to Elaine's.

William could play the piano a bit and had charmed Elaine not long ago by practicing a few easy pieces as a duet with her. But this time he put up a fight.

"Oh, not here in public! Maybe tonight. Your father invited me to dinner."

"Really?" Elaine spun around on her stool with a grin. "How lovely! He nearly died of boredom last night with that awful cousin of mine. Such a bore, you wouldn't believe it! Oh well, you'll see soon enough. She's quite pretty, of course, but otherwise . . . if I were in my grandmum's place, I'd send her to London sooner rather than later."

William had to fight back against his rising displeasure. "Quite pretty?" The girl he had seen the day before was a goddess! And what was Elaine talking about, sending her away? He couldn't let that happen. He . . .

He called himself firmly back to order. What did this girl have to do with him? Kura Warden was absolutely nothing to him; he should not get involved. He forced himself to smile at Elaine. "It won't be all that bad. By the way, you too look particularly pretty this morning."

With that, he took his leave to look for Helen, while Elaine followed him with her eyes, disappointed. "You too look particularly pretty?" She had grown accustomed to receiving more finely polished compliments from him.

When Fleurette O'Keefe learned of Ruben's invitation that afternoon, she was not enthusiastic. She had prepared only a small, informal dinner. Not even Helen had wanted to come out for it. With William as a guest, she would have to put more effort into her cooking and serving, on top of which, Fleurette did not exactly find him easy to please. She had not warmed up to the loquacious young Irishman.

She never knew when William was speaking his mind and when he was merely humoring her or her husband. Besides, she still had not forgotten Lady Chesfield's insinuations. An assassination attempt on the chief secretary for Ireland? If William had really been mixed up in that, he could be dangerous.

Additionally, the looks that every male in the vicinity without exception had directed at Kura thus far had not escaped her. She did not think it was a good idea to lead Elaine's young suitor into temptation. But there was nothing to be done about it now. William had accepted, and Kura-maro-tini had shown remarkable liveliness when Fleurette told Gwyneira and her granddaughter about it.

"I should wear my red dress!" the girl declared. "And I have to clean myself up a bit. Could you send me up a girl to help me get ready, Aunt Fleur? I have difficulty lacing my own corset."

Kura was accustomed to having servants. Though Gwyneira had always tried to manage with a minimum of housemaids and kitchen maids, the manor house of Kiward Station was too big to keep clean herself, and her domestic talents were not especially pronounced. So several Maori girls worked under the aegis of their "butler" Maui, in addition to her head maids Moana and Ani. When Kura was little, they had looked after the child, and Ani, a skillful little thing, had later become a sort of lady's maid who kept Kura's clothes in order and did her hair.

Fleur looked at her niece as though she were not altogether right in the head.

"You can put your own clothes on, Kura! This isn't a large house. We only have a handyman and a gardener who takes care of the stables too. I don't think either of them would care to tie your corset."

Kura did not dignify this with a response and instead moped her way upstairs. Fleurette shook her head and turned to Gwyneira.

"Just what kind of ideas does the child have? She is clearly holding out for something better than us common folk. I've caught on to that. But you don't really allow her a lady's maid of her own?"

Gwyneira shrugged in resignation. "She puts a lot of value on her appearance. And Miss Witherspoon supports her in that."

Fleurette rolled her eyes. "I'd fire this Miss Witherspoon first thing."

As Gwyneira readied herself for a dispute with her daughter like the one she had been having with James for years, she warmed up more and more to Helen's suggestion. Some time in England could only do Kura good! If she was still too young for the conservatory, she could probably find a girls' school. Gwyneira thought of Kura's reaction to uniforms and a strict schedule. Would Kura not hate her for the rest of her life?

William arrived punctually, and his second look at Kura left him just as awestruck as the day before. What was more, this time the girl was not wearing a simple riding outfit but an elegantly tailored dress, red with colorful flourishes. The luscious colors suited her, making her skin look even more radiant and creating a pleasing contrast to her luxurious black hair. She was wearing her hair parted down the middle; Kura had braided a few strands on each side of her face and tied the braids together at the back of her head. The simple hairstyle emphasized her classically beautiful features: her high cheekbones, enticing eyes, and generally exotic mystique. William Martyn could have fallen on his knees before so much beauty.

The rules of decorum dictated, however, that he look after Elaine first, since she had been assigned to him as a dining partner. Because she would already be cooking for so many anyway, Fleurette had begged Helen and her longtime friend Leonard McDunn, the police constable, to join them, so that she would have some of her own friends there. As the stocky, mustached Leonard led Helen very attentively to the table, William hurried to do likewise with Elaine. George, who had lost all interest in his beautiful cousin, was to be Kura's dinner partner. As he adjusted her chair, William realized with delight that George had set her directly across from him.

"Have you habituated yourself to Queenstown yet, Miss Warden?" he asked when decorum finally permitted general table conversation.

Kura smiled. "Please, call me Kura." Her voice transformed even the simplest sentence into the melody of a song all her own. Even Leonard McDunn looked up from his appetizer when the girl responded. "And, to answer your question, I'm accustomed to the expanse of the plains. The landscape here is lovely, but its vibrations are completely different."

Gwyneira frowned. *Vibrations*? Elaine and George each stifled a giggle.

William beamed. "Oh, I know what you mean. Every landscape has its own melody. Sometimes, in my dreams, I hear Connemara sing."

Elaine cast a confused glance at him.

"So you're from Ireland, young man?" Leonard asked, clearly trying to move the conversation back to a more general plane. "What's going to come out of this Home Rule Bill that everyone is talking about? And what is the situation in the country? You appear to have the greatest rabble-rousers under control, of course. The last I heard of the Fenians, they were calling for an invasion of Canada to set up Ireland anew over there. A harebrained scheme, if you ask me."

William nodded. "I agree with you there, sir. Ireland is Ireland. You cannot rebuild it somewhere else."

"Ireland has a musical range all its own," Kura said. "Its melodies are melancholy, but display a stirring merriness here and there."

Elaine wondered whether Kura, too, practiced the art of *whaikorero*. Or had she read that sentence somewhere?

"A sometimes heartbreaking merriness," William affirmed.

"Well, as long as the support for the law doesn't succeed in changing the upper house's mind," Ruben opined, trying to get back to Leonard's topic.

"Which reminds me . . ." Fleurette joined the discussion using the sweet, innocuous tone she always used when the spy within her awoke. "Leonard, have you ever heard anything about an attempt on the life of Mr. Morley of Blackburn? Ireland's chief secretary?" She watched William out of the corner of her eye as she asked the question.

SONG OF THE SPIRITS

The young man almost choked on his piece of roast. Elaine didn't miss his reaction either.

"Is something wrong, Mr. Martyn?" she asked with concern.

William waved the question off impatiently.

The constable shrugged. "Oh Fleur, there's always something happening in that country. From what I understand, they're always arresting would-be terrorists of one kind or another. I occasionally receive wanted posters when the boys get away. But we haven't nabbed any of them here. They all go to America, and normally they come to their senses there. Childish antics—thank God without any serious consequences in the last few years."

William exploded. "You see the fight for a free Ireland as a childish antic?" he asked furiously.

Elaine laid her hand on his arm. "Oh dear, that's not what he meant. Mr. Martyn is a patriot, Mr. McDunn."

William shook her off.

Leonard laughed. "Most Irish are. And they have our sympathy without question, Mr. Martyn. But that's precisely why one can't go around shooting people or blowing them up! Think of the bystanders who so often become casualties."

William did not respond further. It occurred to him that he was well on his way toward behaving poorly.

"So you're a freedom fighter, William?" Kura-maro-tini suddenly asked, her big eyes seeking his. William could not tell whether he melted under her gaze or grew by leaps and bounds.

"I wouldn't necessarily put it that way," he murmured, trying for a humble tone.

"But William did stand up for the Land League," Elaine explained proudly, marking her possession by letting her hand drift over to his arm. Callie growled beneath the table. The puppy did not like it when someone touched her mistress, and the opposite was even worse. "For the tenants on his father's farm."

"Your father has a farm?" Gwyneira asked.

William nodded. "Yes, Mrs. McKenzie, he's a sheep breeder. But I'm the younger son, so there is nothing for me to inherit. I have to set about making my own fortune."

"Sheep. We have some of those ourselves," Kura remarked, as though the animals were a burden.

Fleurette could not help but notice William's rapt expression as Gwyneira went on to describe Kiward Station.

For Elaine, the evening dragged on just as the one before it had. She wasn't usually bored when William was with her, but until that night he had always focused his attention entirely on her—making jokes, furtively brushing his leg against her under the table, or casually stroking her hand. That evening, he was fixated on Kura. Perhaps she should not have told him how much the girl got on her nerves; no doubt William now wanted to distract her. But he could at least have saved up a few kind words for his sweetheart!

Elaine comforted herself with the thought that she would be able to see him out after dinner. He would kiss her under the starry sky as he had many times before, and they would exchange a few intimate words. She would have to put Callie away first, however. The little dog always protested fervently whenever William got too close to her mistress.

If only Kura's musical performance would end. As on the previous night, she played for the assembled family and guests, and William appeared to listen with genuine rapture. Kura played beautifully, without a doubt; Elaine had to grant her that. And that night, Kura was singing Irish songs—for William, it seemed. Elaine felt a pang of jealousy.

"Just sing along," Helen said, noting Elaine's growing frustration. "You know the songs too, after all."

Elaine looked questioningly at Gwyneira, and she nodded.

"That would certainly sound very nice," she said. Gwyneira would also have thought it sounded "nice" to let Callie howl along while Kura played the piano.

Elaine stood up bravely, got her bearings quickly, and then joined in on Kura's recital of "Salley Gardens." To Helen, it sounded very pleasing. Elaine's clear soprano harmonized with Kura's enticingly deep voice. And the girls looked very sweet together. The exotic, black-haired Kura and the petite, red-haired Elaine. The great poet Yeats had undoubtedly imagined just such a red-haired Irish girl when he had written the song's lyrics. Helen said something to William, but he did not seem to hear her. He was too deeply entranced by the sight of the girls—or at least one of them.

Kura broke off after a few measures, however.

"I can't sing when you can't stay in tune," she complained.

Elaine's entire face flushed. "I . . ."

"It was an F-sharp, and you sang an F," Kura continued mercilessly.

Elaine would have liked for the ground to open up and swallow her whole.

"Kura, it's a folk song," Helen explained. "You don't have to stick to the notes obsessively."

"You can only sing correctly or incorrectly," Kura insisted. "If she had sung a G or a G-sharp . . ."

Elaine returned to her seat. "Just sing alone then!" she said sullenly. And Kura did.

The incident had sobered everyone up, all the more so because no one else had noticed Elaine's small mistake. Fleurette silently thanked heaven that the visitors would be moving out the next day. Although she enjoyed having her mother stay with her, she had to admit that she liked Kura as little as she liked William. Which recalled to Fleurette's mind the matter of the assassination attempt in Ireland. Had Ruben noticed William's reaction when she'd brought it up?

As she saw William out, Elaine thought over her situation with him. He did finally put his arms around her, but it was not as intoxicating as usual and felt instead like he was simply doing his duty. And the beautiful words that he mustered for her did not excite her much either.

"That music . . . and my red-haired dear . . . I feel as though I'm in the Salley Gardens." William laughed and kissed her softly. "It's strange, those songs, they bring Ireland back to life for me."

"The vibrations" was on the tip of Elaine's tongue, but she held it back at the last moment. William was not to think she was making fun of him.

"I wish my country was free, and I could return."

Elaine frowned. "Can you not return while the English administer it? They're not looking for you, are they?"

William laughed, though it came out a bit forced. "Of course not. Where did you get that idea? I'd just rather not return to a land in chains."

Elaine remained skeptical. She tried to make him meet her gaze.

"William, you didn't have anything to do with that assassination attempt, did you? On that . . . what was his name? Morley?"

"Viscount Morley of Blackburn," William said, almost threateningly, through gritted teeth. "Chief secretary for Ireland, the highest-ranking oppressor."

"But you didn't shoot at him or plant a bomb, did you?" Elaine asked anxiously.

William glared at her. "If I had shot at him, he would be dead now. I'm a good shot. As for the bomb . . . it's just a shame we never got close to him."

Elaine was shocked. "But you tried to? Or knew about it? William!"

"If no one does anything, my country will never be free! And if we don't show them that we're prepared to do anything . . ."

William trailed off, bristling. Elaine, who had been leaning against him, backed away.

"But my father says Viscount Morley is for the Home Rule Bill," she objected.

"For or against, what does that matter? He's England's representative. By going after him, we'd have struck a blow to the House of Lords and their whole accursed band!"

William felt once again the powerful rage he had felt when he and Paddy Murphy had been stopped at the entrance of the government building. They had found the bomb on his friend—an accident that had ended up saving his life. Though William had freely admitted his complicity, his father had pulled a few strings and talked to the right people. Ultimately, Paddy, a poor farmer's son, had ended up on the scaffold, and they'd let William go. On the unofficial condition, however, that Frederic Martyn would get his son out of Ireland as quickly as possible. William had wanted to go to New York, but that was not far enough away to suit his father.

"I'd probably just hear about new idiocies. It's practically crawling with agitators over there," he said to his son as he booked his passage to New Zealand the next day. To Dunedin on the South Island, far from any nests of freedom fighters.

And now this girl was also objecting that he had tried to kill the wrong man.

"I think there is a difference," Elaine said bravely. "In war you kill only your opponent and not his confederates."

"You don't know what you're talking about!" Riled up, William turned away. "You're just a girl."

Elaine flared up angrily at him. "And girls don't understand such things? It looks like you're in the wrong country, William. Women can even vote here."

"Good things are sure to come of that!" He was immediately sorry after the words burst from his mouth. He did not want to anger her. But she was such a child!

In his head, he heard Kura's songlike speaking voice. Kura understood him. Even if she was technically younger than her cousin, she seemed more grown-up. She was already more developed, more womanly.

He caught himself thinking about Kura's full breasts and wide hips as he pulled Elaine apologetically toward him.

"I'm sorry, Lainie, but Ireland . . . you simply can't tell me about these things. Now, calm down, Lainie. Cheer up!"

Elaine had pulled back angrily from William at first, but then let herself be soothed. Still, she did not return his kiss right away. She did not seem to be in the best of spirits when she finally said good-bye to him.

William waved to her as he began to float down the river in his canoe. He would have to be especially nice to her the next day, even if her sulking got on his nerves, as he wanted to see Kura again. And for the time being, the only way to Kura was through Elaine.

6

Autumn in Queenstown was a sight to behold, with a variety of cultural and sporting events, most of which were organized by the parish. A few of the big farmers in the area threw parties as well, and the O'Keefes were invited, naturally—as were their guests from the Canterbury Plains. William received his invitations through Elaine, just as he had hoped he would. He accompanied her to church picnics and bazaars, musical evenings, and bingo games for charity. To Gwyneira's delight and amazement, Kura usually joined them and seemed to enjoy herself. This, despite the fact that the girl had only honored festivities on Kiward Station and neighboring farms with her presence against her will.

"And here I was worried that Lainie and Kura wouldn't particularly like each other," she told Helen. "But now they're always together."

"Although Lainie doesn't wear the happiest expression," Helen observed keenly.

"Happy? The child looks like an animal in a trap," Daphne interjected. The two "hotel" owners had met for their weekly tea, and Gwyneira had joined them. "I'd intervene, Helen. Kura is after Lainie's boy."

"Daphne! What a thing to say!" Helen recoiled.

Daphne rolled her eyes. "Forgive me, Helen. But I think . . . well, in my estimation, Miss Warden is showing an improper interest in Miss O'Keefe's admirer."

Gwyneira smiled. Daphne knew how to express herself appropriately for the occasion. Kura's interest in William had not entirely escaped her—though she did not quite know what to make of it. Naturally, it was unfair to Elaine, but on the other hand, she liked

William Martyn as her granddaughter's admirer a great deal more than the Maori youth Tiare.

"But thus far, Mr. Martyn has behaved entirely correctly with regards to the girls," Helen noted. "I haven't noticed him favoring one over the other."

"That's just it," said Daphne. "He's supposed to prefer Elaine. She's the one whose hopes he got up, after all. And now, at best, she gets as much attention as Kura. That has to have been a blow."

"Oh, Daphne, they're still children." Gwyneira roused herself to a halfhearted pronouncement. "He cannot properly woo either of them yet."

Daphne raised her eyebrows. "Children!" she snorted. "Don't count on it. You'd do better to watch out—Helen, for Elaine's tender soul and Gwyneira, for your heiress. For even if you're convinced that Kura's charms have not yet caused this William Martyn to lose any sleep . . . he can do other things in bed too. Counting sheep, for example. Lots and lots of sheep."

Kura Warden did not know herself what was wrong with her. Why she went along to these church picnics and let herself be chatted up by countless hicks. Why she listened to third-rate musicians and pretended she enjoyed their dilettante fiddling. Why she wasted her time with boat rides and picnics and found herself spitting out platitudes about the gorgeous landscape around Lake Wakatipu. It was all senseless, made only somewhat attractive because she was with William. She had never experienced anything like it before. She had never cared much for people. They were an audience, a mirror in which to check the effect she produced but never anything more. And now here was this William with his cheeky smile, his dimples, his flashing eyes, and his ethereal, sandy hair. Kura had never seen such a golden-blond person before; the Swedes and Norwegians in Christchurch were closest. But they were mostly pale and light-skinned, whereas William had brown skin that contrasted perfectly with his blond head of hair. And then there were his alert blue eyes, which followed her wherever she went. He made compliments without being at all salacious. His manners were irreproachable. Sometimes too irreproachable.

Kura often wished William would make more amorous advances, as Tiare had attempted to do. Naturally, she would reject his advances, but she wanted to feel the pulse of the earth—if, for example, he put his hand on her hip. The "pulse of the earth" was what Marama called it when a woman felt that tingling between her legs, that languorous ascendance of warmth through her body, the heartbeat of expectation. Kura had only rarely felt it with Tiare, but William unleashed it whenever his leg accidentally brushed her skirts under the table. Kura wished for clearer signs, but William always behaved very properly. Thus far, he had not granted her anything more than the fleeting touch of his hand whenever he helped her out of a boat or carriage. Kura, however, felt that these touches were neither accidental nor innocent. She was certain that their encounters electrified William too—that he burned with desire for her. Kura fanned that flame whenever she could.

She would have been astounded if anyone had told her how much she was hurting Elaine by doing so—she did not even notice her unhappy face and increasingly monosyllabic responses. Not that Kura would have foregone her efforts in order to spare her cousin. Kura did not even think about Elaine, who was just one more of the many unmusical and decidedly average creatures who populated the earth. Then again, it seemed that not even the gods were perfect. Certainly they succeeded only rarely in creating a masterpiece like Kura—or William Martyn. She felt that he was her soul mate, not Elaine's. Kura saw fewer similarities between herself and Elaine than between a butterfly and a moth.

For that reason, she did not consciously register what was going on between Elaine and William. Kura had no qualms about leaving the man she had chosen alone with her cousin. And so William still took Elaine home, and he still kissed her, which was the only thing that held the girl together at all that autumn.

Elaine suffered deeply whenever she heard Kura and William chatting—about music and art, the opera, or the latest books—all subjects that occupied hardly anyone's thoughts in Queenstown. It wasn't that Elaine was uneducated—as Helen O'Keefe's granddaughter, coming into contact with culture had been unavoidable. And now, because William was clearly interested in literature, she made an effort to read all the new publications and attempt to form an opinion on them. But Elaine was a pragmatic person. More than a poem a day made her fidgety, and entire volumes concentrated with poetry overwhelmed her. Elaine also did not like to have to chew over a story before its meaning—and its beauty—became clear to her. She could suffer and laugh with a book's heroes, but endless navel-gazing, lugubrious monologues, and endless descriptions of the landscape bored her. If she were honest, she liked sneaking off with her mother's magazines and reveling in the serialized stories in which women loved and suffered.

But of course she could not say any of that in front of Kura, and especially not in front of William. He had not really struck her as such an aesthete when she had first met him. Now he suddenly seemed to find nothing more satisfying than reciting poems with Kura or listening to her play the piano. His long-winded discussions with Kura spoiled all the picnics and boat regattas and other activities that she usually found so enjoyable. And she never seemed to be able to do anything right! When she leaped up and cheered at the top of her lungs for the eight-oared boat that George was rowing in, William and Kura looked at her as though she had thrown off her bodice on Main Street. And when she let herself be pulled into a rollicking round of square dancing at the church picnic, the two of them went out of their way to avoid her. The worst, however, was that she could not talk to anyone about it. Sometimes she thought she was going mad, since she it seemed that she was the only one who had noticed all of these changes in William's behavior.

Her father was as enthusiastic as ever about his help in the store, and her grandmother Helen found it completely normal for a young man to behave himself "correctly." Elaine could hardly tell her that William had already kissed her and caressed her body parts that . . . well, that a lady should not have made accessible to him. She did not want to turn to her mother, as she knew that Fleurette had never really liked William. As for her grandmother Gwyn, under normal circumstances, she would no doubt have been the ideal person to talk to. After all, Elaine felt that Kura's constant blather about art and her endless speeches about music theory got on her grandmother's nerves too. But Gwyneira loved Kura more than anything. She always reacted to critiques of her granddaughter with icy silence or took Kura's side. And she appeared to sanction William's relationship with Kura; at least, she didn't seem to have anything against the young man. Elaine often saw her grandmother chatting with William. No wonder, since his natural *whaikorero* talent could be just as eloquently employed on sheep as music.

Winter arrived. Snow blanketed the mountains, and an occasional snowstorm passed through Queenstown as well. Gwyneira acquired a fur coat for Kura, which made the girl look like a South Sea princess who had gotten lost. Framed by the wide hood of the silver-fox coat, her black hair and unusual features astounded onlookers and drew all eyes to her once more. Elaine agonized whenever William solicitously helped the clumsy girl across the icy road or laughed with her when she attempted to feel the snowflake's melody. To Elaine, they fell without a sound. By this time, she had nearly been convinced that she had no musical talent whatsoever and no sense of romance. Eventually, she couldn't take it anymore. She planned to ask William if he still loved her.

She found an opportunity to do so the following evening. Helen had arranged a music recital at her hotel. There were a few classical music lovers on the surrounding farms who played the violin, viola, and bass. They liked to come to Queenstown from time to time to play music together and then spend the night at Helen's hotel. Elaine had always played the piano at these concerts. This time, however, it was

Kura who played. Elaine had not dared to play an instrument in her cousin's presence for some time now.

The O'Keefes would also be staying in town that night, as the weather made the long trip back out to Nugget Manor too troublesome. Elaine and William snuck outside after the concert for a few stolen tender moments while the others sat relaxing with a glass of wine. However, Elaine had a feeling the whole time that William had only reluctantly left Kura behind in her circle of admirers. Her cousin was positively holding court: there was no end to the compliments on her musical talent or her beauty. Is William really thinking of me, Elaine wondered, as he pulled her close and kissed her? Or was he imagining that he was holding Kura in his arms?

"Do you still care for me?" The words burst out of her when he finally let go of her. "I mean, really care? Are you . . . are you still in love with me?"

William gave her a friendly look. "You little fool! Would I be here if I wasn't?"

That was precisely what Elaine wanted to know. But he had just offended her again by calling her a "fool."

"Seriously, William. Do you think Kura is prettier than I am?" Elaine hoped her question did not sound like begging.

William shook his head and appeared almost annoyed.

"Lainie, the difference between you and Kura is that she would never ask me such a thing!" With that, he left her standing there and walked back into the house. Did he feel insulted? Because she had suspected him of having feelings he did not? Or was it, rather, because he did not want to look her in the face?

Kura, standing behind a curtain, had observed the entire scene. She saw William kiss Elaine. She had already suspected something between them, but until then had never seen anything. Kura was not angry, however. If William kissed this girl, then surely he was only doing so to get by. Men needed girls. That, too, she had learned from the Maori. When they went a long time without lying with a woman, they became unbearable. But William deserved better. He was a gentleman. Very carefully, Kura would teach him to understand that even the pulse of the earth had a melody—and that it was more beautiful to explore it with someone who could hear it.

In June, Ruben O'Keefe and his family received a strange invitation. The Swedes in the gold-mining camps were celebrating Midsummer—completely disregarding the fact that the twenty-first of June in New Zealand was not the longest day of the year but the shortest and that, flowers were not blooming in the meadows but on windows in the form of ice crystals. A small detail like that did not, however, deter the rough men of the north. Beer and liquor tasted good in this hemisphere too, fires were blazing, and dancing warmed you up—it would just be a bit harder to pick flowers. But that was the girls' job anyway; the men could do without. To ensure that there were plenty of girls, the gold miners sent invitations to Daphne and her crew.

"The easier the girls, the easier it will be for them to jump over the fire with us!" said Søren, one of the unusual festival's organizers. "But there's no need to worry about bringing your daughter, Mr. O'Keefe. We know a lady when we see one!"

Fleurette thought it sounded like fun. She had read about Midsummer customs and wanted, if nothing else, to dance through the Saint John's fire. Ruben would have accepted the invitation anyway since the gold miners were among his best customers. Helen, however, refused to go.

"It will be too cold for my old bones. Let the children dance. Gwyn, we'll have a pleasant evening to ourselves. Daphne can come too, if she likes."

Daphne, however, shook her head and laughed. "Nahhh, Helen. I have to go and keep an eye on my girls," she explained. "So that they don't give themselves to the boys for free, and, who knows, bring a little Swede home in their bellies! It's supposed to be a fertility ritual, jumping through the fire and all, isn't that right? You have to watch out for those."

While Elaine was looking forward to the festival, Kura had mixed feelings. Once again, there would be awfully coarse men and a band that would play every second note off-key; she would freeze and everybody would talk about stupid things. But William would be there, and there would be dancing. There might even be proper dancing, not that hopping around that passed for dancing at the church picnic. Kura had learned to dance—waltzes and the like—from Miss Witherspoon. It would be wonderful to sway with William to real music, to rest in his arms and let herself be carried by the rhythm . . . Kura felt a gentle regret that she did not have a ball gown. But the O'Keefes would have laughed at her anyway, as everyone would be wearing their warmest clothes that night.

The girls at the festival grounds wrapped themselves tight, shivering in coats and shawls. One or two of the Swedish women wore traditional clothing. The scenery had a surreal quality to it, for it had long since grown dark and the moon hung high above the snowy mountains. The girls danced around the midsummer pole, their brightly decorated red hats lit up by the fire. The men did their best to see that no one got too cold. Liquor and beer, as well as mulled wine for the women, flowed freely, creating inner heat. Already rather tipsy, Daphne's little group was flirting with the gold miners. And once the two Swedish women had explained the dance around the midsummer pole to them, the girls got themselves tangled up in the brightly colored ribbons.

Though Elaine surveyed the scene with interest, Kura seemed to be disgusted. Both of them had started off with wine, but as they began to get cold, they grew to appreciate the warm drink, which quickly caused them to forget their reserve. Elaine suddenly decided to join the dancers, and ended up twirling around the midsummer pole and laughing, hand in hand with a towheaded, blue-eyed girl named Inger. Then Inger came up to her and Kura and held a couple of withered plants out to them.

"Here, you don't have any flowers yet!" Inger spoke with a funny accent. "But that's part of Midsummer. A girl has to gather seven different kinds of flowers and lay them under her pillow on Saint John's eve. Then she'll dream of the man she's going to marry."

Elaine took the rather sad bouquet Inger was offering and thanked her. Kura, however, hardly looked at hers. She was once again morose and bored. William was chatting with Ruben and a few gold miners on the other side of the fire, and Elaine had long since stopped trying to talk to her.

"We gathered them by first light this morning, according to custom," Inger explained, although the selection had necessarily been limited. "They're all cooking herbs and houseplants. So if you only dream of cooks and layabouts, you mustn't take it too seriously."

Elaine laughed and asked the girl about Sweden. Inger answered enthusiastically. She had emigrated with a boy she had been madly in love with. But they had hardly reached Dunedin when he found someone else.

"It's *owful*, no?" Inger asked in her funny accent, but it sounded like she was still hurt. "He brings someone else along, and then . . . though of course I was the one who made the money for the trip."

Apparently in the horizontal trade since Inger let it be known that she would have done just about anything for this man.

Elaine looked over at William. Would she do anything for him too? Would he do anything for her?

The festival had taken awhile to get going, but by the time the fire began to die out, it had been fun for everyone—except Kura. She'd had other dances in mind, she explained in a dignified tone when a drunken young gold miner worked up the courage to ask her to dance. In the end, she let William talk her into a jump through the fire. Elaine looked on sullenly. Was that not a custom for those who were in love?

Ruben and Fleurette finally announced that it was time to go, before the festival was completely over. This was when Daphne had to keep an eye on her girls—though she ignored Inger and Søren's kissing. Perhaps Inger will dream of him tonight, Elaine thought, carefully gathering up her bouquet. Søren seemed to be a nice man, and the towheaded girl deserved better than the life of a prostitute.

Ruben and Fleurette wanted to head straight back to Nugget Manor. They did not want to spend the night in town, as their Maori servants were also at a festival and they had left George alone—a situation about which he had complained bitterly. He, too, would have liked to romp through the fire, but there was school the next day. Fleurette wanted to find out if the boy was in his bed as he should be.

Elaine insisted, however, on returning to town with William and Kura. She had left her horse in Helen's stable, riding with the two of them in a carriage, so she had a legitimate reason.

"But you can rent a horse from here," Ruben said, not comprehending. "Why did you leave Banshee in town anyway? You could just have easily ridden behind the carriage."

Fleurette laid her hand on his arm, trying to appease him. How could men be so dense? She understood that Elaine did not want to leave her admirer alone with Kura for even a second.

"I'll explain it to you later," she whispered to her husband, at which point Ruben stopped insisting. "But don't take too long, Lainie. Ride quickly and don't stop for anything!"

William looked indignant. He did not think it ladylike for Elaine to ride such a long way alone at night. Was he expected to accompany her? Elaine merely laughed when he halfheartedly offered to do so. She had come into the hotel for a last cup of tea to warm herself up after the carriage ride, and Helen and Gwyneira were still sitting by the fire.

"William, I ride circles around you. You already complain that I gallop down that 'dangerous path' by day. At night you would only hold me up."

She was no doubt correct, but had not expressed herself particularly well, Helen thought. After all, no man liked to be told he was a skittish rider. William looked correspondingly sour, but Elaine did not appear to notice. She blithely told her grandmothers about the midsummer pole and the flowers she had to lay under her pillow.

She is a child, William mused, and in his heart, he realized that sounded like an excuse for her having just rebuffed him . . . and for his being in love with Kura.

When Elaine left shortly thereafter, he accompanied her outside. That went without saying; he was a gentleman, after all. His good-bye kiss was barely a peck, though Elaine seemed not to notice. So close to her grandmother's watchful eye, she did not dare make any affectionate gestures either, as Helen would know all too well what was going on if Callie started barking. The little dog still did not like it when William embraced her.

With something close to a sense of relief, William followed Elaine with his eyes as Banshee began to trot away. She would let the horse go at a warm-up pace until she had passed Main Street, and then ride briskly home, followed by that crazy little dog. She would probably even enjoy herself. William shook his head. So much of Elaine's behavior would always be incomprehensible to him. In complete contrast to Kura.

Kura-maro-tini crept out of the house. The light in Helen's salon had just gone out. She had been sent to her room, but she was staying on the ground floor. From her window, she had watched as William said good-bye to Elaine.

William was happy that he had not seriously kissed Elaine. It would not have felt right to him if Kura, who was now leaning as if by chance against the wall to the right of the front door, had caught him in the arms of someone else. No one could see Kura from a window. She had thrown on her fur coat but had not closed it, and he could see the dress she was wearing underneath. The top three buttons had already been undone. Kura wore her hair down, and as it flowed over the pale fox fur, the moon made it glow silver.

"I needed some fresh air because it's so hot inside," she said, playing with the fourth button on her dress.

William stepped closer to her. "You look beautiful," he said, awestruck, and then wanted to hit himself for that. Why could he not think of a wittier compliment? Normally he did not find it the least bit difficult to come up with the right words.

Kura smiled. "Thank you," she said quietly, drawing the word out into a tune that promised heaven.

William could not think of a reply. Slowly, almost timidly, he touched her hair. It was smooth as silk.

Kura trembled. Though she seemed to be shivering, had she not just said that she was hot?

"Strange to think that it's summer elsewhere," her voice crooned. "Do you celebrate these festivals in Ireland as well?"

"On the first of May rather than the end of June," William replied, suddenly sounding hoarse. "People used to call it Beltane. A spring festival."

"A fertility festival," Kura said alluringly. She started to sing. "When the summer comes and the trees bloom lovely . . ."

As Kura sang, Queenstown's icy Main Street seemed to sink away, and William found himself in Ireland again, kissing Bridget, the daughter of his father's tenant, feeling her warmth and desire.

And then he took Kura in his arms. It just happened. He had not really wanted to. She was so young, and there was Elaine, in spite of everything, and his job here in Queenstown, but more importantly just then, there was Kura. Her scent, her soft body. Kura was the beginning and the end. He could have lost himself in her kiss. Kura was the earth and the moonlight. She was the silver gleaming lake and the eternal sea. At first, William kissed her slowly and tentatively, but she pulled him closer and returned his tender advances wildly and—evidently—knowledgeably. This was nothing wary or timid like Elaine. Kura was not delicate and fragile, not coy like the girl in the Salley Gardens, but as open and alluring as the blossoms that people heaped on the altar of the goddess at Beltane. As William tugged her dress down a bit to caress the smooth, soft skin of her shoulder, Kura rubbed against him, mussing his hair and placing little kisses, then little bites, on his throat. Both had long since forgotten the need to stay hidden within the cover of the house. It was as though they were dancing with one another on the hotel's terrace.

Elaine had just left Main Street behind and directed Banshee toward the river when she remembered something. The flowers! She had left the flowers that Inger had worked so hard to gather next to Helen's fireplace. Would it still work if she put them under her pillow the following night? Probably not, as it would no longer be Saint John's eve. And Inger might ask her about it. Elaine hoped so anyway. Inger might have been a woman of easy virtue, but she was almost like a friend, and Elaine desperately wanted to whisper and giggle with her about their dreams. If she wanted to know what her future husband would look like, she would have to ride back. If she galloped, she would lose no more than five minutes.

Banshee turned back unwillingly. Elaine had wanted to get home as quickly as possible and had ridden at a correspondingly energetic gallop. And now back to Main Street? That did not suit the mare one bit, but she was an obedient horse and let herself be turned around.

"Come on, Banshee, when I go in, I'll grab you a cookie," Elaine whispered to her.

William and Kura really should have heard the hoofbeats, but the two of them were making their own music that night, and could hear nothing but the other's breath and heartbeat as they felt the pulse of the earth.

Elaine might not even have noticed the couple if they had remained in the house's shadows. She had expected the hotel to be locked and meant to enter through the stables. But Kura and William were standing in the moonlight, captured by a beam of light as though on a stage. Banshee shied back when she saw the two of them, and stamped her hooves into the ground. Elaine's breath caught. She could not comprehend it. It had to be her imagination. If she closed and then reopened her eyes, surely she would not see William and Kura together.

She tried to catch her breath and blink, but when she looked again, they were still kissing. Oblivious, they formed a single silhouette in the moonlight that lit up the street. Suddenly a light went on in the house, and the front door opened.

"Kura! For heaven's sake, what are you doing out there?" It was her grandmother Helen! So it was not her imagination. Her grandmother had seen it too.

Not even Helen could say what had compelled her to go downstairs one last time before going to bed—perhaps it was the flowers that Elaine had forgotten. She had spoken of them with such high expectation, and she knew she would almost certainly come back when she noticed that she had forgotten them. And there were these shadows in front of the house, or maybe one shadow.

And hoofbeats.

Helen saw how Kura and William were fondling each other—and looked for the length of a heartbeat into Elaine's horrified, wide-open eyes before Banshee reared up on her hind legs and galloped down Main Street as if the devil were on her heels.

"You'll come inside this instant, Kura! And you, Mr. Martyn, please seek new lodging immediately. You will not spend another night under the same roof as this child. Go to your room, Kura. We'll speak in the morning!" Helen's lips formed a thin line, and a deep wrinkle furrowed her brow. William suddenly understood why the gold miners had such immense respect for her.

"But . . ." the word stuck in his throat as Helen looked at him.

"No 'buts,' Mr. Martyn. I do not want to see you here anymore."

7

"Believe me, Fleur, I didn't fire him!"

Ruben O'Keefe was growing tired of his wife's inquisitions. He hated that his wife was taking her anger out on him, when he was entirely innocent of the family catastrophe involving Elaine, William, and Kura.

"He quit. Wants to go to the Canterbury Plains, he said. His future requires him to be around sheep."

"I can believe that," Fleurette spat out furiously. "He probably has his eye on ten thousand sheep in particular! I never trusted that boy. We should have told him straightaway to get lost."

Fleurette could tell that she was getting on Ruben's nerves, but she needed a lightning rod. She had heard Elaine come home the night before, but she hadn't said anything. The next morning, the girl didn't come down to breakfast, and Fleur discovered that Banshee had been only sloppily tended to in her stall. Elaine had fed her and thrown a blanket over her, but she hadn't washed or even brushed the mare. The dried-on sweat in her coat spoke of a hard ride, and it was not like Elaine to neglect her horse. When she finally went upstairs to see what was wrong, she found her daughter crying inconsolably in bed, her puppy pressed against her. Fleurette could get nothing out of her. Helen first reported what had happened that afternoon.

That alone was difficult enough to believe. Helen drove out to Nugget Manor alone in a borrowed dogcart pulled by Leonard's horse. She avoided driving or even riding whenever she could. She'd had a mule in the Canterbury Plains, but after Nepumuk died, she had never acquired a new animal to ride. And she had not asked for Gwyneira's assistance that day.

"Your mother's packing," she explained through pursed lips when Fleurette alluded to this. "She's very sorry about all of this, and she understands that it's better if Elaine is spared having to see Kura for a while. Otherwise, she was rather reticent about punishment. There is no longer any question of boarding school in England, or in Wellington, for that matter. Even though that would be the only solution when it comes to that spoiled brat. She has to learn that she cannot have everything she wants."

"You mean she seduced William?" Fleurette asked. She was not disposed to grant the young man extenuating circumstances.

Helen shrugged. "She certainly did not discourage him. He didn't drag her out of the house. She must have followed him and Elaine outside. Besides, there wasn't much seducing to be done. Or as Daphne put it, men fall to that girl's feet like ripe plums."

Fleurette almost had to laugh. She was not used to that kind of expression coming from Helen.

"And now he's going to follow her to the Canterbury Plains. What does my mother say to that?" she asked.

Helen shrugged again. "I don't think she knows about that yet. But I have a rather hateful suspicion. I am afraid your mother may see William as the answer to her prayers."

"Elaine will get over it."

Fleurette heard those words again and again over the next few weeks. William's departure was the talk of the town, of course. Although Elaine had been the only witness to his shared caresses with Kura, several customers and employees had heard rumors. And people, especially the women, were able to put two and two together, at least when the Canterbury Plains were mentioned and with Gwyneira and Kura Warden leaving on practically the same day. Elaine hardly dared go into town, though Fleurette reminded her that she had nothing to be ashamed of. Most people were rather sympathetic. The older citizens of Queenstown had not envied Elaine her suitor, and there were not many respectable girls her own age around who would savor gossip about her bad luck. Nevertheless, Elaine cried unceasingly. She hid herself away in her room and sobbed as if she would never stop.

"What goes around comes around," Daphne said when Helen told her what had happened over tea.

Elaine no longer greeted new guests at the reception desk, and she had stopped helping out in the store. If she was not crying, she wandered the woods with her horse and her dog. Unavoidably, she went past places she had been with William—picnic sites, spots where they had kissed, and so on—with the result that she inevitably broke down in tears again.

"It was her first love. She just has to push through," Daphne said. "I still remember how I howled back then. I was twelve, and he was a sailor. He took my virginity, the bastard, and didn't even pay me. No, he told me he would marry me and take me around the world. What an idiot I was. Since when do sailors take their sweethearts to sea? But he spun his yarn about how he would stow me away in a lifeboat. When he disappeared, my world shattered. I've never trusted another man since. But that's the exception, Helen. Most fall for the next boy straightaway. It would be good for your Lainie to have something to do. Sitting around crying won't do her a bit of good."

So Helen tried to convince Elaine to give up her exile, with Fleurette and Ruben's encouragement. Still, it was a few weeks before she could be lured back to town and talked into working in the store or the hotel.

The girl who displayed fabric and registered guests was no longer the old Elaine. Not only because she had lost weight and looked pale and tired—those came with heartbreak, Daphne explained. More alarming was Elaine's behavior. She no longer laughed with people, no longer walked through town with her head held high, no longer let her locks blow free in the wind. Instead, she tried to make herself invisible. She preferred to help in the kitchen rather than work at the reception desk, and was more inclined to find tasks in the storehouse than to assist customers. When she bought a dress, she no longer chose anything cheery or colorful, but instead opted for something inconspicuous. As for her hair, which William had once described "as though spun from copper by angels"—another line he had never really meant—Elaine had once let it dance around her as though electrified. Now, however, she straightened it impatiently with water before tying it into a bun behind her head.

The girl seemed strangely shriveled. She shuffled about with a sunken gaze and hunched back. Every look in the mirror was a form of torture for Elaine, who saw only an ugly, average face staring back at her. Dumb and lacking in talent, she was nothing in comparison to the wonderful Kura Warden. Elaine saw herself as scrawny and flat-chested, where she had once thought herself slim and petite. "Elfin," William had said. At the time she had thought that a wonderful compliment. But what man wanted an elf? Men wanted a goddess like Kura!

Elaine sank into self-flagellation, though Inger tried repeatedly to cheer her up. The girls had become friends, and the news that her father had hired Søren to take William's place in the store and that the young Swede wanted to marry Inger had drawn Elaine out of her sorrow, for a while at least. But Inger was no real help. Elaine was not exactly complimented when her friend remarked casually that Daphne would chomp at the bit for a girl like her. Sure, she was good enough for a brothel, but a man like William could never love her.

As time went on, William's face began to fade from her memory. She could think about his touch and his kisses without feeling the acute pain that they would happen no more. In short, exactly what Daphne and everyone else had prophesied would happen, did. Elaine got over what William did.

But not what Kura did.

William set out for the Canterbury Plains on the same day as Gwyneira and Kura, though the three of them did not travel together, of course. Gwyneira had packed her light baggage in her buggy and asked Ruben to send the rest of her things along on the next supply transport to Christchurch. Then she had turned her horse northward and trotted off. After bedding down for a night in the gold-miners' camp again, William had to buy a horse before he could be on his way. Ultimately, however, he moved faster than Gwyneira and Kura because, on the return journey the two of them spent the night only on farms that were known to them and therefore had to take occasional detours.

William kept his breaks short. He did not like sleeping in the wild, and the winter weather was biting cold. So he reached Haldon a full two days earlier than Gwyneira, rented a room in a rather dingy local hotel, and immediately began looking for work in town. The settlement did not particularly appeal to him. Haldon consisted only of a single Main Street, which was lined with the usual businesses—a pub, a doctor, an undertaker, a smith, and a general store with a large lumberyard. The entire town consisted of one- and two-story wooden houses, many of which could have used a fresh coat of paint. The street was not well paved, proving muddy in winter and no doubt dusty in summer. In addition, it seemed to be in the middle of nowhere—true, there was a little lake, but aside from that, there was only grassland in every direction, which managed to remain a restrained green despite the cold season. In the distance on a clear day, one could see the mountains. Though they looked near enough, this impression was an illusion. A person would have to ride for hours to come perceptibly any closer to them.

Throughout the wide area surrounding Haldon were numerous sheep farms, large and small, which all lay many miles apart from each other. There was also talk of Maori villages in the area, but exactly where they were almost no one knew, as the natives often migrated from one location to another.

Everyone, however, knew Kiward Station, the Wardens' farm. Mrs. Dorothy Candler, the store owner's wife and apparently the town's gossip center, gave William a comprehensive explanation of the family's history. She reported with reverence that Gwyneira McKenzie was real landed gentry from Wales, and that a certain Gerald Warden, the founder of Kiward Station, had brought her to New Zealand many years ago.

"Just think, on the same ship I came on! God, I was afraid of the passage. But not Mrs. McKenzie, she was happy to come. She was looking for adventure. She came here to marry Gerald Warden's son, Lucas. A pleasant man, Lucas Warden, really an admirable, very restrained gentleman—only he didn't have much to do with the farm. He was more of an artist, you see. He painted. Later he disappeared—to England, Mrs. McKenzie says, to sell his paintings. But it's hard to say if that's true. There were a lot of rumors going around for a while. At some point he was declared dead, may he rest in peace. And Mrs. McKenzie married this James McKenzie fellow. He's a nice man, really. I don't want to say anything bad about Mr. McKenzie, but he was a rustler, you know! The McKenzie Highlands were named after him. He hid out there until a man named Sideblossom caught him. Well, and then Gerald Warden met his end on the same day as Howard O'Keefe. Bad business that, bad business. Mr. O'Keefe killed Mr. Warden, whose grandson then shot Mr. O'Keefe. Later they tried to play it off as an accident."

After a half hour with Mrs. Candler, William's head was spinning. It would take him some time to make sense of all that. But this first impression of the Wardens was encouraging: compared with all the misconduct in this family, a thwarted attempt on an Irish politician's life was rather a venial sin.

Nevertheless, he would have to work hard to make a good impression. After the scandal Helen O'Keefe had made of his few kisses with Kura, Mrs. McKenzie was certainly not going to be speaking well of him. That was why William went straight to work looking for a job. He had to have a secure position before he called on the Wardens. Mrs. McKenzie was not to think he was after Kura's inheritance, after all. An allegation he would be prepared to deny categorically at any time! Financial considerations may have played a small role in his courtship of Elaine, but when it came to Kura, William would have wanted her even if she were a beggar.

The situation did not look promising on the surrounding sheep farms. Management positions were not being offered at all. William would have been able to start as a shepherd, but even those jobs were hard to come by in the winter—and didn't take into account the miserably low wages, primitive lodging, and hard work. Yet his work as a bookkeeper in Ruben's store proved helpful. The Candlers were positively enthusiastic when he inquired about a job. Dorothy's husband, who had only been to the village school himself, reacted almost euphorically to William's educational history.

"I'm always having trouble with the books!" he freely admitted. "It's practically a punishment for me. I love spending time with people, and I understand buying and selling. But numbers? I keep those more in my head than in the books."

Mr. Candler's records reflected that. Even after only a fleeting glance, William found several ways to simplify storage and, even more importantly, to save on taxes. Candler grinned like a Cheshire cat and gave William a bonus immediately. Dorothy, a model housewife, looked around for lodging suitable to William's station. She arranged for him to sublet a room in her sister-in-law's house and invited him almost every day to eat with them—during which time she took the opportunity to parade her sweet daughter Rachel before his eyes. Under other circumstances, William probably would not have said no. Rachel was a tall girl with dark hair and soft brown eyes, a beauty through and through, but compared to Kura, like Elaine, she fell short.

None of the Wardens or McKenzies made an appearance in town for a while. Kiward Station made purchases, of course, but Gwyneira usually sent employees to pick the items up. Dorothy revealed to him during one of their regular, gossip-laden teatimes that Gwyneira bought almost all of her dresses in Christchurch.

"Now that the roads are better, that's not as difficult as it once was. It used to be a trip around the world, but now . . . And the little one, her granddaughter, is really rather spoiled. I can't remember her ever setting foot in our store. She has to have every little thing sent from London."

William found this information disappointing. Of course, it was wonderful that Kura had taste, and the dress selection at the Candlers' store would truly have been beneath her. But he had hoped that he would run into her in Haldon—at first, by chance and later, perhaps, even secretly—and he realized that that was not going to happen.

Nevertheless, Mrs. McKenzie finally appeared, almost six weeks after William had arrived in the Canterbury Plains. She sat on the box of a covered wagon beside a somewhat older but tall and powerful-looking man. They greeted the town's residents self-assuredly, though the man did not give the impression of being an employee. This had to be her husband, James McKenzie. William used his hidden position in the general store's office to get a closer look at the pair. Mr. McKenzie had brown, slightly shaggy hair with a hint of gray. His skin was brown and weathered, and like Mrs. McKenzie, his face was dominated by laugh lines. The two of them appeared to enjoy a harmonious marriage. Especially noticeable, though, were James's alert brown eyes, which looked friendly, but made clear that he was not a man easily fooled.

William considered whether he should seek out James's acquaintance, but decided against it. Mrs. McKenzie might have complained about him. It was better to let things settle down for a few more weeks. He suddenly felt a deep urge to see Kura again, however. So the following Sunday he saddled his horse, which hadn't had much to do since he'd arrived, and rode to Kiward Station.

Like most visitors, William was quite struck by the sight of the manor house set in the middle of the wilderness. He had been rambling along through mostly untouched land, past endless grassy plains, which didn't look as though they'd been grazed and which were only occasionally interrupted by a rock formation or a small crystal clear lake. And then riding around a bend, he suddenly thought he'd been set down in rural England. An immaculately tended entry road carefully covered with gravel led through a sort of avenue sown with southern beeches and cabbage trees, and then opened onto a circular flower bed planted with blooming red bushes. Beyond it lay the approach to Kiward Station. That was no farm; that was a palace!

The house had obviously been designed and built by English architects from the gray sandstone typical of the country, which was only used in cities like Christchurch and Dunedin for "monumental buildings." Kiward Station had two floors, and the facade was enlivened by numerous turrets, oriels, and balconies. The stables could not be seen, but William supposed they were behind the house along with a garden. He had no doubt that this residence had a well-tended landscape garden, perhaps even a rose garden—even if Gwyneira McKenzie had not encouraged the impression that gardening was among her passions. Something like that would appeal more to Kura. William let himself daydream of her, dressed in white with a flower-decorated straw hat, plucking a few roses from the bushes and climbing up the stairs to the house with a basket full of flowers.

But the thought of Kura also brought him back to reality. He couldn't simply barge his way in here. He would never run into the girl "by accident" on this estate, especially since he knew that Kura was not exactly a nature lover. If she left the house, then surely it would only be to visit the gardens, and those were likely fenced in. Besides, the area was probably swarming with gardeners. The carefully maintained approach alone suggested there must be several of them.

William turned his horse around. He wanted to avoid being seen. Lost in his dismal thoughts, he began to circle the estate from a distance. A farm road led from the manor house to the stables and paddocks, where horses were chewing on the sparse winter grass. William did not turn in that direction, as the danger of meeting people who would ask him what he was doing there seemed too great. Instead, he took a narrow footpath through the grassland and stumbled upon a copse of trees. The southern beeches and the lack of underbrush appeared European, and he was momentarily reminded of England or Ireland. A path that looked more worn by people's feet than horses' hooves wound through the thicket. Full of curiosity, William followed the path.

After rounding a bend, he almost collided with a young woman who seemed as lost in thought as he was. She wore an austere dress, which she'd paired with a small dark hat that made her look older. She made the surreal impression on William of an English governess on her way to church.

The young man halted his horse at the last moment and put on his kindest and most apologetic smile. He would have to quickly think up an excuse for being there.

The woman did not exactly look like a specialist in animal husbandry. Maybe she thought he was one of the workers. William greeted her politely and then added, "Excuse me." If he simply rode on right away, the woman would no doubt hardly remember him.

At first, she didn't even lift her head. Only after his apology did she grant him a look. William cursed his upper-class accent. He really ought to try to develop his Irish accent.

"There is no need to apologize. I didn't notice you either. The paths here are an affront." The woman made an indignant face but then tried a shy smile. Her pale-blonde hair, pale skin, and gray-blue eyes made her look washed out, and her face was a little long but finely formed. "Can I offer you some assistance? You don't really mean to be going to visit the Maori?"

The way the woman pronounced the word, one might think she was referring to a tribe of cannibals and that visiting them would be an act of madness. In her plain dark-gray dress and boring black hat, she could have been mistaken for a missionary. She was carrying some sort of songbook under her arm.

William smiled. "No, I wanted to go to Haldon," he claimed. "But this doesn't appear to be the right way."

The woman frowned. "Indeed, you have gotten rather lost. This is the footpath between the Maori camp and Kiward Station. The building behind you is the manor, and you have probably already ridden past the Maori camp, but you cannot see it from the road. Your best option would be to ride back to the house and take the main road."

William nodded. "How could I go against advice spoken from such charming lips?" he asked gallantly. "But what is a young lady such as yourself doing among the Maori?"

This last point truly did interest him. This woman spoke flawless upper-class English, albeit with a slight twang.

The woman rolled her eyes. "I have been asked to, well, to bring some religion to these savages. The pastor asked me to hold a devotion in the camp on Sundays. Their former teacher, Helen O'Keefe, always did that, and Mrs. Warden continued it."

"Mrs. Gwyneira Warden?" William asked, surprised, though he risked his cover by doing so. Gwyneira had not struck him as the godly type.

"No, Mrs. Marama Warden. She is Maori herself, but she married again and now lives at O'Keefe Station in the next camp. She runs a school there." The young lady did not look like the missionary work made her particularly happy. But wait—had she not just mentioned teaching? Could this be Kura Warden's governess?

William could hardly believe his luck—that is, if the relationship between Kura and her beloved Miss Witherspoon was really as close as the girl had indicated in Queenstown.

"You teach the Maori?" he inquired. "Do you only teach there, or—I hardly dare ask—but Miss Warden spoke very affectionately of a Miss Witherspoon."

Kura had not actually spoken about her tutor with "affection," but, at best, with a sense of forced alliance against all the philistines all around them. Regardless, Miss Witherspoon was the only person at Kiward Station with whom Kura enjoyed halfway friendly relations. And the young woman looked like she could use some encouragement.

A wide smile spread over Miss Witherspoon's strict face. "Really? Kura spoke warmly of me? How do you know Miss Warden?"

The young woman looked at him searchingly, and William worked to assume a contrite and simultaneously waggish expression. Could it really be that Kura had not even mentioned him?

Then Miss Witherspoon seemed to come to her own conclusions.

"Wait a moment. You're not . . . ?" Miss Witherspoon's distrustful look gave way to excitement. "But you must be! You are William Martyn, are you not? According to Kura's description . . ."

Kura had described William down to the last detail—his blond hair, his dimpled smile, the radiant blue eyes. Miss Witherspoon beamed at him. "How romantic! Kura knew you would come. She simply knew it. She has been dreadfully depressed ever since Mrs. McKenzie was suddenly called back from Queenstown."

Called back? William realized they had probably not told the governess everything. Even Kura seemed to have confided only a limited amount to her. William decided to exercise caution. However, this colorless creature was his only hope, so he brought his charm back into play.

"I did not wait so much as a day, Miss Witherspoon. After Kura departed, I resigned my position, bought a horse, and here I am. I have a position in Haldon—not a management position yet, I must admit, but I plan to work my hardest! One day I would like to court Kura openly."

Miss Witherspoon's face glowed. That was exactly what she wanted to hear. She obviously had a weakness for romantic stories.

"Thus far, it has proved rather difficult." William did not say why, but the young woman came up with a few reasons of her own right away.

"Kura is still rather young, of course," she remarked. "One has to grant Mrs. McKenzie that, even though the girl does not accept it herself. Kura was quite incensed when she was so suddenly . . . er . . . torn from your side." Miss Witherspoon blushed.

William lowered his head. "It broke my heart as well," he admitted. He hoped he wasn't laying it on too thick, but Miss Witherspoon looked understanding. "Please do not misunderstand me, though. I am well acquainted with the responsibility. Kura is like a flower in its prime that has not yet fully bloomed. It would be irresponsible to . . . too soon . . ." If he said "to pluck her," this young lady would likely die of shame. William simply chose not to finish the sentence. "I am, in any event, prepared to wait for Kura. Until she is of age . . . or Mrs. McKenzie recognizes her as such."

"Kura is quite mature for her age!" Miss Witherspoon expanded on the point. "It would surely be a mistake to treat her like a child."

Kura had indeed been sulking since her return from Queenstown, and just that morning there had been another unpleasant confrontation between her and James McKenzie. It took place during the fifth repetition of the Bach oratorio that Kura was working on while the rest of the family ate breakfast. For James, it was the straw that broke the camel's back.

Kura did not need to have meals with them, he explained, but she should spare them her moods. Either way, he would not listen to that depressing music a moment longer, he said. Even a cow would lose its appetite! While Jack, giggling, had taken sides with his father, Mrs. McKenzie had remained silent, as usual. In the end, Kura fled, insulted, to her room, and Heather Witherspoon had followed to comfort her. At which point she became the next person over whom the storm cloud broke. She was not to support Kura in her folly, Mrs. McKenzie informed her, and was instead to see to her obligations and hold the devotion with the Maori.

William knew none of that, of course, but he sensed Miss Witherspoon's resentment toward Mr. and Mrs. McKenzie. He decided to risk it.

"Miss Witherspoon, would it be possible for me to see Kura just once? Without involving her grandparents? I do not have anything indecent in mind, by any means. I'd just like to get a look at her. A simple hello from her would make me so happy. And I hope very much that she likewise yearns for me." William observed his conversation partner attentively. Had he struck the right note?

"Yearns for you?" Miss Witherspoon asked, flushed, her voice wavering. "Mr. Martyn, she's being eaten up inside! The girl is suffering. You should hear her singing! Her voice has become even more expressive. She feels so deeply."

William was delighted to hear that, though he did not recall Kura being quite so sentimental. He had difficulty imagining her bursting into tears. But if Miss Witherspoon wanted to play the role of a lifesaver who could prevent the suicide of someone with a broken heart . . .

"Miss Witherspoon," he broke in. "I do not meant to push too hard, but is there any possibility, truly?"

The woman finally seemed to consider the matter seriously. And came quickly to an answer.

"Maybe in church," she concluded. "I cannot promise anything, but I'll see what can be done. In any event, go to service next Sunday in Haldon."

"Kura wants to go to Haldon?" James McKenzie asked, dumbfounded. "The princess is prepared to mix with the common folk? Why this sudden change of heart?"

"Now James, just be happy, instead of only looking at the dark side of everything." Gwyneira had just explained to her husband that Miss Witherspoon and Kura intended to attend the coming Sunday service. The rest of the family could ride along or simply enjoy a peaceful Sunday morning without arias and adagios. That alone was reason enough to skip the service.

Wild horses could not have dragged James and Jack to town— even if they were a bit curious about what exactly was drawing Kura to Haldon. Gwyneira, too, was looking forward to an undisturbed family breakfast with Jack—or just alone with James in their room. In fact, she would like that even better. "Kura has been working so long on this strange Bach piece. Now she wants to hear it on the organ. That's understandable."

"And she means to play it herself? In front of every Tom, Dick, and Harry in Haldon? Gwyn, there's something very strange about all this." James furrowed his brow and whistled for his dog. Gwyneira had sought out her husband in the stables. Andy and a few other men were deworming the ewes while James directed the sheepdogs who were driving the ewes to them. At the moment, Monday was contentedly following on the heels of a thick, rebellious ball of wool.

"Who else is supposed to play it?" Gwyneira asked, pulling the hood of her waxed jacket over her head. It was raining again. "The organist in Haldon is terrible." This last point was one of the reasons that Kura had not attended church in Haldon for years.

The winter weather caused James to bring up another objection. "Say, Gwyn, isn't that piece the *Easter Oratorio*? It's August."

Gwyneira rolled her eyes. "As far as I'm concerned, it could just as well be the *Papa Loves Rangi Oratorio*." James grinned at the mention of the Maori creation myth that spoke of the separation of the lovers, Rangi, who represented heaven, and Papa, the earth. "The main thing is that Kura is no longer walking around here with a face like the suffering Christ and is finally moving on."

8

Hearing Kura Warden at the organ in Haldon was an experience. And the Sunday service was better attended than it had been for months. No wonder, since every resident of the town was dying to see and hear the mysterious Warden heiress. Her effect on the service was quite positive, and the prayers were spoken with uncommon zeal that day. All the men fell into various states of prayer as soon as their eyes fell on Kura's face and figure, while the women were overcome by the girl's singing. Kura's voice filled the small church with harmony, and her organ playing was virtuosic, despite the fact that she had practiced only once.

William could not get over seeing her slender figure in the gallery. Kura wore a simple but flattering navy-blue velvet dress. Her hair, pulled back from her face by a velvet band, fell like a dark current down her back. William imagined kissing the delicate yet powerful fingers now flitting across the organ's keys, and he could have sworn he could feel anew how those fingers had explored his face and body that night in Queenstown. Naturally, Kura sat facing away from the congregation as she played. Yet she occasionally lifted her head a bit from the music so that William could see her face. Her equal-parts exotic and aristocratic features and the holy earnestness with which she played put him under her spell once again. He had to talk to her after service. No, he had to kiss her! Just seeing her would be too much to bear. He had to touch her, feel her, breathe in her scent.

William forced himself to smile at Miss Witherspoon, who was sitting upright in one of the front pews, occasionally looking at him, as if for praise. Because she had arranged this meeting? If that was the case, she would probably be willing to do more to bring the lovers together. Or was she merely proud of her highly gifted student?

In the end, Dorothy Candler led William straight to Kura. Like almost every citizen in Haldon, she was dying to see the prodigy up close, and William offered her the perfect excuse.

"Come, Mr. Martyn, let's say hello. You know the girl, do you not? She was just in Queenstown visiting relatives. Surely you were introduced to her."

William mumbled something about her being a "passing acquaintance," but Dorothy had already taken him by the arm and, encouraged, steered him toward Kura and Miss Witherspoon.

"You played exceptionally well, Miss Warden," Dorothy said. "I'm the head of the women's group, and I can assure you on behalf of all of us that it was wonderful. By the way, this gentleman is Mr. Martyn. I believe you've met."

Kura had, until that moment, been staring into the crowd—or rather, through the crowd—with her habitual bored gaze. But suddenly a spark of life flickered into her radiant blue eyes. Her expression of interest was quite restrained, as Kura knew that she was being observed. William could not help thinking about Elaine. At a moment like this, she would have blushed and lost her ability to speak; he was sure of it. But Kura proved her maturity in this situation.

"Indeed, Mr. Martyn. A pleasure to see you again."

"Come along into the hall," Dorothy said. "Every Sunday we have tea after service. And today, since there is something special to celebrate."

Miss Witherspoon looked a bit harried, but Kura acquiesced politely.

"I'd love some tea," she said, giving the shopkeeper's wife a smile. Only William knew it was really intended for him.

In the church hall, he brought Kura tea and cake, but she only took a few sips and crumbled the cake between her fingers. As she politely and monosyllabically answered questions from the reverend and members of the women's group, she cast tiny glances at William from time to time—no more than a heartbeat long—until he thought he could not take it any longer. But then she shuffled past him as she said good-bye to the women's group and whispered a few words to him.

"You know the path between Kiward Station and the Maori camp. Meet me there at sundown. I'll say I'm visiting my people."

Immediately thereafter, Kura excused herself from her enthusiastic devotees in Haldon. The reverend asked her if she would now be playing the organ more often in the church, but Kura replied evasively.

William left the room before she did. He was afraid he would give himself away with a look or a gesture if he formally took his leave. He did not know what he would do with the rest of the day.

Until sundown on the path through the woods. Alone.

That last point proved a false conclusion: Kura did not come alone but with Heather Witherspoon. She did not appear to be enthusiastic about this arrangement, and treated her governess like a burdensome footman. However, she could not be gotten rid of. Decency was paramount to Miss Witherspoon.

Still, William almost expired from bliss when Kura finally stood before him again. Gently, he took her hand and kissed it—that touch alone sent him through a thousand fires that gave him life instead of burning him. Kura smiled openly. He melted under her gaze and could hardly tear himself from the sight of her creamy brown skin. He stroked her cheek with trembling fingers, and Kura rubbed against him like a cat—or rather, like a tamed tiger—moving her face against the palm of his hand and gently biting its heel. William could hardly hide his arousal, and it seemed no different for Kura. Miss Witherspoon, however, let out a cough when the girl raised her lips to him for a kiss. That degree of intimacy was clearly too much for her.

Nevertheless, she permitted a walk, hand in hand, and Kura's fingers teased William's palm as they strolled, fluttering up to his wrist and caressing it with tiny circles. That alone was enough to take William's breath away. It was difficult to have a normal conversation, even one between two people in love, as William and Kura did not want to talk. They wanted to make love.

They exchanged compliments about Kura's concert and William's new job, and Kura complained a bit about her family. She wanted to escape from her grandmother's control as soon possible.

"I could live with my mother, of course," she explained. "But then I would not be able to use the piano. My grandmum has made that very clear. And Miss Witherspoon would not like living in a Maori village, let alone the one on O'Keefe Station."

William learned that Marama and her husband lived on what had once been Ruben O'Keefe's parents' farm. After Howard O'Keefe's death, Helen had sold the farm to Gwyneira, who had passed it on to the Maori as reparation for the irregularities in the sale of Kiward Station. It was an arrangement that the chieftain, Tonga, had only acquiesced to because Kura, the designated heir of the Wardens' land, had Maori blood.

"That's why everyone is obsessed with my holding onto this boring farm," Kura sighed. "I couldn't care less about it, but I hear 'You are the heiress!' three times a day. And my mother is no different, though at least she doesn't care whether I marry a Maori or a *pakeha*. For my grandmum, on the other hand, the sky would fall if I were to choose someone from Tonga's tribe."

William was all but going mad with love and longing. He was listening to Kura's stories as he had once listened to Elaine's babbling. Though her last comment had registered, he would not think about it until later.

Perhaps he and Gwyneira McKenzie had more in common than he had thought. She might not be entirely opposed to a conversation after all.

"I'm missing something, Gwyn, aren't I? You don't really mean to allow her to officially visit with the boy who broke our Lainie's heart?"

James McKenzie was pouring himself a whiskey from the cabinet, which he still did only rarely even after many years as the so-called lord of this manor. During his time as a foreman under Gerald Warden, he had hardly ever been asked into the salon, and the old man had certainly never offered him a drink. That evening, however, he was helping himself generously. He needed a pick-me-up. He had just watched the young man, recently pointed out to him as William Martyn by Dorothy Candler, ride away grandly down the main approach. His name had not been given at the time; otherwise, James would have had a few words to say on the subject of Elaine. He took a big gulp from his glass.

Fleurette's letters still sounded terribly despondent. Even three months after the scandal had broken, Elaine had not recovered from her heartache. James could well understand that; he remembered the burning jealousy he had felt toward Gwyneira's fiancé, Lucas Warden, after she first arrived at Kiward Station. It had broken his heart when she had become pregnant with someone else's child, and he had fled, just like Lucas. If he had only known then that the unfortunate child—Paul—had been the result of Gwyneira being raped by her father-in-law, everything might have turned out differently, even with Paul. And they might not have the insufferable Kura hanging like an albatross around their necks—Kura, whose contact with William Martyn his wife now wanted to make official! Gwyneira could not be serious. James poured himself another drink.

Gwyneira too was worked up enough to make use of the whiskey bottle herself, which hardly ever happened.

"What am I supposed to do, James?" she asked. "If we forbid it, they'll meet in secret. All Kura needs to do is move to the Maori camp. Marama isn't about to impose limits on who she shares her bed with."

"She won't move to the Maori camp, because she can't take her beloved piano with her. That condition was a master stroke, Gwyn—one of the few you've ever made in raising that child." James took another long slug.

"Thank you," Gwyneira growled. "Blame me for everything! If I'm not mistaken, you too lived in this house while she was growing up."

"And you stopped me several times from bending Kura over my knee." James put his hand on his wife's arm and smiled at her. He did not want to fight about Kura's upbringing. That could not be changed, and the subject had already led to enough recriminations between them. But this business with William Martyn was another matter.

"She probably wouldn't give a damn about the piano. She's in love with him, James, head over heels. And he with her. You know all too well that there's nothing to be done about that." Gwyneira returned his tender touch as though to remind James of their own story.

He was not to be soothed, however.

"Don't talk to me about eternal love. Not with a boy who just left his last girl. And charming little Kura likewise just cast off Tiare like an old shirt. Yes, I know that's exactly what you wanted. But when the two of them fling themselves at each other so soon after that, grand romance is hardly what comes to mind. Then there's what Fleur writes about him."

"Oh? And what exactly does she have to say?" Gwyneira asked. "What has he done that's so terrible? He comes from a good family, he's educated and he's apparently interested in culture, which is precisely what makes him so attractive to Kura. So what if he was excited about the Fenians? My God, every boy wants to play Robin Hood."

"But they don't all go straight to bombing the sheriff of Nottingham," James remarked.

"He didn't even do that. I admit it sounds as if he got himself tangled in a bad bit of business. But you especially ought to understand how that can happen."

"Because of my past as a livestock thief, you mean?" James smirked. That subject had not been able to rob him of his composure for some time. "At least I never stole the wrong person's sheep, whereas your William almost killed someone on his own side. Fine, fine, the folly of youth. I don't want to beat a dead horse. But he behaved like an ass to Elaine, and there's no reason to believe he'll treat Kura any better."

Gwyneira drank the rest of her whiskey and held the glass out to James. Frowning, he filled it a second time.

"I'm not afraid for Kura," Gwyneira said.

If James were being honest, he had to admit that she was right not to be. If they had not specifically been talking about William Martyn, he would have been more worried about the man.

"She'll hold on to him as long as she wants him. My God, James, try to look at it another way. As though he had not just left Lainie but some other girl. Or as though you knew nothing about it. Then . . ." She reached nervously for her glass.

"Then?" James asked.

Gwyneira took a deep breath. "Then you, too, would be saying that heaven had sent him. James, he's a proper gentleman who would insinuate himself masterfully into society here. You know these people. Even if the attempted assassination story were to come out, they would only find him all the more interesting. And he comes from a sheep farm. He'll be happy to move in here. We can put him to work. Ruben says he's handy. Perhaps someday he'll run the farm with Kura at his side." Gwyneira sounded more than a little wistful. Her conversation with William that afternoon had gone very smoothly. The young man, who had already been making a good impression in Queenstown, struck her as an ideal match.

"Gwyn, the girl is not going to do an about-face once she's Mrs. Martyn."

"What other choice does she have?" Gwyneira stated flatly. "When she gets married, she ties herself to Kiward Station. Willingly. And more strongly than before. Then she can't simply sell the farm. And she can't flee to the Maori and live in a hut."

"You want to set a trap for her?" James was almost in a state of disbelief.

"She's setting it herself!" Gwyneira declared. "We're not making the match, are we? She's meeting the young man of her own free will. If something more comes out of it . . ."

"Gwyn, she's fifteen!" James said, troubled. "I obviously don't care for her, but we owe it to her to let her grow up."

"And act on her harebrained schemes? James, if she goes to England, and nothing comes of her singing, she'll probably sell the farm out from under our feet." Gwyneira was no longer drinking from her glass but pacing the room nervously. "I've lived here for forty years, and now everything hangs on a child's whim."

"It will be six years before she comes of age," James said in an attempt to appease her. "What about Helen's suggestion to send her to boarding school in England? Fleur mentioned it in her letter, and I thought it sounded entirely reasonable."

"That was before William," Gwyneira said. "And he strikes me as the surest solution. But of course nothing has been decided yet. I have not given him permission to court her, James. He may only accompany her to church."

For two months, Kura was happy with William Martyn's "official accompaniment." Then she grew tired of the situation. It was wonderful, of course, to be allowed to see her beloved without secrecy, but there was nothing more in it than a stolen kiss or a few hastily exchanged caresses. Haldon was more conservative than Queenstown. There were no gold miners or whorehouses here, only the church society and the ladies' socials. Who was "seeing" whom was minutely observed—even if Heather Witherspoon briefly lapsed in her attention, Dorothy Candler or her sister-in-law, or the reverend or his wife stood ready to keep their eyes on the young lovebirds. With overwhelming friendliness, of course. Everyone went out their way to be kind to the gorgeous Warden heiress, who had finally let herself be seen in the community, and the gallant who suited her so well. Dorothy sighed that there had not been such a lovely couple in the area since Gwyneira and Lucas Warden, and she could talk for hours about how as a girl she had served in the wedding.

Kura, however, did not want to sip tea and chat while everyone stared as though hypnotized at her hand held in William's. She was pining away with desire and wanted to try out everything that Tiare had taught her about physical love with William. William, she assumed, likewise had a virtuosic mastery of the game; otherwise, he would hardly have been able to seduce her prudish little cousin into caresses on the lakeshore. If only there were a way to be alone with him for an hour or two! But her previously reclusive life ruled out any chance of that. Kura was afraid of horses—so a ride together was out of the question. She had hardly ever left the area around the main house—so she could not claim to want to show William the farm, the lake, the stone circles, or even the sheep. Not even the piano was in her private rooms. If she invited William to listen to her play, it would be in the salon and, as a rule, in the presence of Heather Witherspoon. Kura had attempted to sneak away a couple of times down the path to the Maori village to meet William there after he had ostensibly ridden home, but Miss Witherspoon always managed to stick close to her. Once Jack and his friends had followed her—and, while they were kissing, shot them with paper wads from their slingshots. The second time, they were caught by a couple of Maori who naturally spread the word immediately that Kura had a sweetheart. When Tiare had words with her about it, she did not deny any of it.

Tonga's fit of choler concerned her more, however. The chieftain was far from pleased about this English immigrant who suddenly wanted to get his hands on the tribal land of his people.

"It is your duty to the tribe to return the land! You should marry one of our own, or at least bear the child of one of ours. After that you can do what you want!"

Tonga, too, knew about Kura's lofty plans to become a professional singer, but the Maori viewed the situation differently. As long as Kura left an heir and did not hit upon the idea of selling Kiward Station while she was in Europe, in Tonga's view, she could go wherever she wanted. However, the Maori chief feared the worst if Kura were left to her own devices. The natives knew nothing about the discipline of being a professional singer. They saw only an extremely sensual girl who already at the age of thirteen had been casting lustful gazes at the tribe's youths. And now there was this Englishman. She had not shared her bed with him only because the *pakeha* had almost forcibly kept her from doing so. If the right man came along, she would give up Kiward Station for him out of simple caprice. Tonga would therefore have been just as happy as Gwyneira to tie Kura to the land—only not by means of a *pakeha* who reminded him painfully of his old rival Paul Warden.

The resemblance didn't stem from their physical appearance, since Paul had been dark-haired and shorter than William, but there was something in the manner of the newcomer, in the way he simply ignored the Maori workers on the farm. There was the impatient hand holding the reins of his horse, his lordly mannerisms. Tonga had a bad feeling about him, and he had made that clear to Kura. Not very diplomatically, as Gwyneira reported to her husband with a grin after Kura had complained earnestly to her about the chieftain. While Gwyneira remained just as taken with Kura's admirer, James made observations along the lines of Tonga's.

Regardless, Kura was disappointed. She had imagined the "official accompaniment" differently. Neither attending the spring festivals on neighboring farms nor dancing in Haldon that October held any charm for her whatsoever.

It was not all that different for William, though he enjoyed the festivals. The invitations to neighboring farms and to Christchurch interested him most of all, as they offered him the chance to get to know new people, who were generally happy to show him their property. In this manner, William gained an overview of the sheep husbandry business in the Canterbury Plains without asking nosy questions. After a few months, he considered himself to be more than capable of managing such a farm and was eager to try his luck as a "sheep baron." His job in the Candlers' shop was noticeably dull by comparison.

Yet, even among his hopes for Kiward Station, it was Kura he longed for above all. He awoke every night from dreams of her, and then had to stealthily change his sheets so that Dorothy's sister-in-law might not giggle and spread word that, unbidden, his firm virility unburdened itself nightly. When he saw Kura, even his beautiful words failed him; at that point, he was nothing more than feeling and longing. Sometimes he could hardly conceal the erection that the very sight of her set off. He had to have the girl. Soon.

"Dearest," he said one day when they were out of hearing range of Haldon's residents. The monthly parish picnic included boating, and William was rowing his sweetheart around Lake Benmore. Granted, always within sight of the shore and at least three other boats, in which other young couples were suffering the same tortures. "If you really don't want to wait, we're going to have to get married."

"Get married?" Kura asked, appalled. Until that moment, she had never considered such a thing. She simply dreamed of living out her passions—and celebrating her triumphs as an opera singer. She had not exactly been wracking her brain about how it would all work together.

William smiled and—something that had only recently been permitted—put his arm loosely around her. "So you don't want to marry me?"

Kura bit her lip. "Can I still be a singer once I'm married?"

William shook his head in bewilderment. "What a question! Love will make your voice come into full bloom for the first time."

"And you'll come to London with me? And to Paris?" Kura leaned back on his arm, trying to bring herself as close to him as she could.

William swallowed. London? Paris? But then again, why not? The Wardens were rich. Why should he not promise her a European voyage?

"But of course, my sweet. With the greatest pleasure. Europe will be at your feet."

Kura turned gracefully, still wrapped in his arm and, facing away from prying eyes for a moment, kissed his shoulder and his neck.

"Then let's get married soon," she purred.

In principle, Gwyneira's entire plan fell into place with William's marriage proposal, but when he formally asked for Kura's hand so soon, she could no longer ignore her conscience. In the end, her love for Kura triumphed over her love for Kiward Station. James was right.

She had to offer the girl the choice between marriage and an artistic career, regardless of her personal feelings on the matter.

So she asked Kura, albeit reluctantly, to have a talk and laid out Helen's plan for her.

"Go to school in England for two years. We're looking for a boarding school where you can take singing lessons. If a conservatory takes you after that, you can study music. You can always marry then too."

Gwyneira was convinced that Kura would forget William after her first year at school, if not well before, but she did not tell her that.

Kura was decidedly unenthusiastic, even though she would have been thrilled if her grandmother had made her a similar offer even just a few weeks earlier. As it was, she stood up defiantly and started pacing around the room impatiently.

"You just want to stop me from marrying William!" she accused her grandmother. "You don't think I can see that. You're no better than Tonga!"

Gwyneira looked at her, confused. Tonga's and her intentions were rather at odds. As far as she could tell, William made the Maori chieftain see red, but perhaps that was still better than Kura leaving Kiward Station.

"I'm just waiting for you to propose turning me into a broodmare too!" Kura kept hurling accusations until Gwyneira could hardly keep up. "But all of you are mistaken. Wild horses could not drag me away from here without William. And I have no intention of getting pregnant right away. I will have both, William *and* my career. I'll show you all!"

Kura looked pretty as a picture when she was angry, but that made little impression on Gwyneira.

"You can't have it both ways, Kura. New Zealand wives don't stand on European opera stages. Especially not when their husbands enjoy the title of 'sheep baron.'"

Gwyneira bit her lip. That last remark had no doubt been a mistake. Which did not escape Kura.

"So you admit it? You think William is after my dowry! You think he wants Kiward Station, not me. But that's where you're mistaken. William wants me—me and only me. And I want him."

Gwyneira shrugged. No one could accuse her of not trying.

"Then you can have him," she said calmly.

"Mr. Martyn?" James McKenzie called out just as William was stepping out of Kiward Station's main house with a radiant look. Gwyneira had just told him that she accepted his marriage proposal. As long as Kura's mother had nothing against it, she would begin the wedding preparations.

James knew that, of course, and had been in a bad temper for days. Gwyneira had asked him to stay out of the matter, but he could not restrain himself from sounding William out one last time as fully as he could. He stepped in front of William and rose up almost threateningly before him.

"You don't have any plans at the moment, do you? Aside from perhaps celebrating your success, I take it. But you'd be celebrating the pig in a poke. You've yet to even see Kiward Station. Would you be so kind as to let me show you?"

William's smile froze. "Yes, of course, but—"

"No buts," James broke in. "It'd be my pleasure! Come, saddle your horse, and we'll take a little ride around."

William did not dare object. Why would he? He had been impatiently awaiting an opportunity to look around Kiward Station for weeks. Though he would have preferred a different guide than Gwyneira's grim husband, nothing could be done about that now. Obediently, he walked over to the stables and saddled his horse, something he no longer usually did himself. Normally some Maori youth working about the stables took over that task. However, he did not think it wise to delegate that day, as James McKenzie would likely have made some snide remark. He waited patiently with his bay horse in front of the stables as William led his horse out.

Without a word, James first set out toward Haldon. Then he turned off the road and started riding toward the Maori village. When William saw the settlement for the first time, he was surprised. Instead of the primitive huts or tents he had expected, he found himself in front of a well-built meeting hall decorated with carvings directly beside the lake. Large stones next to an earthen oven offered places to sit.

"The *wharenui*," James remarked. "Do you speak Maori? You should learn it. And it wouldn't be a bad idea to consummate the wedding ceremony according to the rites of Kura's people, in addition to the regular celebration."

William made a disgusted face. "I don't believe Kura sees these people as her own," he observed. "And I have no intention whatsoever of lying with Kura in front of the whole tribe as their laws dictate. That would go against all decency."

"Not among the Maori, it wouldn't," James said comfortably. "And you wouldn't really have to lie with her in public. It's enough to share your bed with her and then eat and drink with their people. It would make Kura's mother happy. And it would get you started on the right foot. Tonga, their chieftain, is particularly displeased about the fact that you're marrying into this family."

William gave James a lopsided grin. "Well, you and Tonga have that in common then, don't you?" he asked provocatively. "But what does that mean? Should I expect a spear in my back?"

James shook his head. "No. These people aren't generally violent."

"Oh, is that so? What about Kura's father?"

James sighed. "That was more or less an accident. Paul had provoked the Maori to the point of violence. In any case, his murderer wasn't from around here. He was an underage fool from John Sideblossom's farm who'd had bad experiences with the *pakeha* since he was a child. Paul wasn't even paying for his own sins when he died. Tonga has explicitly expressed his remorse for Paul's death."

"Oh, he certainly showed plenty of that," William said.

James did not respond. "I only mean to say that it would be better for all involved if you had a good relationship with the Maori. I am sure it's something close to Kura's heart as well."

In reality, James was of the opinion that nothing lay close to Kura's heart except the fulfillment of her own caprices, but he kept that to himself.

"Then Kura should tell me so," William declared. "For all I care, we could invite these people to the wedding. There will be a party for the workers, won't there?"

James inhaled sharply but said nothing. The young man would learn soon enough that Tonga and his people most definitely did not view themselves as the Wardens' "workers."

At that hour in the afternoon, the Maori camp was largely empty. A handful of old women could be seen preparing dinner and watching the children playing in the lake. The rest of the tribe was elsewhere; some worked for the Wardens, and others were out hunting or in the fields. As it was, William saw only a few wrinkled and tattoo-covered faces, which would have struck fear into him had they belonged to younger people.

"Ghastly, those tattoos!" he remarked. "Thank God no one decided to disfigure Kura that way."

James smiled. "But you would, doubtless, have loved her anyway, isn't that right?" he teased. "Don't worry. The young Maori aren't tattooed anymore—aside from Tonga, who had himself tattooed with the chieftain's symbols to provoke a reaction. Originally, that was how they showed which tribe they belonged to. Each community had different tattoos, like the English nobles' coats of arms."

"No one ever tattooed those into the children though," William said excitedly. "People are civilized in England."

James grinned. "Ah yes, I forgot the English were taught their arrogance in the crib. My people saw things differently. We Scots would paint ourselves blue whenever we went against the occupier. What did the real Irish do?"

William looked as though he were ready to leap at James.

"What is that supposed to mean?" he asked. "Do you mean to insult me?"

James looked at him innocently. "Insult? Me? You? Where did you get that idea? I just thought I'd remind you of your own roots. Besides, I'm only giving you good advice. And the first thing is: don't make enemies of the Maori!"

The men were now riding through the camp, past a long sleeping lodge, several storehouses on stilts—*patakas*, James explained—and a few single-family homes. James greeted the old people and exchanged a few jocular words with them. A woman appeared to ask about William, and James introduced him.

The old women then whispered to each other, and William caught the name Kura-maro-tini a few times.

"You should now say *kia ora* to be polite and bow to them," James said. "In reality, they rub noses together, but I can tell that would be asking too much."

He exchanged a few words with the women, who giggled.

"What did you say?" William asked suspiciously.

"I told them that you're shy." James seemed to be enjoying himself thoroughly. "Now, go on, say hello."

William had turned red with anger, but repeated the greeting politely. The old women seemed genuinely pleased and, laughing, corrected his pronunciation.

"*Haere mai!*" called the children. "Welcome!"

A little boy gave him a tiny piece of jade. James thanked him exuberantly and made William do likewise.

"That's a *pounamu*. It's supposed to bring you luck. A very generous gift from a little boy, one you should plan to be on good terms with by the way. He's Tonga's youngster."

The boy already had the bearing of a chief and accepted the gratitude of the *pakeha* with great majesty. Then the men left the village. The land around the camp had not been put to use by the Wardens, and the Maori had planted a few fields and gardens. A short while later, they rode past some large paddocks, some of which held sheep.

As the rain had set in again, the animals were crowded into the pad-docks' shelters, where hay was provided as fodder.

"There's enough grass in the pastures for most of the sheep even in winter," James explained. "But we feed the ewes more. That way the lambs are born stronger and you can herd them into the highlands earlier, which saves on fodder. This is where we keep the cattle too. We've increased the number we breed since the refrigerated ships have started going to England. Before, the meat could only be delivered to Otago or the West Coast—thankfully, gold and coal miners have always been blessed with a healthy appetite. But now these ships with cooling contraptions sail for England. It's a good business. And Kiward Station obviously has no shortage of pastureland. The first shearing shed is over there."

James indicated a large, flat building that William would not have known what to make heads or tails of a few weeks before. He had since learned from spending time on other farms that this was a dry place for the shearing companies that traveled from station to station in the spring to shear the wool from the sheep.

"The first?" William asked.

James nodded. "We have three in all. And we need the shearers for three weeks. You see what that means."

William grinned. "Quite a few sheep," he said.

"More than ten thousand at the last count," James said, adding, "Happy?"

William was incensed. "Mr. McKenzie, I know what you're insinuating. But I don't care about your damned sheep! I only care about Kura. I'm marrying her, not your livestock trade."

"You're marrying both," observed James. "And don't try to tell me you don't care one way or another."

William flared up at him. "Do I care one way or another? I love Kura. I'm going to make her happy. Nothing else matters. I want to be with Kura, and she wants to be with me."

James nodded, though he did not look convinced. "You'll get her all right."

For the Sake of Man

QUEENSTOWN, LAKE PUKAKI, AND CANTERBURY PLAINS

1894–1895

1

William Martyn and Kura-maro-tini Warden were married shortly before Christmas in the year 1893. Their wedding was the most glorious celebration to be held at Kiward Station since before the death of its founder, Gerald Warden. It was the height of summer, and so the hosts had made it a garden party. Gwyneira had supplementary tents and pavilions set up as a defense against any possible summer rain, but the weather cooperated. The sun competed to outshine the guests, who arrived in great numbers to celebrate the couple. Half of Haldon was present, the perennially sniffling Dorothy Candler chief among them, of course.

"She bawled her eyes out at my first wedding too," Gwyneira told James. The residents of the surrounding farms had come for the festivities as well. Gwyneira greeted Lord and Lady Barrington and their younger children. The older ones were off studying in Wellington and England, and one of their daughters had gotten married on the North Island. The Beasleys, once their nearest neighbors, had died without direct heirs, and their distant relatives had sold the farm. A Major Richland, a veteran of the Crimean War, had taken over the farm's sheep and horse breeding and ran them in just as "gentlemanly" a manner as had Reginald Beasley. Fortunately, he had capable overseers who simply defied the would-be farmer's more absurd orders.

George and Elizabeth Greenwood came from Christchurch, accompanied only by their daughters. One of their sons was still studying in England, while the other was finishing up practical courses at the Australian branch of the family's trading house.

Their older daughter, Jennifer—a somewhat shy blonde girl—lost all ability to speak when she stood face-to-face with Kura-maro-tini.

"She's beautiful," she merely whispered when she saw the bride in her creamy-white gown.

That was undeniable. The dress, which had been tailored in Christchurch, highlighted Kura's perfect form without being indecent. She wore a garland of fresh flowers in her hip-length hair, which she left down. That made a good enough veil on its own. Although she looked almost as disinterested as at any other celebration she had ever graced with her presence, her skin shimmered, and her eyes sparkled whenever they fell on her future husband. When she walked toward the altar, her movements were as graceful as those of a dancer. However, there was one small problem to solve before the bishop, who had traveled from Christchurch, could marry the couple under the flower-decorated canopy.

Jennifer Greenwood, who normally played the organ in Christchurch—"angelically" in the bishop's opinion—had lost her nerve. No wonder, since Dorothy Candler had just described in scintillating detail how the bride and groom had come together after Kura's sensational concert in Haldon.

"I can't do it," Jenny whispered to her mother, her face as red as a beet. "Not now that I've seen her. I'll play something wrong and then everyone will look at me and compare me to her. I thought all those stories about Elaine O'Keefe were exaggerated, but . . ."

Gwyneira, who could not help catching these words, bit her lip. The Greenwoods probably knew every detail of the fiasco that had taken place between Elaine and Kura in Queenstown. Helen was close friends with George and Elizabeth, both of whom had been among her favorite students in their youth. Helen had been George's tutor back in England, and Elizabeth was one of the orphan girls she had accompanied to New Zealand. She kept nothing secret from them, especially from George, who was a successful wool trader and import-export merchant. Without his powerful backing, her husband, Howard, would not have been able to hold onto his farm for long, and Helen's marriage would have taken an even more traumatic course than it already had. Ruben O'Keefe clung to his "Uncle George" with nearly idolatrous love, and he had named his younger son after

George Greenwood. It was quite possible that Ruben's conversations with him—or Georgie's with his namesake—had unveiled embarrassing secrets.

Elizabeth, a blonde, still-slender woman in a simple, elegant dress, tried to calm her daughter's nerves: "It's just 'Here Comes the Bride.' There's nothing simpler, Jenny. You could play it in your sleep! You've even played it in the cathedral."

"But when she looks at me like that, I just want to disappear." Jenny indicated Kura, who was casting a rather merciless look in her direction. The music should long since have begun, after all.

Not that Jenny had any reason to hide. She was a tall, slender girl with golden-blonde hair and a sweet, narrow face dominated by large green eyes. But at that moment, she was doing her best to conceal her face by lowering her head and letting her hair fall over it like a curtain.

"No, we can't have that!" a young man in the last row said as he stood up gallantly. It was Stephen O'Keefe—the only representative of the family in Queenstown. As he was among the closest relatives of the bride, Gwyneira had reserved a place for him in the very front, but he had been hiding in the back.

Fleurette and Ruben had sent him to avoid creating any further scandal that might be brought on by boycotting the wedding altogether. Fleurette had made it clear in a letter that they wished Kura and William all the best, but that Elaine wanted no part in the celebration: "Though she seems to have slowly gotten over Mr. Martyn's rejection, she remains a shadow of her former self. Unfortunately, she places the blame squarely on herself. Instead of being rightfully angry, she makes herself miserable thinking about what she did wrong and how she pales in comparison to her cousin. There is no way we can expect her to watch Kura as a glowing bride."

Stephen, however, was on Christmas break and happy to ride to Kiward Station. Though he had learned from his mother's letters all about what had happened between Kura and Elaine, he had not taken the matter all that seriously. During his next visit to Queenstown, however, he had been quite disturbed by how distraught his sister still appeared to be. He could not pass up the opportunity to get to know the two causes of this tragic change.

"With your permission," Stephen said, smiling. He bowed to Jenny Greenwood and sat down at the splendid grand piano that was serving in place of an organ. It was Gwyneira's wedding present to her granddaughter, even though James had grumbled, "We'll have to clear out half the salon to make room for it."

"You can play?" Gwyneira asked, amazed, having left her seat to see to the delay.

Stephen smiled again. "I'm Helen O'Keefe's grandson and grew up next to her church organ. Even Georgie could manage something as laughably simple as the 'Wedding March.'"

Without further delay, he struck the first notes. He played the piece casually, with almost a little too much verve, as the wedding couple stepped up to the improvised altar. Since Stephen did not know what song was supposed to be played when the couple walked back down the aisle, he played an equally animated version of "Amazing Grace," which earned him an amused look from James McKenzie and a chastising look from Gwyneira. After all, the lyrics "how sweet the sound that saved a wretch like me" were hardly flattering to a young bride.

Nevertheless, Stephen hit every note. Insecurity was alien to him. Jennifer smiled at him gratefully from behind her curtain of hair.

"I've earned myself the first dance after that, right?" he whispered to her, at which Jennifer blushed again, this time with delight.

In the meantime, a group of Maori musicians had assembled in front of the pavilion. Marama sang a few traditional songs with them—at which time it became clear to everyone where the girl had gotten her beautiful voice. Marama's voice was higher than Kura's and possessed an almost ethereal timbre. If the good spirits that Marama conjured with her songs could hear her, they would not be able to resist her; Gwyneira was certain of that. The guests were likewise enraptured.

Only William seemed to find his mother-in-law's performance unsuitable, despite the fact that Marama was wearing a European-style gown and none of the other musicians stood out with unusual clothing or even tattoos. The groom preferred to ignore the natives and looked relieved when the music came to an end. The parade of congratulations that followed appealed to him a great deal more, though he found it a bit strange that the sheep barons of the area congratulated Gwyneira at least as heartily as the newlyweds.

"You've achieved something quite extraordinary," said Lord Barrington, shaking her hand. "The boy is just what you wanted for Kiward Station. It's as if you made him yourself."

Gwyneira laughed. "I did no such thing. It's just how things turned out," she said humbly.

"You didn't pull any strings, then? Never slipped little Kura a love potion, or anything?" asked Francine Candler, Haldon's midwife and one of Gwyneira's oldest friends.

"I would have had to have you brew it for me," Gwyneira teased. "Or do you think the Maori witch doctor would ever have cooked up a concoction that would give the farm an English heir?"

Tonga was present, of course, though he had not ceded his right to wear his tribal clothing, including his chieftain's insignias. He observed the ceremony with a stony face and then congratulated the couple politely. Tonga spoke perfect English with excellent inflection—when he condescended to demonstrate it to the *pakeha*. He, too, had been among Helen O'Keefe's best students.

The other Maori, including the bride's mother, Marama, and her husband, kept to themselves in the background. Gwyneira would have liked for them to participate more fully in the festivities, but they had a fine sense for what the celebration's main couple wanted. Although Kura looked as indifferent as she always did, word of William's skeptical attitude toward the tribes had already gotten around. For that reason, Gwyneira was happy that James joined the Maori guests and chatted amiably with them after the meal. He was not entirely at ease in the illustrious company of the sheep barons and notables of Christchurch anyway. After all, he had only "married in" and had no real claim to

137

the land on which he worked. Several of those men had even come after him as a rustler many years before. Running into each other at society functions only caused both sides embarrassment. Besides, James spoke fluent Maori.

"I truly hope that they will be happy," Marama whispered to him in her melodious voice. She'd had no objections to William, though she felt snubbed by his behavior that day. "And that he won't stand in his own way like Paul did." Marama had loved Paul Warden with all her heart, but her influence on him had always been limited.

"I have heard the name Paul a little too often in connection with this Martyn boy," Tonga remarked grimly.

James could only nod.

William floated through his wedding celebration. He was deliriously happy. Naturally, there had been a few unpleasant moments, including the Maori's unplanned performance and the strong handshake of the young man who represented the O'Keefe family. "Best wishes—from my sister too," Stephen had said, looking William coldly in the eye. He was the first young man William had seen who had no reaction whatsoever to Kura's beauty. Although she smiled at him, he wished her well just as coolly as he had William. And then there had been his piano playing. There could hardly have been anything less suitable than "Amazing Grace."

All of that, however, was more than offset by the sheep barons, who heartily accepted the newcomer into their ranks. William got along beautifully with Barrington and Richland, and he hoped he'd made a good impression on George Greenwood when he was intro-duced to him. He was utterly content with the way the celebration had turned out. The meal was exquisite, the wine first-class, and the champagne flowed in rivers. Even Gwyneira's domestics had proved themselves well trained, though the Maori cooks and maids—as well as the peculiar majordomo Maui, an older Maori man—were somewhat too willful for his taste. But he could see to that. He would talk to Kura about it soon.

In the meantime, the musicians had arrived from Christchurch and began to play. It was time for the dancing to get under way, and William and Kura opened with a waltz. The bride, however, seemed to have had quite enough of the celebration.

"When can we retire?" she whispered, rubbing her body so provocatively against his that the guests could not have helped but see. "I can't wait to be alone with you."

William smiled. "Watch yourself, Kura. You can hold out for another couple of hours. We have to make the rounds here. It's important. After all, we're representing Kiward Station."

Kura frowned. "Why do we suddenly have to represent this farm? I thought we were going to Europe."

William spun her in an elegant turn to give himself time to think. What was she talking about? She didn't really believe that he was going to . . .

"Everything in good time, Kura," he said soothingly. "For now we're here, and I'm as anxious as you are."

That, at least, was the truth. He dared not let himself think about taking possession of Kura that night. That would surely draw embarrassing looks. Just his close proximity to her while dancing aroused him.

"We'll stay until the fireworks; then we'll disappear. That's what I discussed with your grandmother anyway. None of us wants to hear the bawdy comments that will come when we leave."

"You discussed when we would go to bed with my grandmother?" Kura asked indignantly.

William sighed. He was crazy about Kura, but she was behaving so childishly.

"We have to follow the proper etiquette," he said calmly. "Let's go get something to drink. If you keep rubbing against me like that, I'm going to have my way with you right here in the middle of the dance floor."

Kura laughed. "Why not? The Maori would be thrilled. Take me in front of the whole tribe!" She pressed herself even more firmly against him.

William rebuffed her energetically. "Behave yourself," he whispered. "I don't want people talking about us."

Kura looked at him, disbelieving. She *wanted* people to talk. She wanted to be a star, her name on everyone's lips. She loved how the European gazettes wrote about famous singers like Mathilde Marchesi, Jenny Lind, and Adelina Patti. Some day she, too, would travel through Europe on her own luxury train.

Determined to get her way, she threw her arms around William's neck and kissed him right in the middle of the dance floor. A long, deep kiss that no one could miss.

"She's beautiful, isn't she?" Jenny Greenwood repeated her remark, this time to Stephen. She had found him for the first dance, as promised. As Kura kissed William passionately—in anticipation of their wedding night, it seemed—Jenny vacillated between exhilaration and discomfort. The scene was visibly embarrassing for the groom. He looked as though he wanted to disappear and went so far as to rudely push his young wife away from him. A few unkind words followed. It was not a very harmonious start to a marriage.

"And she's supposed to sing beautifully too. My mother sometimes likes to say that all the fairy godmothers gather around some people in their cribs." There was a hint of envy in Jenny's voice.

Stephen laughed. "They say that about Sleeping Beauty too, but as it turned out, one person doesn't always get it all. Besides, I don't think she's that pretty. There's another girl at this party I much prefer."

Jenny blushed and couldn't even look at him. "You're fibbing," she whispered.

George Greenwood had introduced Stephen to his wife and daughter after the ceremony as Ruben O'Keefe's oldest son, soon after which Jenny and Stephen started chatting familiarly with each other.

Though the O'Keefes' last visit to Christchurch had been some ten years before, they had played together as children then. Jenny's little sister, Charlotte, who now scurried around them curiously, had still been in her crib back then.

Stephen lay his hand on his heart. "Jennifer, in important matters, I never fib . . . At least I haven't yet. If I ever find a position as an attorney, that might change. But today, I tell you on my honor and conscience that I see several girls here who I find prettier than Kura-maro-tini. Don't ask me why—I couldn't tell you—but that girl is missing something, something important. Besides, I don't like it when people make others feel small. And you looked completely done in earlier after just one look from her."

Jenny's hair curtain opened a little as she looked up at him. "Are you going to dance with all the girls you think are prettier than her?"

Stephen laughed and gently moved one of her locks out of her face.

"No, just with the girl I find the prettiest."

William realized that the two glasses of champagne Kura had drunk had caused her to completely lose her inhibitions. Not even his cold reaction to her kiss could dampen her spirits. She would not take her hands off him. He breathed a sigh of relief when the fireworks were set off and they could take their leave. Kura giggled unabashedly as they walked toward the house. She wanted to be carried over the threshold, so William picked her up obediently.

"Up the stairs too?" he asked.

"Yes, please," Kura yelled, still laughing.

With great ceremony, William climbed the open, winding staircase up to the second floor, where the family's sleeping quarters were located. William was very pleased with the agreement that had been reached over the couple's future chambers. At first, Kura had wanted to keep her rooms. She had a spacious bedroom, a dressing room, and a "work room" where Miss Witherspoon had tutored her. The suite had once belonged to Gwyneira's first husband, Lucas Warden. They had just added another room for William, but William had been querulous.

"You're the heiress, Kura. Everything here belongs to you, but you make do with apartments that look out on the backyard."

"I don't care where my rooms are," Kura said placidly. "All you can see is grass in any direction."

This last remark made it clear that she had never looked out the window. Kura's rooms had a view over the stables and a few paddocks, and Gwyneira's windows looked out on the gardens, but William had his eye on the rooms that faced the approach and the road.

"Those are the apartments meant for the owner of the manor. And you should have them. You could even set up your piano there." The suite William was talking about was where Gerald Warden had once lived. It had stood empty for sixteen years. Gwyneira had never even touched the furnishings, and James certainly had no interest in them. He was happy with Gwyneira's bedroom and had never wanted a separate one for himself. Jack lived in what had once been Fleurette's nursery.

Gwyneira was surprised when Kura demanded to move.

"Do you two really want to live with all that old furniture?" she asked. Just the thought of living surrounded by Gerald's old furnishings—let alone sleeping in one of the rooms he had inhabited—sent a shudder down her spine.

"Kura can refurnish it," William explained when Kura did not respond. She clearly could not have cared less about the furniture—as long as it was expensive and in keeping with the latest fashion. It seemed that what she feared most was Miss Witherspoon's critique—and so Kura eliminated all her possible objections by leaving practically the entire refurbishment up to her. Heather Witherspoon threw herself giddily into the project, flipping through catalogs and selecting the most beautiful pieces she could find without sparing a thought to cost. William was happy to help her in this endeavor, and the two of them spent entire afternoons discussing the relative merits of native versus imported wood, a question they ended up answering by having all of the furnishings sent from England. Gwyneira did not say a word about the costs, as Kiward Station seemed to be awash in gold.

The freshly wallpapered and newly furnished rooms suited William's taste perfectly. Kura had acquiesced to the decor with her typically apathetic mien.

"We won't be living here all that long, in any event," she had said placidly, almost giving Miss Witherspoon a heart attack. The governess had been certain that Kura would give up her lofty professional goals after the wedding was announced.

"Let my fiancée dream. She's still so young," William had said, sounding indulgent. "After she has a child . . ."

Heather Witherspoon had smiled. "Yes, that's true, Mr. Martyn. But it's such a waste. Kura has such a beautiful voice."

William agreed with her. Kura would sing their children to sleep with the most beautiful voice in the world.

He carried his young wife over the threshold into their common bedroom. There were additional private rooms for each of them, of course. The room was done in warm colors, and the bed's curtains and the drapes were of heavy silk. William saw that someone had made the bed, and Kura's lady's maid stood by, ready to help her undress.

"No, leave us," William said, breathing heavy with arousal. Holding Kura in his arms had only further stoked his passion.

The girl left, giggling. William laid his wife down on the bed.

"Do you want to take off your dress or—"

"What dress?" Kura ripped her neckline open, not bothering with the bodice's many hooks. And why should she? She would never be wearing it again. William felt his excitement grow. Her wildness defied all convention. He tossed his concerns aside and began to tear at the delicate fabric while liberating himself of his pants as quickly as he could. Still half-dressed, he then threw himself on top of her. He kissed her neck and the tops of her breasts, as he untied her corset, which went slowly since the whalebone offered some resistance. Finally, she was naked and stretching toward him with desire.

William had learned that one had to be careful with virgins—his tenants' daughters had occasionally cried after he had slept with them, and occasionally even during their lovemaking. Kura, however, knew no such sense of shame. She seemed to want to feel him inside of her and to know exactly what awaited her. William found that strange. He did not think a woman should be so lusty. But then he gave himself over entirely to her passion. He kissed her and rubbed against her, and then thrust himself into her triumphantly. Kura let out a short cry—William could not tell whether of pleasure or pain—and then moaned loudly when he began to move inside her. She dug her fingernails into his back as though she wanted to force him deeper into her. He exploded in ecstasy as Kura buried her teeth in his shoulder and cried with pleasure at the long-awaited release of her desire. Then she began kissing him again and asking for more.

William had never experienced anything like this before. Indeed, he would not have believed such sensuality was possible. Kura had melted into a stream of melodies and feelings that no aria, no love song had ever been able to release in her. Music had dominated her life up to this point, and there would always be harmonies. But this was something stronger, and she would do anything to experience it again and again. Kura's armor of apathy burst that night, and William fulfilled all her dreams.

James McKenzie observed Gwyneira as she fluttered from one dance partner to another. It was hard to believe that this whirlwind of energy would soon be sixty. But that evening, Gwyneira saw herself fulfilling her dearest wishes—it was very different from so long ago, when James had watched her dance with Lucas Warden. As a seventeen-year-old, she had been formal and stiff, and nervous about her wedding night—during which, it turned out, nothing had happened. Gwyneira was still technically a virgin when she asked James a full year later to help her conceive a child, an heir for Kiward Station. James had done his best, but that lineage had already been replaced. And who knew what it had bound itself to with William Martyn.

James suddenly had an urge to go see Monday. He had left her in the stables—just as Gwyneira had done with her beloved dog Cleo at her and Lucas's wedding. He laughed to himself when he thought of the dog show Gerald Warden had wanted to have the afternoon of the wedding ceremony. He had bought a litter of Welsh border collies, born sheepdogs, and had wanted to show his friends and neighbors how the dogs could revolutionize farmwork. The best, most fully trained dog back then had belonged to Gwyneira, but since the bride could not present the dog herself, James had been asked to show off its abilities for her. He would never forget how Gwyneira had stood there, in a state of excitement in her bridal gown, and the concerned look on her face when she realized Cleo was not minding James's instructions, forcing her to intercede. She then led the dog masterfully through its tasks with her veil flapping in the wind. And she had given James that happy smile that Lucas had never been able to draw out of her. Much later, she had given him Friday, Cleo's daughter, before he had gone into exile. Monday, James's current dog, was also Cleo's grandchild.

James stood up and made his way to the stables. The wedding party would manage without him, and champagne was not his purview anyway. He would prefer to empty a few glasses of whiskey with Andy McAran and the other workers.

The path back to the stables was like a walk into the past. The fireworks were just being set off above the house, and James remembered how he had danced with Gwyneira for the first time on a New Year's Eve many years before. This evening, too, young farmworkers were swinging girls in a circle to the improvised music of a fiddle and an accordion, and just like before, it was infinitely cheerier than the rather stuffy party in the garden.

James smiled when he noticed a couple who did not entirely belong there. His grandson Stephen was blithely leading Jenny Greenwood in a jig. Little Charlotte tried to convince Jack to dance with her, but he was attempting to run away. Jack did not care whether it was a waltz or a jig—he found all dancing strange.

Monday and a few other dogs left Andy and a few of the older workers who were passing a bottle around the fire, and trotted over to James. After greeting his four-legged friends, James accepted the bottle.

Andy McAran pointed to the hay bale beside him.

"You're welcome to have a seat here, if that nice suit can take it—I hardly recognized you today."

James was wearing an evening suit for the first time in his life.

"Gwyn wanted everything to be perfect," he said, taking his place.

"Then I'd have looked around for another son-in-law," smirked Poker Livingston, another veteran shepherd with whom James had shared a decades-long friendship. "That Martyn boy looks good—I'll give him that—but is anything going to come of it?"

James knew that Andy was skeptical. During the six weeks that he and Kura had been engaged, William had occasionally helped out on Kiward Station, giving the men the opportunity to look him over. He had not made the best impression, particularly during the sheepshearing, when every last man was needed and had to bring everything he had. It had soon become clear that William Martyn had never sheared a sheep before in his life—which ordinarily would not have been a problem, but given how often the young man had boasted about his upbringing on a sheep farm, it had caused no small amount of snickering. William had likewise proved himself incompetent with regard to the herding of the animals and the handling of the dogs—and seemed unwilling to learn. He had thought of "helping" more in terms of overseeing. When it was finally revealed that he was a sharp observer and knew how to work with numbers, good-natured Andy had handed over control of shearing shed three. Unfortunately, William had not simply counted the sheep per shearer, as he had been asked to do, but had become seized with ambition. Every year, the best shearing shed was awarded a prize, and in order to win, William had come up with the strangest ideas for shortening the work process. But most of his suggestions were impractical at best. At worst, they proved to be a stretch for the shearing company's workers, who had never reacted well to criticism, given that they saw themselves as an elite force among New Zealand's labor force and had corresponding egos. Andy, James, and finally even Gwyneira had to soothe and conciliate them multiple times—not a good sign for William's future on the estate.

"Man, do you fellas also feel like we've gone back in time tonight? Feels to me like when Gwyn married the younger Mr. Warden, that good-for-nothing," Andy observed casually, taking another sip of whiskey. He passed the bottle to Poker. "But it could have gone worse."

"Oh, come on, the new guy's no better," Poker said. William had really gotten on Poker's bad side.

James reflected, taking another sip of his whiskey as he did so, which made the speech that followed a little unsteady: "If . . . you ask me, both of them . . . were . . . are . . . good-for-nothing do-nothings. Lucas Warden, he did nothing real quiet . . . so no one heard him. But this one here . . . Even if Gwyn doesn't want to see it . . . he does nothing loud and clear. He'll do nothing loud enough for everyone to hear."

2

Ruben O'Keefe was in a bad mood, and Fleurette had not come into town at all. She had excused herself by claiming that there was urgent work to be done around the house for the next few days. This had nothing to do with the fact that Kura and William Martyn's wedding was being celebrated on faraway Kiward Station. Ruben had long since forgotten the young man; in general, he was not one to hold grudges. In fact, his patience for his fellow man knew only one exception: John Sideblossom of Lionel Station. And at that moment, he, of all people, was running about Queenstown, accompanied by his son. Helen had even rented the pair a room, which Ruben almost held against her.

"Now, do not behave like a child!" his mother said resolutely. "That fellow is no gentleman, of course, even though he acts like one. But I can hardly turn him out because he tried to woo my daughter-in-law twenty years ago."

"He tried to rape her!" Ruben clarified.

"There is no doubt that he went too far, but that was a long time ago. And Gerald Warden had encouraged him in his delusion that she would be the ideal wife for him," Helen said.

"And James? Are you going to excuse him for nabbing James too?"

After years of searching for James McKenzie in vain, John Sideblossom had been the leader of the company that had finally hunted the livestock thief down.

"You can hardly blame him for that," Helen said. "He was not the only one nettled by the animal thefts, and James did not exactly cover himself in glory doing that, even though you now paint him as though he were Robin Hood in the flesh. His behavior during the arrest, that

149

was something else entirely. Sideblossom behaved insufferably there again. But that proved to be almost a stroke of luck. Otherwise, they might have seized Fleurette too, and if that had happened, there would be no O'Kay Warehouse today."

Ruben did not like to think about it, but it was true that the initial capital for the business had come from James's thieving. Fleurette had been there with her father when John cornered him, but she had been able to flee during the general mayhem surrounding the arrest.

"You're acting as though I should be grateful to Sideblossom," mumbled Ruben biliously.

"Just polite," Helen said, laughing. "Simply treat him like any other customer. In a few days, he'll move on. Then you can spend the next few months forgetting about him. Besides, you make a lot of money from him every time he comes to town, so don't complain."

It was true that John Sideblossom came to Queenstown no more than once or twice a year. He did some business with a sheep farmer in the area. Then he took the opportunity to all but buy out the O'Kay Warehouse's stock, to which he had recently added orders for building materials and furniture, as he had just gotten married again—the way powerful men so often did. His wife, Zoé, was the twenty-year-old daughter of a West Coast gold digger who had come into money quickly and lost it just as quickly to failed investments. According to the gossip in Queenstown, the girl was gorgeous, but also spoiled and difficult—though almost no one had gotten an actual glimpse of her yet. Lionel Station, the Sideblossoms' farm, lay in a beautiful area, but was a considerable distance from any other settlements on the western arm of Lake Pukaki. It was several days' ride from Queenstown, and John's young wife seemed disinclined to follow her husband on these strenuous expeditions. Naturally, people—and the female population in particular—wondered what such a young woman did up there all alone. But then again, the question was not so pressing to the women of Queenstown that anyone went to the trouble of paying a neighborly visit.

"Did you not bring Lainie along?" Helen asked, finally changing the subject. "With Fleurette refusing to leave the house? We could both use a little help, don't you think? The twins can't exactly split themselves into three."

Laurie and Mary worked as chambermaids at Helen's or as sales personnel at the O'Kay Warehouse, depending on where they were needed.

Ruben laughed. "Then the confusion would be complete. Another completely identical blonde with a name ending in an 'ee' sound. No one would believe it. But you're right. I could use Elaine. It's just that Fleur turns into such a mother hen whenever Sideblossom comes to town. She'd like to wrap Lainie from head to toe or, better yet, not let her out of the house. All that, even though she's become so shy and dresses like a church mouse. Sideblossom wouldn't spare her a second look."

Helen rolled her eyes. "Besides, the man is over sixty. He's in good shape, I'll grant you, but not the type to move in on an underage girl at the reception desk of a hotel."

Ruben laughed. "Fleur thinks him capable of anything. But maybe Lainie will come in this afternoon. She must be starting to get cabin fever at home. And she doesn't like playing the piano anymore." He sighed.

Helen's face turned grim. "I am not a violent person, but I wish the plague on this William Martyn. Lainie was such a fun-loving, happy little thing."

"She'll get over it," Ruben said. "And as for the plague, Georgie is saying William already has it. He thinks William's marriage to Kura is just about the worst thing that could happen to a man. Should I be worried about him, do you think?"

Helen laughed. "Maybe Georgie's showing a keen eye. Let us hope he keeps his good sense regarding people's inner virtues until he's of marriageable age. Do send Lainie over to me if she comes into town, won't you? She can watch the front desk. I have to see to dinner. Both Sideblossoms will be present, so I can't just serve vegetable soup."

Elaine did in fact come to town that afternoon. She had ridden out to a nearby sheep farm to train Callie, as the border collie needed some experience with sheep. Since there were no sheep at Nugget Manor at the moment, Elaine rode out to the Stevers' place. Fleurette was not very keen on this outing. The Stevers, German immigrants, were reclusive people who only rarely let themselves be seen in Queenstown and did not have any friends. Fleurette thought that the middle-aged wife looked unhappy and haggard, but Elaine didn't really concern herself with them. She had met the owners of the farm only a couple of times, and came into contact only with their shepherds, almost all of whom were Maori.

A tribe had taken up residence on the farm a few weeks before, and the Maori welcomed Elaine and Callie good-naturedly. Neither the dog nor the girl was an imposition on them, and they had proved helpful. They often invited Elaine to eat with them or to come to their tribal celebrations, and they frequently gave her fish and sweet potatoes to take back to her mother. Since the incident with William, Elaine had spent more time with the Maori than with the girls her own age in town. Fleurette had noticed this, but was unconcerned. She, too, had grown up with Maori playmates and spoke their language fluently. She even accompanied Elaine sometimes to refresh her language skills and meet her daughter's new friends. The Maori had begun to come into town more often to shop at the O'Kay Warehouse—which caused Mrs. Stever to complain. Her workers had started asking for more money, she explained during her rare visits to Queenstown. Until then, they had always paid their shepherds and maids in produce, cheating them heftily at that.

However, there was little for the Maori to do on Stever Station that day, and what was worse, one of the girls had told Elaine that they were planning to migrate soon. The Stevers' sheep would be up in the highlands for the summer, after all, and Mr. Stever was cheap. He paid his workers only on a per diem basis, when he had a specific need for them. That being the case, the tribe planned to depart for a few months to fish and hunt in the highlands, and then return in the fall to herd the sheep back down to the lowlands. That was of the traditional Maori way, and they seemed to be looking forward to it. But a sad summer lay ahead for Elaine and Callie.

Now they were desperately looking for something to do. On that day in particular, Elaine did not feel like brooding. The wedding was taking place, after all. In its way, it had been touching of her mother not to tell her exactly what time the ceremony was, but of course Elaine had found out anyway. It did not hurt as much anymore. If she had been wise, she would never have gotten her own hopes up. Up against a girl like Kura, she could not help but lose.

Filled with gloomy thoughts, she led Banshee to her grandmother's stables. To her surprise, she found two horses there that she did not recognize, one more beautiful than the other. Both were black, a gelding and a stallion. The stallion was unusual. Most farmers, even the wealthy sheep barons, preferred mares and geldings because they were easier to handle. And yet this fellow here seemed perfectly trained. He hardly stirred when Elaine led Banshee past him. The mare had already been covered, though, and would soon be having Owen's foal.

The gelding, unquestionably of Arab pedigree, was almost as handsome as the stallion, and was likely his son or brother. It was unlikely that someone had bought two such similar animals independently of each other. So it must be two riders who had come to town together. Elaine's curiosity was piqued, and she planned to ask her grandmother about it.

Elaine took the most direct path between the stable and the house, only casually brushing the dirt and horsehair from her riding dress. She did not plan to change her clothes, and she had tied her hair back carelessly. Regardless of whether she would be helping in the kitchen or the store, she did not want anyone to notice her.

One of the twins was waiting at the reception desk, looking through a supply catalog and clearly bored.

"Oh, hello, Lainie! And Callie!" She laughed radiantly and petted the dog, who immediately jumped up on her, wagging her tail. Elaine was convinced that Callie could tell the difference between the twins. She, however, still had to guess. Her grandmother had said

Mary was the more outgoing one. So she was more likely to be at the front desk while Laurie cooked.

She tried her luck. "Hi, Mary!"

The twin giggled. "Laurie. Mary is helping out in the store. Even though we have so much to do. Mrs. O'Keefe has several guests, and we have to cook. But now you're here. Mrs. O'Keefe said you're to take over the front desk, so I can finally get to work in the kitchen."

Elaine was not particularly pleased about that arrangement, as she no longer enjoyed working at the reception desk. On the other hand, she couldn't really take care of the cooking on her own. She didn't even know what Helen wanted to serve. So she obediently took Laurie's place. Callie followed Laurie into the kitchen, where something tasty often fell down for her.

At least Elaine could satisfy her curiosity. The new guests must have written their names down, so she would quickly be able to learn whose horses those were in the stables.

John and Thomas Sideblossom.

Elaine almost had to laugh. If her mother only knew she had just fallen into the lion's den. She knew the old stories about John Sideblossom but did not take them very seriously. Besides, that had all been twenty years ago—half an eternity for a young Elaine. In any event, there was no reason for Fleurette to still be unsettled by him. Elaine had seen him from a distance before and had not found him so terrifying. A tall, muscular man with weathered skin and longish, dark hair that had probably gone gray. His haircut had been somewhat unconventional, but otherwise he did not strike her as so outlandish. Elaine's mother had always talked about his "cold eyes," but Elaine had never gotten that close to him. Nor, for that matter, had Fleurette in the last twenty years. She always barricaded herself in her room as soon as she heard he was coming to town.

Elaine heard steps on the front porch and froze. She would have like to make herself invisible, but she had to smile and receive the hotel's guests. She lowered her gaze as the colorful wind chime that Helen had hung at the entrance announced the arrival of a guest.

"Good evening, Miss O'Keefe! Nice to see you here again."

Thank goodness it was only Mr. Dipps, the older of the two bankers. Elaine nodded at him.

"You're early, Mr. Dipps," she observed, looking for his key.

"I have to go back to the bank later. Mr. Stever wants to discuss a loan and cannot come in during normal hours since he has to see to his animals then. He's complaining that his Maori are taking off, but it's his own fault for not hiring people on for the whole year. Oh well, since I'm going to be working late, I came back a little early. Would it be possible for me to make use of the bathhouse, Miss O'Keefe? Or would that be too much to ask of you?"

Elaine shrugged. "I can ask Laurie, but the twins have their hands full today. It's possible that the stoves have been heated anyway. We have new guests, and they may want to bathe as well."

She ran to the kitchen and looked almost enviously at Laurie cutting carrots. She would have liked to hide away in here, rather than run the risk of seeing John Sideblossom out there. Though, in truth, she was a bit curious about him.

Laurie raised her head from her work and thought for a moment. "The bathhouse? Yes, we heated it. But I don't know if there's enough water for three people. Ask Mr. Dipps to be frugal. As a banker, he should know how to do that."

Mr. Dipps heard the comment—Elaine had forgotten to shut the door—and laughed with delight. "I'll try to do my bank justice. If I use too much, I'll haul up a couple of buckets myself; I promise. Do you have the key, Miss O'Keefe?"

While Elaine was looking for the key to the bathhouse, she missed hearing the wind chime when it rang a second time. When she had finally found the key in a drawer and turned to face Mr. Dipps, she found herself unexpectedly standing before a new guest as well. The tall, dark-haired man standing behind the banker fixed his inscrutable brown eyes on Elaine.

Almost scared to death by his sudden appearance, she lowered her gaze and blushed. At the same, she grew angry with herself. She could not behave like that here. The man must think her a hopeless fool. She forced herself to look at him.

"Good evening, sir. What can I do for you?"

The man looked her over for a moment before deciding to smile at her. His face was chiseled, almost a little square even, and his curly hair was neatly combed. It looked as though he was coming from a business meeting.

"Thomas Sideblossom. My key, please. And the key to the bathhouse. We've reserved it."

Mr. Dipps smiled apologetically. "I have it at the moment. If I might offer to show you the way, we won't need to bother Miss O'Keefe."

"I . . . I could call the bellboy if more water is needed," Elaine stammered.

"I think we'll manage," said Thomas curtly. "My thanks . . . Laurie, was it?"

"No, I should say thank you . . . but I . . . that is, I'm not Laurie." Elaine now looked at the young man more closely, admiring his smile, which softened his features.

"What's your name then, miss?" he asked amiably. He seemed not to have been put off by her stammering.

"Elaine," she said. "Elaine O'Keefe."

Thomas Sideblossom did not have much experience with *pakeha* girls. There simply weren't any in the area around the farm where he grew up, and on his travels he'd had contact only with a few whores. They had proved far from satisfying though. Whenever Thomas thought lustfully of a woman, a brown, wide-hipped figure appeared before his eyes rather than a light-skinned creature. Her hair should be straight and black, long enough to wrap around his fingers and hold in his hand like reins. He banished the image of submission from his mind— a head thrown back, a mouth opened in a scream. He banished the thought of Emere from his mind. Such an image had no place here. For even if he did not know much about respectable *pakeha* girls, the insolent little things in the brothels had made it clear enough to him that he could not come close to expecting of them what Emere did for his father.

So if he ever wanted to get married, he knew he would have to make compromises. And getting married was unavoidable: Thomas needed an heir. He could not risk having his father and his father's new wife potentially produce a little rival. Not to mention the fact that he simply couldn't take it anymore. All these women in the house, all of whom belonged to his father, or were taboo because they . . . No, Thomas dared not think about that either. The only thing he knew for certain was that he needed a woman all his own, who belonged entirely to him and who must never have belonged to another. It had to be a suitable girl, from a good house. But not one of those giggling, overly self-assured creatures occasionally introduced to him by hopeful business partners. The daughters of those sheep barons and bankers were attractive, but he was turned off by the way they examined him appraisingly, almost lasciviously, their frank speech, and their enticing way of dressing.

Which made the little redhead from the front desk, whose whole life story Mr. Dipps was now describing for him, appear all the more refreshing. The banker proved himself loquacious in the bathhouse, and little Elaine had kept the town gossips thoroughly occupied. Naturally, that knocked her out of the running for Thomas. It was a shame, but this girl was obviously no longer unspoiled.

"The fellow broke the girl's heart." Dipps recounted Elaine's relationship to William Martyn with genuine sympathy. "But the girl he cheated on her with was out of her league, of course. It would have been hard for anyone to compete with her, a Maori princess, that one."

This last bit of information was of little interest to Thomas. A Maori girl was out of the question for the heir of Lionel Station. Elaine, however, had made a good impression at first. So sweet and shy in her simple, dark high-buttoned riding dress. And yet nicely shaped, with long, silky hair—silk-lined reins. Thomas allowed himself a reverie of a few seconds, during which he pictured delicate red tresses taking the place of Emere's hair.

Still, he would not have spared the girl a second thought after Dipps's revelations—had his father not mentioned Elaine as well.

"Did you see the redhead at reception?" John Sideblossom asked when the men met later in their room. Thomas had just left the bathhouse and was changing, and John had just arrived after dealing with Herman Stever. It had gone well. The man planned to buy a whole herd of their best ewes, driving himself deep into debt for them. Though of course it could be a good stroke of business for him if he bred the sheep right on schedule and did not skimp in the wrong places. John would have liked to sell him a few rams too, but the obstinate German claimed not to need them. It would be his own fault if the offspring did not meet his expectations.

Thomas nodded indifferently, though an image from his earlier reverie flashed before him. "Yes, I met her already. Her name is Elaine. But she's damaged goods. They say she was involved with an Englishman."

James laughed, but it was his predatory laugh, not the hearty laugh he used among the men with whom he like to recount his conquests in the various brothels he frequented up and down the West Coast.

"Damaged, that one? Never ever. Now, who told you that? She might have been in love, but she's a classy girl, Thomas. She wouldn't go to bed with just anyone."

"I heard she's related to the hotel owner," Thomas said. "And she has the red hair too . . . though she doesn't behave like she grew up in a pub."

John roared with laughter. "You think she's related to Daphne O'Rourke? The madam? I don't believe it! Don't you have any sense for class, boy? No, no, that red hair comes from the Wardens. She gets that from the legendary Gwyneira McKenzie, formerly Warden."

"Gwyneira McKenzie?" Thomas inquired, buttoning the vest of his three-piece suit. "Of Kiward Station? The one who's married to that rustler now?"

"That's the one. This girl's the spitting image of her mother and grandmother. Just looks like a gentler version. Fleurette had a sharp tongue, and old Gwyn no less so. But she was a classy girl, both were classy. You should take another look at the girl. Besides, I still have a score to settle with that family."

Thomas did not rightly know whether he wanted to help settle his father's scores. But what he had heard about Elaine's family intrigued him. He already knew all about his father and Fleurette Warden—everyone in the area still talked about it years later. The only woman to ever resist John Sideblossom, according to the gossip. Who just disappeared after their grandly announced engagement, only to reappear, already married, in Queenstown. It would be difficult to top Fleurette—he was quite certain that this girl Elaine would never behave in such a manner. All the better. Thomas Sideblossom's hunter's instinct was aroused once again.

He skipped the visit he had been planning to Daphne's. How would it look if he satisfied himself with a whore one night and then tried to court a girl from a good house the next day? His hope of running into Elaine at the hotel's dinner table went unfulfilled. However, he learned that she was not an employee, but Helen O'Keefe's granddaughter. Hence the misunderstanding about her being Daphne's relative.

"Elaine is a charming girl, but one has to lure her out of her shell first," Helen revealed. "She was out of sorts earlier because she was so timid at the front desk. She fears you must think her an idiot."

Helen was not entirely comfortable speaking so openly about Elaine to the Sideblossoms and knew that Fleurette would probably have stoned her for doing so. On the other hand, this young man appeared well-bred, friendly, and courteous. He had inquired very politely about Elaine, and he was at least as handsome as William Martyn. And he was rich! Perhaps Elaine would start to behave more like her former self if another distinguished young man courted her.

Nothing would come of it, of course. But a few friendly conversations, a hint of admiration in the boy's dark eyes—Thomas Sideblossom's gaze was less sharp and piercing than his father's, more wistful—might be just the thing to bring Elaine back to life. The girl was so pretty. It was time someone told her so!

"I actually quite like it when a young girl is a little . . . hmm . . . reserved," Thomas said. "I rather liked Miss O'Keefe. If you would pass that along for me . . ."

Helen smiled. Elaine would finally have a reason to blush with joy again, rather than from a lack of self-assurance.

Thomas likewise smiled. "Perhaps I will see her here again. Then I would be able to speak to her at greater length."

Helen had the feeling that things were moving in the right direction.

3

Thomas ran into Elaine again in her father's store when he was looking for fabric for new suits. There were excellent tailors in Queenstown, as his father had pointed out. And they worked at much more reasonable rates than their colleagues in Dunedin. When he really thought about it, there was hardly any reason to make the long trip to Dunedin for every little thing. He liked every aspect of the selection in Queenstown. And the fabrics that Ruben carried were not only of good quality but were also recommended by the most delicate hand.

Elaine was straightening a few bales on a shelf when Thomas entered the textiles department. His father was busy with Ruben O'Keefe at the time. All the better, as Thomas wanted to get another look at the girl on his own.

Elaine turned a flaming red when she saw him coming, but Thomas thought it suited her. He also liked the timidity, almost fear, in her eyes. They were beautiful eyes, scintillating like the sea in the sun with a hint of green. She was still wearing the same riding dress as the day before. One certainly could not accuse her of vanity.

"Good morning, Miss O'Keefe. You see, I made a note of your name."

"It's . . . it's not like I have a twin." The stupid remark slipped out before she could work up something cleverer. Thomas, however, seemed to find her enthralling.

"Thankfully, no. I think you're one of a kind," he responded gallantly. "Would you care to show me a few fabrics, Miss O'Keefe? I need two suits. Something high quality, but not too gaudy. Suited to business in banks and formal evening functions—the livestock breeders' gathering in Dunedin, to be specific."

A few months before, Elaine would have coquettishly replied that livestock breeders tended to go about in leather jackets and breeches. But at that moment, no reply came to her at all. Instead, she simply let her hair fall into her face. She was wearing it down that day, and it was well suited to hiding. When she lowered her head, no one could see her face, though she could not keep track of what was happening around her very well either.

Thomas looked on, amused at the way she fingered through the selection. She really was quite attractive. And she must be red-haired down below too. Thomas had once been with a red-haired whore whose pubic hair had been blonde. It had made him angry. He could not stand it when people tricked him.

"Here, there's this one, and we also have something in brown," Elaine said.

It matched his eyes, she thought, but she could not bring herself to say it out loud. In any case, it would certainly look better than the gray suit he was wearing that day. He had beautiful eyes. There was something mysterious in them, something hidden.

She laid the swatches of material before him eagerly.

"Which would you choose, Miss O'Keefe?" he asked kindly. His deep voice was a bit raspy and almost too quiet to hear, altogether different from William's bright tenor.

"Oh, I . . ." Surprised by the question, she lapsed again into stammering. Finally, she pointed at the bolt of brown fabric.

"Good. Then I'll take that. The tailor will contact you after he's taken my measurements. Thank you very much for your advice, Miss O'Keefe."

Thomas moved toward the exit. Suddenly Elaine would have liked to stop him.

Why did she not just say something? Before that business with William, she had never found it difficult to talk with people. Elaine opened her mouth, but could not overcome her own resistance.

Thomas turned around abruptly.

"I would enjoy seeing you again, Miss O'Keefe. Your grandmother told me that you ride. Would you care to accompany me on a ride?"

Elaine did not mention her rendezvous with Thomas Sideblossom to her parents. Not only because she knew how her mother felt about his father, but even more importantly, because she feared being rejected again. No one was to know about it if another man should take an interest in Elaine O'Keefe. For that reason, she steered Banshee quickly out of town. Thomas behaved like a perfect gentleman. The town's residents would simply think it a coincidence that the black horse and Elaine's white mare had left the stables at Helen's hotel at the same time, and it was to be expected that their riders would exchange a few words in that situation. Only Daphne followed Elaine and Thomas with a searching gaze. It was not easy to pull the wool over her eyes. She saw the interest in his eyes, as well as hers. And she did not like it.

As it turned out, the black gelding belonged to Thomas, the stallion to his father. And the horses were, in fact, father and son. "My father once bought an Arabian in Dunedin," Thomas said. "A fantastic horse. He's been breeding it ever since. He always keeps a black stallion. Khazan is his third. My horse here is named Khol."

Elaine introduced Banshee, but she did not overwhelm Thomas—as she once had William—with a torrent of details about her grandmother Gwyneira's Welsh cob breed. She still hardly spoke a word in Thomas's presence, though that did not appear to bother him. Maybe she had scared William off with her chattering? Elaine was struck hard by the realization that Kura had answered practically every question with only yes or no. She would definitely have to exercise more restraint.

So she rode in silence alongside Thomas, who had no trouble keeping the conversation going on his own. Though he was thoroughly interested in his companion and asked many polite questions, Elaine answered with a simple yes or no as often as she could. Otherwise, she proffered brief comments, always hiding behind her hair. Indeed, she only slipped up once during the whole ride: she suggested a race when they came to a long, straight stretch. She was immediately sorry she'd suggested it though. William had never liked such wild rides, and when she had beaten him, he had become downright angry. But Thomas reacted differently. He even seemed to be quite taken with the idea as he brought his horse up next to Elaine's. He let her give the signal to start. The Arabian Khol beat Banshee effortlessly, of course, but Elaine crossed the finish line only three horse lengths behind him.

"She's pregnant," she explained, excusing her horse.

Thomas nodded, not much interested. "That's what mares are for. But you're a bold rider."

Elaine took that as a compliment. As she rode home much later, she held her head high for the first time since William's betrayal, letting her hair blow in the wind.

When the Sideblossoms extended their stay in Queenstown, Ruben grumbled and Fleurette came up with more work that needed to be done around the house. Only Helen knew of the relationship developing between Thomas and Elaine, whose frequent meetings were no more a secret to her than the first signs of Elaine's recovery. Of course, she felt some degree of guilt, since she was clearly abetting their secret. On the other hand, Elaine was laughing again, and she'd observed that Elaine was wearing more flattering dresses and brushing her hair until it shone.

Helen did not notice that Elaine lowered her head whenever she spoke with Thomas or that she remained largely monosyllabic, weighing each word carefully. When Helen had been growing up in England, all the girls had behaved that way. In fact, she had found Elaine's open manner with William rather shocking. When Helen compared Thomas to William, Thomas was the clear choice. William had been charming and eloquent, of course, but also thin-skinned and impulsive. Helen had always felt when speaking with him at the table as though she were guarding a powder keg. Thomas, however, was polite and reserved, a gentleman from tip to toe. Whenever he rode out with Elaine, he held the stirrups for her.

At the church service on Sundays, which the Sideblossoms attended, naturally, Thomas exchanged only a few polite words with the girl, and not even Fleurette noticed the pair's friendly relations at first. She was too busy trying to make herself invisible. As Ruben and Fleurette had done everything they could to avoid the Sideblossoms, they were surprised when Thomas asked Elaine to join him for a boat ride after the community picnic. The ever-resourceful church society was renting rowboats to young couples to collect money for the construction of a new church.

"I met your daughter in Mrs. O'Keefe's hotel and would be honored if I could treat her to a little something."

Elaine immediately reddened as she all too vividly recalled her last moments of fun with William.

Fleurette looked as though she was about to rudely turn him down, but Ruben laid a hand on her arm. The Sideblossoms were good customers, and Thomas's behavior had never given them cause for complaint. There was no reason to send him away. As Fleurette launched into an argument with her husband, Thomas led the nervous Elaine, with her father's permission, over to the nearest rowboat. Elaine did not notice that he had not even asked her whether she would like to go or that he did not—as William had—let her choose the color of the boat. Thomas simply steered them toward the nearest one and genteelly helped her in.

Elaine, overcome by a flood of feelings and memories, did not say a word the entire time, but looked very sweet in her pale-blue silk dress, with matching ribbons braided into her hair. She gazed into the water, her face averted from Thomas, who had a chance to admire her profile as he fought against his own memories. Emere's silhouette in the moonlight like a shadow play. She never looked the man who took her in the eye. In the sunlight, it didn't seem real. Yet if Thomas were to take a wife, he would also have to deal with her during the day after filling his nights living out his darkest dreams.

But Elaine was quiet and looked easily intimidated. It would be easy to keep her in line. He tentatively began to speak of the Sideblossom farm and Lake Pukaki.

"The house has a beautiful view of the lake, and is comparable to Kiward Station in style, even if it is not quite so big. We have well-tended gardens, and there is plenty of house staff on hand . . . even if Zoé thinks the Maori don't do their work well. She's working hard to rectify that, but a second woman in the house would be a great benefit to Lionel Station."

Elaine bit her lip. Was that meant to be a proposal? Or was he cautiously testing her? She risked a look at Thomas's face and read the expression in his eyes to be serious, bordering on a little anxious.

"I've . . . heard that the farm is in a very . . . lonely place," she remarked.

Thomas laughed. "None of the big sheep farms have neighbors close-by," he said. "There is only a Maori camp near Lionel Station. Queenstown is the nearest town of any size, though there are a few smaller villages closer. But a place is only lonely if you are unhappy."

It sounded as though Thomas, too, was lost in his own sad thoughts.

Elaine looked up at him timidly. "And are you often lonely?" she asked hesitantly.

Thomas nodded gravely. "My mother died when I was still a boy. And the Maori who cared for me never . . . gave me what I needed. Later, I was sent to England to boarding school."

Elaine looked at him with interest, suddenly forgetting her shyness.

"Oh, you were in England? How was that? It's supposed to be very different than here."

Thomas smiled. "Well, there aren't any weta bugs, so you might not think much of it if you couldn't live without the 'god of ugly things.'"

"That's what it means in Maori, right? 'The god of ugly things.' Do you speak Maori?"

Thomas shrugged. "A bit. Like I said, my nannies were natives. That's entirely different from England, as well. There, good nannies

carry the children to bed and sing them lullabies instead of . . ."
Thomas trailed off, and a painful expression swept across his face.

Elaine studied him and felt an upswelling of sympathy within her.
Bravely, she put her hand on his arm. He let the oar go.

"I would not mind living on a farm even if it was a little isolated.
And I have nothing against weta, either." In fact, she had enjoyed
catching the huge insects as a child and racing them with her brother.

Thomas got ahold of himself. "We can talk more about it later,"
he said. Elaine felt a surge of warmth inside her that William, too,
had made her feel when he spoke lovingly to her.

Arm in arm with Thomas, she walked with a spring in her step
back to the place where her parents were sitting.

"What did he talk about with you?" Fleurette asked skeptically
after Thomas had taken his leave with a formal bow.

"Oh, just about weta," Elaine murmured.

⁂

"Your granddaughter is in love again," Daphne said flatly over tea
with Helen. "It appears she has a weakness for men that make my
hair stand on end."

"Daphne!" admonished Helen. "What exactly is that supposed to
mean?"

Daphne smiled. "Forgive me, Helen. I meant to say that Miss
O'Keefe is drawn to men who fill me with a vague feeling of unease."

"Have you ever made a kind remark about any man of your
acquaintance?" Helen inquired. "With the exception of those who . . .
er . . . are in a certain sense self-sufficient?"

Daphne demonstrated a pronounced preference for barkeepers
and bellboys who felt themselves more drawn to the same sex. She
had always spoken very warmly of Lucas Warden; she had gotten to
know him shortly before his death.

She laughed. "I'll remember that expression! Drinking tea with
you is still so informative after all these years, Helen. As for the boys,
homosexuals are simply more practical, since they don't bother the girls.

167

Besides, normal men are boring. Why should I waste kind remarks on people who aren't even clients? These Sideblossoms, however. The boy never comes by, but the old man is not exactly among our favorite guests, and that's putting it mildly."

"I don't want to know about that, Daphne," Helen declared energetically. "Even disregarding the fact that Thomas Sideblossom's behavior here has been above reproach, Elaine is really flourishing."

"It might be a short bloom though," Daphne noted. "Do you really think he has honorable intentions? And even if he does, Fleur won't be happy."

"That goes without saying," Helen said. "But the same goes for her as for you, Daphne. Thomas and John Sideblossom are not the same person. Whatever the elder Sideblossom's failings, he must not have passed them on to his son. My Howard was no gentleman either, but Ruben does not take after him one bit. It could be the same with the Sideblossoms."

Daphne shrugged.

"*Could,*" she noted. "But if I remember correctly, you, too, only discovered the truth about Howard after you were already established in the Canterbury Plains."

Inger was more direct with Elaine, even if she did not go into all the details of her experience with John Sideblossom.

"Daphne would only let him have the experienced girls. There were always discussions about it. He only wanted the very young ones, and, in a certain sense, we wanted that too, because it . . . well, there was always extra money for men like that and we often got a few days off too. But Daphne only gave in once because Susan really, really needed the money."

Inger pointed a little ashamedly at her pelvis, a gesture that Elaine did not know how to interpret, however.

"After that"—to her astonishment, Elaine saw her friend blush for the first time—"but after that, she didn't need the extra money anyway. Her . . . expectation did not survive the night. But Susan was rather . . . that is, she was not well. Miss O'Rourke had to get the doctor. And after, she would always run off when Mr. Sideblossom came. She couldn't look at him anymore."

Elaine found Inger's story very strange. What "expectation" had Mr. Sideblossom destroyed? But she did not want to hear about him anyway. She wanted to talk about Thomas. When she described to her friend in minute detail what they did when they were together, Inger could not find fault with any of it. If there was any cause for concern, in fact, it was that Thomas's behavior was so reserved.

"Strange that he's never tried to kiss you," she said after an excruciatingly long description of a ride during which Elaine and Thomas had done nothing more than exchange glances.

Elaine shrugged. She would not allow herself to admit that it was precisely that aspect of Thomas's behavior that she liked most. After the incident with William, she was anxious about touching. She did not want anything else awakened within her that would find no fulfillment. "He is a true gentleman, you know, and he wants me to take my time. Sometimes I think he has serious intentions." She blushed slightly.

Inger laughed. "Let's hope so! When boys don't have serious intentions, they go after what they want quicker. Not even ladies are spared."

Thomas was still uncertain. On the one hand, Elaine was appearing more and more often in his dreams, and she was, of course, a suitable bride. On the other hand, he felt almost unfaithful—a completely ridiculous feeling, as he had never once touched Emere. She would never have permitted it, not even when he was a little boy yearning for innocent tenderness. Yet it was almost as though a window would close—an era would be brought to an end—if he seriously courted Elaine and ended up bringing her back to Lionel Station. Thomas could not bring himself to make a decision, though he would soon have to, because his father was pushing him. He was more than happy with his son's choice—and was already looking forward with devilish glee to dancing with Fleurette O'Keefe at Thomas and Elaine's wedding—but for the time being, he wanted to return to his farm. Queenstown had run out of charm for him; he had seen to all the business he needed to and visited every whore Daphne would let him. He had also begun to miss his young wife, Zoé, and the work on the farm. It would soon be time to herd the sheep out of the highlands, and he needed Thomas back for that.

"What reason do you have for wanting to stay here?" he asked his son. "Does a Sideblossom hang around a woman's front door like a male dog in front of a bitch's doghouse? Strike while the iron is still hot! Ask the girl and then her father. It'd be better the other way around, but nobody does that anymore. You've got the girl eating out of your hand, don't you?"

Thomas grinned. "The girl is ripe for the picking, though I'm not sure she knows what that means. It doesn't seem that this Martyn fellow could have taught her much, being as timid as she is. How could I ever have doubted that she was a virgin? She shrinks whenever I so much as accidentally touch her. How long will you give me?"

John Sideblossom rolled his eyes. "After you've got her in bed, three minutes. Otherwise, I'd like to leave in no more than a week. By then, I should hope that you will have gotten your yes."

"But I *want* to marry him!" Elaine held her head up defiantly, and almost stomped her foot. For the first time in months, Fleurette and Ruben caught a glimpse of their old vivacious and contentious daughter. They just wished it had happened under different circumstances.

"Elaine, you don't know what you're saying," Ruben said. Unlike Fleurette, who had reacted hysterically to Elaine's announcement of her engagement to Thomas Sideblossom, he tried to remain calm. "Do you really want to marry a complete stranger whose family history is, to put it mildly, questionable at best?"

"One of my grandfathers was a rustler, and the other was a murderer! I think we're quite well suited to each other," Elaine objected.

Ruben rolled his eyes.

"A family with whom we haven't had the best experiences, then," he corrected himself. "If you marry him, you'll be moving off to a farm in the middle of nowhere. Lainie, Nugget Manor is practically on Main Street compared to Lionel Station."

"What of it? I have a horse, and I know how to ride. Kiward Station is isolated as well, and it doesn't bother Grandmum Gwyn. Besides, there are other people there: Zoé, Mr. Sideblossom . . ."

"An old womanizer who just bought a young girl for his love nest!" Fleur cursed him, leaving Elaine speechless for a moment. She would have expected an expression like that from Daphne, but never from her well-bred mother.

"He did not buy Zoé," Elaine said.

"Didn't buy her? Half the West Coast is talking about how he did."

Fleurette had evidently not spent the last few weeks only doing housework, but had also found time to visit her neighbors near and far, during which all the gossip that the South Island had to offer was discussed at length.

"Zoé Lockwood's father was looking at total ruin," she said. "He had completely overreached with his farm and his high living, another self-important braggart who came into a fortune though gold mining but had no idea how to hold onto it. Sideblossom paid Lockwood's debts and offered him a few sheep to breed. He got the girl in a trade. I'd call that 'buying.'"

Fleur glared at her daughter.

"But Thomas and I love each other," Elaine maintained.

"Oh, do you?" Fleurette retorted. "You thought that about William too!"

That was too much. Elaine vacillated between bursting into tears and throwing something at her mother.

"If you won't let me, we'll just wait until I'm of age. But I'll marry him one way or another. You can't stop me!"

"Then wait!" Fleur yelled angrily. "Maybe you'll come to your senses."

"I could elope with him."

Ruben thought with dread of his daughter sulking for several years. He did not think Elaine capricious enough to change her mind. Moreover, he, too, had noted the changes in his daughter. Thomas Sideblossom seemed to have done her quite a bit of good. If only Lionel Station were not so awfully far away.

"Fleur, maybe we should talk about this alone for a moment," he said in an attempt to intercede. "It won't do any good for us to keep yelling at each other. If we arranged a sufficiently long engagement . . ."

"Out of the question!" Fleurette was still haunted by the memory of the night John Sideblossom had cornered her in Kiward Station's stables. Fortunately, her mother had arrived just in time, but then Fleur had crossed paths with Gerald Warden and several of his drinking buddies while on her way through the salon in a torn dress. It was the most mortifying episode of her life.

"Mother, you don't even know him! You haven't said so much as a word to Thomas, but you speak of him as though he were Satan himself," Elaine argued.

"You're right," Ruben observed. "Come on, Fleur, give him a chance. Let's invite the young man over, and hear what he has to say."

Fleurette flared up at him. "Because that worked out so well with William!" she remarked. "In the end, everyone was taken in by him except me. Dinner is no test of human nature. This is about Lainie's future."

"That's right, about *my* future! But you always want to interfere."

Ruben sighed. This could go on for hours. Fleurette and Elaine rarely argued, but when they did, they fought tooth and nail. He could not bring himself to listen anymore. He stood up calmly, went to the stables, and readied his horse. Perhaps he would simply go have a talk with the Sideblossoms himself—something best done with *both* father and son.

Ruben had no public feud with John Sideblossom. True, he did not find him very sympathetic and he continued to hold a grudge against him, but the tall, hard-drinking farmer had never had many friends. He had become famous in the livestock breeders association for hunting down James McKenzie, but he'd likewise been infamous. His behavior back then had routinely offended the gentlemen farmers in the group, but no one could argue that he hadn't been successful. As for Fleurette, she and Ruben had already been a couple for a long time when John Sideblossom had come around to court her. He and Ruben had never been direct rivals. Ruben had heard the stories of how the courting played out. As far as he knew, a great deal of alcohol and even more braggadocio had played a role. And after twenty years, he was prepared to forgive. In addition, John had proved himself a good customer who was able to pay his bills. His mother was right about that. The man did not haggle, preferred quality to cheap junk, and was quick to decide when it came to large purchases.

He came quickly to the point once the men had gathered in the pub.

"I know that your wife is still angry with me, and that saddens me," John Sideblossom declared. "But I don't think the young ones should be made to suffer because of that. Not that we're watching some great love story unfold here. That's not my style. But to my way of seeing things, the match is a good one. My son is a gentleman and can offer your daughter a livelihood appropriate to her standing. Lionel Station is a very grand estate. And, unless my young wife surprises me"—his smile reminded Ruben of a shark—"Thomas is my only heir. So you don't have to worry about anyone being after the dowry this time."

"This time?" Ruben erupted.

"Come on, the rumors about that business with William Martyn are all over town. An ambitious young man like that—do you blame him for choosing Kiward Station over running a branch of a general store?"

Ruben felt his blood beginning to boil. "Mr. Sideblossom, I'm not *selling* my daughter to the highest bidder."

"That's what I'm saying," John said comfortably. "'The greatest of these is love.' Says so in the Bible, no less. Just marry your daughter off without thinking about the finances."

Ruben decided to take a different approach.

"Do you love my daughter?" he asked, turning inquisitively to the younger Sideblossom, who had not said a word so far. Whenever the old man spoke, his son had little to add. Ruben had noticed that already in the store.

As Thomas turned to him, Ruben found himself looking into inscrutable brown eyes.

"I would like to marry Elaine," Thomas declared formally and gravely. "I would like her all for myself, to support her and care for her. Does that tell you what you want to know?"

Ruben nodded.

Only much later would he reflect on how Thomas's "declaration of love" could just easily have justified the purchase of a pet.

4

The O'Keefes and the Sideblossoms agreed on a six-month engage-ment. The wedding was to take place at the end of September, during New Zealand's spring, before the sheepshearing, which required Thomas and John's presence. Fleurette insisted that Elaine visit Lionel Station at least once before the wedding, so that the girl could see what she was getting herself into. Fleurette wanted to accompany her daughter herself, but then her courage failed her. Everything within her bristled at the idea of spending even a single night under the same roof as John Sideblossom. Though she remained steadfastly opposed to the match, she could not come up with any good arguments against it. The men had met with each other and come to an agreement, and neither the elder nor junior Sideblossom had made a bad impression during the meeting.

"So the old man is a scoundrel, everyone knows that. But he's no worse than Gerald Warden. It's that whole generation. Seal hunters, whalers—my God, they didn't make their fortunes in kid gloves. They were roughnecks! But they've settled down with the years, and the boy appears well-bred to me. Those fellows occasionally raise some softies. Just think of Lucas Warden."

Fleurette had only fond memories of Lucas Warden, the man she had long thought to be her father. So finally she, too, declared herself ready to get to know Thomas. When she did, she could not find any objections to the young man. However, Elaine's behavior toward him surprised her. When William had been around her, the girl had been practically glowing—whereas with Thomas, she fell silent. Fleur had grown accustomed to seeing her daughter chattering away cheerily again as she rushed through the house with her skirts and hair blowing about her.

Fleurette finally asked Helen to accompany her granddaughter when she went to visit the Sideblossoms, and Leonard McDunn offered his services as a driver. Fleur thought both of them had good judgment, but they seemed to be of two minds when they returned.

Helen was full of praise for the comfortable house, and its beautiful location and well-trained staff. She found Zoé charming and well-bred. "An exemplary beauty!" she crooned. "Poor Elaine retreated back into herself again when she found herself confronted with that radiant young woman."

"Radiant?" Leonard asked. "I found her rather cold, though she does look like a gold-foil angel. Didn't surprise me at all that Lainie was reminded of Kura. Only this time the girl's not competition. She only has eyes for her husband, while young Sideblossom never looks at anyone but Lainie. As for the servants, those people may be well trained, but they're afraid of their masters. Even of little Zoé! When she's among the maids, that angel turns into a field marshal. Their housekeeper, Emere, is like a dark shadow, that one. I found her downright spooky."

"You exaggerate," Helen interrupted. "You just don't spend enough time around the Maori."

"There's one thing I still haven't gotten over! That flute music, and always at night. It was enough to give you the creeps." Leonard shuddered. He was not normally the nervous type—more the sort of man who kept both feet firmly on the ground—and no one had ever noticed him having any dislike of the Maori before.

Helen laughed. "Oh yeah, the *putorino*. That is true. It does sound a bit eerie. Have you ever heard it, Fleur? It is a very strangely formed flute of hardwood that you can practically play in two voices. The Maori refer to its male and female voice."

"Male and female?" Leonard asked. "To me it sounded more like a drowning cat underwater—or what I imagine the critter would sound like in that case."

Fleurette had to giggle despite all her concerns. "It sounds like the *wairua*. I've never heard it before though. Have you, Helen?"

Helen nodded. "Matahorua could awaken it. It would send an ice-cold chill down your spine." Matahorua had been the Maori witch doctor on O'Keefe Station whose advice on "feminine matters" Helen and Gwyneira had sought from time to time in their younger years.

"*Wairua* is the third voice of the *putorino*," Fleurette explained to Leonard, who was looking on uncomprehending. "The spirit voice. It's rarely heard. Apparently, it involves using a very particular technique to bring it out."

"Or a particular talent," Helen said. "In any event, this Emere is no doubt considered a *tohunga* among her people."

"And that's why she plays the flute after dark until the last night bird stops its twittering?" Leonard asked skeptically.

Fleurette laughed again. "Perhaps her people don't dare visit her during the day," she ventured. "From what I've heard, Sideblossom doesn't have a very good rapport with the Maori. It's quite possible that they only seek out their witch doctor in secret."

"Which still does not answer the question of what a Maori *tohunga* is doing as the housekeeper of such a disagreeable *pakeha*," grumbled Leonard.

Helen waved him away. "Don't listen to him, Fleur. He's only upset because the elder Sideblossom took twenty dollars from him at poker."

Fleurette rolled her eyes. "Then you got off pretty well, Leonard," she said conciliatorily. "He's taken other people for all they were worth. Or did you think he'd made all the money for Lionel Station from whaling?"

Anyone would have found that proposition doubtful. The manor house was too fine for that, the furniture and interiors of the rooms too expensive. Though Zoé had grown up in similar surroundings, Elaine had been almost awed by the home's splendor. While Zoé had handled the expensive porcelain and the crystal glasses with ease, Elaine had needed to concentrate as she reminded herself of her grandmother's long-ago lessons regarding how to use the various spoons, knives, and forks at dinner.

Elaine did not reveal her anxieties about these things. In answer to Fleurette's question, Elaine declared that Lionel Station had been lovely. Though she had been greatly looking forward to exploring the farm, she had not managed to see much of it. But there would be plenty of time for that after the wedding. Thomas had been wonderful, very obliging and polite, and she was still in love with him. Moreover, it had always been a dream of hers to live on one of the grand farms—even as a child, she had been completely taken with Kiward Station. Preoccupied as she had been learning about the house, Elaine had not noticed the spooky housekeeper or the nightly flute playing. Perhaps, she thought, her room had been in a different wing of the house from her grandmother's or Mr. McDunn's. And the sound of the *putorino* did not carry far.

Fleurette herself couldn't pinpoint what it was that she did not like about the upcoming wedding. Perhaps she was just letting her prejudices influence her feelings. For that reason, she restrained herself from expressing her unease. After all, no one had been interested in her vaguely skeptical feelings about William, either. She was therefore surprised to suddenly hear from someone who shared her concerns: Daphne O'Rourke.

The infamous "hotel owner" stopped her on Main Street two months before the wedding. Fleurette noticed that Daphne was behaving in an unusually inconspicuous way and that she was dressed in a relatively reserved dark-green velvet dress without any more flounces than were decent.

"I hope I'm not overstepping my bounds, Mrs. O'Keefe, but I would like to have a word with you."

Astonished but open-minded, Fleurette turned to her. "Naturally, Miss O'Rourke. Why ever not?"

"There's that," Daphne grinned, gesturing with a motion of her hand toward several respectable ladies who were looking over at them curiously.

Fleurette smiled. "If that's the only reason, we can go to my house and have tea. If *you* feel bothered, that is. Let them talk, for all I care."

Daphne grinned even more widely. "You know what? Let's really give them something to talk about and go to my residence. The pub is closed now, so we can sit in there." She gestured to the entrance of her hotel.

Fleurette did not have to deliberate over the invitation for long. She had been in Daphne's establishment before, had even spent her wedding night there with Ruben. So why should she hesitate? Giggling like schoolgirls, the two women repaired to the pub.

It had changed considerably since Fleurette had first arrived in Queenstown many years ago. The barroom was much more sumptuous than before. Nevertheless, it still contained all the same features as practically all bars in the Anglo-Saxon world: wooden tables and chairs, stools at the bar, timber-plank construction, and an arsenal of bottles lined up on shelves. But the stage on which the girls danced had been crafted with markedly more care than the simple wooden dais that had once stood there. Pictures and mirrors also hung on the walls. Though they were a bit frivolous, Fleurette found no cause to blush.

"Come, we'll go to the kitchen," Daphne said, leading Fleurette to an area behind the hotel's front desk. In Daphne's Hotel there was not just whiskey but also small meals to be had.

Daphne prepared tea while Fleurette sat comfortably at the kitchen table. It was a rather long table, and Fleur thought that Daphne probably fed her girls there.

"So, tell me, what is this about, Miss O'Rourke?" Fleur asked as her host set a lovely porcelain cup in front of her.

Daphne sighed. "I hope you don't take it as an intrusion. But, damn it . . . oh, forgive me. Surely you have an uneasy feeling about this situation too."

"About . . . the situation?" Fleurette asked cautiously.

"Your daughter's engagement to that Sideblossom fellow. Do you really want to ship your daughter off to that hermitage on the far side of the Pukaki? Alone with those fellows?" Daphne poured the tea.

"What I want does not seem to matter," Fleurette said. "Elaine is insisting. She's in love. And Helen . . ."

"Is singing the praises of Lionel Station, I know." Daphne blew on her cup. "That's precisely why I wanted to speak with you, Mrs. O'Keefe. Helen, well . . . she is a lady. And what's more, she's . . . let's put it this way, she's perhaps an especially ladylike lady. There are things you can't talk to her about."

"Do you know something about Thomas Sideblossom, Miss O'Rourke?" Fleurette asked nervously.

"Not about the boy. But the old man is . . . well, I wouldn't leave my daughter alone with him. They also say strange things about his marriage."

Fleurette was about to object, but Daphne raised her hand to signal for her to wait.

"I know what you're about to say. The old man has a bad reputation, but the younger one could be different. Helen made the same objection. And I don't mean to say anything against the boy. It's only that"—Daphne bit her lip—"you should probably tell Elaine before her wedding what she can expect."

"I should do *what*?" Fleurette asked, blushing. She loved her Ruben dearly and was not ashamed of what they did in bed together. But to talk about that to Elaine?

"You should tell her what happens between men and women in bed," Daphne specified.

"Well, I think she knows the most important things . . . We all figured it out for ourselves. I mean . . ." Fleurette did not know what to say.

Daphne sighed again. "Mrs. O'Keefe, I don't know how I can express myself more clearly. But let's just say that not everyone figures out the same thing, and it's not always a pleasant discovery. Tell her what *normally* happens between a man and a woman."

Fleurette's conversation with Elaine turned out to be rather embarrassing for both of them and left more questions unanswered than it resolved.

In its most important aspects, she explained to her daughter, the same thing transpired between a man and a woman as between a stallion and a mare. Only the woman would not be having any foals—at least not literally—and that, naturally, it all took place in the marriage bed in the dark and not in public in broad daylight. Owen and Banshee had, after all, felt no compunctions about that.

Elaine turned beet red, her mother no less so. By the end, neither of them could speak, and Elaine preferred to put her questions to a less ladylike initiate. That afternoon she went in search of Inger.

However, her friend was not alone. Inger was chatting in her mother tongue with a pale-blonde girl; Elaine recognized her as one of the new stars of Daphne's establishment. Elaine turned to leave, but Inger motioned for her to stay.

"Maren was just leaving anyway. You can sit with us until she goes. Or does that make you uncomfortable?"

Elaine shook her head. Maren's cheeks, however, had flushed. Apparently, the two women had been discussing rather salacious matters. As they continued, it became rapidly clear how uncomfortable Maren felt.

"Can you translate for me?" Elaine finally asked, annoyed. "Or just speak in English. Maren needs to learn the language if she's going to stay here."

The immigrant girls often did not speak English very well, which was one of the reasons that many of them ended up in brothels instead of finding more suitable employment.

"The subject is a little difficult," Inger said. "Daphne asked me to explain something to Maren that she . . . well, that she would not understand in English."

"Well, what is it?" Elaine's curiosity was aroused.

Inger chewed on her lip. "I don't know if respectable girls should hear it."

Elaine rolled her eyes. "Sounds like it has to do with men," she said. "And I'm getting married soon, so you can just—"

Inger laughed. "Then you *definitely* shouldn't hear it."

"It's about how woman not have babies," Maren said in broken English, looking intently at the ground.

Elaine laughed. "Well, you're an expert on that," she remarked, looking at Inger's stomach. The young woman was expecting her first child in a matter of weeks.

Inger giggled. "To know how to avoid having babies, you first have to know how they're made."

"My mother says it's like between a stallion and a mare," Elaine said.

Maren snorted with laughter. Her English was evidently not all that bad.

Inger laughed too. "Men and women generally do it lying down," she clarified. "And they look at each other while they do it, if you understand what I mean. You can do it other ways too, but . . . well, they're not suitable for a lady."

"Why not? My mother says that it's nice . . . at least when all goes well," Elaine said. "Though if it's so nice, why don't all girls . . . um . . ." She cast a meaningful look at Maren's "uniform," a red dress with a wide neckline.

"I not find nice," Maren said.

"Well, not with strangers. But with the man you love, then it's nice," Inger said, qualifying her friend's statement. "Men always think it's nice though. Otherwise, they wouldn't pay for it. And if you want to have a baby"—she stroked her stomach—"it's unavoidable."

Elaine was confused. "So, how does it work then? I thought you had babies when you did it like . . ." She trailed off, glancing at Callie, who was letting Maren pet her just then.

Inger raised her eyes to heaven.

"Lainie, you're not a horse or a dog," she said sternly and began to repeat in English the speech she had just made to Maren. "Women conceive children when they lie with men exactly in between their bleedings. Exactly between. Daphne gives her girls that time off. They only have to sing and dance or work in the bar on those days."

"But then you would only need to do it at that time," Elaine said. "At least if you wanted a baby."

Inger rolled her eyes. "Your husband won't think that way. He'll always want it. I can promise you that much."

"And when still do in tese days?" Maren did not seem to have understood everything either.

"Then you make a rinse of warm water and vinegar. Immediately after. Wash everything out of yourself even if it burns, and use as much vinegar as you can handle. Then do it again the next day. True, Daphne says it's not sure to work, but it's worth a try. She says it always helped her. She never had to have anything done away with."

Elaine did not dare ask what Inger meant by "done away with." Just the thought of washing the most intimate region of her body with vinegar made her shudder. But she would never have to do that. She wanted Thomas's children, after all.

5

A storm was brewing over Kiward Station, and William Martyn spurred his horse on to try to make it back to the house before the rain started. A tumult was raging inside him similar to the one building in the cloud formation above, which had begun sending powerful gusts of wind across the Canterbury Plains. The foremost cloud suddenly obscured the sun, and a thunderclap crashed and rumbled dully over the land. The light over the farm grew strangely sallow, bordering on ghostly, and the hedges and fences cast threatening shadows. Then the first bolt of lightning whipped through the atmosphere, seeming to electrify the air. William rode faster, but did not manage to leave his anger behind. On the contrary, the harder the wind blew, the more he wished he had the power to fling thunderbolts, to give expression to his rage and disappointment.

As soon as he returned to Kura, he would have to contain his temper. Only then would he have any chance of persuading her to take his side now and again when it came to the interests of the farm. If she would only be willing to more firmly assert her—and therefore his—future claim over the farm! But he was completely on his own in that respect. She did not seem to hear his complaints about the intractable shepherds, the lazy Maori, and the recalcitrant foremen. She merely listened to him with an indifferent expression on her face and answered with non sequiturs. Kura still lived only for her music—and she seemed not to have given up on her dream of performing in Europe. Whenever William informed her of a new slight by Gwyneira or James McKenzie, Kura consoled him with remarks like: "But dearest, we'll be in England soon enough anyway."

Had he really once believed that this girl was rational?

Still in a temper, he steered his horse between the neatly fenced-in pastures, where woolly ewes were feasting on massive quantities of hay, unperturbed by the weather. This despite the fact that there was plenty of grass adjacent to the farm! Though the spring sun seemed fainthearted, there had already been the occasional hot day. All around the lake and the Maori settlement, the grass stood high from the previous year and was still growing appreciably. For that reason, William had given Andy McAran the order to herd the ewes there. But the fellow had simply ignored his order, and, even more infuriatingly, set Gwyneira on him. And she had cut William down to size right there in the cow barn.

"William, *I* make decisions like that, or James does, if necessary. You shouldn't have anything to do with it. The sheep are about to lamb, and we have to keep an eye on them. You can't just send them out on their own."

"Why not? We always did it that way in Ireland. We sent one or two shepherds with them, and then off into the hills they went. And the Maori live there anyway. They can keep an eye on the sheep," William said, defending himself.

"The Maori want the sheep munching on their gardens as little as we do," Gwyneira explained. "We don't use the land around their houses, around the lake where they live, or the rock formations we call the 'stone warriors' for pastureland. Those are holy places for them."

"You're telling me that we're neglecting several acres of the best pastureland because the darkies over there pray to a couple of rocks?" William asked belligerently. "A man like Gerald Warden agreed to such nonsense?"

Over the last few months, William had heard a great deal about Gerald Warden, and his respect for the founder of the farm had grown. It seemed like the man had had style; the manor was proof of that. Surely, he'd likewise had the livestock husbandry and his workers under control. Gwyneira let too much slide for William's liking.

Her eyes flashed angrily, as they did every time William mentioned the old sheep baron.

"Gerald Warden generally knew how to pick his battles!" she said gruffly before continuing in a more conciliatory tone. "I know you mean well, William. Just think things through a little more. You read the paper too, after all, and you know what's happening in the other colonies. Native uprisings, massacres, military occupation. It might as well be war over there. The Maori, by contrast, are soaking civilization up like sponges. They're learning English and listening to what our missionaries have to say. They even sit in our parliament, and all that in less than twenty years! And I'm supposed to disturb this peace to save a bit of hay? And that doesn't even take into account the fact that the stones in the green grass have a very ornamental look to them."

Gwyneira's face took on a wistful expression, though she did not, of course, reveal to William that her daughter, Fleurette, had been conceived in that very circle of "stone warriors."

William looked at her as though she were out of her mind. "I thought Kiward Station already had problems with the Maori," he remarked. "You in particular."

The fights between Tonga and Gwyneira were the stuff of legend.

Gwyneira snorted. "My differences of opinion with Chief Tonga have nothing to do with our nationalities. We would argue even if he were an Englishman . . . Or an Irishman. I'm learning about the obstinacy of those people as well. The English and the Irish fight over things that are just as childish as what you want to start a fight about here. So please, show some restraint!"

William had backed down. What else could he do? But confrontations like that one were becoming more common, with James McKenzie as well. Fortunately, he was absent at the moment, as he was attending his granddaughter Elaine's wedding in Queenstown. William wished the girl much happiness, and her fiancé seemed to be a good match. He would not have been against going to the wedding with Kura to congratulate them and could not understand why Gwyneira had rejected the idea so vehemently. Nor could he comprehend why she was missing the wedding. He would have been able to take care of Kiward Station on his own. He might even have been able to get the workers to pick up the pace.

He was still having trouble with the employees. They were so different from in Ireland, where he had always enjoyed a good relationship with his tenants. In Ireland the tenants feared their landlords and requited every loosening of the reins with gratitude and affection. Here, on the other hand, if William handled one of the shepherds roughly, that shepherd sometimes did not think it necessary to even announce his resignation. He simply packed his things, rode to the main house to collect the rest of his pay, and looked for a job on a neighboring farm.

The old hands like Andy McAran and Poker Livingston were even worse. They just let his outbursts wash over them. William sometimes daydreamed about firing them as soon as Kura came of age and handed the management of the farm over to him. But the workers did not even have reason to fear that. Andy and Poker, for example, had female acquaintances of long duration in Haldon. Andy McAran's friend, a widow, even owned a small farm. They could find shelter there in no time. And the Maori were a problem all of their own. They disappeared as soon as William got loud, simply leaving him in the lurch. They would appear again the next day—or not. They did whatever they liked, and Gwyneira let them.

"Fire!"

William had been trotting along lost in thought, his head with its wide-brimmed hat lowered against the rain, which had begun to beat loudly and powerfully, drowning out all other sounds. But suddenly William discerned hoofbeats and a high-pitched voice behind him. A Maori youth was racing toward him on an unsaddled horse bridled only with a cord around its neck.

"Quickly, quickly, Mr. Martyn! Lightning struck the cow barn, and the steers have overrun the fences! I'm going to get help. Ride quickly! It's burning!"

The boy did not await William's response and instead galloped on toward the house. William turned his horse and spurred it to a gallop. The cow barns lay by the lake and contained several herds of steers and cows. If the animals really were running around, then it was possible the Maori and their holy pastures were going to have company after all.

Indeed, he soon detected the smell of something burning. The lightning strike must have been powerful. The flames were already spreading from the feedlot despite the rain, and mayhem reigned all around the barns. Workers were running about in the thick smoke, trying to free the last, miserably lowing cattle. Gwyneira McKenzie was with them. She burst out, coughing, from the barn, dipped a cloth in a bucket of water, held it to her face, and ran back inside. There did not yet appear to be any danger of the building collapsing, but the animals in the barn could suffocate. The Maori men—the entire village had arrived with lightning speed—were organizing a chain of buckets from the well to the barn; the women and children had formed a second chain to the lake. The loose cattle were running in all directions, trampling the ground into a bog and leveling their paddock fences. Jack McKenzie and a few other boys tempted death by standing in their way but could do nothing to halt the panicked animals. Not that most of them were in any direct danger, as practically all of the barns' stalls had been opened by then. Only a few dairy cows and bulls were still penned up inside—and Gwyneira was attempting at that very moment to free them, along with a few remaining heifers.

"William, go let out the bulls!" Gwyneira called to him, screaming wildly against the wind. She had just emerged for the second time, dragging a cow behind her that seemed to feel safer inside. "That's where we need people who know something about livestock."

William had wanted to manage the bucket chains and encourage the people to work faster, but he turned with trepidation in the direction of the bulls' stalls.

"Get to it!" roared Andy McAran, taking William's horse without asking after William had finally dismounted.

"Come on, Gwyn, we've got enough heifers. We need good riders to herd the steers in. Otherwise, they'll level the Maori village like they did the paddocks." The old farmhand dug his heels roughly into the flanks of William's horse, which seemed to have as little desire to plunge into the tumult as its rider. However, the situation was becoming critical. While the boys held the heifers and dairy cows in check, the young steers had long since been on the move. William observed Gwyneira leaving the cows to other helpers and leaping onto her horse. She rode alongside Andy toward the Maori camp. Her cob mare did not need to be spurred on, seeming to have been waiting for the chance to leave the burning buildings behind.

William finally approached the barn, annoyed at Andy McAran for taking possession of his horse. Why could the cad not release the bulls himself and let William ride off with Gwyneira?

Meanwhile, flames were pouring out of the dairy cows' barn, but the cows were already trotting about outside. Two Maori women who seemed to know what they were doing had freed the last of them and were now drawing them into a paddock that their men were in the process of jury-rigging. The boys were driving the heifers in the same direction. The animals had calmed down significantly, and the rain and thunder slowly abated.

William stepped into the barn, but Poker Livingston held him back.

"Take a rag first and hold it over your nose or you'll breathe in smoke!" The old farmhand then ran back into the barn, directly toward the stamping, roaring bulls. The animals could now see the flames and were panicking in their pens. William began working on the first pen's lock. He didn't feel entirely safe stepping up to the raging monster to untie it, but if Poker thought . . .

"No, don't go in!" thundered Poker, running among the pens. "Haven't you ever worked with cattle before? Those beasts'll kill you if you get in their pens now. Here, come and hold me. I'm going to try and undo the chain from above."

Poker clambered up the stall and balanced precariously on the thin wall. As long as he held tight to a beam, it was fine, but to undo the chain, he had to lean forward and have his hands free. He would have to let go of the cloth covering his mouth too, though the smoke in that area was not overpowering yet.

William climbed onto the wood divider as well, straddled it and held Poker's belt tightly. Poker dangled perilously but kept his balance as he fumbled with the first bull's chain. Both men had to keep a watchful eye to avoid being struck by the mighty animal's horns.

"Open the pen, Maaka!" Poker called to a Maori boy who stood ready in front of the stall. The boy who had just been driving the cattle with Jack ducked behind the gate in a flash as the bull burst forth from his pen.

"Good. Now, onto number two. But careful, Maaka, this one's crazy." As Poker moved to start climbing the wall of the next pen, the bull inside rolled its head about and pawed threateningly at the ground.

"Let me do it, Poker! I'm faster!" The exuberant young Maori had already clambered up the wall before the older man had found the right footing. With a dancer's grace, Maaka balanced on the wooden divider.

William just wanted to be done with the whole business. The flames were coming closer, the smoke was getting thicker, and the men could hardly breathe. But neither Poker nor Maaka seemed to even consider sacrificing the bulls.

William held Maaka by the belt as he had held Poker before, while the old hand went on his own to see to the third bull, a youngster bound to its pen with a rope instead of a chain. Poker used his knife to slice through the rope from above, and Jack McKenzie, who had just entered the barn, opened the stall. As a result, the bull had already stormed out before Poker could even climb back from the feed trough to the gate to set the animal free. Jack and Poker then went to work on the gate of the last pen, which appeared to be stuck. Meanwhile, Maaka was still struggling with the chain on the wild bull, which had only grown more panicked since the other bulls had taken off. The boy leaned forward recklessly, almost floating over the stall's walls.

William did not know whether Maaka was first struck by the bull's horn or his own precarious seat on the divider was to blame, or if the belt that he was holding onto gave way. It could have been the shaking caused by the collapsing haystack that disturbed their balance. William would never know if he felt himself fall or heard Maaka's scream first as the leather belt slid from his hand. But he saw the boy fall between the hooves of the bull as William landed in a corner of the pen himself—safe from an attack as long as the animal was chained up. But then he saw that the bull was free. Maaka must have undone the chain just as he fell. Once the bull realized it was free, it tried to flee, but the pen was still shut. While Poker and Jack struggled with the locking mechanism, the bull ran around its stall in a crazed panic. It stopped short when it caught sight of Maaka, who lay scrunched up on the ground, trying to shield his face. The boy whimpered as the bull's massive, horned head approached him.

"Distract the beast! Damn it, Mr. Martyn," Poker howled, turning the bar on the pen's lock. It hardly budged.

William stared as though hypnotized at the gigantic animal. Distract it? Then the beast would charge at him. He would have to be crazy to do such a thing! But the injured boy was crawling toward him in a panic.

"Look here, Stonewall!"

William saw out of the corner of his eye that Jack McKenzie was waving a blanket in front of the gate to draw the attention of the animal away from Maaka. Dead tired, Jack flung himself against the stall's wall. As he did so, the lock finally gave way, and the door swung open. The bull did not realize this right away, however, and continued to focus its wrath on Maaka. Lowering its horns, the animal was preparing to strike . . . when Jack threw the damp blanket onto the animal's hindquarters and started dancing around behind him like a torero.

"Look here, Stonewall. Come here!"

Poker roared something from the gate, apparently wanting to call the boy back. But Jack stayed where he was and continued goading the bull, which turned around very slowly.

"Come get me! Come on," Jack provoked him—and spun around in a flash when the animal finally began to move. As the wiry boy dove in a single leap over the fence to safety, Stonewall finally saw the opening in the pen. The bull shot out of its stall past Poker Livingston and finally made it outside. The men in front of the barn must have heard the screaming, because helpers streamed inside. Flames had lit up the barn. As William started coughing, he was seized by a couple of strong Maori workers and dragged outside. Two other men carried Maaka away, and a third supported a hacking Poker.

As William, gasping, breathed in the clear late-afternoon air by the lake, he was only peripherally aware that parts of the barn were collapsing behind him.

Although several men were tending to Maaka and Poker, William's helpers didn't even give him a chance to catch his breath before one of them pulled William abruptly to his feet. Once again, his men had markedly failed to show him any respect.

"Are you hurt? No? Then, come, sir. There's nothing more to be done here, but we need to herd the sheep elsewhere. And the cattle have to be put up somewhere. We just got word that Mrs. McKenzie is herding the steers toward the shearing sheds. The sheep needed to go there so that the cattle can go into these paddocks. And we have to work fast. They could be here at any moment." As the man ran to the sheds, he turned around several times, as though to make sure that William was following.

William was wondering why Gwyneira did not herd the cattle straight into the shearing sheds and was about to give an order to that effect. But the words died on his lips when he saw the tiny entrances to the sheds. Of course. The sheep were released more or less one at a time after being sheared and put through a bath, and only then gathered together again in the paddocks outside. The riders would never be able to get a riled-up herd of cattle through those narrow gates. At the moment, the sheep were proving unenthusiastic about the shift into the sheds, which was hardly surprising, as they did not have very pleasant associations with the shearing buildings. But the sheepdogs were doing most of the work anyway. William and the rest of the men merely had to direct the stream of sheep into the correct sheepcotes and shut the gates.

At the time, William didn't know much about how Gwyneira and Andy were herding the cattle, but he heard a great deal about their apparently spectacular efforts later, of course. They had caught up with and stopped the herd of steers just in front of the Maori village, turned it around, and driven it back, with only four riders and a sheepdog. Thanks to their efforts, the damage from the lightning strike was minimal. True, the cow barn was completely destroyed, but a wood building like that could easily be rebuilt, and the stores of hay had been all but exhausted anyway. Only a few of the Maori's fields had been trampled, and Gwyneira would pay the damages. No animals had been lost, and the heifers had only suffered a few scratches and mild smoke poisoning. Only Poker and Maaka had come out of it any the worse off. The old farmhand had some bruises and a dislocated shoulder, while the Maori boy had a few broken ribs and an ugly head injury.

"That could have turned out much worse," mused Andy McAran when it was all finally over, and the cattle were chewing hay in their new paddocks. Jack and his friends had managed to drive the bulls toward the shearing sheds to join the herd of steers and were at that moment walking proudly among the workers. Jack's assertion that in Europe you could make money for making bulls angry by waving a red cloth in front of them while a crowd watched made all the Maori boys want to grow up to be matadors.

"How did that even happen?" Andy asked. "Maaka didn't enter the stall with Stonewall, did he?"

While Gwyneira yelled at her son, accusing him of endless stupidity, Andy McAran began to investigate what had happened. Jack and the other helpers couldn't tell him anything though, since none of them had witnessed the accident, and Maaka himself was still not coherent. Finally, Poker, who sat on a blanket, still coughing, caught Andy's eye.

"The crown prince was a good . . . sorry, a good-for-nothing," commented the old hand with a meaningful smile. Then his face took on a pained expression. "Could somebody snap my shoulder back into place? I promise not to squeal."

"What the hell did you think you were doing?"

Gwyneira had finished with her son and had rewarded the hard-working helpers with a barrel of whiskey. She had given the Maori women a sack of planting seed to thank them for their help. Now she was taking advantage of the walk back to the manor house to lay into William. She was soaked, dirty, in a very bad temper, and looking for a scapegoat. "How could you let the boy fall?"

"I already told you. It was an accident!" William said, defending himself. "I would never—"

"You never should have allowed the boy into the stall! Couldn't you loosen the chain yourself? The boy could have died. And Jack too. But while those two boys tried to let the bull out, you sat in the corner looking on like a spooked rabbit!"

He doubted that Poker had phrased it that way, so that expression must have come from Jack. William felt rage swelling inside him once again.

"That's not how it happened! I—"

"That *is* how it happened!" Gwyneira broke in. "Why would the boys lie? William, you're always trying to secure your position here, which I understand. But then things like this happen. If you've never worked with cattle before, why didn't you say so? You could have helped with the bucket chains or with repairing the paddocks."

"I should have ridden with you," William declared.

"So that you could have fallen off your horse?" Gwyneira asked rudely. "William, wake up! This isn't a business you can run like a country gentleman. You can't simply ride out at your leisure in the morning with your gamekeeper and delegate the work. You have to know what you're doing, and you should count yourself lucky that you have people like Andy and Poker who come to your aid. People like that are inestimably valuable. This isn't Ireland."

"I see things differently," William stated brazenly. "I think it's a question of leadership style."

In the last light of day, he saw Gwyneira rolling her eyes.

"William, your old tenants have been on the land for generations. They don't even need the landlords. They would keep the shop in order on their own—and maybe even do a better job! But here, you mostly have make do with beginners. The Maori are gifted shepherds despite the fact that sheep only first arrived in this area some fifty years ago with Gerald Warden. There is no tradition here. And the white shepherds are adventurers from the four corners of the earth. You have to teach them and no amount of arrogance will help with that. Just listen to me for once and stay quiet for a few months. Try to learn from James, Andy, and the others instead of insulting them all the time."

William wanted to make a retort, but they had reached the house by then and stopped the horses in front of the stables. Gwyneira led her mare in without a second thought and began to unsaddle it. The stableboys had probably left to celebrate with those who had helped put out the fire. The two of them could be grateful, though, that the house servants had not joined the impromptu party.

William saw to his horse himself, wanting nothing more than a bath and a quiet evening with his wife. She, at least, could almost certainly be counted on to treat him with deference. Gwyneira retired early, and if Kura insisted on sitting at her grand piano for hours, William did not have anything against a private concert. He could drink whiskey while she played—and paint a mental picture for himself of the pleasures they would share in the bedroom later that night. In that arena, there were no problems at all. Every night with Kura was a revelation. The more experienced she became, the more refined her ideas for making him happy. She had no shame, loved with all her senses, and offered up her lithe body in ways that sometimes made even William blush. Yet her joy in loving was completely innocent and free. In that respect, she was a child of nature. And a natural talent.

Gwyneira held the door to the manor house open for William and tossed off her drenched coat in the vestibule. "What a day. I think I'm going to pour myself a whiskey."

For once, William agreed with her, but they did not even make it as far as the liquor cabinet.

Because instead of hearing the expected piano music and song emanating from the salon, they heard soft voices and heavy sobbing.

Kura was hunched over the divan in tears. Heather Witherspoon was desperately trying to calm her.

William let his gaze wander searchingly over the scene. On the coffee table in front of the sofa were three teacups. The women had evidently had a visitor.

"You wanted this!" When Kura caught sight of her grandmother, she leaped up and glared at her, flushed with rage. "You wanted this! And you helped!" This last comment she directed at William. "You never wanted to go to Europe. None of you wanted me . . . me . . ." Kura began to sob again.

"Kura, behave like a lady," Miss Witherspoon said, more sternly this time. "You are a married woman, and this is completely normal."

"I wanted to go to England. I wanted to study music," Kura complained. "And now . . ."

"You wanted William more than anything. You told me so yourself," Gwyneira declared curtly. "And now you should get ahold of yourself and explain to us why you suddenly don't want him anymore. This morning at breakfast, you still looked happy to me." Gwyneira poured herself a whiskey. Regardless of what kind of mood Kura was wallowing in, she needed a pick-me-up.

"Really, dearest." William had not the least desire for further complications on this catastrophic day, but he sat down next to Kura nonetheless and tried to put his arms around her. He thought she might ask why he smelled like smoke and was covered in soot, but Kura didn't notice a thing.

"I don't want to . . . I don't want to . . ." She sobbed hysterically. "Why weren't you careful? Why did you . . ." She extricated herself from William's embrace and began to beat on his chest.

"Collect yourself," Miss Witherspoon ordered her. "You should be happy instead of raging about. Now cease this crying and inform your husband of the news!"

Gwyneira took a different approach. She turned to Moana, the Maori housekeeper, who had just come in to clear away the tea set.

"Who came to visit, Moana? My granddaughter has fallen to pieces. Did something happen?"

Moana's entire wide face was beaming. She, at least, did not seem perturbed. "I not listened, mistress," she explained happily. She then lowered her voice as though to tell her a secret. "But was Miss Candler. Miss Witherspoon send for her, for Kura!"

"Francine Candler?" Gwyneira's troubled expression brightened. "The midwife in Haldon?"

"Yes!" sobbed Kura. "I hope you're all happy! You've managed to pin me down to your damned farm! I'm pregnant, William. I'm pregnant!"

William looked from Kura weeping, to Miss Witherspoon embarrassed, to Moana excited. Lastly, he looked at Gwyneira drinking her whiskey, who had a look on her face like the cat that finally got the canary. Then she returned his gaze.

William Martyn realized that at that moment Gwyneira McKenzie forgave him everything.

6

While William Martyn was securing his position on Kiward Station, Elaine O'Keefe and Thomas Sideblossom's wedding was taking place in Queenstown.

The atmosphere was a little tense, however, especially when the bride's mother had to join the groom's father for an obligatory waltz, during which Fleurette O'Keefe acted as though she were being forced to dance with an oversized weta. At least that was how Georgie put it, earning a reprimand from his grandmother Helen. Ruben found the remark quite apt, though he noted that Fleurette had never really feared touching the giant bugs—unlike John Sideblossom.

Ruben, however, enjoyed his dance with Thomas's still-green stepmother. Zoé Sideblossom was hardly twenty years old and was indeed very pretty. She had curly golden-blonde hair, which she wore up for the wedding, since otherwise it would have fallen to her hips. Her face was aristocratic—pale and symmetrical—her eyes a deep brown that seemed to detract from her hair and complexion. The young woman was polite and well-bred. Ruben could not confirm Leonard McDunn's judgment that she was beautiful but ice-cold.

When it came to beauty, though, the bride shone above the rest that day. Elaine wore a sumptuous white gown with a wide skirt that was so tightly corseted at the waist that she could hardly eat a bite of the wedding feast. Her face seemed to shine with an inner light, and her hair gleamed beneath her lace veil and a garland of white flowers. James McKenzie assured her that he had never seen a lovelier bride, except for perhaps Gwyneira, and for Elaine, that was the nicest compliment she could have received. After all, the last bride her grandfather had seen was Kura. Elaine's wedding was on par with

Kura's in both size and grandeur. George Greenwood had come with his whole family—no doubt in part thanks to Jenny's urgent pleading, as she was eager to pursue her acquaintance with Stephen. They hadn't been out of each other's sight since the Greenwoods had arrived.

"Well, I guess we know who the next bride will be," James McKenzie teased Jenny's proud father.

"I would have nothing against it," George said. "But I think the young man wants to finish his studies first. And Jenny is still very young—though that doesn't seem to stop them."

Thomas and John Sideblossom behaved irreproachably throughout the festivities. John even managed an almost-polite greeting to James McKenzie. Fleurette had feared the worst. John, after all, had been the one to corner her father and drag him to court back in his livestock-thieving days. Though James had his own reasons for hating the groom's father, Fleurette had much more faith in her father's ability to control himself. He kept his distance from John Sideblossom, especially as the evening advanced and the whiskey began flowing in streams. Though Fleurette knew that John could imbibe prodigious amounts without anyone being able to tell, she nevertheless kept a watchful eye on his alcohol consumption that night. He behaved quite well, though, only strengthening his grip on his wife's arm from time to time when she dared to talk or dance with another man.

Inger—who had turned down the role of Elaine's "maid" of honor due to her large stomach—noticed that Thomas Sideblossom was behaving similarly with his new wife. He did not let Elaine out of his sight, and he became increasingly possessive as the night went on. Elaine, by contrast, was almost acting like her earlier self. She was boundlessly happy about the successful party, the kind and admiring looks of the guests, and all the compliments she received. But naturally, she was very nervous, as well. Her wedding night loomed ahead of her, after all, and Thomas had booked the largest room in Helen's hotel.

The old Elaine had always expressed her anxiety through unceasing chatter. She simply talked and laughed away her fear. That evening, she tried to do just that. The restraint she had shown since William's scandalous departure was gone. Elaine joked with Jenny Greenwood and her brother, let Georgie tease her, and allowed Søren to lead her in a dance.

Thomas quickly put a stop to that, however. Smiling coolly, he stepped between the pair, who were happily horsing around on the dance floor.

"May I steal my wife away from you?" he asked politely, but Søren could see the serious expression in his eyes.

The young Swede tried to maintain his jocular tone.

"Like you said, she's yours!" he said amicably, releasing Elaine and bowing to her formally. "It has been a pleasure, Mrs. Sideblossom."

When Elaine heard her new name for the first time, she was so delighted that she did not even notice Thomas's bad temper.

"Oh, Thomas, isn't the party wonderful?" she babbled breathlessly. "I could keep dancing forever."

"You've danced enough," Thomas remarked, leading her ably through a waltz while ignoring her attempts to lean into him affectionately. "And with enough men. You're not behaving in a ladylike manner, and it doesn't suit you. It's time we retired."

"Already?" Elaine asked with disappointment. She had hoped there would be fireworks. Georgie had implied as much, and her parents likewise knew that she had always dreamed of fireworks at her wedding.

"It's time," Thomas repeated. "We'll take the boat. I already talked it over with my father."

Elaine knew that was the plan. She had also learned that Jenny and Stephen had spent the whole morning decorating the boat with flowers. The nocturnal boat ride was supposed to be romantic, and Elaine was looking forward to it, but she was nevertheless saddened to think that she would not be taking Banshee along to Lionel Station. The mare was looking after her foal, a beautiful little stallion. The black pony was stocky and sound, and he could have made the journey to Lionel Station alongside his mother without any trouble. Thomas thought the mare and her foal would hold up the trip, but Elaine did not see it that way, since the party would not be moving all that quickly anyway.

Her father was sending a freight wagon with her trousseau and a few purchases the Sideblossoms had made, and Zoé would be riding in a coach. On the largely unpaved paths between Queenstown and the farm, the coach would, in fact, hold them up a good deal more than a strong cob foal and her mother. Thomas, however, persisted in his opinion, and Elaine relented. John could bring the mare after his next visit to Queenstown. On this trip, Elaine would be accompanying Zoé in her comfortable chaise.

Elaine said good-bye to no one. Only Inger smiled encouragingly at her as Thomas led her to the boat hung with flowers. The ride down the river that followed was very romantic—in part because fireworks were being set off at Nugget Manor. Elaine was delighted by the colorful cascades of light and the showers of stars bursting above the dark trees. She could hardly restrain herself from singing the praises of the lights reflected in the river.

"Oh, what a wonderful idea, Thomas, to watch the fireworks here on the water, just the two of us! Hasn't it been a wonderful evening? We should make love right here, out in nature like the Maori do. My grandmother Gwyneira tells such romantic stories. When she was young, she always rode along when the sheep were being herded and . . . Oh, I would like to do that too, Thomas! I'm so looking forward to life on the farm, with all the animals, and Callie is a wonderful sheepdog. You watch, Callie and I will do the work of three men." Elaine radiated with joy and tried once again to snuggle close to Thomas, as she once had with William. He pushed her away.

"What an idea! Sheepherding! You're a woman, Elaine. It is out of the question for you to go fooling around in the stables. Really, I hardly recognize you today. Has the champagne gone to your head? Now move over to your seat and sit still until we get there. This exuberance of yours is unbearable."

Elaine withdrew, soberly, to the bench across from Thomas.

But then music coming from the riverbank broke the tension between the young couple. The boat was just passing the landing by Stever Station. Elaine's Maori friends, who had returned to the area for the upcoming herding, had gathered on the river to serenade the newlyweds.

Elaine recognized a *haka*, a sort of musical play in which the action was represented in dance while men and women sang and played traditional instruments, including the *koauau*, the *nguru*, and *putorino* flutes.

"Oh, can't we stop, Thomas?" Elaine asked enthusiastically. "They're playing for us."

Then she saw the twisted expression on Thomas's face. Anger? Pain? Hatred? Something seemed to be unleashing a rage in him that he was having difficulty controlling. She also detected a strange hint of fear.

Elaine drew back into her corner of the boat as Thomas seized the oars with a taut face. Though the river's current was strong enough to carry them, Thomas rowed on urgently.

Elaine had a thousand questions, but she remained silent. Thomas was very different than she had thought, and she was slowly beginning to dread their wedding night. Up until then, she hadn't been overly anxious about it. After talking with Inger and Maren and, moreover, after William's caresses, she considered herself almost experienced. For some time now, she had let herself think of William again—almost without spite. She remembered his caresses and his kisses fondly. She had been more than willing to be touched and had become wet from excitement. That had been embarrassing for her at the time, but Inger had assured her that it was completely normal and made lovemaking easier for women to bear. As she had sat next to Thomas admiring the fireworks, she had felt that same warmth and wetness below, but the sensation had passed. What if Thomas did not succeed in arousing her again later? Did he even want to do so? At the moment, it looked more like he wanted to tear someone to shreds.

Elaine pushed the thought firmly away. Of course Thomas would take her in his arms, caress her, and be tender to her. And then she would be ready for him.

To her surprise, the twins were waiting for Elaine at Helen's hotel. And yet they had both still been dancing at the wedding when Elaine and Thomas had left.

"Daph . . . er . . . your grandmother thought that we should come home early to take care of you, Miss O'Keefe," Mary twittered.

"Someone has to help you get your dress off," Laurie added. "And help with your hair."

Thomas was not pleased and tried to rebuff them. "Thank you very much, but I would be happy to help my wife myself."

But he had not counted on the obstinacy of the twins—who had, moreover, received clear instructions from Daphne O'Rourke.

"No, no, Mr. Sideblossom, that wouldn't be decent," Mary protested. "A lady's husband must wait until she is ready. We have some nice hot chocolate for you right here."

Thomas gnashed his teeth and kept control of himself only with great effort. "Why don't you bring me a whiskey."

Laurie shook her head. "No hard alcohol under Mrs. O'Keefe's roof, only wine if you must. And we have a bottle here, but it's for later. You can have a drink with Miss O'Keefe when—"

"Before or after . . ." Mary giggled.

Thomas clenched his hands into fists. Who did they think they were, ordering him around? First those flutes on the riverbank—the damned Maori!—which had awoken these feelings in him, these memories. And now these wenches. What did it matter to them what he did with his wife? And Elaine even appeared pleased about the delay.

"I'll be right in, dearest," she said and happily following the twins upstairs. Thomas sat down in a chair and forced himself to be patient. Starting tomorrow, no one would stand in his way.

Mary and Laurie made a grand production out of undressing Elaine, loosening her hair, and brushing it. Finally, Mary helped her into a richly embroidered silk nightgown while Laurie filled a princely goblet with wine.

"Here, drink up, Miss O'Keefe!" she ordered. "It's excellent wine, a wedding present from Daphne."

"Daphne sent you?" Elaine was suddenly nervous. Until that moment, she had believed that Helen had prepared this surprise.

Mary nodded. "Yes, Miss O'Keefe. And she told us you should drink at least one glass of wine first and then another with him before you . . . well, you know. A sip of wine makes it go more easily and nicely."

Elaine knew that as a lady, she should have protested, and she had never needed alcohol to feel safe and comfortable in William's arms. But Daphne undoubtedly knew what she was talking about. She politely drank up the wine, which had a sweet taste. Elaine smiled.

"Please tell Thomas . . ."

"That you're ready!" the twins said practically in chorus. "We'll do that, miss. Good luck!"

Thomas did not want any wine. Elaine had thought it would be lovely to present herself to him as a Roman goddess of love would have, in her becoming nightgown, her hair flowing down her back, and a chalice of wine in her hand to offer her beloved. But Thomas pushed the glass away—any harder and he would have slapped it from her hand.

"What's this all about, Elaine? Are you playing a little game here? Lie down in bed like an obedient wife. I know you're pretty. You don't need to show yourself off like a whore."

Elaine gulped. She stepped over to the bed like a whipped dog and lay down on her back. The sight seemed to please Thomas.

"That's better. Wait while I take off my clothes. You could have helped me, of course, but not when you're already half-naked. That wouldn't be ladylike. Now wait."

Thomas took off his clothes unhurriedly, laying his things neatly on a chair. But Elaine could hear his breathing quicken, and she was startled when she saw his member after he had removed his pants. Inger had said it would swell . . . but that much? Oh God, it would surely hurt when he pushed that into her. Elaine flinched, turned onto her side and scooted a little away from him. Thomas glared at her. He was breathing even more quickly. He seized her shoulder and pulled her sharply back into the right position. Then he threw himself on top of her.

Elaine wanted to scream as he thrust himself into her, but he covered her lips with his mouth. His tongue and member pushed into her at the same time. Elaine almost bit down in terror and pain. She whimpered as he began moving inside her, moaning with pleasure. As his movements grew faster and his breath ragged, Elaine could barely suppress her pain.

"Ah, that was good . . ." He said nothing more as he caught his breath.

"But . . ." Elaine mustered her courage as the pain abated. "Don't you want . . . don't you have to kiss beforehand?"

"I don't have to do anything," Thomas said coolly. "But if you want."

He only needed a little time to recover; then he threw himself back on her. This time, he kissed her—first on the mouth, just as deeply and forcefully as before, then on her neck and breasts, which hurt because he bit her more than kissed her. It felt so very different than it had with William. Elaine seized up this time more than before. She groaned in pain as he pushed into her again, and he didn't stop until he finally released into her. There was fluid again, as there had been first time. Elaine finally understood what the whores washed off with vinegar when they were forced to make love on unsuitable days. And the thought of a little vinegar, or soap and water at least, sounded very attractive to her just then. She felt sore, dirty, and disgraced as she lay rigidly next to Thomas, who soon fell asleep. Trembling, Elaine got out of bed.

The bathroom lay right next to her room. She hoped that no one else would need it; most of the hotel's guests were surely still at the wedding. At *her* wedding.

To Elaine's surprise, there were lamps burning in the room, and the twins were waiting for her with two buckets of hot water and scented soap.

Elaine burst into tears when she saw them. So that had been Daphne's wedding present. She did not have to bear this all alone. And the twins obviously knew what they were doing. For once, they did not twitter, and instead spoke quietly and comfortingly to her as they removed her nightgown and washed her body.

"You poor thing! It will still hurt tomorrow, but then it'll get better quickly."

With a sponge, Laurie gently rubbed the spots that Thomas's hungry sucking and biting had left behind, what he had called "kisses."

"Is it always like that?" Elaine sobbed. "If it's always like that, then I'd rather die."

Mary pulled her close. "Of course not. You get used to it."

Elaine remembered hearing that Daphne had never made the twins get used to anything like this.

Laurie gave her some more wine; indeed, Daphne had sent several bottles. Elaine drank it, thirsty as never before. She had heard you could drink to forget, but what good what that do? What had just happened would repeat itself again the next night.

"Say thank you to Daphne," Elaine whispered when she finally left the twins and returned, laden with fear, her heart pounding, to the room where her husband slept.

"What we should we tell Daphne?" Laurie asked her sister as the women picked up their things. "He wasn't very nice to her."

Mary shrugged. "True. But how many of them are? Daphne didn't ask if he was nice. She wanted to know if he . . ." She went quiet with embarrassment.

Laurie understood without the need for words. "You're right. It just hurts me to see Miss O'Keefe so. But Daphne doesn't need to worry herself about it. As far as anyone can tell right now, he's normal."

7

Elaine was very relieved that she did not have to ride the next day. In addition to the fact that her lower body hurt unbearably, she had slept poorly, rigid with tension, on the edge of the bed. She ached all over, and her face was bloated and blotchy from crying. Thomas did not comment on her appearance, however. Nor did Zoé, with whom Elaine would be sharing a carriage for the next few days and a house thereafter. Elaine had been hoping for a bit of kindness from her—the young woman had to know what she had been through the previous night, after all—but Zoé didn't say a word. And there was no one else Elaine could confide in.

The Sideblossoms wanted to get an early start. Elaine only had a chance to embrace her parents briefly. Naturally, Fleurette could see that something was amiss, but there was no time for questions. Only Helen had a moment alone with her when Elaine helped carry the breakfast dishes into the kitchen. She immediately recognized Elaine's stiff, painful movements.

"Was it bad, child?" she asked sympathetically.

"It was terrible."

Helen nodded understandingly. "I know, dear. But, believe me, it gets better. And you're young. You'll get pregnant quickly. Then maybe he'll leave you in peace."

Elaine spent the whole of that first morning in the carriage making hectic calculations to determine whether the experience the night before could lead to the conception of a child. Everything inside her bristled at the thought that she could have conceived a child that night. In the end, though, she calmed herself. Her last menstruation had been only four days before and, according to Inger, conceiving at this time was not possible.

Although Zoé's chaise was quite well cushioned, the roads around Lake Wakatipu were in poor condition. Elaine groaned every time they lurched across one of the countless deep potholes. She tried desperately to start a conversation with Zoé, but the young woman did not seem to have any interests other than housekeeping and the various luxury objects with which she had decorated Lionel Station. She spoke at length about the furniture and drapes, but never thought to ask about Elaine's taste or preference. After a few hours, Elaine became determined not to let her husband limit her to the house. She would perish of boredom in Zoé's company. She would have to assert herself and establish her role on the sheep farm. Her grandmother Gwyneira had done it, after all. Lost in thought, she stroked Callie, who could tell that her mistress was in need of comfort.

Zoé eyed the animal critically. "I hope you don't intend to bring that mutt into the house."

Elaine felt a wave of anger swelling up inside her.

"She's no mutt. She's a Kiward border collie. They are the most celebrated sheepdogs in New Zealand. The people of Christchurch even wanted to make a monument to Friday, her grandmother. They descend from the Silkham collies, which are famous throughout Great Britain." Elaine drove the point home. "If only every immigrant had such a pedigree."

Zoé's lovely face twisted into a grimace of rage. Elaine had not wanted to offend her personally—her remark was meant as a joke—but Zoé had evidently not had the most respectable ancestors.

"I don't want animals in the house! And nor does John!" she informed Elaine.

Elaine bristled. If Zoé wanted to fight for dominance . . .

"Thomas and I will have our own rooms, of course," she said. "I will arrange those as I choose. You may as well know that I don't like flouncy valances."

Silence reigned in the chaise for the next few hours. Elaine concentrated on the beauty of the landscape. At first, the road followed the lake, but then they turned off and crossed a plain in the direction of Arrowtown. The grassland was similar to that of the Canterbury Plains, though the land was not as wide or as flat and a greater variety of vegetation grew there. It was a center of sheep breeding—or at least was supposed to become one—before a sheepshearer named Jack Tewa found gold almost thirty years before. Gold miners had been flocking to the area ever since, and the town of Arrowtown had grown quickly. Elaine wondered if there really was gold in the passing streams and rivers, whose bucolic wooded banks looked so inviting.

Thomas had told her they would spend the night in Arrowtown, but in reality they rested at a sheep farm whose owner the Sideblossoms knew. The house had little in common, however, with either Kiward or Lionel Station. It was simple, and the guest rooms were tiny. The owner proved to be, like virtually all farmers in New Zealand, an excellent host nonetheless. Garden Station lay rather far from town, after all, and visitors were rare. Elaine did her best to satisfy Mrs. Gardner's need for news from Queenstown and Otago, even though she was not especially in the mood to chat. Indeed, she was both exhausted after the journey and fearful of the upcoming night with Thomas. Her husband had hardly exchanged a word with her, either that morning or during the trip, and even now, the male Sideblossoms conversed exclusively with Mr. Gardner. The women kept to themselves, and Zoé was no help at all. She ate the proffered food without a word. Elaine's fatigue and anxiety prevented her from eating much of anything as she regaled Mrs. Gardner with her stories. Finally, Zoé asked permission to retire. Elaine joined her only too willingly. Mrs. Gardner looked a little disappointed, but showed herself understanding.

"Of course. You must be tired after your wedding, child, and then off on this journey straightaway. I remember being a newlywed like it was yesterday."

Elaine was afraid that a lengthy paean on the delights of marriage would follow, but Mrs. Gardner seemed to be implying something else. When she brought water for washing up, she nonchalantly placed a jar of salve next to the washbasin.

"You may have some need of this," she said, averting her gaze. "I make it myself, out of pig fat and plant extracts. I have marigolds in my garden, you see."

Elaine had never touched herself before in her nether regions, but when Mrs. Gardner left, she reached for the jar of salve, and, her heart pounding against her chest, began rubbing the raw places between her legs with it. The pain eased instantaneously. Breathing a sigh of relief, Elaine undressed and collapsed onto the bed. Thomas was still drinking with Gardner and his sons—he appeared to be as skilled at holding his liquor as his father—and Elaine fell asleep. That, however, did not save her. She woke up, aghast, and screamed in terror when someone grabbed her by the shoulder and forced her onto her back. Callie, who had fallen asleep in front of the door, barked loudly.

"Make that beast shut up," Thomas growled.

Elaine saw that he had already undressed, and he was holding her tightly. How was she supposed to go out and calm the dog?

"Lie down, Callie! Everything's all right!" Elaine tried calling out to the dog, but her voice sounded so terror-stricken that she would not have believed herself. And her dog had a fine sense for her moods. Thomas released his wife, walked over to the door, and punished the dog with a swift kick. Callie whined but continued barking. Elaine no longer feared for herself alone but for the dog as well. She sighed with relief when she heard Mrs. Gardner's friendly voice in the hall. She seemed to be leading the reluctant dog away. Elaine thanked heaven for her hostess and lay still obediently as Thomas turned back to her.

He did not bother with any caresses that night. He simply thrust into his young wife without even bothering to undress her, pulling her nightgown up so violently that it ripped.

Elaine held her breath to keep from screaming—it would have been mortifying if the Gardners heard her. But it did not hurt nearly as much as it had the night before. Furthermore, the salve facilitated Thomas's thrusting. That night, he only entered her once and fell asleep immediately afterward, not even bothering to withdraw from Elaine's body. She could smell his sweat and the pungent stench of whiskey. He must have drunk a great deal. Elaine vacillated between fear and disgust. Would he wake up if she moved out from beneath him? She had to try, as she thought she wouldn't make it until morning in that position.

Finally, she gathered all her courage and pushed Thomas's heavy body to one side. Then she rolled out of bed as quietly as she could, felt for her dressing gown—an elegant article from Dunedin that she had ordered with images in mind of cozy breakfast scenes with her beloved spouse—and slipped out of the room. The toilet was downstairs near the kitchen, and she heard quiet whimpering coming from within. It was Callie. Elaine forgot her original destination, opened the kitchen door, and followed the sound of the plaintive voice. She eventually found the dog huddled in a corner of Mrs. Gardner's pantry. Elaine fell asleep there too, but fortunately, she woke up before dawn. She hastily closed Callie in again and snuck up the stairs. Thomas did not notice a thing. He was still sleeping as before, lying across the narrow bed, snoring. Elaine pulled a blanket out from under Thomas and spent the remainder of the night curled up on the floor. Only when Thomas began to stir groggily did she curl up on a corner of the bed.

If things went on this way, she would die of lack of sleep. Elaine felt wretched. Mrs. Gardner's sympathetic looks the following morning did not help at all.

"Take that ointment along with you. Oh, and let me write the recipe out for you real quick," she said good-naturedly. "It's a shame that you won't give me the little dog there in exchange. Such a nice animal. It would help us out a lot."

In her panic, Elaine almost considered giving her Callie; then the dog would at least be safe. She had feared that Thomas might seriously injure the dog the night before. But she was sure she would find some solution to the problem on Lionel Station. Instead, she considered writing her grandmother Gwyn a letter. Surely there was a Kiward collie that Mrs. Gardner could have. They just needed to see about getting it there. But arrangements could be made. Elaine would have given her kind hostess almost anything that day, even the crown jewels.

The day passed similarly to the previous one. They were following the trail in the direction of Cardrona and climbing higher into the mountains; there was even still snow in places. Elaine, just as weary and sore as before, was freezing in the chaise. She had not thought to unpack her winter coat. Finally, the driver her father had sent—a bright, redheaded young Irishman—stopped to look for blankets and furs in the trousseau he was pulling. Elaine warmed up but nevertheless sighed with relief when they finally reached the hotel in Cardrona where they were to spend the night. It was a simple, low wooden structure with a bar that women were prohibited from entering. Elaine and Zoé were not even permitted to warm themselves at the fireplace, but had to go straight to their rooms, where a maid served them warm beer and something to eat. Elaine drank as much of the beer as she could, despite the fact that it tasted terrible. Aside from a little wine, she had never drunk much alcohol before, but she recalled Daphne's message: alcohol could make it all go more easily.

Unfortunately, the beer did not have the desired effect. On the contrary. That night was the worst she had yet had to endure, for Thomas came to her almost directly after their arrival and was not drunk. Elaine hoped at first that this would make him more patient and gentle, but she trembled at his mere touch. To her horror, that only seemed to arouse him.

"You're adorable when you play hard to get," he said. "I like this a great deal better than that nonsense you were trying before. It suits my innocent little country girl."

"Please, no!" Elaine backed away as he reached for her breasts. She had not yet completely undressed and was still wearing her corset, but that did not seem to bother him. "Not like this, please . . . Can't we be a little . . . nice to each other first?"

She blushed under his mocking gaze.

"Be nice? What do you mean by that? Some little game? Did that whore friend of yours teach you something? That's right, don't try and deny it. I asked around about your acquaintance. So how do you want it? Like this?"

He ripped open her corset, threw it on the bed, and kneaded her breasts. It hurt, and she pulled out of his grasp, but he only laughed and moved to thrust himself into her.

"Or would you prefer something wilder? Maybe like this?"

Elaine whimpered as he turned her around.

Men and women normally looked at each other as they did it, Inger had said. What could possibly be normal about this?

Over the course of the next few days, their path took them out of the mountains. They made good time and it grew warmer. Grass once more grew between the rocks. Yellow and white spring flowers pushed their way out of the ground, unwilling to match Elaine's cheerless mood. She knew from her first trip that the landscape around Lake Wanaka was even lovelier than that around Queenstown. The rocks did not descend so abruptly into the lake, and there were beaches and forests by the shore. For the first time since Elaine's wedding, the weather was beautiful, and the views of the lake magnificent. The lake was a deep blue, with a beach nestled up against it and imposing trees reflected in the water. It appeared to be completely void of people. That was an illusion, however, as the township of Wanaka lay nearby. It was a small town, comparable to Haldon near Kiward Station, only in a much nicer location. The Sideblossoms crossed Wanaka early that afternoon, but then followed the Cardrona River in the direction of Lake Hawea. It was a detour, but this path led directly along the lake through the mountains, and was one of the few roads that could be managed with vehicles.

They spent the last night of their journey in a farmhouse on the Hawea River. Elaine was finally allowed a break there. The men got so drunk on the whiskey that the Irish farmer distilled himself that

Thomas could not even find his way to bed. Elaine finally slept the whole night through and was in considerably better spirits for the last stage of the journey. However, she become increasingly nervous as they approached her new home. Had she really ridden through this unpopulated mountain landscape on her first visit to Lionel Station? The area was gorgeous—the beauty of the deep-blue lake competing for attention with the splendor of the mountains—but she had not caught sight of a house or any sign of human habitation all day. Elaine finally faced the truth: even if she had her horse at hand, it was a full two-day ride from Lionel Station to Wanaka. What she had failed to registered before suddenly became undeniably clear: John and Thomas, Zoé, and perhaps a few workers were the only white people she would see for months at a time.

Lionel Station lay in the Makarora region, west of Lake Pukaki. The estate dominated a bay at the mouth of the Makarora River, and the pastureland occupied by the Sideblossoms' sheep stretched around the manor and along the river up into the McKenzie Highlands. The house servants consisted entirely of Maori, but since no village lay directly adjacent, they slept in provisional shelters on Lionel Station. Even Elaine, who was not all that familiar with Maori customs, understood that this likely meant a great deal of fluctuation in the staff. The Maori were a family-based people, and their tribes drew them back even when they enjoyed working for the *pakeha*. The personnel who were expecting them that day, therefore, consisted of many different members of the tribe than those who were present on Elaine's first visit. Zoé had complained about that en route. She was endlessly occupied with training new people. She seemed to have a talent for it, however, since the new personnel carried themselves impeccably. Then again, the servants were overseen by another Maori.

Elaine recognized an older woman who had been introduced to her previously as Emere. Her face still bore tattooing, but would have appeared fearsome even without the traditional ornamentation of

Maori women. She wore her long gray-laced black hair down, which was unusual for the servant of a mistress as strict as Zoé, who placed value on Western clothing and pinned-up hair and even insisted that the chambermaids wear bonnets. But Emere did not look like she took many orders. She had an air of unflappable self-assurance as she appraised Zoé and then Elaine with bottomless, expressionless dark eyes.

Elaine greeted her as graciously as she could after her long journey. She wanted to establish a good relationship with the staff. Without any friends, she knew she would be lost on Lionel Station.

Thomas did not leave her enough time for a thorough introduction, however.

"Come, Elaine, I'll show you our apartments. I had the west wing arranged for us. Zoé was kind enough to help furnish it."

Elaine, who, after her first restful night, was no longer docile and afraid but angry about the way she had been treated, followed him peevishly.

Thomas came to a stop in front of the entrance. A door in the lavish entry hall led to the west wing.

"Do you want me to carry you over the threshold?" he asked, grinning.

"Save your romantic inclinations for more intimate occasions," she retorted brusquely.

Thomas looked at her, astonished. Then his gaze became wary, and a flicker of anger flashed in his eyes. With unaccustomed courage, Elaine returned his gaze.

As she had expected, the west wing was overflowing with flowery valances and prim, dark furniture, none of which appealed to Elaine. Normally, she would not have cared much, since she preferred to keep busy outside and she hardly noticed her surroundings when she found herself reading an interesting book inside. But just then, she could no longer restrain herself.

"Can I change anything about the furnishings if I don't like it?" she asked, her tone more provocative than she had intended.

"What don't you like about it?" Thomas inquired. "The furnishings meet the highest standards of taste. Everyone who's seen it has been in agreement. You can do as you like, but—"

"My standards may not be particularly fine, but I like to see my hand when it's in front of my face," declared Elaine, shoving the heavy curtains in front of one of the windows resolutely aside. This required a bit of strength as Zoé liked voluminous velvet monstrosities that completely shut out the outside world. "These, at the very least, must go."

Thomas looked at her, and his gaze spellbound her. Had she really believed a week ago that pain underlay his impenetrable expression? His secrets had been revealed since then. Thomas may have felt abandoned as a little boy, but he had found a way to get what he wanted as an adult.

"I like them," he said heatedly. "I'll have your belongings brought up. Tell the servants where you want them to put your things." With that, he turned around, dismissing Elaine, who found herself both frightened and humiliated by the threatening tone in his voice.

What was she supposed to do with an entire wagonful of her trousseau? Because of their confrontation, Thomas had not even shown her into their shared rooms. Elaine looked desperately around her.

"May I help you, madam?" an affected and very young voice asked her from the entrance. "I am Pai, your lady's maid. Or at least that is what Mrs. Sideblossom said I am supposed to be, if it pleases you."

Elaine looked confused. She had never had a lady's maid before. Why did she need one? Little Pai did not quite seem to know, either. She couldn't have been more than thirteen years old and looked lost in her black maid's uniform with its white apron and bonnet. And this formal form of address. Zoé had sent the girl she could most easily do without to her daughter-in-law. Anger and defiance sprang up inside Elaine. But it wasn't Pai's fault. With her wide, unusually light-skinned face, the girl looked innocent and kind. She wore her thick black hair in a tight ponytail that emphasized her heart-shaped face. She was certainly not pure Maori, but mixed like Kura, though far from being such an extraordinary beauty.

Elaine smiled. "How lovely. *Kia ora*, Pai! Do you know these rooms? The men are about to bring a mountain of stuff in here, and we have to do something about it. Do we have . . . Do I have any other servants?"

Pai nodded energetically. "Yes, madam, another maid, Rahera. But she is shy. She does not speak much English. She first came here two weeks ago."

So, it was just as Elaine had thought. Zoé had kept the experienced servants for herself while she had to sort things out with the new arrivals. Well, she would try to hold onto her maids for a longer time.

"That's all right, Pai, I speak a little Maori," she said pleasantly. "And you speak very good English, so we'll get along fine. Go fetch Rahera . . . Or, no, first show me the apartments. I need some idea of where things should go."

So Pai led Elaine around. She felt much better as soon as Pai pointed out her room. It looked like Elaine had a bedroom and dressing room all to herself. She would not have to share her bed with her husband every night then, or at least not have to sleep beside him. In addition to those rooms, there was a salon and a study, one leading into the other, neither of which was very large. It was reasonable to assume that Lionel Station was similar to Kiward Station in that the biggest common room would be used by everyone in the house, and meals would be taken together. The west wing had no kitchen, but did have two amply furnished, extremely modern bathrooms.

Elaine had a gift for quickly assessing a situation and good spatial imagination. She therefore had no trouble figuring out the layout of the apartments, and when the men—the driver her father had sent and a Maori worker—carried in her furniture and chests, she could tell them quite precisely where to put them. Pai likewise proved herself useful. She may not have had much experience, but she knew that as a lady's maid, it was incumbent upon her to take care of her mistress's clothing—and that consequently, it was best that the clothing be placed in the dressing room. So Pai energetically emptied chests of clothing into the dressers and drawers, while Rahera placed silver and crystal ware in the display cases with so much care that it bordered on reverence. The Maori boy assisting with the move introduced himself as Rahera's brother Pita. Normally, he explained to Elaine, he worked as a shepherd. He had only offered his services as a mover to be close to Rahera.

Or rather, Pai, Elaine thought, who had not missed the conspiratorial sparks in the eyes of the boy and girl. But all the better. If Pai found a suitor here, she would not run off anytime soon.

"That be beautiful dog!" Pita said, admiring Callie, who had entered the house with the driver. The dog had spent the previous few nights with him in the covered wagon. Elaine had to find somewhere new for her, not an easy task, and all the more pressing for that reason.

"Good for sheep. Bought Mr. Sideblossom?" Pita's English needed work. Elaine had to find out where these people came from, what tribe they belonged to, and why there was such a difference in the education level between Pai and the others.

"No," she said with a bitter smile. "He came here along with me. Her name's Callie. She's my dog." She pointed to herself when Pita seemed not to understand right away. "Only listens to me."

Pita nodded. "Very beautiful dog. You lend us for sheep."

"Madam!" A sharp voice came from the door. Zoé rushed into the room. The young woman had apparently already taken a bath and changed after the trip. She looked a good deal fresher and cleaner than Elaine felt. She immediately set about correcting the servants. "Repeat after me, Pita! 'If it would be agreeable to Mr. Sideblossom and yourself, we would like to borrow the dog for our work with the sheep, madam.' I don't want to hear this native babble in my house. And above all, habituate yourself to the correct form of address: 'madam.'"

Zoé waited until the terrified Pita had repeated her complicated phrase—doubtless without completely understanding it. Only then did she turn to Elaine. "Is everything to your satisfaction? Thomas said you . . . particularly liked the furniture." The young woman smiled sardonically.

Callie growled at Zoé. Elaine suddenly wished her gentle collie were a snarling rottweiler.

"My own furniture will mix things up a little," Elaine said with steely self-control. "If Pita would be so kind as to help his sister push the drapes out of the way. There's no need to call me 'madam,' by the way, Pita, not in my house."

Pita and Rahera looked at her like frightened rabbits, but Pai suppressed a giggle.

"We will await you at eight o' clock for dinner," Zoé said as she left the west wing carrying herself majestically.

"Goat," growled Elaine.

Pai grinned at her. "What did you say, madam?"

It was almost eight o'clock by the time all the chests had finally been emptied and the furniture distributed among the rooms. Most of it had been placed in Elaine's bedroom and dressing room. To make room, she'd had a few of the original pieces of furniture distributed to other rooms. The living room now looked rather crowded, but Elaine did not care, since she did not plan to spend much time there. She had only ten minutes to change for dinner. She recalled from her visit that dinner had been a very formal affair. Was it John who insisted on that? Or Zoé? It would depend on how strictly the men interpreted the rules. Elaine did not believe that Zoé had as much say in the house as she pretended to. During their journey, she had always proved quite submissive to John.

Nevertheless, Elaine would not have sat down at the table in a dirty traveling dress even in Queenstown. She had to at least provisionally clean herself and put on another dress. Fortunately, Pai was already laying one out for her. But first her father's driver wanted to say his good-byes.

"Do you want to get going already, Pat?" she asked, astonished. "You could leave tomorrow at your leisure. I'm sure there's a bed for you around here somewhere."

Patrick O'Mally nodded. "I'm sleeping in the servants' quarters, Lainie. Pita invited me. Otherwise, I would have slept in the wagon like I did on the trip."

Elaine realized with some regret that none of the Sideblossoms had thought of lodging for Patrick. She thought that inconsiderate, as she knew there had been free rooms in the hotels.

"But I want to get out of here at the crack of dawn. Without a load to carry, and the ladies to hold me up, I'll easily make it to Wanaka." Patrick saw a troubled look cross Elaine's face and corrected himself. "Sorry, Elaine I . . . uh . . . didn't mean it like that. I know you're a fast rider. But that Zoé Sideblossom's chaise and the lame nags pulling it . . ."

Elaine smiled with understanding. She, too, had noted that the noble steeds pulling Zoé's chaise could not keep up with a draft horse like Owen or the cob mare team pulling Patrick's freight wagon.

Patrick could have left it at that, but he seemed to have something else weighing on him.

"Elaine . . . is everything really all right?" he finally stammered. "With your . . ." He cast a side glance at Callie. Elaine had not explained to him why she'd had the dog sleep with him during the journey, but Patrick was not dumb.

Elaine fumbled for words. She had no idea how to answer his question. But just then, Thomas materialized behind Patrick.

"Mrs. Sideblossom, if I may!" he said sharply. "I will not tolerate this intimate form of address, boy. It's disrespectful. Besides, you wanted to be on your way, didn't you? So say your good-byes properly then. I want to see the backs of your horses before the day is done, boy!"

Patrick O'Mally grinned at him. He was not easy to intimidate.

"Gladly, Mr. Sideblossom," he said calmly. "But I didn't realize I was your bondman. So please, don't address *me* too intimately. I don't recall giving you permission to call me 'boy.'"

Thomas's pupils widened, and Elaine saw the abyss in his eyes once again. What would he have done if Patrick did work for him?

Patrick returned the stare with a fearlessness bordering on insolence.

"Good-bye, Mrs. Sideblossom," he said. "What should I tell your father?"

Elaine's mouth was dry, her face pale. "Tell my parents . . . I'm doing well."

8

Thomas did not give Elaine time to make herself presentable for dinner. He ordered her to accompany him as she was. Elaine felt humiliated and dirty in the eyes of the immaculately dressed Zoé and the men, who had exchanged their riding clothes for suits. Emere seemed to notice as well, for the aged Maori studied Elaine with her unfathomable gaze. Disapproving? Assessing? Or merely curious about the reaction of those at table? Elaine, however, could not find fault with Emere's behavior. She was polite and served very skillfully.

"Emere was trained by my first wife," John declared without looking at the tall Maori woman. "Thomas's mother. She died very young, however, and left us with only very few such well-trained servants."

"Where do these Maori come from anyway?" Elaine asked. "There doesn't seem to be a village in the area."

And why was Emere still here instead of married with children? Or seeing to the needs of her tribe? Hadn't her grandmother said Emere was a *tohunga*? If she was able to draw the *wairua* voice out of the *putorino*, she must be regarded as a powerful witch doctor. Now that Elaine was getting a closer look at her for the first time, the wide heart-shaped face reminded her of somebody. But who? She wracked her brain.

"The men hire themselves on here," Thomas explained. "As shepherds. They're the usual ramblers. As for the girls, some of them the men drag them with them; some we get from the mission school in Dunedin. Orphans." He spoke the last word with meaningful emphasis, and appeared to cast a mocking glance at his father.

Elaine was once again confused. She had never heard of there being orphan children among the Maori. It didn't match up with their understanding of family. Helen had explained to her that Maori children called every woman of the appropriate generation either "mother" or "grandmother." The tribe raised the children communally. There was no way it would set orphaned children on the doorstep of a mission school.

Nevertheless, an education at such a school explained Pai's first-class English and her basic understanding of housekeeping. Elaine would ask the girl later where she had originally come from.

Though strongly influenced by Maori cuisine—it consisted mostly of roasted meat, fish, and sweet potatoes—the food at the Sideblossoms' table was exceptional. Elaine wondered if it had always been that way or if Zoé oversaw the kitchen and wrote out the menu. She could hardly remember what she had eaten during her first visit. At the time, she'd only had eyes for Thomas, but she had likewise fallen in love with the landscape around Lionel Station, and just found everything heavenly. At the moment, Elaine wondered how she could have been so blind. And not only once, but twice now, with William.

She would never let anything like this ever happen to her again. She would not fall in love again. She . . .

She was *married*. The realization that there was no way out of her current situation made her stop in the middle of chewing. This was not a nightmare from which someone would rescue her someday. It was immutable reality. There was divorce, of course, but then she would have to have provide serious cause—and she would never be able to bring herself to describe to a judge what Thomas did to her every night. Just the thought of telling someone about it almost made her die of shame. No, divorce was not an option. She just had to learn to live with it. Determined, she swallowed the food in her mouth, despite the fact that it her mouth felt just as dry as earlier. There was wine, at least. Elaine took her glass, but she was careful not to drink too much. She needed a clear head. Callie still needed a place to sleep. Perhaps she could ask Pai, or better still, Rahera. Rahera could take Callie to her brother, and Pita would take care of the dog. And then . . .

Elaine had to try to recall Daphne O'Rourke's many tips, other than the one about seeking oblivion in wine. At least for the time being, the last thing she wanted was to become pregnant by such a brute.

In the first month of her marriage, fate was kind to Elaine. Just before the time of month that would put her at greatest risk for pregnancy, the men left to herd the sheep into the highlands. For the ewes, they liked to use the hidden pastures that James McKenzie had discovered. With the sheep, it was a two-day ride. The return trip would take at least a day, and the men might stop to fish or hunt along the way. With a little luck, the critical days would have passed by then.

Elaine did not dare hope for willing abstention on the part of her husband. Thomas slept with her almost every night, and she saw no way of "getting used to it." She still felt like she was being ripped apart every time he plunged into her. She had long since used up the ointment that Mrs. Gardner had given her, and Elaine had not had a chance to search for the ingredients to make a new one. Whenever Thomas pulled her to him or dug his fingers into her breasts, she was black-and-blue afterward. He was at his worst when she had angered him or not behaved in a "ladylike" manner. He called that "playing games with him" and responded with his idea of play. There were ways of penetrating a woman that Inger had not known about or had kept from Elaine.

Pai regularly reddened when she saw the evidence of Thomas's mistreatment on Elaine's body.

"I'm never going to get married!" she once declared categorically. "I can't lie next to a man. I don't want to!"

"But is nice," remarked Rahera with her soft voice. She was a charming girl of roughly fifteen, short and stocky but attractive. "I like already marry man of my tribe. But cannot. Have to work." Her countenance was sad. As Elaine had since learned, Pita and Rahera were in no way "ramblers" but belonged to a tribe that dwelled predominantly in the McKenzie Highlands. Unfortunately, their tribe's chief had his own reasons for wandering the same territory as the legendary rustler. The tribe had come under suspicion when a herd of the Sideblossoms' best sheep had disappeared. When the animals reemerged a short while later, John held the young Maori boys who were near the herd by chance accountable, knowing that the boys would take flight with their tribe if John informed the constable. Rahera, Pita, and two other youths were now working off their sentence—an interminable sentence that John had determined himself. Elaine knew that the boys' situation would have turned out more favorably if they had gone before the court, and it was unlikely that Rahera would even have been punished.

"You . . . have already?" Pai asked, ashamed. "I mean . . . with a man?" The fact that she had been raised in a mission was obvious. She had never lived among her people and spoke their language only imperfectly.

Rahera smiled. "Oh yes. Named Tamati. Good man. Now works in mine in Greymouth. When free, we will do in *wharenui*. Then man and wife."

For the first time, Elaine saw the sense in the Maori custom of sleeping together in public before the whole tribe. What would the female elders have had to say if they knew what Thomas did to her every night?

Elaine took advantage of the men's absence to get a better look around Lionel Station's stables. That is to say, after only a few days in the house, she was already beginning to go mad with boredom. There was nothing to do in her apartment. She did not do the cooking, and the maids took care of the cleaning. Rahera had no idea how to clean silver or scour floors and seemed to think it all superfluous, and Pai was all the more fastidious as a result. Elaine knew nothing of Pai's faith, but the mission school had done a first-rate job of educating perfect English maids. Pai trained Rahera and made sure that she did everything correctly. Elaine only got in the way. Distractions like books or a gramophone were not to be found in the Sideblossom household. Neither father nor son seemed to read much, and Zoé stuck to women's magazines. Elaine devoured those, but they only came once a month at best, and when they did, she read them within a day.

In the grand salon, however, there was a piano that Zoé didn't use. When it came to Zoé's education as a perfect lady, someone had neglected musical training. So Elaine began to play again. She was a little rusty, not having touched her own instrument since the incident with Kura. Here, though, practicing filled up the many empty hours, and it wasn't long before she was attempting more challenging pieces.

At that moment, however, the path to the stables was clear, and with a happy Callie at her heels, Elaine explored the structures outside. They were extensive, as she'd expected they would be. The horse stables and depot lay directly near the house, similar to Kiward Station. Elaine cast a glance into the clean stalls. Several black horses—along with a bay here and there—whinnied at her. All of them had the small, noble heads of John and Thomas's riding horses, and their exaggerated reaction to every distraction spoke to their thoroughbred status. Elaine petted a small black stallion that was beating its hooves impatiently against the stall door.

"I know how you feel," she sighed. "I don't feel very well today, but tomorrow I'll go for a ride. Would you like that?"

The little horse snorted, and sniffed her hand and then the riding dress she had just taken out of her dresser at Lionel Station for the first time. Could he discern Banshee's scent?

Elaine stepped back out into the sunshine. She followed a farm road out to another cluster of barns and stables. There, she ran into Pita and another Maori boy, who were attempting to herd a few rams that had broken off from the group back into a freshly repaired paddock. The sheep were high-spirited youngsters that would no doubt have liked to follow the ewes and stud rams into the highlands, and they remained unimpressed by Pita's attempt to tame them. A rascally one even attacked the boy.

At first, Elaine laughed at the little ram from which the shepherds fled. But then her heartbeat quickened. Should she intervene? Callie sat panting and tense beside her. The dog wanted nothing more than to herd these sheep. Her training had been patchwork, though; Elaine had only improvised it. What if it didn't work? She would never get over her embarrassment.

On the other hand, what did she have to lose? The two Maori boys might tease her, but she could get over that. With a little luck, she could make a good impression, and if the boys mentioned it later, Thomas might see that she was of much more use outside than cooped up in the house.

Elaine whistled piercingly, and Callie shot out of her holding position like a cannonball. The dog threw herself between the boy and the insolent ram, gave a single curt bark, faced the ram head-on, and made it clear that he did not have a choice. The ram spun around immediately. Callie stuck to his heels before turning her attention to the others. Within seconds, she had gathered all six into a herd and gave Elaine a beaming collie look.

Elaine casually approached the paddock's gate—she did not dare run since that would cause the sheep to scatter. She opened the gate a bit wider and whistled for Callie once more. The sheep trotted into the pen in such an orderly formation that it was as if they had practiced marching in lockstep.

Elaine laughed and praised Callie effusively. The little dog was so proud that she could hardly contain herself. She jumped up on her mistress and then onto her new friend Pita. Callie had indeed found asylum in his lodging in the stables and seemed to be comfortable with the arrangement.

"That good, Mrs. Sideblossom! What wonder!" Pita was enthusiastic.

"Yes, madam! That was extraordinary. I've heard of such sheepdogs before, but Mr. Sideblossom's animals don't work half so skillfully," the other boy said.

Elaine gaped at the boy in astonishment. The boy expressed himself as eloquently as Pai. And was she seeing things, or did they resemble one another? He was unquestionably a mulatto too, but something else about his squared features looked familiar. She had never seen anything like that before among the Maori. She could tell the Maori apart without much effort—which not every white person could manage right away—but she had never been able to identify family resemblances in the few Maori she had gotten to know before.

Wait a moment—family? Those sharp features were not a Maori trait! Elaine had a bad feeling. She had to learn more.

"My dog may herd sheep very well," she said, "but your English is truly exceptional."

"Arama, madam, call me Arama. At your service." The young man bowed politely.

Elaine smiled.

"No need for the 'madam,' Arama. The word 'madam' always makes me think of a matron in a rocking chair. But do tell me where you learned such good English. Are you related to Pai?"

He looked like Pai. And Pai looked like Emere. Emere and . . .

Arama laughed. "Not that I know of. We were both orphans at the mission school in Dunedin. We were left there as babies. That's what the pastor said anyway." Arama winked. He had to be about twenty, so was no longer a child. He must have recognized the resemblance just as Elaine had. There may well be other boys and girls on the farm that were part of the same "family."

Elaine was shocked. Not so much because John Sideblossom was clearly sleeping with, or had slept with, his Maori maids. But because it must have happened before his son's eyes. Thomas must have witnessed at least two of Emere's pregnancies. And had she not been his nanny? How could John have forced the woman to give the children to an orphanage?

Elaine turned pale. "Are there more?" she asked hoarsely.

Arama's face took on a searching expression.

"Sheep?" he asked tentatively. "For the dog? A whole bunch. Please join us if you like and . . ."

Elaine did not answer but let her gaze rest seriously and expectantly on him.

"Mr. Sideblossom has taken five mulatto children from the mission school in Dunedin," Arama said finally. "Two girls as maids and three boys as farmworkers. I've been here four years, and he trusts me. I'm in charge of the farm while he's off herding the sheep with the others. And—"

"Does Thomas know?" Elaine asked without emphasis.

Arama shrugged. "I don't know, and I don't ask. You should do the same. Mr. Sideblossom is not very indulgent. Nor is his son. Would you like to help us with a few other sheep? We're repairing the fences, and there's still some herding to be done."

Elaine nodded. She could think later about what she had just learned. And about what Zoé might know. And about the news Zoé had proudly shared with Elaine that morning: she was pregnant. Thomas would soon have a half brother or half sister—though apparently that was nothing new.

Elaine pushed aside her father-in-law's unique method of increasing his staff and followed Arama and Pai to the other sheepcotes. There was not much work for a sheepdog of Callie's caliber, since most of the sheep were in the highlands. Staying behind were only a few sickly sheep, a ewe that had been covered very late and hadn't yet lambed, and a few dozen sheep that were to be sold. The latter were the most fun for Callie, because it was a larger herd, and the dog enjoyed the challenge. For the first time in a long time, Elaine, too, was something akin to happy when she made her way back to the house that evening.

"You smell like sheep," Zoé complained when they ran into each other at the house's entrance. "I cannot tolerate that in my condition."

Elaine had already heard that remark twice at breakfast. First Zoé had not been able to tolerate the smell of coffee, then she had felt sick at the sight of scrambled eggs. If things continued in this manner, several difficult months lay ahead for Elaine and the female servants.

"I'll wash up straightaway," she informed Zoé. "And the baby should get used to the smell of sheep. Mr. Sideblossom is hardly going to raise his child to be a rose gardener."

With that, Elaine rushed off to her own chambers. She was rather pleased with herself. She was slowly regaining her old quick-wittedness—though she had never been so cutting and mean in the past. *Maybe I should be more patient with Zoé*, Elaine thought, particularly if she's drawn the same conclusions that Arama and I have. It had to rattle Zoé's nerves to live in such close quarters with Emere. Zoé had no avenues of escape like Elaine did in the closed-off west wing. Zoé and John's apartments included the manor's common rooms and were adjacent to the kitchen. And Emere ruled over them all. Cold as ice, with her penetrating gaze. *Zoé was probably in hell.*

Elaine returned to the stables first thing the following morning. Arama and the few men who had stayed behind with him had more work for Callie. After they were done, around midday, Elaine decided to risk an afternoon ride. Arama offered to saddle the small black horse that she had been friendly with the day before.

"His name is Khan," Arama said. "He's just three years old, and has only been ridden for a few months. You can ride, can't you?"

Elaine nodded and told him about Banshee. "My father will send her as soon as her foal can handle itself. I can hardly wait. I miss her a great deal."

Arama looked skeptical, which astonished Elaine. Did he not trust her horsemanship? Or did the thought of a white mare in these dark stables bother him? Elaine did not plan to lock up her horse anyway. Banshee was used to pasturing.

She erased any concerns Arama might have had about her riding ability in short order. She climbed nimbly onto Khan's back without help, and laughed when Arama told her regretfully that he could not offer her a lady's saddle.

"Zoé Sideblossom does not ride," he said.

Now why did he say that so portentously?

No matter. Elaine was not going to read anything into Arama's words. Instead, she set off to investigate her new surroundings. Riding

Khan proved to be a real pleasure. The stallion was spirited but easy to ride, and Elaine, unaccustomed to Arabians, enjoyed the feeling of lightness. When her grandmother's cobs galloped, the earth beneath their hooves seemed to quake. Khan, however hardly seemed to touch the ground.

"I could get used to this," Elaine remarked, patting the horse's throat. "Let's do it again tomorrow."

On her first ride, she had limited herself to the area immediately around the farm, examining the pastures around the house and the shearing sheds. Lionel Station had two, both of which were of an imposing size. There was no cattle breeding, as on Kiward Station, because the terrain was too rocky. She knew that cattle only made a good return on expansive grassy flatlands like the ones in the Canterbury Plains, since they could not be driven up into the highlands in the summer like sheep.

The next morning Elaine set out early after packing a lunch for herself. She wanted to ride along the river in the direction of the mountains and explore the foothills of the McKenzie Highlands. It was her family history, in a manner of speaking. She giggled when she thought of her grandfather and the breakneck ride that had brought her mother to safety back then. Fleurette had come across James while fleeing John Sideblossom—and both of them had nearly fallen into the same trap.

Elaine enjoyed her excursion tremendously. The weather was grand: dry and sunny, with a light breeze, ideal for riding. Khan set off energetically but was more even-tempered than the day before and no longer took advantage of every opportunity to go at a gallop. Elaine could therefore concentrate on the landscape and take in the panorama of the high mountains on both sides of the Haast River. Callie ran happily beside her, only leaving her occasionally to lay fervent chase to a rabbit—which she really should not have done since sheepdogs were normally discouraged from hunting. But the rabbit problem in New Zealand had grown so dire in the last few years that even purists like Elaine's grandmother Gwyneira didn't reprimand their dogs for engaging in a bit of hunting. Brought to New Zealand on some ship, rabbits had multiplied explosively due to a lack of natural predators. In some parts of Otago, they were even making grass scarce for farm animals. Entire plains that would otherwise have served as pasture-land for sheep had been eaten clean by the long-ears. The desperate settlers had finally introduced foxes, lynxes, and other rabbit hunters into the wild. But there were still nowhere near enough predators to significantly reduce the rabbit population.

The rabbits had nothing to fear from Callie, however. True, she set after them enthusiastically, but she never caught any. Gwyneira liked to say that border collies were more likely to herd the rabbits together than to eat them.

Around midday Elaine rested by a stream that flowed down a little waterfall into the Haast River. While Khan and Callie splashed about in the water, Elaine took a seat on a rock. She set her lunch on another, since the stones were arranged like a table with chairs around it. The Maori would like that. Elaine wondered if Rahera's tribe often camped here, but she did not see any trace of them. Well, she would not be leaving any behind herself—the Maori treated the land with care, and Fleurette and Ruben had taught their children to do the same. Khan ate a bit of grass, of course, and his hooves left imprints in the tall grass, but they would be gone in a day. Elaine did not even light a fire.

After eating, she lay in the sun a little longer, enjoying the clear, bucolic day. Where the landscape was concerned, she liked her new home. If Thomas would only behave normally! What did he enjoy so much about torturing and humiliating her? Perhaps there was some kind of fear driving his behavior. She considered trying to speak to him again, to make her point of view clear. If he could only bring himself to confide in her! Here in the sunshine—far from the gloomy apartments she had come to view as a nightmare, and after three days of freedom without Thomas—her situation no longer felt as hopeless.

Filled with renewed optimism, she climbed back onto Khan. She knew that she should start riding back to Lionel Station, but she gave in to the temptation to explore one more bend of the river, just to see what lay behind it. She told herself that she had been going almost entirely uphill, so she would make considerably faster progress on the return downhill. The river now lay far below her in a canyon. It looked as though someone had split the landscape with a knife and then poured water in the gouge. Elaine took in the spectacular view with delight, laughing at Callie who was standing on the ledge and peering down curiously at the river. She wondered where the McKenzie Highlands began and where the famous pass was, through which her grandfather had herded the sheep and where he had kept himself hidden from every pursuer's eyes for so long.

It was late afternoon by the time Elaine decided to turn back. As she did so, Khan suddenly raised his head and whinnied. As other horses answered, several dogs barked, and Callie greeted them in turn. Elaine peered in the direction of the whinnying and recognized John and Thomas and their crew. They had returned much sooner than Elaine had thought they would.

Despite her earlier sense of contentment, the usual shudder of fear and mistrust shot through her when she saw Thomas coming toward her. Her instinct was her to flee. The men might not yet have seen her, and Khan was fast. Then she chided herself for the thought. These people were her family, and she had done nothing wrong. There was no reason to run away. It was time for her to stop acting like a terrified rabbit in Thomas's presence. Elaine put on her friendliest smile and rode toward the men.

"Now this is a surprise!" she called out cheerfully. "I would never have expected to run into you here. I didn't think you'd be back until tomorrow."

Thomas looked at her coldly. "What are you doing here?" he asked slowly, drawing out each word, and not bothering to acknowledge her greeting.

Elaine forced herself to look him in the eye.

"Riding, what else? I thought I'd explore the area a bit, and since my horse isn't here yet, I borrowed Khan. That was all right, wasn't it?" The last question came out like a whisper. It was not easy to act self-assured when Thomas assumed that inscrutable mien. Elaine did not appear to be the only one who felt threatened by the situation. The Sideblossoms' men, almost all young Maori, withdrew perceptibly.

"No, that was not all right!" spat Thomas. "That stallion has hardly been broken in, and that's not even taking into account the fact that it's no horse for a lady. Something could have happened to you. Besides, it's not ladylike, you riding around here alone."

"But Thomas," Elaine said. Despite the tension, his argument was so ridiculous that she almost had to laugh. "There's no one here to see. Since leaving Lionel Station, I've yet to run into anyone who *could* find my behavior unladylike!"

"*I* find it unladylike," Thomas said coldly. "And that's the only one who matters. I have nothing against the occasional ride—together with me on a gentle horse. But you won't be leaving the farm alone anymore. Do we understand each other?"

"But I've always ridden out alone, Thomas. Even as a child. You can't lock me up!"

"Oh, can't I?" he repeated coldly. "I see that we're playing the usual little game. Who knows whom or what you were looking for here. But come along now. We'll discuss this further later."

The men let Elaine into their midst as though she were an escaped prisoner who had to be led back under guard. Suddenly she no longer found the landscape so intoxicatingly beautiful or sublimely expansive. Instead, the mountains felt as though they were closing in on her like a prison. Thomas did not say so much as a word to her, and the three-hour return trip passed in a dreary silence.

Arama and Pita, who had been waiting for her in the stables, took Khan from her. On Arama's face in particular, Elaine detected a look of deep concern.

"You should not have stayed out so long, Mrs. Sideblossom," he said quietly. "I feared something like this, but I did not think the men would return until tomorrow morning. Do not worry, we won't say a word about your helping us with the sheep."

Elaine would gladly have brushed the stallion down herself as she had done the day before, but Thomas indicated that she was to return to the house straightaway.

"Go change your clothes so that you will at least come to dinner looking like a lady!"

Elaine trembled as she fled into her dressing room. Pai had kept a dress of hers ready and quickly helped her to tie her corset tighter.

"Mr. Sideblossom is . . . angry?" she asked tentatively.

Elaine nodded. "I can't take it," she whispered. "He wants to lock me up. I can't—"

"Shhh." Pai caressed Elaine's cheek with her hand as she put Elaine's hair up. "Don't cry. That won't make it better. I know that from the orphanage. Sometimes the children cried, but it never helped. You get used to things, Mrs. Sideblossom. You can get used to anything."

Elaine thought she would scream if she heard that phrase one more time. She would never get used to this life. She would rather die.

Zoé was waiting for everyone with a sanctimonious smile.

"And you're back as well, Elaine! How nice. Perhaps you'll be offering me a little more company over the next few days. Spending all your time with the workers and the dogs can't be any fun."

Elaine ground her teeth. Thomas gave her an icy look.

"I used to ride out a bit before too," Zoé continued cheerfully as the food was brought out to them. That evening, she supplied most of the dinner conversation herself. Thomas was silent, and John seemed to find it interesting to observe the young married couple. "Just think, Lainie, I had a horse when I came. But I eventually no longer cared to go riding. Our men hardly have any time to accompany a lady on a ride anyway. Then John sold the horse."

What was that? A warning? Or was Zoé already looking forward to the fact that Thomas would surely sell Elaine's beloved Banshee as soon as the horse arrived at Lionel Station? Elaine now understood why the mare had not been allowed to join them for the journey.

It had not been about saving the foal from the long trip but about shackling Elaine to the house.

Emere served as silently as ever. But even she had her eyes on Elaine. That night she played the *putorino* flute. Elaine tried to shut the spirit voice out, but it sounded closer than ever, and not even the thickest curtains could block it out.

It was that ghastly night that Elaine tried the vinegar rinse for the first time. She groaned with pain as she washed herself. She could hardly walk to her bathroom as it was, after Thomas had driven the "little games" out of her more wildly and forcefully than ever. Emere's eerie flute playing had only appeared to heighten his rage.

When he finally left her, Elaine would have most liked to crawl under her blankets until the pain eased, but then she remembered Inger's directions for avoiding an unwanted pregnancy. For she would not have a child. Not ever.

9

William and Kura's marriage had taken a very strange turn ever since Kura learned she was expecting. The young woman appeared to take offense at practically everything the residents of Kiward Station did. She spent most of her day alone, or with Heather Witherspoon, if necessary. She hardly played the piano anymore, and had not sung for weeks. Though Gwyneira was worried, James and Jack found it restful.

"Peace and quiet!" James said happily, sprawled in an armchair on the evening of his return from Queenstown. "And I used to like music so much too! But now . . . oh, don't make a face like that, Gwyn! Let her sulk. Maybe it's because of the pregnancy. Women can behave very strangely when they're expecting, they say."

"Thank you very much," Gwyneira returned. "Why didn't you bring that to my attention earlier? When I was expecting Jack, you always said that pregnancy made me more beautiful! There was no talk of 'strange' behavior."

"You remain the notable exception," James said, laughing. "That's why I fell in love with you at first sight. And Kura will calm down again too. She probably only just realized that marriage isn't a game."

"She's so dreadfully unhappy," Gwyneira sighed. "And she's furious at all of us, me most of all. Though I did give her the choice."

"Having our wishes fulfilled doesn't always make us happy," James said wisely. "But there's nothing to be done. I almost feel sorry for William. He must bear the brunt of it. But it does not seem to bother him much."

This equanimity mostly had to do with the fact that Kura's bad temper and reclusive tendencies were limited to daylight hours. She seemed to forgive William everything at night and was at times an even more exciting lover than before. It was as though she were saving up all her energy to give herself and William the greatest possible satisfaction at night, and so one climax followed another. During the day, William saw to the work on the farm—which he felt quite a bit better about. Gwyneira mostly left him in peace these days. Even if something did not suit her, she generally took William's side, sometimes even in confrontations with James McKenzie. James was by nature an easygoing person, and he had never thought of Kiward Station as his, so he accepted William's occasional poor decisions without commentary. The young man would most likely be the master of the farm one day, so James might as well get accustomed to William bossing him around.

Poker Livingston, however, retired. He claimed that his wounded arm kept him from doing any more hard work, and he moved in with his friend in town. William took Poker's place triumphantly, overseeing the maintenance and repair work that had to be done over the course of the summer. Shortly thereafter, the Maori tribe that resided on Kiward Station departed on a long journey. James merely rolled his eyes and hired white farmhands in Haldon.

"This grandson of yours is expensive," he said to Gwyneira. "Maybe you should have encouraged a Maori father for Kura's baby after all. Then the tribe wouldn't be fleeing now. And if they were, they might have just dragged Kura along, and we wouldn't need to see that accusing face of hers every day. She acts as though *we* were the ones to get her pregnant!"

Gwyneira sighed. "Why is it that William can't get along with the Maori? Back in Ireland, he had trouble because he was too nice to his tenants, but here he disrupts the natives."

James shrugged. "Our William likes for people to be grateful to him. And that is well known to be an alien sentiment to Tonga. Not that he owes William anything. Look at the facts straight, Gwyn. William can't deal with people on his own level. He wants to be the boss, and woe to anyone who doubts him."

Gwyneira nodded despondently, but then managed a smile. "We'll send the two of them off to the sheep breeders' conference in Christchurch," she said. "Then our country gentleman can feel important. Kura will enjoy a change of scene, and you can mend the fences. Or did you want to go the conference yourself?"

James waved that suggestion away. He thought livestock breeders' conferences totally unnecessary. A few speeches, a few discussions about current problems, and then plenty of drinking, during the course of which the proposed solutions to said problems became increasingly nonsensical. The year before, Major Richland had actually voiced the idea of starting a drag hunting society to fight the rabbit plague. The fact that drag hunting did not actually involve hunting animals—but merely following an artificial trail—had completely escaped him.

James, for one, did not need any of that—not to mention that the Livestock Breeders Society of Christchurch had first convened to deal with a certain livestock thief. A circumstance that Lord Barrington invariably brought up after his third glass—if not sooner—in James McKenzie's presence.

"Well, I hope they don't talk William into any dumb ideas," James murmured. "Otherwise, we might soon find ourselves breeding hunters rather than sheep."

William enjoyed the trip to Christchurch, and seemed two inches taller upon his return. Kura had spent a fortune at the tailor's, but was otherwise in even worse spirits than before. William's friendly and natural acceptance into the circle of sheep barons had finally opened her eyes to the truth: her marriage and her child shackled her to Kiward Station. William had never had any intention of following Kura through the opera houses of Europe as a sort of male muse for her. Perhaps as a vacation sometime in the future, but certainly not for a longer stay, and never for her to study at a conservatory. During the long, lonely daylight hours, Kura raged against her husband and herself—only to sink back into William's arms again at night. When William kissed her and caressed her body, she forgot all her other wishes and needs. His worship was equal to the applause of the masses, and when he pushed into her, he fulfilled her more than the elation she derived from any singing. If only it weren't for the endless days, and if only she were not forced to watch with a wary eye as her body changed. William thought that pregnancy had made Kura even more beautiful, but she hated her new roundness. Everyone assumed she must be overjoyed about this baby, but Kura was indifferent about it at best.

When fall came, the men rode into the highlands to herd the sheep down to the plains. William brought eternal shame upon himself by getting lost in the mountains while searching for a runaway sheep. It took a search party until the next day to find him.

"We all thought he'd picked up and left," Andy reported with a grin to the sneering James. Neither of the McKenzies had ridden along this time. Gwyneira had thought Kura could use some company, and James's bones had begun to hurt when he spent the entire day in the saddle and his nights on the hard ground. He had started to imagine leaving Kiward Station to William someday and moving into a small, cozy house with Gwyneira. A few sheep, a dog-breeding business, and a warm fireplace in the evening that he lit himself instead of leaving it to a servant. Gwyneira and James had dreamed of such a life when they were both young, and James saw no reason not to make it a reality. Giving up the farm would make him a little sorry, but only for Jack's sake. Though his son was still young, he would be the perfect stock farmer—and Andy was full of praise for the boy.

"Jack has a sixth sense for the work. He finds every sheep, and the dogs listen to him almost before he speaks. Is there really no chance of his taking over the farm?"

James shook his head. "He's not even a Warden. If Gwyneira had inherited the farm, it would have been somewhat different. Stephen, George, and Elaine would have preceded Jack in order of inheritance, but we could have come to some agreement with them. Stephen and George don't have any interest in it, after all, and Elaine has her own sheep farm now."

"But Kura doesn't have any interest either," Andy objected. "It's a shame you couldn't marry her off to Jack. Yeah, it'd be a bit incestuous, but good blood."

James laughed heartily. "Jack wouldn't do such a thing for all the sheep in the world, Andy! Even if Kura was the last girl on earth, he'd become a monk!"

As Kura's delivery approached, her mood became noticeably worse. William did everything he could think of to lift her spirits, but without much success. Ever since he had stopped reaching for her at night—to keep from harming the child—she had treated him with icy disdain, sometimes becoming so angry that she threw things at him. There no longer was anyone who could cheer Kura up even for a short time. She did not want a baby. And Kiward Station was the last place she wanted to be.

Marama was worried that Kura's anger could harm the child, and Gwyneira, too, was occasionally reminded of her own pregnancy with Paul. She had likewise rejected her child. But Paul had been fruit borne of a rape while Kura awaited a child borne of love. Gwyneira was almost relieved when Kura's labor finally began. Marama and Rongo Rongo, the Maori midwife, arrived straightaway to be at Kura's side; Gwyneira also sent for Francine Candler, so that she would not feel insulted. The baby was already born, however, by the time the midwife arrived from Haldon. Kura had an easy delivery and was in labor for only six hours before bringing a very small but healthy girl into the world.

Marama's whole face glowed when she presented the baby to Gwyneira.

"You're not angry, are you, Gwyn?" she asked, sounding concerned.

Gwyneira smiled. Marama had asked the same question when Kura was born.

"Of course not, we're maintaining the female line," she said as she took the baby from Marama's arms. She looked searchingly into the tiny face. She could not yet see whose features the baby had inherited, but the down on her little head looked more golden than black.

"What does Kura want to name her?" Gwyneira asked, rocking the baby. The infant reminded her of Fleurette as a newborn, causing a wave of tenderness to wash over her as the baby awoke and gazed at her with big blue eyes.

Marama shrugged unhappily. "I don't know. She's hardly spoken, and she didn't even really look at the baby. All she said was, 'Take her to her grandmother,' and 'I'm sorry it's not a boy.' When William said, 'Next time, my love!' Kura almost went mad with fury. Rongo Rongo just gave her a sleeping potion. I don't know if that was the right thing to do, but with her raving like that . . ."

William was likewise disappointed. He had been counting on a son. Tonga nevertheless sent a present for the birth, since the Maori recognized female inheritance.

Gwyneira did not care whether it was a boy or girl. "As long as she's not musical," she said to James, laying the baby down in her crib. Since no one had given it any thought of it before, she had turned Kura's little salon into a nursery. James had retrieved the cradle from storage. It seemed that no one had even thought about a name.

"Name it after Kura's favorite singer," James advised. "What are their names, again?"

Gwyneira rolled her eyes. "Mathilde, Jenny, and Adelina. We can't do that to the child! I'll ask the baby's father. Perhaps we can name her after his mother."

"Then she'll probably have a name like Mary or Birdie," James said.

It turned out that William had, in fact, thought of a name for his daughter.

"It has to be a special name," he declared, already a little addled by whiskey when Gwyneira had found him in the salon downstairs. "Something to express our triumph over this new land. I think I'll name her Gloria!"

"I suppose there's no need to explain it to Tonga that way," James said, grinning, when Gwyneira told him the news. Jack had joined him, and father and son were busy affixing a mobile over the baby's crib. James explained to his son that the baby couldn't really see much just then, but that in time the little dangling bear would distract and calm her.

"What is she anyway? My aunt?" Jack asked, as he peered, fascinated, at Gloria in the crib.

"You can touch her if you're gentle," Gwyneira encouraged him. "But good question. What is she? You and Kura's father would have been half brothers. So Kura would have been your half niece. And the baby is your great—half niece. It's is a little complicated."

Jack smiled at the baby. His face mirrored the expression that his father showed when looking at newborn animals: incredible astonishment, almost something like devotion. Finally, he stuck his hand in the crib and felt carefully with his finger for Gloria's small hand.

The baby opened her eyes for a brief moment before closing them again. She blinked at Jack, apparently fascinated. With a tight grip, she closed her tiny hand around Jack's finger.

"I think I like her," said the boy.

Over the next few days, the care of little Gloria became a major point of contention among the women of Kiward Station. Marama and Kiri, the cook, were dead set against taking responsibility for the child away from Kura. Years earlier, after Gwyneira's unfortunate pregnancy, Kiri had cared for little Paul and now, looking back, thought that a mistake. Gwyneira had never worked on building a relationship with her son and had never really loved him as a child—or as an adult. Had she simply let Paul cry, Kiri argued, Gwyneira would sooner or later have been forced to nurture the baby—and then she would have developed natural maternal instincts toward him. It would be the same with Kura and Gloria, Kiri maintained.

Gwyneira, however, felt that she had to take responsibility for her infant great-granddaughter. If for no other reason than that no one else was doing it. Kura, for one, did not seem to feel obligated to pick up her baby just because it was crying. She simply retreated into another room to avoid hearing her cries. Putting little Gloria in her salon, the most remote room in her suite, had proved to be a mistake. The nursery was connected to a corridor, so Gloria's crying did not remain concealed from the other residents of the house. But when Kura withdrew into her bedroom or dressing room, she heard next to nothing. As for Heather Witherspoon, the screaming clearly rattled her nerves, but she was afraid of dropping Gloria if she picked her up—and after Gwyneira observed her holding the baby, she shared that concern.

"My God, Miss Witherspoon, that's a baby, not a doll! Her head isn't screwed on; you have to support it. Gloria can't hold it up herself yet. And she's not going to bite you if you lay her on your shoulder. Nor will she explode—you don't have to hold her like a stick of dynamite."

Heather Witherspoon had kept her distance ever since. As did William, who had nevertheless engaged a nanny, a certain Mrs. Whealer. He refused to have a Maori girl looking after his daughter. Though Mrs. Whealer was quite competent, she could only start work at nine o' clock in the morning since she came from Haldon, and she liked to be home before dark. James grumbled that they could just train the man who drove Mrs. Whealer to change diapers and it would cost the same.

Regardless, there was no one to comfort and feed Gloria at night, and as often as not, it was Jack who went to his parents' room to tell them that the baby needed them. The boy slept in the room next to the newly furnished nursery and was therefore always the first to hear the baby. The first few times, he simply took the baby out of her crib and laid her next to him like he did the puppy he had gotten for Christmas. However, he tended to feed the puppy before he went to bed, which meant the dog slept soundly, whereas Gloria could not sleep because she was hungry.

This left Jack no other choice but to wake his mother. Out of a sense of duty, he always tried to wake Kura first, but she never stirred. From her bedroom, she never responded to his knocking, just as she never responded to Gloria's crying, and the boy did not dare to barge into her private rooms.

"What is that boy William doing anyway?" grumbled James as Gwyneira got up for the third night in a row. "Can't anybody explain to him that it's not enough just to make a baby?"

Gwyneira threw on a dressing gown. "He doesn't even hear it. Nor does Kura. Heaven only knows what they're thinking. In any case, I can't imagine William with a milk bottle in his hand, Can you?"

James was just about to reply that William would first have to let go of the whiskey bottle, but he did not want to worry Gwyneira. She was so busy with the baby and the farm that she hadn't noticed, but James had seen a marked reduction in the alcohol stores. William and Kura's marriage no longer seemed to be as happy as it had been early on—or even as in the early months of her pregnancy. The two no longer turned in early for the night, exchanging loving glances as they once had, but now seemed rather to be living alone together. William often remained in the salon long after Kura had retired. Sometimes he stayed there chatting with Heather Witherspoon—James would have loved to know what they had to talk about. Yet he often brooded there alone, always with a full glass of whiskey at his side.

Indeed, William's relationship with Kura had not improved as he had hoped it would after Gloria's birth. Ever the gentleman, he had allowed his wife the traditional four weeks of recovery after the birth before attempting to join her in bed again. He had expected to be warmly welcomed there. After all, Kura had accused him for weeks of no longer wanting her on account of her big belly. She certainly appeared to enjoy his kisses and caresses and aroused him almost to the point of climax. But when he wanted to enter into her, she pushed him away.

"You don't really think I'll let that happen a second time," she said coolly as soon as he had regained enough control over himself to complain. "I don't want any more children. We're done with that. We can, of course, do anything else that won't make me pregnant."

At first, William had not taken her seriously, but when he tried again, Kura remained firm. Once again, she applied her ample skill to arouse him to the height of ecstasy, but then retreated at the last moment. She did not seem to think anything of his frustration. In fact, it rather seemed to please her that William lusted after her almost to the point of madness.

One night, however, he lost control and took her against her will, overpowering her resistance and laughing as she struck and scratched at him. Though her resistance soon abated, it was an unforgivable act. William apologized immediately that night and then three times over the course of the following day and appeared to be genuinely contrite. Although Kura said she accepted his apology, that night, he found her door locked.

"I'm sorry," Kura said, "but it's too risky. We would end up going through this over and over, and I don't want another child."

Instead, she resumed her singing and piano playing, practicing for hours, as she had at the beginning of her marriage.

"You should be careful what you wish for," sighed Gwyneira, rocking little Gloria. Apparently, her prayer that the child be wholly unmusical had been heard: Gloria erupted in violent screaming as soon as the piano sounded.

"I'll take her with me to the stables," Jack said cheerfully, likewise taking flight from Beethoven and Schubert. "It's perfectly quiet there with the dogs; she even laughs when Monday licks her. What do you think—when can we teach her to ride?"

It drove William mad to see Kura every day, to observe her figure once again assuming its old captivating form, her movements once again becoming graceful like a dancer's. Everything about her aroused him, from her voice to the dance of her long fingers on the piano keys. Sometimes just the thought of her was enough to arouse him. As he sat alone drinking his whiskey, he replayed their nights together in his mind's eye. He recalled every position, thought yearningly of every kiss. Sometimes he thought he would explode with desire. He imagined it was the same for Kura—he had noticed her prurient looks—but she kept an iron grip on herself.

Kura did not yet know what turn her life would take, but the idea of remaining on Kiward Station—having one baby after another, becoming fat and unattractive, and waddling around like a duck each time she got pregnant—was too unspeakable to fathom. The few months of passion in between did not make up for the disadvantages. And Rongo Rongo had given her no illusions on the subject: "You could have three children before you're twenty—and who knows how many in all."

Chills ran down Kura's spine at the mere thought of three screaming brats. She did think Gloria was adorable, but she had no idea what to do with her, any more than with all the puppies, kittens, and lambs that Gwyneira and Elaine found so enthralling. She certainly did not want any more of them.

Nevertheless, denying William's love made her more and more irritable. She needed something, whether it was music and applause or satisfaction and love. Music was the less dangerous option, so she began to practice the piano again, she sang, and she waited. Something had to happen.

10

Roderick Barrister was not exactly a virtuoso singer. True, he had graduated from the musical program of a somewhat renowned institute, and he had slogged through the most important tenor parts in the operatic repertoire. Moreover, he was rather handsome, with thick, straight black hair that he wore long, adding flair to the operatic heroes he played. His delicate face, so much softer than classical chiseled features, touched female hearts, and his eyes flashed black and fiery. His outward appearance alone consistently landed him engagements in smaller ensembles and at recitals. However, that was not enough for a career on the grand stages. Roderick no longer fooled himself on that point.

Though he loved the audience and yearned for stardom, he was not stupid. For that reason, he seized the opportunity to become a big fish in a small pond when a New Zealand businessman who was putting together an ensemble to tour through Australia and New Zealand approached him. In doing so, George Greenwood, a wealthy man who was no longer young, was evidently pursuing altruistic goals rather than simply filthy lucre. Though he would make a little money in the deal, it was, more importantly, a kind gesture for his wife, Elizabeth. The couple had spent a few months in England years before, and his then–still–young bride had succumbed to the charms of the opera. On New Zealand's South Island, there was still no opera house, so admirers of virtuosic singing had to content themselves with gramophones and records. George wanted to help remedy that and was using another stay in London to put together a company of singers and dancers.

Roderick was among the first to apply, and he quickly realized that he could put his organizational skills to work for profit. George Greenwood knew nothing about music and had only a slight interest in it. He found it tiresome to have to judge singers and dancers in addition to his other work, and had difficulty selecting the best ones. He therefore readily accepted Roderick's offer to help with the selection process, and Roderick suddenly found himself in the role of an impresario.

He fulfilled his role conscientiously, though he did hire the most beautiful and compliant ballerinas while choosing male dancers who were drawn to their own sex. He did not have to take competition with him overseas, after all. When it came to the singers, he was careful not to hire anyone who would make his voice or appearance look worse by comparison. Though a kind person, his frequent partner, the first soprano, was consequently average in both looks and singing talent. Sabina Conetti knew as well as Roderick that great art was beyond her. She was thankful for the well-paid engagement, always ready to take care of Roderick when the ballerinas were not in the mood, and generally willing to pull anyone to her ample bosom who confided their woes to her, all of which helped Roderick a great deal. He was able to ignore all of his ensemble's personal problems, the kind that so often meant sleepless nights for other impresarios. Peace and harmony reigned in his little company, and, as it turned out, the public was not demanding. On board the ship, a steamer that made the journey in a few weeks, the troupe gave a few concerts, and the passengers heaped praise on the artists and the immensely satisfied George Greenwood.

Buoyed by their admiration, Roderick looked ahead calmly to their first performance in the Canterbury Plains. Sabina Conetti in person was presumably still a good deal better than a recording of Jenny Lind, he thought.

Christchurch was a pleasant surprise. The singers and dancers had expected a hick town at the ends of the earth, but the city was evidently striving to be an English metropolis. The main attraction in that regard was the brightly painted trolley, in operation since 1880, which jingled through the city's dapper streets. Christ's College attracted students from throughout New Zealand, adding a youthful flair to the city. And the city hardly looked as miserly as they'd expected. Sheep breeding and, more recently, meat export had brought great wealth to Christchurch, and the city fathers poured tax money enthusiastically into impressive public buildings.

There still was no opera house, however. As a result, the performance was to take place in a hotel. Once again, Roderick thanked heaven for Sabina. While she wrestled with the singers' complaints about the poor acoustics in the White Hart's ballroom and the dancers' concerns about the small size of the stage, he had a look around the town. Then, shortly before the performance was to begin, he peeked out curiously into the audience—a crowd of finely dressed people, looking full of anticipation, who would soon be celebrating Roderick Barrister as though he were Paul Kalisch himself. It would be a dream come true! And then he saw the girl.

It was Heather Witherspoon who had drawn William and Kura Martyn's attention to the opera ensemble's guest performance. Although George Greenwood had informed Gwyneira, she had completely forgotten about it—helped by the fact that neither James nor Jack wanted to attend.

"Opera is quite beautiful," Gwyneira said, trying halfheartedly to change her son's mind. She wanted to give him a comprehensive education, which was not always easy in New Zealand, and James generally tried to help her in this regard. The McKenzies had been thrilled to attend a performance of the Royal Shakespeare Company that had toured New Zealand the year before, though Jack had found the sword fights more exciting than Romeo and Juliet's love poetry. It looked as though opera may have been definitively spoiled for Gwyneira's family, however.

"What are we supposed to do with Gloria?" Jack asked. "She cries a good deal when we're away for long, and she'll be miserable if we take her with us. She doesn't like all that noise."

The boy had begun to make a habit of carrying his "great–half niece" around with him like a puppy. Instead of a stuffed bear, he had a hoof pick dangling over the baby basket that he'd placed in the stables, and when Gloria reached out into the air, he put a few stalks of hay or a horse brush in her hand to play with. The little girl seemed to like that. As long as her mother was not singing, she was a peaceful child—and since Jack had learned how to warm milk as well as any nanny, she now slept through the night.

Gwyneira had not informed Kura or William about the upcoming opera performance at least in part because the family on Kiward Station had taken to living more and more separate lives. Kura's evening concerts on the grand piano in the salon drove James and Jack into their rooms early, and even when she finally retired for the evening, no one cared to keep William company while he drank his whiskey. Except Heather Witherspoon, of course.

"Is there something between the two of them?" James asked mistrustfully at one point. "They can't be spending every evening chatting about her boarding school education, can they?"

Gwyneira laughed. "Jack claims that Kura and William 'aren't doing it anymore.' That's exactly how he phrased it. Could it be that you're having a bad influence on him? Helen would be horrified. In any case, he claims that he hears them arguing every night. He didn't tell me that, though. I heard it from his friend Hone and only caught that bit by accident. The two of them have recently developed an interest in girls. Although Hone is considerably more precocious than Jack in that regard. Our boy's been scared off women by Kura, and will probably end up a monk."

James grinned. "I think that's unlikely. He's a good shepherd, but I think it would upset him if he couldn't shear his two–legged flock and herd them around as he liked. Besides, no father confessor I ever met would employ a border collie as a guardian of public virtue."

"Maybe it wouldn't be a bad idea." Gwyneira giggled. "Do you still remember how Cleo used to bark whenever you touched me?"

James cast a probing look at Monday, who lay in her basket next to their bed.

"The current guardian's asleep. Let's not pass up the opportunity at hand."

Kura was naturally all in favor of a trip to Christchurch, and Heather Witherspoon no less so. William headed off willingly, though he was quite a bit more interested in speaking with other livestock barons than in the music. Gwyneira gave the governess the time off against her will. She remained dissatisfied with Miss Witherspoon's work with regard to Jack and the Maori children's education. Yet Heather so rarely asked for leave that Gwyneira could hardly deny it.

"Maybe she'll fall for a singer and decamp," James said hopefully.

That, however, was not to be. Heather's feelings had long since been spoken for. For, even if William had yet to show any interest—still dreaming as he was of once more conquering "Fort Kura"—there was a reason she sat with him nearly every evening. At some point, he would recognize the woman in her. At least she hoped that would be the case. In the books and magazines that she read, it always came about by accident. A woman only had to be soft, patient, and, above all, available until the right moment presented itself.

So Kura, William, and Heather traveled to Christchurch, and upon Roderick Barrister's first glance into the audience, his gaze fell on Kura-maro-tini.

"I'll be damned, have you seen the girl down there?" Roderick simply had to give voice to his awe.

Bored, Sabina peeked through a hole in curtain to where he indicated. "Which one? I see at least ten. And after the performance they'll all be eating out of your hand. Do you want to do the Tamino first or the Don José?"

"We'll start with the Mozart," Roderick murmured without thinking. "But how can you see ten girls out there? Next to this one the entire hall fades into nothingness! That hair and that face, there's something wonderfully unusual about her. And the way she moves, she looks like a born dancer."

You do have a weakness for dancers," Sabina sighed. "Brigitte and Stephanie will soon be clawing each other's eyes out over you again. Try to restrain yourself. Now go get your makeup put on. The 'nothingness' is waiting to be entertained!"

The company performed scenes from *The Magic Flute*, *Carmen*, and *Il Trovatore*. From the last, they sang the famous quartet from the final scene, which no one in the ensemble could perform very well. The troupe's mezzo-soprano in particular—a young girl who was primarily a dancer and who had only studied a bit of singing on the side—made a horrendous Azucena. However, she could hardly be heard as the men were doing their best to sing loudly to make up for the fact that they could not sing well. Sabina had already declared that she planned to take the stage with her ears plugged the next time. Her Leonora could certainly not sound any worse.

In the entire complaisant Christchurch audience, only one listener noticed the weakness of the performance, and she was concentrating on the women's voices. So that was opera? You needed do nothing more than sign on to an international ensemble? On the one hand, Kura was disappointed; on the other, she was seized by hope. This girl who was cawing Azucena, who had also squawked Carmen like a crow, was far less talented than Kura. And these sopranos! But Kura liked the tenor. Though he did not hit every note, she thought that might be due to his partners. In any event, he made Kura's heart sing—she would have loved more than anything to join him when his duet from *Carmen* failed miserably, and she was confident that she would have performed Pamina better than that soprano. Besides, the man was handsome, exactly as she had pictured Manrico and Tamino and all the others. Although Kura knew the performance was third-rate, she had never wanted anything as much as she wanted to stand on the stage here.

Heather Witherspoon could likewise have judged the quality of the singing, but she was too preoccupied with being in love. William sat between Kura and her—how easy it was to imagine that he belonged to her and that she would be escorting him to the reception George Greenwood had arranged for the performers and the most important guests afterward. Only William and Kura had been invited, of course. Nevertheless, for two hours, Heather enjoyed dreaming of an alternate world, and she could not have cared less whether the people up on the stage were singing in key or not.

William would very much have appreciated her company at the reception as well. As it was, he was hopelessly bored because, aside from the Greenwoods, there were hardly any worthwhile people present. The sheep barons of the plains were evidently not interested in song and dance, at least around sheepshearing time. The shearing companies had already arrived at the Richlands', George was telling him.

"After that, I imagine they'll head on to Kiward Station," the merchant said. "Won't you be needed there, Mr. Martyn?"

William could have blushed. Gwyneira had not said a word to him about when the shearing would be getting under way. Letting him come all the way to Christchurch was probably just another attempt to get him out of the way. By the time he got back, all the sheep would have been herded in and ready for shearing—and the workers would be running their mouths about the young master who preferred the opera to work.

William boiled with rage, and Kura's behavior did nothing to placate him. Instead of staying at his side like a good wife—which she normally did out of indifference toward the other guests—she was flitting from one singer to the next. One dark-haired pretty boy in particular seemed to have caught her eye.

"Really? You sing, Miss . . . ?" the man asked, with that covetous expression that every man's face assumed whenever Kura was present.

"Warden . . . Oh, no, Martyn. Mrs. Martyn." Kura's marital status only seemed to occur to her at the last moment. The singer appeared disappointed. William could have beaten Kura.

He wondered whether he should continue to eavesdrop on their conversation but decided not to torment himself further. Instead, he headed to the bar. A whiskey would perk him up. And he could keep an eye on Kura just as well from there. It was not that William was jealous; he knew that every man fell for Kura at first sight. Why should it be otherwise for this singer? If he challenged every fellow who cast covetous looks at Kura to a fight, he would hardly have time to sleep. William trusted Kura: if she would not let him into her bed, she would not grant the honor to someone else. And as soon as she left this room, he would be at her side again, as long as the idea of shutting him out of their shared hotel room did not cross her mind.

For the moment, however, Kura was smiling at Roderick. She had a breathtaking smile.

"I wanted to be a singer. I'm a mezzo-soprano. But then love got in the way."

"And robbed the world of a wonder like you? The muses should not have allowed such a thing to happen," Roderick said. He did not for a moment believe that she had an extraordinary gift. She was just another of these women who far overestimated the few hours of piano classes they had taken, though several of them had shown themselves willing to share in his genius for a few hours at least. "In case you should reconsider," he said indulgently, "we're here for another week. You're welcome to sing for me."

Kura was beaming as she practically danced through the hotel's corridors at William's side.

"William, I always knew it! I knew I could sing opera, and the impresario thinks I should audition. Oh, William, I should! First thing tomorrow! Maybe I don't need to do all that tedious studying. Maybe we could just go to London, and I could audition, and then—"

"Sweetest, I would be more than happy to let you audition, but we must return to the farm tomorrow." William had decided that rather spontaneously after his third whiskey. "I just learned that the shearing companies are on the march, and I'm needed there. I can't leave all the shearing work to Gwyneira and James."

"Oh, they've managed for twenty years without you," Kura told him, not incorrectly. "Please, let me have just one day! Let me sing for this Mr. Barrister, and then—"

"We'll see." Kura had taken his hand, and William began to hope for a dreamy night in her arms. He kissed her when they entered the room, and felt his hopes confirmed when she kissed him back hungrily. He let his lips drift slowly down her throat, kissing the tops of her breasts that her evening dress revealed, and began to run his hands down her dress.

"My God, Kura, you're so beautiful. People would pay any price to see you onstage whether you sing or not," he whispered huskily. Kura let him undress her. Then she was standing naked before him, allowing him to caress and kiss her body, and finally she sank down on the bed with him, where his mouth explored the interior of her thighs and then teased her most intimate body parts. She moaned, letting out tiny cries, and quickly came to climax. She embraced him happily, stroked his hair, and began to tease him, finally moving to straddle him while caressing his chest with her hair.

"Wait," William cried. "Wait, I need to take my pants off." He felt that his member might soon burst through his trousers. He ripped them off and set himself free, wanting Kura on top of him, above him, to take him into her, to become one with her, as she had done so many times before. Kura withdrew firmly.

"Kura, you can't," William said, mustering all his willpower not to seize her long, unbound hair and pull her to him, not to grasp her shoulder and take her by force. It was too much. It was simply too much.

But Kura only looked at him, uncomprehending. "I already told you that I don't want to any more babies. Especially now that it's probably going to work out with my singing. I don't want another baby!"

William tumbled out of bed. If he stayed there even a moment longer, he would take her against her will. No one could expect him to let her arouse him to just before the point of climax and then sleep beside her as though they were brother and sister. His erection was ebbing slowly, but he needed to leave. He would find the bathroom and give himself relief, and then see if there was another room available. Though it would be so embarrassing to ask for one at the front desk.

On the way to the bathroom, he ran into Heather Witherspoon. Normally that would have been awkward for him, half-dressed as he was, but she only smiled casually at him. She was far from formally dressed herself. William let his gaze wander over her. Her hair fell over her shoulders, and her feet were bare. And her face lit up when she saw him.

"Mr. Martyn! Could you also not sleep? How was the reception?"

Heather was wearing only a light dressing gown over a silk nightgown. Her breasts stood out underneath it. Freed from her eternal corset and boring old spinster dresses, her feminine figure was clearly recognizable. Her gaze was inviting, her lips trembled, and her eyes sparkled.

William did not have to consider long. He wrapped her in his arms.

The next morning, William hardly gave Kura time to eat breakfast. When he had returned to her bed late the previous night, satisfied from making love with Heather and drunk on whiskey, she had been sound asleep. Kura did not know jealousy. She was too self-assured for that. Though she was strongly protesting against the rushed departure, she could not get a word in edgewise.

"He doesn't really want to listen to you. He simply wants to ogle you," William explained to his complaining wife. "I don't care whether he does that or not. However, they can't start the shearing without me. That is, they could, but I would lose respect in front of the workers. How would that look? The future master of Kiward Station hanging on the train of a would-be diva while others do the work."

He hurt Kura deeply with his "would-be diva" comment, which at least granted him a peaceful return trip. She maintained a huffy silence, only exchanging a few words with Heather. They made good time, as William had two cobs pulling the light chaise, and the roads had improved considerably in the last few years. It had long been unnecessary to stop for a night's rest between Christchurch and Haldon.

The travelers reached Kiward Station early that evening, and William reported almost triumphantly for the sheepshearing. The very next morning he would oversee the assignment of the sheep to their sheds. He began the evening with a few glasses of whiskey, however—and ended it in Heather Witherspoon's bed.

Heather, deeply satisfied from making love with William, did not know how to react to Kura's complaints about the missed audition. She didn't want Kura to go to England—at least not with William. Kura had made it clear that she would not consider leaving Kiward Station without him. However, a great deal had changed in the interim. As Kura's confidante, Heather knew very well that Kura had not allowed her husband into her bed since Gloria's birth. Everything that had transpired after that—in particular, Kura's initial attempts to return her sexual relationship with William to the harmless kissing and caressing she had once enjoyed with Tiare—had not reached her ears, but she didn't care about the details. In Heather's opinion, Kura's marriage to William was virtually over. Maybe Kura would, in fact, accept the reality of that and leave her husband. The audition in Christchurch could be the first step. For that reason, she tentatively advised the girl, "You shouldn't get your hopes up too much, of course. But listening to what an expert has to say certainly couldn't do any harm."

"I would have had to stay in Christchurch for that. William is so cruel!" Kura began that lament anew. Heather had already been obliged to listen to her complaints all morning. But then Heather had a stroke of genius. They should find the music for some of the pieces they had heard at the performance. Kura began to practice with determination, singing the parts of Carmen and Azucena parts over and over again.

"I would have stabbed Carmen no later than in the second act; or better yet, the first scene," James mumbled as the "Habanera" rang out through the salon for the third time while he was attempting to unwind after dinner.

He was already out of sorts as it was. He had not figured William's early return into his plans. Which had not been helped by the fact that the young man had appeared with a hangover that morning and still stiff from his ride the day before. In an ill humor, William had pushed the workers around and then set the sheep into confusion by suddenly changing the herd assignments, all of which had brought James to a boil. And now he had to listen Kura sing for hours on end about love and rebellious birds. The same pieces, over and over again.

"What's this all about?" he asked. "Didn't she say just three days ago that she desperately needed to practice her German, because she couldn't sing Schubert's songs in English for some reason? But now she's singing in French, right?"

Kura had learned French from Heather Witherspoon.

"They heard that piece in Christchurch, and the singer is supposed to have been horrendous," Gwyneira explained. She then went on to tell him about the audition. "Kura wants me to put a driver and a carriage at her disposal, so that she can meet this singer, this 'impresario,' again. But we can't really spare anyone at the moment, except maybe William. He could have just stayed on with her there."

"I wouldn't have let her audition either, had I been in his place," James remarked grumpily. "It's clear what that other fellow wants.

Do you truly believe that he's going to foist a girl on his other singers who has never seen the inside of a conservatory before?"

Gwyneira shrugged. "I don't know, James. I don't the first thing about all that, and to be honest I don't care. I would just like to be rid of Carmen. And to make Kura happy."

Kura had just started the aria again from the beginning. James rolled his eyes.

"Not again," he muttered peevishly. "Look at it this way, Gwyn: You've been trying to make Kura happy for sixteen years. Now it's William's turn. They should figure out how to get her to Christchurch, and if all goes well, he'll stay there to hold her little hand while she sings. No doubt he'd prove grand at negotiating her contract and driving the others crazy when she sings too loud or quietly. But that's not your concern anymore. It's bad enough that neither of them looks after their child. Which reminds me, we need to tell Jack that he can't bring the baby into the sheds during the shearing. The air in there won't be good for her. Even if it means she cries all day."

Gwyneira sighed. That again! The nanny would surely resign. Gwyneira would be overseeing one of the sheds as she always did, but if Kura sang all day, making Gloria cry all day, Mrs. Whealer would quite likely lay down her arms.

Kura sang as if possessed, and the more reliable her mastery of the lyrics and notes, the more confident she grew that she would meet Roderick Barrister's standards. She had to get to Christchurch; she simply had to! And the week had almost passed; she only had two days left, one of which would be wasted on the trip there. Perhaps she could talk to William once more. Or more than talk. If she let him back into her bed after all this time, he would be putty in her hands. Naturally, there was a risk. But if she whipped William from one climax to another, he would promise her anything. She would simply have to take the risk. Besides, she had heard rumors among the dancers at the reception—something about a stroke of bad luck that had befallen one of them, but it had evidently been possible to straighten it all out. So, if worse came to worst, she could ask the girl how she'd resolved the matter. Or Roderick Barrister. He couldn't have his singers and dancers running around with protruding bellies, of course.

And so Kura did not spend her afternoon at the piano but instead devoted herself to making herself pretty for William. She did not sing again until that evening for him and Heather Witherspoon. Gwyneira and James had retired early, and Jack had barricaded himself with Gloria and his dog in his halfway-quiet room.

Kura did not pick up her opera music that evening, but instead practiced the Irish songs that had always enchanted William. And, indeed, no later than "Salley Gardens," she saw the light of desire in his eyes. She sang "Wild Mountain Thyme," to rekindle his lust, and promised her love in "Tara Hill." By the time she finished her last song, she thought him sufficiently aroused. She stood up slowly, making sure he did not take his eyes off of her, and walked to the stairs, her hips swaying.

"Don't stay up too late," she breathed, filling her voice with enticement and promise. William's breath seemed to have quickened. Kura climbed the stairs, certain that she would soon hear him knocking at her door.

But William did not appear. At first, Kura was not particularly unsettled. He had to finish off his whiskey and to extricate himself from Heather Witherspoon's chatter. Heather seemed to have fallen a bit in love with him. How absurd!

Kura undressed at her leisure, perfumed herself, and wrapped herself in her loveliest nightgown. Only then did she begin to grow impatient. She wanted to get under way soon, if for no other reason than that they needed to get an early start the next day. She wanted to reach Christchurch before nightfall. Ideally, she thought, she would audition briefly for Roderick Barrister that evening, so that they could work out a time for her to take the stage the next day.

After almost an hour had passed, Kura had had enough. If William would not come of his own accord, then she would just go get him.

She pulled on a dressing gown, combed her hair once more and stepped out onto the grand staircase leading to the salon. She wanted him to see her coming, an enchanting—and lonely—beauty in her nightclothes.

Kura floated down the stairs.

But William was not in the salon. Indeed, the light had been turned out, and it looked as though everyone had gone to bed. Had William really retired to his bedroom without knocking on her door even once? After that performance? Kura decided not to hold it against him and instead to feign a little remorse. After all, she had rebuffed him so often that it was understandable if he had given up all hope. It would only make her strategy that night all the more effective.

Kura slipped with feline movements into William's apartments. She would kiss him awake and be on top of him when he opened his eyes. But no one's head rested on the pillows. William's bed lay untouched. Kura frowned. The only other possibility was the nursery. Maybe William had wanted to take a look at Gloria or was comforting her while she cried. Kura had never seen him do such a thing, but she did not know where else he might be spending the night.

A moment later, she knew. Silence reigned in the nursery, and no sound was coming from Jack's room next door. She did, however, hear laughing and moaning coming from Heather Witherspoon's room. Kura did not hesitate. She ripped the door open.

"She's gone? What do you mean, 'She's gone'?" Gwyneira asked, bewildered. She had come down to breakfast still a little sleepy. She and James had drunk a bottle of good wine to put Carmen behind them, and enjoyed a lovely night after that. And now, here was William, wanting something from her first thing. "Come, William, Kura doesn't know how to ride, and she doesn't drive. She can't even have left Kiward Station."

"She was a little hysterical yesterday. She might have misunderstood something." William hemmed and hawed.

In truth, Kura had only cast a burning glance at him and Heather in bed, a glance that expressed something almost like hate. Or rather, disappointment, an unwillingness . . . William did not quite know how to gauge her expression. He had only seen it for a fleeting instant. After she had grasped what she was seeing, she had stormed out of the room. William knocked on her door immediately thereafter, but she had not answered. Nor when he tried again, or again after that. Finally, he gave up and retired to his own room, where he tossed and turned. Only at dawn did sleep finally overpower him.

When he'd woken up, he wanted to try once again to speak with Kura. When he went to her room, however, he found her doors wide open. And she was gone.

"Did you have a fight?" Gwyneira asked, groping for an explanation.

"Not exactly . . . Well, yes, but . . . For heaven's sake, where could she be?" William appeared almost frightened. Kura had behaved so strangely. And though he would not admit it, he had found a letter she had written on the table in her dressing room.

It isn't worth it.

Nothing more and nothing less. But Kura would not have done anything to herself, would she? William thought with horror about the lake next to the Maori village.

"Well, I would probably start by looking for her in Christchurch," James said casually as he came down the stairs in excellent spirits. "Isn't that where she wanted to go?"

"But not on foot," William objected.

"Kura rode off with Tiare," said Jack, who had just entered the room followed by his puppy. Apparently, he had already been out checking on things in the stables. "I asked if she wanted to say good-bye to Gloria, but she didn't even look at me. Felt guilty, I bet, since Tiare was taking Owen without asking."

"Maybe she looked in on Gloria earlier," said Gwyneira, in an effort to make her granddaughter not appear to be such a horrible mother.

Jack shook his head. "Nah, Gloria slept with me. I just left her with Kiri in the kitchen. And Kiri didn't say anything about Kura."

"And you just let her take the horse?" William flared up at him. "That Maori boy comes here, takes a valuable horse and—"

"How was I supposed to know they didn't ask?" Jack said calmly. "Tiare will definitely bring him back anyway. I'm sure they only drove to Christchurch for that absurd audition of Kura's. They'll be back tomorrow."

"That I not believe," Moana remarked. The housekeeper had been setting the table for breakfast when William had come downstairs with the news of Kura's disappearance. Moana had gone straight upstairs to inspect Kura's things. She felt no need to hold back, having served in the house for forty years and having raised Marama and Paul. Kura was like a very spoiled granddaughter to her. "She took big bag, all beautiful things, also evening dresses. Looks like big trip."

Roderick Barrister rounded up the ensemble for a rehearsal shortly before their last opera recital in Christchurch. They needed to practice the quartet from *Il Trovatore* again. It had become an embarrassment, and his Azucena was only getting worse. The girl felt too much was being asked of her; she was suffering from the other dancers' ridicule, and then there was this other business . . . Something would have to be arranged soon. Roderick asked himself how it could have happened. He had never impregnated any of his many lovers before. At least no one had ever told him if he had.

The girl's failure in *Il Trovatore* was still bearable—worse was the scene from *Carmen*. It would be best to strike it altogether from the program and look for something else. *La Traviata* perhaps. He could stage that with Sabina. Although then she would be overtaxed in that role too, and she did not have a suitably consumptive look about her.

"Maybe if we place the ladies a bit further forward," he considered, "Then a bit more of the song will come across."

"Or, the men could just sing a bit more softly," Sabina commented peevishly. "Piano, my friend. That should also extend into the higher range if you call yourself a tenor."

The giggles of the dancers, who were slowly gathering for their entrance, mixed with the ensuing cries of protest from the man playing the role of Luna, as well as Roderick's own objections.

And then a sweet voice suddenly sounded from the auditorium. "*L'amour est un oiseau rebelle, que nul ne peut apprivoiser . . .* "

The "Habanera" from *Carmen*. But sung by a much stronger voice than that of the little dancer. Though this singer was not perfect either, all that was lacking was polish, voice formation, a little education. The voice itself was magnificent.

Roderick and the other singers, in a state of excited confusion, looked into the room. Then they saw the girl—wondrous in an azure-blue dress, her hair held in place with a Spanish comb just as Carmen herself must have worn. A Maori boy waited behind her.

Kura-maro-tini sang her aria to the end calmly and with great self-assurance—did she already recognize the amazement in the eyes of her spectators? Regardless, the singers onstage and the dancers backstage could not contain themselves. They applauded enthusiastically when Kura finished—the little mezzo-soprano who saw an end to her suffering—Roderick most of all. This girl was a dream—pretty as a picture, with a voice like an angel. And he could shape her.

"I need work," Kura finally said. "But it looks like you need a mezzo-soprano. Can we come to an arrangement?"

She licked her lips lasciviously and held herself upright like a queen. Her hands played imaginary castanets. She had studied her Carmen. And she would wrap this impresario around her finger just as the gypsy had Don José.

11

Elaine's determination to avoid becoming pregnant at all costs consumed her whole life. It sometimes seemed an irrational obsession, since, viewed objectively, a pregnancy could actually have improved her standing in the Sideblossom household. John, for one, did not seem to believe in pestering pregnant women with nightly visits. Indeed, he was increasingly absent as Zoé's stomach grew rounder. His "business" sometimes took him to Wanaka, sometimes to Dunedin and even as far as Christchurch.

When he was home, he followed Emere with his eyes and occasionally touched her possessively. Though she cast looks of barely concealed hatred at him when he did so, Elaine suspected that she always obeyed his summons at night. Whenever she lay awake herself, she often heard noises in the corridors, ghostly sounds, as though someone were being dragged outside. Though Emere always moved gracefully, with swaying hips and measured step, on the days after the sounds, she appeared a little stiff. And whenever she left the house, she played the *putorino*—clear evidence that it really was she who slipped outside after nightfall rather than disappearing after dinner into the shelters with the other servants.

Emere elicited strange, almost human sounds from the exotic little instrument, which unsettled Elaine and made her anxious, as though the flute were mirroring her own torment. She hardly dared move when she heard it, out of fear that Thomas would awaken, for Emere's music seemed always to rouse a particular rage in him. When he heard it, he would stand up, close the window abruptly, and try to further muffle the sound by drawing the heavy curtains. Though they could no longer hear the flute after that, Thomas would pace the room like a caged tiger, and whenever Elaine dared to speak to him or draw his attention, he took his rage and excitement out on her. Elaine had tried insulating the room against every sound in advance. But then the air would become sticky and hot, and Thomas would wrench the window open after having his way with Elaine. Then she had to fear Emere's playing all over again.

That, too, came to an end. Emere's form began to grow round just like Zoé's, and John left her alone.

Elaine's relief did not last long, as John trained his lustful gaze on her next. He occasionally stroked her hip when he passed by or even casually touched her breast, pretending he was brushing a leaf or blade of grass from her hair. Elaine found his overtures detestable and did all she could to withdraw from his touch. When Thomas became aware of his father's advances, he glared at his father and took his revenge out on Elaine afterward. From his perspective, she was encouraging practically every man she saw, and the fact that she was now trying to ensnare his father was the very pinnacle of insolence. She could deny it all she wanted. It was no use. Thomas was pathologically jealous. Elaine became increasingly nervous and haggard because of it. She never got used to his nightly visits and fits of jealousy—how could anyone get used to torture? Elaine knew this couldn't be normal for married life, but she found no remedy for it. Even when she attempted to be inconspicuous and not create any friction with Thomas for which he would feel he had to "punish" her, it was at best only less bad—it was never painless.

It also proved nearly impossible to avoid the "dangerous" days, though Elaine made every effort to do so. Sometimes she would eat nothing for several days to render herself pale and fake a febrile illness. Or she would stick her finger down her throat, vomit several times, and declare that there was something wrong with her stomach. Once she even stooped low enough to eat soap because she had read that doing so would produce a fever. She did, in fact, become violently ill for two days—and hardly had energy on the third for her vinegar douche after Thomas had "visited" her again. The solution seemed to be working though. Elaine had yet to conceive.

She occasionally tried to talk Thomas into visiting Queenstown. She had to do something. She could not spend the rest of her life in Thomas's prison! Perhaps she would find the courage to confide in her mother—and if she could not manage that, Inger or even Daphne. She would certainly know of something to make Elaine's nights more bearable.

Thomas vetoed the idea outright. Elaine began to suspect that he was reading her mail. After she had woven a few hints of her boredom, her pent-up state in the house, and the unpleasantness of her nights into a letter to her mother, Thomas had descended on her with terrible savagery. He would run the boredom out of her, he declared to her, though she had never complained to him. Elaine suspected that Fleurette never received the letter.

She could only hope that her parents would come up with the idea to visit her themselves —but she knew how difficult that would be for them. Business was booming in Queenstown, making Ruben, at least, practically indispensable, and Fleurette would hardly travel so far alone to place herself under the roof of her old enemy, John Sideblossom, if there was not an urgent reason to do so. Thomas's censorship kept Elaine from giving her such a reason.

Sometimes Elaine thought that a pregnancy might even help. Her parents would come for the birth, or no later than the baptism. But she rebelled wholeheartedly against the idea of bringing another life into this hell, not to mention the fact that a baby would shackle her to Lionel Station without hope of escape. So she carried on and hoped for a miracle. Although none was forthcoming, Patrick O'Mally returned to Lionel Station almost a year after her wedding.

The young Irishman was driving a heavy team that had just dropped off a heavy load of supplies in Wanaka.

Now, however, the wagon was empty, and a white horse was following him at a proud trot.

"Since I was already in the area, I thought I'd pay you a visit, Elaine, and bring you your Banshee. It's a shame, her just standing around and you without a horse. The little stallion has been on its own for a while now and is filling out beautifully. Oh, and your mother says you should write more often—and not just these small-talk letters. She's almost getting a bit worried. Then again, no news is usually good news, right?" Patrick looked at her inquisitively. "Isn't that right, Elaine?"

Elaine looked around her fearfully. Arama and Pita were taking care of the horses nearby. Pita had been the one to call her when Patrick arrived. But Thomas would not be away for long. He was overseeing some sort of work with the ewes and would undoubtedly coming storming back as soon as he learned of Patrick's arrival. The young driver seemed to sense this, not even unharnessing his team. He wanted to be on his way home before getting into a fight with Thomas Sideblossom. But for the moment, Elaine was alone with him—and he was asking prying questions. Elaine wondered if he could see how unhappy she was. She knew she had lost weight and that her face looked sallow and was often marked by tears. She should say something. Patrick seemed only to be waiting for her confirmation. But she couldn't confide in this young man! Her shame kept her from saying anything explicit, but perhaps she could manage a few hints.

"Sure, though . . . I'm often bored inside the house," she beat around the bush.

"Then why do you stay inside?" Patrick asked. "Your mother thinks you should already have taken over the sheep husbandry here like your grandmother did at Kiward Station. And this little dog needs something to do!" Patrick was petting Callie.

Elaine blushed. "That would be nice. But my husband doesn't want me—"

"What doesn't your husband want?" Thomas's booming voice interrupted Elaine's stammering. He had appeared as if from nowhere on his stallion, looming like a vengeful god in front of Elaine and young Patrick. Pita and Arama disappeared forthwith into the stables.

"I was just explaining that you don't want me helping with the sheep," Elaine whispered. Thomas was not going to believe this harmless explanation, but unless Patrick was both blind and deaf, he would have to notice what was going on.

"I see. And perhaps your husband doesn't want you flirting with errand boys either. I know you, boy; you accompanied her here. So there's something between the two of you, is there?"

Thomas had sprung from his horse and was now approaching Patrick with a threatening look. Elaine was terrified when he grabbed Patrick by the collar.

It did not seem to scare Patrick at all, however. He looked prepared to pay Thomas back in kind. Yet Elaine couldn't help but project her own panicky fright onto the young man. Thomas could hit Patrick, could kill him, and then . . .

Elaine's fright erased her ability to think rationally. Frozen with fear, she observed the fight brewing between the two men. Thomas and Patrick exchanged angry words, but Elaine did not catch any of them. It was as though she were in a trance. If Thomas did anything to Patrick, if he were to make Patrick disappear, her parents would never know. There was no hope and . . .

Elaine trembled, thinking feverishly. Then something occurred to her. Ruben O'Keefe did not send his men out on the road completely defenseless. Although the South Island was not exactly a den of thieves, a supply wagon loaded down with valuable merchandise and occasionally with spirits could awaken covetousness. For that reason, a revolver lay under the seat of each of the O'Kay Warehouse's delivery wagons. It was easily accessible there, and the driver could draw it with a single motion.

Awaking from her paralysis, Elaine moved closer to the delivery wagon's box. Thomas and Patrick took no notice of her. They were still jostling and abusing one another—not really anything dangerous, but to Elaine's overexcited imagination, their actions appeared quite threatening. She prayed the weapon was there, and it was: her hand touched cold steel right away. If I only I knew how to use the thing, she thought.

Then, suddenly—while Elaine was still weighing the weapon in her hand—the men backed down and their faces relaxed. Patrick O'Mally had evidently realized that it made little sense to get into a public-house fistfight with a sheep baron on his own farm. He thought

Thomas's reaction to be way out of line, crazy even, but knew that it was best just to keep one's distance from people like that. He would certainly tell Ruben O'Keefe about it though. It was high time someone with more influence than a driver looked into what was going on here.

Patrick said placatingly, "Fine, fine, now get ahold of yourself, man! I didn't touch your lady, just brought her horse. We weren't even alone. Your stableboys—"

"My stableboys are a no less lustful mob," Thomas ranted, but he let Patrick return to his wagon. "You get out of here, you understand? If I ever see you on this farm again, I'll put a load of lead in your hide!"

Elaine was still standing next to the box, but she stepped back hastily—hiding the weapon in the folds of her dress. It was not worth thinking about what Thomas would do if he found it on her. She should have given it back to Patrick, but the revolver felt good in her hand. It gave Elaine security—even if she did not yet know how to use it. At least she had it. She could hide it in one of her chests and figure out how it functioned later. Silently, she observed Patrick as he climbed onto the box and got the horses moving after a brief parting word accompanied by a meaningful look. Patrick had understood, she thought—he would send help.

In the meantime, however, Elaine's situation worsened. Patrick's visit seemed to have intensified Thomas's madness. He hardly ever left Elaine unattended anymore. She panicked when she found the west wing locked the next day. She was even close to climbing out the window at one point.

Thomas avenged himself mercilessly for her brief conversation with the young driver. The day after Patrick's visit, her body was so black-and-blue that she could not get out of bed. Pai and Rahera were beside themselves when they brought her breakfast.

"That's not good!" Rahera said. "Not happen in my tribe."

"In the orphanage we saw that," Pai explained. "We were always beaten when we did something wrong. But not . . . you did not even do anything, Mrs. Sideblossom."

Elaine waited until the girls were gone before dragging herself over to her chest of drawers and pulling out the revolver. It fit almost comfortingly in her little hands. Tentatively, she put her finger on the trigger. Could she manage to fire a weapon this big? But why not? She had observed men at target practice before. Though most of them used one hand, some of them aimed with both hands for greater accuracy. She could do that too. Elaine raised the revolver and aimed it at the ugly curtains. Wait, first she had to take the safety off. That was easily done. The gun was a primitive instrument. Elaine then figured out how to load it. Not that it mattered. She would not be getting more than the six cartridges already in their chambers anyway. And she knew that she would never be able to fire off more than one before Thomas took the weapon from her. So there could be no test firing. Elaine put the weapon back.

But from that moment on, she thought about it every hour of her miserable life. Until then, she had always held out hope that help would come, like for the girls in the penny novels and magazines or even the heroines in famous books. However, she was no character in a novel but a person of flesh and blood. She did not have to wait for a knight to come to her rescue: she had a gun, and she had a horse. She did not seriously consider shooting her way out of there, but with the revolver in her bag, she would feel stronger, just as she had already felt stronger with it hidden in the chest in her room—despite all the abuse she suffered. She would shoot Thomas dead before she let him beat her to death. She felt the wish to do so every night. But of course it was ridiculous to think she could take the weapon out while Thomas abused her. Elaine would have to hide the thing under the bedsheet, and she lacked the courage for that. She dared not think about what would happen if she made a mistake and the weapon did not fire. No, it was better to look for a moment when she could escape unnoticed. She would ride to Queenstown and attempt to get a divorce.

Elaine's fear exceeded her sense of shame. It would be embarrassing to confide in a judge—but she now feared for her life.

While Zoé awaited the birth of her child and Emere practiced playing her flute again—though there were no more "visits" from John Sideblossom, perhaps she was conjuring magic for her unborn child—Elaine forged her plans for escape. Maybe she would leave when the sheep were being herded back down from the highlands. Thomas would be gone for at least two days. The stableboys were on her side, and Zoé and Emere would not be able to stop her if she rode away with enough determination. But that was still a long way off. Elaine forced herself to be optimistic. It was possible that help would come from Queenstown first.

But only a week after Patrick's visit, an opportunity to leave Lionel Station presented itself. The day before the shearing companies arrived, Thomas and John had their hands full. Each of them would be overseeing a shearing company, a task they were loath to give to anyone else, despite the fact that the "orphans" could count and write perfectly. Zoé complained that John was abandoning her when her time was nearly at hand. She did not look well and demanded the services of the entire house's staff. To Elaine's annoyance, even Pai and Rahera had been summoned to help, this despite the fact that her maids generally had no involvement with Zoé. On the other hand, Elaine suddenly found herself entirely unsupervised for the first time since her arrival at Lionel Station. She immediately began to think about saddling Banshee and trying to flee. But it struck her as too risky. Thomas's horses were faster than Banshee. If she only had a three- or four-hour advantage, they would catch up to her.

Then her luck turned in her favor: Zoé's labor began around midday. The young woman began to bleed heavily and started to panic.

Emere sent for John to receive instructions, and then she withdrew, as she said, to ask the spirits for a happy delivery.

When John heard about Zoé's labor, he unleashed his rage on nearly every Maori girl or woman present, then sent frantic messengers off to Wanaka to drum up a midwife somewhere. He posted himself in Zoé's room, apparently seriously concerned about his wife—or at least the baby, who he surely assumed would be a boy. Between the two of them, husband and wife kept the entire house and kitchen staff occupied. Zoé alternated between asking for tea or water in a weak voice and screaming hysterically whenever she was seized by a labor pain. She was obviously terrified and called crossly for Emere, who did not appear.

Everyone seemed to have completely forgotten about Elaine. No one was watching over her, and Thomas hadn't locked her apartments that day. The farm could not spare him. Since his father was keeping watch outside Zoé's bedroom—having emptied half a bottle of whiskey and alternatingly cursing and lamenting—the management of the sheepshearers had been left to Thomas and his foremen. And since the Sideblossoms did not trust their foremen, Thomas would hardly move from the shearing sheds.

While Elaine pretended to be doing some needlework, her thoughts were racing. Could she bring herself to do it? If she could get Banshee out of the stables unnoticed, she could be in Queenstown in three days. She was not even worried about the route, because the horse would undoubtedly be able to find the path back to its old home. The mare did not yet feel at home in the Sideblossoms' stables, and if she were allowed to have free rein, she would probably race home as fast as she could. It wouldn't be easy to escape the pursuers who would follow later, but with a six- to eight-hour advantage, she could do it. Banshee was strong. She would not need to rest long. The prolonged ride would be harder on Elaine than the horse. But that was of no consequence. Elaine would have ridden day and night to get home. Whatever else happened, she would never return to Thomas. Her parents would undoubtedly support her. After all, Fleurette knew from her own experience what kind of people the Sideblossoms were.

A new succession of cries issued from Zoé's room. Everyone in the house was distracted.

If she did not do it now, she never would.

Elaine ran to her bedroom and threw a bundle together. She did not need much, but she had to take a cloak and riding dress. She did not have the time to change just then, but she did not want to brave a three- or four-day ride in her housedress, especially not in the mountains where it was still quite cold. Though she would have liked to bring along some provisions or at least firewood, it was too risky to sneak into the kitchen, and she would not dare start a fire in the wilderness.

The only other thing that Elaine took before running out was the revolver, which she slid into the pocket of her housedress. She did not look back. Her grandfather James McKenzie had once told her that brought bad luck. Anyone who left a prison had to keep looking forward.

Elaine made it to the stables unseen. Banshee and little Khan whinnied greetings at her as soon as she entered. Banshee pawed impatiently as Elaine hurried past her stall in the direction of the tack room to let Callie out. Pita shut Callie up in there when he was working and could not watch her. Otherwise, the little dog would go in search of Elaine right away, and, as of recently, she was no longer allowed in the house. Zoé had ostensibly developed an animal allergy during her pregnancy.

Now that was all behind her. Elaine felt a surge of joy and the desire for adventure rising within her. Hopefully, Patrick had thought to bring Banshee's saddle, as the Sideblossoms' horses were all thinner than her horse. She found the saddle was hanging there—and thankfully not the lady's saddle, which would have turned the hours of galloping into torture. There was no time to clean her horse, but Banshee had not gotten dirty in the stables anyway. Elaine bridled and saddled her while the horse was still in her stall. She tied her baggage to the saddle's leather straps. She was ready. They just needed to make it outside and head toward the river, giving the shearing sheds a wide berth. With a half hour, they would be out of Thomas's sphere of influence.

It was a shame she didn't know where Emere had gone off to for her spirit summoning. Elaine didn't trust her. Though Emere appeared to hate the Sideblossoms, she had served them loyally for years. There had to be a reason she continued to allow John Sideblossom to sleep with her instead of running away. Did she love him, or had she loved him once? Elaine did not want to think about it, but either way, she would have felt safer if the old Maori woman had been far away. It would be much better if no one saw her.

But then she heard the flute. Emere was once again playing in that confusing hollow-sounding tone with which she conjured the spirits. Evil spirits, from the looks of things. But none of that mattered now. Elaine sighed with relief when she heard the flute. The music was coming from somewhere in back of the house, and as long as Emere continued to play, it would be easy to avoid her.

Elaine led her mare into the aisle of the stable—and stopped, aghast, when she saw Thomas at the entrance. His shadow loomed threateningly, framed against the sunlight outside. He was rubbing his forehead—as he so often did when he heard Emere's flute. But that day he had no need of spirit voices to whip himself up into a frothing rage.

"Hey now. Another ride? I knew it was worth checking up on that sweet wife of mine. With all the sheepshearers on the farm, one doesn't leave such a lusty little thing unattended." Thomas grinned sardonically, but his hand moved as if by force to his ear in an apparent attempt to muffle the sound of the flute.

Elaine squared herself. She needed to gather her courage. There was no going back.

"I'm not interested in your sheepshearers," she said calmly, guiding her hand slowly toward the pocket where the revolver was stored. Emere's playing sped up. Elaine felt the heavy pounding of her heart. "And I'm not going for a ride. I'm leaving you, Thomas. I don't want any more to do with your jealousy and your strange . . . little games. Now let me out!"

She moved to lead her horse past him, but Thomas stood with legs spread in front of the exit.

"Well, look here, your puppy's growling!" he yelled, laughing.

Callie began to bark wildly as though on command. She easily drowned out Emere's flute playing, which seemed to relieve Thomas. He took a step toward Elaine.

Elaine drew her weapon.

"I'm not joking," she said with trembling voice. She would not relent. She could not! It was not worth thinking about what he would do to her if she went back now.

Thomas's laugh boomed. "Oh, a new toy!"

He pointed to the revolver. Callie barked even louder, and, in the background, the notes that Emere was drawing from the flute were vibrating.

Then everything happened in a flash. Elaine, terrified, removed the weapon's safety just as Thomas lunged at her. But his attempt to take her by surprise came too late. Elaine pulled the trigger, uncertainly, holding the gun in one hand. She did not know if she hit him, but Thomas froze with a look of disbelief. She grasped the pistol with both hands, and with ice-cold concentration, she aimed it at her husband again. She meant to hit his chest, but the revolver seemed to develop a life of its own when she pulled the trigger. The recoil forced the barrel upward. And then she saw the blood spray. Thomas's face exploded in a fountain of red before her eyes. He did not scream even once. He just fell to the ground as though struck by lightning.

"You shall be damned!" Thomas heard Emere's voice. He knew he was not supposed to follow the spirits' song. Had she not always told him that he would only be safe in his nursery when she called the spirits? But he was curious, and he was now eight years old. At that age, a boy had to summon the courage to stand up against threats. At least that is what his father had told him. And so he had followed Emere one night when she mistakenly believed he had fallen asleep to the deep, hypnotic sound of the flute. However, Emere

was not meeting with any spirit. It was his father who approached her in the garden. She seemed strangely unsteady, as though she did not know whether she should stay or run away. And then his voice.

"Didn't I call you?"

Emere turned around to face him.

"I come when I want."

"Oh? So you want to play these little games."

What Thomas saw next was burned into his memory forever. It was repugnant, but also . . . thrilling. It was almost as if this secret observation allowed him to share in his father's power. And what power it was. His father received the affection Thomas yearned for so desperately. Emere embraced him and kissed him. But she had to be forced, subdued, in order to do it. Thomas longed to possess his father's power, longed to be able to force Emere like that. Finally, his father left her lying there. She whimpered. She had been punished . . .

And then the flute sounded. The spirit's voice. Thomas should have fled. Then Emere would never know that he had seen her defilement. But he stayed, stepped nearer even. He would have liked to . . .

And then she turned to face him.

"You saw everything? And you're not ashamed? You have it in your eyes already, Thomas Sideblossom. You shall be damned!"

Thomas's face exploded.

Out of the corner of her eye, Elaine saw a red pool spreading around Thomas's head. She didn't dare move, though she no longer felt fear, only horror and cold. Callie whined, hiding in a stall. She was afraid of loud noises. Emere's flute warbled unceasingly, its hollow notes swelling and ebbing.

"He's dead; he's dead." The thoughts tumbled over each other in Elaine's brain. She vacillated between the morbid desire to go to Thomas to be sure and the longing to run and hide in a corner of her room.

But then she realized that she would do nothing of the sort. She would do exactly what she had planned: take her horse and disappear.

Elaine did not look at the man lying on the ground again—not even when she had to lead Banshee over him. His mutilated face horrified her, and she already had enough horrible memories of Thomas to last her a lifetime. Banshee snorted, but then stepped over the body as though it were a log in the woods. Elaine thanked heaven that she did not step on him; that would have been too much. It was bad enough that Callie sniffed at him curiously. She had to reprimand the dog sharply to keep her from licking his blood. They reached the barnyard unseen, though Emere must have heard the shot. She could not have immersed herself that deeply into her flute playing. Elaine would have that gunshot in her ear forever.

Though Emere did not appear, the flute had ceased by the time Elaine left the stables. Was that a coincidence? Or had the old Maori woman gone off in search of help? Elaine did not care. She only wanted to escape. Swinging herself up on Banshee, she took off at a gallop. The mare wanted to take the most direct path to Wanaka, and Elaine no longer needed to avoid the shearing sheds.

Then the realization struck her, like a knife into her soul: she had shot her husband. She had aimed a pistol at an unarmed man and pulled the trigger with icy coldness. She could not even plead self-defense. It was no longer possible to flee to her parents and hide out there. She was now a murderer on the run. By the following morning, if not sooner, her father-in-law would file charges, and then the constable would be after her. There was no question now of riding back to Queenstown or even to the Canterbury Plains. She had to forget her friends and family, change her name, and start a new life somewhere else. How and where were a mystery, but flight was her only option.

Elaine turned her rather unwilling mare in the direction of the McKenzie Highlands.

Flight

CANTERBURY PLAINS AND GREYMOUTH

1896

1

"My God, William, of course we could bring her back!" Gwyneira's voice struck an impatient note, but she was having this conversation with her grandson-in-law for the umpteenth time. "This ensemble's touring schedule is hardly a secret. They're on the North Island, not in Timbuktu. But the question is whether that would do any good. You read her letter: she's happy. She's exactly where she wants to be and doing what she's always wanted to."

"But she's my wife," William objected—not for the first time either—pouring himself a whiskey. It was not his first of the evening. "I have my rights."

Gwyneira furrowed her brow. "What kind of rights? Do you want to take her by force? Theoretically you could, I suppose; she's still a minor. But she would never forgive you. Besides, she would just run right away again. Or do you want to lock her up?"

William had no answer to that. Of course he didn't want to lock Kura up, not that he would have been able to find a prison guard on Kiward Station. The McKenzies had accepted Kura's departure—and the Maori did not get overwrought about this sort of thing. He could not even count on Tonga's help. After all, there was a new heiress, in Gloria. Tonga had lost the game for this generation. Gwyneira, on the other hand, had triumphed and appeared to be almost happy for her granddaughter. Kura's letter from Christchurch—delivered by George Greenwood after the troupe had already left for Wellington—had sounded euphoric, overjoyed. The opera ensemble had taken her in with open arms. Naturally, she wrote, she still had a great deal to learn, but the impresario, Roderick Barrister, was instructing her personally, and she was making rapid progress. They had even allowed her onstage on her very first night; she had sung the "Habanera" and earned a standing ovation.

Kura's success, as Gwyneira silently mused, might also be traced to her outward appearance, but in the end it did not matter. Kura was enjoying herself and making money. As long as her success lasted, she would not spare Kiward Station a thought.

"Give her a little time, boy," James said appeasingly, holding his glass out to William. Gwyneira had not noticed, but William had just drained his third whiskey. James had been listening to the dispute for half an hour and felt that he had earned a drink. "Running after her now won't do any good. Besides, you obviously had a fight before she took off, isn't that so?"

William and Heather were still the only two who knew what had happened the night Kura set out, and neither wanted it to become common knowledge. Kura's departure had marked the end of their relationship, at least for the time being. William had not touched the governess since his wife had left him and did not feel inclined toward any intimate conversation with her. No one seemed to suspect any-thing—and William knew that it was in his best interest to keep it that way.

"Exactly! Just let her take part in this tour," Gwyneira said. "After that, we can see. The other singers' return trip is already booked anyway; George assured me of that. The organization is bearing all the travel expenses. If Kura wants to go on to England afterward, she will either have to pay using her own wages or ask me for money. We can revisit the matter then. But peacefully, William. I don't want to lose another granddaughter!"

This last comment made everyone go quiet. She was referring to the tragic story of Elaine, which Gwyneira and James had only recently learned about. Gwyneira had gotten very worked up but hadn't condemned Elaine at all. The same thing could have happened to her; after all, she too had stood before John Sideblossom with a gun in pointed at him. Though the circumstances had been different, Gwyneira was convinced that Elaine must have had good reason for defending herself in such a manner. But she didn't know why the girl had not sought her help. Kiward Station was isolated. They could have hidden Elaine for a while as they looked for a solution. An escape to Australia or even England could have been arranged. Elaine's disappearing without a trace wore on Gwyneira's nerves. It was out of the question that they should also lose contact with Kura!

William took a few, somewhat smaller, gulps of his whiskey. He would have liked to chase after his wife now rather than later—that sly Roderick Barrister was not letting her sing out of the kindness of his heart. He was undoubtedly hoping for something in return for allowing Kura onstage so soon. And he was "instructing" her himself. In what art? Not only was William's pride wounded, but he was also seething with jealousy.

On the other hand, he could hardly counter Gwyneira's arguments. Yes, it was embarrassing to sit there as an abandoned husband. But if he forced Kura to return, the first thing she would do was tell everyone why she had left—and William would be dead to the McKenzies.

"What am I supposed to do in the meantime?" he inquired, drunk and nearly in tears. "I mean, I . . . ."

"You continue on as before, though you would be most welcome to care a bit more actively for your child," Gwyneira informed him. "Beyond that, challenge yourself to learn your work properly and make yourself useful. Let us assume that Kura is just taking a trip. She is getting to know the world a bit, exercising her gifts, and will return in a few months. You must look at it that way, William. Anything else would be nonsense."

That was easy for Gwyneira to say, but if William's life on Kiward Station had already had its perils before Kura's departure, it now became unbearable. The workers, who had once mocked his failings as a sheep baron with some degree of discretion, now leered openly. Apparently, or so they whispered, the "crown prince" lacked certain skills outside of the stables too—he didn't appear to have what it took to hold onto a gem like Kura for long.

"Good-for-nothing!" said Poker Livingston, who had been showing up at the farm more regularly. The more easygoing Andy McAran
listened to William's orders and ideas with a neutral expression, but
then just did whatever he thought was right.

To William, the Maori were the worst. When the tribe had
returned from its migration, the men resumed their work at Kiward
Station. William, for his part, ignored them. They had always accepted
him, however begrudgingly, as a member of the local *pakeha* tribe, but
with Kura's departure, he lost all authority. It didn't matter whether
William expressed his demands calmly or by screaming—most of the
Maori simply looked right through him.

That drove William mad, all the more so because he was getting
less and less sympathy from Gwyneira. She had noticed that he was
drowning his anger in whiskey and had taken to criticizing him for
that.

"How do you mean to provide an example to the men when
you show up late and hungover in the morning? I don't like it either,
William. Above all, I don't know how I should act. If I defend you,
I turn myself into a laughingstock and lose authority with the men.
But if I concede that the men are right, you hold it against me and
sink deeper into your whiskey. It has to stop, William! I've had a
drunk on the farm before, and I won't let it happen again as long as
I have any say in the matter."

"And what do you mean to do, Gwyneira?" William asked mockingly. "Throw me out? You could do it, of course, but then you'd lose
Gloria. Because, naturally, I'd take her with me."

Gwyneira forced herself to remain calm. "Then start learning to
cook porridge," she replied nonchalantly, "and think about who will
want to give you a job when you've got a baby in tow. How do you
even mean to travel with Gloria? Do you plan to stick the girl in a
saddlebag?"

Her speech struck William dumb, but later, Gwyneira confessed
to her husband that his threat had filled her with fear.

"It is true that we have no right to the child. If he were to take her with him, we would have to support them, maybe send him money each month to pay for a nanny and an apartment."

James shook his head. "Gwyn, dear, don't panic," he said, attempting to soothe her by stroking her hair. "You're being absurd. Thank God our Billyboy didn't hear you say that. But you don't seriously believe that our would-be sheep baron would allow himself to be supported by you? Where would he go with Gloria once word had gotten out? And what would he do with her? Dear God, he doesn't even know how to hold her. He would never take her with him, especially since our Mrs. Whealer is no serf he can simply order to accompany him. Besides, the girl still has a mother. You could turn to Kura. She must care enough for her daughter to hand custody over to you. Any court would decide in her favor. So don't drive yourself mad." James pulled Gwyneira into his arms, but he did not altogether succeed in calming her. She had felt so sure of her position. But William was getting out of control.

For the first few days after Kura's departure, Heather Witherspoon had slunk around like a whipped dog. She could not understand why William had suddenly rebuffed her and, moreover, so rudely. It was not her fault that Kura had caught them. On the contrary, she had easily figured out Kura's strategy that night and made hints to William about it. But he had been too drunk to understand and unwilling to let himself be manipulated by his wife.

"I don't come crawling whenever she whistles!" he had declared in a state of drunken agitation. "And . . . and I'm certainly not going to take her to Christchurch. She can swing her hips until the sky falls. I'll take her when I want and not when it suits her."

Heather had not tried to persuade him further. No one could ask that of her. She loved him, after all. It was not right to lay all the blame on her.

Yet Heather had long since learned that life did not always work out according to what was right, and so she fell back on her tried-and-true strategy: she would wait. William would eventually come around; at some point he would need her. She did not believe that Kura would return. She was basking in success for the first time in her life, and if she needed a man, she would look for one where she was. Kura-maro-tini was not dependent on William Martyn. And if Heather did believe in love, it was in the love *she* felt.

Kura had already found her man—even if she would not have described her feelings for him as love. But she certainly admired Roderick Barrister: he embodied the fulfillment of all her dreams of success and career. For one, he could initiate her into the mysteries of opera singing, much more deeply and intensively than Heather Witherspoon ever had with her three music classes in Switzerland. In addition to that, he had power—the ensemble followed his orders with a devotion like nothing Kura had ever seen before. There were masters and servants on Kiward Station, of course, but Kura had taken for granted the high-handedness and self-assurance of the workers that had so confounded William. Slavish obedience was not wanted on sheep farms; whoever worked there had to be able to make decisions for themselves. In Roderick Barrister's ensemble, however, only one person's opinion counted: his. He could make ballerinas happy by promising them another solo, and even fully trained singers like Sabina Conetti dared not contradict him when he put a novice like Kura before them. Roderick Barrister's favor, Kura quickly learned, had much to do with the physical exertion of the ensemble's female members. The ballerinas often spoke of how Brigitte was allowed to sing the Carmen piece only because she let the impresario have his way with her. A close-lipped midwife in Wellington did away with the unwanted consequence of the affair.

Afterward, Brigitte could not dance for several weeks and repeatedly sobbed through the night, a routine that initially got on Kura's nerves because she was sharing a hotel room with the dancer. However, after only a few nights, Kura began to slip out shortly after bedtime to visit the impresario herself. Brigitte did not hold this against Kura and pretended not to notice a thing. She was relieved to be rid of the singing parts that were hopelessly beyond her, and she certainly had no further interest in Roderick.

Kura found herself strongly attracted to the handsome tenor. She did not have to fake her enthusiasm when she succumbed to his advances. He did not bother long with kisses and harmless caresses though. And when Kura expressed her fears about becoming pregnant, he only laughed.

"Nonsense, child, I'll be careful! Nothing will go wrong with me. No worries."

Kura wanted to believe that, and she noticed that Roderick pulled out of her more quickly when making love than William had. But the situation with Brigitte nagged at the back of her mind. Finally, with a thumping heart, she confided in Sabina Conetti. Although she was a bit concerned that the singer did not particularly like her—Roderick was now rehearsing the soprano roles with his new discovery—Kura trusted her more than anyone else to have insights into women's problems. And Sabina did instruct Kura in what little she knew about these matters.

"You can stay away from him on the dangerous days. But that is never a sure thing; nothing ever is," she said. "Least of all the fellows' promises they'll marry you if things go wrong, or anything else they say. Believe me, Roderick will promise you the moon and the stars now, but you shouldn't count on that. For the moment, he thinks himself a Pygmalion, but in the end, he's the same as the rest. Once he has no more need of you, he'll drop you.

This warning was wasted on Kura, however. For one thing, she knew nothing about Greek mythology, and second, she was firmly convinced that Roderick meant to do right by her. If he was so egotistical, he would not be giving her ever-greater roles or singing lessons every day for free. He spent half the afternoon on the piano with Kura while the other members of the ensemble enjoyed their freedom, exploring towns like Auckland and Wellington, and taking trips to visit the region's natural wonders.

Kura was at his service at night as well. Though she enjoyed herself, Roderick paled in comparison to William as a lover. Kura missed the ecstasy, the breathless climaxes her husband had driven her to, and was occasionally irked that Roderick did not compensate her in the same manner for the risk of becoming pregnant. But she forgot all that when she stood onstage in the evenings, basking in the audience's applause. And Roderick proved to be anything but vain. On the contrary, he let her shine, sending her repeatedly in front of the curtain on her own to receive the ovations of the crowd and handing her flowers onstage. She was exquisitely happy then, and after the performance, overwhelmed with gratitude toward Roderick, she covered him in caresses.

"Our rooster seems to have found true love!" whispered Fred Houver, the baritone, to Sabina Conetti one evening. "And the girl is really improving. She still has trouble with her breathing, but one day she'll make has-beens of the rest of us—and him first of all."

The singers were standing in the background while Roderick bowed to Kura onstage for the fifth time. They had served as the chorus while Kura and Roderick had played Carmen and her matador.

Sabina nodded at Fred Houver's words and looked at Kura's radiant face. There was no question that Roderick had fallen for the girl. But would that save her when the day of reckoning came?

William had had enough. It had been another one of those days when he would have liked to leave Kiward Station sooner rather than later—if only he could imagine some alternative. Gwyneira had sold a flock of lambs to Major Richland and asked William to herd them over to him. Since the weather had looked promising, the major had decided to ride along and had spent the night before at Kiward Station. He had tippled with William for quite a while after Gwyneira and James had retired, which meant they were both hungover and in a bad temper the following morning. It didn't help that it was now raining and that the Maori shepherds Gwyneira had assigned to William had not appeared. Only Andy McAran was hanging about in the stables. William asked him to accompany him and the major, as he did not trust himself to find the selected sheep on his own. Andy, who saw that he had no other choice if the whole endeavor was not to degenerate into a complete disgrace, condescended to come along, but kept up a grueling tempo and ignored William when he asked him to slow down on account of his older guest. Major Richland, however, held his own just fine on his thoroughbred, his spirits rising with every drink from the flask he carried. William ended up drinking, too, though Andy declined with a shake of his head.

"Not on the job, Mr. Martyn. Gwyn doesn't look kindly on that."

William, sensing that he was being reprimanded, tried to ride with Major Richland, but as it turned out, he could not hold his liquor half as well as the old soldier. He failed miserably at herding the sheep together. His dog refused to listen to him, instead pressing itself to the ground in fear as he yelled at it. Then his horse shied away from a thick-headed young ram that broke through the shepherds' lines, and William found himself sprawled in the wet grass.

Andy McAran kept an iron grip on himself, maintaining his composure, but Major Richland teased his host mercilessly the rest of the way back to the farm. In addition to that humiliation, the rain was still pouring down and the men were soaked to the bone. The major did not want to return home that evening, and instead planned to spend the night at Kiward Station, undoubtedly entertaining the McKenzies with the tales of William's misadventures. The whole undertaking had turned into a fiasco. If only Kura would return. But in the enthusiastic letters that she occasionally sent to Gwyneira, she sounded as happy as ever. She had not once written to William.

Naturally, there was no stableboy in sight when the men finally rode into Kiward Station's farmyard, and William had to tend to his horse himself. Andy McAran did not insist that William accompany him to the sheepcotes where the sheep were to be kept overnight.

Stinking of wet wool and lanolin, William decided he hated working with sheep more than anything in the world.

Gwyneira and James were expecting the major and William in the salon, but they made no move to offer the men a drink. They could tell from their red faces and unsteady steps that enough alcohol had already flowed that day. Gwyneira and James exchanged looks: there would be no alcohol before dinner if this was to be a pleasant evening. They sent the men upstairs to bathe and change. The butler carried the hot water to the guest's room first.

William would have liked to lie down in bed with a bottle of whiskey, but when he entered the rooms he had so lovingly furnished for his life with Kura, there was a surprise waiting for him: the aromatic scent of fresh tea wafted from the little salon. A samovar was keeping it warm, and beside it were two glasses and a bottle of rum.

William could not restrain himself. He reached for the rum bottle and took a long slug. But who might have prepared all this for him? Certainly not Gwyneira, nor Moana or Kiri to be sure. The Maori women had little sense for such things, and the servants were busy with the houseguest anyway.

William looked around skeptically. Then he heard an effervescent laugh coming from the bathroom.

"What a horrible day! I had to teach school for the Maori, and the water came through the roof. How could they have thought to cover that hut with palm leaves? And then I thought of you out there. You must have been frozen to the bone."

At the entrance to the bathroom stood Heather, with a radiant smile on her face and an apron over her dark dress like a well-trained housemaid. With a motion of her hand, she directed him to the bathtub, which was already filled with hot, fragrant water.

"Heather, I . . ." William vacillated between gratitude, desire, and the knowledge that it would be madness to let himself be seduced by her. But Kura had been gone a long time.

"Come, William," said Heather. "We have an hour before dinner is served. Mrs. McKenzie has to keep an eye on the kitchen, Mr. McKenzie is lounging by the fireplace, and I've given Jack enough

homework to keep him quiet. There's nothing to fear. No one saw
me come in."

William wondered fleetingly if she had carried the hot water up
here herself, which he could not imagine. But then he stopped thinking and succumbed to the temptation to submerge himself in the hot
water, let her massage his shoulders, caress him, and finally lead him
to bed.

"I don't want anyone to notice us either," purred Heather. "But
it's difficult enough as it is here. We don't have to live like monks."

After that evening, William and Heather rekindled their relationship.
He forgot his qualms and his fears as soon as he lay in her arms, and
moreover, he assuaged his self-recriminations. Kura was certainly
not leading a completely chaste life either. And besides, he saw only
Kura's face and body when he took Heather in a dark room or with
his eyes closed.

Elaine O'Keefe strolled down Main Street in the little town of Greymouth on the West Coast. What an ugly little town, she thought peevishly. The name fit! Although she had once heard that the town was named for the mouth of the Grey River, Elaine felt it was nothing more than a gray abyss threatening to swallow her whole. That was due in large part to the fog that enveloped the town. In sunnier weather, the town would surely not look so forbidding. After all, Greymouth was idyllically placed on a narrow strip of coast between the river and the sea, and the one- and two-story houses that lined the street appeared just as new and tidy as the buildings in Queenstown.

Greymouth, too, was a rapidly developing community, although it drew its wealth not from the gold mines but from the professionally run coal mines that had opened a few years before. Elaine wondered if there was coal dust hanging in the air or if it was only the fog and the rain that made it hard to breathe. Either way, the atmosphere struck her as altogether different from that of her lively, optimistic hometown. In Queenstown, of course, all the gold miners hoped to get rich quick, while the coal-mining trade only brought its operators good money, damning the pitmen to a hard life underground.

Given the choice, Elaine would never have sought this town out herself, but after several weeks of riding through the mountains, she'd had enough. During the first few days after fleeing Lionel Station, she'd had good luck with the weather. At first, she had ridden along the Haast River—in the water as often as possible to cover her tracks. Not that she believed they would employ bloodhounds. Where would they get them? And even if Elaine had taken a different route, Banshee's hooves hardly left imprints on the dry ground. It had not rained for a few days prior to her departure, and the weather remained clement until she reached the McKenzie Highlands. Then it grew cold, and Elaine froze horribly even after wrapping herself up in all the clothes she had brought with her. Banshee's saddle blanket helped, but it was usually wet with the mare's sweat. Added to all that was her gnawing hunger.

Elaine was quite fluent in the plants of her homeland —Fleurette had often taken her children on "adventure rides," and James McKenzie had likewise played the "survival in the wilderness game" with his grandchildren that Gwyneira had found so wonderful in her youth. But Elaine had no shovel for digging and no knife for peeling roots or gutting fish, or more importantly, for making fishing line or hooks. She occasionally succeeded in making a fire by striking two stones together—but that became hopeless after the first rain. She had managed to catch a few trout with her hands and then roasted them, but she always worried that the fire might give her away. For the same reason, she was afraid to shoot at the ubiquitous rabbits. Not that Elaine was likely to hit anything. After all, she had missed Thomas's chest when he was standing only six feet away. How was she supposed to shoot a rabbit?

Callie did catch a rabbit once. It was a lucky day all around, since Elaine discovered a dry cave in the mountains and managed to make a fire that night. Stewed with its skin and hair, the rabbit was no culinary wonder, but at least it filled Elaine's stomach. The days after that were bad, as nothing edible seemed to grow on the West Coast. There were only ferns, and they also offered some protection from the rain. At one point, Elaine ran into a Maori tribe who took her in hospitably. Their cooked sweet potatoes had never tasted so good.

Finally, the Maori showed her the way to Greymouth—or Mawhera, as they called it. It had a long history as a Maori stronghold, but had been in the hands of the *pakeha* for many years. Nevertheless, the Maori indicated to her that the area was very safe—probably another story having to do with the spirits. Elaine did not care. One town was as good as another to her, and she had to give up her wandering sooner or later. So she decided to follow her new friends' advice and look for work in Greymouth. It was the largest town on the West Coast, and it would not be all that easy for people to find her there. More than anything, she needed a proper bed and clean clothes. Even Banshee seemed excited about the prospect of a dry stall.

Paying for a stall was Elaine's first transaction, which she handled with a heavily beating heart, because she could not pay up front. The owner of the stables did not ask for any payment though, and instead directed the mare right away to a clean stall strewn with straw and gave it an abundance of hay.

"She's a little scrawny, the sweet girl," he remarked, which was no surprise. The meager grass in the highlands had been inadequate nourishment for the horse. She wasted no time eating her fill. Elaine still had no idea how she was going to pay for Banshee's luxurious accommodations. The proprietor had already looked her over meaningfully, as though to let her know that the horse's rider looked just as ill-cared-for as the horse. Elaine asked him where she might be able to find a job and a place to stay. The man thought about it.

"There are a few hotels on the quay, but they're expensive. Only the rich folks who make their money with the mines stay there." It was clear that he did not think Elaine fell into this category. "As for the Lucky Horse, well, I wouldn't especially recommend that one, though they'd probably welcome you with open arms if you don't care what kind of work you do." He grinned significantly. "But the widow Miller and the barber's wife rent rooms. You could ask there; both of them are good women. If you don't have money though . . ."

Elaine took the hint. The man didn't know of any positions for single, respectable women. But that did not mean anything. Elaine set out bravely up the street through the center of town. She would find something.

The town did not look very promising, however. And Elaine's determination to ask for work in every single store fell apart as soon as she reached the Chinese laundry. The billowing steam robbed her of even more of her breath, and then the proprietor hardly seemed to understand her request. Instead, he tried to buy Callie from her—even though he did not have any sheep. Elaine remembered the rumor that the Chinese ate dogs, and she turned on her heels immediately.

The barber's wife had a vacant room, but no work. Elaine had been nursing hopes that she might. After all, she was thoroughly familiar with the sort of work done in a hotel. But Mrs. Tanner kept the three rooms she rented clean herself, and she didn't need help cooking those extra three diners.

"Come back when you've found something," she told Elaine, who took the hint: until she found a source of income, there would be no bed and nothing to eat.

The next business was a coffin maker, which Elaine ruled out with a guilty conscience. But what was she supposed to do there? Although the general store gave her a spark of hope, it was run by a family with five bright kids. There were enough helping hands. A tailor worked next door, and Elaine desperately wished she could sew. But she had always hated handwork, and Fleurette had not forced it upon her. She had learned a little sewing from her grandmother Helen, but her skills hardly went beyond sewing buttons. Nevertheless, Elaine stepped into the store and asked about work. The tailor was kind but only shook his head.

"There aren't many people here who can afford a tailored suit. The mine owners, sure, but they like to shop in the bigger towns. They only come to me for alterations, and I manage those on my own."

That was in essence what she heard from all the other honorable tradespeople of Greymouth. All that were left were the grand hotels, where Elaine could apply as a chambermaid. But that was unlikely to work out, given how tattered she looked at the moment. Maybe she should try her luck in a pub. As a waitress or a cook? Her cooking skills were rudimentary, to be sure, but she could certainly try. She had passed by an inn and considered going back to ask. But the entrance had looked so ugly and sleazy. As Elaine argued with herself, she found herself once more in front of the Lucky Horse Inn.

Elaine was very much reminded of Daphne's establishment. The entrance was colorfully painted and looked almost inviting—at least to men, for the offer was directed at them. For girls, however, it seemed to offer the only opportunity to make money—if not in an honorable way.

Elaine shook her head energetically. No, anything but that. Not after she had just run away from a nightly hell. On the other hand, it could hardly be worse than her marriage to Thomas. If she stooped that low . . . Elaine almost had to laugh. She was a murderer. It didn't get much lower than that.

"Move along or come in. Or do you have something important to do out there in the rain?" The voice came from the pub's half-open door. Callie must have slipped in. She was being petted by a woman who was looking Elaine over inquisitively. Callie's gaze, however, was begging, or rather, calculating, as the odor of something frying drifted out of the pub. Whatever it was made Elaine's mouth water as well. Moreover, it was warm and dry inside.

Elaine suppressed her qualms. The blonde, light-skinned woman in heavy makeup did not look dangerous. On the contrary, her large breasts, full hips, and wide, good-natured face gave her a rather maternal look. A very different sort than Daphne.

"So, out with it! Why are you looking at my door like a mouse at the trap?" the woman asked. "Never seen a nice, well-kept whorehouse before?"

Elaine smiled. Daphne would never have called her establishment a "whorehouse."

"Sure," she said. "But I've never been inside." She did not want to reveal what she knew about Daphne's "hotel."

The woman smiled. "In a whorehouse or in a trap? To be honest, you look like you just fled from one."

Elaine turned pale. Was it that easy to tell that she was running from something? And if this woman could see it, what would the respectable matrons whisper about her?

"I'm . . . looking for work. But not . . . like that. I could clean perhaps, or . . . help in the kitchen. I'm used to that. I mean . . . uh . . . my aunt ran a hotel." At the last moment, it occurred to Elaine that it was probably best not to mention her grandmother. The more of her previous life that remained hidden, the better.

"Child, you're too cute to clean! The boys wouldn't keep them-selves clean long, if you see what I mean. Besides, I have a room free. And my girls earn good money; you can ask. Everyone's satisfied here. My name is Clarissette Baton, by the way. Pronounced the French way, if you please. Just call me Madame Clarisse." Madame Clarisse took a familiar tone with the girl.

Elaine reddened.

"I can't. Such work . . . I can't. I don't like men!" This burst out of her like a cry and made Madame Clarisse erupt in booming laughter.

"Well, well, dearie, don't tell me you were thrown out of your fine home because you like girls! I don't believe it. Although there are ways to make money there too. An old friend of mine had two girls dance, twins. They did crazy things, but nothin' dirty. The boys ate it up, even though they weren't allowed to touch. But you look too respectable to me for something like that."

Elaine blushed even more. "How did you know I came from a fine home?"

Madame Clarisse rolled her eyes. "Sweetheart, anyone could see that you've been sleeping in your clothes for weeks, and unless he couldn't see the nose in front of his face, they'd see they were expen-sive too. Besides, this little dog here is no street dog. It comes from a sheep farm. I hope you didn't steal it. Sometimes those fellows come after their mutts faster than their women."

Elaine saw her hopes fading. She seemed to be an open book to this woman. And others would draw the same conclusions about her that Madame Clarisse had. If she took a room at Mrs. Tanner's, the whole town would be talking about her in no time. On the other hand, there was Madame Clarisse's offer . . . No one whispered about Daphne's whores. Respectable women did not seem to care where they'd come from, nor where they went when they left.

Madame Clarisse smiled at Elaine, but a probing gaze lay behind it. She could tell that the girl was seriously considering her offer. Would she do as a barmaid? No doubt she'd had bad experiences with men, but she would hardly be an exception in that regard. And yet . . . there was something in this girl's eyes that went beyond "not liking." Clarisse recognized the fear and the hatred, to be sure. And that murderous glow in Elaine's eyes that drew some men like moths to a flame, but which, in the end, only ever led to complications.

Elaine let her gaze drift across the barroom. Her first impression from outside was confirmed. Everything was clean and orderly. There were the usual tables and wooden chairs and a few dartboards on the wall. People evidently liked to play and gamble here, too, as she saw a board posted with information on the outcomes of the horse races in Dunedin.

There was no stage as there was at Daphne's, and it was less elegantly furnished—perhaps to suit the customers. Coal miners, not gold seekers. Men with their feet on the ground and fewer "stars in their eyes," as Elaine's grandfather James would have put it.

And then Elaine saw the piano. A beautiful, apparently brand-new instrument. Elaine bit her lip. Should she ask? But she would never be so lucky.

"What, starin' at the piano?" Madame Clarisse asked, "Can you play? We just got the thing. The fella who mixed the drinks here used to talk wonders about how well he could play. But we hardly got the hunk of junk before the guy up and disappeared. No idea where, but suddenly he was gone. So now we have a decorative piano. Looks nice, huh?"

A hopeful expression spread across Elaine's face. "I play a little."

Without waiting to be asked, she opened the instrument and hit a few keys. It sounded wonderful. The piano was perfectly in tune and not cheap.

Elaine played the first piece that came to mind.

Madame Clarisse let out another booming laugh. "Child, I'm happy you can bang some notes out of that thing. But let's give it a rest. How about we make a deal? I'll pay you three dollars a week to play. We open at dusk, close at one. You don't need to go to bed with any fella if you don't want, but in exchange, you'll never play 'Amazing Grace' for me again!"

Elaine had to laugh too. She thought of something and tried "The Hills of Connemara."

Madame Clarisse nodded, satisfied. "Much better. I was just thinking you were Irish, with the red hair and all. Though you don't talk like it. What's your name, anyway?"

Elaine thought for the blink of an eye.

"Lainie," she said. "Lainie Keefer."

An hour later, Elaine not only had a halfway-decent job, but also a room and, most importantly, a full plate in front of her. Madame Clarisse fed her meat, sweet potatoes, and rice, without asking half as many questions as Elaine had feared she might. She did, however, advise her strongly against asking for a room at Mrs. Tanner's again.

"That old bag is the town gossip. And more virtuous than Mary herself. When she hears how you make your money, she'll likely kick you right back out. And if she don't, she'll soon have half the West Coast talking about the highborn girl fallen off the straight and narrow. Since that's what y'are, isn't it, Lainie? I don't want to know what you're runnin' from, and I don't think Mrs. Tanner needs to either."

"But . . . but if I move in here"—Elaine tried not to talk with her mouth full, but she was too hungry to stop—"then everyone will think . . ."

Madame Clarisse gave her another piece of meat. "Child, they'll think it anyway. You can only have one or the other: a job or a reputation. At least for the ladies. The boys are different. They'll all have a go at trying to make you, but when you turn 'em down, it'll be fine. And if it isn't, then they'll have me to deal with, so don't you worry. You just can't count on the understanding of the Mrs. Tanners of the town. It's simply beyond their comprehension that you could see thirty fellas a night and not go to be with a single one of 'em. They still think *I'm* a seductress!" Madame Clarisse laughed again. "These honorable women have a funny understanding of virtue. So grow yourself some thick skin. Besides, you'll like it here better than with the old dragon. I'm a better cook, guaranteed, and the food's free. And we have a bathhouse too. So, what do you say?"

Elaine felt as if she would not have passed on the bathhouse that day for anything on earth. She had hardly finished her dinner before she was lying in a tub of steaming hot water—and getting to know one of the girls who worked for Madame Clarisse.

A buxom and black-haired nineteen-year-old helped Elaine wash her hair. Her name was Charlene, and she talked freely, telling her story.

"I moved to Wellington with my family, but I was still a baby and can't remember much of it. All I recall is that we lived in the most appalling shacks and that my daddy beat us every night after he'd done his level best to load my mum up with the next baby. By the time I was fourteen, I'd had enough and eloped with the first boy who came along. A true Prince Charming, I thought at the time. He wanted to go looking for gold to make us rich. After scraping together every last bit of money for the crossing, he headed to the North Island, since things had taken off there with the gold find. But he had no talent for the work, or luck either. He only had me, and he made good use of me too. He rented me out to the boys in the gold-miner camps, which, God knows, was no fun. They'd share the ticket as often as not, and then I'd have two or three of them on me at once. I never saw any of the money myself. It all went to whiskey, though of course he told me he was spending everything on equipment to develop his claim. I was eighteen when I finally realized *I* was the claim. I took off one night, and here I am."

"But . . . but it's the same thing all over again," Elaine objected. "Only now you do it for Madame Clarisse."

"Sweetheart, I would've liked to marry the Prince of Wales, believe me. But I don't know how to do anything else. And I've never had it as good as I do here. I've even got my own room! When I'm done with the boys, I change the sheets, spray a little rose oil, and then it's nice and comfortable. Then there's the bathhouse, always plenty of water to wash up, enough to eat . . . Nah, I'm not too bent on finding someone to marry. Wouldn't be hard, though, there're hardly any single women here, and the miners aren't picky. Last year, they married three girls away from Madame Clarisse. Now they can't get

309

enough of the respectable life, even though they live in disgusting shacks without a toilet, and one of them already has her second brat hanging off of her. No, I like this better. If I ever get married, he'd better really be a prince."

Charlene brushed Elaine's freshly washed hair. She did not seem to think it strange that the newcomer had not brought any baggage with her. Madame Clarisse's hotel was a sort of depot for lost girls.

"You still need a dress. But mine are too big for you. Wait here, I'll ask Annie."

Charlene disappeared briefly and returned with a low-cut sky-blue dress decorated with lace and a thousand flounces.

"Here. Annie doesn't have anything at the moment, so it'll have to do for today. You can wear something underneath if the cleavage is too indecent for you. But I'm sure we can find a shawl for you. The fellows aren't supposed to be ogling you, after all."

Elaine looked the dress over. It was so much flashier than anything she had ever worn before that it almost scared her. When she looked at herself nervously in the mirror, however, she was pleased. The azure-blue material went with her eyes. The black lace at the neckline emphasized her pale coloring, and her glowing-red hair highlighted it. The matrons of Queenstown might find her outfit outrageous—and she dared not think what Thomas would have said about it—but Elaine thought she looked beautiful.

Madame Clarisse whistled when she saw the girl. "Sweetheart, if I offered you double, wouldn't you do two or three a night? The boys would lick their chops for you."

Elaine looked worried, but Madame Clarisse's tone was jocular. She even lent Elaine a black shawl.

"Tomorrow we'll have a dress made for you. The tailor'll sure be delighted. But it's not free, sweetheart. I'm taking it out of your pay."

Madame Clarisse asked for rent for the little room too, but Elaine thought that only fair. At first, she had been worried she would have to live in a room on the first floor, where the men "visited" the women. However, Madame Clarisse showed her to a tiny servant's room near the stables. A stableboy was meant to live there, but Clarisse had no need for anyone like that. Her customers left their horses there only for a few hours and cleaned up after themselves. Still, the stables were very roomy, and there was a run in the back courtyard. Elaine asked timidly if she could house Banshee there.

"So we have a horse too," Madame Clarisse said, frowning. "Dearie, dearie, if you didn't have such a respectable face . . . You promise me you didn't steal the nag?"

Elaine nodded. "Banshee was a gift."

Madame Clarisse raised her eyebrows. "For an engagement or wedding? I'm not judging, sweetheart, but I'd like some warning if next thing I know a husband is going to show up on my doorstep in a rage."

"Definitely not," declared Elaine. "Not a chance."

Madame Clarisse noted the girl's strange undertone, somewhere between guilt and satisfaction, but she could not pinpoint it. Regardless, the girl did not appear to be lying.

"Well, all right. Then bring your horse over here. Otherwise, the stables'll take half your pay. But you have to feed and clean up after it yourself."

Elaine decided to wait until the following morning to retrieve Banshee. She could afford one night in the stables. In the meantime, she washed her clothes and hung them up to dry in her tiny room. Outside it was still raining, and the air was cool and uncomfortable. Elaine still did not like the town—there was no comparison with Queenstown, which was so often sunny and where rainstorms rarely lasted long. Though the winters were appreciably colder there than on the West Coast, they were clear and snowy rather than gray and damp.

Despite the weather, the pub did good business. The men entered like wet cats out of the rain, and Madame Clarisse hardly knew what to do with all the soaked-through jackets and coats. Elaine thought of Gwyneira's waxed jacket—the coal miners could have used something

311

functional like that, but it seemed they could not afford it. It was quite a long way from the mines to town. They must have been in great need of a little warmth and entertainment to brave such hardships after their shift.

"You should see how they live out there," Charlene said when Elaine mentioned it to her. "The mine owners place sheds in the mining compound for them to use, but they're hardly more than a roof over their heads. They don't even have proper washrooms, mostly just an iron bucket. And those swine charge them extra for water, so we end up with coal dust on our sheets."

Most of the customers did, in fact, look badly in need of washing. Their faces were covered in a smeared layer of gray. Since coal dust was greasy, the men could not completely remove it from their faces, no matter how hard they scrubbed.

Elaine felt a bit sorry for them, but to her amazement they seemed happy despite their hard lives. Though the majority of the men came from English and Welsh coal-mining regions, she heard all and sundry dialects. Almost all of them were immigrants—second- and third-generation New Zealanders did not slog it out underground.

The men applauded enthusiastically when Elaine played an old Welsh song that her grandmother Gwyn had taught her. A few of them sang along, while others grabbed girls to dance, and soon the first whiskey was placed on the piano in front of Elaine.

"I don't drink whiskey," she objected when Madame Clarisse pointed it out to her and to the man who had bought it for her. A squarish Englishman from outside Liverpool.

"Try it first," Madame Clarisse said as she winked at her, and when Elaine hesitantly took a gulp, she discovered it was cold tea. "None of the girls here drink, or they'd be too drunk to stand by ten. But you get half of every glass the boys buy you."

That sounded like a good deal to Elaine. She sipped her "whiskey" and smiled at her benefactor. He came right over to the piano and asked for a rendezvous later. However, he took it calmly when Elaine refused and disappeared with Charlene a short while later.

"You're livenin' the place up," Madame Clarisse said as she brought Elaine her third drink. "We do good business on Tuesdays. It generally peters out by Thursday and Friday, because the boys are out of money. But Saturday is payday, so things really pick up, and then the mines're closed on Sunday, so everybody winds up here to drink the world into a better place."

As the evening wore on, Elaine even began to enjoy herself. She had never had as gracious an audience as these miners, and in truth, no one gave her cause for offense. In fact, they seemed to view her with a measure of respect. The men never called her by her first name like the other girls but always politely said "Miss Keefer" when they asked for a particular song or asked if they could buy her another drink.

She was deeply satisfied when she closed the piano for the night, while Charlene and the others said good-bye to the last men. It was long before closing time, but the first workers went down at four in the morning, and the work underground was not without its dangers. No one wanted to risk a hangover.

"But wait for the weekend. Then the booze flows in streams," Charlene declared.

⚜

The next day, Elaine walked over to retrieve Banshee, and the stable owner complimented her on her piano playing. He had stopped by the pub briefly and listened. He no longer wanted payment.

"No, forget it. But let me have three songs, all right? And you're not allowed to laugh at me when I begin to howl at 'Wild Mountain Thyme.'"

The tailor, too, had heard about Elaine's new job and was delighted to take her measurements for a dress.

"Not too wide a neckline? But that will mean fewer tips, miss. You should know that," he teased her. "And you have to have a little lace. You don't want to look like a nun."

But Elaine would have liked to look like just that when she ran into Mrs. Tanner on Main Street. After looking her over from head

313

to toe, she did not deign to greet Elaine as she passed. Elaine could understand that to some extent. Even she did not feel right in Annie's clothes. On the street in the bright light of day, the dress looked much more salacious than it had the night before in the pub, where all the girls were similarly attired. Her own clothes were not yet dry, however, and it was raining again. She would eventually need a few new dresses, but she was considerably more optimistic about getting them now. Three dollars a week was not much, but the side money from the "whiskey" would bring in almost twice that.

That Saturday evening was quite demanding. The pub was full to bursting. It looked like every miner from far and wide, as well as several businessmen and workers from town, had found their way there.

"Even more than usual!" Madame Clarisse rejoiced. "It seems these rascals prefer music to dogfights."

Elaine learned that the other coal-miner pub in town specialized in entertaining its customers with gambling. Dogfights and cockfights took place in the courtyard every weekend. Elaine's stomach turned at the mere thought. Though a few bookmakers did some business at Madame Clarisse's, they placed bets on dog and horse races in Dunedin, Wellington, and even England.

The men sang, drank, and danced on Saturday until closing time—if they did not fall over first, that is. Several customers approached Elaine with unmistakable intent, but she firmly rejected every intrusion, and the men accepted her answer without complaint. Whether Madame Clarisse's admonishing gaze or the look in Elaine's eyes, which flitted between panic and rage, was responsible for their leaving her in peace, she did not know.

Instead, the revelers soon began to take the girl at the piano for some kind of mother confessor. Whenever Elaine took a break, a young man would appear beside her, wanting more than anything to pour his—usually tragic—life story out to her. As the evening wore on, the confessions became more openhearted. Elaine vacillated between disdain and sympathy when lanky Charlie from Blackpool told her between sobs that he did not want to hit his wife, but it just came over him, while Jimmy from Wales, a bear of a man, revealed in a halting voice that he was afraid of the dark and died a thousand deaths every day in the mine.

"And the noise, Miss Keefer, the noise. Every sound echoes through the shafts, you know. You hear every blow of the pickax a dozen times. I sometimes think my eardrums are going to burst. Play 'Salley Gardens' one more time, Miss Keefer. I want to listen to it close, so maybe I'll hear it down below."

By the end of the evening, Elaine's head was booming, too, and when the men had finally left, she drank a whiskey with Madame Clarisse and the girls.

"But just the one, girls, I don't want you to smell like booze in church tomorrow."

Elaine almost had to laugh, but Madame Clarisse really did lead her flock to Sunday service, the whores following along with sunken heads like a line of chicks behind a hen. It did not seem quite right to the priest, a Methodist, but he could hardly turn the penitent sinners away. Elaine was glad to be able to wear her riding dress, whose neckline closed high up, and even dared to look Mrs. Tanner in the eye.

Over the next few weeks, Elaine grew more accustomed to Greymouth, and she had to admit that Charlene was right: it was not the worst life—nor was it the worst town. Since she only worked at night and her little room did not require much housekeeping, Elaine had a good deal of time during the day to saddle up Banshee and explore her new surroundings.

She wandered through the mountains and fern forests and looked in awe at the lush green of the occasionally junglelike landscape that resulted from the almost daily rainfall on the gray river. The sea fascinated her, and she was enraptured when she stumbled upon a seal rookery one day. It was incomprehensible to her that the Coasters had slaughtered these animals and sold their fur only a few decades before. People had turned to industry and coal mining in the Westport area since then. There was even a railroad, which on bad days Elaine watched pass by full of longing. The Midland Line connected the West Coast with Christchurch. After just a few hours' ride, she could be with her Grandmum Gwyn.

Elaine only rarely allowed herself such musings. It hurt too much to think about what her parents and relatives must think of her now. After all, she had never had a chance to tell anyone about Thomas's cruelty. No one could possibly have any compassion for her.

Whenever Elaine thought about the deed itself, however, she felt no remorse. In fact, she had no feelings at all about that morning in the stables and instead viewed the events from a peculiar distance, almost as though it were a scene in a novel. The roles had been assigned just as clearly as they were in those stories: there was only good and bad. If Elaine had not killed Thomas, sooner or later he would have killed her. For that reason, Elaine considered her act to be a sort of "preventative self-defense." She wouldn't have done anything differently had she been given the chance.

She was nevertheless astonished that the spectacular story of the husband who'd been murdered on the Pukaki River had not made it to the West Coast. She had expected news of that kind to spread quickly, and had been afraid that they might send out a wanted poster with her name on it and maybe even her picture. But nothing of the sort happened. Neither the whores nor the respectable ladies gossiped about a murdering spouse on the run. Elaine accepted it as a stroke of good luck. Slowly, she adjusted to life in her new home. She did not want to have to flee again. People greeted her on the street now, the men politely and the women fleetingly and somewhat reluctantly.

Regardless, Elaine could no longer be ignored, since she had finally found the courage to speak to the priest about a second instrument in town, orphaned until then. Inside the church stood a brand-new organ, but the parish had been torturing itself without accompaniment through church songs, which often came out far off-key.

Having long since heard that the young pianist in the pub was not "for sale," the priest did not long hesitate before accepting Elaine's offer to play.

Though Elaine could not see her from the gallery, when she opened her first Sunday service with an energetic rendition of "Amazing Grace," she thought she could feel Madame Clarisse's smile on her back.

3

While Kura traveled through Australia with the opera ensemble, William and Heather continued to go bed together ever more brazenly. No one seemed to care what the two of them did at night, especially since William kept his distance from the bar for a few weeks. Though she did not make the connection to his love life, Gwyneira observed with relief that he had become more even-tempered, and he rarely picked a quarrel with the workers, even the Maori. Though he continued to demonstrate little talent for farmwork, he occasionally even allowed the workers to teach him something instead of simply giving orders. James thought this was a result of William's disgraceful sheepherding debacle with Major Richland. In any case, James kept William busy with routine work, freeing himself up for more important matters and enabling him to enjoy his hard-won peace. A few things struck James as odd, however. For instance, the grand piano in the salon was being played again. Though no one really cared to hear it, Heather offered to play for the family. William alone encouraged her, claiming to feel closer to Kura through the music. He had her face and form before his eyes again, he explained, which caused Heather's features to narrow disapprovingly. The two of them resumed their evenings together in the salon, and William renewed his consumption of whiskey.

"Can't we get rid of that Miss Witherspoon?" James groaned as he genteelly held the door to their apartments open for Gwyneira. Heather had been playing Schubert songs downstairs for hours. "We don't really have a use for her anymore now that Kura's gone."

"Who is going to teach Jack and the Maori children?" Gwyneira asked. "I know, I know. She doesn't exactly excel at that, but if we send her on her way, we'll have to find a replacement. Which means advertising in England again, waiting for applications to arrive, and then my having to make another guess."

"We'd have one criterion less at least," James said grinning. "Neither Jack nor Gloria have any interest in the piano. But seriously, Gwyn, I don't like William spending half the night alone with Miss Witherspoon in the salon. Especially now, when Kura is away. She's clearly trying to seduce him."

Gwyneira laughed. "William the gentleman with that plain little thing? I can't imagine it. That would be a real downgrade after Kura."

"But the plain little thing is at hand," James offered for consideration. "We should keep an eye on it."

Gwyneira laughed. "Wouldn't you rather take advantage of the fact that I'm at hand?" she teased. "All those love songs have made me quite sentimental." She undid the buttons of her dress, and James kissed her softly on her bared shoulder.

"Then all that noise at least did some good," he murmured.

While William and Heather's relationship was good for his acclimatization to life on Kiward Station, Heather's own efforts to ingratiate herself to her employers grew rather lax. The longer her love for William persisted, the more secure she felt. With every month that ticked by without Kura's return, she grew more hopeful of binding William to herself forever. He would eventually grow tired of waiting for Kura, particularly since he did not feel at home on Kiward Station. Then surely their marriage would be dissolved, and the way would finally be clear for William to commit himself fully to Heather. Besides, more than three years had passed since William had left Ireland. His deeds there had undoubtedly long since passed into oblivion, and he would surely be able to return. Heather saw herself striding into his parents' house at his side. They would no doubt be delighted by their son's choice, for she had been given a first-class education and was from a good family, though fallen on hard times. She would exert a moderating influence on William, who would certainly not get involved in any further scandals on his father's land. Perhaps he would even find a position in the city—Heather would like that even better.

In any event, she obviously considered teaching dirty native children to be beneath her dignity and made even less of an effort toward them than before. She could not neglect Jack, of course. He was meant to go to Christ's College and could not be allowed to fail the entrance exam. But she taught him strictly and without enthusiasm. Jack completed his assignments but took no joy in doing so. That didn't strike Gwyneira as particularly unusual, as she, too, had hated her lessons as a girl. James, however, who had never enjoyed the benefit of a first-rate education, thought it a shame and continued to insist on dismissing Heather Witherspoon as soon as possible.

"Look, Gwyn, of course I understand that Jack doesn't want to learn Latin. But he's always been interested in history, and animal and plant biology. He used to say he'd love to be a veterinarian. I could definitely see him pursuing that if he doesn't take over Kiward Station. But Miss Witherspoon is driving out all his interest in books. And she'll do the same to Gloria. Get rid of her, Gwyn. Just get rid of her!"

Gwyneira continued to hesitate. Then, however, Heather Witherspoon's lack of interest in her work did one day—if by a detour—result in her and William being discovered.

Gwyneira McKenzie frequently sold sheep for breeding, sometimes entire flocks, to other farmers. Gerald Warden had begun the practice after he had created the ideal wool producer for the Canterbury Plains by crossing Romney, Cheviot, and Welsh Mountain sheep. His animals were robust and self-sufficient, and the ewes and their lambs spent the whole summer loose in the highlands without any significant losses. They produced wool of consistently high quality, and were easy to feed and simple to handle. It was no surprise that other breeders were chomping at the bit to enrich their own flocks with these animals. In fact, many of the sheep that grazed throughout the Canterbury Plains and Otago could be traced back to Gerald Warden's breeding stock.

No one in the remote northeastern part of the South Island had ever shown any interest in Gwyneira's sheep. Husbandry was still in its infancy there. But a certain Mr. Burton of Marlborough suddenly contacted her. Though he was a war veteran like Major Richland, he obviously had more ambition with regard to informed sheep breeding. Gwyneira immediately took a liking to the lively old gentleman. Slim and sinewy, Burton was a spirited rider and a good shot—he surprised his hosts straight off with three rabbits, shot "in anticipation."

"They're yours. I shot them on your land," he grinned. "I presume their death does not aggrieve you too much."

Gwyneira laughed and had the animals brought to the kitchen.

"You didn't have to bring your dinner with you," James joked. "Do you have a rabbit problem up north too, or are the foxes taking hold there?"

It wasn't long before Mr. Burton and James were deep in conversation—for once, William did not dominate. Gwyneira noticed how animated James was as he chatted and joked with the farmer from Marlborough. Finally, here was someone who did not know about his past as a rustler and who simply accepted him as the foreman of Kiward Station. Jack, too, seemed to like Mr. Burton from the first, and asked him all about the animals in the jungles around Blenheim and the whales in the Marlborough Sounds.

"Have you really seen one, Mr. Burton?" he asked eagerly.

Mr. Burton nodded. "But of course, young man. Since they stopped hunting the critters so much, they've become rather trusting. And they really are big as houses. I would never have believed it. You read about it, of course, but when you encounter one in a boat suddenly made tiny by comparison, you learn respect for the whalers who throw the harpoon instead of running away!"

"The Maori hunted them from their canoes," Jack informed him. "That must have been exciting."

"I found whaling loathsome and disgusting," James said. "When I arrived on the West Coast years ago, whaling was considered the surest way to make money fast, and I gave it a try, but I didn't have it in me. Like you said, Mr. Burton, the whales are too trusting, and I just couldn't bring myself to jab a spear into something that just wanted to hold out a friendly flipper to me."

Everyone laughed.

"Do they have flippers?" Jack wanted to know. "They're mammals, after all."

"You should come visit sometime and see for yourself, young man. Perhaps you can help herd the sheep our way after your mother and I talk business tomorrow." Mr. Burton cheerfully raised a glass to Gwyneira. He did not seem to have any doubt that they would reach an agreement.

Indeed, they did raise their glasses to the acquisition of a stately flock, and Mr. Burton repeated his invitation. Jack and his friend Maata had already helped herd the sheep together for him, and the boys' use of the sheepdogs had impressed Mr. Burton. He acquired two border collies straightaway—and, winking cheerfully at Jack, claimed to desperately need help with their training. The boy could hardly contain himself.

"I can go, can't I? Right, Mum, Dad? Maata can come too. It'll be an adventure. Just wait, we'll bring a baby whale back and put it in our lake!"

"The whale's mother will be thrilled," Gwyneira said. "Just as I will be. You have school, Jack. You can't just go on holiday."

Heather, who had kept to herself until then, nodded dutifully. "We have to start on French soon, Jack, if you want to pass the entrance exams in Christchurch."

"Psh," Jack grumbled. "We'd only be gone two weeks at most, isn't that so, Mr. Burton?"

"You were supposed to have started French six months ago," Gwyneira retorted. She understood Jack's dislike of the language. Her French governess had driven her mad when she was a girl. Fortunately, the woman had had a dog allergy that the younger Gwyneira had used to her advantage. Unfortunately, she had once told Jack that story—so the boy knew she would not insist on making him learn the language.

And then he received an unexpected vote of support from his father.

"He'll learn more on the trail to Blenheim than Miss Witherspoon can teach him in six months," James growled.

Heather wanted to protest, but his dismissive hand gesture quieted her.

"The coasts, the forests, the whales, you have to see those things. They make you ask questions, and then you go find the answers in books. You, my dear Miss Witherspoon, could use that time to seek out some of that knowledge yourself and teach it to the Maori children. That is, they would be surely enjoy reading something other than the Bible and *Sara Crewe* for once. If nothing else, they would learn a thing or two about whales."

"Oh yes, I can go! It'll be wonderful, Mr. Burton! Mum, Dad, can I go down to the village and tell Maaka right away? We're going to get to see whales!"

Gwyneira smiled as he ran off excitedly to surprise his friend with the news. No one doubted that Maaka would receive his parents' permission. The Maori were born nomads and would be happy for the boys. "But you're responsible for making sure they leave the critters where they are, Mr. Burton. I've gotten used to wetas in the playroom, but I have no intention of getting used to whales in the pond."

Andy McAran and Poker Livingston would also accompany the sheep. An overjoyed Poker took advantage of the opportunity presented by this excursion. The quiet life with his female friend was already becoming dull to him. The preparations had to be made quickly, as Mr. Burton wanted to leave soon.

"You can keep one of your workers, Mrs. McKenzie," he said, "and I'll practice working with the dogs on the way."

Gwyneira did not tell him that either Andy or Poker could have effortlessly handled the trail with just the two dogs—and James or herself with just one. But she did not want to dampen either his or the boys' excitement.

Only one thing bothered Jack about the plan: what would Gloria do without him?

"If I'm not here, no one will hear her when she cries at night," he said. "She hardly does anymore, but you can't be sure."

Gwyneira cast an accusatory glance at William. It should have been his job to reassure them that he would look after his own daughter. But William remained silent.

"I'll put her in our room," Gwyneira said to assuage her son.

"Perhaps Miss Witherspoon could take some responsibility for her future pupil," James jeered.

Open war had broken out between the tutor and James after his comment about her useless lessons.

Heather did not dignify him with a glance.

"In any case, Gloria will be fine," Gwyneira said. "Though she'll miss you, of course, Jack. Maybe you can bring her back a picture of a whale and then show her in the yard how big one is."

Jack was in high spirits when the riders finally set off. Gwyneira, however, was struggling with visibly low spirits. Her son had only just left, and she already missed him. The house did in fact seem to have lost some of its vitality. Jack's cheerful chattering and his little dog who had always seemed to be in the way were greatly missed at dinner. The evening meals passed more formally than usual, now that the air between James and Heather had become perceptibly frosty, and William contributed little to conversation. One evening, James, sensing Gwyneira's disheartened mood, went in search of a particularly good bottle of wine and suggested to his wife that they retire for the evening.

Gwyneira gave him her first smile of the day, but then something disrupted their plans. A young worker in the stables needed help caring for one of the horses that had fallen ill. Normally he would have alerted Andy, but in his absence, the worker preferred to turn directly to the McKenzies rather than take a risk. James and Gwyneira left the table to go see what was wrong with the mare.

Heather took the opportunity to pinch a bottle out of the normally locked cabinet.

"Come along, William, let's do what we can to have a pleasant evening," she said enticingly as he was still deliberating over whether tagging along with the McKenzies might not be more conducive to familial peace. On the other hand, he was not exactly a specialist in equine illness—and he had already spent the entire day outside under the incessant rain. He'd had enough for one day.

He was surprised when Heather did not lead him toward her room as usual but headed directly for the rooms he had once shared with Kura.

"I've always wanted to sleep in this bed," she declared blithely, placing the wine on the night table. "Do you remember when we selected it? I think that's when I fell in love with you. We had the same taste, the same ideas; these are really *our* rooms, William. We should finally take possession of them together."

William did not especially care for that idea. For one thing, though he had very concrete memories of that bed, they had less to do with its selection than with the bliss that he had experienced with Kura there. To sleep in that same bed with Heather almost felt like a desecration. He sensed that his adultery would then be complete. Until that moment, he had used Kura's refusal to sleep with him as an excuse for his relationship with Heather. But now—it did not feel right to him to intrude on Kura's private rooms.

Heather merely laughed and uncorked the wine.

"Are there no glasses in here?" she asked, disbelieving. "Did the two of you never"—she giggled—"need a little encouragement?"

William could have answered that he had never had to loosen Kura's inhibitions with wine. But instead, he obediently went to fetch glasses. What would be the use of angering Heather, after all?

He nevertheless made one attempt at retreat.

"Heather, we really shouldn't do it here. If someone were to come—"

"Now, don't be a coward," Heather said, handing him a glass as she took a sip herself. The wine was exceptional. "And who's going to come? Mr. and Mrs. McKenzie are in the stables, Jack is gone . . ."

"Gloria might start crying," William said, even though they would not have heard anything in that part of the house.

"The baby is sleeping in their apartments. She said herself that she would take her in. So enough of this nonsense, William. Come to bed."

Heather undressed, which she did not normally like to do while the light was still burning brightly. In her room, she lit nothing more than a candle when they made love, and that was only right to William, who still dreamed of Kura as he caressed Heather's body. In here, however, she let the gas lamp burn. It seemed that she could not get enough of admiring these rooms that she had decorated herself.

William did not know what other objections he could raise. He took a deep gulp of the wine. Maybe it would help him forget the shadows Kura had left in the room.

The horse in the stables had colic, and Gwyneira and James spent quite a while getting it to take a purgative, massaging her stomach, and leading her around to get her bowels working again. After more than an hour, the worst had passed and Gwyneira was suddenly struck by the thought that no one in the house was looking after Gloria. Usually she could count on Jack, but she knew that neither William nor Heather Witherspoon would think to keep an eye on the child, and Moana and Kiri had already left for the evening before the McKenzies had been called to the stables.

Gwyneira left further care of the mare to James and the young worker and ran back to the house to check on Gloria. The girl was almost a year old and slept through the night most of the time, but she might be missing Jack and upset because of that. When Gwyneira arrived, she did, in fact, find Gloria awake but not crying; she was merely murmuring contentedly, as though having a conversation with herself. Gwyneira laughed and picked her up.

"Well, and what are you telling your doll?" she asked sweetly, handing Gloria her toy. "Wild stories about whales eating our little Jack?" She rocked the baby, enjoying her warmth and scent. Gloria was a sweet and easy child. Gwyneira remembered that Kura had cried so much more, even though Marama had carried her everywhere, whereas Gloria spent, if anything, too much time on her own. Kura had always been demanding. And even as a baby unusually attractive. She had not passed that on to Gloria. Though the baby was sweet, she was not as adorable as her mother had been at that age. Gloria had porcelain-blue eyes, and it seemed rather certain that they would stay that color. Her still-scant hair did not seem able to decide, however, whether it wanted to be dark blonde or light brown. There was not the smallest hint of red in it, and it was not straight and strong, as Kura's had already been when she was an infant, but curly and downy soft. There was nothing exotic about her features; instead, she showed a slight resemblance to Paul and Gerald Warden. Her resolute chin was most definitely a Warden inheritance. Otherwise, her features were rather softer than those of her grandfather, evidence of William's features pushing through.

"You're pretty enough for us," Gwyneira teased her great-grand-daughter, rocking her gently. "And now you're coming with me. We'll take your basket along, and you can sleep in your grandmum's room tonight."

As she carried the child out of the room and crossed the dark hall, she was unable to miss the light coming from Kura's rooms.

Gwyneira frowned. William had apparently already come upstairs, since she had not seen anyone in the salon. But what was he doing in Kura's rooms? Reviving old memories? His own bedroom was located at the other end of the hall.

Gwyneira chided herself for her nosiness and was about to continue on to her own quarters when she thought she heard moaning and giggling coming from the rooms. William? Suddenly she remembered

James's mistrust of Heather Witherspoon. Until that moment, she had always thought his suspicion absurd, but now . . .

Gwyneira wanted to know. Whoever was enjoying herself in there was not allowed to do so. This was still her house.

Gwyneira put the basket down but kept Gloria in her arms. Then she yanked the door open. She heard the whispering and moaning much more clearly now. In the bedroom.

Gloria began to howl when her great-grandmother opened the bedroom door, and the light shone brightly in her eyes, but Gwyneira could not concern herself with the baby just then. Almost in disbelief, she stared at William and Heather in Kura's bed.

Heather froze. William slid hastily out from under her and tried to cover his nakedness.

"Gwyneira, it's not what you think."

Gwyneira could have burst out laughing. She was tempted to make a snide remark, but her fury won the upper hand.

"I don't need an explanation, thank you. I just got one. Is that why Kura left, William? Did she discover what was going on right under her nose?"

"Kura . . ." William did not know how to formulate his explanation. He could hardly tell his mother-in-law that Kura had been refusing him. "She, she didn't want . . ."

Gwyneira looked at him coldly. "Spare yourself your excuses. I know, and I could slap myself for not realizing it sooner. It was the same with Elaine, after all, wasn't it, William? You cheated on her with Kura, and now you're cheating on Kura with this . . . Start packing your things, Miss Witherspoon! This instant. I want you out of this house tomorrow as well."

"As well?" William asked, confused.

"Yes, 'as well.' Because I don't want to see you around here anymore. And don't you even dare mention your daughter. No judge will award her to an adulterer." Gwyneira had begun to rock the child in her arms, which had calmed Gloria immediately. The little girl now looked at her father and Heather with curiosity. "It's bad enough that she has to see this."

"But I love Kura," whispered William.

Gwyneira rolled her eyes. "Well, you certainly have a strange way of showing your love. Frankly, I couldn't care less whom you love at the moment. If you think it would help, you can track Kura down and beg her forgiveness. But I won't have you hanging around here, drinking my whiskey and seducing the staff. Go, get out of this room! And be gone from Kiward Station by daybreak!"

"You can't really—"

"Oh, can't I?"

Gwyneira stood there with a rock-hard countenance until William and Heather had made themselves halfway decent. She even took the trouble of turning away while the two climbed out of bed and gathered their things. Then she turned out the light and locked Kura's room behind them.

"You'll be gone by daybreak tomorrow," she declared again. "Miss Witherspoon, I'll leave your remaining pay on the table in the salon. I'm coming down to breakfast at nine. I don't want to see either of you then."

With that, she walked off, leaving the humiliated couple to themselves. Gwyneira still needed to go to her office to count out Heather's money. Then she needed a whiskey.

James was just leaving the stables, tired and frozen through, as Gwyneira poured herself a glass. Gloria was asleep in the corner of a sofa with her thumb in her mouth.

James cast an astounded look at his wife.

"Did you knock the kid out with booze?" he asked with a grin.

Gwyneira poured him a glass as well, and turned her pale face to his. "More like I'm trying to knock myself out. Here, take this. You'll need it too."

Sleepless and chalky pale, Heather waited in front of the stables for William. When he arrived around six o' clock in the morning with his saddlebags packed, he cast an astonished look at the young woman and her luggage.

"What are you doing here?" he asked coldly. "Wouldn't it be better to wait on the road to Haldon? Someone is sure to pass by today. If you're lucky, they might even take you as far as Christchurch."

Heather looked at him in disbelief. "We . . . we aren't traveling together?"

William frowned. "Together? Don't be ridiculous. How is my horse supposed to carry all this stuff?"

Tears shone in Heather's eyes. "You could rent a chaise. We . . ."

William felt a surge of rage bubbling up inside him.

"Heather, there is no 'we!' I've tried and tried to make that clear to you, but you don't seem to want to understand that. I'm married, and I love my wife."

"She left you!" Heather yelled.

"And I should have gone after her straightaway. Granted, we had our differences, but all that happened between you and me, that was a mistake. We shouldn't make it any worse. Can I help you carry your luggage to the road?" William set his saddlebags down and reached for her suitcase.

Heather flared up at him. "I can manage on my own, you . . ." She wanted to insult him, to scream and curse him, but people had instilled in her from a young age that a lady did no such thing, and so she could not even find the words to voice her rage.

Heather convinced herself that at least she maintained her dignity that way. She bit her lip but did not cry as she dragged her bags down the road.

"Good luck, William," she managed. "I hope you find Kura and are happy."

William did not reply. By the time he reached the point in the road where it forked to Haldon or Christchurch half an hour later, Heather was gone.

4

Over the next few months, William learned a great deal about sheep, cattle, and panning for gold, but more than anything else, he learned about himself.

His search for work that both suited him and brought in enough money to eke out a living led him throughout the entire South Island—and nearly beyond it, for at first he was pursuing his goal of finding Kura again. But the opera ensemble was in Australia, and William lacked the funds for the crossing—in addition to the fact that he did not possess a precise tour schedule and would therefore never have known how to locate Kura in that giant country. He comforted himself with the knowledge that the singers would return eventually. George Greenwood had received special prices for the boat trip from Christchurch to England, so Christchurch would be the certain end point of the ensemble's tour. Since the singers would be visiting several other towns on the South Island, William only had to fill a few weeks.

Those weeks, however, proved to be more difficult to fill than he'd expected, since his pride forbade him from asking for work in the area around Kiward Station. The sheep barons had known him as their equal, after all. So he directed his horse's steps in the direction of Otago, toward the sheep farms around the McKenzie Highlands. There was always work to be had there, but William did not stay in any one place for long. It was as he had suspected on Kiward Station: he didn't have a talent for handling the animals himself, and the farms' owners either oversaw the work themselves or entrusted it to their long-standing farmhands. Besides, William could not stand the workers' lodgings. He hated sleeping out in the open, and he found the men's bawdy jokes, often at his expense, more insulting than entertaining.

Thus he moved from farm to farm, even doing a stint at Lionel Station, where he learned the details of Elaine's tragedy. William had come to regret the matter deeply. He knew that James McKenzie for one, and surely the rest of Elaine's family as well, blamed him for her rash marriage. Elaine had never completely gotten over him. In addition, he had long since come to the conclusion that Elaine would have been the smarter match for him. Assisting in the O'Kay Warehouse had suited him much better that his work on Kiward Station, and though Elaine had not been as exciting, she had been much more reliable and far gentler than Kura.

Nevertheless, his heartbeat quickened whenever he so much as thought about anything that was somehow connected to Kura. He had truly loved her—he loved her still, damn it! And he would have taken on anything, even the challenges of the farm, if only she had stayed with him. Why could she not be happy with what she had?

He was surprised that Elaine had not found happiness, either. Though William found John Sideblossom repellent, Lionel Station was a beautiful property. And Elaine had always dreamed of living on a sheep farm.

William did not stay on Lionel Station for long. The atmosphere was gloomy, and John paid poorly—it was no wonder, he had created his own stream of endlessly renewable cheap labor. Ever observant, William had immediately noted the similarities between the Maori workers and their employer. The man had more trouble producing legitimate children. Zoé Sideblossom's first child had died during delivery, and she had just suffered a miscarriage.

William had no luck at the gold mines of Arrowtown. And seal hunting on the West Coast repulsed him more than it attracted him. Hunting seals had become a downright exhausting business anyway. The animals had become more skittish and ceased to wait on the beach by the hundreds for their hunters, as they used to do. William tried his hand helping out a coffin maker, but the work was too morbid for him. As it was, the coffin maker was the first boss to regret his departure. Once William had started advising the customers, they had begun paying considerably more money for beautiful and elaborate coffins.

Finally, he was drawn to Westport, once again hoping to find Kura. Though he had heard that the West Coast would be one of the tour's last stops, he saw nothing about any touring opera ensembles when he arrived. People were looking for workers for the coal mines. Though it was apparently well-paid work, William dreaded the prospect of backbreaking labor in the mines. In his view, you had to be born a coal miner. So, instead, he headed off with his gold-miner gear to the Buller River, where he finally had a bit of luck. He pulled about thirty dollars' worth of gold dust from a stream in a single day. Since William had no claim himself, the owner of the claim pocketed half. Still, fifteen dollars was enough for a few nights in a hotel, some good whiskey, and access to a bathhouse. William moved into what was reputedly a properly well-run inn and ordered himself a drink first thing. While the owner filled his glass, he let his gaze wander over the room—and what he saw astounded him.

The barroom was not full of men drinking whiskey and playing cards or darts, as was customary. That day, the center of attention was a man tinkering with a strange machine that he'd placed on a table. He was giving a presentation while running the rumbling little device by means of a crank on its side. His audience was even more astounding, for it consisted entirely of excitedly twittering women and girls. Respectable women, by the looks of them, wearing simple dresses. The older women kept an eye not only on the machine but also on their daughters, who had likely entered a pub for just the first time in their lives. The girls, however, couldn't have been less interested in the pub decor or the few lonely drunkards in the corners. They only had eyes for the elegant young man, who was explaining the finer points of the machine.

"You see, where a practiced seamstress makes fifty stitches, this little work of wonder manages three hundred. In any woman's hands. Would you like to give it a try?"

The man let his gaze wander over the circle of women and girls who stood around him like a class of eager schoolgirls. He finally selected a darling little blonde girl. She blushed immediately.

"Can I really?" she said hesitantly.

The young man ran a hand through his curly dark hair with a smile.

"But of course, my lady. You can do the machine no harm. On the contrary! In such beautiful hands, it will run without a hitch."

Flattered, the girl sat down in front of the machine and began to crank the lever. She did not appear to be too successful however, and let out a shocked cry when something went wrong.

"Oh that's nothing, my lady. The thread occasionally breaks when you're just getting started. But we'll fix that in no time. Look here, we simply thread it through, and here, and here, and then through the needle again. It's that simple. Now try again. But this time, don't hold tight to the material. Just guide it. With a gentle touch. That should come easily to you."

While the girl gave it another try, William approached, his glass in his hand. He was taller than most of the girls and could easily see over them. The little machine looked a bit like a large insect bending its head hungrily over its prey and biting its teeth into it repeatedly. The "prey" proved to be two pieces of fabric and the teeth, a needle that was pushing through the material at lightning speed, binding the pieces with a clean stitch. Things did not appear to be going well for this seamstress, however.

"Let me try," said an older woman, and the girl made room for her. As the woman turned the crank at a more relaxed tempo, the needle slowed its dance and made a series of straight, even stitches. The man could hardly contain his enthusiasm.

"There you have it. You're a natural talent, my dear woman. A few days' practice, and you could be sewing your first dress. Well done!"

The woman nodded. "Truly, it's a wonder. But a hundred dollars is a lot of money."

"Tut, tut, my dear woman. Do not look at it that way. Naturally, the expense seems daunting at first. But think of what you'll save!

You'll be able to sew your whole family's clothes. You'll be able to sew curtains, linens, and even spiff up older items to make them like new. Take a look!"

The man took his seat at the machine, drew out a simple child's shirt and some lace from a stack of materials he had at hand, and measured the length with skilled movements. Then he placed the lace and the shirt under the needle of the machine. After rattling away for a few seconds, the neckline of the shirt had a tidy band of lace. The women reacted with astonished cries.

"There, is that not good as new?" trumpeted the man. "And think what a lace shirt costs. No, no, a sewing machine is not an indulgence. It pays for itself in no time. Many of my customers even make a little business out of it and are soon sewing dresses for their friends and neighbors. Besides, you don't have to pay for it all up front. My company offers installment plans. You pay something now and then a few dollars each month after that."

The man spoke with an angel's tongue until every woman and girl was perishing to try the device. The salesman patiently let them use the machine, one after another, and had a flattering word for each of them. He laughed at their little mistakes and praised their tiny successes to high heaven. William found it exceedingly entertaining to listen to him.

In the end, three women placed orders, and two others explained that they first had to talk to their husbands.

The man looked very pleased when the group finally dissolved. William approached him while he was packing the machine away.

"That's a fascinating machine," he remarked. "What do you call it?"

"A sewing machine," repeated the man. "A certain Mr. Singer invented it. Well, he didn't invent it so much as introduce it to the market. At affordable prices. In installments even, when that's what the ladies want. Sew now, pay later. Brilliant!"

William could only agree.

"You don't build the machines yourself then? Might I buy you a drink, Mr. . . . ?"

"Latimer, Carl Latimer, at your service. And I'd gladly take a whiskey." Carl Latimer pushed his neatly packed sewing machine aside and made room for William and the bottle of whiskey. Only then did he answer William's question.

"I don't build the machines myself, of course. Nobody could do that for a hundred dollars. It's quite a complicated box of parts. How many patents do you think went into that? The inventors are to some extent still fighting it out over who stole what idea from whom. I don't bother with all that though. I'm a sales representative. I just bring the thing to the people, specifically the women."

William poured him another glass.

"Sales representative?"

"Like a Bible salesman," Carl Latimer responded, smiling. "I did that for a while too, but it was not nearly as interesting or as profitable. But in the end, the same principle applies: you go from house to house and tell the people that buying this product will lead to their everlasting happiness. In the towns, you can spare yourself the time-consuming house-to-house work. Like you just saw, the women in town come to my demonstrations entirely of their own accord. But I generally travel from farm to farm and show the machine to the women there individually."

"But then you don't sell as many, do you?" William asked.

Carl Latimer nodded. "That's right, but you do away with the costs of food and lodging. The ladies are always delighted to offer me their guest rooms—and you would not believe how often there's a sweet little daughter or servant girl on hand to make the night more pleasant. And the sales really aren't so bad. It's all about picking the right farms. The smaller operations usually lack money, but they often latch on to the installment plan. If the woman thinks she can earn a little extra on the side with the machine, then she'll be enthusiastic right away. On the bigger farms, they have money like hay, but the women are often bored and lonely. So I always show them a few French fashion magazines and lure them in with the idea that they could make those dresses themselves. I don't mean to brag, but I always bring two or three women around. It's a question of eloquence."

William nodded. The voice of the banker in Queenstown was in his ear again: "Stick to something you know."

"Tell me," William said, raising his glass. "How does one become a sales representative? Do you need an education for it? Starting capital? Where did you even learn to use this machine anyway?"

William earned the starting capital at the overjoyed coffin maker's, honing his sales technique simultaneously. The demonstration model itself had to be purchased from a representative, and since he could not transport it on his horse, he would need a light wagon.

Shortly after applying for a position with the company Carl Latimer worked for, he received an invitation to an introductory training in Blenheim. He learned the principle of the sewing machine, how to take the machine apart and put it back together, and how to make repairs in emergencies. Naturally, the future representatives—all, without exception, young, good-looking, and charming men—also practiced producing perfectly straight stitches and quickly learned to fabricate and decorate small articles of clothing.

"It's not enough to just sew. You need to astound the women, excite them—and nothing works better than putting a child's dress together in a few minutes," the teacher explained. But William was only half listening. He knew he would have no trouble convincing his customers. After all, he had always been able to talk. What had Elaine called that art? *Whaikorero*?

William had finally found something he could do better than anyone else.

Kura had always sensed that she could sing better than anyone else. Now her conviction that she was a gifted singer grew with each passing day.

Although Roderick had ended their singing lessons—despite her efforts and compensation, he had lost interest and now preferred to take

her on excursions to the local attractions in the towns they were staying in—she outperformed the other singers effortlessly. She managed
greater highs and lows, and her voice now encompassed almost three
octaves. She held her notes longer and never tried to overcompensate
by singing more loudly than was indicated in the score. Even in the
performance's weakest piece, the *Il Trovatore* quartet, during which the
other singers practically screamed at each other, her Azucena was not
drowned out. Kura's strong voice came through at normal volume,
without strain, giving her the chance to fill her role theatrically as
well. The audience bestowed her with a standing ovation every night,
and her confidence soared. Kura, who had almost come to the decision
that she would travel back to England with the ensemble, was shocked
when Brigitte revealed that the ensemble would dissolve after the tour.

"We were only engaged in New Zealand and Australia," said the
dancer, who had regained her old form. Kura felt something close to
respect for Brigitte, who exercised with as much determination using
the back of a chair for a barre as Kura practiced her scales.

"You don't really think anyone would want to see us in Europe,
do you? Most of the singers are disasters, even if only Sabina knows it.
After this, she intends to give it up and teach voice. As for the dancers, a few of the boys are talented, but most of the girls are just pretty.
Roddy probably only chose them for their looks. A real impresario is
critical in that respect. He wouldn't be interested in your smile. He'd
only care how you danced."

Or sang, thought Kura with a rush of fear. But she still firmly
believed that she would make it in London too. After all, she was not
alone; Roderick would certainly continue to help her. He undoubtedly had contacts in England and would probably be putting another
troupe together for a new tour.

And so Kura was in good spirits when they had finally left Australia
and their boat arrived in Wellington. From there, they returned to
the South Island; their ferry landed in Blenheim. Kura had no idea
that William was sitting in a drafty warehouse on the edge of town,
fighting with the obstinacy of a hand-powered sewing machine, at
the very moment that the singers were disembarking and preparing

themselves for the journey on to Christchurch. She did know, however, that he was no longer at Kiward Station. She had written to her grandmother sporadically and received the occasional letter from her when they stopped in one place for any length of time or when George Greenwood saw to the forwarding of their mail. She had not been informed of the exact circumstances of William's departure, but her grandmother had written that Miss Witherspoon had likewise left the farm.

Jack now has a new tutor, a very nice student from Christchurch. He only comes on the weekends, but he actually manages to get Jack and Maata excited for the Bello Gallico, *whatever that is. And Jenny Greenwood is currently instructing the Maori children! Ostensibly, she's thinking about taking a teacher's exam, but if you ask me, she only applied for the position because Stephen O'Keefe wants to come visit for the summer. Do you recall how the two of them were whispering to each other at your wedding?*

Kura did not recall, nor did she care. Heather Witherspoon would not have been able to teach her anything more anyway. As for William, during the day she found no time to think about him, but at night she still missed him, even when she was sharing her bed with Roderick. That was happening less and less, however. Kura was losing interest in her older and rather dull lover. She no longer revered him as she had at first. She had become informed enough to recognize the weaknesses in his own singing and to know that he did not have any special talent. Even as an instructor, he was not as good as she had initially believed. When by chance she overheard a singing lesson that Sabina was giving Brigitte, she understood much better what she had to do. Nevertheless, she remained at Roderick's disposal when he wanted her. She still needed him, after all. He was her ticket to London!

Roderick Barrister was seriously considering taking Kura to England. The girl was exceptionally talented and, moreover, a joy in bed. When his partner took the stage, there could be no doubt where the real talent lay. Although her full potential had yet to be reached, she already sang far better than he did. The Australian audiences had given Kura her due by granting her more curtain calls. Roderick could live with that, but he had no illusions about London; people would boo him off the stage. If he took Kura with him to England, he would have to build his future on her as her teacher and impresario. Roderick was confident that he could make her sufficiently reliant on him that she would not take on an engagement or sign a record contract without his advice. After all, the girl was barely eighteen. She needed a paternal hand to guide her and negotiate her contracts. That could bring in a good deal of money, probably more than Roderick would ever earn as a singer. Indeed, everything pointed in its favor—if only it were not for his overwhelming desire to be onstage himself!

Roderick loved the stage. He was addicted to the feeling of expectation when the curtain rose, the hush in the audience before the music began, and the applause—more than anything, the applause! If he cast his lot with Kura now, he would never again experience that. At least not directly. He could imagine standing backstage and enjoying the delirium with her. But it would not be the same. It would be a secondhand life, a performance from the second row. And if Roderick were honest with himself, he was not ready for that. Not yet. Maybe if he had come across Kura five years later. But he still had his good looks, which were enough to get him engagements. He was young enough to withstand tours like this. Perhaps another one would come his way in the future. He should make it a point to look for one. Maybe he would eventually tour through India or Africa.

When Roderick stood on the stage, all his plans and thoughts left him. The applause was better and more satisfying than anything he had ever experienced, even more beautiful than sex. As he fell further behind Kura vocally and people looked at him less, his love for Kura dissolved—insofar as it had even been love and not lust.

After their last performance, he decided not to take Kura with him. She should make her career in New Zealand, he thought; she would manage that without question. And if she came to London someday, there might be a second chance for them then.

He didn't want to anger her, though, so he determined it was better not to tell her too soon.

Gwyneira attended the final concert in Christchurch together with Marama. She had wanted to bring James, Jack, and most of all, Gloria. Marama agreed that it would be good to bring Kura and her child together. James, however, refused categorically to pay to hear Kura's singing, and Jack strongly opposed exposing Gloria to it.

"She'll probably cry when Kura sings," the boy said. "But I suppose we haven't tried it in a while. She might stay quiet, and then Kura might think she has talent. You never know what will run through her head. What will we do if she suddenly wants to take Gloria to England?"

"She is her mother," Gwyneira objected halfheartedly.

James shook his head reluctantly. "When the boy's right, he's right. She's never cared for the child, but Gloria's bigger and prettier now, and Kura could get some crazy idea in her head. It's better not to take the risk. If Kura wants to see her daughter, she can come to Kiward Station. The ship is not leaving for England first thing tomorrow."

Though Gwyneira considered that a sound argument, Marama remained of the opinion that they should at least try to get Kura to take an interest in Gloria. Erring on the side of caution, Jack found his own solution to the matter: he disappeared with the little girl on the day of the trip. He had recently started setting her in front of him on his horse, so looking for them would be useless. The pair could be miles away.

"I'll bend him over my knee when he gets back," James said when the women finally departed, with a wink at Gwyneira. He would more likely congratulate his son instead.

Marama had only been to Christchurch a few times and quickly forgot about the minor disappointment once they were on their way. The women chatted about the weather, the sheep, and Gloria's development, but they did not have much in common anymore. Marama had completely melded into her tribe, teaching some reading and writing, but she mostly focused on dance and music. The newest books out of England, the latest discoveries, and current events no longer interested her as much as they had when she had lived with Kura on Kiward Station.

The excursion was nevertheless quite congenial. They arrived in Christchurch early and had time to freshen up before the concert. Naturally, they would have liked to have visit with Kura, but they did not get a chance. Apparently, the singer needed to concentrate before she made her entrance. Instead, Gwyneira met Elizabeth Greenwood in the lobby of the hotel with her youngest daughter, Charlotte. Gwyneira had to smile. The light-blonde, delicately framed girl was almost a perfect replica of the little Elizabeth she had met so many years before on the *Dublin*.

"I'm so excited to see Kura," Elizabeth said cheerfully when the women had sat down to a cup of tea. "Everybody is raving about how beautifully she sings."

Gwyneira nodded, but she felt uncomfortable. "People have always raved about her," she said guardedly.

"But George thinks she's further developed her talent. At least that's what the impresario says. George doesn't really understand anything about music himself. He thinks the man is going to take her back to England. What do you think about that? Are you still her guardian?"

Gwyneira sighed. So people in Christchurch were already talking about Kura and the "impresario." Well, William had seen that coming. But now she had to answer with some diplomatic tact.

"Strictly speaking, I'm not her guardian anymore. She is married, after all. So you would really have to ask William what he thinks. In fact, I would quite like to know that myself. I was almost certain he would come today, but he hasn't booked a room."

"Maybe he's only coming to the concert. But in all seriousness, Gwyneira. I'm not just asking you all these questions because I'm curious—at least that's not the only reason." Elizabeth smiled coyly, and Gwyneira was reminded of her shy expression as a child. "George wanted to know what you thought about it. After all, he booked passage on the ship for the other singers. If Kura wants to go with them now, he can arrange that—or if you don't want her to go, he can set up some 'difficulties.' George could claim there were no more cabins on board the ship, and that she would have to take the next one. Then you would have some time to work on her."

Gwyneira was touched by the Greenwoods' concern. George had always been a good friend and had a talent for diplomacy. However, she did not rightly know what to think.

"Let me talk to her first, Elizabeth. We'll see her after the concert, and before that, we'll hear her sing. Not that I understand much more on that subject than George, but I think anybody should be able to tell if she can hold her own with the other singers or not."

Elizabeth understood the implication: Gwyneira was alluding to whether Kura would truly be accepted as an artist or merely as the mistress of the impresario—and consequently, whether Roderick truly believed in her career or simply could not resist her body.

"Just let us know first thing tomorrow," Elizabeth said kindly.

5

Kura-maro-tini was in a rage. This was to be their last concert in New Zealand, and all of her relatives and acquaintances would be sitting in the audience, and yet Roderick had struck two of her solos. Ostensibly, the performance would be too long. A cast party for the ensemble thrown by George Greenwood was to take place following the concert, so it was important that the recital not run too late.

Roderick didn't even talk to her before the concert—it was Sabina who had told her about the changes. And then this cast party! All of the other artists had received formal invitations; only Kura had been excluded. She would still go, of course. Sabina, Brigitte, and all the others had explained that there must have been a mistake, and everyone offered to take Kura as their personal guest—everyone, that is, except Roderick. He had not shown himself all day. Kura decided to make a scene that night in bed.

She took a moment to look into the audience—and felt insulted once again when she saw only Gwyneira and Marama in the first row. It wasn't that she cared much for James or Jack, but after both of them had complained about her music studies for years, she would have liked to savor her triumph in front of them now. It did not occur to her to miss Gloria. Kura would never have even considered bringing the baby to a concert. She might cry! But where was William? On this point too, Kura had let her imagination run wild; naturally, he would come to Christchurch to see her once more. He would beg her forgiveness and entreat her to stay, but she would tell him once more to his face what she had written when she left: "It isn't worth it!" She could not entomb herself in Kiward Station just because she loved William. And then? In Kura's dearest fantasies, he embraced her at this point, told her that she was far more important to him than all the sheep in the world, and booked a cabin straightaway on a steamer bound for England. Naturally, there would be romantic rivalries. Oh, it would be glorious to play Roderick and William against each other a bit. But in the end, she would have them both: William and her career. Just like she had always wanted. Except that William had put a spoke in her wheel. The concert would begin in a few minutes, and he had not arrived yet. Well, there was always Roderick. Kura left her peephole in the curtain. He would be getting an earful!

Gwyneira was right. One did not need to be a music connoisseur to judge Kura's performance. It was clear to everyone after the first few notes that the young singer was not only a match for her colleagues but that she outsang them by a considerable margin. Kura met every note with expression, singing with verve and expression—pleading, enticing, and crying with her voice. Even Gwyneira, who had never thought much of opera, and Marama, who was hearing operatic arias for the first time, understood what was motivating the characters onstage, even when Kura was singing in French, Italian, or German.

Marama had tears in her eyes during the *Il Trovatore* quartet, and Elizabeth could not stop clapping after the "Habanera." Roderick Barrister paled in comparison to his partner. Elizabeth Greenwood no longer knew why she had been so enthusiastic about his singing after the first concert in Christchurch.

After the final curtain—the audience had cheered frenetically for Kura one more time—the women stayed in their seats and looked at one another.

Finally, Elizabeth congratulated Marama. "You have to send the girl to London! I always thought they were exaggerating about Kura's talent. But now . . . She doesn't belong on a sheep farm; she belongs on an opera stage!"

Gwyneira nodded, if somewhat less euphorically. "She can go if she wants. I, for one, won't stand in her way."

Marama bit her lip. She was always a little shy when she found herself the only Maori surrounded by whites. All the more so because she was not an exotic beauty like Kura but more typical of her people: short and, now that she was getting older, a bit stocky. She had put her straight black hair up that night and worn English clothes, but she nevertheless attracted attention among the people in this room. And she never was sure whether Gwyneira was embarrassed by her Maori daughter-in-law or not.

"Could you still send her to a school, Gwyneira?" Marama finally said, risking a remark in her beautiful, songlike voice. "What is it called again? A conservatory, right? She sings wonderfully. But this man, I don't think he taught her everything he knows. Kura could be even better. And she needs a degree. It may be enough merely to sing beautifully here, but among the white people, you need a diploma to become a *tohunga*."

Marama spoke impeccable English. As Kiri's daughter, she had practically grown up in the Wardens' household, and she had always been among Helen's best students.

She was right. Gwyneira nodded. "We should talk to her straight-away, Marama. It would be best to go straight backstage before twenty people are standing in line in front of us to tell her how irresistible she is."

Kura did like to hear how irresistible she was, and there were already plenty of admirers in the troupe's provisional dressing area to reassure her. Roderick, however, was not among them this evening. He had not even granted her a curtain call of her own, but had stepped forward with her every time to accept the applause. Only a few weeks before, he had been giving her roses. Kura could hardly wait to give him a piece of her mind. But her mother and grandmother were waiting, and she planned to savor her triumph. When she asked the two of them into her dressing room, Brigitte, with whom she shared the room, tactfully withdrew.

"Well, did you enjoy it?" Kura asked almost regally.

Marama embraced her. "It was wonderful, dear," she said tenderly in their language. "I always knew you could do it."

"You weren't quite so sure," Kura said to Gwyneira.

Gwyneira once more suppressed a sigh. Kura might sing better than before, but dealing with her had not gotten any easier.

"I don't know anything about music, Kura. But what I heard tonight really impressed me. I can only congratulate you. You're bound to enjoy great success in England too. The money for the passage and the conservatory should not be a problem." Gwyneira likewise wrapped the girl in her arms, but Kura remained cool.

"How gracious of you," she remarked mockingly. "Now that I've done it without help, naturally you're ready to oblige me in every respect."

"Kura, that's not fair," Gwyneira protested. "Before your wedding, I offered—"

"But only if I gave up William. If I had only gone with him to England then . . ." Kura glared at her. She was evidently determined to hold her grandmother responsible for the failure of her marriage.

"Do you really think you would have made it then?" Marama asked softly. She hated the endless discussions that the whites seemed to love having about guilt and innocence, cause and effect. Her daughter was a master at the art of dragging these bitter, useless conversations out for hours—for which Marama blamed Gwyneira. She had not learned it from the Maori, that was certain.

"You sing beautifully," Marama said, "but do you believe that they're waiting for you and you alone in London?"

Kura's face took on an expression of extreme indignation.

"I can't believe it! Are you trying to tell me I'm not good enough?"

Marama remained calm. She had played the lightning rod for Paul Warden often enough as well. "I'm a *tohunga*, Kura-maro-tini. And I've listened to your records. You could become as good as the greatest singers, to be sure. But you still have to learn."

"I have learned. I've practiced like crazy these last few months. I was on the North Island and in Australia, Mother, but I saw nothing of the scenery. Only my piano and my music."

"You've improved, but you could learn even more. You should not go with this man. He's no good for you," Marama observed, gazing calmly at her daughter.

"You're one to talk! A Maori who wants to forbid her own daughter from choosing her own companion."

"I'm not forbidding you from doing anything. I—"

"I'm tired of all of you," Kura upbraided them. "I'll do what I want, and thank God, I don't need to ask anyone permission anymore. Roderick will take me with him. We'll look for engagements in London, or we'll put together another troupe like this one and go on tour. I'm not sure yet. But I don't need your money, Grandmum, or your advice, Mother! Go herd your sheep on your beloved Kiward Station. I'll write you from time to time from England!"

"I'll miss you," Marama said lovingly. In spite of everything, she wanted to take Kura in her arms and kiss her good-bye, or rub her nose against Kura's, as was customary among their people, but Kura stiffened this time as Marama approached.

"*Haere ra*," Marama whispered. "And may the gods bless and guide you in your new country."

Kura did not answer.

"She didn't even ask about Gloria," Gwyneira said as the two women left the dressing room, shaken.

"She's sorrowful," Marama remarked. "She's tense. Something is not going as she had hoped. Perhaps we shouldn't leave her, Gwyneira."

Gwyneira rolled her eyes. "You can stay here and play her doormat, for all I care, Marama. But I've had enough of her arrogance, her heartlessness, and her men. She should go to London if she wants. I only hope she really does earn enough there to make a living or looks for a man who can support her for a change. She's the last person we need on Kiward Station!"

Kura looked beautiful when she was angry and Roderick's determination almost faltered when she came into the ballroom with eyes flashing, cheeks flushed with excitement and nearly bursting with pent-up emotion. He was dancing with Sabina just then and would have liked to break away from her to greet the girl, touch her, perhaps coddle her a bit, to make things go more smoothly later. He thought that would be a mistake, though, so with mild regret, he turned to Brigitte after his dance with Sabina. But he had not counted on what Kura would do. Infuriated by his indifference, she wedged herself between him and the dancer.

"What are you trying to do, Roderick? Avoid me? First you don't let anyone see you all day, then you strike half my performances, and now you act as though you don't know even me. If this continues, I'll have to think hard about whether I'm going to share a cabin with you on the trip."

Kura's hair was down that night but she was wearing it held back with a headband decorated with flowers. She had chosen a red dress with a neckline that emphasized a necklace of azure-blue gems. Her large matching blue earrings made her eyes shine even brighter.

Roderick squared himself. It was truly a crying shame.

"What trip?" he asked amiably. "To be honest, lovely, I have in fact been avoiding you today. I can't bear the pain of parting." He smiled regretfully.

Kura glared at him. "Do you mean to say you don't plan to take me to England? But that's settled."

"Oh, Kura, my sweet, we might have talked about it—or dreamed about it, to be more precise. But you weren't really counting on it, were you? Look, Kura, I don't even have any engagements lined up for myself over there."

Roderick noticed to his dismay that others were gathering all around them. His confrontation with Kura was attracting attention. He had not pictured it playing out this way.

"But *I* will find an engagement," Kura said self-assuredly. "It can't be that difficult. You yourself said I have more than a little talent."

Roderick rolled his eyes. "My God, Kura, I've said a great many things the last few months. You do have talent, of course, and look, here in New Zealand, you have a truly great gift. Over there, however . . . The conservatories in England alone produce dozens of singers every year."

"Are you suggesting that I'm no better than dozens of others? But all these months . . ." Kura was unsettled.

"You have a sweet voice. In this troupe of rather . . . washed-up singers . . ." At this, a storm broke out among the bystanders, but Roderick paid it no mind. "In this troupe, you almost stand out a bit. But in Europe? Really, dear, you're getting a bit ahead of yourself."

Kura felt alone, as though on an island surrounded by her inept, petulant colleagues. If she had been paying attention, she might have heard that Sabina and a few others were taking her side and praising her voice. But she felt struck down by Roderick's words. Could she have so completely misunderstood him? Could he have lied so shamelessly just to get her in bed? Were the audience's countless standing ovations worth nothing at all? Had she been just another third-class singer raping the art of song in front of dilettantes?

Kura became taut with anger. No, it couldn't be! She would not allow it to be!

"Look, Kura child, you're still very young," Roderick added in a patronizing tone. "Your voice is still developing. If while you're here—"

"Where?" Kura asked brazenly. "There's no conservatory here."

"Oh, girl, a conservatory—who ever mentioned such a thing? But within the limited scope of your potential, you can bring a lot of joy to people."

"Within the limited scope of my potential?" Kura spat out the words. "What about the limited scope of *your* potential? Do you think I can't hear? Do you think I didn't notice that you can't hold a note any higher than an A when singing piano? Or that you modify practically every aria so that it will be easier for the great Roderick Barrister to sing?"

The people around them laughed; a few even applauded.

"In those respects, I am considerably less 'limited' than you are," Kura crowed.

Roderick shrugged. "If you say so. I can't stop you from trying your luck in Europe. The money you've earned should certainly suffice for the passage."

He just hoped she wouldn't actually take him up on it. Spending six weeks at sea with Kura breathing fire would be hell on earth.

Kura considered. The money she had earned would most certainly not be enough. Perhaps for the crossing, but after that she would not have a penny left to support herself while she looked for an engagement in England.

She could ask Gwyneira for money, of course. If she were willing to admit that Roderick did not want her. If she conceded that Marama had been right in her appraisal of Kura's level of education. If she groveled.

"In any event, I'll be standing onstage when the only use anyone will have for you is to carry set pieces," she spat. "In England, and everywhere else in the world, for that matter." With that, she turned and walked quickly from the room.

"Well done. You showed him," Brigitte whispered to her.

"Don't be fooled," Sabina said. She was about to add a few other bits of advice, but Kura did not want to listen. She did not want to listen to anything or anyone anymore. She wanted to be alone. She could no longer bring herself to look at Roderick. Or more precisely, she never wanted to see him again. The ship to England had not even arrived in Lyttelton yet, so the troupe might be lodged in the hotel in Christchurch for another few days.

Kura ran through the corridors to her room, blinded by tears. She had to pack up and leave. As quickly as possible.

At the crack of dawn the next morning, she was in the stables asking for a horse. Gwyneira's chaise was still there; her grandmother and Marama had also spent the night at the White Hart. Yet Kura would not condescend to discuss her situation with them. She had decided the night before that she wanted to continue the tour alone, or rather, to repeat it. The audience had loved her, after all. Of course people would be happy to hear her again. And she had enough money to pay for a small carriage, a horse, and the printing of a few placards. That would have to be sufficient for a start. She would undoubtedly start earning much more than before, since she would be able to keep all of the profits.

The owner of the stables was more than happy to sell her a horse and a two-wheeled gig. Though it had little space for her luggage, the carriage had a canopy top, which was important to Kura. She only just managed to fit her bag with her stage costumes in it. As for the horse, the dealer assured her it was a docile animal. Kura was relieved, and indeed, she got off to quite a good start with it. However, she did not advance very quickly; the little bay did not compare with Gwyneira's cobs. Although Kura found that reassuring at first—given her fear of having to drive herself—it soon got on her nerves. She tried to goad the horse on, but to no avail.

She did not reach Rangiora that first day, as she had hoped to. The ensemble had given a guest performance there on the way to Blenheim several months before. At the time, they had traveled in comfortable coaches with fast teams, and the miles had simply disappeared under their hooves. Kura's more easygoing bay only got her as far as Kaiapoi, a village that did not even boast a proper hotel—only a grimy brothel. As a result, Kura slept in the stables, curled up on the carriage seat, so as not to catch any fleas from the straw. The owner of the stables had helped her to hitch and unhitch her horse without acting put upon. He did, however, ask who she was and where she was going. Her answer, that she was a singer on tour, seemed to amuse him more than impress.

It took Kura three days to reach Rangiora. At that rate, it would take her several years just to make it all the way around the South Island. By the last evening, she was both desperate and exhausted. The horse and carriage had been expensive, and she had not counted on so many nights' lodging. So she gave in to the hotel proprietor's request to entertain his guests with a few songs. Though the place was clean, Kura viewed it as a demotion to have to perform in a pub. Since the listeners undoubtedly had no idea how to appreciate operatic arias, Kura sang a few folk songs and gazed dourly, almost contemptuously, into the crowd as the men roared with excitement.

Rangiora itself was also a disappointment. When the ensemble had sung and danced in the church hall, Kura had thought that the hall had been made available to them free of charge. However, it looked like rent had to be paid. In addition, the priest first had to be persuaded to hand the room over to the singer on her own.

"You won't be performing anything indecent, will you?" he asked skeptically, though he remembered Kura from the previous guest performance. "You didn't sing much that night; you mostly stood by the others and looked pretty."

Kura assured the wary clergyman that she had just joined the singers at the time and hadn't had much stage experience yet. To assure him that things were different now, she sang a rendition of the "Habanera," which was enough to convince him. Still, she worried about whether she would have enough money left over after paying for her hotel, the stables, the church hall, and a boy to hang up her placards.

Fortunately, almost all the seats for the first concert were filled. Rangiora was not exactly a bastion of high culture, and artists rarely performed there. But the audience proved less enthusiastic than they had been during Kura's performances with the ensemble. Though no one had known much about music, the colorful costumes, the variety of the offerings, and most of all, the dance scenes that took place between the operatic arias had kept people chained to their seats. Kura, swinging her castanets in the middle of the chorus, had been a high point. But a girl who sat alone at the piano and sang?

After a half hour, people were already getting restless and beginning to whisper and fidget in their seats. At the end, they applauded, but more politely than exuberantly.

Only ten people attended the second performance. Kura canceled the third.

"Perhaps if you were to sing something happier . . ." the priest advised. If nothing else, Kura had won him over: he was enthusiastic about her voice and her interpretations of the various arias. "The locals are simple people."

Kura did not deign to respond. She simply continued up the East Coast, headed for Waipara. With the ensemble, she hadn't sung again until Kaikoura, but she could not afford such long stretches between performances; she was traveling too slowly. She surveyed every town along the way to assess whether it offered performance opportunities. She found it most pleasant when a reputable hotel put its rooms at her disposal. Then she usually did not have to worry about the cost of lodging, and the fees for performance space were lower than those of the church halls. Concerts increased drink sales after all. The hotel owners often tried, in fact, after her first evening to talk her into becoming part of the regular program.

"No one here wants to hear that nonsense, missy!" the hotel pro-prietor in Kaikoura explained, although he had been thrilled by the ensemble's performance. "Sing a few love songs, maybe something Irish. Those are always well received. There are a good number of Germans here too. You do sing in different languages . . ."

Kura compromised a little and included a few Schubert songs in the program. A portion of the audience was deeply touched, which was not to the owner's liking.

"Child, you're supposed to get them to drink, not wail. God, you're pretty as a picture! Why don't you dance a little too?"

Kura angrily explained to him she was a singer, not a barmaid, and she continued onward the next day. Her tour was not going as smoothly as she had imagined it would. When she finally reached Blenheim three exhausting weeks later, she had still not made enough money for passage to the North Island.

"What else can we do? We'll stay and continue our way around the South Island," she told her horse. Another fall from grace!

She used to mock Elaine for talking to Banshee for hours and insisting that the mare understood every word. But Kura missed having someone to talk to—as long as he did not constantly contradict her, give her well-meant but impossible advice, or attempt to throw himself at her. In the past few weeks, she'd had to rebuff the advances of countless pub owners and ostensible "music lovers." She had not experienced anything like that during the performances with the troupe. She had always been treated with the utmost respect.

"Should we go to Picton or Havelock?" she asked her horse. "One is as good as the other."

When William finished his introductory training in Blenheim, he bought a brand-new sewing machine as a demonstration model. As a beginner, he could not expect to cover the most coveted sales regions, like Christchurch, Dunedin, or their environs. He was counting on a placement somewhere on the West Coast or in Otago. But then, to his great surprise, he learned that he had been posted to the North Island, to a region in the north around a town called Gisborne. Though he imagined it was probably a rather sparsely populated area, it was virgin soil in the realm of sewing-machines sales, as no representative from his company had ever been there.

In good spirits, William boarded the ferry from Blenheim to Wellington. Though he fought heroically against seasickness on the stormy water, he buoyed his spirits with the thought that he would make it as a salesman. He had shone during his training, and some of his teachers had been quite enthusiastic about his creative sales strategies. None of the other participants had received as positive an assessment. William approached his new assignment optimistically. Whether it was coffins or sewing machines, if they made them, he could sell them!

6

Timothy Lambert was incensed, but at least he now understood why his father usually rode his horse the relatively short distance from their house to the mine. It clearly disgusted the mine owner to cross on foot the cesspool in which his men housed themselves. It was not that Timothy had never seen slums in Europe. Coal-mining camps were hardly oases of paradise in England or Wales either, but there was no comparing the filth his boots stomped around on in his father's mines with anything he had seen abroad. The settlement had clearly not been laid out with any plan.

The miners had simply placed one shelter right beside the other. The huts were made of waste wood and damaged formwork boards that had obviously been rejected from the mine. Most of the shelters lacked a chimney, with the result that if someone lit a fire inside, the smoke must have made it nearly unbearable. Toilets were so rare that the men simply went around the corner to answer nature's call. The rain that fell almost daily in Greymouth then washed the excrement and waste into the muddy streets between the shelters. Those "streets" had turned into stinking streams, and it cost Timothy a great deal of effort to make it through with dry feet.

At the moment, the settlement looked deserted. He could hear only some sniffing and coughing coming from a few huts—probably the "absences due to illness and laziness" that his father complained about. Among miners in general, instances of black lung and consumption were on the rise, but the area around the Lambert Mine had been hit particularly hard, especially since it seemed that no one was caring for the sick. Clearly, there were few families living there and hardly any women to see to a minimum of order and cleanliness in the huts.

The vast majority of the miners were single and preferred fleeing to the pub to making their quarters habitable. Not that Timothy could blame them. Anyone who had spent ten hours in a dark mining shaft digging coal was ready for a few beers in a friendly atmosphere. Besides, the men perhaps lacked the money for renovations.

Timothy absolutely had to speak to his father about this. The mine could at least make the construction materials available. Ideally, the miners would tear it all down and rebuild it following sensible plans. The newly founded labor unions overseas were demanding more humane worker camps, although so far with little success.

Timothy had reached the mining compound itself by this time. As he passed through the main gate, he noted that the roads improved immediately. The freight wagons in which the coal was transported could not be allowed to become stuck in the mud, after all. Timothy wondered why there was still no rail connection to the train tracks, enabling the coal transport to be executed more quickly and cheaply. Another subject he needed to bring up with his father.

Timothy stomped his boots clean and entered the flat, ground-level office building that sat across from the mine entrance. His father's office offered a good view of the headframe and the building complex, which had space for both a steam engine and a storehouse. He could likewise observe the men entering and exiting the mine, as well as the aboveground workers. Marvin Lambert liked to have his eyes on everything.

There was a row of mines around Greymouth that belonged either to individual families or joint-stock companies. The Lambert Mine was the second-largest private company of this sort, and Marvin Lambert fought tooth and nail with his rival, Joshua Biller. Both men scrimped on labor and mine safety in whatever ways they could. In this matter, Marvin Lambert and his rival saw eye to eye. Both thought that coal miners were idle and greedy by nature, and modern mining techniques only captured their interest when they offered higher returns. But Timothy suspected that the mine owners might be judging their workers too hastily.

To be fair, his father had already helped himself to the whiskey by the time Timothy had arrived late in the evening. Timothy had been home only since the day before, and after his long journey, he might have been a little tired and grumpy. Eight weeks by ship to Lyttelton followed by the train ride to Greymouth had left their mark. At least he had not had to take the train from the East Coast. The newly built rail line made the trip to the West Coast both faster and more comfortable.

New Zealand had changed since his parents had sent Timothy to Europe ten years before. First to a private school, then to study mining techniques at various universities, and finally to tour the most important coalfields of the Old World. Marvin Lambert had financed all of that willingly. Timothy was his heir after all, and he was supposed to take over the mine for the family someday and increase its profits. Today was his first day of work—or at least that's what he assumed. He planned to explore the town later.

Greymouth had grown considerably since he'd left the area at the age of fourteen. Back then, the Lamberts' villa had stood rather isolated on the river between town and the mine. Now the construction reached almost to their doorstep.

The mine's office revealed Marvin Lambert's parsimonious nature. On the whole it was spartanly furnished, and bore no resemblance to the palaces that European mine owners built for themselves. Marvin raised his head from his papers and gave his son a cross look.

"What are you doing here already?" he asked. "I thought you'd keep your mother company for a bit longer. After all that time she had to do without you."

Timothy rolled his eyes. In truth, his mother's maudlin complaints had already gotten on his nerves. Although Nellie Lambert had wept with joy when he first arrived, she had soon begun hurling accusations at him because of his long absence. She seemed to feel that he had pursued his studies abroad only to worry her.

"I can go home early, of course," Timothy said, untroubled. "But I wanted to see the mine. What's changed, what needs changing. You have an idle mining engineer standing before you, Father. I'm dying to make myself useful." He smiled almost conspiratorially.

Marvin Lambert cast a glance at the clock.

"In that case, you've arrived rather late," he grumbled. "We start at nine here."

Timothy nodded. "I underestimated the trip—above all, its condition. Something absolutely must be done about that. At the very least, we have to clean up the streets in the camp."

His father nodded grimly. "The whole cesspit has to be demolished. How does it make us look? And right next to the mine! Someday I'll have those 'houses' torn down and the area closed off. Nobody gave those fellows permission to put those huts up there."

"Where are they supposed to go?" Timothy asked, astonished. Since the mine's compound had been painstakingly wrested from the fern forests, the men would have to clear new land if they wanted to build a settlement outside of the compound. And if they were to do that, they would be a good distance from the mine. That was why workers were typically housed in the immediate vicinity of the mine's entrance.

"I couldn't care less. Anyway, I've had enough of those shit holes they call houses. Unbelievable that they can live like that. I'll just come out and say it—they're scum. They send us everything from England and Wales they can't find a use for."

Timothy had already heard all this the night before and had heartily reproved his father. He had, after all, just returned from England and knew that emigration from the European coal mines to New Zealand was viewed as a way to a better life. The men hoped to earn a better living there, and only the best and most entrepreneurial managed to save up for several months for the passage. They did not deserve that hell outside.

Timothy held his peace for now, however. Having that discussion again just then would not change anything. It would have to wait until his father was in a better mood.

"If it's all right with you, I'd like to go down in the mine and have a look around," he said in order to avoid addressing Marvin's grumbling. It had to be done, though one look out the window was sufficient to rob Timothy of any desire to do so. The mine entrance itself did not make a trustworthy impression. His father had not even bothered to put a roof over the washhouse, and the headframe looked rudimentary and outdated. What would it look like inside?

Marvin Lambert shrugged. "As you like. Although I remain of the opinion that you'll be needed more in distribution and logistics than underground."

Timothy sighed. "I'm a mining engineer, Father. I don't know much about business."

"You'll learn that here real quick." That, too, had already been discussed. Marvin thought the skills that Timothy had acquired in Europe were of limited value. He did not want an engineer as much as a capable salesman and crafty businessman. Timothy wondered why his father hadn't had him study business instead of mining techniques. Either way, he would have refused to work as a salesman. He knew he had no natural talent for that.

Timothy tried again to make his role and his intentions clear to his father. "My job is to oversee the work in the mine and to optimize the excavation methods."

His father frowned. "Oh?" he said, apparently taken aback. "Have they found some newfangled way to swing a pick and hammer better?"

Timothy remained calm. "There'll be machines doing it soon enough, Father. And there are already more effective ways to ship coal and spoils now. There are more modern ways to reinforce the shafts and drill air shafts, and the whole mine drainage—"

"And in the end, that will all cost more than it brings in," Marvin broke in. "But fine, if it makes you happy. Go have a look. Breathe in a little coal dust. You'll have had your fill of it soon enough."

He turned back to his papers.

Timothy said a few words in parting and left the office.

Though he was greatly interested in geology and engineering, he didn't actually like much about the coal-mining industry. Left to his own devices, he would probably have chosen a different profession. The work underground and the many dangers associated with it distressed him. Timothy loved to spend his time out in nature and would have preferred building houses to digging tunnels. Railroad engineering, too, appealed to him, particularly in New Zealand. But because he would someday be inheriting a mine, he had buried all personal predilections and pursued an education in mining; he'd even received a certain degree of recognition in Europe as a specialist in matters of safety. Given his great fear of mine collapses and gas explosions, his primary interest had always been in figuring out how to prevent such catastrophes. But it was the nascent, still-loose associations of coal miners who sought his expertise rather than the mine operators. The latter generally invested in the safety of their miners only after some accident had occurred, and probably more than one of those operators had breathed a sigh of relief when a scaremonger as pushy as Timothy Lambert had left their office. Let him drive up his father's costs. Certainly none of them shed a tear when he left England.

Timothy asked the two gloomy men at the shaft winder to have the foreman sent up. He did not want to enter the shaft without a guide, and so he waited patiently until the message had been delivered. As the winder was finally set in motion, creaking and rattling, Timothy wondered, with a mild case of goose bumps, how often the cable was changed. A rather young man who spoke with a Welsh accent, the foreman appeared to be somewhat hostile toward the mine owner's son.

"If it's about the delivery rate again, I've already told your father that it can't be increased the way we're currently operating. I can't work the men any faster, and it won't do much good to get more men down there, either. They're already stepping on each other's feet as it is. Sometimes I'm afraid we're going to run out of air."

"Has no one seen to adequate ventilation?" Timothy grabbed a helmet that fit and a Davy lamp, which made him frown. More current models had been around for a while. Timothy preferred benzine lamps. Not only did they provide light, but their aureole also revealed the amount of methane gas in the air.

The foreman noticed that Timothy seemed accustomed to being underground, and became somewhat less frosty. "We're doing our best, sir. But air shafts don't build themselves. To dig them, I'd have to reassign men, and then the shafts would have to be reinforced, running up material costs. Your father would give me hell for that."

It was plenty hot. Though the day outside was rather chilly, the temperature rose as they descended in the hoisting cage. When they reached the deepest level, Timothy noted the stale air and the stifling heat.

"Dead air," he remarked competently before greeting the men, who were pushing carts of coal to the hoisting cage in preparation for transport. "Something has to be done about that—and straightaway. It's not even worth thinking about what would happen if gas started seeping in here."

"That's what he's here for." The foreman pointed to a cage where a tiny bird hopped dismally from one bar to another. "If that bird falls down, that's the signal to get going."

Timothy was horrified. "But that's medieval! Birds are used all over the world because they can't be beat as an early warning signal, but they're not meant to be a replacement for adequate ventilation. I'll speak with my father. The working conditions here have to be improved. The men will be able to dig more effectively then too."

The foreman shook his head. "Nobody could dig more effectively. But you could spread out the supports and do a better job reinforcing them."

"And we need to improve the spoils transportation," Timothy said. "It can't really be true that the men are hauling the debris away in baskets. And did I really see black powder outside? Please don't tell me you're not using safety explosives yet?"

The foreman replied that they were not. "We don't even have explosion barriers. If anything goes off, the whole mine will burn."

An hour later, Timothy had finished his inspection of the mine and had made a new friend in his foreman. Matt Gawain had attended a coal-mining academy in Wales, and his ideas about modern extraction techniques and mine safety had a lot in common with Timothy's. With respect to the most current ventilation techniques and shaft construction, however, Timothy was quite a bit more knowledgeable. Matt had been working in New Zealand for three years, and coal-mining techniques were constantly evolving. They made plans to meet in the pub later to continue their conversation over a beer.

"But don't get your hopes up about making it all happen," Matt said. "Your father is like most bosses, and only interested in fast money. Which is important, of course," he rushed to add.

Timothy waved that off. "Thinking about the future is just as important. It costs more money if a mine collapses because no one properly secured it than to renovate at appropriate intervals. Not even to mention the cost in human lives. Besides, the union movement is on the march. Eventually, people won't be able to avoid creating better conditions for their workers."

Matt grinned. "At which time I have no fear that your family would be robbed of so much as a morsel of bread."

Timothy laughed. "You'll have to ask my father about that. He won't waste any time telling you that he's already ruined, and that every day a miner takes off from work brings him closer to starvation."

He sighed with relief when the mine released him, and he saw the light of day again. His prayer of thanks to Saint Barbara had been sincere, even though he actually believed that preventing mining accidents was not the task of patron saints, but that of mining engineers.

"Where we can we wash up?" he asked.

Matt laughed. "Wash? You'll have to go home to do that. You won't find washrooms with ceilings or hot water around here."

Timothy decided not to go home. On the contrary. As grimy as he was, he intended to go to his father's office to have a very serious talk with him.

That afternoon, Timothy directed his horse toward the center of Greymouth. He wanted to order materials right away for the improvements to the mine he had wrested from his father. It was not much, however. Marvin Lambert had agreed only to the construction of a new air shaft, as well as a few explosion barriers, and he'd done even that much only to meet the minimum standards of the national mining authority. Timothy's argument that his rival could discover and expose his safety violations—"He only needs to ask one of your miners, Father"—had convinced the old man. Timothy was determined to look over the regulations once more in detail over the next few days. Perhaps there was something else in there he could use for his purposes. But for the time being, he was enjoying the ride in the unusually pleasant spring weather. Though it had rained that morning, the sun was now shining through, and the meadows and fern forests glowed green in front of the mountain backdrop.

At the entrance to town, he passed the Methodist church, an attractive wood building. He contemplated whether he should go in and say a few words to the priest. The man was charged with the spiritual well-being of his workers after all, even if many of them were Catholic and did not attend service there. But then he saw that the pastor already seemed to have a visitor. A short and stocky white mare was tied up in front, and a three-colored collie waited patiently nearby. Just then, the church door opened. Timothy watched as the priest stepped outside to see his guest off. He held the door open for a red-haired girl with a few songbooks under her arm. An exceptionally attractive girl in a worn-out gray riding dress. She wore her long, curly hair in a braid, but a few strands had freed themselves and played about her narrow face. The priest waved amiably to his visitor as she walked over to the white horse and packed the sheet music in a saddlebag. The little dog appeared beside itself with joy at the sight of her mistress.

Timothy rode closer and greeted her. He had thought the girl had already spotted him as she left the church, but when she heard his voice, she started and spun around. For a moment, Timothy thought he detected something almost like panic in her eyes. The girl looked around hastily like an animal caught in a trap, only calming down when Timothy made no move to leap at her. She seemed to take comfort in the proximity of the church. She tentatively returned Timothy's smile but lowered her eyes immediately, and then limited herself to casting a few suspicious glances at him.

However, she returned his greeting in a quiet voice, climbing skillfully into the saddle as she did so. She looked like she was accustomed to mounting her horse without help.

Timothy realized they were headed the same way when the girl turned her horse toward town.

"You have a lovely horse, miss," Timothy remarked after they had been riding beside each other for a little while. "It looks like the ponies I saw in Wales, but the bigger ones are rarely white."

The girl risked a somewhat longer glance in his direction. "Banshee has Welsh Mountain blood," she explained, a little hesitantly. "Hence her white coloring. Otherwise, you're right, it's rare among cobs."

An astoundingly long speech for so obviously shy a creature. The subject of horses seemed to be right on the mark. And she clearly knew something about them.

He continued his questions. "Welsh Mountains are the ponies, right? The ones that are also used in the mines?"

The girl nodded. "But I don't think they make good mining horses. They're too willful. Banshee, at least, wouldn't let herself be cooped up in a dark mine shaft." She laughed nervously. "She would probably make plans the first night to build a ladder."

Timothy remained serious. "It would probably hold more weight than the hoisting cages in some of the local mines," he said, thinking of the rickety elevator he had been in earlier that day. "But you're right, the ponies used in the mines are normally from Dartmoor or New Forest. Fell ponies are often used as well, though those tend to be a bit bigger."

The girl appeared to be overcoming her shyness. She looked him over for a while. Timothy was struck by her beautiful eyes and freckles.

"Are you from Wales, miss?" he asked, though he doubted it. The girl did not speak with a Welsh accent.

She shook her head but did not disclose any further information. "How about you, sir?" she asked instead. It did not sound as if she were genuinely interested though, rather that she simply wanted to keep the conversation casual.

"I worked in a mine in Wales for a while," he informed her. "But I'm from here, in Greymouth."

"So you're a miner?" This question, too, came out casually, but as she asked it, she was eyeing his tidy clothing, his valuable saddlery, and his handsome horse. Miners could not usually afford such things and generally got around on foot.

"Mining engineer," he said. "I studied in Europe. Mining engineers concern themselves with the mining facilities and—"

"And they make all that," she said, indicating the headframe towers and spoil piles that disfigured the landscape around Greymouth with a wave of her hand, her facial expression reflecting her opinion of it.

Timothy smiled at her. "They're ugly things. You can go ahead and say it, miss. I don't like them any better than you do, but we need the coal. It gives us warmth, makes steel production possible . . . No coal, no modern life. And it creates jobs. In Greymouth alone, it feeds a large portion of the population."

The girl could have said a thing or two to that. Furrows formed on her forehead, and her eyes flashed indignantly. If she had lived in the area for any length of time, she might be familiar with the miners' slums. Timothy felt guilty. He was still fumbling for further explanations when they reached the first houses on the edge of town. He almost thought he could feel the girl next to him relax. She seemed considerably less anxious after receiving and returning the first greeting from a passerby. So she had felt uncomfortable alone with him despite their pleasant chat. Timothy wondered: since when had he become someone women felt they had reason to fear?

The building materials trader was among the first shops they came upon, and Timothy explained to the girl that he was stopping there.

He introduced himself quickly. "By the way, my name is Timothy Lambert."

He did not get a reaction.

Timothy gave it another try.

"It was nice chatting with you, Miss . . ."

"Keefer," the girl murmured.

"Well, good-bye, then, Miss Keefer."

Timothy removed his hat and directed his horse into the trader's yard.

The girl did not reply.

7

Elaine could have slapped herself. It had not really been necessary to behave like that; the young man had only been trying to be polite. But there was nothing she could do about it: as soon as she found herself alone with a man, everything inside her closed up. She felt only hatred and fear. Most of the time, she couldn't utter a word. This man had succeeded in luring her out of her reserve only by speaking so knowledgeably about horses. On the other hand, it could be dangerous to have him know Banshee's breed. He may have heard of Kiward Station's Welsh cobs and could make a connection between Elaine and them.

She chided herself for her mistrust. The man was a mining engineer. He didn't know any sheep farms in Canterbury. He probably couldn't have cared less about Banshee. He had simply wanted to have a friendly conversation with her, and she had not even managed to say good-bye. This had to stop. She had been in Greymouth for almost a year, and no one had come after her.

Not that she intended to fall in love again, of course, but she had to be capable of speaking with a man without completely seizing up. This Timothy Lambert fellow would have been a good start. He didn't appear dangerous; in fact, he looked like a rather nice fellow. He had curly brown hair that he wore rather long, and he was slender and of average height. Neither as lanky as William nor as strapping as Thomas, he was not the sort of man who immediately caught one's eye. But he sat comfortably on his horse and managed the reins with a light hand. He didn't look like the type who spent all his waking hours in an office—but not underground either. His skin was sunbrowned and clean, not pale and grayed by coal dust like that of most miners.

Elaine had avoided looking him in the eye, but she thought his eyes were green. An unimposing brownish green. His eyes didn't shine like William's, nor were they secretive like Thomas's. They were the peaceful, friendly eyes of a completely normal man who wouldn't hurt a fly.

But she had thought the same of William. And of Thomas.

She vigorously chased away every thought of her recent companion. Upon reaching Madame Clarisse's stables, she unsaddled Banshee and fed her. Callie followed her into their tiny room, which she had made more inviting with bright curtains and an attractive plaid bedspread. She had to change her clothes, as the pub would be opening in a half hour. It was a shame that she had not made it back sooner. She would have liked to try out the new music the priest had given her for the Sunday service. But Madame Clarisse did not like it when Elaine played church songs in the pub. In the mornings, it didn't matter much, but by this time of day, most of the girls would be in the barroom having a bite to eat before work.

"You're not going to convert me," Madame Clarisse had explained, shaking a finger at her.

Elaine now laughed easily at such jokes. She had also grown accustomed to the girls' talk and no longer blushed when they talked about their customers. Their stories, however, only confirmed her suspicion that she wasn't missing anything by staying away from men. It was true that the girls who could be bought earned a great deal more than she did at the piano, but the life of a whore was not an enviable one, especially not to a married woman.

Elaine selected a pale-blue dress that emphasized the color of her eyes, unraveled her braid, and combed her hair. She made it to her piano on time, followed, as always, by Callie. The little dog had long ago stopped barking just because her mistress was playing the piano. But she growled whenever a man came too close to Elaine. It made Elaine feel safe, and it did not seem to bother Madame Clarisse. Elaine wasn't afraid of talking to the men in the pub. That was part of the job, and there was no danger, since the pub was often full. As a rule, she would have preferred to avoid any conversation there as well, but if she was too prickly, the men would not buy her drinks—and Elaine depended on the extra income. Her first "whiskey" arrived on the piano shortly after she had begun to play. Charlene, who had placed her drink there, nodded at her.

"He'd like you to play 'Paddy's Green Shamrock Shore,'" she said. Elaine nodded. An evening like any other.

After flipping through several catalogs and discussing the merits of various building materials, Timothy had managed to convince the salesman that the Lambert Mine wanted the best materials rather than the cheapest this time. The man was utterly astonished and offered to buy Tom a beer when they were done. Another new friend. Timothy was very satisfied with what he'd accomplished and quite happy to finish his evening at a pub. It was just a shame that his plans with Matt were so vague. He didn't even know where the young foreman liked to go to drink his beer, but he suspected it was not any of the upscale hotels and restaurants along the quay. The first of the miner bars, the Wild Rover, did not look like a wholesome place. The customers already appeared to be drunk, and the atmosphere was tense. Timothy heard belligerent voices coming from inside. If Matt spent his free time there, Timothy would have had to be wrong about him. So he looked for the other pub, the Lucky Horse Inn; he knew that the local brothel was also located there, but bars and brothels often went hand in hand. That fact did not necessarily reflect on either the atmosphere in the barroom or the quality of the whiskey.

Timothy was about to tie his horse in front of the inn when another rider who had just arrived informed him that there were stables.

"Otherwise, that fine saddlery of yours'll get soaked pretty quick," he explained while visibly looking the horse over. The spring weather that afternoon had proved to be an unreliable ambassador for the summer, as it had begun to drizzle again. "And that'd be a shame. English work, right? Where'd you buy that? Christchurch?"

The man turned out to be the local master saddler, and the stables were a small but clean and dry annex to the bar. A white mare whinnied. Timothy placed his horse next to the mare and stroked her nose. Wasn't this the girl's cob? His gelding seemed to recognize the mare too and made a few fainthearted advances. Banshee responded enthusiastically.

The saddler, Ernie Gast, gave the horses some hay and tossed a few cents on a tray for the recently acquired stableboy. Timothy wanted to ask him about the mare, but he forgot about it when he entered the barroom.

It was warm in Madame Clarisse's, and it smelled like tobacco, fresh-tapped beer, and grilled fish. Timothy immediately felt better than he had at its competitor's, though this place was rather noisy too. Here, however, people were singing rather than brawling; three Welshmen had formed a small chorus around the piano. At some of the tables, men were chatting with girls in low-cut dresses, others were playing cards, and a group of mine workers was competing at darts. In a corner, sitting somewhat apart from the general commotion, Matt Gawain waved cheerfully at the newcomers.

"Over here, Mr. Lambert. It's quieter. It's better if the men don't realize their foreman is here, let alone their boss. That'll make a lot of them nervous. I don't think they understand that our kind has a dry throat after a day in the mines too. They probably think I'm counting their drinks."

"They'd hardly be able to afford many during the week anyway," Timothy said, sitting down. A barmaid approached, and he ordered a beer. Ernie Gast did likewise. Matt had offered him a seat as well, and the two of them seemed to know each other.

Matt shrugged. "A few of them afford themselves far too many. Most of their pay goes toward drink, and that's why they never come to much. But can you blame them? Thousands of miles from home and still no future, their filthy houses, the constant rain."

"Still, it's no good to have drunks underground," Timothy said, taking a sip of his beer and a closer look around the pub. The men were not drinking outrageously just then. Most of them had beer glasses; only a few had ordered whiskey, and they didn't look like miners. The music suddenly took a more cheerful turn. The sad Welshmen had cleared away from the piano, and the pianist was playing an Irish jig.

The pianist?

"Who the devil is that?" Timothy asked, astounded, when he recognized the girl on the piano.

It was without a doubt the shy little thing he had met that afternoon. She was no longer wearing her unremarkable riding dress, however, but a flouncy, pretty blue dress that emphasized her narrow waist. The color was a little too intense for a girl from a good home, but it was relatively high-cut and far from being as salacious as what the barmaids and whores were wearing. Her hair, hanging down over her shoulders now, seemed to be in constant motion. Her locks were so fine that even the tiniest breeze blew them about.

Startled, Matt and Ernie looked in the direction where Timothy was pointing. Then they laughed.

"The cutie on the piano?" Ernie asked. "That's our Miss Keefer."

"The Saint of Greymouth," Matt joked.

Timothy frowned. "Well, she doesn't look like a saint to me," he remarked. "Certainly not here of all places."

Matt and Ernie chuckled.

"You just don't know our Miss Keefer," Ernie said soothingly. "They also call her the 'Virgin of Greymouth,' but the ladies don't like to hear that, because it makes it sound like she's the only one."

There was roaring laughter, this time from the neighboring table as well.

"Will someone please fill me in?" Timothy asked in a surly tone. He didn't know why, but he did not appreciate the way the men joked about the girl. The little redhead looked remarkably sweet. He watched her delicate fingers flying over the keys as she strung together the difficult passages of the melody, a deep furrow between her eyes, a sign of her intense concentration. The girl seemed to forget the pub and the men all around her, forming an island of . . . innocence?

Matt was finally moved to pity and told Timothy what he knew.

"She says her name is Lainie Keefer. She popped up here about a year ago, in pretty bad shape and looking for work. Respectable work. She even made an attempt to rent a room in a decent hotel. The barber's wife still gets worked up about how she almost let someone like Lainie into her house. But she had no money. Well, as you can imagine, Greymouth is not exactly a hub of female labor. Madame Clarisse finally hired her as a pianist. Naturally, we all took bets on when she'd fall. In this sort of environment, how is a girl supposed to stay clean?"

"And?" Timothy asked. He watched as one of the barmaids placed a whiskey on the piano for the girl. Miss Keefer knocked the drink back in one go. Not exactly the hallmark of an innocent country girl.

"And nothing!" replied Ernie. "She plays the piano and chats with the men a bit, but otherwise—nothing."

"And she keeps the chitchat limited to work hours," Matt added. "Otherwise, the only man she speaks to is the priest."

"She talked to me this afternoon," Timothy remarked.

The girl was now playing "Whiskey in the Jar," apparently by request. One drink, one song.

"Oh, you've met her already," Matt said, laughing. "Well, I bet the conversation was limited to the weather. She doesn't manage much else."

"We talked about horses," Timothy said absentmindedly.

Ernie laughed. "Well, you're a quick one. Gave it a try too, eh? And not a bad one at that. Horses are just about the only thing she'll talk about—with dogs a close second. Joel Henderson claims she once managed three sentences on two versions of an Irish song with different sets of lyrics."

"What was I trying?" Timothy wasn't really listening. Elaine's piano playing had a much stronger grip on his attention.

"Well, to land her," Matt said, rolling his eyes. "But that's hope-less, believe me. We've all tried. The miners too, but they never have any luck either. What girl wants to move to their place? But even the landowners and their sons, the artisans like Ernie here and the smith. Not to mention yours truly, as well as foremen of the Blackburn and Biller mines. All love's labors lost. She doesn't spare anyone a glance."

That was indeed the case—in the strictest sense of the word. Timothy thought of Elaine's lowered gaze during their whole conversation.

"Do you know what the other girls say about her?" Ernie asked. He seemed a little tipsy by this time, but it might be that the thought of his botched courtship of Elaine gave him a melancholy aspect. "They say Miss Keefer is afraid of men."

Timothy waited for the conversation to move on to other topics. Then he slowly stood up and went to the piano. This time, he made sure that Elaine saw him. He did not want to startle her again.

"Good evening, Miss Keefer," he said formally.

Elaine lowered her head, and her hair fell like a curtain in front of her face.

"Good evening, Mr. Lambert," she replied. So, she had taken note of his name.

"I just placed my horse next to yours, and the two of them are flirting like schoolchildren."

Elaine's face flushed slightly.

"Banshee likes company," she said stiffly. "She's lonely."

"Then we'll want to cheer her up from time to time. Perhaps she'd like to take a walk with Fellow sometime." Timothy smiled at the girl. "Fellow is my horse, and I assure you he has only the most honorable of intentions."

Elaine continued to hide behind her hair.

"No doubt, but I"—she looked up briefly and he thought he saw a twinkle in her eye—"I don't let her go for walks unattended, you see."

"We could both chaperone the horses, of course." Timothy tried to sound casual.

Elaine eyed him carefully. Timothy was looking at her with sincerity, neither salaciously nor lustfully. He appeared to be kind, and he'd presented his invitation to a ride together in the most diplomatic manner. The other men had probably warned him. And now there was probably a bet over whether he would get her to come around.

Elaine shook her head. No excuse came to her; she simply blushed and bit her lip. Callie growled beneath the piano.

Madame Clarisse finally took matters into her own hands. What was this stranger doing to Elaine? Was he trying to cozy up to her? He seemed to be driving the girl to distraction.

"Miss Keefer is only for looking at," she explained resolutely. "And listening to. If you've got a favorite song and want to buy her a drink, she'll play it for you. Otherwise, stay away from her, got it?"

Timothy nodded. "I'll get back to you," he said amiably but without clarifying whether he meant the invitation or the song.

Matt and Ernie received him with a grin.

"Nothing, eh?" the saddler asked.

Timothy shrugged.

"I've got time," he said.

Timothy went to the pub again the following evening, sat down near the piano, and watched Elaine. He drank a beer slowly, then a second, and exchanged a few words with his new friends, but aside from that, he did nothing but stare the girl at the piano.

At the end of the evening, he said good-bye politely to Elaine and Madame Clarisse, who was a little embarrassed about her gruff behavior the day before, having since learned who he was. Timothy came again the following night. And the next. On the fourth evening, a Saturday, Elaine could not take it anymore.

"Why do you sit down there every night and gawk at me?" she asked, aggravated.

Timothy smiled. "I thought that's what you were there for. At least that's what your boss told me. 'Miss Keefer is only for looking at.' So, that's what I'm doing."

"But why? If there was a certain song you wanted to hear, you could ask, you know?" Elaine looked at him helplessly.

"I'd be happy to order you a tea if that's what this is about. But as for songs, that's difficult. Drinking songs are too loud for me, and you don't put any feeling into the love songs."

Elaine blushed at the mention of tea. "How did you know?" She indicated the whiskey glass on the piano.

"Oh, it's not hard to guess," Timothy said. "You've had five drinks since I arrived. If that were alcohol, you'd have long since been quite drunk. You should give it a try though. It might ease the problem with the love songs."

Elaine turned even redder.

"I get half," she said flatly. "Of the whiskeys."

Timothy laughed. "Then we should just treat ourselves to a whole bottle. But what would we do for a song? How about 'Silver Dagger'?"

Elaine bit her lip. It was a song in which a girl swears off love. She sleeps with a silver dagger in her hand to keep the men away from her.

It awakened very concrete memories in Elaine, and she had to force herself not to tremble.

Madame Clarisse approached.

"Now, let the girl work in peace, Mr. Lambert. The poor thing gets nervous when you stare at her the whole time. Behave like an upstanding gent and go drink with your friends. You can meet with the girl at church tomorrow and politely ask her if she'll let you walk her home. That strikes me as much more respectable than sharing a bottle of whiskey with her."

Timothy was not sure, but he thought he saw Elaine stiffen at the mention of church. Whatever the reason, the red in her cheeks faded to a waxy pallor.

"I think I'd prefer the whiskey," she said softly.

The next morning Timothy did indeed meet the girl in front of church, but she slipped away at once—which was easily done since she played the organ and was separated from the rest of the congregation. During the service, Timothy did what he was now used to doing: he watched her. This time, it was his mother, rather than Madame Clarisse, who chided him. He hoped that he would have a chance to see Elaine after the service, but she disappeared as soon as the last notes had sounded.

Charlene explained to him that Elaine was eating lunch with the priest and his wife.

"They invite her to join them occasionally, but I think she invited herself today. Church is not the best place to pursue her, Mr. Lambert. She's had some bad experience with that."

Timothy wondered where he could go about pursuing her then, but his determination had been awakened once and for all.

He continued to visit the pub regularly over the next few weeks. Though he did not stare at the girl as noticeably as he had the first few times, he always sat nearby. Sometimes he exchanged a few words with her before requesting the same song every time and ordering her a drink. She would then smile shyly and play "Silver Dagger" while Charlene served her "whiskey."

Several weeks passed in this manner without his making even modest progress. But then Saint Barbara's Day approached.

"Your father's really putting on a festival?" Matt Gawain asked Timothy as soon as they entered the pub. The horse race at the Lambert Mine was the only thing anyone was talking about at the Lucky Horse that evening, and the young foreman was hungry for any details.

Timothy had arrived a little later than usual and had just gotten through his exchange of formalities with Elaine—"Good evening, Miss Keefer." "Good evening, Mr. Lambert." Only then did he approach his regular table and sit down next to Matt.

"The festival wasn't my idea if you're really asking me why there's money for entertainment but not for safer explosives," Timothy replied reluctantly. He had just been fighting with his father over the matter, and had made no headway as usual.

"A festival is much more important to these miners than their working conditions," Marvin Lambert had insisted. "Bread and games, my son, even the ancient Romans knew that. If you build them washrooms, tomorrow they'll want a new hoisting cage or better mine lamps. But if you offer them a proper horse race, roast an ox, and let the beer flow in rivers at your own expense, they'll be singing the praises of it all for weeks."

"That's not what I'm asking," Matt said, trying to placate Timothy. "It's just not at all like the old boss to put on a big festival for Saint Barbara's Day. It's never happened before, and I've been here three years."

Timothy shrugged. "We've talked about it before. The unions are making progress. People have heard about the uprisings in England, Ireland, and America. It would just take the right leader and we'd be in trouble." Timothy emptied his beer faster than usual and ordered a whiskey. "My father thinks he can prevent that with bread and games."

"But a horse race? We don't even have any racehorses," Matt said as Ernie and the smith, Jay Hankins, joined them at the table.

Timothy raised his eyebrows.

"We don't have any greyhounds either," he remarked calmly. "So we also couldn't have a dog race. Unless we had Miss Keefer's Callie run against Mrs. Miller's poodle." Timothy smiled and cast a glance at the small dog underneath the piano.

Callie heard her name, stood up, and trotted over to him, tail wagging. If nothing else, he had won Callie's heart over the course of the last few weeks, though not by being above bribery. Callie loved the little sausages Timothy's mother enjoyed serving for breakfast.

"But there are undoubtedly a few horses around here that can gallop, and my father means to offer the people something to gamble on. If we don't want to stoop to cockfights, horse races are our only option. Besides, they're easy to organize. The roads that lead around the mining complex are relatively flat and good for riding. The whole area around Lambert Mine is called Derby, after all. Anyone can compete, anyone can bet, and the fastest horse wins."

"Then let's do it ourselves," Jay Hankins, said grinning. He owned a long-legged mare, and Timothy's gelding had thoroughbred ancestors.

"I can't ride in the race," grumbled Timothy. "How would that look?"

This was another discussion he'd had with his father. The elder Lambert was not only of the opinion that his son should participate in the race but that he had to win it as well. The way he saw it, the miners should bet on a Lambert and triumph with him. That was supposed to create a feeling of common purpose and help the men develop a sense of loyalty to their employer. Marvin Lambert was even seriously considering purchasing an extra thoroughbred.

"How should it look?" Ernie asked surprised. "You have a horse and you're competing—like everyone else in town whose nag can still manage to trot around the mine, I imagine. You wouldn't want to miss out on that, would you?"

For the miners, it wouldn't all just be good fun. Timothy knew that they were planning to place large bets. A week's pay could be lost in a flash, and no one could know who would win such an unconventional race.

"Well, our Lainie's competing anyway," Florry, the barmaid, remarked as she placed new pint glasses on the table. She had been listening to the conversation.

The men laughed.

"Miss Keefer with that pony?" Jay scoffed. "We're dying of fear!"

Florry looked at him disparagingly. "Just wait until you're eating Banshee's dust," she spat. "We're going to bet everything on her."

"That won't make the little horse go any faster," Matt teased. "Seriously, though, where did she get the idea to race?"

"Lainie can ride better than any fellow here," Florry crowed. "She told Madame Clarisse that she'd like to, and Madame Clarisse said if she wanted to, she should. We're going to put colorful bows in Banshee's mane, and then she'll be a running advertisement for the Lucky Horse. Lainie was a bit uncertain about it at first, but we're all

382

going to be rooting for her, and Banshee's definitely going to be the prettiest horse there."

"And Miss Keefer the prettiest rider," Timothy said with a smile before Matt and the others could tease the barmaid further. Florry was not the cleverest girl in the room, and she may not have grasped the difference between a horse race and a beauty pageant. But to Timothy, this was an interesting development. During the race, Elaine would have to talk to him, jockey to jockey so to speak. He raised his glass and drank to his friends.

"All right, fine. Tomorrow I'll put my horse on the list too. May the best man win!"

Or the best woman, thought Elaine. While playing a few simple songs, she, too, had been following the men's loud conversation. And she had no intention of making herself the laughingstock of the mine. She had checked out the course the day before. The race covered three miles over varied terrain—hard and soft, wide and narrow, uphill and downhill. It would not simply come down to who was fastest; it would also hinge on the sure-footedness and condition of the horse and the skills of the rider. Elaine cast a glance at Timothy Lambert, flushing when he noticed and winked at her.

All right, fine. He wanted a ride together. On Saint Barbara's Day, he would get one.

8

The fourth of December, dedicated to the patron saint of mining, landed at the height of the New Zealand summer. Even in rainy Greymouth, the sun had appeared, and it was beaming down on Marvin Lambert's men, who had transformed the mine compound into festival grounds. Decorated with garlands, little flags, and balloons, the offices, headframe towers, and piles of coal did not look as dilapidated as usual, and the compound roads in between were finally dry. Decorations were also strung from temporary stalls, where beer was being given away, along with tea for the ladies. Whole oxen were being roasted on the spit over large fires. Men were competing at darts and trying their hand at horseshoe-throwing and nail-hammering competitions.

But the paddock for the horse race formed the main attraction, and people had begun to camp out there several hours ahead of time. Many of those wanting to place bets would wait until the last minute to choose the horse and rider they considered most likely to win. The start and finish lines were located right in front of the mine entrance, as was the improvised betting office. It was being managed by Paddy Holloway, the proprietor of the Wild Rover. People could place their bets near the beer stands and follow the end of the race later.

They had selected the patient local pastor as judge—and he had only accepted the job so that he might deliver a sermon about the dangers and godlessness of gambling before the race. For a man of God, he demonstrated exceptional flexibility in declaring himself prepared to hold a service on the morning of the festival in front of the mine, even though, as a Methodist, he had nothing to do with Saint Barbara. But Reverend Lance took a pragmatic perspective: the men in the Lambert Mine surely needed divine assistance in their daily lives. What they wanted to call this friendly power, he left to them.

Elaine played "Amazing Grace," a song which—except at weddings—was always a suitable choice.

By that afternoon, as race time approached, the revelers had satisfied their hunger and most of them were a little tipsy.

As Elaine rode her mare into the paddock, she noticed that the audience was overwhelmingly male. Madame Clarisse's girls, in their colorful, low-cut summer dresses, stood out among the men like flowers in a meadow and cheered her on as she rode past. The few other women in the crowd kept silent. They consisted largely of haggard miners' wives who had stuck around mainly to keep their men from gambling away all the money. A few of the local matrons sat next to their husbands near Marvin Lambert on the dais. They were already gossiping mercilessly about the presence of the easy women and—even more shocking—about Elaine competing in the race. They had come to the unanimous opinion that it was indecent. But good Miss Keefer had never taken decency all that seriously.

Elaine, who knew perfectly well what the women were whispering about, waved triumphantly at them.

Timothy noticed that and grinned to himself. Elaine could be so self-assured and blithe. Why then did she shrink back like a whipped dog whenever a man spoke to her?

Even now, she lowered her gaze when he greeted her—though she could not hide herself behind a curtain of hair that day. She had put her hair up and had even donned a bold little hat—presumably on loan from Madame Clarisse. Its gray color matched Elaine's riding dress, and someone had wrapped an indigo-blue ribbon around the brim. Banshee's mane and tail were likewise decorated with colorful ribbons.

Elaine noticed Timothy's gaze and begged his pardon with a smile. "The girls insisted. I think it looks indescribably absurd."

"Not at all," Timothy said. "On the contrary, it suits her. She looks like a Spanish matador's horse."

"Were you in Spain too?" Elaine asked. She steered Banshee up alongside Timothy's horse and appeared relaxed compared to her usual self. She was in a crowd of people, and so no more alone with Timothy now than in the pub.

Timothy nodded. "Spain has mines too."

By this time, the paddock had filled. In all, nine men and one woman were prepared to ride against each other. The field was as diverse as Timothy had expected. He recognized Jay Hankins, the smith, on his high-spirited mare. The stable owner was on a tall, big-boned gelding into whose pedigree a thoroughbred might have erred some years back. Two youths from a farm were riding their father's workhorses. Two young foremen from the Biller and Blackburn mines had rented horses just for the race. Though one of them sat very skill-fully in the saddle, the other appeared to be more of a novice. Ernie, the saddler, naturally, would not be denied a chance to participate, though he hardly stood a chance of winning with his well-mannered old gelding. The last rider, Caleb Biller, however, was a surprise. The son of Marvin Lambert's main competition, sitting astride an elegant black stallion, was greeted with cheers. His mine's men would undoubtedly put all their money on him.

"And that may not be such a bad place for it," Timothy remarked. He was riding next to Jay. Elaine had moved back when she found herself stuck between the two men.

"Biller's horse looks grand, a real thoroughbred. It's sure to leave us all in its dust," Timothy said as he scratched Fellow's throat.

Fellow was looking around nervously for Banshee. After months of spending practically every evening in the stall next to hers, Fellow did not want to let her out of sight.

Jay shrugged. "The horse alone can't win a race though. It comes down to the rider. And that young Biller . . ."

Elaine, too, mustered her competitive instincts. Until that moment, she had believed Fellow to be her most dangerous opponent. Timothy Lambert's gelding was a lively dapple gray with undeniable Arabian ancestors. There was no question he would be faster than Banshee on the straightaways. But this blond young man—she had never seen Caleb Biller before—sat astride a true racehorse. However, he did not appear to feel completely comfortable with it. Horse and rider were clearly not a well-rehearsed team.

"Old man Biller bought that nag for him especially for this race." Ernie Gast and the stable owner were discussing the same subject. "He came out of England but he's already run the racetrack in Wellington. They want to win by hook or by crook. That will put a little fear in old Lambert. If after this he has to hand the trophy over to his arch-nemesis . . ."

There were three miles to go before that, Elaine thought, though she, too, had lost her nerve a little at the sight of the powerful black stallion.

Elaine found a starting position on the outside right, which proved a good choice. A few of the horses, already nervous from being cramped together in the paddock, shied at the starting shot. They did not want to run past the man with the still-smoking pistol and ended up in a kerfuffle at the starting line. The two youths on their workhorses and the foreman on his rental horse could not make their horses do anything. The latter fell off his horse almost immediately but was lucky enough not to end up among the trampling hooves. Jay Hankins was less fortunate. His mare suffered a blow to its fetlock joint and foundered. For him the race was over before it had even begun.

Elaine, however, came out of it well, as did Timothy. The two of them found themselves racing beside one another behind the farm boys, who set out at a sprint, followed by Caleb Biller on his stallion. It would have been madness to tear through the pack at full speed. The path was lined with cheering men, and it would have been too dangerous for Elaine to give her horse free rein. Madame Clarisse's girls had posted themselves right around the first curve, and they started cheering as soon as they saw Elaine and Banshee coming.

Florry was wearing a colorful floral dress and bouncing up and down like a rubber ball. She was waving two flags, which promptly caused two of the other horses to shy, Caleb Biller's stallion among them.

"Watch out," Ernie called to the young man when Ernie's gelding almost ran into Caleb's rearing black stallion. "Ride, damn it, before that nag jumps into the crowd!"

The shocked spectators along the edge of the path scattered, screaming. Terrified, the younger Biller gave his horse his spurs—at which the horse shot off at a gallop, passing the farm horses and the foreman on his rented horse, and disappearing around the next curve.

"There he goes," a frustrated Ernie remarked. "We won't see him again before the finish line."

"Oh, I don't believe that," Timothy returned. "He won't be able to keep up that speed for three miles. That horse has never had to run that far. Even the big track races aren't much more than a mile and a half long. Just wait; we'll be seeing him again before you know it."

Timothy's strategy matched Elaine's very closely. He took the first two miles at a brisk but not breakneck pace, and his gelding galloped contentedly alongside her mare. Elaine did not fight that and wondered a bit at herself. Despite the proximity of Timothy and Ernie, who caught up to them initially but soon fell behind, she began to enjoy the ride. She even managed to return Timothy's smile as they passed the frustrated stable owner. His horse had tried to keep pace with Caleb Biller's stallion and was now completely exhausted after barely a mile.

It was no different for the farm boys. Their naturally sluggish workhorses gave up after another half mile. Banshee and Fellow, by contrast, still showed no signs of tiring, and their riders were both still fresh.

Timothy looked over at Elaine with admiration. He had always found her attractive but never as charming and vivacious as now. She had lost her little hat immediately after the race began, and her tight hair bun had likewise fallen apart after the first mile. Only the headwind was keeping her locks out of her face. It looked as though she were waving a red flag behind her, and her face seemed to glow with an inner light. Riding this fast made her happy, and for the first time, her eyes did not assume an expression of suspicion when her gaze met Timothy's.

Because the woods reached right to the mining compound's fence, the course followed the inside fence for quite a while. But they were now approaching the miners' quarters, and the course by necessity turned outward. The turn in front of the mine's southern gate was rather tight—when Timothy had studied the course, he only hoped that every competitor had taken the time to ride over the course ahead of time. Anyone who tried to take this stretch at a full gallop ran the risk of falling off.

Timothy and Elaine slowed their horses well ahead of the turn; again, it was as though they had agreed on it beforehand. Elaine brought Banshee all the way down to a trot, which proved to be a wise move. Caleb Biller was in the middle of the road, limping miserably toward them and leading his handsome horse by the reins.

Elaine observed without pity that at least the horse was all right. In fact, the stallion was not even dirty. So it seemed he had thrown his rider from the saddle.

"He shied," Caleb complained. The cause of the accident was easy to ascertain. In the middle of the road—despite three straight days of sun—was a large puddle, something that would have been unthinkable on an English racing course. The stallion had never seen such a thing, and, after taking the sharp turn, had panicked.

"Bit of bad luck," Timothy replied to his defeated opponent. He did not sound especially sympathetic.

"Why doesn't he just climb back up?" Elaine asked when they'd resumed galloping. "The horse is fine; he could still win."

Timothy grinned. "Caleb Biller isn't the bravest rider. Even as a child, he was scared to death on top of his pony. I've been wondering all day how his old man got him up on that stallion."

Elaine giggled. She felt strangely light and almost drunk. She had not had such fun in years—and that despite the fact that she was competing against a man. It must have been the exceptional circumstances of the race. Regardless, at that moment, she was not the least bit scared of Timothy Lambert. On the contrary, she was cheered by the sight of him, his slim but strong frame on his dapple gray, his brown hair flying in the wind, his friendly eyes and his frequent laughter, which carved dimples into the corners of his mouth.

They had reached the last mile of the course, and only one opponent was still ahead of them: Blackburn's foreman on his rental horse, a dark horse in the race, since he wasn't expected to win. The steed—actually light brown—appeared to be quite tough and the foreman was an experienced rider. As Elaine and Timothy moved to overtake his clearly fatigued gelding, the rider began to zigzag and hold his riding crop far out to the side. Fellow was afraid of passing him. Elaine tried to overtake him on the other side, but the road was narrow and the brown horse did not want to let her pass. He threatened Banshee and bit in her direction. Frightened, the mare fell back.

"That bastard won't let us pass," Elaine cried, her countenance flashing with anger and outrage.

Timothy had to laugh. He was not used to such words coming from the "Saint of Greymouth."

Timothy yelled at the rider in a voice well accustomed to giving commands, but the foreman did not even think of giving way to the heir of the Lambert Mine. He kept his eye on his pursuers and continued zigzagging across the course.

Elaine deliberated feverishly. It was probably a thousand yards or so to the finish line, and the road would stay narrow; in addition, it would soon be lined with spectators, making any attempt to overtake him even riskier. There was only one place where the road widened, at the point where they reentered the mine complex. The course led through the main gate, in front of which was a sort of parking area where freight wagons were usually deposited. That area should be empty now, unless people were standing there. There was enough space to overtake him there, but it was a very short stretch. Unless . . .

Elaine decided to risk it. When the road widened, she firmly directed Banshee to the left—there were only two or three little clusters of people, who scattered quickly when Elaine yelled, "Clear the way!" Banshee caught up with the other rider, but she would not manage to overtake him before the gate and get back onto the road.

Timothy, who had sped up after Elaine as well, did not realize at first what she had in mind. Only when she made no move to cut in front of the other rider—instead, spurring Banshee on straight toward the fence—did he understand. It took all his courage not to rein in Fellow. But the white mare had already flown over the fence and returned to the course by then, leaving the astonished foreman on his rented horse behind her. Timothy had no time left to think. Fellow was already leaping into the air and clearing the fence as effortlessly as Banshee. Timothy closed the gap between himself and the mare and looked breathlessly over at Elaine. She was beaming. Her face was flushed, her eyes sparkling.

"We showed him!" she called out excitedly, spurring Banshee on to full speed.

Timothy would have been only too glad to slacken the reins, or at least pass the finish line right at her side. But then he pulled himself together. None of his men had bet on Elaine. If she lost, Madame Clarisse's girls would be out a few cents, but if she won, dozens of miners would have lost their hard-earned money. Timothy hesitated.

"Do it now," Elaine called to him. "Your horse is so much faster than mine." She laughed. Maybe she had been thinking the same thing.

Timothy struck Fellow with his crop. Unwillingly, the horse pulled ahead of Banshee, crossing the finish line half a horse's length ahead.

Timothy hardly managed to bring Fellow to a stop. The crowd of spectators had erupted into screaming and cheering. He sat astride his excitedly prancing horse and accepted the ovations of his men. Elaine looked at his the elated expression on his face, framed by brown locks of hair, and his peaceful eyes. They were very bright just then, which highlighted the green flecks in them. His gaze reflected no disapproval of an excessively wild ride, as William's had, nor any gloating triumph, as Thomas's certainly would have. No, Timothy was simply happy and wanted to share his joy with others. Laughing, he brought Fellow alongside Banshee, spontaneously taking Elaine's hand and holding it in the air.

"Here's the real winner, people! I would never have dared to jump over that fence on my own."

Elaine had been beaming and feeling as free and buoyant as Timothy, but when he touched her, it all came back in a flash. Thomas's hands on her body, her panic at his strong grip. Those caresses of William's that she had trusted, and which had only turned out to be lies.

Timothy sensed her tense up, all the delight and confidence draining from her. She didn't say anything. She even attempted to hold a cramped smile, but when he let go of her hand, she pulled away as though she had burned herself. In her eyes was that same panic he had seen flare up that first day in front of the church.

"Forgive me, Miss Keefer," he said, dismayed.

She didn't look at him.

"Don't worry about it. I need to fix my hair . . ."

Elaine's narrow face, so recently flushed from the hard ride, had turned pale as death. With trembling fingers, she tried to put her hair back into a bun, but it was hopeless, of course.

"It looks wonderful as it is, Miss Keefer," Timothy said, fumbling for words that would soothe her, but the girl now appeared to retreat when he even so much as looked at her.

She shook her head when a cheerful Jay Hankins wanted to help her from the saddle. A deeply satisfied Marvin Lambert directed the first three finishers to dismount and climb the small winners' podium he'd had built. Elaine slid out of the saddle as she tried to get ahold of herself. She climbed the steps alongside Timothy and then stood there, looking alarmed and ready to bolt, nothing like the exultant, self-possessed girl she had been a few minutes earlier.

Marvin Lambert handed over the winner's trophy, and a drunken guest filled the rather large silver cup with whiskey. "To the winner," he cheered as he held up his glass. The men in the audience did likewise. Timothy laughed and took a sip. Then he handed the trophy to Elaine. When she gripped it, she accidentally brushed his hand and nearly let the trophy fall.

"To you, Miss Keefer," Timothy said. "It was wonderful to ride with you."

Elaine drank deeply and tried to pull herself together. Timothy Lambert had to think she was crazy. And now the old man was approaching to congratulate her, making as if to kiss her. She couldn't. She . . .

"No, Father," Tim said calmly.

Astonished, Marvin Lambert left the girl alone.

"Is there some objection to a kiss for the second-place winner?" he said grumpily.

"Miss Keefer sets great store by her reputation," Timothy explained. "The ladies . . ." He indicated the matrons on the dais who were already gossiping about Elaine's unexpected second-place finish.

Marvin Lambert nodded soberly and merely reached his hand out to Elaine to congratulate her. As she accepted a check for a small money prize, she smiled, but she looked as if she were in pain.

The mine owner winked at Elaine. As he moved on to the third-place finisher, he said, "But after this, you'll dance with me."

Timothy knew that it would never happen. She would not come within a mile of the dance floor. Under no circumstances would she allow a man to put his arm around her.

He met her a short while later by the horses. He had broken away from the others as quickly as he could—which had not been easy since everyone wanted to drink with him that day—and it was just as he had expected. Elaine had given Banshee an hour to catch her breath and was saddling her again.

"Are you going home already, Miss Keefer?" Timothy asked cautiously at the entrance to the tent that had been put up in lieu of stables. He had not wanted to startle her, but he did anyway. "Fellow will be lonely without Banshee."

"The . . . the pub isn't open today," Elaine remarked in an apparent non sequitur.

But then Timothy understood what she meant. She wanted to avoid having him accompany her home.

"I know," he said. "But I thought . . . There's going to be a dance this evening."

"There's a band playing. They don't need me to play piano."

As Elaine spoke, she kept her gaze averted. She was intentionally misunderstanding him.

Timothy didn't let it go. "I would have liked to dance with you, Miss Keefer."

"I don't dance." Elaine fastened her saddle girth hastily.

"Can't or won't, Miss Keefer?"

Elaine did not know how to respond. She stared at the floor before looking up helplessly as though looking for a way out and knowing that there wasn't any.

Like an animal in a trap . . .

Timothy yearned to free her.

"I'm sorry, Miss Keefer. I don't want to impose on you."

What he wanted was to go to her, take her in his arms, and remove all her fears, to stroke and kiss away everything that weighed so heavily on her. But that would have to wait. As would the dancing.

Elaine bridled her mare. Then she hesitated. She had to pass Timothy to leave the stable. Her face drained of color again, and her eyes flickered.

Timothy moved away from the door. He calmly walked over to Fellow, intentionally leaving space between himself and the girl.

Elaine relaxed visibly. She led Banshee out, and then stopped once she believed herself be out of harm's way.

"Mr. Lambert? About before . . . with your father. Thank you."

She did not give him a chance to reply or ask her any questions. Timothy could only watch as she swung up on her horse in front of the tent and rode off.

A strange girl. But Timothy was almost happy as he returned to the festival grounds. She had spoken to him. And someday he would put his arms around her and dance with her. At their wedding.

9

Kura Martyn had realized long ago that she'd made a mistake. It had been wrong of her to snub Gwyneira, and running away had made everything worse. She had taken to cursing her stupid pride every day. She could have long since been in England, either performing or continuing her study of music. Either way, she would not have been wasting her time struggling on her own through the South Island's most remote backwaters. It was no longer a matter of artistic fulfillment, but of sheer survival. Kura did not plan any more concerts or have any more posters printed. Most of the small towns she passed through did not even have town halls or hotels through whose rooms well-reputed citizens led their festively attired wives. As a rule, there was only a pub—that with luck would boast a piano. Kura hardly even got upset anymore when the instrument was desperately out of tune. Sometimes there was not even that. In those cases, she would sing without accompaniment or, recalling her Maori roots, she would play the drum or the *koauau* flute between her vocal performances. This music was considerably better received by the small-town locals than her operatic repertoire.

Once, a few Maori shepherds even invited her to sing and play for their tribe. Kura enjoyed this concert, which took place in conjunction with the tribe's *tohunga*. Accompanied by musicians on *putorino* flutes, she performed various *haka*. At the end, the tribe honored her with a gift of a *putorino* of her own, and from then on, Kura incorporated the unusual instrument into her performances as well. She had learned to play it from her mother, and she could even conjure the *wairua* voice. The elusive technique had always come easily to her, but then again, she had begun as a little girl.

Unfortunately, her listeners were not very appreciative of the art-istry involved. Because even if they preferred Maori music to opera, what the men really wanted to hear whenever Kura entered a pub were the songs of their homeland. So Kura sang ballads and Irish and Welsh drinking songs, irritated by her audience, which occasionally sang along or danced. The money she made from her efforts was only enough to keep her and her horse alive.

Kura had to deal endlessly with presumptuous men who believed that a singer was naturally also a whore. She spoke with a silver tongue to honorable matrons who rented rooms, but not to "wandering entertainers." She tried to convince pastors that she would introduce their flocks to valuable culture if she could use their church hall to that end, free of charge if possible. Sometimes she even gave concerts in village churches proper. Had she really once believed it beneath her dignity to give the Bach oratorio in Haldon?

After almost a year on her own, Kura was worn-out. She did not want to be on the road anymore; she did not want to pull more clothes clammy from rain out of her mud-covered suitcase. And she did not want to negotiate with sleazy bar owners ever again.

Occasionally, she considered settling down somewhere, at least for a few months. If only she could find a proper engagement. That was only an option, however, if she was prepared to entertain the men in other ways too.

"Why don't you just do it?" asked a girl in Westport who was probably twenty, but who looked forty. "A girl like you'd make money hand over fist. You could choose the fellows you went to bed with."

As far as that went, Kura sometimes felt almost tempted. She missed making love. She often yearned for a solid male body. She dreamed of William almost every night, and on long journeys across the country she daydreamed about him. Where could he be now? He had long since left Kiward Station. With Heather Witherspoon? Kura could not imagine that Heather Witherspoon would be able to hold onto him for very long. William had been a mistake for Kura too, and yet she still believed she could be happy with him. If only it had not been for that farm, goddamned Kiward Station. The farm had taken William from her.

If it had just been the two of them, they would have settled in London ages ago, and Kura would be celebrating resounding success. She dreamed of performances in front of packed houses and nights in William's arms. Roderick had never been able to hold a candle to him. Or Tiare. During her visit to the Maori camp near Nelson, stimulated by an evening of music and song, and, moreover, by the sensual dancing of the Maori, she had given in to her longing and shared her bed with a young man. It had been pleasant but nothing more. It did not compare to the ecstasy she had felt with William. As for the men at her concerts—the generally homesick sailors and miners who tried to impress her—a few had lovely, well-exercised bodies. But they were dirty from working in the mines or stank of blubber and fish. Kura had not yet been able to overcome her reluctance, though a few dollars more would sometimes have been extremely welcome.

The girl in Westport took Kura's silence for serious consideration. "This place here is the worst, of course," she noted. "Not up to your class. I'm getting outta here soon myself. But there's supposed to be a proper brothel in Greymouth. Belongs to some lady, they say, another moll naturally, but now she runs a hotel. She's supposed to've whored out here herself before, but back when this place wasn't so run-down."

Kura didn't think "a proper brothel" would be falling all over itself for the Westport girl, but she didn't say anything. Greymouth was already on her route, so she would hardly be able to avoid the woman's pub anyway. She was hoping for something else from the town, however. She remembered Greymouth from her first tour with the ensemble. At the time, she had stayed in one of the nicer hotels on the quay. The town notables—mine owners and businessmen—had paid homage to her, and the group had received several standing ovations. And Kura most of all. The hotel owners might remember her.

Kura headed into Greymouth in the best of spirits, but she had a very different impression of the place this time. Greymouth was no clean, idyllic town lined mostly with decent hotels and respectable bourgeois homes. Of course, Kura did not arrive by ferry from across the Grey River this time, but up the coastal road from Westport. As a result, the first thing she passed was the miners' camps, followed by the dilapidated city center, which consisted of a meager row of wooden buildings, smaller stores, a barber, and a coffin maker. The whore in Westport had clearly exaggerated about the brothel—the Wild Rover looked just as inhospitable and seedy as the rest of the bars on the West Coast.

Kura was relieved when she found herself in the more respectable parts of town again and rejoiced when she came upon the facades of the elegant hotels. However, when she asked about work, she was quickly disappointed. One artist, on her own? Without the endorsement of some respected member of the community or a concert agent? A girl, granted a beautiful one, but in threadbare clothes with a few flutes for props? One after the other, the hoteliers turned her down with a thank-you and suggested that Kura would do better to try her luck in the miners' quarter.

Crestfallen and humiliated, Kura slunk away. She had hit rock bottom. It could hardly get any worse. She had to make a decision soon. To crawl back to Gwyneira on her knees or to sink even lower and sell her body.

For the time being, she directed her step to the Wild Rover. She had to eat after all.

The pub's owner introduced himself as Paddy Holloway. His establishment was as shabby inside as out. The counter was sticky and grimy, the walls last painted many years before. The barroom stank of stale beer from the day before, and the piano looked like it hadn't been played for a hundred years, let alone tuned. Paddy Holloway himself looked anything but well-groomed. He had apparently yet to shave that day, and his stubble revealed traces of grease, beer, and sauce. The only thing that set the short, rotund man apart from most of the other bar owners Kura had come across was his blatant enthusiasm for the idea of having Kura perform in his establishment. And for him, it actually seemed to be about the music. True, he looked at Kura lustfully, but almost every man did that. Kura had gotten used to being shown the door when she did not prove to be suitably compliant. Paddy Holloway, however, rushed about her as though he were receiving a visit from the Queen herself.

"Of course you can sing here. It'd be a pleasure, miss. The piano's not the best, but if you decide to extend your stay, I'd get you a new one right quick. You wouldn't care for a longer . . . whaddaya call 'em . . . engagement! Would you?"

Kura was astonished. Had she misheard or was the barkeep offering her a respite from the tiny shows and life on the road? Without any grand ulterior motives either, since it looked like he only operated a bar and not a brothel.

"You see, I've been looking for a pianist for a long time," he continued excitedly. "And then one blows right in through the door. And such a pretty one too. And you sing, miss? They don't have that at the Lucky Horse! The boys'll flock to us in swarms."

Kura was only half listening. She was tired and felt run-down. She would have liked to collapse straight into bed rather than sing at all that night. It was only a question of what bed. All of her instincts, honed by her time on the road, told her it was better not to sleep under the same roof as Paddy Holloway, even if he offered her a room just then. The fellow was an odd one anyway. Why was he looking for a girl who played piano? Most barroom pianists were men. If Paddy needed someone, he would only have had to advertise in Christchurch or Blenheim.

The Lucky Horse seemed to be the only competition—probably the cathouse the girl in Westport had mentioned. Kura considered whether she should ask around there first before signing on with Paddy Holloway. But she was too exhausted for that. She would be happy enough if she succeeded in scaring up an acceptable room and entertaining the Wild Rover's customers enough to be able to afford it.

"Could you play something for me, miss?"

Kura's persistent silence seemed to be irritating the proprietor now. Was he buying a pig in a poke?

Kura sat down on the rickety piano bench and played "Für Elise."
That did not appear to be to Paddy's taste. So he wasn't a true, highly
educated music lover that fickle fortune had driven into this backwater.
That hardly came as a surprise to Kura. She had long since stopped
believing in such fairy tales. She mostly trusted her first impressions
and was rarely disappointed that way. It did not matter what Heather
Witherspoon had told her when she was a child. A frog was a frog,
not a prince.

The owner made a face and interrupted her performance.

"Sounds a little dead," he remarked. "Can't you play anything
livelier? Something Irish? 'The Wild Rover' maybe?"

Kura had grown rather accustomed to people speaking to her
overly familiarly after the third sentence and no longer got upset about
it. Nevertheless, she marshaled all her pride once more and sang the
"Habanera" from *Carmen* instead of the requested drinking song.

Against all expectations, Paddy Holloway was rather taken by it.

"You can really sing," he said enthusiastically. "And you can play
the piano too. I'd almost say even better than that timid little Lainie
Keefer at Madame Clarisse's. What do you say? Three dollars a week?"

Kura thought about it for a moment. That was more than she
usually made. If she stayed there for a few weeks, she could recover
a bit and think her future through. There was only the question of
suitable lodgings. And surely, there must be some money to be made
on top of that.

"Nothing less than four dollars," she finally told the owner and
did her eyelash-batting routine.

Paddy Holloway nodded willingly. He would have offered her
five dollars, no question.

"And twenty percent of every drink the boys buy me," Kura added.

The bar owner nodded again. "But tea instead of whiskey," he
specified. "If you want real liquor, I won't make anything."

Kura sighed. She did not want cold, unsweetened tea, but right at
that moment, that didn't matter. "Then we're in business. But I still
need lodging. I don't intend to live here in the pub."

Paddy Holloway had no idea who was renting rooms in town. When he had customers who were on the road, he let them sleep in the stables—after an evening in the Wild Rover, they couldn't tell a pile of straw from a bed anyway. He explained to Kura with a grin that the nearby "hotel" was out of the question, his facial expression telling her everything she needed to know. Kura had expected as much. When it came to hotels, she no longer hoped for respectable but affordable establishments like the White Hart in Christchurch.

Since Paddy could not be of further help, she took her leave and set about looking for a place to stay. Maybe there would be a sign on the street somewhere that pointed the way to rooms for rent.

Kura made her way slowly through town on her horse and quickly located the Lucky Horse. She noted its freshly painted colorful facade, well-swept porch, clean windows, and the sign over the entrance: Inn. The girl in Westport had been right. Though it was without question a pub with a whorehouse attached, it was decidedly among the best of its kind.

Kura felt a pang of regret. The Lucky Horse looked a great deal more attractive than the Wild Rover. Could she never do anything right? She wearily guided her horse to the stables and arranged proper lodging for her horse at least. As in most towns, the stable owner was able to help her find lodging for herself. Kura thanked him, took her suitcase and sought out Greymouth's two private renters. She felt good about her prospects, having had a good deal of experience wrapping ladies like that around her little finger by then. She decided to see the widow Miller first, while holding Mrs. Tanner's rooms in reserve. Mrs. Tanner was the barber's wife after all, and married women were loath to take Kura into their homes.

Mrs. Miller melted as the young woman described her triumphs as a singer. Mrs. Miller had once heard an opera in England when she was young and could still talk about it at length. The local priest, too, she assured Kura, was a great lover of music. No doubt he would he let her use the church for a concert. Of course, Mrs. Miller would rent this beautiful, well-bred girl a room. Kura didn't mention the Wild Rover for the time being.

It wasn't long before the people of Greymouth were talking about her; her first evening in the pub created a furor. Kura was astounded. Sure, men ate from the palm of her hand; that had always been the case. She was all but drowning in song requests and double entendres. But more than anything, the men seemed to be making comparisons. Kura was so much prettier than Miss Keefer, some of them commented, and what was more, she could sing. Others seemed to be taking bets on whether the Rover would be filled with regulars of the Horse the following Saturday.

"Even Tim Lambert will probably wander over," one coal miner remarked, and the others could hardly contain their laughter. "This one sings. She by necessity opens her mouth twice as often as Miss Keefer."

Only one slender blond man seemed more interested in Kura's music than how she compared with "Madame Clarisse's timid little mouse," as Paddy liked to put it. Kura had noticed him as soon as he entered. He was considerably better dressed than the other customers, and the miners, instead of greeting him amiably, eyed him with suspicion. The owner, on the other hand, welcomed him in a manner bordering on reverence.

"Would you like to place any bets, Mr. Biller?" Paddy inquired. That, too, was strange. He had called all his other regulars by their first names. "We're having a dogfight on Saturday. And there's a race in Wellington on Sunday. I have the starting list right here. All of it is very reliable, as you know, sir. We'll have the results by Monday evening. I still haven't been able to convince Jimmy Farrier to tap out the telegrams on Sunday."

"Monday's fine," the young man said in a distracted tone. "Just leave the program here, and bring me a whiskey, single malt."

A few of the men sitting nearby rolled their eyes. Single malt—that stuff cost a fortune.

The young man spent the next few hours slowly drinking three glasses of whiskey, watching Kura all the while. That did not surprise her, as she was used to that sort of admiration. What took her aback was the look in the man's eyes. Though he observed her face, hair, clothes, and her fingers dancing over the piano keys with interest, he did not have a lascivious look in his eyes. Instead, he appeared to be appraising her objectively. Sometimes she got the impression he wanted to get up and come talk to her, but then he would change his mind. Was he shy? He didn't seem like he was. He neither flushed at every provocation, nor drank to bolster his courage, nor grinned idiotically when Kura looked over at him.

Finally, Kura decided to draw him out of his seat. The man looked like an indubitably well-bred concertgoer interested in the technical aspects of her performance. Perhaps he knew how to appreciate talent. Indeed, he was all but gaping when she sang the "Habanera." He finally approached her.

"Bravo!" he said enthusiastically. "That was *Carmen*, wasn't it? Wonderful, simply wonderful. You sang it last year when you visited with the Greenwood ensemble. At first, I wasn't sure it was you. But now, that voice . . ."

The man looked almost ecstatic, but Kura felt a little insulted. Could she have changed so much that a concertgoer from a year ago could not recognize her? What was more, a *man*? Normally she made an unforgettable impression on men.

In the end, Kura decided to blame it on her makeup. Every entertainer had made themselves up heavily before going onstage, and, as Carmen, she had worn her hair up whereas she was now wearing it down. Perhaps that was what had confused the man. In any event, she gave him a gracious smile.

"How flattering that you remember me."

The young man nodded energetically. "Oh of course, and I remember your name too. Kura Marsten, was it not?"

"Martyn," she said, correcting him, but nevertheless impressed. A peculiar man. He remembered her voice, her name—but not her face?

"I thought you a great talent even back then. But I thought the troupe had returned to England awhile ago. My name is Caleb Biller, by the way. Forgive me for not immediately . . ."

The man bowed as though neglecting to introduce himself before exchanging a few words with her had been a major faux pas.

Kura took a closer look at him. He was tall, slim, and quite handsome; his face was perhaps a little pale and expressionless, almost childishly innocent. His lips were thin but well shaped, and he had high cheekbones and blue eyes. Everything about Caleb Biller looked a little colorless. He had, however, been well brought up.

Kura smiled again.

"Is there any song in particular you'd like me to sing for you, Mr. Biller?" she asked. Perhaps he would order her a single malt too. For twenty percent of a drink in that price range, she could get used to drinking cold tea.

"Miss Martyn, every song that comes from your lips thrills me," Caleb said politely. "But, tell me, what is that?"

He was pointing at the *putorino* Kura had laid on the piano.

"Is that one of those Maori flutes? I've never held anything like it before. May I?"

Kura nodded, at which Caleb carefully picked up the instrument and cast an expert eye over it.

"Would you play something on it?" he asked. "I would love to hear it, especially the spirit voice."

"*Wairua*?" Kura smiled. "I can't make any promises here, as the spirits do not generally pass through pubs. It's beneath their dignity."

Telling a few mysterious stories about the spirit voice always went over well. Yet in secret Kura wondered how he knew about the spirit voice. Only a few *pakeha* knew about the instrument's peculiarities. This young man here must be interested in Maori culture.

Kura stood up and played a simple song, first in the high-pitched female voice of the instrument. A few customers booed. Without question, the majority wanted to hear more drinking songs, not Maori music.

"Without accompaniment, it sounds a little thin," Kura said apologetically.

Caleb nodded fervently. "Yes, I see. May I?"

He gestured to the piano bench, and a confused Kura made room for him. Right away, he began playing a lively accompaniment. Kura followed him with the flute, switching from the female to the male range, to which Caleb responded with lower notes. When they finished, the miners applauded.

"You don't play the tin whistle by chance?" a drunken Irishman asked.

Kura rolled her eyes.

"But perhaps you could play something else in the style of the Maori?" Caleb inquired. "Their music fascinates me. And the dancing, the *haka*. Wasn't it originally a war dance?"

Kura explained a few peculiarities of Maori music to him and sang an illustrative song. Caleb seemed excited. Paddy Holloway less so, however.

"Now stop that racket," he yelled, decidedly upset after three songs. "The men want to hear something lighthearted. They get enough whining from their wives."

Kura exchanged a look of commiseration with Caleb Biller and returned to the drinking songs. The young man did not stay long after that.

"I must take my leave," he said politely, bowing again formally to Kura. "It was exceptionally stimulating to be permitted to listen to you, and I would very much like to do it again when an opportunity presents itself. How long will you be staying in Greymouth?"

Kura explained to him that she planned to stay in town for at least a few weeks. Caleb expressed his delight.

"Then we'll most certainly find an opportunity to make music together," he remarked. "But now I must be on my way. I have to be up early in the morning. The mine."

Caleb left unsaid to what degree the mine was dependent on him but bowed once again and disappeared.

Kura decided to ask Paddy about him. The opportunity soon presented itself when he placed another "whiskey" on the piano for her.

"That fellow a miner?"

Paddy roared with laughter. "No, dear, he's on the other side. The Biller Mine belongs to his dad, one of the two biggest private mines in town and one of the oldest in the district to boot. Very rich family. If you land that one, you're set. Doesn't seem to be easy though. They say he don't like girls."

A few months before, this explanation would have confused Kura, but after the tour with Roderick's ensemble, she had learned about life's diversity.

"He seems to be interested in music," she said.

Paddy grinned. "A nail in the coffin of his old man. The boy's interested in just about anything except coal mining. He would have liked to study medicine, but in the end, they settled on geology. Devil knows what that is, but it's supposed to have something to do with coal. The foremen say the younger Biller knows nothing about mining and is a good-for-nothing as a businessman too. And if he bets on a horse, you can be sure it'll come in last. That boy'll be costing his old man money until hell freezes over."

"But does he come to the pub often?" Kura asked. In her experience, regular visits to the pub did not fit with a man who avoided the society of women. Men seemed to recognize such proclivities in other men immediately and singled the bearer of those proclivities out for universal ridicule. Sometimes, there were even serious hostilities. A dancer in Roderick's group had once been beaten in a pub.

Paddy shrugged. "Every now and then, he'll walk in and place a few bets. I don't know if that's what he really feels like doing or if his daddy chases him out of the house. Occasionally, they stop in together, and then the old man buys a few rounds for everyone and acts chummy. But that seems to be more awkward for the boy than anything. When he comes alone, he drinks his malt whiskey—I always keep a bottle ready for him—and doesn't talk to anyone. Strange guy.

Makes you almost feel sorry for the elder Biller. But like I said, keep at it! The post of Mrs. Biller is still up for grabs."

Kura rolled her eyes. Trading her sheep farm in the Canterbury Plains for a mine in Greymouth did not appeal to her in the slightest. Whatever problems Caleb Biller had—Kura-maro-tini was not interested.

10

The relationship between Elaine and Timothy had, according to a gossipy Matt Gawain, markedly improved since the Saint Barbara's Day race. Their recent evening exchange of greetings no longer consisted entirely of "Good evening, Miss Keefer" and "Good evening, Mr. Lambert." Instead, Timothy braved a "Good evening, Lainie," which was answered with a more or less indifferent "Good evening, Timothy."

"If things keep up like this," Ernie Gast chimed in with a grin, "it won't be five years before you're allowed to sit next to her in church."

Timothy Lambert let his friends tease him. He himself felt— and had provoked—many subtle alterations in their interactions. For example, after Saint Barbara's Day, he had ceased to request "Silver Dagger" every night. Instead, he asked for a different ballad—"John Riley"—which was about a young sailor who, after seven years at sea, finally woos his beloved.

At first, Elaine had thought it was just a passing mood. But after three days, she asked him.

"'John Riley' again? What happened to 'Silver Dagger,' Timothy?" Elaine looked a little braver and more approachable that day. It was the Saturday after the race, and Timothy had ordered a round for everyone in the Lucky Horse to celebrate his win and hers.

"To our beautiful Lainie, the real winner of the Lambert Derby!"

Naturally, Elaine had been expected to drink with them, and was now tipsy. She had even eyed Timothy a bit mischievously over the piano when he placed his musical request.

Timothy laughed and winked at her conspiratorially.

"The 'Silver Dagger'? Oh, I'd rather you learned to do without it, Lainie. It would make me nervous to have my wife always carrying a dagger around."

Elaine frowned. "Your wife?"

Timothy nodded seriously. "Yes, Lainie. I've decided to marry you."

Elaine, who had been just about to take a sip of tea from her whiskey glass, almost dropped it.

"Why?" she asked flatly.

Timothy rescued the glass. "Watch out for that good whiskey of yours. I think I might have to order you a real one. You look a little pale."

"Why?" she repeated. The continuous alternating of her face between flush and pale reflected her inner turmoil.

"Well," Timothy finally said, his eyes twinkling as he spoke, "I've had my eye on you for a few weeks. You're beautiful, you're smart, you're brave, you're the woman I've dreamed about my whole life. I've fallen in love with you, Lainie. Should I get down on my knee in front of you now, or shall we wait a bit?"

Fear shone in Elaine's eyes, which she suppressed only with great effort.

"I'm not in love," she blurted out.

Timothy nodded.

"That's what I thought," he said calmly. "But that will change. And I'm not looking for a straw fire. Just take your time falling in love, Lainie. Don't get all worked up."

"Not in this lifetime!" Elaine's voice now sounded a bit shrill. She hid herself behind her curtain of hair and lowered her head over the piano keys. Timothy was concerned. If he didn't manage to draw her out of her reserve now, he was afraid she would withdraw back into her shell.

Timothy pursed his lips, but his eyes smiled. "That makes things a little more difficult, of course," he said. "I'll have to talk to the priest about our prospects for getting married after the resurrection. Perhaps we'll exchange our vows on a cloud? And yet I imagine a married life like that would be rather monotonous. And indiscreet. I wouldn't care to have the whole world eyeing me on the cloud."

He cast a side glance at Elaine, who was sitting up straight now.

"So it might work out better if we picked a different religion," he continued. "One that grants us more than one life. They believe in reincarnation somewhere. In India, right?"

Elaine blinked behind her hair. "But you'd probably be born again as an animal. As a horse or a dog."

Her voice sounded normal again. She had clearly decided not to take Timothy and his proposal seriously.

Timothy sighed with relief and laughed. "That would be pretty romantic too. I can picture it now: a couple that doesn't find its way together in life on two legs is reunited in the stables. Like Fellow and Banshee."

Elaine had gotten ahold of herself and found her wit to boot. She brushed her hair from her face and gave Timothy Lambert a sweet if dishonest smile. "Then watch out that someone doesn't make a gelding out of you by mistake," she said loudly.

Timothy let the roaring laughter of the men wash over him and ignored all the other mockery brought on by his apparently hopeless flirting. He lived for these moments, when Elaine's true self flared up from behind her facade. Lively, intelligent, and mocking, but sensual and loving too. Her defensive walls would collapse someday. And Timothy would be there when they did.

"Who's going to sacrifice himself and go spy on the Wild Rover?" Madame Clarisse was asking around just as Timothy sat down at his regular table where Ernie, Jay, and Matt were already sitting.

All the customers could talk about that day was the mysterious new pianist in the pub down the street. It was supposedly some Maori girl with the voice of an angel. That seemed as strange to Madame Clarisse as it did to those few among her customers who had seen a bit more of the world than most miners. Maori girls did not generally learn to play the piano, and they rarely traveled alone outside of their tribe. Even in the brothels, one rarely came across a Maori girl, though there were a few girls of mixed birth with tragic histories.

Madame Clarisse's curiosity had been awakened. The restless bordello owner set a pitcher of beer down in the middle of their table and filled the men's glasses, grinning at them. "Of course, I'm only speaking to the morally sound and devoted regulars of the Lucky Horse. Anyone else exposed to Paddy Holloway would run the risk of falling into gambling. I could never look the pastor in the eye again if I let that happen." Madame Clarisse clutched her hand to her heart theatrically.

"That the boys might become regulars over there never crossed your mind, of course," Matt teased her. "You're only worried about our eternal souls, isn't that right, Madame Clarisse? Thank you, we appreciate the concern."

"But what about fornication, Madame Clarisse?" Jay inquired. "Isn't that a sin too?" The smith looked at her with apparent sincerity, clutching his hand fearfully to his own heart.

Madame Clarisse could only shake her head disapprovingly. "Where is this fornication happening, Jay?" she demanded with a note of moral outrage. "I only see a group of marriageable young gals gettin' to know in their openhearted way a group of marriageable young men. I manage a highly successful matchmaking service. Just last month, I lost another girl. And what's with you and Charlene, Matt? There's sparks there; admit it. And don't forget Mr. Lambert and Lainie."

The men snickered. Charlene, who had just been about to sit down next to Matt, blushed. Something did indeed seem to be developing there.

Timothy raised his beer glass to Madame Clarisse. "In that respect," he said with a grin, "Mr. Gawain and I are sound enough for an evening at Paddy Holloway's. Tomorrow we'll embark on a secret mission."

Elaine only caught scraps of the conversation, but she too had heard of the Maori singer at the Wild Rover, of course, which caused the image of her cousin to flash unavoidably before her eyes. But that could not be. Kura lived with William on Kiward Station. And she would never lower herself to singing in a bar for coal miners.

Kura derived little joy from her job at the Wild Rover. The customers were difficult. The men drank more as the weekend approached, making them correspondingly importunate. Paddy Holloway only halfheartedly kept them from touching her. He evidently didn't want to offend anyone and was very lenient with the boys as a result. Kura had to fend him off too when she didn't manage to slip out of the pub with the last wave of guests at closing time.

The only bright spots were the almost daily visits of Caleb Biller—though the young man still puzzled her as much as ever. Caleb always appeared early in the evening, apparently drinking to give himself more courage before coming over to join her in playing music. If the pub was not packed, and the men did not protest, Paddy allowed Kura to play the *putorino* while Caleb took over the piano accompaniment or to sing traditional Maori songs that Caleb would take and transform into ballads. Kura's respect for Caleb grew from one day to the next. He was highly gifted without question. He was quite a decent pianist, but as an arranger and composer, he had an extraordinary talent. Kura liked working with him and wondered whether there might be other opportunities to do so away from the sleazy Wild Rover and its out-of-tune piano.

One Friday afternoon, several hours before the pubs would open, Kura made her way to the Lucky Horse. From outside she could hear someone playing the piano—though it wasn't exactly what she would have expected to hear in a pub. Someone was practicing church songs. Rather ambitiously too. The pianist was attempting Bach's *Easter Oratorio*—and doing a mediocre job of it. A few months earlier, Kura would have accused it of being "horrendous." Since then, however, she had learned that she had always set the bar too high. Most people did not share her pursuit of artistic perfection. Kura had always known that, but it no longer filled her with pride and disdain. Perfect pitch and musical perfection did not sell around here. She had been blessed with a gift no one knew how to appreciate. And so there was no reason to puff herself up about it too much.

Kura pushed the swing door open and entered Madame Clarisse's establishment. Everything was as tidy and clean as she had expected, the tables scrubbed, the floor swept—and off to the side, a red-haired girl was sitting at the piano.

Kura did not believe her eyes. She froze, but the pianist seemed already to have noticed her.

Elaine turned. She blinked, as though hoping to drive away an illusion. But the girl standing before her in a worn-out red traveling outfit was Kura, without a doubt. A little slimmer perhaps, somewhat paler—her face no longer as haughty but more determined and harder. But her skin tone remained flawless, her hair glossy, and her eyes as captivating as ever. Her voice, too, was as finely modulated as always.

"You?" Kura asked, her eyes widening in surprise. "I thought you were married somewhere in Otago?"

"And I thought you were living happily ever after with William on Kiward Station!"

Elaine was determined not to let Kura browbeat her. Her first impulse had once more been to act small and humbled, but then she felt her long-suppressed anger rising within her, against Kura, the cousin who had so casually destroyed her life.

"What do you want, Kura Warden? Or rather, Kura Martyn? Let me guess. You don't like it over at the Wild Rover. First you took my lover, and now you want my job!"
Elaine glared at her.

Kura rolled her eyes.
"You've always been too sentimental, Lainie," she said, sneering. "And a little too possessive. 'My lover,' 'my job.' And yet William never belonged to you. And this job here . . ." Kura let her gaze pass derisively over the furnishings of the Lucky Horse. "Well, it's not exactly the most prestigious post in the British Empire, wouldn't you say?"

Elaine did not know how to reply. She felt only a surge of instinctual rage, and for the first time since that awful morning on Lionel Station, she wished she had a weapon. Although this was the moment she most needed her confidence, she instead found herself begging—and she hated herself for it.

"Kura, I need this job! You can sing anywhere."

Kura smiled. "But maybe I want to sing *here*," she answered. "And the wife of Thomas Sideblossom certainly doesn't need a job in a whorehouse."

Elaine balled her fists helplessly. But then she heard a sound on the stairs. Charlene was on her way downstairs and must have caught those last words.

Elaine's blazing fury turned into ice-cold terror. *The wife of Thomas Sideblossom*. If Charlene had heard those words and told Madame Clarisse . . .

Charlene, however, only looked Kura up and down, using the steps to full advantage. The buxom, dark-haired harlot assessed the potential competition mercilessly and without shame.

"Who's this, Lainie?" she asked nonchalantly, without deigning to greet the newcomer. "The replacement for Chrissie Hamilton? I'm sorry, dear, but Madame Clarisse is looking for a blonde. We have enough black-haired girls. Unless you can do something special." Charlene licked her lips.

Kura flared up at her. "I'm a singer," she said, incensed. "I don't need to—"

"Aha, the Maori girl who bangs away on the piano at Holloway's." Charlene rolled her eyes. "That is, of course, the springboard for international success. You know how to pick your jobs, sweetness, I'll give you that. You clearly have excellent taste."

Kura had regained her composure. She had never been shy, and in Roderick's ensemble she had learned to make herself heard. Especially among women.

"I'd be happy to play for you if you have any say in what happens around here," she said. "I fear, however, that you're just another whore."

Charlene shrugged. "And you're just another piano player. Sure, we might be better than average, but the customer'll only notice in bed. In my case anyways; he won't notice at all in yours. For the boys here, one set of ivories is as good as another. So don't get melodramatic. Scoot off to your dream job now. Madame Clarisse won't have anything to do with girls who make scenes as soon as they step through the door."

Kura turned around, her head raised regally. "I'll be seeing you, Elaine," she said.

Just then Charlene flew down the remaining stairs with lightning speed, flitted past her, and blocked Kura from walking out the door. Her gaze was cold with anger, her fingers bent into claws.

"Her name is Lainie," she said calmly. "Lainie Keefer. She isn't anyone's wife, never was. So don't be spreading lies, and we won't talk about you, either. Because you're running from something too, same as all of us, lovely. And if I want to, I'll rat out what it is you're running from. Besides," Charlene extended her claws, "beauty isn't everlasting."

Kura glared at her. But she fled and gave up any thought of ever speaking to the madam of the Lucky Horse again. She had never met a girl like Charlene before, but she had heard the dancers talk about them. Girls who fixed their dance shoes so they would slip and fall. Girls who scratched their rival's face, slept with their partners, and convinced the boys to drop them during dangerous routines. And Charlene was not the only one. Madame Clarisse's whole brothel might be filled with aggressive filth defending their position. And Elaine's.

Elaine burst into tears as soon as Kura had left.

"I didn't want to . . . I wanted to throw her out straightaway or rip her hair out. But it was all so sudden, and she . . ."

"She's an ice-cold beast," Charlene declared, taking her friend in her arms. "But don't worry. Whoever you were married to and whatever your real name is, I won't tell a soul. And you can be sure that little goat won't either. I scared her. Besides, Madame Clarisse couldn't care less. She likes you. And I like you. And the customers like you, and Tim likes you."

Charlene rocked the convulsively sobbing Elaine in her arms like a child. She had felt the girl relaxing at first and then how she tensed up the moment Charlene mentioned Timothy Lambert's name. Charlene sighed. If only she had known earlier that there was history between Elaine and this Maori girl. Though this Kura was certainly not pure Maori—one of her parents must have been white. Those eyes alone! And unless Charlene was completely mistaken, she shared some vague similarities with Elaine. Charlene considered whether she should ask right now or whether it was better to wait until Elaine had calmed down. That might take some time. Though the girl was no longer crying, she still seemed preoccupied. She claimed that she wanted to practice for her Easter performance at the church, but she sat motionless at the piano, staring into space. Charlene brought her some hot tea, followed by a proper whiskey.

"Here, you look like a ghost. Drink that. That Tim of yours will be coming later and then you can horse around. Speaking of which, that was sweet yesterday, flirting about being horses in the next life. Now give us a laugh, Lainie."

Elaine drank, but she did not think she would find anything to laugh about that day. Timothy Lambert was going to the Wild Rover that night, and he would stay there. As would Matt Gawain. Once they saw Kura, the men would forget Elaine and Charlene at once. She asked herself vaguely why that bothered her. After all, she should be glad to be rid of Timothy—hadn't she complained often enough about his being too persistent?

Just as she was supposed to, Elaine started to play when the customers began to arrive. But she played mechanically and distractedly, and the men appeared to notice. That evening, there were hardly any drinks for Elaine and no music requests. Elaine only vaguely registered the fact, but it hardly surprised her. After all, Kura-maro-tini was playing a few houses down the street. Why would people want to listen to her?

Elaine's face was pale and indifferent. She seemed to be looking through the piano and the pub's wall—into other worlds and other times. Closing time approached agonizingly slowly. All Elaine wanted to do was disappear into her little room, bury herself under the blankets with Callie in her arms, and put the day behind her. The next day she would have to make plans. Maybe another town, another pub. But no other Timothy Lambert.

"Good evening, Lainie," Timothy's cheerful voice pulled her out of her lethargy.

Elaine broke off from the piece she had been playing and turned around in disbelief. "Good evening, Timothy."

Her voice sounded flat.

Timothy Lambert looked at her inquisitively. "Is something wrong, Lainie?"

Elaine shook her head. "It's only . . . It's nothing," she said decisively, and she began to play again. She felt the color returning to her cheeks, and her heart beat wildly. Then she remembered that Timothy had to stop by the Lucky Horse one way or another. After all, he had promised to inform Madame Clarisse. Elaine hoped to catch a few words of what he said to her, but Friday evenings were very loud in the pub. Madame Clarisse betrayed her curiosity by immediately indicating a table to Timothy and Matt and bringing them a bottle of whiskey. A bottle of the good stuff.

"I'm sorry that took so long," Timothy said to Madame Clarisse, sniffing the expensive drink with pleasant surprise. "But we ran into Caleb Biller and, naturally, used the opportunity to sound him out about his dad's mine." They must have drunk some whiskey while they did so as they appeared less than fully sober.

"Yeah, old man Biller is having all of his air shafts renovated," Matt reported. "They had a gas leak a little while back, and Biller's been scared stiff ever since. Little Caleb was whining about how he had to oversee the whole project."

"Whereas we'd be *thrilled* to oversee something like that if my old man could only bring himself to do the same." Timothy looked despondently into his glass.

Madame Clarisse rolled her eyes. "Boys, did I send you two down to the Rover because I'm so desperate to know about Biller's air shafts? No! So, what about the girl? The little piano player?"

Elaine slumped down. She wondered how much Charlene had told their boss about Kura's afternoon appearance. It was unlikely that she had kept the whole thing to herself.

Timothy shrugged. "She's pretty," he reported.

Matt turned his eyes to the ceiling. "Only someone who's seriously in love could put it that way. Madame Clarisse, the girl is beautiful. When she was born, all the evil fairies must have been out of the room. She's a dream."

Madame Clarisse frowned, and Charlene, who was just then prancing toward the table, glared at him.

"As far as I know," she remarked sarcastically, "most men prefer women made of flesh and blood."

Matt grinned at her. He was obviously enjoying her jealousy.

"Oh, she knows flesh all right, Charlene. When you hear her sing, there's passion there. A volcano beneath a gentle exterior."

"Gentle?" Charlene asked. "Sometimes I wish men weren't so easily fooled."

"Then you wouldn't make as much," Madame Clarisse said, laughing. "But go on, boys, what's all the fuss about? Didn't you boys flirt with her a bit? Who is she and where is she from?"

"Now, now, Madame Clarisse, you wouldn't want us seducing the little thing." Matt was enjoying himself royally. "What kind of language is that anyway? Tim and I would never flirt with a strange woman."

"Besides, we would have had to get past Caleb Biller first," Timothy added. "Which wouldn't be hard. But if he's taken an interest in a girl . . ."

The men laughed, as did those at the next table. The men who came to Madame Clarisse's were predominantly from the Lambert and Blackburn mines. There was a long-standing competition between them and Biller's men that never erupted into open fighting but led

421

to teasing on both sides. The effeminate Caleb Biller was a favorite target.

"She's from the Canterbury area. Though she had not explicitly told Caleb as much, he had inferred it from her history." Timothy coolly told them all he knew about Kura; clearly he had not only sounded Caleb out about his father's mine. "She traveled around with an opera ensemble for a while. South Island, North Island, even Australia. But she didn't want to go with them to England afterward. Or they didn't want to take her. That seems more likely to me. She's been on the move ever since—a tough customer. Caleb is convinced her life is grand, but even if she doesn't complain, you only need to look at where she washed up. The Wild Rover is about the bottom of the barrel. Though she does sing and play really well. She finished by playing together with Caleb. He's not bad either. He plays piano a good deal better than he rides, that's for sure—not to mention mining."

Elaine stopped listening. Of course he was impressed with Kura. And she had gone on to sing opera, even though everyone had doubted she was good enough. But these English musicians had not taken her with them. She could always use that as ammunition if Kura came back this way. She had to learn to fight back! She had to be strong, more like Charlene, who did not seem to make much of Matt's swooning over Kura. Elaine breathed a sigh of relief when the evening came to an end.

That Saturday night was as busy as ever in the pub, and Elaine sat at the piano in her prettiest dress, playing one request after another. She forced herself to be more cheerful—and even smiled when the door opened around nine and Timothy Lambert entered.

It had been raining all day, and he had left his raincoat and sou'wester in the stables. After only the short walk from the stables, the clothes he was wearing were completely soaked through. Timothy laughed and shook himself off like a dog before sauntering over to Elaine. Elaine had to admit he looked handsome, despite his wet hair and the raindrops on his eyelashes, which slowly dripped off by way of his laugh lines. He finally rubbed the water from his face with his shirtsleeve. He seemed carefree, young, and alive.

"Good evening, Lainie."

She nodded at him and felt at once as though a load had been lifted from her. "Good evening, Timothy. Is there something I can play for you?"

Timothy smiled. "You know what I want to hear, Lainie. Conjure up for me again those seven years that John Riley had to wait for his love."

Elaine frowned. "Wasn't John Riley the one who made his love wait?"

Timothy grinned. "Now there's something for you to think about," he said with mock seriousness. "But excuse me for a moment. I have to speak with Matt tonight before he drowns himself in whiskey. He's got reason enough. As do I."

Elaine looked at him inquisitively. "Is there something wrong at the mine?"

Timothy nodded. "My father once again shot down Matt's proposal to widen the air shafts. We only have one new one, and it works well, but if there *is* ever a gas leak, it's much too narrow. And if Caleb Biller can be trusted, we're running an acute risk. Darn it, old man Biller is just as greedy as my father. If *he's* spending money on safety measures . . ." Timothy looked seriously concerned.

"Aren't there those gas masks?" Elaine asked. She had heard of them before and even seen drawings of them in a magazine. The men wearing these protective masks looked like giant, ugly insects.

Timothy was clearly delighted by her interest. "We don't have those either, Lainie. Besides, they wouldn't help much. With gas leaks, the real danger is explosions. It's usually just methane gas, which isn't poisonous, but it's flammable and catches fire quickly. You can only be halfway sure to prevent it by reducing the amount of coal dust in the mine, by sprinkling water for example and securing the air circulation. And we don't do either of those things sufficiently well."

Elaine looked at him with concern. "But you don't go underground that often yourself, do you?"

Timothy beamed. "You've just salvaged my day, Lainie. You're worried about me. That will keep me going for hours."

With those words, he left her and was soon involved in an animated discussion with Matt Gawain. His foreman was close to tendering his resignation. Marvin Lambert had made Matt look ridiculous in front of his men, declaring that improving safety would only be possible by lowering their hourly pay. The miners had to decide if they were hungry or cowardly. Naturally, no one had voted to sacrifice their pay.

Timothy returned to Elaine later, to toast while she gave another great rendition of "John Riley." As the evening had worn on, she had regained her confidence. As far as she could tell, no one had switched from the Lucky Horse to the Wild Rover, and hardly anyone was still talking about the singer in the next pub over. Perhaps it would not do any harm to ask Timothy a few questions. Elaine made an effort to be diplomatic, but her tone sounded provocative.

"Did you request 'John Riley' last night too?" she inquired.

"Last night?" Timothy pretended he had to think about what had been so special about the day before. But then he winked mischievously. "Oh, you mean at the Wild Rover. This evening's just getting better and better. First you're worried about me, and now you're jealous."

Elaine chewed on her upper lip. "No, seriously," she blurted out. "Didn't you think . . . the girl was beautiful?"

Timothy looked at her curiously when he heard the insistence in her voice. The delicate, translucent skin on her face flushed, then turned pale, then flushed again. Her lips trembled slightly, and her eyes flickered.

Timothy wanted to wrap his arm around her shoulders and lay his hand on hers, but he sensed her instinctive reluctance, and he touched the edge of the piano instead.

"Lainie," he said softly, "Of course she's beautiful, and she sings beautifully too. Any man who isn't blind and deaf could tell that. But you're much more beautiful and play much more touchingly, and for that reason, I would never let another girl play 'John Riley' for me."

"But, I'm not as pretty as she. I . . . ." Elaine turned away. If only she had not asked.

"You're prettier to me," Timothy said seriously. "You have to believe that. I want to marry you, after all. That means I'll still think you're pretty when you're seventy years old, gray-haired, and wrinkled."

Elaine hid behind her hair again. "Don't talk like that," she whispered.

Timothy smiled. "You can't deny me that. Now, please play me a cheerful song and forget the girl at the piano in the Wild Rover. I already have."

Elaine brushed her hair back and smiled shyly. She played a few trivial tunes, but people could tell her mind was not on the music. And when Timothy Lambert finally took his leave, a small miracle occurred.

Timothy said his usual "Good night, Lainie," but Elaine took a deep breath and looked at him shyly. Almost afraid of her own courage, she decided to smile.

"Good night, Tim."

Healing

GREYMOUTH

Late 1896–Early 1898

1

Timothy Lambert was in the best of spirits when he rode to his father's mine on Monday. And that despite the fact that they had not yet reached an agreement over the necessary renovations. Timothy had fought fiercely with his father about them on Sunday, but Marvin Lambert considered further investment in the safety of his mine superfluous and declared the elder Biller crazy.

"He's probably blown a gasket with that boy of his playing piano in the pub every night. No wonder the old man is coming up with ideas to keep Junior busy—in something at least vaguely related to coal mining.

Timothy had then suggested that he could start taking piano lessons himself. Maybe they could use him in the pub since his suggestions on matters of workplace safety were unwanted. Why in heaven's name had his father had him study mining engineering if he was just going to ignore every recommendation? The whole conversation had then escalated into their usual discussion about how the mine did not need an engineer as much as it needed a savvy businessman and that Timothy could easily acquire those skills if he would duck into the office more often.

Timothy had been furious, but at that moment, in the bright sunshine that made the landscape around Greymouth appear freshly washed, he forgot his frustrations. Instead, he entertained himself with the thought of what Elaine would say to having him for a piano student, and as he pictured Elaine in his mind's eye, his spirits rose even more. He would see her again that night. He would walk up to her, smile at her, and say "Good evening, Lainie." And maybe she would smile again and call him "Tim." It was a small step forward, but an important one. Perhaps the ice had now broken. Elaine had looked so relaxed and cheerful after he had put to rest her silly ideas about the other pianist.

That was a strange matter, though. Why did the girl react with such panic about a rival she didn't even know? Or was there history between her and this Kura person? It was possible. The Maori girl had traveled around a great deal. Had the opera ensemble brought all of its musicians along from Europe? Maybe Elaine had played piano for the singer and there had been a fight. Perhaps Kura knew who had caused the girl so much pain that she had been afraid of men ever since. Timothy briefly considered speaking to the singer himself, but that struck him as a breach of faith. He could speak to Caleb Biller, however. It was true that the boy was a bit effeminate, but Timothy had nothing against him personally. On the contrary, he was much easier to get along with than his domineering father, and he was not stupid. If Timothy told Caleb about Elaine, perhaps Caleb would cautiously sound out Kura on the subject and then tell Timothy what she had said.

Timothy whistled to himself as Fellow trotted through the miners' camp. He had achieved a few small successes here at least. The streets had been drained for Saint Barbara's Day, and one could travel them easily. The cleanup had also been a step forward for mine safety. There had hardly been any traversable emergency roads to Greymouth before. However, it was not even worth thinking about what would happen if the workers' camp caught fire. Or the mine itself.

Timothy studied the headframe tower and the other mine buildings coming into view with a mixture of pride and repugnance. They could make a model operation out of it, a modern mine with high safety standards, with connections to the rail network. Timothy also had a plethora of ideas about increasing the delivery rate, about new, more efficient delivery techniques, and the expansion of the shafts. He suspected that would have to wait for Marvin's retirement. Nevertheless, his father had agreed to go on another tour that day. At the very least, Timothy wanted to show him from above where ventilation was lacking and what possibilities there were for expanding the shafts—if he was willing to invest the money and labor, that is. Brimming over with vim and high spirits, he almost believed he would convince his father.

Marvin Lambert looked crankily at his son.

"Typical case of Monday disease," he complained. "There's no end to the people skipping work today. Ten percent of the lazybones in the camp didn't show up. The freight-wagon drivers are complaining because their carts are getting stuck in the mud—this damned rain! I should just have built the roads to the train line instead of that street through the camp. And the foreman took off too. Yeah, that's right, took off, without even asking if I thought it proper for him to see to this plank delivery himself, which still hasn't arrived. And then the fellow actually refused to carry on with the face until—"

Timothy's good spirits drained away. "Father, without support beams, he *can't* carry on with the face. I explained that to you yesterday. And the high percentage of sick workers is probably the result of all the rain we've had. It gets to the men's lungs, especially if they're already weak. But the sun is shining today, so they'll be doing better by tomorrow. Just watch, the men'll be here for the next shift. They need the money, you know. But for now, come, Father. You promised you'd look at the plans for the mine expansion."

Marvin Lambert would have liked to finish his tea. Timothy could smell that his father had added a splash of whiskey to it. In the end, however, he gave into his son's importuning and followed him into the bright sunshine.

"Look, Father, you have to think of it like air circulation with an open window. A single window isn't sufficient, nor is a second one on the upper floor of the house. If the entire house is to have fresh air, you need to have several openings. If we continue adding to the face of the shafts, expanding the house so to speak, we have to dig new air shafts. And the greater the risk of a gas leak, the more circulation there has to be. Especially with our weather here. The outside temperature and air pressure play a role as well." Timothy explained all of this patiently, but he doubted his father was listening. The longer his presentation lasted, the more desperate he became to make it clear to his father how complicated and dangerous the network of underground shafts and tunnels really was.

Then he heard a rumbling, almost as though a storm were brewing somewhere. Marvin, too, looked at the sky, irritated, and ducked his head back inside to avoid getting wet. But there wasn't a single cloud over Greymouth, the mountains, or the lake. Timothy was alarmed. That sound wasn't coming from above. It was right under their feet!

"Father, the mine. Something is going on down there. Did you order anything? A blasting? Or . . . you didn't order a shaft expansion, did you? With the old explosives? Is anything out of the ordinary happening today?" Timothy's expression was one of extreme urgency and concern.

Marvin waved his hand calmly. "That young foreman, Josh Kennedy, is extending tunnel nine," he said almost proudly. "He's no hemming-and-hawing do-nothing like Gawain. He was right there when . . ."

Timothy looked alarmed. "When you ordered the extension of tunnel nine? My God, Father, we haven't done any test drilling in tunnel nine! And Matt suspected there were hollow spaces in the rock down there. We have to sound the alarm, Father. Something is going on down there!"

Leaving Marvin standing there, Timothy raced to the mine entrance, but the explosions beat him to it. Though the mine complex continued to look still and unchanged under the spring sky, an infernal noise was erupting beneath the earth. It sounded as though one stick of dynamite after another was going off underground. First once, then a second time, before Timothy reached the entrance of the mine.

Standing at the entrance tunnel, pale with fear, the men who operated the hoisting cage had already set the cage in motion to ascend.

As the cable began to move, there was a third explosion underground.

"That's not right below us," one of the men yelled. "That one's further away, more to the south."

Timothy nodded. "That's tunnel nine. Or it was. There can hardly be much left of it. I hope the men made it out and there weren't any gas or water leaks. I need to get down there. Fetch me a lamp." He looked at the men at the winch. One of them was an old Welsh miner with badly damaged lungs who no longer entered the mine. The other was a young man. Timothy thought he had seen him underground before. "Aren't you normally in tunnel seven? What are you doing up here? Are you sick?"

The man shook his head—and prepared to enter the mine without being asked.

"My wife's pregnant. She thinks the baby's coming today, so the foreman said I should help up here. Tunnel seven was halted anyway because of the shipment of boards, so the foreman told me I could stick close to my wife."

Timothy bit his lip. The unborn child may have just saved his father's life. And now he was putting it in danger again.

"I'm sorry, but you have to come along anyway. It might be too late by the time other help arrives."

Timothy boarded the hoisting cage before the expectant father. The old miner made a motion of prayer, and Timothy caught himself calling out to Saint Barbara. This was a calamitous situation, and the deeper the elevator sank into the mine, the more dire it seemed. With the exception of the noise of the hoisting cage, a deathly silence prevailed underground. Instead of the usual sounds—the constant hammering, the rattling of the carts on the tracks, the shoveling of the spoils, the voices of the sixty to a hundred men working down there—all was quiet.

The young man noticed it too. He looked at Timothy, his eyes wide with fright, and whispered, "My God."

They came upon the first bodies in the relatively wide space in front of the hoisting cage. Two men. They must have been fleeing, but it had been too late to call the elevator.

"Gas," Timothy whispered hoarsely. "It must have been released here, since the ventilation is still functioning here. But they had already breathed in too much of it."

"Could also have been some kind of blast," the young man suggested. "What are we going to do now, sir? Do we continue on?"

Timothy knew the young man would have liked to leave immediately. And he was probably right. If there were dead here, it was highly unlikely that anyone had survived farther into the mine. But what if there were survivors? What if some of them had found air bubbles?

Timothy bit his lip. "I'll take a closer look," he said quietly. "But you can go back up if you want."

The man shook his head. "I'm coming with you. These are my buddies down here."

Timothy nodded. "What's your name?" he asked as they walked through the pitch-black and deathly still shaft.

"Joe Patterson."

The lamps on their helmets bathed the immediate vicinity in a sallow, ghostly twilight.

"Look, there are two more," Joe said.

"Three," Timothy whispered.

It looked as if two of the men had been attempting to support a wounded third.

"Joe, we need to split up to cover ground more quickly. You go to tunnel seven. I'll take nine."

The tunnel forked here. Timothy wondered whether the men had been coming from the right or the left. In the end, he went right. Reluctantly, Joe turned down the left tunnel—continuing alone obviously made him uncomfortable. But there shouldn't have been many men in tunnel seven. Timothy thanked heaven for the wood shipment's delay.

In shaft nine, he found more bodies—and then the first holes. He knew he had found the origin of the explosion, whose blast had dispersed gas and a torrent of rubble all over the place. Silence still reigned. Eventually, Timothy could no longer stand it, and he began to call out.

"Is anyone there? Is anyone still alive?"

And then a young voice, childlike and full of fear, suddenly answered. "I'm over here! Help! Please! I'm over here."

The appeal ended in sobbing.

Timothy grew hopeful again. So there were survivors! "Help's on the way! Just stay calm," he called into the darkness. Even before the explosion, tunnel nine had not been laid out very clearly. The boy could be anywhere. "Where are you exactly? Are you injured?"

"It's so dark!" The boy sounded hysterical. Timothy followed the sound of the voice ever farther down a blind tunnel, hoping the boy had not been trapped under rubble. In their haste, he and Joe had not even brought mining tools down with them. The boy's voice wasn't muffled, and Timothy could tell he was getting closer.

"Stay where you are, boy, but keep talking," Timothy called. "I'll come get you."

Just then he spotted the wide-eyed boy. Roly O'Brien—Matt had introduced him to the boy a few days before. Only thirteen years old, Roly had just started in the mine as an apprentice. His father had been working there for years. A chill ran down Timothy's back. Where was Frank O'Brien?

Roly sobbed with relief and almost leaped around Timothy's neck.

"It cracked," he reported, trembling. "I was inside here. They sent me in because I was supposed to practice digging a bit more. I'd only hold things up in the main tunnels, Dad said, but in here I could help remove the spoils from the face."

This tunnel—which was connected to the others but a bit out of the way—was more or less mined out. The men had never liked it. Since it lay deeper than the other tunnels, the air in it was always stale. However, that might have been precisely what saved Roly's life that day. It seemed that no gas had streamed into that tunnel and that nothing had collapsed there either. Though half-paralyzed with fright, Roly was completely unharmed. When all the lamps had been extinguished, he had not been able to orient himself, so he had crouched in the corner until he heard Timothy calling.

"It will all be all right, Roly. Calm down." Timothy did not know whether he was trying to comfort himself or the shivering boy. "But now tell me a little more. Were you the only one here? Where were the others? What caused the explosion? Did you hear anything after that?"

"My dad and the foreman were fighting," Roly reported. "The new foreman, not Matt. Maybe, maybe that's why they sent me away. Josh . . . er . . . Mr. Kennedy sounded angry. My father too. Mr. Kennedy wanted to extend the tunnel. With explosives. But my father thought there might be a cavity. He thought we shouldn't just blow it up, because we needed to make a . . . a . . . ."

"Test drilling." Timothy sighed. "What happened then?"

Roly sniffled. "Then my father said Mr. Kennedy should do it himself and sent me over here. I think he went into the other tunnel across the way. And . . . and then I heard something, sir. Clearly. When I was here alone."

Timothy's mind worked feverishly. Could somebody else be alive under the rubble? The entrance to that tunnel had collapsed during the explosion. He had seen that as he passed by. But before or after the gas had streamed in there?

"What did you hear, Roly?"

The boy shrugged. "Knocking. Voices?" His voice sounded unsure. He might have imagined it. Nevertheless, Timothy reached for the pickax and the other tools Roly had brought with him into the tunnel. The boy sobbed when he saw the collapsed tunnel entrance.

"My dad's in there, I know it."

Timothy cleared some of the rubble to the side experimentally. It was quite loose, so he could dig a bit. Perhaps then he might get a little closer to whatever sounds Roly had heard. However, he didn't really believe there were any survivors. Though the tunnels were not far apart, solid rock lay in between them. It was unlikely that Roly had been able to hear knocking from the next tunnel over. On the contrary, in this grave-like stillness . . .

Roly, next to him now, grabbed a pick. He was astoundingly strong for his age and his slight build. Soon he was chipping away more quickly than Timothy, and it started to sound hollow when the pick struck against the rubble. So the tunnel was not completely caved in.

"Easy, Roly," Timothy warned as the boy worked feverishly. "If someone is buried in there, you might hurt him. Besides . . ." Timothy still felt a nagging doubt. What if they released a gas bubble here? They needed to proceed carefully: it was better to leave the mine, fetch more help, and carry out a test drilling. Damn it, maybe they could even borrow some gas masks from some less penny-pinching mine in the area.

Just as he was about to tell Roly to stop digging, the boy let out a cry.

"A man, there's someone here, a man!"

With trembling fingers, the boy cleared the earth and stone away. Timothy saw there was no hope. If the man had not died immediately when the tunnel collapsed, he must have suffocated under all that rock. But Roly was frantically digging the man out. He uncovered the man's shoulder, took him by the arm, and pulled with all his might. The tugging set the rubble covering the body in motion.

"Run, boy—it's collapsing!"

Timothy tried to pull the boy away, at first worrying only that they might be struck by falling rock. But then he noticed that it was getting more difficult to breathe.

"Roly . . ." Timothy had only just managed to turn his back to the newly exposed cavity when he heard the explosion and felt himself being hurled through the air. He fell to the hard ground and worked his way onto his knees. Roly was wheezing beside him. Timothy pulled him to his feet.

"Quickly—the gas!"

It was a repetition of the earlier nightmare, but this time Timothy was caught in the middle of it. This time the rumbling of collapsing rocks was not coming from a safe distance aboveground but from all around. Flames began blazing behind him, and he fled just as desperately as the men whose corpses they had discovered earlier must have done.

They would not reach the hoisting cage in time. The gas was now escaping through the main shafts. He hoped it wouldn't catch Joe Patterson. Timothy silently prayed that Joe was already aboveground again.

As Timothy pulled Roly through the tunnels, he kept an eye out for a side tunnel, one like where he had found the boy. But there were none. The new air shaft was their best bet. It was in a spot where Matt and Timothy had been planning to expand the mine. If they were lucky, and Timothy's calculations were correct, there would be fresh air there.

Roly stumbled, but Timothy was now running with single-minded focus. Behind them, he could hear further explosions. Roly wanted to run straight toward the hoisting cage, but Timothy pulled him into the new tunnel. He saw the air shaft, stumbled toward it, took a breath of fresh air, and felt immediate relief.

And then the world collapsed.

2

The news of the explosion in the Lambert Mine spread at lightning speed. Matt Gawain heard about it in Greymouth and began to organize rescue provisions at once. They would need a doctor, a rescue party, and the other mine owners' help. At times like this, there was no competition. Everyone would send people and material to dig out those who had been buried. Matt was under no illusions about the scope of the catastrophe. He knew that it wasn't just one shaft that had collapsed. If explosions could be heard all the way at the surface, there would be casualties—possibly even dozens. Matt informed the doctor in Greymouth and arranged for messengers to be sent to the Biller and Blackburn mines. He also had the wood trader informed. Support material might be needed, no matter what the price.

When he finally reached the mine, it was already swarming with men. However, they looked confused and leaderless.

"Tim Lambert and Joe Patterson went below about an hour ago," the old miner responsible for the hoisting cage explained. "And ten minutes ago, we had another explosion. So I wouldn't send anyone down if I were you, Matt. Of course, that's up to you. Or Mr. Lambert, but he's no good to anyone at the moment, raving around about what madness it was for his son to go down below. He doesn't sound like he's capable of giving any orders whatsoever."

Matt nodded. "First we're going to check the air shafts to see whether they're still open and if there's been a gas leak. Then we'll see. I hope Blackburn has a few gas masks. That's a big mine, so they ought to have modern equipment, even if we don't. I know they have the new mining lamps that don't set off any gas and warn you of methane leaks. Biller has those too, Caleb told me recently. When they get here, I'm going in. Gather up some volunteers and equip the men accordingly. The people up here should make themselves useful and clear out some sheds. We'll need them for the casualties. And we need blankets and beds of some kind. Someone should ride over and inform the pastor. He'll be needed too. And the women's association. And the girls at Madame Clarisse's. Oh God, Tim is down there. What will Lainie say? Has anyone notified his mother?"

Matt tried to keep a clear head, and it wasn't long before he had transformed the confusion in front of the mine into an organized workforce. The first helpers from other mines began to arrive, Caleb Biller leading the way with entire wagons full of miners who had brought mining lamps, rope, and stretchers. Matt's esteem for Caleb rose considerably. He might not have a knack for mining, but he had his men's interest at heart. Or was old man Biller more reasonable than his competitor in that respect too?

Matt would have been happy to share the leadership over the rescue effort, but Caleb waved the idea off with horror at the very mention of it.

"I know nothing about mining, Mr. Gawain. And to be honest, I don't even want to know what transpired down below. I certainly won't go down there. I'm claustrophobic in mines under the best of circumstances. Perhaps I could make myself useful in another capacity?"

We don't need a piano player, Matt thought. But that was not constructive—he couldn't change Caleb Biller. And maybe the young man could do some good aboveground.

"Then see to the emergency hospital until the doctor gets here," Matt suggested. "Figure out what building would be suitable for that."

"The offices," Caleb said, without thinking long. "The sheds lack heating, so we could only bring . . . I mean, there will be dead, won't there?"

Matt nodded wearily. "I'm afraid so. All right, good. I'll talk with old man Lambert. I'll give him an earful while I'm at it. It'll be a pleasure to throw him out of his office.

Marvin Lambert was pacing back and forth aimlessly in his office, evidently numbing himself with whiskey. When Matt entered, Marvin looked as though he were about to leap on him.

"You! If you had been here, my son wouldn't have gotten involved in this madness. But you just had to go messing around, leaving the mine of your own volition. You . . . I'm . . . letting you go!"

Matt sighed. "You can let me go tomorrow," he replied. "But right now I'm going to try to save your son. And any others who might still be alive down there. You, meanwhile, should get outside where the people can see you. The men have all come to help their pals, even the ones who are sick. They need a few words of encouragement—at the very least, you could show your gratitude."

"Gratitude?" Marvin Lambert swayed. "That lazy bunch left me in the lurch this morning and—"

"You should be thankful for every man who didn't enter the mine this morning, Mr. Lambert," Matt said angrily. "Myself included. It doesn't even bear thinking about what it would be like if there was no one here who knew his way around down there. If you don't want to give a speech, fine. Just stop guzzling whiskey! Besides, the younger Biller wants to turn your offices into a hospital. So . . ."

Matt did not listen as Marvin began to lament that Caleb Biller surely only wanted to use the opportunity to get a look at his business's books. Someone must have informed Nellie Lambert by now. Perhaps Timothy's mother would rise to the occasion.

Caleb was just stepping into the office as Matt exited. Two strong-looking men followed him. Caleb glanced around with a look of authority.

"I'm having beds brought in, but before we do that, let's make some space here. This facility isn't very large."

Matt nodded. Caleb could sort out the details with Marvin Lambert himself. As for the number of sickbeds they would require, if the gas leak had been as big as he feared, they would probably not need many.

The doctor pulled up in front of the office building with a wagon full of blankets, bandages, and medicines. Matt greeted him, greatly relieved. Dr. Leroy was a veteran of the Crimean War, so an improvised hospital was not likely to scare him. Moreover, he had brought his wife, who had likewise been tested by war. Berta Leroy had been trained as a nurse by the legendary Florence Nightingale and had met her husband while working on the front. On a quest for peaceful surroundings, they had emigrated to New Zealand and managed their practice together in Greymouth for years. The women in the town maintained that Berta Leroy was at least as knowledgeable as her husband. And she was not afraid to get her hands dirty. She had brought Madame Clarisse and three of her girls along. Charlene burrowed into Matt's arms at once.

"I'm so relieved to know you're alive," she said quietly. "I thought you . . ."

"A lucky accident, my dear Charlene, for which you should thank God thoroughly at the appointed time," Berta Leroy commented. "But we have other things that need doing at the moment. In your profession, you should know how to make beds."

Berta shooed Charlene and the two others into the office. Dr. Leroy smiled almost apologetically at Matt. "My wife prefers working with the girls from the Lucky Horse to the respectable ladies. They simply know the male anatomy better. Her words, not mine."

Matt couldn't help but grin.

"How bad is it, Matt?" Madame Clarisse asked before following the doctor and his energetic wife into the office. "Is it true that Timothy Lambert has gone missing?"

Matt nodded. "Tim Lambert undertook the first rescue attempt. But then there was another explosion. We don't know whether it got him and his helper, but there hasn't been any sign that they're alive yet. We're just getting the rescue operation under way now. Wish us luck, Madame Clarisse." He looked around. "Where is Lainie, anyway? Does she know?"

Madame Clarisse shook her head. "We sent her to inform the pastor as soon as we heard about the accident. With her horse and my wagon. We didn't know about Mr. Lambert at the time, but she should be here any moment. I'll tell her gently."

Matt wondered how you could tell someone news like that gently. Several of the wives of the men in the mine had assembled in the yard outside the mine entrance. One of them, the petite Cerrin Patterson, became the first patient in the Leroys' hospital. Her labor began as soon as she received the news about the accident. As the irony of fate would have it, the first thing to emerge from this place of death would be a newborn.

Nellie Lambert arrived to help, but she seemed more in need of a doctor than likely to make herself useful to one. She was sobbing hysterically, and Matt sent her over to her husband. The least Marvin Lambert could do was look after his own wife.

Then, finally, there was information from the mine.

"Mr. Gawain, we've gone through the air shafts," one of the miners reported. "The ones serving tunnels one through seven are untouched. Two collapsed in the areas of tunnel eight and nine, and one is still intact. And the new one is also in working order . . . But you should probably take a look at that one yourself. One of the boys who checked on it thought he heard knocking sounds."

Elaine directed Madame Clarisse's carriage toward the mine, while the pastor followed with his own. Four respectable ladies from the women's association rode with them, as well as two prostitutes. Their presence had required the pastor to deploy his best diplomatic skills. On the one hand, the ladies saw their eternal souls being endangered by sharing a ride with Madame Clarisse's girls; on the other hand, Madame Clarisse's carriage was much more comfortable than the pastor's box wagon. In the end, they had opted to huddle together, groaning, on the loading bed of the pastor's wagon and left the transport of the piles of quickly donated foodstuffs to Elaine and the girls. Mrs. Carey, the baker's wife, had contributed basketfuls of bread and pastries. The rescue workers had to be fed after all, and no one that day would be dividing the time into shifts and going home to eat in between. The victims' dependents, if there were any, would need looking after—at which point Madame Clarisse and Paddy Holloway's donations might come in handy. They had both contributed several bottles of whiskey.

As Elaine goaded Banshee on, she thanked heaven for the newly paved road between Greymouth and the mine. She was anxious about the men she knew. Naturally, her thoughts circled around Timothy Lambert above all. Since he was not a miner, she could be almost certain that he had been sitting in the office when the mine exploded. But she would not feel truly relieved until she saw him with her own eyes standing aboveground. Indeed, she even imagined herself running into his arms, though she pushed the daydream away at once. She did not plan to let herself fall in love again. Not with Timothy or with anyone else. It was too dangerous. It was out of the question.

The mining complex was a hive of activity. The wives and daughters of the buried men had gathered in a corner. They were staring in silence and horror at the mine entrance, where a rescue party was just preparing to go down. Some of the assembled slid rosaries through their fingers, while others held tight to each other. Some wore expressions of resignation, others of desperate hope.

The pastor attended to them straightaway, while plucky Mrs. Carey assigned her women to make tea.

"Find out where we can set up a soup kitchen," she directed one of her assistants, intentionally ignoring Madame Clarisse's girls, who were unloading Elaine's vehicle. Elaine could not concentrate on anything herself. She was looking around for Timothy, and she found Fellow tied to the stand in front of the office building. That meant Timothy had to be there. Inside, no doubt—or was he planning to go down with the rescue company?

Elaine turned to the men tying on leather aprons, putting on helmets, and familiarizing themselves with the newfangled miner lamps from the Biller Mine while they waited for the hoisting cage.

"I'm looking for Tim Lambert," she explained, blushing. If the men ever told him that she'd asked after him, he would tease her mercilessly.

One miner shook his head seriously. "All we know, Miss Keefer, is that he went down there with Joe Patterson after the first explosions."

Elaine suddenly felt an icy-cold sensation that began at her core and quickly spread, threatening to freeze her to the spot. Timothy was down there in the mine.

The world seemed to be spinning. She reached for an iron railing to support herself and watched in a daze as the hoisting cage rattled into motion. Unexpectedly, it was not empty. The men were bringing up the first corpses.

"They were lying right at the entrance . . . Gas," explained the assistant foreman, who had come up with the men carrying the bodies. "Three more are coming on the next lift. We still have to dig the others out."

Elaine stared into the contorted faces of the dead men being carried out of the lift. She recognized the first two—and then saw Joe Patterson.

"Didn't you say that Joe . . . had been with Tim Lambert?" Elaine asked, stammering, though she knew exactly what the miner had said.

The assistant foreman nodded. "Yes, Miss Keefer. Damn it, and his wife is having a baby any minute. Matt made a point of keeping him out of the mine today. And now this." He ran his hand helplessly over the face of his young comrade, who was covered in dust.

"But don't lose hope, miss!" said one of the rescue workers as he stepped back into the hoisting cage. "Someone heard knocking sounds in an air shaft. Or thinks he did. So there just might be survivors . . . Miss, you look as white as a sheet . . . Someone take this girl away. She's much too close to the mine for my comfort anyway. Women in the mines bring bad luck."

While the cage rattled back into the depths, someone gently led Elaine away. The question of how much bad luck she could still bring to this mine cycled through her head repeatedly.

Madame Clarisse received her in the hospital, where there was still not much to do.

Berta Leroy and Charlene were caring for Cerrin Patterson, who was in the middle of giving birth. Charlene evidently knew more than just men's bodies.

"Helped my mum out with runts nine through twelve when I was a little girl. No one else came to help us," she explained coolly.

So far, Dr. Leroy had handled only the occasional fainting spell of a few family members of those trapped in the mine. He cast a quick glance at Elaine, prescribed a glass of whiskey for her, and motioned to the women and children in front of the mine.

"The people out there are trying to be as patient as they can. There's nothing to do but wait."

As the identities of the first dead were made known, the frozen silence gave way to crying and lamentation. Mrs. Carey directed her women to let the families help wash and lay out the dead. The pastor said prayers and tried to offer them comfort. Not many of the people in front of the mine continued to hold out hope. The wives of the older miners, who had followed their husbands there from England, could evaluate the situation realistically: if the gas had reached as far as the hoisting shaft, there was hardly any chance that the men deeper in the mine had made it. A few young girls, however, latched onto the news about the knocking sounds.

Elaine, too, remained desperately hopeful. Perhaps someone was still alive. But how many? And how many men had gone down that morning? No one knew.

"Someone must have written it down somewhere," Elaine said. "The men are paid by the hour, aren't they?" After a lengthy search, which, if nothing else, kept her busy for a while, she located an office assistant. The man directed her to Timothy's father.

"Mr. Lambert noted down the numbers today. At the time, he was upset that there were so few. You can ask him, if he's still lucid enough, that is. I was just talking to him myself. Someone from the mine's management absolutely has to speak to the women. But Mr. Lambert's utterly disoriented at the moment."

Marvin Lambert was not merely disoriented; he was drunk. He stared into space and muttered incomprehensibly while his wife Nellie sobbed beside him, repeatedly calling Timothy's name out. No one could get through to the Lamberts; at least Elaine had no luck. She planned to send Mrs. Carey to speak with them, or the pastor, but first she needed to find the list of miners. She found a notebook on Marvin Lambert's desk.

20th December 1896

This was it. An orderly list of the workers who had shown up for work that morning followed. Ninety-two in all. And Timothy.

Elaine took the book with her—earning a bit of praise when she informed Caleb Biller about it. The young Biller seemed out of place amid all the mayhem. Unlike most of the other men, who were end-lessly descending into the mine, he was clean and well dressed. And just like the day of the race, he gave the impression that he would rather have been elsewhere. Nevertheless, he appeared to be informed about the most crucial matters and seemed good at coordinating tasks.

"That is an invaluable help, Miss Keefer," he said politely, taking the record of roll call. "The men will at least know how long to keep looking before they have found them all. However, it is hardly likely that all ninety-two of them entered the mine. Some of them were surely working at the hoisting cage or loading the freight wagons. I shall try to ascertain how many."

Elaine glanced at the mine entrance. More bodies were just being brought up.

"Can it be that there are still survivors, Mr. Biller?" she asked quietly.

Caleb shrugged. "Probably not. But one can never be sure. Sometimes there are cavities in the rock, air bubbles, even during gas explosions. However, things do not look good."

SARAH LARK

A short while later, it had been determined that sixty-six men had entered the mine that morning, not including Joe and Timothy, who had gone down later. They had already found twenty dead, most of them in the vicinity of tunnels one through seven, which had not collapsed. They were now digging near tunnels eight and nine. The hours ticked by slowly.

Afterward, Elaine could not have said how the day passed. She helped make tea and sandwiches, but she was hardly aware she was doing so. At one point, the pastor asked her to drive into town to retrieve more provisions. Though the families of the victims could not bring themselves to eat anything, the miners were devouring untold quantities of food. Roughly a hundred men were now working in the mine, working in shifts to avoid stepping on each other's toes. Several sections of the tunnel had collapsed completely, and the quantity of rocks and dirt was massive. Dead bodies were continually being brought to the surface.

As Elaine bridled Banshee, she once more came upon Fellow, saddled and still waiting. It seemed no one had the heart to take him away. The rescue workers probably thought that was another bad omen. Elaine, too, struggled with the ludicrous hope that Timothy might appear at any moment and swing up on his horse, as long as Fellow was waiting. But then she gave herself a kick, removed the gelding's saddle, and led him into the mine's stables.

"Your master will find you here too," she said quietly. Suddenly she felt tears spring to her eyes. She cried softly into the horse's mane. Then she steadied herself and made her way back to town.

Greymouth had been numbed by the catastrophe in the Lambert Mine. The Lucky Horse was closed, and over at the Wild Rover, all was still. The rest of the ladies in the women's association had been cooking. Although two of them joined her, Elaine wondered what there would be for more workers to do. At first, they had all thought they would be caring for the wounded, but so far Dr. Leroy had been needed only for the minor injuries of the rescue workers. All the men the workers had brought up from the mine were dead.

As Elaine passed the Wild Rover, she saw Kura. The young woman had come to work but found the pub empty inside. She seemed to be weighing whether she should go back in when she caught sight of Elaine.

"I heard about the mine," Kura said. "Is it bad?"

As Elaine looked at her, she felt, for the first time, neither anger nor envy nor admiration.

"That depends on what you think 'bad' means," she said through her teeth.

Kura looked as impassive as ever. Only in her eyes could Elaine detect something like fear. That day, it occurred to Elaine for the first time that her cousin could express her feelings only through song. Perhaps that was why she needed music so desperately.

"Should I come along?" Kura asked. "Do you need help?"

Elaine rolled her eyes. "As far as I know," she said gruffly, "you possess none of the qualities needed at the mine at the moment. Neither the art of seduction nor operatic arias are going to be of any use."

The ladies in Elaine's wagon pricked their ears noticeably.

Kura's conciliatory tone vanished.

"And yet I have a rather enlivening effect on men," she said in her darkest, most lascivious voice, tossing her hair back gracefully.

Kura's bravado would have left Elaine speechless the day before. But now she looked at the girl coolly.

"In that case, you actually could put yourself to good use. So far we have thirty-three dead. If you'd like to give it a try . . ."

Elaine gave Banshee a quick flick of the crop, and the horse pulled away with verve. Kura hung back silently. Elaine had won the duel of words, but no feeling of triumph washed over her. On the contrary, she felt tears welling up as she directed her horse toward the mine.

As the rescue operations dragged on into the night, the only bright spot was the birth of Cerrin Patterson's baby. A healthy boy, who would hopefully offer his mother some consolation for the loss of her husband. No one had told Cerrin yet that her husband was dead, and when Elaine heard that, she looked fearfully over the rows of victims laid out in one of the sheds. Perhaps they had already found Timothy and were keeping it secret from her and the Lamberts.

That was not the case, but Elaine was deeply shaken by all the dead. She found Jimmy among the victims, the coal digger who admitted to her on his beer-soaked nights that he was afraid every day before he entered the mine. Charlie Murphy's wife was weeping hysterically over her husband's death, even though he had beaten her often and then regretted it bitterly afterward. Elaine saw apprentices among the dead, boys who had proudly drunk their first beer at the Lucky Horse after their first day of work, and ambitious young workers who had tried their best to court her when she had first started at the pub. One day he would be a foreman, Harry Lehmann had told her with pride. Then he would be able to offer her a good life. Now he lay there, limbs shattered, like so many of the dead who had finally been recovered.

The rescue operations were now pushing into those areas where the explosions had first been triggered. The pitmen there had not died of gas poisoning but struck by rock or burned. Timothy could hardly have made it so far into the mine. In fact, he should have been among the first dead retrieved.

Around eleven o' clock that night, Matt Gawain finally emerged from the mine. He had exhausted all of his strength, and the men had finally forced him to take a break.

Elaine found him in Mrs. Carey's improvised tea-and-soup kitchen, where he was pouring tea down his throat and spooning stew into his mouth like a starving man.

"Matt! Still no news about Tim?"

Matt shook his head. His face was sunken, and black with coal dust. He had not bothered to wash. None of the pitmen had. There was no point, since they were just lurching into the kitchen to recover for a few minutes before their next turn.

"We're slowly making our way into the area where we heard the knocking, if there was any. We haven't heard anything for hours. But if there are survivors, that's where they'll be, near the new air shaft. Those are newly dug tunnels with their own ventilation system, or they're supposed to be. But it's tough. The passages there have completely collapsed and they're often still burning hot after the fires. We're doing our best, Lainie, but we might get there too late." Matt choked down a piece of bread.

"But do you think that Tim . . ." Elaine almost resisted getting her hopes up again.

"If I had been in his place, that's where I would have tried to get to. But who knows if he made it? There are still tunnels we haven't dug out. Theoretically, someone could still be there. In any event, we'll get to the air shaft soon. If we don't find him there . . ." Matt lowered his head. "I'm going right back in, Lainie. Wish us luck."

Matt did indeed go back in, though Dr. Leroy would have liked to prohibit him from doing so. After all, he was swaying with exhaustion. However, he wanted to be there for the last shovelful—and to potentially carry out test drillings if a suspicious hollow appeared. The danger in the mine was far from over.

3

Elaine moved aimlessly about the mining complex, where the victims' families and many of the volunteers from the village had settled down to rest a bit. Mrs. Carey and Berta Leroy were asleep on the beds that had been prepared for the wounded. Dr. Leroy was dozing in Marvin Lambert's armchair. He'd had cots brought into a side room for the Lamberts themselves. Marvin had ended drinking himself into a fitful half sleep, and Berta, no longer able to stand Nellie's histrionics, had put her to bed with laudanum. Timothy's mother was now sleeping peacefully beside her husband, who tossed and turned restlessly, appearing to curse in his sleep.

Most of the wives and children of the victims had been taken home. Some of them were holding wakes. Those who still had loved ones below continued to wait by the mine's entrance. It was a warm night. Though the women were trembling, it was more from fear and exhaustion than cold. Mrs. Carey had nevertheless had blankets distributed.

Madame Clarisse ordered her girls home. There was nothing more they could do there, and she did not like to leave them unattended at night. Even exhausted men were men, and they would see the prostitutes as fair game. The pastor took them back to town in a freight wagon. Elaine, however, had only shaken her head when Madame Clarisse asked her to bridle Banshee again.

"I'm staying here until they . . . until they . . ." She did not finish, afraid to break down in tears. "No one will try anything with me," she added once she had regained her composure.

She ended up collapsing in the stall next to Banshee and Fellow, snuggling into a bale of hay with Callie in her arms. It seemed to be her fate to find solace only in animals.

But then, as the morning dawned, a yell started her from her half sleep.

"They found someone!" a jubilant voice announced. "There's a sign of life. Someone is clearing away rubble from the other side."

Elaine rushed from the stables without even shaking the straw out of her hair. In the yard she saw a young man surrounded by a cluster of women.

"Who is it?"

"Is there more than one?"

"Are they injured?"

"Is it my husband?"

"Is it my son?"

Over and over the same questions. Is it Rudy, is it Paddy, is it Jay, is it . . .

"Is it Tim?" Elaine asked.

"I don't know! I don't know!" The young man could hardly hold back the tide. "So far there have only been noises. But they're digging there now. Maybe another hour."

Elaine remained near the other women, shaking, crying, and praying right along with them. They were weak with exhaustion and fear. And this was their last chance. They knew that the men were not likely to find other survivors.

It took more than two hours for the message to make it to the surface.

"It's one of the boys, Roly O'Brien. Let his mother know! The boy's a bit done in but he's unharmed. And . . ."

The women rushed to the entrance of the mine and looked expectantly at the hoisting cage.

"The other is Timothy Lambert. But let the doctor through, quickly now, it's urgent."

Elaine stared in a state of disbelief at the stretcher on which Timothy was carried into the fresh air. He was unconscious, but he didn't look as though he were sleeping. His body lacked any rigidity. Elaine felt like she was looking at a marionette whose joints had been flung carelessly any which way. But he had to live, he simply had to!

Elaine wanted to come closer, but Dr. Leroy was already tending to the injured man. Elaine watched anxiously as the doctor felt for his pulse, listened to his breathing, and delicately felt his body.

Finally, the doctor straightened. Elaine attempted to read his stonelike face.

"Doctor," she said desperately. "Is he alive?"

Leroy nodded. "Yes. But will that be good news to him in his condition?" Leroy bit his lip when he saw Elaine's horrified face. "I need to examine him further." The doctor averted his gaze and turned to the men with the stretcher. "Take him in and lay him on one of the beds, but be careful. This man's broken every bone in his body."

"Now, don't drive yourself mad with worry, my dear," Berta Leroy said, watching the girl sway as the men lifted Timothy's stretcher. "My spouse tends to exaggerate sometimes. It may not be so bad after all. After such a short examination, he can hardly know anything for certain. Just let us take a closer look first."

"But he'll get better?" Elaine asked anxiously, supporting herself gratefully on the older woman's arm. "I mean, the broken bones."

"That'll work itself out, my girl," Berta reassured her. "The main thing is that he's alive. Mrs. Carey, could you give me a hand here? Do you have some tea for the young lady? With a drop of brandy in it, perhaps?"

Berta gently pried Elaine's clammy hands from her sleeves and followed her husband and Timothy into the office. Elaine got a grip on herself and started after them. She did not want to be left behind. She knew it was irrational, but she felt that nothing could happen to Timothy as long as she was near.

"No, not you," Berta said, shaking her head firmly. "We won't have any use for you in there. We need to inform his parents now too, and you—don't take this the wrong way, but you're not his official fiancée. And we don't want any trouble with the Lamberts."

Although Elaine's brain accepted that logic, she nevertheless had an overwhelming urge to hammer on the door as it closed before her.

Then she saw Matt Gawain and some of the other members of the rescue party. They surely knew the circumstances of Timothy's rescue. After all, they were just then leading the second survivor into the office. Roly O'Brien entered the makeshift hospital on his own legs. Though he was a little shaky, he was wholly unhurt; his mother was at his side, crossing herself and sobbing with joy. He looked a bit disoriented, but after awhile he would undoubtedly be basking in the general attention. Already questions were pouring in from every side.

Matt did his best to shield Roly from the deluge of inquiries. "The boy urgently needs to eat something," said the foreman. "Can you see to that, Lainie? We did find these two near that air shaft, by the way. They managed to escape the gas, but the rocks that fell after the explosion caught Timothy. The boy was sitting safe and sound in the tunnel, however, and actually had quite a bit of space. He might have gone mad from loneliness, but he would have survived for days."

"It was so dark," Roly whispered. "It was so horribly dark. I . . . I didn't dare move. At first, I thought Mr. Lambert was dead, and that I was all alone, but then he woke up."

"He was awake?" Elaine asked excitedly. "Was he the one knocking?"

Roly shook his head. "No, that was me. He couldn't move; he was buried up to here." The boy indicated the middle of his chest. "I tried to pull him out, but it didn't work, and he told me to stop; it only hurt him. Everything was hurting him. But he wasn't afraid at all. He said they'd dig us out for sure. He told me I just had to find the air shaft, by following the movement of the air, and hit against the wall with a rock. Right below the shaft. So that's what I did."

"And he was conscious the whole time?" Elaine clung to this hope. Timothy could not have suffered any serious internal injuries if he had spoken with the boy all day and half the night.

Mrs. Carey placed a cup of tea and a plate of sandwiches on the table in front of the boy. Roly drank thirstily while simultaneously trying to shove the food in his mouth, causing him erupt in a fit of coughing.

"Eat slowly, child," Matt grumbled. "Nothing else is going to fall on you today, and if my nose doesn't deceive me, the ladies are warming up some soup for you."

Elaine waited impatiently for the boy to swallow.

"Roly, how was Mr. Lambert?" she asked impatiently. She would have liked to shake the boy.

"He went in and out the rest of the time. He was awake for a while at first, but then he wasn't doing as well. He moaned and talked about how dark it was, and I was crying too. But then I heard them digging somewhere in the tunnel, and I thought they were getting us out, so I screamed and drummed on the walls, but Mr. Lambert wasn't really aware of what was going on at that point. They really need to give him something to drink!" That only just seemed to occur to Roly, and he looked almost guiltily at his teacup. "He kept talking about how thirsty he was."

Roly's words did nothing to soothe Elaine's uneasy heart. She heard loud voices and crying coming from the office next door. Matt noticed it too and looked concerned.

"His heart was still beating strongly," he said in an effort to comfort Elaine.

She couldn't stand it anymore. Determined, she went to the door and let herself in. Let Dr. Leroy toss her out—at least she would see whether Timothy was still alive.

But the doctor and his wife were too busy just then to even notice Elaine. Berta was seeing to Nellie Lambert, who was crying pitifully, while Dr. Leroy tried to calm Marvin Lambert.

"That was just like Timothy! Nothing but nonsense in his head. I always tell him that those boys aren't worth sticking your neck out for. But he was always trying to save them. At the risk of his own life! Couldn't he have led the rescue operations from out here? That foreman, that Matt Gawain, he was smarter. He didn't go storming into some adventure without thinking only to come back a cripple."

"Matt Gawain has been in the mine for hours," Dr. Leroy said, seeking to appease him. "And your son could not have known there would be further explosions. Other people would say he was a hero."

"Some hero!" Marvin mocked. "He probably wanted to dig the buried men out himself. We can see where that got him." He sounded bitter, but Elaine could smell the whiskey fumes. Perhaps the old man was trying to make himself feel better, albeit in his own vicious fashion.

Elaine followed the elder Lambert's gaze to Timothy's slender frame on the bed. Thank God he was still unconscious so that he was spared his parents' reactions. His face looked gray, as did his hair. Although someone had done a quick job of washing the coal dust from his hair, a layer of greasy dirt was still lodged in his pores and the laugh lines that were so characteristic of him. To her relief, Elaine saw that his chest rose and sank evenly. So he was alive. And now that someone had spread a blanket over him, he didn't look quite so disjointed and shattered.

Marvin Lambert held his tongue for a moment as his wife launched into a new fit of hysterics.

"And now he'll be lame for the rest of his life. My son, a cripple!" As Nellie Lambert sobbed, Berta Leroy looked as though she had reached the limits of her patience.

Nellie collapsed over Timothy's bed, and he groaned in his sleep.

"You're hurting him," Elaine said, feeling a violent urge to tear the hysterical woman away from her son. Instead, she pulled herself together and gently drew Nellie Lambert away before Berta could intervene more firmly. Nellie fled into her husband's arms.

Elaine gave Dr. Leroy a pleading look. "So what's wrong with him, really?" she asked quietly.

"Complex fracture of the legs," Berta answered quickly. She seemed to want to prevent her husband from giving a more precise diagnosis that would send yet another person into hysterics. "And a broken hip. It caught a few of his ribs too."

"Is he paralyzed?" Elaine asked. The word "cripple" was seared into her brain. She had stepped closer to Timothy's bed and wanted to touch him, to run her hand over his forehead, or to wipe the dirt from his cheek. But she did not dare.

Dr. Leroy shook his head. "He's not paralyzed. He would have had to break his spine for that, and it looks like he managed to avoid that. Though you have to ask yourself whether that was a blessing. If a person is lame, at least he no longer feels pain. But in this condition . . ."

"But broken bones heal, don't they?" Elaine objected. "My brother broke his arm once, and that healed in no time. And my other brother fell out of a tree and broke his foot. He was in bed for a while, but then . . ."

"Simple fractures can heal without complications," Dr. Leroy broke in. "But these are comminuted fractures. "We can splint them, of course, but I don't even know where to start. We'll have a specialist come up from Christchurch. They'll undoubtedly heal one way or another."

"And he'll be able to walk again?" Elaine asked hopefully. "Not right away of course, but in a few weeks or months?"

Leroy sighed. "Child, be satisfied if he can sit in a wheelchair in a few months. This broken hip bone—"

"Now stop all the doom and gloom, Christopher!" Berta Leroy was at her wit's end. Her husband was a good doctor but a chronic pessimist. And even if he was usually right, there was no reason to scare Timothy's friends and family. This red-haired girl, who was somehow connected to Madame Clarisse but apparently not a whore, already looked like the slightest breeze would knock her over. When her husband had mentioned the wheelchair, all the color had drained from the girl's face.

Berta gripped Elaine's shoulders energetically. "Take a deep breath, dear. You won't be helping your friend any if you go fainting on us too. Like he said, a specialist is on his way from Christchurch. Until he gets here, there's nothing we can say with certainty."

Elaine halfway regained control of herself. Of course, she was being absurd. She should be happy that Timothy was still alive. If only she did not have that image from the horse race constantly before her eyes: Timothy as a radiant victor, smiling as he leaped from his horse, climbing the winner's podium fleet of foot, and embracing Fellow before swinging back into the saddle. She could not imagine the same man in a wheelchair, condemned to inactivity. Perhaps the doctor was right, and he would find it worse than death.

But she would think about all that later. First she needed to ask Berta Leroy what she could do for Timothy, if there was anything that might keep her occupied.

Berta, however, had moved on to Nellie Lambert. "Now, madam, would you get ahold of yourself," she hissed at Timothy's sobbing mother. "There are a lot of women outside who lost their husbands and sons today. And, what's more, they don't even know how they're going to scrape together the money to bury them. You, on the other hand, have your son back. You should be thanking God instead of crying your eyes out senselessly. Where is that pastor anyway? Madam, go see if you can find someone outside who will drive you home. We're going to wash and feed this boy, and then put him to bed while he's still unconscious. He's got enough pain ahead of him. Christopher?"

His wife was pleased to see that he was already sorting his splints and bandages. She then turned back to Elaine.

"Feeling better, dear? Good. Then go look for Mrs. Carey. We need someone else here who knows how to do the work." Berta turned to Timothy's bed and moved to air the sheets.

Elaine followed her. "I can help."

Berta Leroy shook her head. "No, not you. The last thing you need tonight is to be changing the dressings on your sweetheart's legs and yanking on them. Then you really will faint on me."

"He's not my sweetheart," Elaine whispered.

Berta laughed. "No, of course not, dear; you're as cold as a dog's nose! Completely indifferent. You've just stuck around by chance because you know Tim Lambert in passing, right? Tell it to someone a little more gullible. But before that, bridle that little horse of yours. Madame Clarisse's carriage is still here, right? Find someone to take the seats out. We need to be able to fit a stretcher in there."

"You want to send the man home tonight, Berta?" Dr. Leroy asked reluctantly. "In his condition?"

Berta Leroy shrugged. "His condition is hardly going to change in the next few weeks. Besides, he'll wake up tomorrow, and then he'll be able to feel every pothole. This way, we spare him that torture."

Elaine began to see who in the Leroys' practice was really in charge.

"But the family—"

Berta, interrupting her husband, turned to Elaine.

"What are you waiting for, girl? Off you go to the stables."

Elaine ran outside. Deep down, she knew that Dr. Leroy was right. If she brought Timothy to the Lamberts' house, his father would assail him with accusations, and his mother would hardly be able to look after him in her distressed state. She now understood why Timothy spent every evening in the pub. It must have been hell to have his parents cast helplessly upon him.

Banshee and Fellow whinnied as Elaine entered the stables. Several miners had collapsed in the straw, exhausted after the rescue operations. She had not noticed the men before, or she would never have gone to sleep there so fearlessly. She had to shake a few of them awake, as she would never manage to prepare Madame Clarisse's carriage to transport Timothy on her own. She chose two of the older, more easygoing fellows she knew in passing from the pub. Although the men were not especially enthusiastic, they acknowledged the urgency and fetched their tools.

Unfortunately, they left dirty fingerprints all over Madame Clarisse's red velvet upholstery. Elaine would have to clean it afterward. She sighed. Would the day ever end?

When Elaine pulled up in front of the office building with the modified carriage, the Leroys were still quarreling. Berta seemed to want to treat Timothy at their medical facility, which had a small two-bed hospital. The doctor, however, was of the opinion that a nurse hired by the Lamberts could do just as much for Timothy at home. And Timothy was going to require months of care.

Berta shook her head at such male lack of understanding. "The nurse would be able to wash him and change his bandages, but what else? You've seen what the Lamberts are like. If you send him into that, you'll have a serious case of depression on your hands. And do you think any of his friends would brave that place to visit him? Matt Gawain maybe, every three weeks in his Sunday suit. There's always something happening at our place, though. His chums can pop in, all of the town's respectable ladies will send their daughters by, and Madame Clarisse's girls come by unchaperoned, anyway." Berta smiled when she saw Elaine standing in the doorway. "Especially that one," she added, "who doesn't think much of him."

Elaine blushed.

Dr. Leroy gave up. "All right, fine. In our hospital then. Do we have two men to carry the stretcher? And we'll need at least four people to maneuver him onto it."

Timothy's body, including his chest, was wrapped in bulky bandages. His arms, however, looked unharmed. That gave Elaine hope. She turned pale again, though, when the Leroys and their assistants raised him from the bed, and he groaned loudly.

"I've lined the carriage with blankets," she said.

Berta nodded and followed the stretcher-bearers to the carriage. "Very nice, you think ahead. I'll ride with you and try to keep him soothed. Who does that second horse belong to?"

Elaine had tied Fellow to the back of the carriage.

She pointed to Timothy. "His. The Lamberts forgot about him. But he couldn't just stay behind here."

Berta grinned. "You really are a saint. Caring for a man nothing ties you to and even looking out for his nag. It's exemplary! Maybe the pastor should give a sermon about that sometime."

Elaine directed Banshee to walk the entire way, but she did not manage to avoid every pothole in the dark. Even in his unconscious state, Timothy cried out softly every time, and Elaine gradually came to understand why Berta Leroy had insisted on transporting him that night. As the men carried Timothy into the doctor's office, Elaine took care of the horses. She followed the Leroys into the house once Banshee and Fellow were contentedly munching on hay.

"Can I help with anything else?"

Berta Leroy cast an appraising eye over the petite girl in her soiled riding dress. Though Elaine looked pale and deathly tired, she had a look in her eyes that told Berta she would not be getting any sleep over the next few hours anyway. Berta herself, however, needed a bed. She would sleep like a rock.

"You can stay by his side, dear," she said after thinking it over briefly. "Someone should be there when he wakes up. Nothing can happen. His life's not in danger. And if something comes up, just wake us."

"What do I do when he wakes up?" Elaine asked hesitantly, following the doctor's wife into the sickrooms.

Timothy lay motionless on one of the beds.

Berta shrugged. "Talk to him. Give him something to drink. And if he's in pain, he should take this." She indicated a cup filled with a milky liquid next to a water carafe on the nightstand. "He'll go back to sleep again soon after that. It's strong medicine. Just encourage him a little."

Elaine pulled a chair up to the bed and lit the lamp on the little night table. Berta had already turned off the main light. Not that Elaine would have minded sitting in the dark. But when Timothy woke up, it shouldn't be dark. She still had Roly's words in her ear: *He moaned and talked about how dark it was.*

Timothy looked exhausted. Elaine only then realized how sunken his cheeks were, how dark the circles around his eyes. And the coal dust was everywhere. Elaine took a washbowl that she found in the room and poured some water into it. Then she washed the dust out of the corners of his eyes and ran the washcloth gently over all the lines that made his face look so rakish when he laughed. She was fastidious about touching him only with the cloth. She reeled back as though struck by lightning when her fingers inadvertently stroked his cheek.

She had not touched a man since those horrifying nights with Thomas, nor had she even been alone with one. Certainly not at night in a dark room. She had never wanted to do such a thing again. But now she almost smiled, thinking about her fears. Timothy presented no danger at the moment. And Timothy's face felt pleasant. His skin was warm, dry, a little raw.

Elaine set the cloth aside and tentatively ran her hand over his forehead, his eyebrows, his cheeks. As she brushed the hair out of his face, she learned how soft it was. Finally, she played her fingers over his hands as they lay still on the sheet. Strong, sunbrowned hands capable of a firm grip. Yet she also recalled how lightly he'd held Fellow's reins during the race. Timothy's fingers were dark from coal dust, his nails broken off. Had he actually tried to dig out the buried men with his own hands?

Elaine stroked the backs of his hands. She finally took his right hand—and issued a muffled cry when his fingers closed around hers. It was madness, she knew, but even his weak grip was enough to make her draw her hand away and leap up, out of reach.

Her cry caused Timothy to open his eyes.

"Lainie . . ." he said quietly. "I'm dreaming. Who just screamed? The boy?" Timothy looked around, confused.

Elaine chided herself for her nonsensical reaction. She stepped closer and increased the lamp's brightness.

"No one screamed," she said. "And the boy is safe. You . . . you're in Greymouth at the Leroys'. Matt Gawain dug you out."

Timothy smiled. "And you took care of me."

With that, he closed his eyes again. Elaine reached for his hand. This time she would hold it tight until he awoke again, and then she would smile at him. She needed to master her absurd fear. She must only take care not to fall in love again.

Morning had just begun to dawn the next time Timothy gained consciousness. Elaine was no longer holding his hand, having fallen asleep in the armchair. She started awake when he said her name. A male voice that ripped her from her sleep. It had always begun that way when Thomas . . . But this was not Thomas Sideblossom's hard, domineering voice. Timothy's voice was higher pitched, kinder, and—at the moment—very weak. Elaine managed to smile at him. Timothy winked in the morning twilight.

"Lainie, can you . . . do you mind . . . the window . . . light."

Elaine turned the wick of the lamp.

"The curtains." Timothy's hand twitched on the sheet as though he wanted to open them himself.

"It's still quite dark outside," Elaine said. "But it will soon be morning. The sun is rising."

Nervously, she got up and drew the curtains aside. The early light of morning cast a weak glow into the room.

Timothy blinked. His eyes were inflamed from the coal dust.

"I was thinking I'd never see you again, or the sun . . . Lainie?" He tried to move, but winced with pain. "What am I missing?" he asked quietly. "It hurts like hell."

Elaine sat down again and reached for his hand. Her heart was beating wildly, but Timothy enclosed her fingers very carefully.

"Just a few broken bones," she claimed. "Here, if you . . . if you drink this here . . ." She reached for the glass on the night table.

Timothy tried to sit up and reach for it, but even the smallest movement sent pain shooting through his body. Though he held back a cry with some effort, he could not suppress a small whimper of pain. Elaine saw drops of sweat on his forehead.

"Wait, I'll help you. You need to lie there without moving." She carefully slid a hand beneath his head, raising him lightly, and put the cup to his lips. Timothy drank with effort.

"That tastes terrible," he said, trying to smile.

"But it will help," she said.

Timothy lay still and looked out the window. He couldn't see much from his bed, not much more than the silhouettes of the mountains, one or two roofs, and a headframe tower. But it was getting light quickly.

Elaine washed the sweat from his brow.

"In a moment, it won't hurt anymore," she said, trying to comfort him.

Timothy looked at her inquisitively. She was keeping something from him. But she was there. He opened the hand he had balled into a fist at the rush of pain and held it out to her.

"Lainie, even if it isn't bad, it feels pretty bad. Could you . . . could you maybe just hold my hand again?"

Elaine blushed but laid her hand in his. And then they watched in silence as an exceptionally beautiful sunrise bathed the town outside the window, first in fiery reds and then in radiant sunlight.

4

The sun rose over a shaken, grieving town. The citizens of Greymouth, including the traders and artisans who had no connection to the mine, seemed worn out and disheartened. Life went on in fits and starts, but it was as though the people and vehicles were moving in a thick fog.

Most of the private mines did not close, however. And the workers who had helped dig the day before had to enter their own mines again unless they wanted to forfeit their meager pay. Profoundly exhausted, they signed in for their shifts and could only hope that an understanding foreman assigned them to an easy job or put them to work aboveground.

Matt and his colleagues, however, did not want to stay aboveground. If the men remained idle too long, the images of the victims would sear into their minds, and they would fear the mine from that point on. A few men always quit after mining accidents, but the majority continued to enter the mine day after day, some of them full of fear, though few would admit as much. Most of these men came from generations of mine workers. Their fathers and grandfathers before them had toiled in the mines of Wales, Cornwall, and Yorkshire, and their sons would enter for the first time at thirteen. All the Paddys, Rorys, and Jamies could not imagine anything else.

Matt and his people dug the last corpses out that day. It was a demanding and arduous job, but there were still women and children in front of the mine waiting for a miracle.

The pastor attempted to stand with them while simultaneously trying to make arrangements for the sixty-six dead. He sent the ladies of the women's association to visit the families of the dead—and pacified them when they returned afterward, horrified at the conditions of the miners' residences. The grime, the poverty, and neglected-looking children were all conditions for which Greymouth's matrons held the miners' paltry wages and the cupidity of the mine owners less responsible than the miners' wives' lack of domestic skills.

"No sense of aesthetics whatsoever!" Mrs. Tanner exclaimed, becoming riled. "And yet you can make even the poorest shack cozy if you only place a cushion here and there and sew some curtains."

The pastor held his tongue and thanked heaven for Madame Clarisse, who was offering meaningful assistance to the two widows who had once worked for her as prostitutes. She loaned them both money for the burial, then promised the younger one another job in the pub and the older one, who had three children hanging from her apron strings, a position in the kitchen. Clarisse's girls also helped identify the dead who did not have any family. The parish would have to scrape together the money to bury almost half the victims. In addition, their affairs needed to be placed in order and their relatives in Ireland, England, and Wales identified and informed. It would be difficult, tedious, and bitter work.

More than anything, however, the pastor dreaded visiting Marvin Lambert. Whether the man liked it or not, he needed to take some responsibility for the victims' families. The women and children needed support. Of course, Nellie Lambert would likely be mourning only the great calamity that had befallen her own family—this despite the fact that the younger Lambert's life was no longer in danger, according to Dr. Leroy. The pastor had taken a detour through town specifically to ask about Timothy.

"Naturally, anything could still happen," the pessimistic doctor informed him. "He'll be in bed for quite a while, which promotes lung infections. Nevertheless, he's a strong young man."

When he arrived at the Lamberts' home, the pastor did not bother with lengthy explanations, and instead simply attempted to placate Nellie Lambert with the news that her son was doing well under the circumstances. The message did not get through to her, however, and Marvin Lambert likewise proved unreasonable.

"Let's await the results of the investigative committee first," he grumbled. "I'm not going to promise anyone money before that. That would be an admission of guilt. We can consider a donation fund later."

The pastor sighed and hoped to be able take care of the most urgent expenses with the collection. The ladies of the parish were already fervently planning the first bazaars and picnics to raise funds in addition to taking up their own collections.

The mining authority didn't take long to appear—in fact, the inspectors arrived at the very moment that Matt Gawain, after working for two days straight without a break, was about to finally go home to bed. Instead, he led the men through the mine and he did not mince words. Though the final report chastised the mine operator for a lack of safety precautions, it found that he had not flagrantly violated the standard regulations. The new air shaft that he had so reluctantly granted Timothy—and to which he owed his son's life—had saved him in that respect as well. Only a small monetary fine was levied, because the mining teams were insufficiently equipped.

Marvin Lambert went into a rage when he read that, as the inspectors could not have known that from their tour of the mine. Someone had talked—he suspected Matt Gawain—and naturally, Marvin was indignant. He threatened to let Matt go several times, not seeming to recognize how much the prospect of losing Matt frightened his remaining workers.

"Many of them are already asking about work in the other mines," Matt complained. He had finally gotten some sleep and was visiting Timothy before returning to work. "Until now, I never really noticed, but your father lives in another world."

Timothy nodded. His father had blamed everyone and everything for the accident except his own apathy toward safety measures in the mine. He did not recognize that any of the fault was his and refused to consider changing his approach for the expansion of new tunnels.

"But this time he won't be able to get his way," Matt declared with conviction. "We'll need to hire at least sixty new people. That will be hard enough in itself now that we have the reputation for being the 'Death Mine.' If we keep on this way, Mr. Lambert will have to dig his coal himself."

Timothy remained quiet. He had enough to do in his own encumbered condition. To fight with his father on top of that was more than he could bear. Besides, Marvin rarely visited him. He seemed to want to ignore the misfortune that had struck his son as much as his responsibility for his remaining workers.

Matt Gawain wondered bitterly whether Marvin Lambert believed that Timothy would someday return fit as a fiddle or if he had simply written his son off. Though he did not discuss these thoughts with Timothy, he brought it up one night at the pub when he was getting drunk with Ernie and Jay. Shaken by Timothy's condition, they ordered one whiskey after another.

The Lucky Horse had reopened the day after the accident, as had the Wild Rover. Business was quieter, and neither Elaine nor Kura played the piano. The men chatted in lowered voices and drank more whiskey than beer, as though hoping to numb their own anxieties.

Over the next few days, the miners returned to their routines. They did not celebrate Christmas that year. Nor did they mark New Year's Day. No one felt festive.

Matt began looking for new workers and complained that he could hardly find any experienced miners. The few applications he did receive came from men who had done just about everything short of having seen the inside of a mine, from whaling to digging for gold. These men would have to be trained first—an arduous and tedious business.

The pastor held the memorial for the victims of the catastrophe on the following Sunday so that everyone could take part.

"The mines should have given the men a day off—Lambert's at least," he declared to Elaine. "But at this point, I'd rather just give in than have to get into it again with him about it."

Elaine nodded. "What should I play?" she inquired, looking for her music. She had come to the church to give the pastor the money that Madame Clarisse had gathered for those left behind. That had sparked another dispute.

The women's association normally had a monopoly on donations, and the ladies had discussed heatedly whether they could accept the brothel's "sinful money." The pastor and the more practical Mrs. Carey had been for accepting it, particularly as it represented a considerable sum. Madame Clarisse had collected nearly three times as much as the respectable ladies.

"Let's just look at it this way," Mrs. Carey had finally declared to general acceptance. "Madame Clarisse has merely made restitution for the money that the dearly departed previously left in the pub. That should also absolve the men of a few sins before they stand before their creator."

Elaine flipped through the liturgy for funerals. "'Amazing Grace' is always a good choice," she suggested.

The pastor bit his lip. "Don't strain yourself, Miss Keefer. I hope you do not take offense, but I have already planned the ceremony with Miss Martyn."

Elaine glared at him. "With Miss Martyn? Well, thank you for telling me."

The pastor turned away. "We did not want to pass you over, Miss Keefer. Certainly not. But Miss Martyn plays Mozart's *Requiem* so exceedingly movingly. I haven't heard anything like that since I left England. And I thought that since you've already done so much, and continue to do so . . ."

Elaine stood up. She was so angry that she wanted to leave before she screamed at the pastor or, if nothing else, revealed her cousin's true marital status.

"And what exactly am I doing that's so much?" she asked angrily. "I didn't raise the money, and I'm not cooking for the ceremony like the ladies on the church council. But of course I will acknowledge that I cannot hold a candle to 'Miss Martyn' on the organ, whenever she condescends to let the lesser folk take part in her angelic playing. Just take care that Mrs. Tanner does not sing out of key again. 'Miss Martyn' can become rather difficult when that happens."

With that, Elaine stormed out. She felt more than a little inclined to have a talk with Kura, but decided against it. Kura would only derive pleasure from her outburst and probably make a few pointed remarks about her rival's organ playing. Elaine knew, after all, that she did not play perfectly. Kura would lend the funeral ceremony a much more solemn air since she displayed no emotion except in her eyes.

So Elaine rode to the Leroys instead and visited Timothy, as she did every afternoon. She knew that the people in town talked about it. Though some were of the opinion that she was merely doing her Christian duty, others whispered that Miss Keefer no doubt wanted to hook the rich mine owner's son. Even as a cripple, he was a good catch.

The miners took it the most calmly. They had often seen Timothy standing next to the piano, and a few of them even knew about his tenacious but thus far unsuccessful courtship. Now they asked Elaine every day how he was feeling.

Elaine encouraged the men to visit Timothy themselves, which many of them then did. Berta Leroy's plan was working out exactly as she'd hoped. Timothy was not cut off from the world in this little hospital, and his friends' visits cheered him up. That was proving to be of the utmost importance. He was still awaiting the expert from Christchurch. Although the doctor kept delaying his arrival, Timothy had nevertheless set his hopes on him.

He'd learned of Dr. Leroy's provisional diagnosis, despite the fact that Elaine and Berta had expressed themselves only vaguely on the subject and that even Dr. Leroy had held back his worst prognosis. Timothy's mother, however, knew no such scruples. Nellie Lambert visited her son every day and seemed to view it as her duty to cry unceasingly for an hour. When the sixty minutes were up, she took her leave in haste, often bumping clumsily into Timothy's bed. Timothy tried to view this with a sense of humor, but that was not always easy considering the great pain he suffered whenever he moved even the smallest bit. It took hours for the sensation of knives cutting through his body to abate. Berta was well aware of that, as she too inevitably caused him pain during his daily care. But when she offered him morphine, Timothy categorically refused to take it.

"I may have shattered legs, but that's no reason for me to cloud up my brain. I know that there comes a time when you can no longer do without it, Mrs. Leroy, and I don't want that for myself."

Sometimes, however, the pain was so unbearable that it took all his strength not to scream. Berta gave him a dose of laudanum whenever that happened, while Elaine sat still beside him, simply waiting or tentatively taking his hand. Timothy bore her tender, trembling touch better than anyone else's. She never gripped him hard. Even when she gave him something to drink or dried his forehead after he had broken out in a sweat, her gestures were featherlight.

One day, Timothy was in especially good spirits; the specialist from Christchurch had finally agreed to come the day after the funeral service. Timothy was looking forward to the doctor's visit and smiled at Elaine's anger at Kura and the pastor.

"You'll have to tell me someday what it is you have against that Maori girl who plays for Paddy Holloway," he teased. But he stopped immediately when Elaine's expression turned stonelike. She reacted that way whenever he asked her anything about her past. "Look at it positively, Lainie, you don't have to go cry at the funeral service; you can keep me company instead. It would make Mrs. Leroy happy. She's always worrying that I'll fall into a depression if she leaves me here alone. And as the doctor's wife, she can't miss the service. She was on the verge of asking my mother if she wouldn't stay with me. But my mother would never pass up the opportunity to show off her new black lace dress as she bows her head in sorrow. She already wore it yesterday when she paid me a visit. I hope she doesn't make a habit of it."

Elaine did stay with Timothy during the service, which the town's gossip-craving matrons didn't fail to remark upon. Berta caught two ladies in the act of discussing the matter and took them angrily to task.

"That man can barely move! You should be ashamed of yourselves to even consider the possibility of any untoward happenings."

Mrs. Tanner smiled knowingly. "Mrs. Leroy, there are certain things men can always do," she maintained. "And that girl was already a little suspect to me when she showed up here in her ragged state."

Kura came out ahead this time with respect to who had the best reputation. Both Mrs. Miller and Paddy Holloway basked in the glory of her presence. The young singer endowed the funeral service with such a poignant air that even the most hard-bitten fellows had tears in their eyes. Kura herself also cried, thus winning every heart to her side. No one wasted an uncharitable word when Caleb Biller congratulated her on her wonderful performance and offered to accompany her to the interment that followed. Kura made an appealing picture at his side. Even his mother, Mrs. Biller, looked more intrigued than hostile.

Elaine, meanwhile, sat beside Timothy, who was in a terrific mood, seeming to expect miracles from the specialist from Christchurch, who was supposed to straighten the fractures and make casts. It would probably take the doctor several hours, but Timothy was firmly convinced that he would heal quickly afterward.

"I've always been healthy, Lainie. And I've broken my arm before, when I was a boy. That was back in working order again just a few weeks later."

Elaine knew that Dr. Leroy expected Timothy to be in casts for a few months, but she kept it to herself. As she put away the newspaper that she had been reading to Timothy and closed the curtains, he protested. "I can't possibly sleep now, Lainie. It's the middle of the day, and I'm not an infant. Come, read me some more or tell me a story."

Elaine shook her head. "You need your rest, Tim. Dr. Leroy said that tomorrow will be difficult for you." She brushed a lock of hair out of his face. Timothy could move his arms, but his broken ribs made any other movement of his upper body painful. Elaine assisted as much as she could, though Timothy hated it when she helped him eat or drink. He only let Berta Leroy perform the unavoidable hygienic functions, and that was mortifying enough.

Elaine straightened his sheets carefully. She was so anxious that she could have cried. She could not share Timothy's optimism. Dr. Leroy had not actually said tomorrow would be "difficult" but "painful." Straightening the fractures would be excruciating, and there was no way Timothy would want her to be present for that. Elaine hoped that Berta Leroy would succeed in keeping Nellie Lambert away too.

Timothy smiled at her, as irresistibly as ever. The image of a healthy Timothy at the horse race flitted across her mind. She stroked his forehead soothingly.

He winked at her. "I get my best rest when you hold my hand," he claimed. Suddenly Elaine saw a spark in his eyes, the very one that she had so often seen—and learned to fear—in Thomas Sideblossom's expression. "It's more exciting when you stroke my forehead that way. I'm still a man, after all, in spite of everything."

He felt for her hand, but then he saw her face and could have slapped himself. The soft, trusting expression in Elaine's eyes had turned to suspicion and fear. She drew her hand back as though she had burned it. Naturally, she would stay with him; after all, she had made a promise to Berta. But she would certainly not be resting her hand in his that day.

The next day, however, she asked herself ruefully how she could feel such fear toward Timothy and why, moreover, she had not succeeded in masking it. She had treated him coolly the rest of the day, and he had been visibly deflated when she left him—this despite the fact that he could have used all the hope and optimism he could get. Elaine sensed the calamity before she even saw him. She ran into Nellie Lambert, who was sitting next to Berta Leroy and crying into her teacup.

"He'll never be healthy again," she whimpered to Elaine. Over the last few days, the two women had run into each other several times in the doctor's office, but Timothy's mother evidently had no idea what Elaine's relationship to Timothy was. Nor did she seem to really notice Elaine, who might just as well have been a piece of furniture in the little hospital.

"The doctor from Christchurch has the same fears as my husband," Berta said. "He put casts on the broken bones, but they're splintered and compressed. And of course we can't look inside—at least not yet, although some man named Röntgen is supposed to have recently invented a machine in Germany that can do just that. Dr. Porter was very excited about it, but alas, it won't help anytime soon. So righting the broken bones comes down to a matter of luck, and the likelihood that everything will hold together perfectly is practically zero. He hopes he got the hip in place right at least, which should enable him to sit again. But we'll just have to wait and see. Tim was very brave though. Go on in to him, Lainie. He'll be happy to see you."

"But don't upset him," Nellie Lambert demanded. "I don't actually think he should receive any more visitors today."

The first thing Elaine did upon entering the darkened room was pull the curtains open. It was not late, and it was summer—why the devil did Timothy's mother always feel the need to block out the sunlight?

Timothy looked at Elaine gratefully but did not manage a smile. His eyes were glassy. Though he had taken morphine that day, it did not look like it had been sufficient to mask the pain, for he appeared drained and sick. Even immediately after the accident, he had not looked so haggard.

Elaine sat next to him but did not touch him, since she sensed that *he* was the one who would shrink from any contact that day.

"What did the doctor say?" Elaine finally asked. The new plaster casts around Timothy's legs were covered with a blanket, but they seemed much bulkier than Dr. Leroy's splints. She knew that Timothy would refuse to show them to her, so she did not even ask.

"A load of nonsense," Timothy said gravely. The morphine made him seem sleepy and subdued. "Just another pessimist like our good doctor. But what do we care about that, Lainie? I'll be able to walk again someday. We can't have me being wheeled through the church. I want to dance at our wedding, after all."

Elaine did not answer. She did not even look at him. But Timothy almost found that comforting. It was much better than the indulgent and empathetic looks that his other visitors gave him whenever he contradicted the doctor's prognosis. Elaine seemed, rather, to be fighting with her own demons.

"Lainie," Timothy whispered. "About yesterday . . . I'm sorry."

She shook her head. "There's nothing to be sorry about. I was being ridiculous." She raised her hand as though she wanted to stroke his forehead but then could not bring herself to do it.

Timothy waited until he could no longer bear it.

"Lainie, today was a . . . rather hard day. Could we maybe . . . try it again? With the hands and going to sleep, I mean?"

Without a word, she took his hand.

5

Kura-maro-tini was vexed. She could give several reasons why. For one, she had hardly earned a cent the previous week. There was no business during the mourning period after the mining accident, but she'd heard that Madame Clarisse's girls continued to get paid. Paddy Holloway's did not; if Kura did not play, there was no money to be had. The problem was that Mrs. Miller still wanted her rent, as did the stable owner. Kura had considered selling the horse, but she had grown fond of the animal.

Though she was irresolute and restless, she was relieved that the funeral service was over. She had enjoyed playing the organ—all the more so since she had been able to get the better of her obnoxious cousin Elaine—but it had been a genuine pleasure to play music again seriously. Even if Caleb Biller was the only one who rightly knew how to appreciate what she was capable of.

Perhaps, Kura conceded, her distressed state of mind had something to do with Caleb. Kura was far from being in love with him, but she yearned for a man. While she had been on the road, preoccupied with finding lodging and organizing performances, she had been able to repress it. But now not an hour went by that she did not think of William and the joy she had found in his arms. Looking back, she even recalled Roderick Barrister in a better light. This Caleb Biller who seemed to admire her was likewise interesting.

The boy was peculiar, though. One the one hand, he had behaved very gallantly at the funeral service; on the other, he had remained as cold as a fish, even when she leaned on him in apparent need of consolation. During her tour, Kura had come across men who preferred

"Greek love," as people whispered. But Caleb did not behave like they did. Perhaps he just needed a little push.

He turned up again as soon as Kura had resumed her place at the piano, and once again required his two glasses of single malt to work up the courage to talk to her.

"Miss Martyn, I must once again thank you for introducing me to Maori flute playing. It made quite an impression on me. I find the music of the . . . of the 'natives' fascinating as a whole."

Kura shrugged. "You don't need to sound so apologetic about the Maori being natives," she replied. "Besides, it's not even entirely true. They emigrated here in the twelfth century from an island in Polynesia they called Hawaiki. Though no one knows precisely which one it was, the names of the canoes they arrived in have been passed down. My ancestors, for example, came to Aotearoa on the *Uruau*."

"Aotearoa is their word for New Zealand, right? It means—"

"Big white cloud," Kura said, bored. "The first settler here was a man by the name of Kupe, and his wife, Kura-maro-tini, compared the island to a cloud as they approached it. In answer to your next question, yes, I'm named after her. Can I play something for you?"

Caleb's eyes were radiant, though his response seemed to have more to do with the information she had relayed than with her person. The man was a puzzle to Kura.

"Yes . . . No. So, I don't imagine anyone has written down the music of your people, have they?"

"In music notes?" Kura asked. "No, not that I know of."

Though her mother was one of the best musicians on the island, Marama could not read music. Even Kura had only ever learned her tribe's songs by ear. She had never thought to write them down. Besides, her talent in that area was limited. Though she could write down a simple melody in notes, most of the tribe's repertoire for multiple voices would have been beyond her.

"That's a shame, don't you think?" Caleb inquired. "Might I ask you to perform a war song for me? What are they called again? *Haka*, is that correct?"

"A *haka* is not necessarily a war song," Kura replied. "It's more a sort of musical play. You express feelings through song and dance, and often there is a simple plot as well. As a rule, the song features multiple singers."

"Then you must simply sing all the parts for me one after another, Miss Martyn," Caleb said eagerly. "Though it would naturally be difficult with the male parts. Or are there *haka* that are performed only by women?"

Kura nodded. "There are all sorts of *haka*. Usually with shared roles." She played a few notes on the piano. "This one, for example, is performed at burials. There's no special choreography. Everyone dances however they want, and the singers can either be both men and women, or just men or just women."

She then began to sing in her enchanting voice. The melody suited the current depressed mood in the pub. Kura's voice expressed the sorrow of the song so poignantly that all conversation in the Wild Rover soon came to a stop.

When Kura finished, an old miner raised his glass to the victims of the Lambert Mine. After that, the men requested "Danny Boy."

Caleb waited patiently until every last alcohol-addled Irishman had given voice to his sorrow. It took hours. Kura, however, was not displeased. The endless string of sad songs got on her nerves, of course, but the men were buying her drink after drink. That evening, she would refill her pockets.

"Have you thought about it, Miss Martyn?" Caleb finally asked, casting an almost fearful look at the door.

A strapping blond man of a ripe age entered and greeted Paddy in a booming voice.

"Holloway, you ol' scoundrel! I heard the caterwaulin' out on the street, and I thought I'd better grab my son before he gets weepy. It is a tragedy, all that business with the Lambert Mine, but the boys only have themselves to blame. They could have signed on with me after all. Like all the good, sensible coal miners in this pub! A round for the men of the Biller Mine!"

With these last words, he turned to the drinkers in the pub, savoring the predictable applause. Kura recognized him: Joshua Biller, Caleb's father. She had seen him briefly at the funeral service. Caleb, however, did not look enthusiastic about his sudden appearance. He gave the impression of wanting to disappear with his whiskey glass from where he was standing near the piano.

Joshua Biller drank a quick toast to his men and then joined Caleb. He seemed to quite like what he saw.

"Well now, boy, I thought you were playin' accompaniment to the general whining. Pardon me, miss, but whenever my son reaches for the keys, it always sounds like a funeral. You, however, are a sight for sore eyes at least, and I'd wager you could play something more cheerful too."

Kura nodded stiffly. This man was just the type who almost always tried to fondle her, after building up to it so crudely that even a more sociable girl would retreat into her shell.

"Of course," she said. "Your son and I were just speaking about the music of the Maori, particularly the *haka*. This, Mr. Biller, is an example of a joyful dance. It tells the story of the rescue of Chief Te Rauparaha, who hid in a hole in the ground to escape his foes. At first, he expects to be cornered by them, but then a friend—who is represented in some versions by a woman—tells him that the men have left. The song expresses first his fear and then his joy."

Kura struck the keys and began to sing: *Ka mate, ka mate, ka ora, ka ora . . .*

Caleb listened rapturously, his father indifferently.

"The way it sounds, even the Maori write about nothing other than dark holes and tunnels underground. But your little friend is lovely, Caleb. Aren't you going to introduce me?"

Kura could hardly believe it, but Caleb did indeed rise to the occasion to present Kura to his father.

"Kura-maro-tini Martyn."

"Josh Biller," boomed the old man. "Very pretty indeed. Can I get a whiskey, Paddy?"

Joshua Biller drank three glasses of scotch in no hurry, never taking his eyes off Kura and his son. Although Caleb behaved irreproachably, he made Kura nervous. However, she had plenty to keep her busy. The miners wanted to hear more sentimental folk songs; Caleb evidently no longer thought it wise to ask for more *haka*. After an hour, the two Billers formally took their leave. As Joshua stepped outside, he nodded at Kura once more.

"A very pretty girl, Caleb!"

Kura found both men very strange. But that was nothing compared to her surprise the next day. She slept late into the morning—as she always did when she had played until late at the pub the night before. Then she would normally skip breakfast and just eat a few sandwiches for lunch. But that day, Mrs. Miller's shy Maori maid knocked on her door and passed on an invitation.

"Mrs. Miller has visitors and would like you to come to tea."

Kura looked at the decades-old grandfather clock that so often kept her awake with its loud ticking and noted the time.

Eleven o' clock. The perfect hour for a courtesy call by respectable ladies. Heather Witherspoon had explained to her that any earlier would be improper, since the lady might still be sleeping. And any later would interrupt the preparations for lunch.

Although all of her dresses were rather worn out, Kura put a little more care than usual into her appearance. She would have to begin saving money to have something new made. When she arrived downstairs, the girl did not lead her into the breakfast room where Mrs. Miller generally "received" but into the salon.

Mrs. Miller sat in an armchair with an expression like a well-pleased cat. On the sofa, a simply, but expensively dressed woman balanced her teacup. The woman instantly reminded Kura of Caleb. She had the same long, somewhat expressionless face. But unlike Caleb and his father, she had brown hair.

"Miss Martyn, this is Mrs. Biller. I've been keeping her company here, but she really came to see you." She beamed as though she had done something particularly nice for Kura.

Kura greeted the woman politely, sat down gracefully on the seat offered to her, and picked up her steaming cup of tea just as elegantly as her visitor. Naturally, decorum forbade her from inquiring directly what it was Mrs. Biller wanted. So she made conversation first.

Yes, it was terrible what had happened in the Lambert Mine, above all to Timothy Lambert. A tragedy. The town would need time to get over it, of course. And had the pastor's funeral service not been moving?

"Naturally, you in particular caught my eye, Miss Martyn," Mrs. Biller said, finally coming to the point. "Your wonderful rendition of Mozart. I couldn't hold back my tears. Where ever did you learn to play like that, Miss Martyn?"

Kura was on her guard, but she had rehearsed her story so often that it came out of her mouth almost automatically.

"Oh, I grew up on a farm in the Canterbury Plains. A little out of the way, very quaint. My father was very interested in high culture. My mother died when I was young, you see, and his second wife was originally from England. She had been a governess on one of the larger farms, but the two of them fell in love, and she raised me. She was a gifted pianist. And my mother is still considered a legend among the Maori with respect to dance and music."

This last bit was not a lie. But the first part of the story—about her supposedly dead mother—never failed to make Kura feel guilty.

"How extraordinary!" Mrs. Biller seemed satisfied. Kura had often observed that when she asked pastors and church councils about the use of their hall, they often paid close attention to whether she depicted her birth as legitimate or illegitimate. It appeared to be no different for Mrs. Biller. Her eyes had lit up at the mention of "his second wife."

"What I wanted to ask, Miss Martyn—I'm having a small dinner party, nothing special, just family—and I wondered if you would like to come. My son would be delighted if you could join us. He's always speaking of you with such high esteem."

"We have a common interest in music," Kura remarked politely, hoping to convey that she had no further interest in Caleb.

"So, might I count on you?" Mrs. Biller inquired, clearly pleased.

Kura nodded. A strange beginning for an affair. But fine, if Caleb wanted to introduce her to his intimate family circle.

She resolved to prioritize the purchase of the new dress. Once Mrs. Miller had informed her best friend, the tailor's wife, about her prospective relationship with the Biller family, she would certainly receive some credit.

At first, Caleb appeared to consider the invitation a source of embarrassment, but once he had gotten over it, he asked Kura to come even earlier and bring her flutes along.

"Perhaps I could write down the first part of the first *haka*?" he asked eagerly. "I take this project very seriously and hope to persuade you of its value. Perhaps we could even publish a book together."

Kura made her entrance at the Billers' dinner in a new burgundy dress that highlighted her magnificent skin tone. Joshua's eyes shone like those of a child peeking beneath the Christmas tree as he greeted the lovely girl. Caleb's eyes likewise sparkled. However, Kura did not detect the smallest gleam of desire in his gaze. Although he paid her a few polite compliments, his father made several insinuations that caused Caleb to blush even more than Kura. He led her quickly to the grand piano to free her from his father's company.

At the sight of the instrument, Kura beamed, then thought with a pang of regret of the gorgeous grand piano in her house's salon that was no longer played by anyone. Perhaps her daughter had taken an interest in music. But Gloria was no doubt still too little to learn anything. Although Kura still had no interest in the child, the memory of Gloria's conception conjured an image of William's face, and she almost thought she could feel his touch. Could Caleb not be any more sensual?

Yet his fingers seemed almost tender as he placed them on the piano keys and played a short song. Astonished, Kura recognized the main theme of the mourning *haka* she had sung in the pub. The man was unquestionably very talented musically, and Kura grew quite excited as he began to write her singing and flute playing in musical notation. Caleb wrote notes from "dictation" the way others wrote letters. By the time his mother finally called them to dinner, he had already recorded three vocal parts and the flute part and was combining them into a sort of orchestral sheet music.

"It's coming along beautifully, Miss Martyn!" he said enthusiastically as he led Kura to the table. "It's only a shame that we cannot record the dance, though you did say that this piece has no prescribed steps. It's truly a shame that we lack the resources of the big libraries in Europe. No doubt we'd be able to write out the choreography, but I simply don't know how it's done."

Caleb chattered on about sheet music and compositions until his mother discreetly indicated to him that he was boring the whole table. Aside from Kura, there were only family members present, and it seemed that they had hardly anything to say to one another. Caleb introduced her to his uncle and his uncle's wife, and to his cousin Edmund who had recently married the silent blonde girl at his side. Kura learned that both uncle and cousin worked in the mine as well—the uncle in the office, the cousin in management, like Caleb. Unlike Caleb, however, Edmund seemed to actually be interested in his work and chatted at length with Joshua about the shortfalls and geologic conditions that had led to the accident in the Lambert Mine. For the Biller ladies, that proved just as dull as Caleb's thoughts on contemporary opera.

For that reason, the three Biller ladies concentrated their conversation on Kura. Caleb's mother was apparently making every effort to represent the young singer in the best possible light. The aunt and cousin's questions, however, could almost have been described as taunts.

"It must have been interesting to grow up as a native," said Edmund's young wife, batting her eyes innocently. "You know, we hardly have any Maori in our social circle. I've heard"—she giggled—"that they have rather liberal customs."

"Yes," Kura answered shortly.

"It must have been difficult for your mother to adjust to life on an English farm, was it not?" the aunt inquired.

"No," Kura stated.

"But you don't wear traditional dress, do you? Not even during your performances?" The young female cousin eyed Kura's bodice as though Kura were about to tear it off and dance a *haka* bare-breasted.

"That depends on the performance," Kura said patiently. "When I sang as Carmen, I wore a Spanish dress."

"Miss Martyn performed for an opera," Caleb's mother interceded. "She was on tour with an international ensemble. On the North Island and in Australia too. Isn't that exciting?"

The ladies assented but adopted such a patronizing a tone that it sounded as though they were assuring a wandering prostitute that she had no doubt led a varied life.

"I'm sure you got to meet some fascinating men," the aunt remarked right away.

Kura nodded. "Yes."

"Our little Greymouth must look rather shabby in comparison," tittered the cousin.

"No," said Kura.

"What are you doing here anyway, Miss Martyn?" the aunt inquired, sweet as sugar. "I mean, working in a pub can hardly compare with the great art of the opera stage."

"Hardly," Kura confirmed.

"Although you have no doubt met interesting men here as well," the cousin said with a smile, casting a meaningful look at Caleb.

"Yes."

Up to that point, Caleb had listened without saying a word, gazing at Kura almost as adoringly as he had in the pub when she sang the "Habanera." Her ability to bring all conversation to a dead halt obviously impressed him as much as her musical talent.

Now, however, he felt he had to intervene.

"Miss Martyn is traveling the South Island to collect and catalog the musical heritage of the various Maori tribes," he explained. "It's very interesting work, and I feel exceptionally honored to be allowed to take part. Would you like to do a bit more work on that *haka*, Miss Martyn? Perhaps another of the flute parts? Our audience here might enjoy it."

He winked at her as he extricated her from the ladies. Kura seemed as unflappable as ever.

"I'm mortified, Miss Martyn. My relatives seem to be insinuating something about you. You . . . er . . . and me," Caleb said, reddening.

Kura gave him her most charming smile.

"Mr. Biller, let your relatives think what they like, but marrying you is probably the last thing on earth I would want to do."

Caleb's astonished expression reflected both relief and mild affront.

"Do you find me so objectionable?"

Kura burst into bright laughter. Could this man really be so dense? Her gentle advances at the memorial service, her flirtation at the pub, and the fact that she had even come to dinner that day should have been enough to convince any man of her interest. She raised her hand and caressed him slowly and lasciviously, starting at his forehead, down over his cheek to the corner of his mouth, where she traced a small circle before letting a finger trickle down to his throat. Caresses like that had driven William mad. Caleb, however, did not seem to know exactly what to make of it.

"I don't find you at all objectionable," Kura breathed. "But marriage is out of the question for me. As an artist."

Caleb nodded energetically. "Naturally. I had that same thought. So, you won't hold all their talk against me?"

Kura rolled her eyes. She had touched this boy, caressed him, tried to excite him. And all he could think about was social convention.

When he led her out and politely said his good-byes a short while later, she gave it another try. She pushed herself up against him, smiling, her face right in front of his, her lips slightly parted.

Caleb blushed but made no move to kiss her.

"Perhaps we could continue with our work on the *haka* at the pub tomorrow afternoon?"

Kura nodded, resigned. Caleb was a hopeless case. But she enjoyed making music with him. She found it fascinating to watch the Maori recitatives suddenly take a readable form on paper—in the process becoming understandable and playable for other musicians. It might be even more interesting to arrange the music for European instruments. Kura had never been interested in composing before, but this spoke to her.

Over the next few weeks, the work with the songs of her ancestors filled her days, but her nights remained lonely, no matter what she did to try to encourage Caleb. She finally got her hopes up when he asked her to make contact with a local Maori tribe.

"I can well imagine how a *haka* like this sounds. You bring the various voices together beautifully, after all, Miss Martyn. But I would love to hear them in their native environment and see the dancing. Do you think the tribe would perform a *haka* for us?"

Kura nodded. "Yes, of course. It's part of the greeting ritual when honored visitors introduce themselves. Only I don't know where the nearest tribe lives. We might be on the road for several days . . ."

"If that's not a problem for you," Caleb said, "I'm sure my father would let me have the time off."

Kura had already learned how exceedingly generous Caleb's father was with his son's time—at least when he spent it with Kura. She often wondered how the mine could possibly spare his help almost every morning or afternoon, since the work on the *haka* could only take place when the pub was closed. Mrs. Biller had begun to invite Kura regularly to tea—a wasted effort, really, but Kura found it far more enjoyable to work on Caleb's perfectly tuned piano in his salon than in Paddy's smoky pub. So she often made plans to work on music with Caleb first and then to drink tea afterward with his mother. As a pleasant ancillary, Mrs. Biller served exceptional delicacies with tea. Kura ate enough to last her the rest of the day.

"I do like it when young people help themselves heartily," Mrs. Biller said enthusiastically as Kura devoured great quantities of sandwiches and cakes, but always with the most graceful of movements.

"Thank you," said Kura.

They tracked down the nearest Maori tribe in the area around Punakaiki, a tiny village between Greymouth and Westport. The nearby Pancake Rocks formation was famous, Caleb explained excitedly as soon as Kura told him the location. Although he took little interest in anything practical—such as mining—he was nevertheless an enthusiastic geologist and suggested making a side trip to view the rocks while they were they were in the area visiting the tribe. There might even be a hostel nearby where they could spend the night.

"The tribe will invite us to spend the night there," Kura replied.

Caleb nodded but looked a little nervous. "I don't know. Would that be decent? I wouldn't want to offend them."

Kura laughed and tried once more to draw him out of his shell by stroking his hair and neck. She even rubbed her hips against him, but he only looked embarrassed.

"Caleb, I'm half-Maori. Anything that is decent to my people is acceptable to me as well. You will have to have to acquaint yourself with the customs of my people. After all, we mean to ask the tribe to make its defining repertoire, its own special tribal *haka*, available to us. And that won't happen if you treat them like exotic animals."

"Oh, I have the greatest respect . . ."

Kura did not listen further. Perhaps Caleb would finally let himself go, out of respect for the customs of her people. For the time being, however, she continued to spend her nights touching herself and dreaming of William.

The journey to Pancake Rocks took almost a full day with Kura's coach and their horses. She had hoped for a faster team from the Billers' stables. But Caleb knew almost as little about horses as she did, so they were both quite relieved to hear that it was better to hike the Pancake Rocks than to attempt the difficult path with a carriage. Moreover, the weather was stormy, which was making the horses jittery.

However, it was ideal weather for the Pancake Rocks, the bartender at the inn in Punakaiki had explained.

"The effect becomes truly spectacular when the sea swells. Then it looks like the 'pancakes' are being grilled over geysers!" the man said, laughing happily as he pocketed the money for two single rooms. He was, of course, convinced that the young couple really only wanted one. And though he could not have cared less where the two of them ended up spending the night, that had not stopped him from asking sternly for their marriage certificate when they arrived. The success of this ploy had raised his spirits, and after that he was delighted to play tour guide.

A short while later, Kura and Caleb found themselves ambling among the strange pancake-round rock layers along the edge of the roaring sea. Kura's loose hair flew in the wind, and she looked ravishing. That had no effect on Caleb, however; he merely lectured, enthralled, about the density of limestone and the impact of hydraulic forces.

Kura's beauty did attract two young Maori men, who, after speaking briefly with her, invited the two hikers to visit their tribe. It turned out that they had already heard of Kura. Since her guest performance for the tribe near Blenheim, she had become known as a *tohunga*, and the young men gave the impression that they could not wait to hear her music. The looks they gave Kura's breasts and hips, though, indicated more, Caleb noticed with embarrassment. He insisted that they not

491

accept the invitation immediately and instead head over to the Maori village the next day.

"Those two boys do not look very trustworthy to me," he said, concerned, as he led Kura back to the inn. "Who knows what they would have attempted if we had simply followed them into the wilderness. Besides, it will be dark soon."

Kura laughed. "They wouldn't have attempted anything with us, although no doubt they would have liked to attempt something with *me*. Oh, don't look at me like that, Caleb. It's flattering. They probably would have spent the whole trip displaying their daring in an effort to lure me out of your bed and into one of theirs."

"Kura!" Caleb looked at her indignantly.

Kura giggled. "Don't be such a prude! Or should I have said we were married? Then they would have left me alone."

Caleb looked like he was in agony, and Kura did not provoke him further. Though he still did not touch her that evening, he proved extremely generous by treating her to the best food and wine Punakaiki had to offer. That wasn't saying much, but ever since Kura had embarked on her largely penniless nomadic life, she had learned how to appreciate small gestures.

The next morning, Kura followed the Maori's directions to their *kainga* and found the village straightaway. Caleb was surprised by its size. Until then, he had apparently been under the impression that the Maori lived in tepees like some Indians in America. The diversity of houses, sleeping halls, cooking houses, and storehouses astounded him.

Kura wondered, not for the first time, how some *pakeha* children grew up so sheltered from reality. Although it was true that there was no fixed Maori settlement right next to Greymouth, as far as she knew, Caleb had visited several cities on the South Island, as well as Wellington and Auckland. Had there really been no opportunity to learn about Maori culture there? However, Caleb had still only been a child at the time. He, like Timothy Lambert, had spent almost his entire youth in English boarding schools and universities.

As Kura had expected, they were convivially received and did not even have to ask the villagers to show them the most important *haka*.

"These tribal *haka* have an unusual story behind them," Kura explained to Caleb while the men and women demonstrated their personal dance. "Originally, they were composed by rival tribes and meant to mock the tribe. But then the tribes adopted the *haka* themselves, out of pride that anyone had enough fear or respect for them to compose a defensive song."

Naturally, Kura spoke fluent Maori, and the villagers were excited to see that Caleb had already picked up quite a few phrases and learned several more over the course of the day. Even Kura was surprised at how easily it came to him. Though she had learned a bit of French and German during her singing lessons, she had never succeeded in repeating the words with no accent as Caleb now managed to do with the Maori language.

Eventually, the two of them found themselves seated in the splendidly carved meetinghouse with the villagers, passing around the whiskey bottle they had brought with them. It wasn't long before Kura was tipsy. To everybody's amusement, she selected one of the strapping young dancers and disappeared outside with him. Caleb assumed an indignant expression, but not a jealous one. Kura grew a little annoyed when she noted it, and the Maori were rather surprised.

"You not . . . ?"

Kura observed the man beside Caleb making an obscene gesture. Caleb turned red.

"No, we're only . . . friends," he stuttered.

The man followed this with a remark that caused a great deal of laughter.

"He says, 'We Maori don't do it with enemies either,'" his wife translated.

The next day, Kura explained to the still slightly indignant Caleb that she had only wanted to elicit a special love song from her companion. The young dancer was happy to sing one for Caleb too, after he had finished laughing. The thought of singing a love song for a man seemed more than a little strange to him. But then he sang and danced with almost exaggerated gestures, and Kura observed that Caleb was so lost in admiration that he hardly managed to notate the music. When his eyes lit up, it clarified to Kura once and for all why all her charms were wasted on him. Later, when he insisted that she translate the text for him, Kura took a few liberties with its obscene content.

Shortly before the two of them started upon their return to Greymouth, Kura had another encounter that preoccupied her a great deal more than Caleb's obvious preference for the male sex.

The chief's wife, a strong, resolute woman who had always danced the *haka* in the first row, spoke to Kura as she was packing her things away.

"You come from Greymouth, is that right? Do you know if the girl with the flaming hair is still there?"

"A redheaded girl?" Kura thought immediately of Elaine but pretended to be unsure.

"A delicate little creature who even looks a bit like you—if one has good eyes," the chieftain's wife said, smiling as an incensed look appeared on Kura's face.

Kura nodded. "Elaine? She's still there. She plays piano in a pub. Why? Do you know her?"

"We found her awhile ago and sent her to Greymouth. She was doing rather badly, having wandered through the mountains for days with her little dog and horse. I would have liked to keep her with us, but the men thought it was too dangerous. And they were right to be cautious. He's still looking for her. But as long as she stays where she is, she should be safe."

The woman turned away. Kura checked her curiosity and held back her questions about what made Greymouth so much safer than any other backwater on the West Coast and who was looking for Elaine anyway. Probably the husband she had fled. But that was a long time ago. He should have long since accepted the fact that Elaine would not be coming back.

With respect to love and marriage, Kura had been entirely shaped by her mother's culture. A girl sought out the man she wanted to belong to, and if he did not meet her expectations, she took another. Why did the *pakeha* always have to combine that with marriage? Kura cast a cross look at Caleb. His parents would eventually push him to get married.

Kura hardly wanted to picture the afflicted girl's wedding night.

6

William Martyn had practically flooded the North Island with sewing machines. At first, he had been assigned to a rather unattractive region on the East Coast. However, true to the teachings of the sales genius Carl Latimer, who had himself unloaded masses of sewing machines on the women-starved West Coast of the South Island, William had ridden complaisantly from farm to farm. Along the way, he informed himself of the most important gossip so that he always had something to chat about with the mistress of the house before he unpacked his wonder machine.

The ladies' covetousness was then quick to awaken—Carl Latimer had not exaggerated on this point. Though it was true that the more isolated regions comprised a smaller market for his machines, he was always offered a free, and occasionally even heated, place to sleep. In those cases, William used every tactic at his disposal to close the deal. Sometimes he wondered if the women—especially the well-off but lonely women on the bigger farms—bought his machines only so they could avail themselves of his "maintenance services" the next time he stopped in the area.

He won over the more impoverished women and girls with arguments for saving money by sewing their own clothes and the possibility of making some extra money by touching up clothes for the neighbor women. It wasn't long before his sales figures demolished all expectations, and the firm moved him to the much more attractive area around Auckland, where William additionally suggested that the machines might be used for the industrial production of articles of clothing. Instead of only inviting women to his demonstrations, he also passed out flyers to men—immigrants looking to establish themselves in their new country. By purchasing three or four sewing machines, according to William, anyone could produce clothing in bulk and earn a profit. William promised to provide the training himself on his next stop in the area, and he did just that. Although most of the businesses soon failed due to a lack of business savvy, two or three of the small companies operated successfully. One of his clients ordered new machines every few months as his business continued to expand.

The notion of ridding themselves of several machines at a time in this manner caused something of a sensation among the sales management. They invited William to give presentations on the concept in the North Island's training center and entrusted him with another interesting sales area. William had begun driving a carriage appropriate to his standing with an elegant horse to pull it. He dressed in the latest fashion and enjoyed his new life. The only thorn in his side was the fact that he had not been able to track down Kura and the opera ensemble—though, truth be told, he did not know how his life and hers could be brought back into harmony. Sewing-machine marketing and opera singing were hardly compatible, and he knew that Kura would never have wanted to give up her career so soon.

As he directed his horse through the lively streets of Wellington on the lookout for his company's main New Zealand offices, he contemplated that the opera singers must long since have been in Australia, the South Island, or even back in Europe. Had they taken Kura with them? William did not believe they had. The troupe's director had given the impression that he wouldn't tolerate any gods beside himself. And Kura certainly had what it took to be a star in Europe. Even if her gift was not enough for the grand opera houses, her appearance alone would have smoothed her path.

William finally located the office and found a place for his horse behind the building. The company's sales director had personally invited him to an interview, and William was looking forward to it but not concerned. He knew his sales numbers and was expecting a bonus, not an admonishment. Perhaps there would be new assignments too. He tied his horse up and took the folder with his latest balance sheets out of the carriage before brushing the last bits of dust from his gray three-piece suit. The suit fit him admirably—though it had not actually been finished, as he always claimed, in one of the new factories using Singer sewing machines but by one of Auckland's best men's tailors.

Daniel Curbage, the sales director, greeted him amiably.

"Mr. Martyn! Not only punctual to the minute but also with a pile of new sales contracts under his arm!"

The man seized the contents of William's folder at once. "I have to tell you how much your efforts never cease to impress us. May I offer you something? Coffee, tea, something a little stronger?"

William decided on tea. No doubt the whiskey would be excellent, but he had learned long ago that successful negotiations required a clear head, not to mention the fact that it always made a better impression when one did not reach for the bottle immediately.

Daniel Curbage nodded, clearly pleased, and waited for his secretary to bring the tea. Only then did he get down to business.

"Mr. Martyn, as you are well aware, you are one of our top workers—and naturally, during your training, you were singled out for possible advancement within the company."

William nodded, though he hardly remembered that period. Back then, he had spent more time grappling with hemstitching than career planning.

"From a position as sales director for one of the larger districts, you could climb up to . . . well, up to my position," Daniel Curbage said, laughing heartily as though the latter were a rather daring leap of the imagination. "And I had actually already selected you for a management position here in the office." He looked at William, expecting appreciation.

William made an effort to look appropriately enthusiastic, though in truth, he was not crazy about the prospect of a desk job. The post would have to be very well compensated to lure him off the road.

"However, the board of directors in England—you know how those people are—think that after only a year's experience, you might still be a little too . . . well, too green for such an assignment. Besides, the gentlemen seem to believe that the machines more or less sell themselves in cities like Auckland."

William wanted to object, but Daniel Curbage gestured with a conciliatory motion of his hand to stop. "You and I both know that's not the case. But then again, we both come from the practical side of things. The directors, however . . ." The sales director's expression made it clear what he thought of the pencil pushers in far-off London. "Well, it's not worth talking about. All that matters as far as you and I are concerned is that I must now burden you with a sort of field test. Please don't take this as an affront, let alone a punishment. On the contrary, consider it as a springboard. Your predecessor, Carl Latimer, recently received the commission to take over the training center on the South Island."

William's thoughts raced. "Carl Latimer? Who used to travel the West Coast on the South Island?"

Curbage nodded, beaming. "You have an excellent memory, Mr. Martyn. Or do you know him? You're from the South Island as well, aren't you? Well, perhaps you'll be delighted then to return."

William bit his lip.

"Mr. Curbage, Latimer blanketed the West Coast with sewing machines," he dared to object. "The fellow is a genius. He put a Singer in the hands of practically every human being, even the ones who only looked feminine."

Daniel Curbage laughed. "Well, that leaves you the fifty percent of the population that's male," he joked. "And here in Auckland, you've already shown how that's done."

William suppressed a sigh. "Do you know the West Coast, Mr. Curbage? Probably not, or you would have placed the male percentage higher. I think it's more like eighty or ninety percent of the population. And those are tough Kiwis: seal hunters, whalers, coal miners, gold miners, and the like. As soon as they have a cent in their pockets, they take it to the nearest pub. None of them will take to the idea of a sewing machine, I guarantee you that. Where's any ambitious business-minded fellow going to scrounge up enough seamstresses? If a girl's not a prude, she makes a lot more in a cathouse."

"Another possibility for expansion, William," Curbage said, switching over to a more familiar form of address. "Save these women from themselves! Make it clear to these girls that it's infinitely more worthy of them to strive for a respectable life as a seamstress than it is for them to continue pursuing a life of sin. Besides, more and more coal miners are flocking to the area, some with their entire families. Their wives should be delighted at the prospect of making a little extra money on the side."

"Only they don't have the hundred and fifty dollars for the machine. That's how much they cost now," William noted drily. "I don't know, Mr. Curbage."

"Please, call me Daniel. And don't look so gloomy. As soon as you get to know your new area, something will come to you. Besides, I'm working on a new payment option especially for miners' families. Make the most of your new assignment, William. Make me proud. So, how about that drink now? I have some top-notch whiskey."

William felt a little deflated when he finally left the office. This new region had little appeal for him. And he would have to start all over again. Even if he were to take his horse and carriage along to the South Island, his fiery horse and sleek little chaise were ill suited to the muddy roads of the West Coast, as was his elegant, urban clothing. He would need to equip himself with boots, leather bags, and waxed jackets again. Three hundred rainy days a year and hardly any sheep farms with lonely mistresses—instead, he could count on hotels with exorbitant prices that usually only rented their rooms by the hour. William especially dreaded vermin-infested lodgings. However, he needed to put a positive spin on this new plan or he could forget about making any sales. After all, Carl Latimer had sold a reasonable number of machines on the West Coast, and the towns there were prospering. That meant there would be more women—and, therefore, more customers for William.

The young man squared his shoulders. His competitive spirit had awakened. They probably would not leave him on the West Coast any longer than a year, and during that time he would do his best to top even Carl Latimer's miraculous numbers. And what about the Maori? Had anyone ever tried to sell a Singer to a native?

Later that same day, William asked about ferry connections to Blenheim. A week later, he handed over his region to his successor, selling the man his horse and carriage in the process. Then, his old demonstration model in hand, he set off for the South Island. Though there were more modern models on the market now, he did not want to exchange his machine for one of them. His old machine had brought him luck. William was determined to conquer the South Island. Surely, he would hear something from Kura there too. In fact, he could even write Gwyneira again and ask about Gloria. She would certainly know where Kura was these days. And she probably didn't have a sewing machine yet.

Gwyneira was open to almost anything—just not a sewing machine. She might have warmed up to the idea though, if William's letter had contained even a hint of her granddaughter's location. Still, she was quite pleased to hear that Gloria's father made no further claims on the child. It was clear that William knew as little about Kura's whereabouts as she did. The only thing they could be fairly certain of was that Kura had not traveled to England with the opera ensemble.

"She doesn't appear on my receipts," George Greenwood had explained to her. "And Barrister would have tried to pawn her costs off on me, I guarantee you. That man knew all the tricks. If she did make the journey, she didn't travel under her own name, at least according to the shipping company. Then again, she might have given a different one. They don't register these things very exactly."

"But why should she do that?" Gwyneira had asked nervously. "Perhaps because she was still a minor?"

"They would hardly have checked up on that," George had mused, but he had promised to send out feelers in England.

A few weeks later, he had brought Gwyneira the results of his inquiries.

"There's no Kura-maro-tini or any other Maori girl involved in the serious London music scene," he informed her. "My people found Barrister at a rather seedy theater in Cheapside, and Sabina Conetti is singing in a musical—a kind of operetta, lighthearted entertainment. Two of the dancers from the ensemble ended up there too. But no news of Kura. She is definitely not in England. That leaves only the West Coast, the North Island, Australia, and the rest of the world."

Gwyneira had sighed. She worried about Kura almost as much as Elaine.

James did not share her fears. "If it were about her virtue," he'd said drily, "I could understand. But that's not worth a damn. And when it comes to bare survival, I'm not worried about Kura. The girl is resilient, even if she was sheltered."

Gwyneira had admonished him for being heartless, but deep down, she hoped he was right. She could not care less about Kura's virtue. She just wanted to have her back safe and sound as soon as possible.

In the end, it was Marama who picked up a trace. Though Kura's mother had mourned the disappearance of her daughter, she did not worry about her life.

"I would know if anything happened to her," she had said with conviction—and her expectations were finally proved correct. A migrating Maori tribe spoke of a *tohunga* who stayed for a few days in their village near Blenheim. Kura had sung beautifully, enjoyed herself with them, and told them about her heritage in Marama's tribe. There could be no doubt about her identity. But what else she was doing, where she had come from, and where she was going, they had not asked. And when exactly the encounter had taken place the Maori no longer knew.

"The ferry to the North Island is in Blenheim," Gwyneira said with resignation. "So Kura has probably crossed over. But what is she doing there? And what is she trying to prove? My God, she could just come home and—"

"She's not even nineteen yet," Marama remarked. "She's pigheaded and still a little childish. She wants to have everything, and when something goes wrong, she stamps her foot and screams. Never mind that she always plays the adult. At some point, she will come to her senses and return. You just have to wait patiently, Gwyneira."

Waiting had never been Gwyneira's strong suit. But while Kura's disappearance merely challenged her patience, the entire family was deeply concerned about Elaine. Ruben O'Keefe had a private detective searching for her on the North Island, with the utmost discretion.

"We don't want to play into Sideblossom's hands—or the police's, after all," he sighed. "Old Sideblossom is looking for her too. There's no way he'll leave everything to the constable—at least not after what happened with James."

John Sideblossom had wanted a much harsher punishment for James McKenzie after he had caught him rustling animals so long ago. However, James's prison sentence had not been especially arduous, and then the governor had commuted his lifetime banishment. In the end, James had spent a little time in prison followed by a stint in Australia, but he had then returned. John Sideblossom had never gotten over that. He no longer believed in the justice system and would have loved to take the law into his own hands—in Elaine's case as well. But there was still no trace of the girl.

Fleurette O'Keefe lacked Marama's rock-hard faith in the transcendental connection between mother and child. In her nightmares, she saw Elaine dead—sometimes lost and frozen in the mountains, sometimes struck dead and buried somewhere by John Sideblossom, sometimes abused and murdered in some gold-miners' camp on the West Coast.

"Sometimes I'd rather be sure than paint a new horror for myself every night," she wrote to her mother and father, and James McKenzie nodded. He'd had his own dealings with the Sideblossoms, after all, and could well imagine what his granddaughter was running from.

The first person William Martyn recognized on the South Island belonged to someone he thought had long been in England. But there could be no doubt: the young woman strolling along the coastal road with two pretty little girls holding her hands was indeed Heather Witherspoon. She turned her head immediately too, when, without giving it much thought, William called her name. At least there was no hatred in her eyes when she recognized him.

"Redcliff," she immediately said, correcting him with a certain degree of pride. "Heather Redcliff. I've married."

As William looked her over more closely, he saw that marriage suited her well. Heather's face looked rounder and softer, her hair was no longer pulled back so tightly, and the style of her clothing had completely changed. She wasn't wearing the gray or black skirts with silk blouses that she used to, and she no longer seemed as strict as an old spinster. In a pale-blue coat with a pink blouse underneath, she looked quite fashionable even. Her high-laced shoes had a small heel that made her stride look more graceful—and she was wearing proper gold jewelry.

"You look wonderful," William said. "But you could not possibly have two little girls already, though they do bear some resemblance to you."

Indeed, the children were also blonde and blue-eyed. The older one was on course to develop less washed-out-looking features than Heather, and the younger one had light curls that played around her round, childish face.

Heather laughed. "Thank you. I hear that a lot. Annie and Lucie, be polite and say hello to Mr. Martyn. Don't stare at him like that; it's not ladylike. Now, Annie offer him that little hand of yours."

Though the little girl—she might have been five—still got her left and right mixed up, she proved compliant and offered William the correct hand after she had resolved her confusion. She slipped a bit on her curtsy, but Lucie, probably all of eight years old, greeted him in perfect form.

"The girls are my stepdaughters—absolutely wonderful children. We're very proud of them." Heather ran her hand through the younger one's hair. "But would you rather continue this conversation indoors? It will begin to rain again soon."

William nodded. He had just put a hellish crossing behind him and could now confirm all the horror stories he had heard about the unpredictable seas between the two islands. Some tea in a cozy room sounded perfect to him just then. But where did one take respectable ladies here?

Heather had her own ideas about where they should go. "Just come along home with us. We only live two streets away. It's a shame you won't get to meet my husband, but he's away on business. Will you be in town for a while?"

William told her a little about what he'd been up to as he followed Heather and the girls down a peaceful residential street where the family lived in a mansion. William did not need to worry about Heather's reputation either: a housemaid opened the door for the two of them, curtsied, and took his coat. Heather watched, rather pleased, as he deposited his card in the tray laid out for that purpose.

"Bring some tea and cake to the salon, Sandy," Heather instructed the maid. "The children will take their tea in their room. Please keep an eye on them after you have served us."

The maid curtsied. The entire scene struck William as a bit surreal.

"It's such a relief not to have to deal with Maori domestics," Heather chattered as she led William into her expensively furnished salon. The room was at least as tastefully decorated as the rooms at Kiward Station, though he could tell that it had not been done by Heather herself. After all, William knew her taste from their work together on Kura's apartments. She had truly found her golden-egg-laying hen in this Mr. Redcliff. "True, Sandy is a simple girl—she comes from a coal-mining family in Westport—but at least you can speak to her in English, and you don't have to constantly be reminding her to put on shoes."

Although William had never thought the Maori domestics on Kiward Station particularly uncivilized, he nodded encouragingly at Heather. Perhaps she would finally tell him how she had ended up in Blenheim.

"Oh, it was just dumb luck," she explained when the tea was finally in front of them, and they were nibbling on little cakes. "After you showed no interest in continuing to travel with me"—she gave him a cold look, at which William lowered his eyes guiltily—"I found a coach to take me from Haldon to Christchurch. I wanted to return to London, but the next ship wasn't scheduled to leave for a few days, so I rented a room in the White Hart in the meantime. That's where I met Mr. Redcliff. Julian Redcliff. He spoke to me in the breakfast room, exceptionally politely, only after having the hostess ask whether he might speak with me. Julian is very concerned that everything be done properly."

She gave William another meaningful look, who made an effort to look even more contrite, as he had quite understood her unspoken message: *Unlike you, Mr. Redcliff is a gentleman.*

"In any event, he wanted to ask me to look after his daughters on the passage to London. They were scheduled to travel to England to attend a boarding school." Heather fidgeted with her coiffure until a lock of hair broke loose and slid down over her right ear.

She looked quite pretty. William dared an admiring smile.

"The little girls?" he asked incredulously.

"It broke Mr. Redcliff's heart too, of course," she declared energetically. "But his wife had died a short time before, and he works for the railroad."

"Not laying the tracks, I suppose," William observed, letting his gaze wander over the room.

Heather smiled proudly. "No, managing the construction. They're now connecting the East Coast with all the coal-mining regions on the West Coast. It's a massive project, and Mr. Redcliff works in a position of responsibility. Unfortunately, it means he must travel a great deal. It would be absolutely impossible for him to raise the children on his own."

William saw where this was going. "Unless he had a trustworthy, well-reputed governess."

Heather nodded. "He was delighted when he heard my references, and I was instantly taken with Annie and Lucie. They are . . ."

. . . very different from Kura. William completed her thought in his mind. Heather's fondness for her stepchildren was obviously real.

"So we did not go to England, neither the children nor myself. Instead, I took over the management of Mr. Redcliff's household, and our feelings for each other began to grow. After his year of mourning had passed, we married," Heather concluded, beaming at William, who returned her smile. He thought about this Mr. Redcliff. He could hardly be the most passionate of men—if after all this time, he still could not get his wife to address him by his first name.

"So you're no longer mad at me?" he finally asked. He liked this house. It was warm, the bar was no doubt well stocked—and Heather was prettier than ever. Perhaps she would be interested in reviving their old acquaintanceship. William leaned a little closer to her. Playing with her hair, Heather released another lock.

"Why should I be mad at you?" she replied. She seemed already to have forgotten the cool looks she had been giving him earlier. "Looking back, it was actually a very lucky twist of fate. If we had stayed together, where would I be then? The wife of a salesman?"

It sounded a bit deprecatory, but William merely smiled. She was, of course, boasting about her new wealth. Now *she* was the owner of the manor. His station was beneath hers, no matter how well he sold sewing machines. He would probably never own such an estate himself—certainly not if he continued to climb the Singer hierarchy.

He had other qualities, though. William laid his hand lightly on Heather's and played with her fingers.

"You would, however, have been one of the first women on the South Island to own a sewing machine," he joked. "They're little miracle workers, and unlike working with needle and thread, your hands remain as soft and delicate as they are." He caressed each individual finger as he counted off in a soft voice how many stitches the latest Singer saved the manicured woman's hand, and he finished by explaining to her more concretely, but with somewhat heavy breath, what other wonderful things a person could do with the time they saved.

In the end, Heather's cook and housemaid unexpectedly received the evening off, the children a nighttime drink flavored with a tiny drop of laudanum, and William an exceedingly pleasant first night back on the South Island. Heather remembered everything he had taught her—and seemed starved for love. Julian Redcliff was doubtless a gentleman but a cold fish nevertheless.

"The maintenance falls to you, doesn't it?" Heather asked as they parted from each other one last time before the sun rose. "I can turn to you if anything about this . . . um . . . sewing machine breaks?"

William nodded, stroking her still-flat stomach. Julian Redcliff seemed not yet to have planted another child, but Heather had told William they were doing their best. She might have just gotten somewhat closer to that goal.

"For normal customers, I come by whenever I'm in the area next," William whispered, his hand feeling its way lower. "But for special customers . . ."

Heather smiled and arched toward his hand.

"Naturally, I still need a more thorough introduction."

William's fingers played with her soft blonde pubic hair. "Introductions are my specialty."

Heather needed two afternoons in his hotel room before she had completely mastered the technique. After that, she signed the sales contract for a sewing machine.

William sent it triumphantly to Wellington. His stay on the South Island had gotten off to an excellent start.

7

Timothy Lambert lay in his plaster casts for five months. He had withstood the raging pain of the first few weeks and the acute boredom of the last weeks, which made him restless and insufferable, and endured all the weeks in between. In the meantime, things were not going smoothly in the Lambert Mine. Many opportunities to renovate and improve the mine after the accident were not implemented during the repair work. Timothy was impatient to get involved again. But whenever his father even bothered to make an appearance—he seemed to have to work up some Dutch courage first—and then peered at his son through glassy eyes, he answered Timothy's questions about the mine with vague platitudes. His remarks filled Timothy with rage, but he put up with his father's ignorance and his mother's caterwauling—and moreover, even managed a smile, a joke, and a little optimism when Elaine came by in the evenings.

Berta Leroy observed with fascination that Timothy never took his bad moods out on Elaine—as he did on other regular visitors. And no matter how bad the pain was in the beginning or how desperately he sometimes dug his fingernails into the sheets, he always enfolded Elaine's hand with his fingers as warily as if she were a timid little bird. For her part, Elaine seemed to spend her entire day gathering stories with which to cheer Timothy up. She laughed with him and commented on the town gossip with sharp and pointed words, read to him, and played chess with him. It surprised Timothy that she had such a command of the game. Not that he believed her story about her origins—Elaine like to claim that she was from a working family in Auckland. He'd only had to ask her about two important building projects in Auckland to determine that the girl had clearly never seen the city.

Elaine's daily visits kept Timothy going. Still, as the weeks stretched on in torturous boredom, he grew increasingly impatient for the day when he would finally be free of his casts. When the expert from Christchurch finally fixed a date and announced that he would be appearing in the middle of July, Timothy could hardly contain his joy.

"I can't wait to see you again at eye level," he said, laughing, when Elaine came to see him that afternoon. "It's horrible having to look up at people all the time." They had become much more familiar with one another over the last few months. Fortunately, the girl could manage familiarity.

Elaine frowned. "If you were as short as I am, you would have gotten used to it a long time ago," she teased. "Besides, Napoleon is supposed to have been a pretty short fellow."

"At least he could sit on a horse. What is Fellow up to these days? Is he looking forward to seeing me again?"

Elaine had held onto Timothy's gelding after the accident. None of the Lamberts had ever asked about the horse, so Fellow had simply remained in Madame Clarisse's stables. Madame Clarisse did not complain as long as Elaine took care of the feeding costs, and the grain dealer had put that on the Lamberts' tab at Timothy's behest anyway. Banshee was delighted to have the company, and Elaine took turns riding the horses. Timothy looked forward to her daily reports, and that alone made the extra effort worth it.

"Of course," Elaine said. "But do you think you'll be able to ride right away?"

Elaine would have loved to share Timothy's optimism, but the doctors' bad prognosis still rang in her ears. What if Timothy's bones had not healed as well as he hoped? If he could not walk again at all or had to always use crutches at best? She did not want to remind Timothy of Dr. Leroy's fears, but she was as fearful as she was hopeful when she thought about the day his casts were to be removed.

"The day I can't ride anymore is the day I die," Timothy said, and Elaine had to laugh. She knew that expression from her grandmother

Gwyneira; she would have so much liked to tell Timothy about the tough old woman. But caution made her keep it to herself. It was better not to let anyone in on her true life story. And one did not need to be all that clever to know that a laborer's daughter from Auckland did not have a sheep baron for a grandmother.

"It doesn't have to be right on the first day," she said vaguely.

While Timothy spent the following weeks doing nothing but making plans for after his liberation, Berta Leroy looked on in an increasingly concerned frame of mind. On the day before the specialist's visit, she took Elaine aside.

"Be here tomorrow when they remove the casts. He'll need you," she said grimly, with an almost threatening undertone.

Elaine looked up at her in confusion.

"He doesn't want me there," she said with some regret. "I'm not supposed to come until afterward."

"He thinks he'll be able to walk to you smiling," Berta remarked bitterly, pointing to a pair of crutches that leaned next to the door to Timothy's hospital room. "The carpenter made them from pictures in a catalog since Dr. Porter had not wanted to bring any. Nellie Lambert told Tim they would be too cumbersome to transport, but she never knew how to work the truth."

"Work what truth?" Elaine felt an ice-cold tingle down her spine. "Wasn't it that no one could know exactly how well the fractures would heal? And now, Tim's so sure. He hasn't had any pain for weeks."

"Child," Berta sighed as she pushed Elaine gently in the direction of her living quarters behind the doctor's office. "I think we'd better have some tea first, and then I'll try and help you understand what to expect. Tim doesn't want to hear it of course, and Nellie . . ."

Elaine followed the doctor's wife uneasily. She had known that it would not be as simple as Timothy hoped. But this sounded far more serious than she had thought.

"Lainie"—Berta finally spoke when they had two steaming cups of tea in front of them—"even if Tim's right to be optimistic, which I hope with all my heart . . ."

But don't believe, Elaine continued in her head.

"Even if everything has healed perfectly, he still won't be able to walk tomorrow. Not tomorrow, not the day after, nor in a week or even in a month." Berta stirred her tea.

"But my brother could walk right after he broke his leg," Elaine objected. "Sure, he limped a little, but—"

"How long was your brother bedridden? Five weeks? Six weeks? Probably not, you can't keep a boy inside. Let me guess. After three weeks, he was happily up and about on two crutches and one good leg, was that it?"

Elaine smiled. "After one. My mother just wasn't supposed to know."

Berta nodded. "There you have it. My lands, Lainie, you can't be that naïve. That horse you're always telling him about, you give it exercise. Why do you do that?"

Elaine looked confused. "So that it doesn't get out of shape. If horses just stand around, they lose muscle."

"Don't you see?" Berta said, satisfied. "And how much muscle would a nag lose laying about for five months?"

Elaine laughed. "Then he'd be dead. Horses can't lie down for that long." Suddenly she understood what Berta was trying to tell her, and her expression turned serious. "You mean, Tim will be too weak to move?"

Berta nodded again. "His muscles have withered, his tendons shortened, his joints stiffened. It'll be awhile before that's all back in working order. And it won't happen on its own, Lainie. The last few weeks were a cakewalk compared to what Tim has ahead of him if he really wants to learn to walk again. He'll need an unbelievable amount of courage, and strength, and maybe even someone who—pardon the expression—kicks him in the rear occasionally. Every last thing is going to hurt at first, and he's going to have to fight for every inch he can move his joints. There's no chance that he'll be working or riding right away. And that's all going to hit him tomorrow all of a sudden. Just be there when it happens, Lainie. Just be there." Berta's voice was both concerned and serious.

"But he wants to go home straightaway," Elaine said. "I—"

"What an idea!" Berta snorted. "I can't bear to think of delivering him to Nellie in his condition. She's long since come to terms with babying him, and she seems to like it better and better. She's bored to death in that big house. If she had someone there whose nerves she could get on whenever she wanted, she'd really come into her own. She's already hired a nurse for the more unpleasant work. She's coming tomorrow with Dr. Porter. With a wheelchair too. She's already started calling Tim 'baby.' Lainie, if we leave Tim to his parents, he won't be there two weeks before he's numbing himself with anything he can get his hands on. I'm not giving him any morphine, but Nellie has more than enough laudanum, and men tend to prefer whiskey anyway."

"But what am I supposed to do?" Elaine asked, discouraged. "I can ride to the Lamberts' place, but . . ."

"First you need to be there tomorrow," Berta explained. "Let's see what happens then."

Elaine watched from inside the pub as the coach with the doctor from Christchurch left the little hospital, followed shortly by a chaise containing Nellie Lambert and a squarely built young woman dressed as a nurse. Then she walked over. Berta Leroy was waiting for her in the anteroom, alternating between rage and despair.

"Go to him, Lainie," she said without inflection. "They want to take him tomorrow. Dr. Porter and my husband both declared him unfit for transport today."

"Did it heal that badly?" Elaine asked quietly.

Berta shook her head. "Not at all. Quite well, actually. Dr. Porter is very enthusiastic about the hip, even if it's still a little out of line. But otherwise, he thinks Tim has every reason to hope for the best. Though his best hope right now consists of taking two steps on crutches between the bed and the wheelchair. Yes, my Christopher put it that starkly. Tim is, naturally, shaken to the core. We had the usual waterworks from Nellie. Don't put morphine or anything else in his hand that he could use on himself. I'm afraid he's capable of anything."

Elaine fought back her tears as she opened the door to Timothy's room. But she reached for the crutches with determination and took them in with her.

She had to blink when she entered the room. Timothy lay in half darkness—as he so often did whenever Nellie left him. Usually, he called Berta right afterward and asked her to open the curtains again. But now he could reach the lamp on the night table himself. He was not lying in his bed as usual but reclining in a half-sitting position, leaning back on his pillows. He did not even turn his head when Elaine entered, and instead continued to stare, motionless, at the wall across from him.

"Tim." Elaine felt a sudden urge to sit on his bed, but then she saw his face, and the familiar expression of pain and strenuous self-control. He would not be able to stand being touched at the moment.

"Tim." Elaine placed the crutches next to the bed and drew the curtains open. Timothy's face was deathly pale and his eyes had an absent look to them. Elaine smiled at him. "You're looking better already," she said kindly. "It's almost like you're sitting up. You don't even need to work to be at eye level when I sit down too."

A weak smile passed over Timothy's features.

"Little more will come of it," he said quietly. "I'll never be able to walk again." He turned his face to her.

Elaine caressed his forehead gently. "Tim, right now you're tired and disappointed. But it's not all that bad. Mrs. Leroy was very optimistic, and look what I brought with me." She pointed to the crutches. "Just watch, in a few weeks—"

"I won't be able to do it, Lainie. Would you all just tell me the truth!" Timothy wanted to sound angry, but the words came out choked. Elaine saw the tears in his eyes and noticed that they were ringed with red. He must have been crying when he was alone. She once more fought the urge to take him in her arms like a child. She must not think of him like that! If everyone treated him like a hopeless cripple . . .

"The truth depends on you alone," she stated firmly. "It's a question of how long you exercise, how much you can take. And there's almost nothing you can't take. Shall I help you lie back down? You're in pain right now, aren't you? Why did you let them leave you like this?"

Timothy managed a brief smile. "I threw her out. I couldn't bear it anymore—so both doctors declared me of unsound mind. That's the only reason I'm still here. Otherwise, they would have packed me up in that thing straightaway."

A burning rage seized Elaine when she spotted the wheelchair that Nellie Lambert and the nurse had deposited in a corner of the room. It was a voluminous thing with a headrest and flower-print cushions. Elaine would have picked something like that out for an old woman who was only ever going to be pushed from one room to another. Wheeling it with one's own arms, as she had occasionally seen the lame do on the streets of Queenstown, would be almost impossible in such a contraption. With those soft cushions, Timothy would be forced into more of a reclining position than a seated one.

"My God, didn't they have anything else?" she exclaimed.

Timothy shrugged. "This was apparently exactly to my mother's taste," he said bitterly. "Lainie, I'll never get out of that thing. But maybe you can actually give me a hand me now. If I lie down, at least I won't have to look at it anymore."

Supporting his head, Elaine tried to gently remove the pillows out from under his body to lower him back into a supine position. It was not easy, however. His upper body was heavy, and she ended up putting her arm so far around his head that he rested on her shoulder. She felt his presence more strongly than she ever had, and it was pleasant to hold him and feel his warmth. Before she let him slide back onto the pillows, she turned her head to him and gave him a shy kiss on the forehead.

"You're not alone," she whispered to him. "I'm here. I can just as well visit you at home as here. After all, I still have two horses."

Timothy smiled, though it was clear he was still in pain.

"You're awfully meddlesome, Lainie," he teased as he freed himself with perceptible unwillingness from her embrace. "What will my fantastic new nurse, Elizabeth Toeburton, have to say about that?"

Elaine stroked his cheek. "Nothing, I hope. Otherwise, I'll get jealous."

She tried to imitate his jocular tone, though she felt like crying. He looked so tired and helpless, and yet here he was trying to cheer her up. She would have liked to embrace him again—and all at once she could picture being embraced by him someday.

Elaine took a deep breath. "Or do you want to marry Miss Toeburton now?"

Timothy looked at her, and his expression suddenly turned serious. "Lainie, what does that mean? You're not saying that out of pity, are you? I'm not misunderstanding you, am I? And you won't take it back tomorrow, will you?"

She shook her head. "I'll marry you, Timothy Lambert. But that thing there," she said, pointing at the wheelchair, "I won't marry that. So see to it that you don't need it for long. Got it?"

Timothy's exhausted face lit up.

"You know what I promised," he said hoarsely. "I'll dance at our wedding. But for now I want a proper kiss. Not on the forehead or on the cheek. You have to kiss me on the mouth."

He looked at her expectantly, but Elaine hesitated. She suddenly remembered William's deceptively sweet kisses. And Thomas's violent entry into her mouth and body. Timothy saw the fear in her eyes and wanted to take his request back. But then she overcame her fears and kissed him, hesitantly and tentatively. Her lips had barely brushed his when she pulled back and looked around almost in a panic.

"Callie?"

Confused, Timothy watched her as she searched for the dog, which had curled up under his bed as soon as she had entered the room. Berta Leroy did not like having the dog in her sickrooms, which Callie seemed to understand. Normally she kept out of the Leroys' sight, but now she came out, and, wagging her tail, pushed her face against Timothy's dangling hand. For some reason, it seemed to calm

Elaine to see him scratch the dog between the ears before holding his hand out to her. Elaine approached him again and entwined her fingers trustingly with his.

"It'll all get better, Lainie," he said sweetly. "We just need to practice dancing and kissing a bit."

And as he held her hand and watched the stars slowly appear in the little piece of sky he could see outside his window, he considered that Elaine's path to dancing at their wedding might be just as long and hard as his.

When Elaine stopped by the doctor's office the next day around noon, she did not find Berta in the clinic as usual. But the doors were not locked, and Elaine knew she would be welcome in Timothy's room. However, she was not prepared for the sight that awaited her there. Timothy had disappeared, as had his wheelchair. Instead, she found Berta Leroy lying on the bed, propped up by cushions, and Roly O'Brien putting his arm awkwardly around her. He let her head slide to his shoulder, reached for her waist . . .

Elaine stared openmouthed at the old nurse. But before she could slam the door in horror, Berta caught sight of her and let out a booming laugh.

"Good God, Lainie, it's not what you think!" she chuckled. "Oh, you should see your face. I can't believe it. Did you really think I was up to no good with a half pint like this one?"

Elaine turned a glowing red.

"Hello, Miss Keefer," Roly said. He appeared to grasp neither the situation's suggestive nature, nor the comedy of it.

"Let me reassure you, child. This is only a nursing course. We couldn't find any volunteers who would pretend to be patients. My husband didn't really need to leave for the Kellys' this morning—he just wanted to get out of doing this. He has the same feelings about male nurses as Nellie Lambert has."

"Maybe Miss Keefer could volunteer?" Roly inquired hopefully, casting a covetous eye over Elaine's slim body.

Berta leaped up. "You'd like that, wouldn't you! And then afterward, you'd tell the whole pub Miss Keefer let you feel her up. Now get out of here. We'll continue in an hour or so. Maybe my husband will be back by then and spare us any surprises like the one we just had." She chuckled again, and it struck Elaine that it had been a long time since she had seen Berta so happy. "Perish the thought if Mrs. Carey or Mrs. Tanner saw us like that. Come have some tea with me, Lainie. I want to know what you did to Tim."

After Roly had left the room, Berta closed the office temporarily and shooed Elaine into her apartment.

"If someone wants something, they can ring. Now tell me. How did you do it?"

Elaine's head was spinning. "A male nurse?" she asked. "For Tim?"

Berta nodded, beaming like a child under the Christmas tree.

"Tim was like a changed man today. When they came for him this morning, they wanted to carry him out on a stretcher, but he insisted that they seat him in that monstrosity of a chair. He said he hadn't suffered here for five months just to be carried out like he was brought in. And then the first thing he did was dismiss his nurse."

Elaine smiled. "The Miss Toeburton I've heard so much about?"

Berta laughed. "One and the same. She said something to him like 'And now we're going to lay this nice, soft pillow under your hip, Tim,' to which he answered that he hadn't given her permission to call him by his first name. That awful mother of his looked at him like an ornery three-year-old and said, and I quote, 'Now, be polite, baby.' Then he exploded. And I tell you, a dynamite blast is nothing compared to what I witnessed. He had let Nellie's caterwauling bounce off him for five months, but that was too much. They heard him roaring all the way out on the street, and I enjoyed every word. First, he sent his nurse packing. She's leaving right away with the expert from Christchurch after he fits Tim with leg splints, though he thinks it's too soon or too senseless to bother with them. But my husband took Tim's side. If Dr. Porter didn't want to put on the splints, he'd do it himself, he said. And naturally, Dr. Porter didn't want to risk letting a town doctor take the credit. After that, Tim asked for a male caregiver. If there weren't any available, we'd just have to train one. And that's just what I was doing with Roly. Now, tell me how you did it, Lainie. I'm dying of curiosity."

Elaine, however, was still preoccupied with the idea of a male nurse. "How did you decide on Roly?"

Berta rolled her eyes impatiently. "Mrs. O'Brien was in the office next door when the bomb went off. And like I said, you couldn't get away from Tim's yelling, no matter how indiscreet you thought it was to listen in. Mrs. O'Brien came up to me rather shyly afterward and asked if we couldn't give Roly a try. The boy hasn't wanted to go down in the mine since the accident. You can't blame him, but naturally it puts the family in a rather difficult spot financially. The father dead, the oldest son without a real job. Roly's been getting by as an errand boy, but he makes next to nothing. He wouldn't think anything of it if the others teased him for being a nurse. Not when it's for Timothy Lambert. You already know how he worships Tim."

Roly was among Timothy's most dedicated visitors. The boy was convinced he owed Timothy his life, and he would do anything for him.

"Now, tell me, Lainie. What happened yesterday between you and Tim? You stayed for a while, didn't you? I had to leave with Christopher, you know."

Dr. Leroy had been called away to a difficult birth, and Berta always accompanied him to those.

"I stayed until he fell asleep," Elaine said. "But that wasn't all that long. He was deathly tired."

"There was nothing more to it?" Berta asked incredulously. "You only held hands a bit, and then all was well again?"

Elaine smiled. "Not quite. While we were at it we . . . might have gotten engaged."

8

"You must help me, Kura! You're the only one who can!" Caleb
Biller appeared in the Wild Rover on a Thursday just before
midnight, much later than usual and completely out of sorts. He was
also more elegantly dressed than he usually was for a visit to the pub.
His gray three-piece suit was better suited to a formal dinner party.
Though he could hardly wait for Kura to finish the piece she was
playing, he nonetheless managed to gulp down a whiskey.

"What is going on, Caleb?" Kura asked, amused. As she had gotten to know Caleb better over the last few months, she had grown
accustomed to his occasionally peculiar reactions to more or less
petty, everyday problems. Since the dance in the Maori village, she
had done everything she could to quell her desire for physical love
from Caleb. She understood that he shared the predilection of some of
the members of Roderick's ensemble who were more drawn to their
own sex. Kura acknowledged this utterly without judgment. After
all, having grown up the sheltered heiress of the Warden estate, she
had never been confronted with resentment against homosexuality.
And she had learned about this aspect of human nature for the first
time among artists, where it was accepted as normal. Kura did not
understand why Caleb made such a secret about it, but she had come
to understand her role in the Biller household: Caleb's parents were
willing to accept even a bar singer with Maori ancestry, as long as it
was a girl.

"They want me to get engaged," Caleb blurted out. Much too loudly
really, though the pub was fairly quiet at that hour on a weeknight.
The mine workers had already left, and the few remaining drunks at

the bar appeared to be immersed in their own troubles. Only Paddy Holloway looked over with a smirk, which Caleb didn't even notice.

"Seriously, Kura, they didn't say it in so many words, of course, but there were these intimations! And the girl, the way she behaves. As though she already knew with certainty that she would be the future Mrs. Biller. Everything has been arranged and . . ."

"Slow down, Caleb. What girl?" Kura exchanged a look with Paddy that let her know that he had nothing against her closing the piano for the night. Instead, he brought two glasses over for Kura and Caleb at an out-of-the-way table.

"Her name is Florence," Caleb said, swallowing down the second whiskey. "Florence Weber, of the Weber Mine near Westport. And she is quite pretty, well educated; you can converse with her about anything, but . . ."

Kura took a sip herself and noted with delight that Paddy had poured her a single malt as well. The barkeeper clearly thought she could use it.

"So, once more, Caleb. Your parents had a dinner party today. Is that correct?" That was not difficult to deduce from Caleb's clothes. "For this Weber family from Westport. And they introduced the girl to you then."

"Introduced? They presented her like a debutante. In a white dress, even. Well, not all white, there was a touch of green on it too. Appliqué around the neckline, you see."

Kura rolled her eyes. That was also typical of Caleb. He could never manage to concentrate on what was most important, because he was always being captivated by the details. This trait was helpful when it came to their work together—and the Maoris greatly appreciated it. Over the last few months, Kura and Caleb had sought out other villages where they could study *haka*, and Caleb could lose himself for hours working with some *tohunga*, discussing, for instance, the stylization of a fern in a typical carving. He had picked up the Maori language very quickly and took special note of unusual words—almost more than common words like "water" or "village." Caleb's meticulous nature did not make him particularly well suited to daily life, however, and in situations like this, he could drive his listener to distraction.

"Get to the point, Caleb," Kura admonished.

"In any case, they never stopped talking about the mines, the Webers' or ours, and their common distribution lanes. And she looked me over with such a resigned expression. It was as though she weren't even at the horse market, but had already been stuck with a lame nag and decided to try to make the best of it."

Kura had to laugh. "But you're no lame nag," she remarked.

"No, but a 'queer fellow,' as they say," Caleb whispered, sinking his head far over his glass. "I don't like girls."

Kura furrowed her brow. "People refer to that as being a 'queer fellow'? I hadn't heard that. But it's hardly a surprise."

Caleb looked up at her, confused. "You . . . you knew?" His long face turned red as a beet.

Kura had to laugh. It was inconceivable that this man had not noticed her attempts to seduce him. But it would do no good to tease him about it. So she nodded and waited for Caleb to cease struggling to breathe and for his face to resume a halfway-normal coloring.

"As I said, it hasn't escaped me," she said finally. "But what do you plan to do now? Should I . . . I mean, would you like me to sleep with you? That won't work; I can tell you that straightaway. Bernadette, one of the dancers in the ensemble, was in love with Jimmy, but he was . . . like you. Bernadette tried everything: made herself pretty, fondled him, got him drunk. But nothing worked. Some are just one way, others another."

Kura had no trouble accepting that. Caleb considered her again with pained, if also slightly embarrassed, looks.

"I would never importune you in that manner, Kura," he assured her. "Even to think about it would be indecent."

Kura could hardly hold back her giggling. She hoped Paddy Holloway was not listening and spreading this conversation around the pub.

"It's only . . . Kura, would you get engaged to me?"

There. He had said it. Caleb looked at her expectantly, but the hopeful light in his eyes went out when he saw the expression on her face.

Kura sighed. "How would that help, Caleb? I won't marry you, absolutely not. Even if I could, I mean, even if I could warm up to the idea of getting married. I would want something out of it. I wasn't made for a platonic marriage. You're better off asking this Florence girl. *Pakeha* women are often brought up rather prudish."

"But I don't even know her." Caleb almost sounded like a child, and it struck Kura that he was scared to death of the Weber heiress. "And I wasn't even thinking of marrying. Just of . . . er . . . being engaged. Or pretending that were the case. Until I think of another solution."

Kura couldn't help but wonder what solution Caleb could possibly think of. However, he was highly intelligent. Perhaps he would find an answer once he had calmed down a bit.

"Please, Kura," he said. "At least come to Sunday dinner. If I invite you formally, that's practically a sign."

Kura saw it more as a declaration of war, but the likes of Florence Weber did not scare her. The girl would probably look for the closest hole to crawl through as soon as she laid eyes on Kura. Kura knew how girls typically reacted to her, and she would do with Florence Weber just what she had done with Elaine O'Keefe.

"All right, fine, Caleb. But if I'm going to play your fiancée, you must stop being so formal with me."

Florence proved to be of an entirely different caliber than Elaine. A person would require both Caleb's kind disposition and his lack of instincts about female beauty to even call the girl "quite pretty." Florence was short and of a shape that, though still appealing now, would assume the roundness of her mother after her first child. The pale-red freckles on her oval, almost doughy face did not exactly suit her thick brown hair. Though her dark tresses looked just as unruly as Elaine's, they seemed to be smothering her face rather than dancing playfully around her features. Added to which, the girl was nearsighted—which was perhaps one of the reasons the sight of Kura had not completely demoralized her.

"So, you are Caleb's . . . friend," Florence remarked as she greeted Kura. "I've heard you sing." Florence emphasized the words "friend" and "sing" as she spoke, as though they demonstrated a total lack of propriety. However, the fact that Caleb kept company with barroom singers did not seem to shock her. Kura came to the conclusion that Florence Weber was not so easily shaken.

"Florence took a few singing lessons herself," Mrs. Biller piped. Though she had emphasized Kura's attractive qualities at the last dinner party, she had apparently since decided to advocate for the Weber heiress. "In England. Isn't that right, Florence?"

Florence nodded, with eyes cast down demurely. "But merely to pass the time," she said with a smile. "You can enjoy an opera or chamber music concert so much more when you have some understanding of how much work and how many hours are poured into a production of that sort. Don't you agree, Caleb?"

Caleb could only nod.

"But you never really *studied* singing, did you, Miss Martyn?"

Kura remained composed on the surface, but she was angry. This girl did not have even a modicum of fear or respect for her. And she would not be satisfied with Kura's usual monosyllabic answers. Florence seemed to know that trick and only asked questions that required that Kura to answer in complete sentences or with as many justifications as possible.

"I was privately educated," Kura explained briefly.

At which point Mrs. Biller, Mrs. Weber, and Florence all pointed out the undeniable advantages of a boarding-school education.

Caleb listened with a pained expression on his face. His boarding-school education had helped him to understand his predisposition early in life. He had admitted as much to Kura later on that night in the pub, but of course he could not use that as an argument here. Instead, he presented such a theatrical demonstration of his love for Kura that it was almost embarrassing. A gentleman would never have put his feelings on display in that manner, but in this case, Caleb lacked his sense, usually so fine, for what was appropriate.

Kura reflected that any other girl would surely have run screaming from the room if presented with such a candidate for marriage. Florence Weber, however, observed the performance with a stoic smile and ironclad composure. She chatted affectedly about music and art, effortlessly managing to make Caleb look silly and lovestruck, and Kura like Jezebel herself: "I understand that you particularly love *Carmen*, Miss Martyn. I'm sure you lend her a very convincing . . . air. No, I don't think Don José is really to be blamed. If sin comes in such a seductive guise as that gypsy. And besides, he gets over her in the end. If by . . . well, rather drastic means." She smiled at that, as though she would be ready at any time to sharpen the knife that would finally be thrust between Kura's ribs.

Kura was thrilled when she could finally make her escape; Caleb, however, remained prey to Florence Weber. The Webers were the Billers' houseguests while they looked for their own residence in Greymouth. Mr. Weber had acquired a share in the new train line and wanted to put his business affairs in order. It was quite possible that the Webers would reside with the Billers for several weeks before they returned to Westport, during which time they obviously hoped that Florence and Caleb would feather their own nest.

The young man showed up at the pub again the next day in a dejected state and told Kura his sorrows. While his mother had dealt with him harshly that very evening after dinner, his father had gone about it more subtly. The next morning, he had asked his son to come into his office to say a few serious words to him, man to man. "Boy, naturally you're attracted to that Kura girl. She's without a doubt the loveliest thing you could imagine, but we have to think about the future too. Give Florence a couple of kids to keep her busy, and then find yourself a pretty mistress."

Caleb looked so desperate that even Paddy had some sympathy and waved Kura away from the piano.

"Cheer the boy up a bit, girl. No one wants to see a sad sight like that. But get him to buy a bottle of the single malt while you're at it, got it? Otherwise, you'll have to make up the difference in what we make."

Kura rolled her eyes. Paddy was probably already taking bets on when and whether a milksop like Caleb Biller would ever succeed in getting Florence Weber pregnant.

"She's awful," Caleb mumbled, seeming to tremble at the very thought of the girl. "She wants to smother me completely."

"That can happen," Kura said drily, imagining the corpulence she expected of Florence someday. "But you don't have to marry her. No one can make you. Look here, Caleb, I've been thinking about it."

She had actually been doing just that and, in the process, had gotten involved in someone else's problems for the first time in her life. Kura could hardly comprehend it herself, but then again, the results of her efforts might work out favorably for her as well. She poured Caleb a large glass of whiskey and laid out her thoughts.

"You could never, ever live here in Greymouth with another man," she explained. "People would never stop talking about you if you did such a thing, and your parents would drag one Florence Weber after another into the house. You'd eventually get worn down, Caleb. That simply won't work. You would only be left the life of a bachelor. But you're an artist. You play the piano very well, and you've got a talent for composing and arranging music. There's no reason for you to make your gifts public only after you've gotten drunk in the pub."

"Kura, please! Have you ever seen me drunk?" Caleb looked at her indignantly before pouring himself a third glass of whiskey.

"Well, no, not drunk, but tipsy," Kura replied. "But an artist needs to have the courage to sit at the piano without whiskey. What I'm getting at is that we could put a recital together, Caleb. You arrange a few of the *haka* and songs we've collected for piano and voice. Or for two pianos with vocal accompaniment, or for a duet on one. The more voices, the better it will work. We can test it out here and in Westport, and then we can go on a tour. First around the South Island, then the North Island. Then Australia, England . . ."

"England?" Caleb looked hopeful. After all this time, he still dreamed of his friends from boarding school. "Do you think we could be that successful?"

"Why not?" Kura was full of confidence. "I like your arrangements, and the Londoners supposedly love anything exotic. It's worth a try, at any rate. You just need to trust yourself, Caleb. Your father—"

"My father won't be enthusiastic." Caleb chewed his lower lip. "But at first, we could perform at charity events. My mother is involved in those, as is Mrs. Weber."

Kura smiled sardonically. "*Miss* Weber will undoubtedly be more charmed than anyone. So, shall we do it? If you want to do it, we can practice in the evenings, after the mine closes and before the pub opens."

As expected, Florence Weber put on a brave face and pretended to be quite enthused by the music of the Maori. Fortunately for Caleb, the Webers had begun renting a house in Greymouth by this time, and Florence and her mother spent a great deal of their time furnishing it. Mrs. Biller raved every day about the taste and skills that Florence was developing in the process.

Kura noted with amusement that Caleb actually enjoyed it when Florence flirtatiously asked for his advice about wallpaper colors and seat covers. Caleb was an aesthete. He could find something to enjoy in every artistic endeavor, though his first love was music.

For her part, Florence studied the sheet music with a serious expression, though Kura doubted the girl could read the notes. Being of a rather practical nature, however, she soon made a habit of accompanying Caleb to his practice sessions.

Naturally, that ignited the town gossip, which vexed Caleb to no end. Kura observed it all calmly. Her new partner needed to get used to playing in front of an audience one way or another. He might as well start with the most difficult test. And that was Florence Weber, without question. She criticized them without compunction. Even if her critiques were meant more unkindly than constructively, she was right more often than not and Kura adopted many of her suggestions.

"Shouldn't you accompany this song with a few . . . how should I put it . . . descriptive gestures?" she inquired about the love song given to them by Kura's friends at the Pancake Rocks.

It had become both Kura and Caleb's favorite piece. Caleb's arrangements sounded artful and playful, in stark contrast to the straightforward lyrics. Caleb had eventually learned what the words meant but had never translated them for Florence. Yet Kura's expressive voice and Caleb's ebullient and occasionally provocative accompaniment gave Florence a good sense of what they were about. Caleb blushed deeply when Florence asked questions about the songs with apparent innocence, but Kura merely smiled. When she sang the song again, Kura started swinging and thrusting her hips so enticingly that Paddy Holloway's eyes nearly fell out of his head. And Florence Weber's even more so.

"I'll hold myself back a little in front of the pastor, of course," Kura said to Caleb afterward when Florence had disappeared—for once—with a beet-red face.

They had already arranged to perform their first concert in Greymouth at the church picnic. The proceeds would benefit the families of the victims of the Lambert Mine accident. In addition, thanks to Mrs. Biller's assistance, they had a performance planned in one of the hotels on the quay. Though Kura was looking forward to the concerts, Caleb was anxious.

"Now, don't be like that. You're an artist," Kura teased him. "Think of the beautiful body of our Maori friend and how nice it would be if he were here now and could dance to your song. Just don't start thrusting your hips when you do or you'll knock the piano over."

William Martyn ignored the bigger towns on the West Coast for the time being. He assumed that Carl Latimer would already have sold a sewing machine to any remotely interested woman who could pay for one in those urban areas. That left only the miners' wives, and he was not likely to do much business with them. Instead, William concentrated on the single-family settlements; he also enjoyed unexpected success in the Maori villages. Gwyneira had once told him that the Maori tended to adopt the customs of the *pakeha* very quickly. Most Maori wore Western clothing, so why shouldn't the women learn to use sewing machines too? Naturally, money was an issue. However, the tribes had come into some money by selling land, and that money was usually administered by the chief.

William quickly developed a way of explaining to the tribal leaders that they would rise in the Maori ladies' graces and could, moreover, acquire the *pakeha*'s respect by no longer shutting out the blessings of the modern world. When he demonstrated his Singer sewing machines, the entire tribe usually stood around him enthralled, watching with wide eyes as William sewed the child's dress together and then staring at him as though he had conjured it out of thin air. The women quickly mastered the machine, and it wasn't long before owning a Singer became a status symbol. It was rare for William to leave a tribe without a sales contract. In addition, the Maori being as hospitable as they were, he had no room-and-board expenses.

William occasionally cursed his poor knowledge of the language, however, as he would have liked to ask about Kura and pick up her trail, which had gone cold after Gwyneira's search among the Maori of Blenheim. As it was, he had to make do with English. Most of the Maori spoke some broken form of the language of the *pakeha*, and they understood almost everything. William often got the impression that the people were not telling him everything, becoming distrustful that a stranger was asking about a member of their tribe.

This was especially noticeable with a tribe located between Greymouth and Westport. People there withdrew almost immediately when William asked in his poor Maori about a girl who had run away from her *pakeha* husband and was now making music. Whereas other tribes had simply laughed loudly as soon as he mentioned Kura's escape from the marriage, these people became nervous and quiet. The chieftain's wife finally cleared up the situation.

"He does not want anything from the flame-haired girl. He's asking about the *tohunga*," she explained to her tribe. "You're looking for Kura? Kura-maro-tini? Has she leave the husband who no like . . ."

The tribe let out a roar of laughter at her explanatory gesture. William, alone, looked confused, as well as a little insulted.

"Is that what she said?" he inquired. "But we—"

"She was here. With tall blond man. Very smart, makes music too. Also *tohunga*. But shy."

The others chuckled again but evidently did not want to reveal anything more about Kura's visit. William had his own ideas about that. So Kura was with another man, again! Though not with Roderick Barrister. She had replaced him, just as quickly as she had left him, William, for the opera stage. And now for a shy blond musician.

William's desire to find his wife again and give her a piece of his mind—before wrapping his arms about her and convincing her of his own incontestable advantages—grew with each passing day.

Elaine was worried about Timothy, who looked more haggard and exhausted each time she visited. The laugh lines around his mouth had turned into deep gouges, the kind that testified to the constant overexertion and weariness of many miners. Of course, he was still always happy to see Elaine, but he had greater difficulty joking and laughing with her. That might also have had to do with a certain estrangement—the old familiarity between the two diminished with every day they did not see each other. And those days had become more frequent, though it was not for lack of effort on Elaine's part. The distance was not the problem; the Lamberts' house lay only two miles from the center of town, and Banshee or Fellow could trot that distance in twenty minutes. But then Elaine had to get past Nellie Lambert, and that was proving to be a much more difficult hurdle.

Sometimes Nellie would not open up at all when Elaine knocked with the heavy copper door knocker. Roly and Timothy did not hear it, as the sound only reached to the parlor, or at best the salon. A maid or Nellie herself should always have been within earshot, but Elaine believed that they were simply pretending not to hear. If Elaine did manage to cross the threshold, Nellie found a thousand excuses to keep her son's "friend"—the word "fiancée" never crossed her lips, even though Timothy made no secret of his intentions—from him. Timothy was sleeping, Timothy did not feel well, Timothy was out being pushed by Roly and she had no idea when they would come back. Once she nearly scared Elaine to death when she declared that Timothy could not receive her because he was lying in bed with a heavy cough. Elaine had rushed back to town and emptied her heart out to Berta Leroy in a panic.

Berta, however, had allayed Elaine's fears.

"Nonsense, Lainie, your Tim's not going to catch a lung infection any faster than you or I. True, he was in more danger as long as he was lying in bed, but from what I understand, he's moving around today more than the rest of us combined. We'll hear about it firsthand in a moment, since Christopher is at the Lamberts' right now. Nellie is driving him crazy too. Supposedly, Timothy felt some pain while he was coughing, so of course Christopher had to rush off to see about it. I hope he doesn't catch his own death in this rain."

It was storming heavily outside, and after her fast ride, Elaine, too, was completely soaked. Berta rubbed her hair dry and pointed her to a seat by the fire while she made tea. However, Elaine was still shivering when Dr. Leroy finally came home in a furious state.

"I'm charging that woman double from now on, Berta, you'd better believe it!" he blustered, pouring a touch of brandy into his tea. "Four miles through this storm for a mild cold."

"But . . ." Elaine wanted to object, but Dr. Leroy shook his head.

"If it hurts when the boy coughs, it's because his muscles are overworked by his excessive training regime. When I arrived, he was lifting weights."

"What for?" Elaine asked. "I thought he wanted to learn how to walk again."

"Do you know what those leg splints weigh, which he has to lift with every step?" Dr. Leroy poured himself another cup of tea and poured a spot of brandy in Elaine's cup as well. "In all seriousness, girl, I've never seen a man work as hard and with as much discipline as Timothy Lambert. I no longer have any doubt that he will meet you at the altar on his own legs. What I saw today—despite all the coughing and sniffing—you've got to respect that. Nevertheless, I gave him two days of bed rest to recover from the cold and the worst of his muscle cramps. Whether he sticks to it is a different matter. Nonetheless, I told him you would come by tomorrow to check on him. And I said it in the presence of that dragon he calls a mother—so she can hardly turn you away."

Nellie Lambert would have preferred that Elaine come to the Lambert household only on special occasions and at her personal invitation. Roughly every two weeks, she received the girl for tea. These were miserably stuffy events that Elaine loathed—in part because the Lamberts bombarded her with questions. About her supposed childhood in Auckland, about her relatives, about her ancestry in England. Elaine entrapped herself in an increasingly complex web of lies, whose details she kept forgetting. Then she would have to improvise, squirming not only under Nellie Lambert's merciless gaze but likewise at Timothy's amused winking.

Timothy clearly saw through her fibs, and Elaine feared that he viewed them as a sign of a lack of trust in him. She was always expecting him to bring them up, which made her anxious and tense when she was alone with him.

For his part, Timothy hated to sit across from Elaine in a wheelchair or to have her push him around. His barbell exercises were bearing fruit, and he could now move his monstrosity of a wheelchair a few yards on his own, but turning, and even the simplest maneuvering around furniture, was still exceptionally difficult. Timothy hated more than anything for people to view him as a "cripple." Whenever Elaine visited him in his own rooms, Roly usually helped him into an armchair. However, the chairs around the dinner table in the dining room were uncomfortable, and the sofas and armchairs in the salon too low. So Timothy sat there in his wheelchair, so discouraged and tense that he could not manage a normal conversation.

Disappointed and helpless, Elaine sometimes cried into Banshee's or Fellow's mane on her way home after these visits, while Timothy released his frustrations on the barbells in his room, training all the more tenaciously.

Thus both of them were dreading the solemn Christmas meal to which Nellie Lambert had formally invited Elaine.

"A small party, Miss Keefer. I hope you have something suitable to wear."

Elaine fell into a panic at once, because of course she had no evening gowns. The invitation had been sent very late, so she had no time to have something tailored, even if she'd had enough money for it.

She tried on one dress after another in desperation until Charlene finally came upon her in tears.

"Everyone's going to look down their nose at me," Elaine sobbed. "Nellie Lambert will get to display to all the world that I'm nothing but a barroom girl without etiquette. It will be horrible!"

"Don't get ahead of yourself," Charlene said, soothing her. "It's not even a dinner invitation. It's only to lunch. Besides, the whole world's not going to be there. She didn't even invite me, for example."

Elaine raised her head. "Why should she?"

"As Mr. Matthew Gawain's official fiancée!" Charlene beamed and twirled proudly in front of the mirror. "Look at me, Lainie Keefer. Here stands a respectable young lady. I've already talked to Madame Clarisse: as of today, I'll still be serving in the pub, but I won't be taking the fellows upstairs anymore. I'm afraid Matt will still have to pay for that until the wedding, but I don't want to know the details. At any rate, we'll be getting married in January! How's that for a surprise?"

Elaine forgot her troubles and embraced her friend.

"I thought you didn't ever want to get married," she teased.

Charlene smoothed out her dark hair and wound it into a tight knot, the way Berta Leroy wore her hair, to see how that looked.

"I didn't want to become respectable at any price, but Matt's a foreman. He'll be sharing the management of the mine with Tim at some point. The two of them have already worked that out. So I haven't got a pauper's life in a hut with ten children pulling at my apron ahead of me; I'm really moving up. Just wait, Lainie, in a few years the two of us'll be leading the church's charity bazaars. Besides, I love Matt—and that's made more than one person change her mind, isn't that right, Lainie?"

Elaine laughed and blushed.

Charlene continued. "Mother Lambert still can't tolerate the sight of me," she said as she looked over Elaine's collection of dresses. "That's why Matt's getting the cold shoulder too, and hasn't been invited to join them. He's real sore about it." She grinned. "Here, put this on." She held up the pale-blue summer dress that Madame Clarisse had had tailored for Elaine when she had first arrived. "And wear my new jewelry with it. Here, look—Matt's engagement present." Charlene proudly held a jewelry case out to Elaine that contained a delicate silver necklace with lapis lazuli stones. "I've always thought you were more of an aquamarine type, but that all looks very nice. The neckline may be a little low, but it's summer, so who cares?"

Elaine's heart was beating in her throat. She lowered her eyes as she extended her hand to Timothy's parents and wished them a merry Christmas. She gave Timothy, who was sitting unhappily in his wheelchair, an appropriately cool and reserved kiss. He was already sweating in his three-piece suit, which etiquette evidently demanded that he wear to this event despite the high-summer temperatures. Moreover, his mother insisted on covering his legs with a plaid flannel blanket—as though they were something offensive that had to be kept out of sight.

Elaine would have liked to comfort Timothy and make some kind of confidential gesture to show he was not alone. But once more, she felt as though she were frozen—particularly after she was introduced to the other guests. Marvin and Nellie Lambert had invited the Webers and the Billers—since the two families were friends, it could hardly be avoided. This last fact, however, seemed to please neither Marvin Lambert nor Joshua Biller. The two of them had already given themselves a dose of Dutch courage, and their wives would spend the rest of the afternoon carefully maneuvering them so that they would avoid starting a fight over something trivial.

The Webers looked composed and distinguished, though both wife and daughter eyed Elaine's somewhat inappropriate dress with equal disapproval. They then whispered about it to Mrs. Biller, which resulted in further critical looks. Elaine's attire was completely forgotten, however, the moment Caleb introduced a real scandal. Nellie Lambert had intended for Florence Weber to sit across from him, but he appeared instead with his supposed "fiancée," Kura-maro-tini Martyn.

Elaine nearly choked on the champagne the maid had just served her.

"Just keep your mouth shut," Kura hissed to Elaine as Caleb formally introduced her, and the two cousins halfheartedly clasped each other's hands. "If you insist, I can explain everything to you another time, but you need to play along today. I'm already sitting on a powder keg."

Elaine quickly understood who held the fuse. The icy coldness between Kura and Florence Weber was unmistakable—and Florence promptly extended her antipathy to Elaine as well. Since both girls worked as pianists in bars, she assumed they were friends, and Kura's friends were automatically her enemies. However, to Elaine, Florence's attacks were completely unexpected. She was just about to hide behind her hair, blush, and freeze as she used to do, but then she looked into Kura's annoyed face and remembered there were other options.

"So do you also have ambitions for the opera, Miss Keefer?" Florence asked.

"No," Elaine answered.

"But you are likewise paid to play the piano. And is the Lucky Horse not moreover . . . how should I put it . . . a 'hotel'?"

"Yes," Elaine confirmed.

"I've never been inside such an establishment. But"—Florence cast an embarrassed side glance at her mother as though to be sure that she was not listening—"one is curious, naturally. Are the men very importunate? I know, of course, that you would never, yourself, but—"

"No," said Elaine.

Kura looked over the table at her, and both girls had to stifle a smile. Elaine could hardly believe it, but she felt something like complicity with her oldest enemy.

The conversation was advancing rather arduously among the other guests as well. Mr. Weber asked Marvin about the reconstruction of his mine after the accident—and when Timothy answered, Mr. Weber stared at him as though surprised that the Lamberts' invalid son could still speak. Marvin Lambert himself no longer could, after several glasses of whiskey, champagne, and wine, causing Nellie, Mrs. Biller, and Mrs. Weber to take the lead in the conversation. The ladies chattered at length about their ideas for furnishing and English furniture—looking at Caleb as if he were some kind of monster when he naïvely joined in. A man who knew anything about "wallpaper" belonged in the cabinet of curiosities as much as a mining engineer in a wheelchair. Elaine had the greatest sympathy for Timothy, whose countenance expressed both exasperation and exhaustion. Kura, on the other hand, found Caleb amusing. He acted like a scolded child.

And above the fray sat Florence Weber, who chatted with equal poise about lampshades, new uses of electricity, Italian opera, and the efficiency of ventilation shafts in coal mines. The latter appeared to interest her most; however, her interest only resulted in the gentlemen smiling condescendingly and the ladies holding their tongues indignantly.

"I have to get out of here," Timothy whispered to Elaine as she pushed him into the study after the meal. Nellie had actually asked her husband to do it, but Marvin would hardly have been able to manage without ramming Timothy into the furniture. Timothy had given Elaine such an urgent, imploring look that she had quickly interceded. Accidents with this wheelchair were painful and not without their dangers. A few weeks before, Dr. Leroy had treated Timothy after his mother had succeeded in overturning the chair, as heavy as it was unstable, with Timothy in it.

"What do you want me to do?" Elaine asked desperately. She could hardly maneuver the chair forward on the Lamberts' thick rugs. "We could say we were going out to the garden, but I'd never in my life be able to get this thing out there. Where's Roly anyway?"

"He has the day off," Timothy said, gnashing his teeth. "It is Christmas after all. He was here this morning, though, and he'll come back this evening. That boy is as good as gold, but he has family of his own, you know."

At these last words, Timothy furrowed his brow as though he thought a family no more worth striving for than a toothache. He went quiet when Caleb approached.

"May I assist you, Miss Keefer?" the young man asked amiably and without a hint of embarrassment. "I think an after-lunch constitutional in the garden is a capital idea. If it would please you, Tim."

Caleb took hold of the wheelchair's handles without hesitation and pushed Timothy—for whom this was anything but pleasing—out of the stuffy rooms and into the roaring-hot summer day. Elaine thought Caleb was being very considerate. He raised the wheelchair carefully over the steps and cautiously avoided bumps on the garden path.

Kura followed, casting nervous glances over her shoulder.

"Freedom," she remarked, catching up with Elaine. "We've successfully escaped Florence Weber. Probably only for a few seconds, but one must be thankful for small blessings." She flung back the luxurious hair that she was provocatively wearing down. Kura's neckline was also too low and her burgundy dress cut too alluringly to really be ladylike, but she nevertheless looked breathtaking.

"Still, at least now I understand why she behaves like that," Kura expounded, falling into step very naturally next to Elaine. "For weeks now, I've been asking myself what drew her to Caleb. She had to realize that he doesn't give a fig about her. But now I see that she wants his mine—whatever the cost. She would probably give her life to inherit from her own dad, but she's 'just a girl' after all. Caleb, however, would be wax in her hands. If she gets him to the altar, the Biller Mine is hers. Tim Lambert would also be an option, of course. Better not leave him alone with her."

Coming from Kura's mouth, that advice struck Elaine as a little hypocritical, but, to her own surprise, she couldn't help laughing.

"You're the expert after all," she remarked pointedly—and observed to her astonishment that Kura looked struck. She even seemed to have tears in her eyes. Until that moment, she had always assumed that Kura had left William. Was it perhaps the other way around? Elaine decided to speak with her cousin sometime.

It was late afternoon before most of the guests finally left. Nellie Lambert threw herself immediately into overseeing the cleanup work while Marvin retired to his study with one last drink.

Elaine was torn. On the one hand, they were surely expecting her to likewise take her leave. On the other, Timothy looked so weary in his chair that she could not bring herself to go. Earlier, he had chatted enthusiastically with Caleb about the Biller Mine, but he had hardly said anything else in the last few hours. It looked as though he had to muster all his strength just to hold himself upright. Not that his father, Joshua Biller, or Mr. Weber had seen him anyway. They didn't even bother to offer him a glass of whiskey or a cigar when they all disappeared into the study to partake of those indulgences. Florence, who had followed the men into the study, was the one who finally gave Tim a glass and a cigar. Apparently, she could no longer stand chattering about curtains and bathroom furnishings. The talk about coal marketing held considerably more allure for her.

Elaine had peeked jealously into the study through the open door and noticed Florence exchanging a few words with Timothy—probably because the rest of the gathering was ignoring the two of them equally. Timothy's heart, however, was not in it. Elaine recognized with concern the agitation of his hands on the wheelchair's rests. He had tried repeatedly to change his position on the overly soft cushions, and winced in pain every time he did not succeed. Now he was sitting by the window, staring ashen-faced into the garden and looking as though he were waiting desperately for the sun to sink below the horizon.

Elaine could take it no longer; she strode quickly into the study and pulled a chair up to Timothy, moving her fingers hesitantly over his hand.

"Tim . . ."

He removed his hand from hers and began to unbutton his jacket.

"May I?" he asked politely.

Elaine stood up to help him, but he rebuffed her gruffly.

"Leave it. I have hands enough."

Disheartened, she moved back and made several attempts at conversation while he fumbled awkwardly with one after another of the many buttons, eventually managing to cool himself off a little.

"Caleb Biller is a nice fellow . . ."

Timothy pulled himself together and nodded. "Yeah, but both of his girls are too much for him." He smiled with difficulty. "I'm sorry, Lainie. I didn't mean to be abrupt with you. But I'm not doing very well."

Elaine stroked his shoulder gently before quickly opening the buttons of his vest. She thanked heaven for her light summer dress—formal menswear at these temperatures looked like pure torture. Though the other men had removed their jackets after lunch, Timothy would have needed help to do so, and he would rather have died than ask for that.

"It was a long day. And the people were awful," she said quietly. "Is there anything I can do?"

"Maybe you could . . . you could ride to the O'Briens' and ask Roly to come a little earlier? I . . ." He tried once more to shift his position but fought hopelessly against the deep cushions.

"Maybe I can help you?" Elaine asked, blushing. She didn't want to give Timothy the impression that she wanted to undress him and take him to bed, but perhaps he would let her help him out of that damned chair. "I can't lift you, of course, but . . ."

Timothy smiled, and for the first time that day she saw something like joy, even triumph, in his eyes.

"Oh, you don't need to lift me. I can almost do that on my own. Only standing up from this thing is difficult. Worst of all, I don't see any possibility of making it to my room."

Moving the wheelchair proved to be the most difficult part. It became easier, however, once they had left the salon and its voluminous rugs. Timothy had lived on the upper story before, where his parents had their bedrooms too, but when he had returned home after the accident, he had moved into what had formerly been the servants' quarters between the kitchen and stables. Nellie had already shed many tears over it, but Timothy was not put off by the fact that it sometimes smelled a little of hay. Elaine pushed him into his small salon, where he generally received her when she visited.

"Can you help me onto the sofa?" he asked her in a distracted voice.

Elaine nodded. "What should I do?" she inquired, freeing him from the hated flannel blanket.

"You have your splints on!" she said, astonished. Upon seeing the steel framework around Timothy's legs for the first time, she suddenly understood the reason for his weight training. "Aren't they uncomfortable?"

Timothy smiled through his pain. "I wanted to keep an avenue of escape open. Unfortunately, I didn't count on my mother." He pointed to his crutches leaning against the wall of his room.

Elaine felt a surge of hot rage toward Nellie Lambert. Even if Timothy could only have taken one or two steps, it would have meant the world to him to greet the guests standing up.

"If you could just hand them to me, please." Timothy squeezed the crutches under his arms and attempted to lift himself out of the chair, but the right crutch slipped out from under him and he reached for Elaine's arm to catch himself. Elaine put her arm around him, supporting him until he made it to his feet. And then, for the first time in a year, he stood next to her. When Timothy realized this, he was so startled that he dropped his other crutch. As Elaine held him, he, too, wrapped his arms around her.

"Tim, you can stand! It's a miracle." Elaine looked at him, beaming. She did not have a chance to worry that a man was holding her. It was simply nice to have Timothy upright beside her and to see his smile brighten as it had that day at the race so long ago.

Feeling Elaine in his arms, Timothy couldn't help himself. He lowered his face to hers and kissed her—first, softly on the forehead and then, having gathered his courage, on the mouth. And then the real miracle occurred. Elaine opened her lips to his. Calmly and naturally, she let him kiss her and even timidly returned the kiss.

"That was wonderful," Timothy said happily, "Lainie."

He kissed her once more before she reached for his crutches. Then he showed her that he could make the two steps to the sofa without overexerting himself.

"My record is eleven," he boasted, smiling, before sinking onto the sofa with a sigh. "But from one end of the church to the other, it's twenty-eight. Roly tried it out for me. So I need to train a little more."

"Me too," Elaine whispered. "Kissing, I mean. And as far as I'm concerned, we could start on that right away."

9

Timothy was so determined to push himself that he was nearly bursting by the time Roly O'Brien came to work the next day.

"We'll start by doing the usual exercises today," he explained to the astonished boy, who had been expecting a relaxing morning. The night before, Timothy had looked content but profoundly exhausted, and Roly believed that he should take it easy that day.

"And then," Timothy said, "you'll pick up Fellow from Lainie at noon."

"Your . . . er . . . horse, Mr. Lambert?" Roly sounded uncertain. He wasn't comfortable with horses, having never had anything to do with any animal bigger than a goat or a hen.

"That's right. My horse. It might be hard for Lainie to part with it, but there's nothing I can do about that. Walking is taking too long for me, Roly. Starting today, we ride."

"But—"

"No buts, Roly! Fellow won't hurt you. He's a good chap. And I absolutely have to find some way of getting out of here. I want to have Lainie to myself for once, to do something with her. I want to be alone with her." Timothy sat up impatiently. He could hardly wait for Roly to help him out of bed.

"Maybe you should try driving the coach first?" Roly suggested nervously.

Timothy shook his head. "So that I can ask her to push me around in my wheelchair afterward? No. No arguments. I want to meet the lady for a ride like a gentleman. I don't want to have to wait anymore for her to visit me, or for my mother to let her through."

Roly rolled his eyes, resigned. Of course he thought Elaine was attractive, but he could hardly comprehend the effort Timothy was expending on her. What was more, his boss could simply receive visits and pampering from one of the girls from Madame Clarisse's establishment. Such thoughts had recently begun to cross into Roly's daydreams, but it would probably be years before he scraped together enough change. It would probably be more economical for him to try courting Mary Flaherty next door a bit.

Elaine shook her head when Roly retrieved Fellow from her.

"This is crazy. Tim can't even sit without something to lean on," she objected.

Roly shrugged. "I just do what he says, Miss Keefer," he said, defending his actions. "If he wants to ride, he gets to ride."

Elaine would have liked to go back with the boy to oversee Timothy's dangerous attempt at riding. But she could only too well imagine Timothy's reaction. So she stayed where she was, and began fretting once again.

And not without reason. Timothy's first attempt to get himself in the saddle nearly took a catastrophic turn. Climbing the improvised ramp that Roly had built for him out of boards and straw bales was difficult enough in itself. But when Timothy tried to support himself on the saddle, the irritated horse took a few steps to the side and Timothy fell forward around Fellow's throat and cried out with pain. He had not put so much weight on his freshly healed hip before, and his suddenly overtaxed muscles and tendons protested fiercely.

"Shall I help you down, Mr. Lambert?" Roly was almost as fearful of approaching the horse as he was of his charge falling and breaking a bone again.

"No . . . I . . . Just give me a few minutes." Timothy made every effort to settle himself in the saddle, but it was hopeless. He finally gave into Roly's insistence that he get down and did not even fight it when Roly made him lie down and relax. He nevertheless sat up a short while later and reached for pen and paper.

When Roly returned from the stables, where, despite his fears, he had divested Fellow of his saddle and bridle, Timothy held a sketch out to him.

"Here, take that to Ernie Gast. You know him, the saddler. Ask him if he can make a saddle like this. And as quickly as possible. Oh yes, and Jay Hankins should take a look to see if he can forge some box stirrups like these."

Roly looked the drawing over skeptically. "That looks funny, Mr. Lambert. I've never seen a saddle like that."

The saddle in the picture looked more like an armchair than a riding saddle, with a higher pommel and cantle, which would brace the rider and hold him fast in his seat. Yet it hardly had knee rolls. Tim would be able to dangle his legs, which would be supported by wide stirrups.

"I have," Timothy said. "In Southern Europe saddles like that are practically the standard. They used similar models in the Middle Ages. Knights, I mean."

Roly had never heard of knights before, but he nodded politely.

Timothy could hardly wait for Roly to come back the next day with Ernie's response.

"Mr. Gast says he can build it, but that it ain't a good idea. He says the thing will hold you like a vise, almost like a sidesaddle. If the horse ever stumbles, and you don't get out, you'll break your back." He pointed to the saddle's "backrest."

Timothy sighed. "Fine. Inform him that, for one thing, Fellow won't stumble, and, for another, every English lady rides in a sidesaddle. England's most important families have yet to die out, so the risk can't be all that great. As for breaking my back, two doctors have assured me that at least you don't feel any pain if that happens. And these days, I'd almost find that worth the effort."

Timothy's hip hurt immensely, but he nevertheless had Roly bring him back to the stables that afternoon so he could repeat his attempt to sit on Fellow. The horse remained calm this time and trotted obediently over to the ramp.

Though the special saddle didn't work any miracles, Timothy's determination eventually triumphed over his body's pain and stiffness. Six weeks after his first attempt to get on his horse, he proudly directed Fellow out of the yard. Though he was still in pain—going faster than a walking pace was out of the question—he was upright and somewhat secure.

The feeling of crossing town high on his steed more than compensated for all the exertion. Though there were not many people out and about that afternoon, everyone who knew Timothy beamed at him and cheered him on. Mrs. Tanner and Mrs. Carey said some hasty prayers, and Berta Leroy scolded him for being "short on sense," but her eyes were sparkling.

"Someone should probably go tell the princess that her knight is here," she said. "'Cause he still can't dismount."

Timothy had to admit that was indeed the case. He could not wear his leg splints on the horse, so he needed Roly's help to mount and dismount, and to attach and remove the splints.

The news of his adventure had traveled faster than Fellow could take him, and Elaine was already outside when Timothy turned his horse toward the pub.

She looked up at him, stunned. Though he could not bend down to kiss her, she took his hands and pressed up against his leg and good hip.

"You're hopeless," she chided. "Where do you get these ideas?"

Timothy laughed. "Don't you remember? The day you can't ride anymore is the day you die. May I invite my most sanguine and beautiful lady for a ride with me?"

Elaine put his hand to her cheek and then pressed a shy kiss into it.

"I'll go fetch Banshee," she said with a smile. "But you are not to try and seduce me if I go with you without a chaperone."

Timothy looked at her with feigned shock. "You're not taking a chaperone? Why, that's indecent. Come, let's ask Florence Weber. She'll surely ride along."

Elaine laughed lightheartedly. She didn't bother to saddle Banshee, and instead simply swung from the mounting block in front of Madame Clarisse's inn onto her horse's bare back. The people on the street applauded good-naturedly.

Elaine waved to them as she directed Banshee down Main Street. A year ago, she would have been afraid of riding from the church to town with Timothy Lambert. Now, however, she enjoyed having Banshee walking tranquilly beside Fellow—and seeing Timothy look as radiant as he had been at the race. As they left town, she held her hand out to him and smiled. It was like in a fairy tale. A princess and her knight.

"I didn't realize you had such a flair for the romantic," she teased him. "Next time we'll ride along the river and have a picnic."

Timothy made a face. "I'm afraid I'd have to eat in the saddle," he replied. Only then did Elaine realize what she had said, and she reddened.

"I'll think of something," she promised when she parted from him at the Lamberts' house, "for next Sunday."

Sunday was her only day off from the pub, and she had no other obligations. She had handed the position of church organist over to Kura, and that Sunday was the first time she was not angry about it. Let Kura play the organ—Elaine would rather be doing something with the man she loved.

She suddenly felt wonderfully free and impetuous. She directed Banshee to stop next to Fellow, and Elaine kissed Timothy, long and tenderly, like they had practiced on Christmas.

Timothy was pleased about Elaine's new confidence, but he sighed with relief when she declined his invitation to come in for tea afterward. That way, she did not have to see how difficult it was for him to get out of the saddle. Dismounting remained a somewhat debasing process. Timothy planned to have mastered it soon, however. Jay Hankins was already working on a ramp that would enable him to mount and dismount more easily.

Though Elaine thought that it was premature of Timothy to be riding, she knew his reason for doing so made sense. They needed to find some way of seeing each other outside of the Lambert house, as Nellie's aura was crushing.

For their Sunday outing, they ended up renting a light two-wheeled gig. Although it was not an ideal vehicle—having little in the way of cushioning—it was low to the ground, so Timothy would be able to get in and out without much help. Besides, they would be able to sit next to each other comfortably, as there was no separation between the box and the passenger space like in most other carriages.

Timothy smiled conspiratorially when she pulled up in the little vehicle.

"A gig! If my mother only knew." He smiled and tried to defend himself from Callie, who leaped up on him joyfully. Until recently, even that would have caused him to wobble, but he had become quite adept with his walking aids. "How fortunate that my mother no longer insists on my accompanying her to church." Not going to church had been a source of frustration for him. Though he survived the week even without the reverend's benediction, he hated to be shut out of regular activities just because Nellie considered him to be too weak to participate.

"Alas, because she was likewise going to church, I couldn't persuade Florence Weber to ride with us." Elaine giggled. "Though it is her Christian duty to keep an eye on the morality of her neighbor. But God will forgive her that sin, just as He no doubt turns a blind eye to the various doings of a certain Kura-maro-tini Martyn."

Timothy would have liked to ask what Elaine thought Kura had on her tally sheet, but he restrained himself. If he pursued the matter, she would probably just withdraw back into her shell.

"We have our own penance to pay, for I have stolen," he remarked in lieu of questioning her. "Here, take my bag, but carefully; some of my father's best wine is in there."

Elaine thought fleetingly of how she had once plundered her own father's stores for her adventures with William. But she wanted to forget that now.

"I have some too, and I even bought mine. It wasn't expensive though," she admitted. "It's probably awful."

Timothy laughed. "If that's the case, we'll pray for the vintner's soul."

Banshee stood perfectly still as Timothy got into the little carriage's seat. It worked quite well, and Elaine felt quite proud of her idea once he was sitting happily at her side.

"Where are you taking me?" Timothy asked as they set out. He tried to relax, but the thinly cushioned vehicle was only marginally more comfortable than Fellow's saddle.

"To the river just beyond your mine. It's not far, and the roads are tolerable. And I just happen to have found a gorgeous little spot there."

In fact, she had spent the entire week looking for it, and the out-of-the-way spot set off a little ways from the main gravel road between the mine and the train line was truly ideal. Elaine reached it just a few minutes later and helped Timothy out.

"I could keep driving, but it would get bumpy. So I thought we'd better just come back to get Banshee and the carriage. Let's walk to the river. It's exactly eleven steps on the direct path through the trees."

Her conscientiousness made Timothy laugh, but he could in fact now make between fifteen and twenty steps without too much difficulty. The going on his crutches was tough here, though, and he stumbled through the underbrush. However, the picnic spot itself was magical: a tiny beach on the riverbank with a sort of grassy clearing at the edge of the fern forest. Ferns as tall as trees hung their green fronds over the river. And whenever the gentle breeze rocked the giant plants, their strangely shaped shadows danced in the sunlight.

"How beautiful," Timothy said.

Elaine nodded as she spread out a picnic blanket.

"Here, sit down while I fetch Banshee and the carriage. Not everyone who passes by on the road needs to see them."

Though there were not likely to be many people on a Sunday, Elaine still wanted to play it safe. Kura might not think of such things, but Florence Weber might very well force Caleb to come to the river for a picnic. And Charlene absolutely raved about such outings with Matt.

Timothy blushed. "I don't know if I could get back up if . . ."

"You can support yourself on that rock there. See, I thought of everything, Tim. And if you still need help, Banshee will pull you up. My grandfather told me how his horse once pulled him out of a mudhole. He simply held onto the tail, and the horse scrambled out. I practiced that with Banshee when I broke her in. Yes, I know, I'm like a child," she smiled abashedly.

Timothy was not thinking about whether she had been absurd or not, but about her adventurous grandfather. A construction worker in Auckland might fall into mudholes under certain circumstances, but there was no way he had a horse to pull him out.

Timothy did not voice his thoughts aloud, though, and instead settled himself down on the blanket and felt better at once. He undid the leg splints and scratched Callie while Elaine skillfully drove the carriage into the clearing and unhitched her horse.

"Banshee is very upset with you for taking Fellow away," Elaine remarked as she sat down, placing the picnic basket between them. "She feels lonesome all alone in Madame Clarisse's stables."

"They'll be back together soon enough. When we marry, you'll bring her along when you move in," Timothy said.

Elaine sighed. "Wouldn't you rather move into Madame Clarisse's?" The prospect of sharing a house with Nellie Lambert scared her almost as much as the marriage itself.

Timothy laughed and took her face between his hands. "No, that would be a little unsuitable." He kissed her. "But I could imagine a little house of our own. Perhaps closer to the mine—which will make it easier once I'm working again. Of course, my father refuses to hear a word about that at the moment. But let's talk about more pleasant things. The cheap wine or the stolen wine first?"

They drank the cheap wine while they ate. Then Timothy insisted on opening the good wine. It did not quite suit the whiskey glasses Elaine had brought with her from the pub, but they both just found that funny. After they had practiced kissing a bit more, they lay down beside each other. Elaine propped herself up on her elbows and lightly caressed Timothy's chest.

"You have very nice muscles."

Timothy made a face. "I do lift weights every day." He gestured at his leg splints with his hand.

Elaine observed the play of his muscles beneath his light silk shirt. But at the very moment he reached for her, wanting to pull her close, she suddenly saw Thomas's strong arms in front of her again, the muscles she had sometimes helplessly struck against or which she had dug her fingernails into when she was overcome with pain. Thomas had only laughed.

Timothy recognized the flickering in her eyes—and then her old familiar retreat from his touch.

He sighed and, supporting himself on the stone, he sat up a bit.

"Lainie," he said patiently, "I don't know what horrible thing some man did to you, but nothing could be further from my intentions than hurting you. You know I love you. Besides, I'm quite helpless. If you don't help put those things back on later, I can't even get to my feet. Even if I wanted to, I couldn't do anything to you. Can't you at least put your trust in that, even if you think the worst of me?"

"That's not what I think at all." Elaine said, reddening. "It just happens. I know, I'm being stupid." She burrowed her face into his shoulder.

Timothy stroked her arm. "You're not being dumb. It's just that something awful happened to you. Don't deny it. There's no other explanation. But you do love me, don't you, Lainie?"

Elaine raised her head and looked him in the eye. "I love you very much. Believe me, I . . ."

Timothy smiled and pushed her gently onto her back. Then he kissed her face, her lips, her throat, and her neckline. He carefully opened her blouse and caressed the tops of her breasts. Elaine tensed up at first, but then she realized that he wasn't hurting her but merely bathing her skin in breathy kisses while whispering endearments.

Elaine had to help him undo her corset, both of them laughing shyly. Then she lay there, her breath quickening as he traced the contours of her figure with his fingers. Timothy told her how beautiful and delicate she was, caressing and kissing her until there rose in her that languorous, warm feeling she had almost forgotten. As Elaine felt herself grow wet, she once more withdrew a little. Timothy realized that and left off touching her.

"We don't need to keep going," he whispered gingerly. "We . . . we can certainly wait until our wedding night."

"No!" Elaine almost screamed the word. Lying once more in bed in a new nightgown waiting for a husband? Trembling at the thought of what he might do to her? Delivered up to him helplessly? Everything in her seized up at the mere thought.

"No, what?" Timothy asked lovingly and began once again to caress her softly.

"No wedding night," Elaine exclaimed. "I mean, not one like that. It's better that we get it out of the way."

Timothy kissed her. "You make it sound like I'm pulling a tooth," he joked gently. "Are you still a virgin, Lainie?"

He could not imagine she was, though she was more timid than any other girl he had ever loved. All the others had been nervous, but also curious. Elaine was only fearful.

She shook her head.

Timothy kissed her again and once more caressed and fondled her breasts, her stomach, and her hips before finally playing with the frizzy red hair between her legs. Elaine did not stir, nor did she completely tauten. Timothy pressed on, arousing her with tender touches and kisses. Only when she began to tremble with desire and her body no longer seemed tense did he slowly and carefully enter her. He remained still inside her for a moment before beginning to move very gently. When he could no longer hold himself back, he released himself in an eruption of passion. Then he sank down beside her.

Elaine heard his panting and stroked his back anxiously. "What's wrong? Are you in pain?"

Timothy laughed. "No, Lainie, not today. Today I'm just happy. It was wonderful. But how was it for you?"

"It didn't hurt at all," Elaine said seriously. She sounded amazed, almost incredulous.

Timothy drew her to his shoulder and stroked her hair.

"Lainie, it's not supposed to hurt. Only a little bit the first time, but after that it's supposed to be beautiful, for you and for me, as though everything beautiful that you've ever experienced comes rushing over you at once, gradually mounting into fireworks."

Elaine frowned. Fireworks? Well, she had felt a sort of tingling.

"Maybe we just need to practice more."

Timothy laughed. "That we must. In all seriousness, there's a sort of art to it. You just need to let yourself go, have a little more faith in me. You're not to be afraid anymore."

He held her in his arms and rocked her while his breathing returned to normal and the heavy beating of his heart slowed. Elaine now seemed completely relaxed and trusting. He contemplated trying to arouse her once more, but then decided to venture out onto even thinner ice.

"Won't you tell me, Lainie?"

The body of the exhausted girl in his arms tightened.

"Tell you what?" she asked breathlessly.

Timothy continued stroking her. "What happened to you, Lainie? What scared you so awfully, what you drag around with you like a weight? I won't tell anyone. Ever. But you have to tell someone eventually before it tears you to pieces."

Elaine loosened herself from his grasp a little, she but didn't completely pull away. Evidently what she had to say was so important that she could not say it casually while they lounged arm in arm in the sunshine. Timothy understood and propped himself up a little too. He had been expecting her to sit up across from him, but she leaned her head back on his shoulder again without looking at him. Her demeanor was no longer relaxed and trusting; instead, it expressed resignation.

Elaine took a deep breath.

"I'm not Lainie Keefer of Auckland. I'm Elaine O'Keefe of Queenstown, Otago. I was married to Thomas Sideblossom of Lionel Station. And I shot my husband."

Voices of the Spirits

GREYMOUTH, OTAGO, BLENHEIM, AND CHRISTCHURCH

1898

1

B ut it was self-defense, Lainie! No one would condemn you for that." Timothy Lambert had listened calmly to Elaine's entire story—without giving the smallest sign of repugnance or horror at her violent act. He had dried her tears and soothed her when she shook uncontrollably while describing her most awful experiences. Finally, she lay there, utterly exhausted, curled up against him, clinging to his arm with one hand. With the other, she held Callie. The little dog had come to her immediately, whimpering quietly, when Elaine had begun to tell her story.

"It wasn't self-defense," Elaine insisted. "Not in the true sense of the law. Thomas had only spoken to me that day; he hadn't even touched me. When I shot him, he was more than two yards from me. That could be demonstrated, Tim. No judge would let me go with that."

"But the man had threatened and hurt you repeatedly before. And you knew he would do it again. Is there no one who will confirm that for you? No one who knows the truth?"

Timothy pulled the blanket over his and Elaine's bodies, as it was getting cool. In early spring, the midday sun did not provide warmth for long.

"Two Maori maids." Elaine's answer came quickly, suggesting she'd had this same conversation a thousand times in her head. "One of whom barely speaks English and works like a slave for Sideblossom because he caught her tribe rustling. Grand witnesses. If they would even dare to provide a testimony. And two stableboys could confirm that my husband had forbidden me to ride, which hardly amounts to a reason to shoot him."

"But it was deprivation of freedom." Timothy did not give up so easily. "The fellow practically locked you up. One can hardly fault you for breaking out, and in doing so . . . well, someone got hurt in the process."

"I would have to prove that, which would be impossible without witnesses. And Zoé and John Sideblossom would hardly corroborate my story. Besides, it's not like I was kidnapped. I was Thomas's wife. It's probably not even illegal for someone to lock up his wife." Judging by Elaine's grim countenance, she seemed to be reconsidering her marriage to Timothy.

"And this Patrick? Your father's driver? He saw how Sideblossom treated you."

Timothy turned the event over and over in his mind. It could not be that Elaine was completely helpless.

"No, he didn't see how Thomas beat me. And what's more, at the moment I shot, I wasn't being threatened. Naturally, Thomas would have killed me later. But there's no such thing as 'preventative self-defense.' Don't strain yourself, Tim. I've spent whole nights thinking it through. If I take the stand, and the judge believes even some of what I have to say, maybe I won't end up on the gallows. But I'd be guaranteed to spend the rest of my life in jail, and that has little allure for me."

Timothy sighed and tried to move his leg into a different position without disturbing Elaine. The weather was gradually turning inclement. Elaine noticed it too. She kissed Timothy lightly as she rolled out of his arms and began to gather up the picnic things.

Timothy wondered whether he should speak his mind. It would undoubtedly distress Elaine. But he went ahead anyway.

"If we want to keep things a secret, that will lead to complications in our personal life," Timothy said. Though he had spoken in a calm voice, he unleashed an explosion.

Elaine spun around. Her face contracted, and she held the empty wine bottle as though she wanted to hurl it at him. "You don't have to marry me, you know!" she spat. "Maybe it was a good thing that we talked about it beforehand."

Timothy ducked and made a placating gesture. "Hey! Now, don't scream at me like that. Of course I want to marry you. More than anything in the world. I just mean that you can never be fully secure here. You may be able to hide from the world as a barroom pianist but not as Mrs. Timothy Lambert. The Lamberts are businessmen, Lainie; we keep an open house. The papers write about the Lambert Mine. You'll have to engage in charity work, and with every public appearance, the risk of your being discovered will grow. What did you want to do about your parents? Never talk to them again?"

Elaine shook her head wildly. "I thought I might let another year pass, and then I'd write them. And now that we want to get married—"

"Now that we *will* get married," Timothy said.

"I wanted to write them right after the wedding. 'From: Mrs. Lambert.' Then nothing could go wrong." Elaine went over to her grazing horse and took it by the halter.

"You think someone is checking your parents' mail?" Timothy asked. "You're going to drive yourself crazy."

"What am I supposed to do then?" she asked, disheartened. "I don't want to go to jail."

"But perhaps you could imagine living with me somewhere else?" The idea had just come to him, but the more he thought about it, the more attractive it seemed. "In England, for example. There are a great many coal mines there. I could look for a job. If not at a mine, maybe at a university. I'm a very good engineer."

Elaine was touched. She sat down next to him again, pushing Banshee away, who all of a sudden seemed to think that the best grass was under their blanket.

"You would really leave everything behind for me? This country, your mine?"

"Hah, my mine. You saw at Christmas what my father thinks of me. And that unspeakable Mr. Weber. If I stayed here in my wheelchair, I could sit and watch my father run the mine into the ground. It looks pretty bad, Matt thinks. We've been showing big losses since the accident."

"But Weber and Biller looked at Caleb the same way," Elaine said. "And Florence when she tried to get involved herself."

Timothy gave a tired smiled. "Get involved? Florence Weber speaks more knowledgeably about coal mining than my father and the elder Biller together. There's no question the girl is a pain in the neck, but she knows a great deal about running a mine. If she only learned that from reading books, she deserves all the more respect. Still, their situation can't be compared to mine. Caleb knows nothing, and no one takes Florence seriously because she's a woman. But their situation will change the moment she marries Caleb and discreetly takes the reins. If Caleb begins to make constructive suggestions out of nowhere, his old man will listen to him; count on it. But I'll be lame forever, Lainie. My father will look at me as an invalid until the sun burns out." He petted Callie. "What do you think of Wales? There's as much rain as there is here, lots of mines, lots of sheep."

"Lots of cob stallions," Elaine said, laughing. "Banshee would love it. My grandmother is from there. Gwyneira Silkham of—"

"The grandmother who's married to the grandfather who was pulled out of the mudhole by a horse?" Timothy asked. He was fighting doggedly with his leg splints.

Elaine nodded and brought Banshee into position to help him up. Both of them laughed as he gripped the horse's tail.

"That's the one."

Elaine was elated not to have to lie anymore. It was wonderful to be able to tell Timothy about the grand love of her grandparents Gwyneira and James, and about her parents' flight to Queenstown. It was good not to be alone anymore.

Timothy wanted to set the wedding date in the middle of winter, but his mother was dead set against it. Though she had accepted that she could not stop her son from marrying a barmaid, she felt that, if it had to happen, it should not be a hastily thrown-together affair.

"Otherwise, it will look like you *had* to get married," she remarked with a stern look at Elaine's flat stomach.

Before a wedding, she lectured her son, came an engagement. With a party and announcements and presents—in short, much fuss and fanfare. They could talk about the wedding in a few months. Summer would best, and the celebration would be more enjoyable that time of year anyway.

"Why not right on the anniversary of the mining accident?" grumbled Timothy when he was alone with Elaine later. "It will be completely inappropriate for us to celebrate anything around then for years to come. But my mother has no concept of that. She's long since forgotten the miners who died."

"I don't mind going ahead with an engagement first," Elaine said. It was all the same to her. On the contrary, the longer she could put off sharing a house with Nellie Lambert, the better. Besides, at the moment she was enjoying her life with Timothy just the way it was. He was still doing his utmost to walk and ride more easily as quickly as possible, but he did not exert himself as tenaciously as before. When he had finished his training program in the morning, he treated himself to rest in the afternoon—or at least relaxation. As a rule, that began with Elaine cooking for him. She had rediscovered the domestic side that William had briefly awakened in her. Then they would end up in Elaine's bed, first for an afternoon nap but later for other activities.

It did Timothy good to be coddled. He put on weight, and his face lost its strained expression. His laugh lines returned, and his eyes once again sparkled as waggishly as they had before. Though he could not dance yet, he was becoming ever more confident on his horse. A special mounting block had been placed in Madame Clarisse's stables—Jay Hankins, the smith, had thought ahead. Often Elaine would pick up Timothy in the gig, no matter how sour Nellie looked. And Roly had recently been practicing driving it. The boy was often in as much of a hurry as the horse, Fellow indeed being too lively for pulling a carriage. But when Roly was a sufficient distance from the horse's hooves and teeth he still feared, the now fourteen-year-old enjoyed his role as a fearless carriage driver. The two-wheeled carriage he had found in the Lamberts' wagon depot leaped wildly over sticks and stones, and Timothy was generally barely hanging on by the time he arrived at Madame Clarisse's.

"I might just as well gallop here on my horse," he moaned, rubbing his sore hip. "But Roly enjoys it tremendously, and he needs to let off steam from time to time. He gets teased enough for being a 'Mister of Mercy.'"

Timothy began once again to take part in the town gossip and jokes. His friends greeted him at their regular table in the pub. Madame Clarisse made a grand production out of replacing the hard chairs around the table in the corner with comfortable armchairs.

"A special service for our most loyal customers," she remarked, "normally reserved only for the gentlemen waiting for our ladies' company." The armchairs had originated in a waiting room on the second floor. "Make yourselves right at home."

Ernie, Matt, and Jay played along as they took their seats in their special "den" with big gestures and even bigger cigars and glasses of whiskey. Timothy was grateful. He stood out enough already with his crutches. He could hardly make it through town or the barroom without people asking how he was doing.

In contrast to his status among the mine owners, the miners' respect for him had risen since the accident. Everyone had followed his long battle for recovery under Berta Leroy's regimen, and even the new miners had been told first thing how the mine owner's son was the first one to enter the mine after the accident and how he had attempted to dig the men out with his own hands, risking his own life. Ever since then, Timothy had become one of them. Someone who knew who knew how dangerous their living was, and the degree of fear and insecurity they lived with each day. For that reason, they greeted him respectfully, occasionally asking his advice or asking him to intercede against a foreman or the mine's management on their behalf. Unfortunately, in these latter instances he had to disappoint them. Timothy's influence over his father remained weak, and the Lambert Mine was hardly in a position to be doing its men any favors these days. Matt increasingly entered the pub with a troubled face and described the business's catastrophic financial situation.

"It all goes back to our not getting enough new workers. 'Lambert pays bad, and the mine's dangerous.' That's the first thing that every recruit hears. And that's not going to change either. Your father has lost any support he had from the workers. The assistance he offered the families of the victims was a joke. It hardly covered the burial costs, and the wives and children have had to rely on charity since then. Not to mention the total lack of decision making. We need to rebuild, invest money, and modernize everything down to the last mining lamp. But nothing's happened. Your father is of the opinion that he needs to make it out of the red first before he can think about investing. But that's the wrong way to go about things."

"Particularly when he continues to invest his money in whiskey." Timothy sighed. He knew that he should not speak so familiarly with his employees, but Matt had to smell the boss's alcohol fumes. "By the time he comes home at noon, he's usually already drunk. Then he starts up again in the afternoon. How's he supposed to make sensible decisions like that?"

"The only solution would be to hand the running of the mine over to you as soon as possible," Matt mused. "Then we'd hardly know what to do with all the workers who'd come running, and a bank loan surely wouldn't be a problem, either."

"Are things so bad that we need a loan from the bank?" Timothy asked, alarmed. "I thought my father had cash reserves?"

"From what I understand, those have been stuck in a rail line that, for the moment at least, is sinking in the mud," Matt murmured. "But I'm not sure. He hasn't given me much detailed information about his finances."

When Timothy looked into the matter afterward, he was rather shocked. Naturally, Lambert's investment in the rail lines would pay off someday—railroad construction was a sure win—but until that day came, they were more or less broke. The modernization of the most important mining structures would indeed have to be financed with a loan—which shouldn't be a problem since there was plenty of collateral, after all—but could Marvin Lambert still get credit from the bankers of Greymouth?

When he spoke to his father about it, another serious fight ensued. Timothy was on the verge of booking passage to London right away.

"And then to Cardiff, Lainie! We'll skip all the theatrics of an engagement and the rest and we'll marry in Wales. I have contacts there. So we could find a place to stay if the Silkhams don't want to open their doors. Just imagine your grandmother's surprise when you send her a card from her old homeland."

Elaine merely laughed, but Timothy was almost entirely serious. For a while now, it had ceased to be solely the mine and his anger at his father that robbed him of sleep; he was now also concerned for Elaine. She had told him all about her family, and he was scared to high heaven just thinking about it. Sheep barons in the Canterbury Plains, a trading house and a hotel in Otago, connections to the most widely known families of the South Island, and finally, the strange story with her cousin Kura, who had ended up in Greymouth too, of all places. Someone was eventually bound to recognize Elaine, especially if she looked as strikingly like her mother and grandmother as she claimed. Perhaps nobody took a second look at a barroom pianist, but it would be perfectly normal to assume that a Mrs. Lambert had connections to the country's best families. Someone was sure to notice the resemblance and ask Elaine about it. Perhaps even at this engagement party that was looming in their near future. Timothy would have liked to ship off with Elaine to Cardiff at the earliest possible moment. He felt as if he could hear a bomb's fuse sizzling.

"Still nothing from Westport?"

John Sideblossom had not offered his informant any whiskey, but he was drinking a second glass himself as he spoke. Not only were his investments in the railroad not proving profitable, but no one had heard a thing about his fugitive daughter-in-law. John Sideblossom, by now almost completely gray-haired, slammed his fist angrily into the table.

"Damn it, I was so sure she would show up on the West Coast. Dunedin is too close to Queenstown, she'd stick out like a sore thumb in Christchurch, and I've had an eye on Blenheim since the start. I even have the ferries to the North Island being watched. There's no way she can have escaped."

"You're still not looking at every corner of the country," the man said. No longer young, he was a typical Coaster in worn-out leather pants and a dirty waxed jacket that he had worn during his stints whaling, seal hunting, and gold mining. His features were hard and weathered, his eyes bright blue and alert. John knew why he paid him. Nothing got past this fellow. "She could be on some farm or among the Maori."

"I've checked the farms," John explained coolly. He hated when people doubted his competence. "Unless she's holed up at Kiward Station. But I doubt that's the case; otherwise, George Greenwood wouldn't be casting about for her too. The McKenzies are just as in the dark as I am. As for the Maori, something tells me she hasn't been wandering around with them for two years. If for no other reason than that they don't wander for two years at a time. They always come back to their villages. Of course they could pass the hussy from one tribe to another. But that doesn't fit; that's beyond their level of thinking. No, I'd swear she's taken up residence in some gold-miners' camp or coal-mining backwater. Probably in some whorehouse. Westport, Greymouth—"

"Since you mention Greymouth . . ." The man felt around in the pocket of his raincoat. "I know you have your own man there. But this was is in the paper a few days ago. It probably doesn't have anything to do with our girl, but it did strike me as funny. The names are so similar."

Mr. and Mrs. Marvin Lambert of Lambert Manor in Greymouth would like to announce the engagement of their son, Timothy Lambert, to Lainie Keefer of Auckland.

John Sideblossom read with furrowed brow.

"Marvin Lambert. I know him a bit, from the old days on the West Coast."

He also knew the man in front of him from that wild time in his life. But unlike John Sideblossom and Marvin Lambert, fate had not been kind to this man. As though he had just been reminded of that fact, John raised the bottle and finally poured his informant a glass of whiskey. As he poured, he thought, and his eyes took on an almost febrile gleam.

"'Lainie,'" he mumbled. "That fits. Her family called her that. 'Keefer,' hmm. Well, it's an interesting possibility, if nothing else. I'll look into it." John grinned sardonically. "Who knows, maybe I'll pay this engagement party a surprise visit."

Satisfied, he filled his glass once more before counting out the man's pay. He considered including a bonus, but then decided a small gesture would suffice.

"Take the bottle with you when you go," he declared, giving the whiskey bottle a tap so that it rolled in the visitor's direction. "I think we'll be seeing each other on the West Coast."

After the man had left, John Sideblossom read the engagement announcement again.

"Lainie Keefer." It was possible; indeed, more than likely. He considered whether to set out for Greymouth right away. He felt the thrill of the hunt start to burn within him, just as he had when he set after James McKenzie. But he needed to keep a cool head. This bird would not fly away; it felt too safe in its nest for that.

Mr. and Mrs. Marvin Lambert of Lambert Manor in Greymouth would like to announce the engagement of their son . . .

The old Coaster gnashed his teeth. Elaine must feel herself to be quite secure to agree to an announcement like this. But he would catch her and rip the birdie from her nest.

John closed his fist around the newspaper sheet. He crumpled it into a ball before ripping it into little pieces.

2

William Martyn had had enough of the Maori. It wasn't that he didn't like them. On the contrary. They were gracious hosts, generally good-natured, and were clearly making every effort not to irritate the genteel *pakeha* with customs that made him uncomfortable. On the West Coast, William had followed his usual strategy of demonstrating respectability by maintaining an air of aloofness. Indeed, the Maori spoke English with him as much as possible, imitated his gestures and expressions, and loved tinkering with his sewing machine. After two weeks of traveling to three different tribes, however, William had had his fill of their *haka*—their long stories told with great gesticulations whose gist he could only inadequately grasp—and their flavorful but repetitive food: sweet potatoes and fish followed by fish and sweet potatoes.

William yearned for a proper steak, a couple of glasses of whiskey in the company of drunk Englishmen, and a decent bed in a private hotel room. The following day, he would organize a demonstration in a pub or church hall. The town of Greymouth seemed big enough to offer him both. There was probably even a hotel worthy of the term that didn't rent its beds by the hour.

Though it was raining when he reached Greymouth, the small city revealed itself to be more than a midsized settlement and even seemed to boast high-class neighborhoods. A passerby William asked about a hotel at least had to give it some thought, suggesting that there must be a range of options.

"Are you looking for something nicer, with a porter and everything? Or just an inn?"

"Clean, but affordable." William shrugged.

The man likewise shrugged. "Then Madame Clarisse's Inn might suit you," he mused. "But are you looking for lodging for the *whole* night?"

Just as soon as he set out in the direction the man had indicated, he came upon the lighted inn sign, but the brightly painted facade and the adjoining pub, the Lucky Horse, made no promises of a quiet night. However, he might be able to get a steak.

William could not make up his mind. But then the music coming from inside the pub urged him on. The people in there crooning "Auld Lang Syne" to middling piano playing were assuredly more than a little drunk. Of course, it was Saturday—not a bad time to arrive, all things considered. William could attend church first thing the next morning and speak with the pastor about the church's gathering space.

First though, he spurred his horse on. Maybe there were other, quieter pubs.

A few streets farther down, there was indeed another bar, the Wild Rover. Music issued into the street from this place as well. But something was unusual about it . . . William halted his carriage and secured his horse. As he tossed a rain blanket over the animal, he listened more closely to the curious sounds coming from the barroom. A piano, played by a virtuoso, and a flute. A Maori instrument.

The music was different from the relatively primitive *haka* that William had heard so many of in recent weeks. Granted, there were parallels, but someone had tinkered with the melody and expression. The dialogue between the instruments had a rousing quality at times, a touching one at others. William recognized a *putorino* as the flutist brought out its feminine voice. It was high and demanding, almost angry, and yet wooing and unquestionably erotic. The piano answered duskily, representing the masculine voice in this conversation. The instruments seemed to be flirting and teasing each other before uniting in a common end note. Then the flute abruptly ceased, as though holding its tongue, while the pianist performed masterful runs into higher registers. Then the *putorino* answered again. A new dialogue, a quarrel this time. Lengthy explanations, interspersed with short, brusque responses, coming together and apart—and, in the end, a break. A lamenting, dying piano, the flute pausing, only suddenly to begin again.

William listened, fascinated. The spirit voice. He had heard about it many times, but had yet to come across a tribe whose musicians knew how to wring that third voice from their instruments. And now here were these notes drifting out of a dingy pub in Greymouth. Curious, William approached. The spirit voice seemed to be conjured from the building's own depths. It sounded cavernous, ethereal. He thought he was hearing the voice of the aboriginal spirit world, the whispering of ancestors, the lapping of the waves on the ancient beach of Hawaiki.

As William entered the pub, he let his gaze wander over the smoky room. The customers had just begun applauding, and some were giving the musicians a standing ovation. The strange song had moved even these stolid men. Then William saw the pallid blond pianist, whose stiff nod took the place of a bow, and a girl, who stood motionless, as if she were still listening to the flute's voice.

"Kura!"

Kura looked up. Her eyes became saucers at the sight of William. As best he could tell in the dim light of the pub, she appeared to turn pale.

"William . . . it's not possible . . ." She stepped closer, looking at him with an expression that suggested she was still held too tightly in the grasp of her music's magical realm to comprehend reality. "When we arranged this song," she said finally, "I was thinking about us. Of what brought us together . . . and tore us apart. And then I sought to have the spirits call you back. But it can't really be! It's just a song . . ." She stood as though frozen, the flute still in her hand.

William smiled.

"You should never underestimate the spirits," he said, placing a friendly kiss on her cheek. But then her skin and her scent took him prisoner once again, and he could not resist. He put his lips to hers.

The men all around clapped and cheered.

"Encore!"

William was not averse to letting her play again, but the pianist had stood up in the meantime. He was tall and thin with a long, blank face. Her lover?

"Kura?" Caleb asked, confused. "Would you . . . care to introduce us?"

A gentleman. William could only just keep from laughing.

Kura seemed abstracted. She had returned William's kiss, but the situation was so unreal.

"Do pardon us, Caleb," she said. "This is William Martyn. My husband."

The pianist stared at William, stunned; then he collected himself and reached out his hand.

"Caleb Biller."

"Miss Martyn's fiancé," Paddy Holloway noted.

"It's not what you think," Kura whispered into the awkward silence.

William decided to maintain his composure. Whatever was going on, it needed not be aired in front of everyone. And it could no doubt wait until later.

"That can wait, my sweet," he whispered back, reinforcing the embrace in which he still held Kura, as though ready to kiss her again. "We still need to discharge our divine duty first . . ."

Smiling, he released her and turned to Caleb.

"It was a pleasure making your acquaintance. I would have enjoyed speaking with you at greater length. But the spirits, you understand. At best, they shall remain here but one or two hours." William fished two one-dollar bills out of his pocket and laid them on the piano. "You are welcome to a whiskey on my tab. But, alas, I must steal my wife away from you for a moment. As I said, the spirits . . . one should not resist their call for too long."

William seized the hand of the confused Kura and left a completely flabbergasted Caleb behind. On the way to the door, he put a bill in Paddy's hand as well. "Here, friend, best bring the boy the whole bottle right away. He looks a tad pale. We'll be seeing you."

Kura couldn't help giggling as he led her from the pub.

"William, you're terrible."

He laughed. "I'm no worse than you. Might I remind you how you yourself behaved in the old days? I just have to think about that kiss on the middle of the dance floor at Kiward Station. I thought you were going to rip my clothes off then and there."

"I wasn't far from doing just that." Kura rubbed her body against his, thinking feverishly as she did so. She could not possibly take him to Mrs. Miller's. Gentleman callers had been expressly forbidden; it probably would have made no difference even if she could have produced her marriage certificate. The stables? No, then they might as well do it in the middle of the road. In the end, Kura pulled her husband in the direction of the Lucky Horse. Madame Clarisse's stables! As far as Kura knew, Elaine's pony was the only horse there. And Elaine would be at the piano for at least another two hours.

Kura and William tittered like children as Kura ran through the rain to the stables. She jiggled the door, and on the second attempt, the lock released and the two of them slipped inside. William kissed a raindrop from Kura's nose. He was dry himself, having yet to remove his waxed jacket.

In the stalls there were actually other horses in addition to Elaine's gray one. They likely belonged to pub customers; the Lucky Horse's clientele consisted of not only miners but also craftsmen and small businessmen who might own horses. Kura briefly considered whether she should take her chances, but William was already kissing her shoulders and moving to pull off her dress.

Kura made it to a haymow in a partitioned-off stall before succumbing to his advances. William threw his jacket off and opened her bodice. And then Kura forgot everything around her, and gave herself over completely to feeling and burning and loving.

Roly O'Brien, hearing moaning and laughing, stared astonished at the couple in the hay. Matt Gawain had sent the boy to the stables to grab a few papers from his saddlebags. And then he'd come upon this . . . Roly retreated quietly, but not so far back that the couple was hidden from view.

Naturally, as a coal miner's son who had grown up in a shack he shared with his parents and five other children, he was not completely surprised by what he was seeing. But the imaginative play of these two had little in common with the fast, embarrassed lovemaking of his parents that he had often overheard.

Roly tried to make out who the two lovers were. Long, dark-black hair—no, that wasn't any of Madame Clarisse's girls taking her pleasure here. And though he could see that the man was blond, Roly could discern little else about him. Finally, he saw the girl's face. Miss Martyn! The pianist at the Wild Rover.

Roly did not know how long he hid out, enthralled by the two of them, but he eventually recalled that Timothy Lambert and Matt Gawain had rather urgently wanted the papers in the saddlebags. If he did not return presently, they would send somebody after him. With regret, Roly pulled himself away and felt his way as quietly as possible over to the horses. Matt's chestnut mare was easy to recognize even without a stable lantern. In order not to make any noise, Roly did not rifle through the saddlebags but instead hastily untied the leather straps and took the bags with him. He was able to slink back out without being seen. He grinned like a Cheshire cat as he stepped into the barroom.

"What took so long?" Matt asked grumpily as Roly laid the bags in front of him on the table. "Couldn't you find the plans?"

Roly lowered his eyes abashedly, though a smile played at his lips. "No, Mr. Gawain . . . er . . . I mean, Matt." It was still hard for him to call the foreman by his first name. "It's just that . . . I wasn't alone in the stables."

Timothy rolled his eyes. "And who else was there exactly? Did you need to have a long chat with Fellow? Or Banshee perhaps?"

Roly giggled. "No, Mr. Lambert, but I didn't want to bother them. That is . . . the piano player from the Rover is doing it with a blond man. And they're doing it right!"

The men at the table looked at each other—and then burst out laughing.

"Let's just say it," commented Ernie Gast. "We have all completely underestimated Caleb Biller."

Although Elaine was troubled when she saw William again, she felt far less hurt than she had feared she would. Perhaps it helped that she was high on her horse while he was walking on foot down Main Street. And it was unquestionably helpful that Timothy was riding at her side. Besides, she was not shocked by the sight of him, as the story of Kura Martyn's husband's sudden appearance had spread like wildfire. Matt had heard it in the morning from Jay Hankins, who had been dropping off a delivery of iron parts to the mine. When Timothy had heard the story from Matt around noon, he had dropped everything and asked Roly to saddle Fellow. He had wanted to find Elaine before she ran into William. He'd ended up rousing her from her bed, the previous night at the pub having been a long one. Elaine had been happy for the visit, but she'd paled when Timothy relayed the news.

"Something like this was bound to happen eventually. I've been telling you that for weeks." Timothy had stretched out next to her. He had managed to keep Fellow going at a gallop for almost half the distance and then to dismount and get to Elaine's room without assistance. He liked to tie his crutches securely behind the saddle now. However, this business with William had so preoccupied him that he felt no particular pain or pride with respect to his accomplishment. "Now we have one more person in town who knows the truth, and who knows if the fellow can keep quiet."

"He was with the Fenians, the Irish terrorists. Of course he can keep quiet."

Elaine had been preoccupied by quite different questions. How would she react when she saw William again? Would she choke on her words because of the beating of her heart? Would she blush and turn pale? She hated herself for her inability to suppress her feelings.

And how would William react? He must know that she had killed Thomas Sideblossom. Would he condemn her for it? Perhaps push her to turn herself in?

"Well, then I hope he's got enough mud on his own boots," Timothy had said. "But this is the beginning of the end. If the two of them settle down here, they'll reestablish contact with your family. Especially if these performances continue."

Kura and Caleb had now successfully performed their musical program, "*Putorino* Meets Piano," in Greymouth, Punakaiki, and Westport. Since their performances were always part of charity events, the papers had not yet written about them. Though there were not any big papers on the West Coast, the two of them were first-class musicians, and their program was something very different and new. Kura had indicated to Elaine that their future plans included a tour through New Zealand, Australia, and England. So far, further performances had failed to work out, however, due to a lack of contacts and, perhaps, Caleb's stage fright. He was sick with fear before almost every performance.

"If things continue this way, he'll have stomach ulcers before we even make it to Auckland," Kura complained. She did not take Caleb particularly seriously. However, Mrs. Biller and the Weber women—on whom Kura and Caleb were dependent for their charitable society contacts—were aware of his discomfort and refused to organize any further concerts for the time being.

"If Caleb and Kura go on tour, they'll be gone, you know," Elaine had noted, caressing Timothy. "You worry too much. Look, I've been here for more than two years, and nothing has happened."

"Which surprises me," Timothy had grumbled, letting the subject drop, though, and kissing Elaine. He would do his best to erase all her memories of William Martyn.

Elaine was accompanying Timothy home when they ran into William. The young man was in high spirits. He had just rented a room at Mrs. Miller's, meeting her best friend in the process, and had sold her friend's husband, the tailor, a sewing machine first thing. He knew it would take an eternity for Mr. Mortimer to make any use of it, as he seemed rather old-fashioned, but William had explained to him that one had to keep up with the times, even in his profession. After all, he did not want to fall behind the competition. Mr. Mortimer forgot that he did not have any competition in the vicinity of Greymouth, though William planned to change that in time.

William felt properly happy when he came upon Elaine O'Keefe—or rather, "Lainie Keefer," William reminded himself. Everyone had his, or her, secrets.

"Lainie!" He beamed at the girl, trusting the time-tested power of his smile to pardon him for all past slights. Though they had not exactly parted as friends, Elaine could not still be holding anything against him.

"Kura told me that you were here, but I could hardly believe it. You look wonderful." William spontaneously stretched his hand out to her. If she had not been sitting on her horse, he probably would have kissed her on the cheek in greeting.

Elaine noted with confusion that his kiss would have left her just as cold as his smile. Although she still thought him a good-looking man, his appearance no longer excited her. On the contrary, she now recognized the flash of flippancy in his eyes, his superficiality, and his egotism. Once she had taken all that for adventurousness, and at the time it had been wonderfully exciting and a bit dangerous. But playing with fire no longer held any attraction for her. In fact, it had never truly satisfied her. Elaine wanted to feel loved and secure—and safe.

Elaine returned William's handshake, but her smile was for Timothy.

"Allow me to introduce you to Timothy Lambert, my fiancé."

Was she the only one to see it, or was that admiration—or even a hint of displeasure—that flared up in William's eyes? Did it not suit him that little Elaine had an exceedingly presentable fiancé? No ragged gold miner but the heir apparent of a coal mine? Elaine's claws sprang out immediately.

William started to extend a hand to Timothy, but Timothy only nodded politely. It may have appeared a little arrogant, but Timothy could still not manage to bend down to pedestrians from his horse. William withdrew his hand.

"Then congratulations are in order," he stiffly.

"They are indeed!" Elaine remarked, sweet as honey. "We're celebrating our engagement on the sixteenth of August. At Lambert Manor. You and Kura are both invited, naturally. Please let her know, since we didn't send her a formal invitation. After all, we thought she'd be coming with Caleb."

With that, she gave him a radiant smile and gave Banshee a gentle kick. "I'll be seeing you, William."

Timothy laughed once they were out of sight. "You're turning into a real little minx, Lainie. I'll have to watch out when I'm married to you. Where is that pistol anyway?"

3

Kura listened with astonishment to the story of William's career as a sewing-machine salesman and watched his demonstration in the church's common room. The whole presentation suffered a bit due to the fact that the two of them could still hardly keep their hands off each other. William struggled considerably more than usual to tease his female audience believably. Nevertheless, he sold two machines to housewives and landed a rather large coup by convincing the pastor to found a sewing workshop for the widows of the mining accident.

"Just watch, sir, I'll instruct the ladies considerably more thoroughly than usual—I shall be staying in the area with my wife for some time— and afterward they should be fit to earn a living for themselves and their families. You must, of course, come to an agreement with your charity committee over the organization of the enterprise," William said, nodding to Mrs. Carey, who had just purchased a machine herself, "over whether you hire the ladies to a fixed position or hand over the machines on consignment, so to speak . . . No, it's not worth trying with any fewer than three machines, and for five I could offer you a proper price reduction."

"You're irresistible," Kura said in amazement as the pair rode back into town together holding hands, both of them on the lookout for a chance to leave the road and make love somewhere in the grass. "People really eat out of the palm of your hand. Do you really think Mrs. Carey will figure out this funny machine?"

William shrugged. "Sometimes there happen signs and wonders. Besides, I don't really care. After she's paid for it, she can sew with it or clean her shoes with it. As long as I get my commission. And the ladies didn't seem unhappy, did they?" He grinned.

Kura burst out laughing. "You've always known how to make women happy," she said, kissing him.

William couldn't stand it a moment longer. He drove the wagon down a side road and pulled Kura under the canopy. Although it was not exceptionally comfortable, they could stretch out, and it would simply be too cold to venture outside at that hour. He had occasionally slept in his wagon during his travels, and he wasn't any the worse for wear.

As far as a shared room went, their situation was hopeless. Neither Mrs. Tanner nor Mrs. Miller would allow it, and a suite in the nicer hotels on the quay would be too expensive. William had even thought about renting a room in the Lucky Horse by the hour, but relations between Kura and Madame Clarisse's establishment were a little tense.

"What happened to your enthusiasm for sheep?" Kura asked, running her fingers over the back of William's neck.

"An obvious dead end," he replied. "My family has been in animal husbandry for a long time, so I thought I must have a talent for it. But in truth—"

"In truth it was really your tenants doing the work, and when you came to realize that sheep manure stinks, you lost your ambition." Kura did not speak much, but when she did, she put things into words very aptly.

"You could look at it that way," William admitted. "And what happened to your enthusiasm for the opera?"

Kura shrugged. Then she told him about Roderick Barrister and her failed efforts to stand on her own two feet as an opera singer. "It's the wrong country for opera," she sighed. "The wrong country, the wrong time, what do I know? New Zealand apparently has no use for *Carmen*. I should have accepted my grandmother's offer. But I didn't know that then."

William grinned. "Back then, you believed more than anything that Roderick Barrister would lay the world at your feet."

"You could look at it that way," Kura replied, smiling before shutting his mouth with a kiss.

After stormily making love, Kura told William of her project with Caleb Biller. William roared with laughter at the story of their "engagement."

"We need to bring the boy up to the level of an 'artist' soon, lest people start whispering that you broke his heart. Or he marries this fabulous Florence Weber. I'd be scared to death of her too." Florence had attended the sewing-machine demonstration and asked several probing questions.

"Oh, Caleb truly is an artist. You heard him on Saturday. He's the best pianist I know, and he has perfect pitch." Kura would not let anything ill be said of Caleb.

"But when he has to play before more than three people, he's scared out of his wits. Grand. Besides, I only heard you on Saturday, which was lovely. But I don't think I'll miss Caleb Biller tonight. Shall we pay a little more homage to the spirits?"

Caleb Biller and William Martyn got along astoundingly well. At first, Kura had worried that William might tease or mock her partner. As it was, however, he recognized Caleb's potential within a very short time. The pub was always very quiet on Mondays. The few drunks who showed up didn't have any music requests and either drank away their gambling winnings from the weekend in silence or attempted to drown their losses in whiskey. Kura and Caleb therefore had time—and Paddy's blessing—to perform their entire program for William. Kura sang and played the *putorino* as well as the *koauau*, a hand-sized, heavily decorated flute played with the nose. Caleb accompanied her on the piano, occasionally losing the rhythm because having a knowledgeable listener made him nervous.

It was not Caleb's piano playing that impressed William anyway. He might normally have performed better, but one could find pianists of Caleb's caliber in any of the better music schools. However, when it came to the arrangement of the pieces, Caleb was without a doubt a master. The way he had combined the *haka*'s simple melodies with the complicated passages on the piano, the conversation between the different instruments, the musical bridge between the cultures—all of that sprang from the creative spirit of Caleb Biller. Kura was an exceptionally gifted interpreter; she could perfectly embody the soul of any music. But to create that soul—to work it out note by note and even open the ears of laypeople to it—required more than voice and expression. Caleb was unquestionably an artist, though unfortunately one plagued by stage fright.

"You'll have to get over that," William said after he had told them how impressed he was. "Last time, when I listened to it outside, it was much better. And you, of all people, don't have reason to be nervous. What you do is sensational. You won't just create a furor with that music; you'll conquer Europe!"

Kura gave him a disbelieving look.

"It's not enough to be sensational," she said. "Even though that's what I used to think. But organizing concerts isn't easy. You have to rent spaces, advertise, and negotiate for good terms. You need an impresario like Roderick Barrister." She sighed.

William rolled his eyes. "Sweetheart, just forget that Roderick Barrister of yours. He didn't do anything but hire a few third-rate singers and a couple of pretty dancers and distribute a few flyers. That's not enough though. Someone has to talk to the press. You have to attract patrons, draw the right people to the concerts—in your case, perhaps get local Maori tribes to participate. George Greenwood was the one who organized the entire opera tour, and that's why it was so successful. You need a businessman at your side, Kura, not a choirboy. And no charity dames or pastors—they always send a hint of 'would but can't.' You need grand rooms, hotels, and convention centers. After all, you want to make some money while you're at it."

"You sound as though you know something about all that, Mr. Martyn," Caleb remarked hesitantly. "Have you done anything like that before?"

William shook his head. "No. But I sell sewing machines. In certain respects, that's also a show—and we certainly had a few people during training who had proper stage fright. I'll teach you a few tricks, Mr. Biller. And you can always give your shows a charitable aspect."

"Like you did with the factory for the wives of the mine victims?" Caleb asked, smirking.

William nodded seriously. "First and foremost, you have to remember that you're selling something. In order to sell sewing machines, I need a cheap room for the demonstrations and reasonable accommodations for my horse and myself. But none of it can look shabby. Over time, you develop a sense for it. I can tell from one glance which pubs I can host a sales show in and which ones no honorable woman would set foot in. I would never allow the two of you to perform at the Wild Rover, for example. No one brings his sweetheart here for cultural entertainment. Nor the Lucky Horse, of course. Here in Greymouth, the grand hotels would be the only places even worth considering. But all in all, it's not the right town." William's last words sounded almost wistful. He seemed already to be planning the tour, reviewing in his mind which of the towns he knew would fit the bill.

Kura and Caleb looked at one another.

"Why don't you try selling us for a change?" Kura finally asked. "Show us how it's done. Organize a big concert in a proper hall in a big city."

"Well, the South Island doesn't exactly have the biggest cities," William said, "and I don't have the contacts that someone like George Greenwood does, of course. But very well, we'll start in . . ." He furrowed his brow. Then his face lit up. "We'll start in Blenheim. I know a lady there . . . Really, we both know a lady there, Kura, who is in desperate need of something to do."

So I feel, my dear Heather, that you would find great fulfillment in such a task. In addition, you should keep in mind that the position of your husband

will force you sooner or later into social or cultural engagement of one kind or another. The prestige that comes with being a celebrated patroness of the arts surely eclipses that of being a simple member of the local orphanage's advisory board. Finally, your exceptional education predisposes you to a calling that goes above and beyond purely charitable endeavors. The presentation of our project, "Ghost Whispers—Haka Meets Piano," would make an excellent debut since you have personally contributed significantly to the musical development and formation of Kura-maro-tini's artistic character. I am certain that your husband would agree with me in this matter. I remain, with most humble regards,

Your,
William Martyn

"How does that sound?" William looked—as though asking for praise—from Kura to Caleb, who was just ordering his third whiskey.

Caleb thought Kura's husband was inspiring and his way of talking irresistible. But Caleb felt like he was being pulled into a whirlpool in which he would inevitably drown.

"*Whaikorero*, the art of beautiful speech," Kura said. "You're a master, no question. Is Heather Witherspoon really married to a wealthy railroad magnate and living in a mansion in Blenheim?"

"The spirits have willed it so," William said dramatically. "So, should I send it? Then you can't back out, Caleb. If Heather agrees—and she will, I trust—you'll be playing in front of a hundred or maybe even two hundred people. Will you manage?"

No, thought Caleb, but he said yes.

At that, Kura ordered a round of whiskey. She wanted to drink with the men, too, that day. Perhaps her career would finally take off!

William looked at Caleb skeptically. The man was too nervous, too pale, not charismatic enough. They would have to replace him eventually. He would never last through a tour of Europe. Still, they would have to make do with him in the beginning. They needed a starting point, a rousing success.

William blew his wife a kiss as he stood up to grab the drinks. It would not be whiskey much longer. If everything went well, Kura would soon be drinking champagne. William was finally prepared to keep the promise he had made to Kura before their wedding. He would go to Europe. With her.

Heather Redcliff's answer came almost as soon as they'd sent the letter. She expressed her joy that William had found Kura again and said that the prospect of smoothing the path to success for her former student appealed to her. After all, she had always believed in Kura and would be happy to tell that to the local press. Indeed, she had already mentioned it—at her last reception on the occasion of the opening of a new wing of the hospital. While Heather had long been engaged with the local charities, art lay closer to her heart. William had been quite astute to recognize that. All of Blenheim society was now waiting rather impatiently to meet Kura-maro-tini. And she, Heather Redcliff, would consider it an additional and special pleasure to see William again.

William smiled. He left out the last line as he read the letter to Kura. Their active future patroness had booked a concert hall at once. Located in the city's best hotel, it comprised some one hundred fifty seats. A reception for invited guests would follow. And the evening before, Mr. and Mrs. Redcliff would take the liberty of introducing the artists to the city of Blenheim's notables. Sunday, the second of September, would be suitable, would it not?

"There you have it, Kura. All you need to do now is sing," William remarked.

The light in Kura's eyes was otherworldly. William had not seen her so inwardly radiant since their wedding. Nor had she kissed him so happily and sincerely since then. William returned her kiss, relieved. He knew then that Kura forgave him everything. The lies and stalling techniques before the wedding, the unwanted pregnancy meant to bind her to Kiward Station—even his affair with Heather

Witherspoon. William and Kura would begin anew, and this time it would be just like in Kura's dreams.

If only it were not for Caleb. He had not smiled but instead turned pale as William read Heather's letter.

William did not like how Caleb had been behaving recently. He had become increasingly agitated, making so many mistakes on the piano that even Kura grew vexed at him. In fact, Caleb couldn't even start to loosen up until he'd had his first or second whiskey and he was certain that William would not be hearing from his prospective patroness in Blenheim that day. But now Heather's letter had come. This was serious. Caleb withdrew from the table, muttering his apologies as he exited the pub. He looked to be in even rougher shape when he returned.

"These hundred and fifty seats, there's no way they'll sell out, will they?" he asked, playing with an empty glass.

William wondered whether he should lie, but there would be no sense in that. Caleb had to rise to the occasion.

"Blenheim sees itself as an up-and-coming city, Caleb, but between us, it's a backwater. A little bigger than Greymouth and more developed. But it's no London. Blenheim isn't exactly filled cheek by jowl with cultural offerings. If one of the city's leading ladies presents a few artists, people will be falling over themselves to get tickets to the concert. We could probably have another show the very next day."

"But—"

"Now be happy, Caleb," Kura yelled. "And if you're too scared to be happy, then think about what comes next. You'll be a famous artist! You'll be able to live like you want, Caleb. Think of the alternative."

"Yes," Caleb said weakly. "I'll be able to live like I want."

He did indeed seem to be thinking about it, but William could tell just how despondent Caleb was.

As the day of Timothy and Elaine's engagement party neared, Elaine had the sense that she was in the eye of the storm. Nellie Lambert had been a bundle of nerves for weeks, spending entire days planning the decorations and the order in which the various courses would be served—or would a buffet be better? She booked a band to play during the dancing, though she almost found it inappropriate since she thought, naturally, Timothy and Elaine could not open the dance. Timothy nonetheless trained tenaciously. Poor Roly ceased his role as a male nurse only to take up that of dance partner.

Timothy almost had a panic attack when he saw the engagement notices in the various West Coast newspapers. He would have liked not to let Elaine out of his sight, and every stranger in town put fear in his heart. Timothy was now seriously planning their emigration. Although he could certainly have started working in the mine's office for a few hours a day by then, his father continued to veto all of his attempts to do so.

Timothy no longer traced that back to his disability. Marvin Lambert was hiding something. The balance sheets were probably even worse than Matt had suggested. The mine was losing money, and the railroad would surely make little progress during this very wet winter. They couldn't count on quick profits from Lambert's investment—and Nellie was spending every penny to show off with this engagement party. If things continued in this manner, there would be nothing left to save. Timothy expected that the mine would have to be shut down while the most important renovation work was being done, which would mean further enormous losses. They would have to declare the losses to the bank, and Timothy's father was not making any effort even to apply for the loan they so desperately needed. In addition to all that, there was the continual danger in which Elaine found herself.

Timothy had had enough. He wanted to leave—before the wedding if possible. Or right after a small, secret ceremony and a round with his friends at the pub. The passage to and organization of their new life in England or Wales would be simpler if they were already married.

Elaine, however, had only just begun to get excited about the engagement party. She could not help herself; she was looking forward it—in part because Nellie Lambert was finally taking her seriously. The women still hadn't completely warmed up to each other, and they were clashing about Elaine's dress for the celebration. Nellie wanted to have Mr. Mortimer tailor it or, better yet, to order an outrageously expensive tulle-and-silk confection from Christchurch. Elaine, on the other hand, wanted to entrust Mrs. O'Brien and her new workshop with their first really big contract.

Here, too, there had been bad blood in recent weeks. The sewing machines had arrived, and William had instructed the women from the miners' camp on how to use them, as he had promised. When it came time to decide who would manage the enterprise, however, the more-than-capable Mrs. Carey got into it with the no-less-capable Mrs. O'Brien. Roly's mother was a skilled seamstress, and she had the necessary business savvy. Hence, she began right away with the production of simple children's clothes that were so reasonably priced that it was not worth it for even the poorest miner's wife to sew the clothes herself. Mrs. Carey, however, was in favor of finishing the seamstresses' training first thing and then "giving a bit of soul," as she put it, to the factory rooms—for which, against his will, Marvin Lambert had placed an old shed near his mine at their disposal.

"I'm not going to spend weeks sewing curtains for this shed," Mrs. O'Brien complained to the pastor. "And we don't need to paint the walls either, least of all in a 'warm antique pink.' If anything, whitewash 'em. I need money, reverend. I've got enough 'soul.'"

Mrs. O'Brien got her way in the end. And though Mrs. Carey was insulted and spoke of her "ingratitude," the women in the workshop looked on calmly. Business was going well. If things continued that way, they would be able to pay the church council back for the sewing machines in one or two years.

Mrs. O'Brien took Elaine's measurements and was enthusiastic about the blue velvet the girl had selected for her engagement dress.

"It's beautiful, and I can wear the dress again later," Elaine explained, justifying her choice to Timothy. "Unlike those silly things from Christchurch."

"At our wedding, for example," noted Timothy. "Give elope-
ment some thought, Lainie. I have a really bad feeling about this
engagement."

William Martyn also had a bad feeling when he saw Caleb Biller
in church the Sunday before the engagement party. The young man
looked even leaner and more nervous than usual, and he seemed to
have become, if possible, even paler. Caleb was leading Florence
Weber on his arm. While the girl looked exceptionally pleased with
herself, Caleb looked utterly defeated. The Biller and Weber parents
followed the couple proudly. William suspected bad news.

Kura observed Caleb's entrance from her seat at the organ and
could hardly wait until after church to hear what had happened. She
was a little embarrassed about that, as she normally prided herself
on being above such things. But the look on his face was so strained
that she couldn't help but be nervous. After all, Caleb had still been
successfully evading Florence the Sunday before.

When the pastor finally dismissed his congregation, Kura joined
Elaine, William, and Timothy. The three of them were chatting at the
edge of the crowd while Timothy waited for Roly, who was flirting
with little Mary Flaherty in the cemetery. Timothy looked to be in
in no particular hurry. He had already taken his seat in the carriage,
where he was laughing with Elaine—and beaming with pride. At
their wedding rehearsal, Timothy had easily managed to cross the
church on his own legs.

"Just a few more dance steps, Lainie, and we can have this wedding. Don't take too long to think about it. A ship leaves for London
on the fifteenth of September—a steamship. We could be in England
in less than six weeks."

Elaine did not respond. Her eyes were focused on Caleb and
Florence.

"What's going on there between the two of them?" she asked
Kura. "I can't help looking. They look awfully official."

William followed Elaine's and his wife's eyes.

"No, it doesn't look good. But he's coming this way. If you're not sure what to do, hold yourself back, Kura. If you make a scene, the town will write it off as jealousy."

Caleb, who had indeed separated from Florence, was walking toward the group with his eyes lowered. Perhaps he had chosen this particular moment precisely to avoid being alone with Kura and William. Florence watched him, a little concerned but more triumphant than anything.

"Mrs. Martyn, Mr. Martyn, Miss Keefer. How are you, Mr. Lambert?"

Timothy smiled. "I'd say I'm doing a good deal better than you. You were quite a sight hauling that Florence Weber of yours through the church."

"Since when is she 'that Florence Weber of yours'?" Kura asked.

Caleb blushed. "Well, how can I put this . . . you see, Miss Weber and I became engaged yesterday."

The news did not particularly come as a surprise William. To Timothy, even less so. The girls, however, stared at Caleb without fully comprehending.

"It's like this, Kura. I spoke with her," Caleb began, breaking the awkward silence. "We talked it over, so to speak. And she doesn't care."

"She doesn't care about what? That you're a qu—"

"Kura, please!" William jumped in.

"She says she would give me every freedom in our marriage as long as I . . . well, let her have a greater role in running the mine than is customary for women."

"She'll undoubtedly do an excellent job," Timothy said kindly. "One can only congratulate the Biller Mine on that. But you don't look too pleased yourself."

"Well, you know how it is," Caleb said vaguely. "But I can continue to dedicate myself to my interests. Music, art, Maori culture. It's not just the music that interests me, as you know. As a private scholar, so to speak, I will—"

"Very nice." William interrupted Caleb's rambling speech. "We were just talking about that recently. Everyone should live as he chooses. My hearty congratulations. Perhaps you'll continue arranging songs for Kura. And you're not going to leave us in the lurch for this concert in Blenheim, are you? We're counting on you for that. We won't be able to find a replacement on such short notice."

Caleb bit his lip. He was visibly struggling with himself, but then he shook his head.

"I'm sorry. But I can't. I tried. Really, I did, but you can hear it yourselves; I hardly hit a right note anymore. My nerves just get the best of me. I'm not made that way. And Florence thinks—"

"Go ahead, put this on her," Kura said wrathfully. "Then you don't need to admit that you're not only queer but a coward to boot. A coward above all. There's nothing wrong with the other."

Elaine pressed closer to Timothy.

"What does she mean by 'queer'?" she whispered.

While Timothy struggled not to laugh, Kura struggled in vain against her tears. For the first time since Elaine had known her, Kura began to cry—in public, moreover. She sobbed wildly and uncontrollably. The usually cool and self-possessed girl was virtually unrecognizable.

"You're ruining my life, Caleb, can't you see that? If we cancel the concert now, my chance won't come again. Damn it, I planned it all for you! The entire program was initially intended to show you off as an artist. I didn't leave you in the lurch when you wanted to play at being engaged. But you—"

"I'm sorry, Kura," Caleb said, deeply embarrassed. "I'm truly sorry."

With that, he turned away. He gave the impression that a great weight had fallen from him as he returned to his family. Florence shoved her arm into his—and showed at least enough decency not to look at Kura.

"Will you really not be able to find a replacement?" Timothy asked. He did not care much for Kura, but seeing the girl cry so desperately moved him to pity.

"In three weeks? On the West Coast? In Blenheim? Maybe if we went there straightaway. But then the novelty element would be gone. If we appeared there without a proper plan, with a local, hastily instructed pianist . . ." William shook his head.

"Mrs. Redcliff could play," Kura said hopefully.

"But she won't. We just encouraged her to embrace her career as an art patroness. She won't take to the stage now. Besides, what would her husband say to that? Forget it, Kura." William put his arms around his wife.

Elaine chewed on her upper lip.

"I haven't heard what you've been working on over there," she said, "but is it all that difficult? The piano part, I mean?"

Kura looked at her, and Elaine recognized a hopeful illumination in her eyes. "Not extremely difficult. A little unconventional in places, with some rapid passages. The player should have at least a few years of experience performing on the piano."

"Well, I've been playing piano for ten years. Not at your level, naturally, as you've done me the kindness of making clear several times. But if I practice for three weeks . . ." Elaine's smile took the edge off her words.

"You've gotten a great deal better," Kura replied. "But seriously, Lainie—would you do it? You'd come with me to Blenheim to play accompaniment?"

"If I can handle the pieces."

Kura looked as though she wanted to fling her arms around her cousin's neck.

"And she's very pretty too," William remarked. "It'll make a much more attractive picture than Caleb."

Elaine looked at him skeptically. Did he say "pretty?" Three years before, her heart would have danced at the word; that day, however, her gaze wandered from William's youthful features to Timothy's face—which no longer looked amiable and amused, but contorted in pain.

"Lainie, you can't do that, no matter how much you want to help Kura. Of course you'd play infinitely better than Caleb Biller and look more beautiful doing it than all the pianists in the world, but Blenheim? The travel, the city, the risk."

"When did you become so anxious?" William inquired. "Compared to the risk your wedding represents—"

"And what exactly is so dangerous about getting married?" Elaine snapped. "You looked at me so strangely the last time it was mentioned."

William rolled his eyes. "Well, you are both surely aware that you're committing a crime by marrying. And even if you don't care, you'll probably want to have children someday."

Elaine laughed, though it came out a bit forced. "Heavens, William. My children won't care whether their mother's maiden name was O'Keefe or Keefer. We could even pass it off as a spelling mistake."

William frowned and looked at her almost in disbelief. "But your children will certainly care when they find out someday that their name is Sideblossom, not Lambert, and that they're going to inherit a farm in Otago, while their mine will go to some distant relatives. This marriage is illegitimate; that has to be clear to you!"

Elaine turned pale. Her pupils widened.

Timothy shook his head. "But Thomas Sideblossom is dead," he said calmly.

"Oh?" William asked. "Since when? He may indeed wish he were dead every day, but as far as I know, he's just as alive as you or I." William let his gaze move from one to the other. Was it possible that Elaine and Timothy were playing dumb? But he came to realize that at least the horror in Elaine's face was real.

"I . . . I shot him in the face," she whispered.

William nodded. "You can tell. The bullet entered here." He pointed to his left cheek. "It passed rather smoothly through the nose and into his head. You shot upward from below, probably aiming at his chest but without accounting for the recoil. In any event, you successfully put him hors de combat. He's paralyzed on his right side, blind in his right eye, and almost blind in his left. The bullet's supposedly still in there pushing on the optic nerve. But he's not dead. You have to believe me, Lainie."

Elaine raised her hands to her eyes. "That's so horrible, William! Why didn't you tell me before?"

"I thought you knew," William said. "You did, didn't you, Kura?"

Kura nodded. "I didn't know the details, but I knew he wasn't dead."

"And you let me get engaged?" Elaine tried to sound angry, but incomprehension was fighting with relief and hope in her head. "I've been scared to death for two and a half years."

Kura shrugged. "Sorry, Lainie, but no one gave me a detailed account of your affairs. I was a little surprised, but you could have been divorced, for all I knew. Or Thomas Sideblossom might have died in the meantime. Isn't he not in his right mind?" She turned to William.

"Not as far as I know. Although he goes to great lengths to drink his mind away, on top of taking morphine. He does suffer from constant headaches and hallucinations. But with all that morphine and whiskey, I probably would too."

"You've seen him?" Elaine clenched Timothy's hand as she stared at William in horror. "You're sure?" Her face was pale as death, and her eyes looked huge, seeming to consist entirely of pupils.

"Good Lord, Lainie, don't stare at me like that. Of course I'm sure. I was on Lionel Station for two or three weeks awhile back, and I saw him once or twice. They can only rarely convince him to go out. Apparently, he can't stand the light of day. But you can't fail to hear him. He roars at the workers, screaming for his whiskey and his medicine. A distinctly unpleasant patient, if you ask me. But not quite crazy, and what's more, certainly not dead."

"That changes everything, of course," Timothy said calmly, pulling Elaine to him. She was now shaking uncontrollably and crying. "As long as you're officially Mrs. Sideblossom, we can't get married. But you haven't murdered anyone either. So calm down. In principle, that's good news. You'll turn yourself in and confess. You can say it was an accident. The weapon just went off. We'll talk to a lawyer about whether it makes more sense for you to tell the whole story or to feign remorse. In any case, they won't hang you for it. You can get a divorce and then live with me completely legally. Here, or in Wales, or wherever."

"I'd rather go to Wales," Elaine whispered. She suddenly felt an urgent need to put as many miles between Lionel Station and herself as she could. Part of her was relieved not to be a murderer, but she had felt safer when she believed Thomas Sideblossom was dead.

"Can't we just run away without my turning myself in first?"

Timothy shook his head. "No, Lainie. William's right. We can't let our children grow up as the official offspring of Thomas Sideblossom, no matter where we raise them. We'll see this thing through, Lainie. You and I together. Don't be afraid!"

"But not until after the engagement party. Right, Tim? Please. I won't be able to handle it if everything implodes just now. Your mother, the whole town will be talking about us." Elaine was crying uncontrollably. It was all too much.

Timothy stroked her and rocked her in his arms. "Certainly, after the engagement party is fine with me. Although I don't like it. I'm worried about this celebration."

"But it's taking place in Greymouth," Kura burst out. "As long as Elaine is in Greymouth, nothing can happen to her."

Three confused pairs of eyes stared at her.

"Are the spirits saying that, dear?" William asked, attempting a joke.

Kura shook her head. "A Maori woman told me that a few weeks ago. They were still looking for Lainie, she said, but she was safe in Greymouth."

4

Elaine clung to the words of the Maori chieftain's wife indicating that she would be safe in Greymouth. But part of the message unsettled Timothy: *They were still looking for Lainie.* And on the sixteenth of August, the Lamberts would present her to half the West Coast as his bride-to-be. Timothy tried to keep Elaine in sight. Although it scandalized his mother, he slept at Elaine's place in the pub and tried to persuade her to leave her room as little as possible.

Naturally, that did not work. Elaine had to go to her last dress fitting. And Nellie Lambert expected her help with decorating the house. The town slowly filled with strangers that Marvin Lambert had invited. All the rooms in Greymouth had long since been booked. Guests were staying as far away as Punakaiki and even Westport. It was impossible to get a good look at all of them before the celebration. Timothy would first see the guests when they lined up to greet the couple at the party, and he'd be meeting many of them for the first time; his father had invited a whole slew of old acquaintances. All of this greatly wore on Timothy's nerves. Overly anxious, he took up his last battle with his mother before the event. In all seriousness Nellie had asked him—for the sake of appearances—to forgo his leg splints and crutches and greet the guests in his wheelchair.

"You needn't be ashamed of the fact that you can't walk, son."

"I *can* walk!" Timothy replied, agitated. "My God, Mother, I'm standing right in front of you! Do the two of you really not understand that I just want to be normal?" Timothy limped out of the room, wishing he could slam the door behind him. For a few seconds, he considered asking Roly to do so, but then he saw the humor in it and he smiled grimly.

"Get Fellow ready, Roly. I'm fleeing to the pub. Or, no—hitch him to the carriage. You look like you could use a beer too. You've been helping out in the house all day, haven't you? How many garlands did you hang?"

"Too many, Mr. Lambert." Roly grinned. "We stopped counting after Mrs. Lambert had us rehang them for the fifteenth time. Your suit for tomorrow is pretty big, by the way, Mr. Lambert. You could probably wear your splints underneath."

"Not a chance," Timothy spat. "My mother's right about one thing. I don't have anything to feel ashamed about."

In addition to preparing for the engagement party, Elaine spent a great deal of time on the piano, which Timothy found somewhat reassuring. He had persuaded Madame Clarisse to let Kura and Elaine practice their music when the pub was closed, which kept Elaine off the streets for several hours a day. He hardly dared think about the performance in Blenheim. However, he hoped by then they would have made it through the worst. After all, Elaine had promised to turn herself into the authorities right after the engagement party. The constable might not even let her go to Blenheim though. Elaine and Kura did not seem to have considered this possibility, as they were too deeply immersed in their work on Caleb's scores.

To her relief, Elaine had determined that the piano part was not too difficult. She could sight-read it fluently right from the start and soon knew it by heart. Unfortunately, she was lacking in virtuosity. Although she was the more sentimental of the two girls, Elaine didn't have the least sense of nuance in music. She did not pick up on the soul of the piece; her playing was technically correct but without any expressiveness or special emphasis. Where Caleb had instinctively created accents through tiny variations—a barely perceptible vibration, or a slight hesitation in the piano's answer to the flute—Elaine simply followed the notes. Kura almost drove herself to distraction trying to explain the distinction to Elaine.

"A rest? I should wait first instead of playing? For how long? A quarter rest?"

"A heartbeat," Kura said, sighing. "A gust of wind."

Elaine gave her a confused look. "I'll try an eighth note."

Kura eventually gave up. Their rendition wouldn't be perfect. But at least Elaine did not suffer from stage fright, and she was certain not to play a wrong note. Besides, the audience in Blenheim would not be terribly discerning. And Elaine's playing was certainly better than most of the opera arias Roderick and his ensemble had defiled on the hotel stage.

Elaine's dress was finally ready. She looked magnificent. Mrs. O'Brien had made an Alice band for her hair out of the same azure-blue velvet fabric as the dress. Elaine planned to wear her hair down, keeping it out of her face with the simple headband.

"You look like a fairy, Miss Keefer," Mrs. O'Brien said adoringly. "You have such wonderfully soft hair. It floats about you as though a breeze were constantly wafting over you. Back home in Ireland, we chose a Queen of Spring every year, and I always pictured a girl like you." Mrs. O'Brien was as proud of Elaine in her beautiful dress as if she were her own daughter.

"I don't know. Fairies and elves are so helpless," Elaine muttered, immediately recalling her first encounter with William. "I think I'd rather be a witch. But this dress is wonderful, Mrs. O'Brien. Soon every woman in town will have you making something for her. Mr. Mortimer will be in a huff."

Mrs. O'Brien snorted. "Mr. Mortimer doesn't have five children to feed. He has a nice house in town and makes ends meet. I don't feel too bad about it."

When the day of the celebration finally arrived, Roly picked up Elaine at the Lucky Horse in Timothy's two-wheeled chaise—and to her surprise, Timothy had accompanied him on Fellow. He was already wearing his evening suit, but he looked vexed.

"I know I should have restrained myself, particularly on this occasion, but I just got into a fight with my father," he said to Elaine. "He's been drinking since he woke up this morning, and I didn't know why. I finally told him he was going to make a rather bad impression on our guests if he was drunk. Well, then he admitted to me—today of all days—that he's looking for investors for the mine! Partners, you understand. With that, he's shutting me out once and for all. And if my own father thinks I'm a failure, there's certainly no stranger who will hire me." Timothy looked miserable and hurt.

"In any case, I'm resolved now. As soon as we've finalized your divorce, Lainie, we'll disappear. I'm fed up with all of it!"

Fellow pranced beneath his impatient rider as though he would have liked to embark on the journey right then on his own hooves. If this continued, Timothy would be completely exhausted before the celebration even got under way. Even on the calmest of days, riding required a good deal of effort on his part.

Elaine soothed Fellow and gently removed Timothy's clenched hand from the reins. "First come down from that horse. Your mother will have a fit if your good suit smells like the stables. Roly can take Fellow back, and you can drive me in the chaise—it will be wonderfully romantic. It's a full moon too. We can make stops along the way and practice kissing as official fiancés."

Timothy smiled weakly, and Elaine pressed a soft kiss into his hand.

"First things first, we need to make it through this evening," she said. "Everything else will sort itself out." She took her seat in the chaise, draping the wide skirt of her dress picturesquely over the bench. Timothy rode over to his mounting block in the stables and accomplished the feat of sliding from his horse, getting his splints from the saddle, attaching them, and returning to Elaine all on his own.

"You heard her, Roly," Timothy said to his slightly indignant servant. "The lady would like you to ride Fellow back home while I drive her. Lainie, do you really want to bring Callie, or should Roly take her to the stables?"

The little dog hopped about around the carriage excitedly, clearly enthusiastic about the trip. Timothy petted her as she leaped up on him.

"She doesn't bother me," he said, "but you know my mother."

"She'll have to learn to live with the dog. Callie is the touchstone for true love, you know. If she barks at the decisive moment, I won't marry you," Elaine said, laughing nervously. "What is it, Roly?" She turned to the unhappy-looking boy standing next to the carriage.

"I don't know how to ride," Roly said, his eyes pitiful. "I'll have to walk the whole way."

His peevish countenance even cheered Timothy up a little. "Roly, if you can't ride, you're already dead," he informed him, using a slight variation on Elaine's favorite saying. "I, on the other hand, would be overjoyed if I could walk the two miles. So take the horse home. I don't care who or what does the carrying or the leading."

Roly did not dare climb in the saddle and instead walked the two miles through the light rain. By the end of his walk, he was feeling cross. His new suit was wet, and he had missed Mary Flaherty. He had wanted to meet her at the kitchen door and entice her with a few treats from the buffet—in hopes of putting her in a receptive enough mood to exchange a few kisses with him. Then, one of the Webers' grooms he knew in passing called out to him. The young man waved a bottle of whiskey.

"Come on, Roly, let's celebrate a bit too. That Mr. Lambert of yours isn't going to need a nurse tonight!"

In general, Roly was not so irresponsible, but that evening, he left Fellow saddled in front of the house. With the intention of returning to fetch him later, of course. But then he forgot. The gray gelding waited patiently. Someone would come for him eventually. Until that time came, he snoozed in the misting rain. No one paid any attention to him until he received some company—much later.

After the sixtieth or seventieth guest had been led past the young couple and greeted with a few words, Timothy almost began to long for his wheelchair. Whose bright idea had it been to have them stand in the salon for hours greeting each and every guest with a handshake? His mother called it a "reception line." Until that evening, Elaine had thought such things only happened in royal courts. Though for her it was merely boring, for Timothy it was very tiring. He cast envious looks at Callie, who was curled up behind them on the carpet and sleeping soundly.

"How many has it been all together?" Elaine asked, pushing somewhat closer to him. She hoped that he might be able to support himself on her, but in reality she was too petite for that.

"Almost one hundred and fifty. Pure nonsense," Timothy muttered, forcing himself to smile for the Weber family. When Florence floated in on Caleb's arm, Caleb lavished words of gratitude on Elaine. He described vividly the heavy stone that had been lifted from his heart when he had heard that she would be standing in for him at Kura's concert.

"Never remove the stone from a geologist's heart," Timothy joked wearily when the couple finally moved on. "He'll analyze every detail of what it consists of, why you were able to remove it, and how many component parts it contained."

Fortunately, the next guests to arrive were Matt and Charlene— the latter wearing a ravishing green dress, another of Mrs. O'Brien's creations—followed by Kura and William. Thankfully, all were feeling more hungry than talkative.

"Where is the buffet?" Kura asked. The time she had spent on the road had taught her never to turn down a free meal. William plied her with champagne, and Elaine and Timothy turned to the next guests.

As luck would have it, not all the guests arrived right on time. When the receiving room stood empty for a few minutes, Timothy decided to put an end to his suffering. He sat down with relief in one of the armchairs in the salon.

"I need to rest up a bit before the dance," he murmured, scratching Callie, while Elaine went to get some champagne.

Elaine pushed her way through the crowd to the buffet, which was set up in the study, chatting briefly with Charlene and Kura and thanking several guests for the compliments they paid her. Though everything seemed to be in order, she nevertheless felt a vague sense of unease. Perhaps, she thought, it was too much like a fairy tale. She knew all too well that she would be forced to snap back to reality the next morning in front of the constable. Elaine smiled at the sheriff and the justice of the peace, who happily returned her greeting. For now.

Glasses of champagne in hand, Elaine began to make her way back to Timothy—and that was when she spotted the tall gray-haired man who was entering the salon with Marvin Lambert. The sight of him turned her to stone. Every instinct told her to run. But no, that was absurd; she must be mistaken. It simply could not be. She shouldn't recklessly take flight. No, she had better get a closer look first and assure herself that there was no way it could be John Sideblossom.

Elaine forced herself to move forward.

Just then, the band began to play in the salon. People began to push their way into the room, blocking Elaine's view of the new guest. Her heartbeat slowed as she let herself be carried by the crowd. It was undoubtedly nonsense. She eventually made it back to Timothy, who was struggling to his feet.

"So, beautiful, will you dance with me?"

Elaine wanted to reply, but she felt a cold breeze at the back of her neck. She turned around nervously, and Timothy's inviting smile froze when he saw the look of panic on her face. Elaine looked like she wanted to flee—but she seemed incapable of budging an inch. Within seconds, all the color had drained from her face.

"Lainie, what is it?"

"He's . . . he's . . ."

"Ah, there they are," Marvin Lambert's booming voice rang out. "Allow me to introduce you to a surprise guest. A very old friend of mine. How long has it been, John? This is John Sideblossom!"

Elaine stuck out her hand mechanically. Maybe this was all just a bad dream. Maybe she was hallucinating.

"My soon-to-be daughter-in-law, Lainie, and my son, Tim."

Elaine felt as though the room were spinning around her. Perhaps fainting wouldn't be such a bad idea. But then John Sideblossom took her hand, and the riotous fear that came over Elaine sharpened her senses.

"Lovely, lovely Elaine," he said. His voice sounded hoarse. "I knew I'd find you. Someday, and under such pleasant circumstances. Mr. Lambert." He smiled his predatory smile as he turned to Timothy. "What an enchanting conquest. What a shame that there are still defenders in place. You should not raise your flag over the castle until you've razed it."

Though Elaine did not understand his words, she grasped the threat they contained. And then she could no longer stand it. She wanted to murmur an apology, but she only managed a gasp. She bolted in a panic, almost running into the study, from which there was no way to get outside. Elaine couldn't think; she wasn't looking where she was going—and she crashed into Kura, who was just entering the salon with two glasses of champagne. The drinks sprayed onto her cousin's dress. Kura was about to curse, but she held her tongue when she saw the horror in Elaine's face.

"Lainie, what's wrong with you? Did you have a fight with Tim?" Kura looked at her quizzically. No, that couldn't be it. Not even when Elaine had caught Kura with William on the street in Queenstown had she looked so pale and drawn, her eyes so big. The eyes of an animal in a trap.

"John Sideblossom. He . . . he . . ." Elaine took off, out of the salon and through the receiving room. She needed air. Gasping, she reached the brightly illuminated entrance, fled from the light, and saw Fellow, tethered along with two other horses that were pulling a wagon. Callie barked. Elaine had not noticed that the dog had followed her. She bent down mechanically to stroke her . . . and heard footsteps behind her. She tensed up. John Sideblossom, she thought. But then she saw Callie's tail wagging and recognized the sound of thudding crutches and Timothy's typical dragging step.

"Lainie, there you are." Timothy leaned on the beam to which the animals were tethered and took her in his arms. "My God, you're shaking like a leaf. Now calm down."

"I can't calm down." Elaine suddenly felt cold, as the sweat dried on her body. "That's John Sideblossom . . . He's . . . he's going to . . ."

Timothy was scared too, but he had a capacity for quickly evaluating and mastering critical situations. In a mine, that could mean the difference between life and death. He stroked Elaine's hair and spoke soothingly to her.

"Lainie, he's not going to do anything tonight. At the very worst, he'll ruin this party. But if he had wanted a scandal, he would have gone about it differently. He probably won't make his move until tomorrow, or he'll take it up with my father presently."

"He'll take it up with the constable, and then they'll lock me up," Elaine whispered. And then she suddenly realized that being arrested didn't scare her. She was not afraid of a night in a cell. On the contrary. She would feel safer there.

"Look, Lainie, the constable is among our guests. We greeted him earlier. The same goes for the justice of the peace. If you'd like, I'll call them over. We can retire to my apartments without making a scene, and you can give your testimony there."

"Now?" Elaine asked. "Right now?" She vacillated between hope and fear.

"That way we'd cut Sideblossom off at the chase. Your divorce request could go out first thing tomorrow. Nothing more could happen to you after that. Calm down, Callie!"

Timothy turned impatiently toward the dog, who was suddenly barking wildly. Elaine pulled back from Timothy when she heard Callie's yelping. Her face once again assumed an expression of despair as she stared over Timothy's shoulder.

"What if my son does not want a divorce, Mr. Lambert?"

John Sideblossom stepped out of the shadows. He must have left the house by one of the side exits. He wore a long dark coat over his evening attire. It looked as though he were ready to leave. Timothy sighed with relief. Callie yapped.

"What if he's hoping for a family reunion instead? That has been his greatest wish, Lainie, since that unfortunate accident."

Elaine could not utter a word. She backed up in horror as John Sideblossom approached.

"But Elaine wishes for a divorce, Mr. Sideblossom," Timothy said calmly. "Please be reasonable. Lainie very much regrets what she did, but your son unquestionably gave her every reason to do it. Please, leave us alone now."

"No one asked you," John roared before turning his raspy voice on Elaine again.

"You owe him, Lainie. From now on, you're going to be an obedient wife to him. Thomas was always a little . . . hmm . . . weak. So I'll keep an eye on you too." He reached for Elaine, but then dodged backward as Callie sprang in between them, barking hysterically.

Timothy leaped in front of Elaine. "Not so fast, Mr. Sideblossom," he said, his voice firm. "It's time for you to take your leave."

John grinned. "Or what? Are you trying to stop me from taking back our property?"

He struck without warning. His fist hit Timothy's chin with force, knocking him to the side. Timothy, in no way prepared for the blow, fell to the ground heavily. When his injured hip hit the ground, he could not suppress a cry of pain. John kicked at Callie, who was still barking.

"Tim!" Elaine forgot all her fear. She knelt down next to him—an opportunity John took advantage of at once. More than that, he seemed to have figured it into his calculations. With lightning quickness, he yanked Elaine's hands and bound them behind her back. Then he clamped a strip of cloth between her teeth so that she could not even scream.

Timothy turned on the ground, attempting desperately to get hold of something, but he could only watch helplessly as John hauled Elaine to her feet, picked her up, and threw her into the wagon.

"Just forget about her," he said, sneering, as he untied his horses.

Timothy tried to roll into his way and stop the horses, though John would surely not have had any scruples about running them over him. He gave Timothy a kick to the ribs.

"You don't really mean to fight me?" he said, laughing, and seemed to consider whether he should go after him again. However, he simply left Timothy lying there. He would not beat up a cripple. At least not any more than necessary.

John had come in a light delivery wagon that had a small cargo bed and a raised driver's box in front. Elaine lay in the back without moving. John supposed he had hurt her when he threw her on the wagon. Well, he could worry about that later. The main thing was that she was still. He calmly turned his team. Why attract attention? If only that damned dog would stop its yapping. He felt for his gun, but realized that if he shot the beast, the people inside the house would hear. It was better to leave the mutt behind. He brought his horses to a gallop.

Kura was looking for Elaine and Timothy, but found only William, who was chatting at the bar with someone. She took him aside.

"Lainie is completely beside herself! She thinks she saw Sideblossom. And I can't find Tim anywhere either."

"Well, Tim can hardly run away," William said. He was no longer entirely sober.

"William, this is serious! Elaine was wild with fear. Heaven knows where she is."

"If I had to guess, behind Madame Clarisse's piano. Elaine always runs off when something scares her; you know that. And how is Sideblossom supposed to have come here? He's paralyzed and as good as blind."

Kura shook him. "Not the younger one! The old one! Now come on, William. We need to find them. If it was a false alarm, all the better. But I'm telling you. Elaine saw somebody. And if it wasn't John Sideblossom, then the way she looked, it must have been the devil himself!"

William pulled himself together. He still thought it unlikely that John Sideblossom could have made an appearance. On the other hand, the fellow was an old Coaster just like Marvin Lambert, and one could not entirely rule out an acquaintanceship.

But running around heedlessly like Kura, who had already darted off, was senseless. William reflected briefly. What he had said about Elaine was true. She did not face her problems; she ran. If she really had seen John Sideblossom, she would already be on long gone. But where to? To Madame Clarisse's? Or farther away? William made for the front door. And then he heard Callie barking. It wasn't very loud. In fact, it sounded like the barking was growing more distant. William broke into a run.

"Over here, help!"

William was standing in the entrance, trying to get his bearings, when he heard Timothy calling. He looked over to the left of the lighted approach. Timothy was trying desperately to pull himself up on the hitching post. He appeared to be hardly able to move his left leg.

"Wait, I'll help you . . ." William was going to pick up the crutches, but he was suddenly struck by an awful suspicion. If Timothy had merely fallen over, he would have had the crutches nearby.

"Leave me!" Timothy shooed William away vehemently. "Go after Lainie! That son of a bitch stole her away. A transport wagon, two horses, headed to Westport. You can catch up to them. Take my horse!"

"But you—"

"Don't mind me. I can help myself. Now, get going!"

Timothy groaned. Fiery knives seemed to be shooting through his hips. It would have been utterly hopeless for him to try to catch up to John Sideblossom on his own, even if he could have somehow gotten on a horse. "Go!"

William set a hesitant foot in the strange stirrups.

"But Westport? Wouldn't he be headed south—"

"For the love of God, I saw him drive away! And how should I know what he wants in Westport! Maybe he has accomplices there. Or in Pukaiki. Go find out! Go!"

Timothy lost his grip on the hitching post and fell back to the ground, but William was finally swinging himself into the saddle. When he dug his heels into Fellow's flanks, the horse grunted fractiously. The heavy box stirrups stuck painfully into his sides. Fellow flung himself around and dashed off at a full gallop. At first, William was out of control. The lightning start had knocked him completely off balance, but falling out of that special saddle was as good as impossible. Timothy thought momentarily of Ernie's concerns when making the saddle. He prayed Fellow did not stumble now.

Fellow did not stumble. By the time he passed by Greymouth's last houses, William had steadied himself on the horse's back. The saddle did not offer much freedom of movement, but he found the stirrups gave him an astoundingly secure hold. Fellow ran as though the Furies were on his tail, but he was compliant once William finally managed to straighten the reins. At first, the well-paved road offered traction, but that soon changed. As the path turned into the coastal road toward Pukaiki, a beautiful stretch with breathtaking views of the sea, it became curvy and uneven, and it could be slippery after the rain. William braced himself, but Fellow showed no concern at all. He hardly lessened his tempo when they reached the unpaved road and began to make up for lost time. No team hitched to a transport wagon could be as fast as the fiery gray horse.

William wasn't worried that John Sideblossom had turned off somewhere, as the moonlight offered decent visibility and also reflected off the road, wet from rain. William would have seen the tracks if John had tried any evasive maneuvers. Besides, he could now hear Callie's barking growing louder. He was getting close.

Fellow took a curve at breakneck speed, and the path began to slope downward. William looked ahead and saw an unlit wagon being pulled by two horses and followed by a little black shadow yapping its lungs out. William knew he would catch up to them in a few minutes. Fellow was pushing himself hard, the possibility of racing with his own kind driving him to a life-threatening speed.

Clinging to the saddle, William only just then began to think about a strategy. It had been madness to simply take off after John Sideblossom. The man was undoubtedly armed and probably had no scruples about putting a bullet in William. Or Fellow. If the horse fell at this speed, the rider could hardly expect to survive.

On the other hand, it would surely be impossible for him to aim properly moving so quickly on uneven ground. He was likely to have his hands full just driving his team. If he did not avoid the potholes, he risked breaking an axle. William's only chance consisted of passing the wagon, stopping the horses, and overpowering the man before he could draw his weapon. Unquestionably, he had the element of surprise on his side. Callie was still barking like mad, so John would not be able to hear the hoofbeats of his pursuer. Fellow had closed the distance and was now galloping alongside the wagon. William grew alarmed when he registered that he and his horse cast long shadows in the moonlight that could not remain concealed from the driver.

And he was right to be alarmed. John suddenly turned around and saw the rider coming up alongside him. William could see him clearly. His opponent had no gun in his hand—only a whip. He began to lash out at William.

Callie's barking restored Elaine to consciousness, that and her body being tossed mercilessly back and forth on the wagon's hard cargo bed. Although there were a few blankets, John had clearly intended for them to hide her rather than to provide comfort. Her head hurt. She realized she must have hit it somewhere and been briefly knocked out. But she had to ignore that for the time being. She had to think, had to do something. Maybe she could somehow loosen her constraints. If she had her hands free, she might take the risk of jumping out. Though it was true that she might fall to her death at this speed, anything would be better than being delivered to Thomas Sideblossom again.

Elaine rubbed her hands back and forth in her bindings. Although the rope dug painfully into her flesh, it did in fact loosen quickly. In his hurry, John had not pulled it tight enough. Elaine rubbed her little hands together, trying to stretch and wiggle them out of her fetters. Then she saw the silhouette of a horse and rider appear next to the wagon.

She recognized Fellow's noble head. Timothy? No, that was impossible. John had knocked Timothy to the ground. She desperately hoped that he had not broken anything again. Elaine struggled to recognize the rider . . . William! And suddenly he was overtaking the wagon, coming up alongside the driver's box.

William had no way to defend himself. He didn't have a crop with which to strike back, and in the rigid saddle, he couldn't duck John's blows. And Fellow was beginning to slow down rather than accelerate. As the blows of the crop struck the horse on the head and neck, he dodged and tried to fall back. When William spurred him on, Fellow only became confused at the contradictory signals.

He had to try something else. In a last-ditch effort, William steered Fellow as close to the box as possible, determined to grab the riding crop the next time John tried to strike him. William saw the face of his opponent for the first time: the man's features were contorted with rage. He loosened his grip on the reins, stood up, and put all his

611

energy into striking at William, evidently hoping to knock him out of the saddle. William looked back at him cold-bloodedly, fixed his eyes intently on the blow that was descending on him and bravely caught the crop. As soon as he felt the leather strap in his hand, he slung it around his wrist instinctively so as not to lose it. If he could just summon the strength to pull the other end of the crop out of his opponent's grasp.

Just then Fellow spooked. Taking fright at the sight of the dancing shadow of the crop above him, the horse jerked to the side. William felt an enormous pull on the leather strip in his hand. Under other circumstances, it would have ripped him off his horse, but Timothy's special saddle held him. John would have to let go, as the crop was being wrenched from his hand. Suddenly, though, the pull subsided. And then everything happened at once.

A scream sounded, followed by a loud rumble. William wanted to look around, but the startled Fellow had sped up again. Once again, William remained securely in the saddle. He freed his wrist from the leather strap, and the crop fell to the ground. Fellow calmed down at once. His heart beating powerfully, William finally looked back.

John's horses were following him at breakneck speed, but the box was empty. The man must have lost his balance and fallen. God alone knew what had happened to him.

William enjoyed a fleeting moment of relief before he realized that Elaine was in no way out of danger. The team pulling the wagon was racing along out of control, and the curvy road had begun to slope steeply upward. William tried to direct Fellow to stop, but even that was risky. The path was too narrow for the wagon and the horse side by side. If Fellow stopped now, and the horses pulling the wagon did not or could not stop because the force of the heavy wagon was too much for them . . . William could already see himself ripped from the saddle, crushed by the wagon, or thrown off the cliff.

Elaine struggled with her restraints. She had seen John fall and knew the danger she was in. Though she could not see the precipitous, curving road before her, a runaway team was perilous on even an ordinary path. Besides, something was wrong with the wagon. Something seemed to be blocking the front left wheel. If the axle broke . . .

But then, all of a sudden, the ropes gave way, loosening just enough for Elaine to be able to stretch out her right hand. The girl just managed to pull herself up, holding onto the bolt. She dragged herself along the wagon's bed and attempted to climb onto the box. She managed to catch hold of one of the reins and began to soothe the horses. Then she finally caught the second. Still half kneeling on the wagon bed, she straightened the reins and gave the horses the first signals to slow them to a halt. If only the road were not so steep! With a last surge of effort, Elaine struggled up onto the box and pulled the brake. The wagon lurched a bit, but the horses were well trained. Now that the wagon was no longer bearing down on them, the horses reacted to Elaine's signals. She reined them in to a trot and then to a walk. Still in front of them, William brought Fellow in step with them until Elaine finally stopped them altogether.

Suddenly everything was still; even Callie was no longer barking, though her panting could be heard as she leaped up on the box to lick Elaine's face.

"My God, Lainie . . ." William felt his heart racing. William was only just realizing how close they had come to death—or at the very least, a serious accident.

Freeing herself from the last restraints at her wrists and the gag in her mouth, Elaine was laughing and crying simultaneously. She hardly managed to shoo Callie away.

"Sweet Callie, good dog. Now down, that's enough. You got me back."

William eyed her with concern. Elaine appeared unnaturally relaxed, almost as though what had just happened were a little mishap.

"Can you take a look to see what's wrong with my front left wheel?" she said. "Something is making it stick."

"My God, Lainie . . ." William repeated his words from a moment before, but his voice sounded hoarser this time as he looked down at the wagon's front left wheel.

Elaine started to move as if to climb down and see for herself.

"No, don't look! Don't do that to yourself," William gasped. The least he could do was spare her that.

In the spokes of the wheel hung the remains of John Sideblossom, held by the tatters of his long waxed jacket. William dropped from his horse and lurched to the side of the road to vomit.

Elaine remained obediently on the box. She had read in William's face what he had seen. Abruptly, she became aware of the entire situation, and she began to shake uncontrollably.

William lifted her down and carried her to the side of the road. Elaine tried to stay focused on the horses. If she thought about anything other than how to take care of the horses, she feared she would go mad. William was already looking at her as though she had lost her mind. He grabbed the blankets. After wrapping Elaine in one, he threw one over the corpse, which would have to be dislodged from the wheel before the wagon could move again. William, confronted with this task, could not bring himself to do it.

"Would you please cover the horses?" Elaine said, staring straight ahead.

It was true; he ought to tie up the horses first. It was not worth thinking about what would happen if the team ran away again, dragging the body with them. William noticed some trees a few yards away. However, since he couldn't lead them there with the wagon, he would have to unhitch them. He started fumbling with the harnesses.

Fortunately, the horses stood quietly, panting, with trembling flanks. Only Fellow made any move, taking a few steps toward Elaine. She took hold of his reins. William saw to the other horses. He worked mechanically . . . Just don't brood on it, he thought. Just don't think about what happened.

"Tim," Elaine said. "Have you—"

"I spoke with him, Lainie. He's fine."

Or maybe not. William thought about Timothy's face, contorted with pain. Just don't think. He put his arm around Elaine. Callie began to bark.

Lainie pulled the blanket closer.

Suddenly Fellow's ears pricked up and the wagon team began to stir.

"Hoofbeats," Elaine whispered. She began trembling more again. "Do you think he—"

"Elaine, John Sideblossom is dead. There's nothing more he can do to you. I imagine that Tim sent people after us . . . Could you get that dog to be quiet? Why does she bark so much whenever a man touches you?"

William stood up.

"She doesn't bark at every man," Elaine whispered.

5

On his long-legged mare, Jay Hankins, the smith, was the first to reach Elaine and William. The constable, the justice of the peace, Ernie, and Matt were not far behind.

"Good heavens, Mr. Martyn! How did you stop the wagon here?" Jay asked, looking at the sharply sloping path. "And where's the fellow who—"

William pointed at the blanket, which had soaked through with blood.

"It was an accident. After he fell, Lainie stopped the wagon."

Elaine looked at him in amazement. Where was the boastful William who had nearly single-handedly freed Ireland from its English oppressors?

"Nevertheless, you were really very brave, Mr. Martyn. The man must have had a weapon. Are you all right, Lainie?" Matt helped the trembling girl to her feet. Callie did not bark this time.

"I think there are still a few things that need to be cleared up," said the constable, lifting one corner of the blanket and making a face. "But first we need to clear away this . . . everything here. Do we have two men with strong stomachs? And how are we getting the girl home?"

Elaine leaned on Matt Gawain. "How's Tim?" she asked.

Matt shrugged. "I don't know, Lainie. The doctor is tending to him. But he was awake and responsive and he told us what happened. We'll send Hankins back with that racehorse of his. He'll fetch a coach, and then you'll be back with Tim again soon. Maybe Jay will be able to learn some new details."

Elaine shook her head firmly. She was cold and miserably scared, but waiting by the side of the road for an hour would hardly improve her condition.

"I have a racehorse myself," she said, pointing to Fellow. "He'll manage the road one more time."

"You mean to ride, Miss Keefer?" the constable asked. "In your condition?"

Elaine looked down at herself. Her dress was dirty and torn, her wrists raw from the restraints, and given the way her head felt, she knew she that her face must be scraped and bruised. But she wanted to get to Timothy.

Then she thought of her grandmother. Though Elaine tried to smile, her words came out sounding serious: "The day I can't ride anymore is the day I die."

Elaine would have liked to gallop, but showing consideration for Fellow, she limited herself to a light trot. Matt and Jay, who were accompanying her, nonetheless shook their heads at her pace as she set forth.

"You can't do anything for him, Lainie," Jay said.

Elaine gave him a murderous look but did not say anything. She was too tired and frozen to talk. Really, she just wanted to cry. However, she kept an iron grip on herself. She was even prepared to put Fellow in the stables when she finally reached the Lamberts' house, but Matt took the horse from her.

"Get going now."

Elaine stumbled through the salon. Though there were still guests there chattering away in a state of agitated confusion, she hardly noticed them. She finally made it into the corridor and then Timothy's rooms.

Elaine burst into tears when she saw Timothy lying in his bed as still and pale as the first day after the accident. It couldn't be, not when he'd come so far! She began sobbing hysterically, unable to hold herself upright any longer.

Berta Leroy caught her.

"There, there, Lainie, now, don't want to exhaust yourself. Roly, is there any whiskey here?"

"Lainie." Timothy's voice.

Elaine pushed Berta away and dragged herself over to Timothy's bed. He sat up as she sank onto her knees beside him. "That hopeless case William actually pulled it off? My God, I thought I was going to have to beat him with my crutches to get him on the horse. And then he wanted to argue about which way to go!"

"Tim, you . . ." Elaine rubbed her face against his hands, then looked over his body. There were no bandages, though he started a bit when she touched his left side.

"Pretty bad contusions," Berta said, handing Elaine a glass. "But nothing's broken, don't worry."

Elaine began to cry again, but this time with relief. She sipped at her drink and shook herself.

"That's not whiskey."

"No, that's laudanum." Berta said, forcing her to finish the glass. "I changed my mind about the booze. You two would just get chatty—not to mention touchy. But you need some sleep. You too, Tim. Otherwise, I'll take my husband at his word and prohibit you from going to the hearing."

Still, the group that met in the constable's office the next morning had gotten little sleep.

Despite the laudanum, Elaine had awoken early, well before dawn, and stumbled directly out of her nightmares into Timothy's bed. Timothy, who, in spite of the morphine, had lain awake brooding, scooted willingly aside and held her in his arms while she told him, through stammers and sobs, a rather confused version of the events surrounding John Sideblossom's death. When she finally fell asleep on his shoulder, he dared not stir. But he could not get comfortable for the rest of the night and looked correspondingly drawn in the morning.

Elaine still had a headache when she woke up and kept bursting into one fit of tears after another. The composure she had managed to maintain immediately after her kidnapping had given way to the total opposite. She cried at the sight of her ruined dress and then burst into fresh tears, of gratitude, when Charlene appeared with a change of clothes.

"Now, don't cry! Mrs. O'Brien will make you a new dress," Charlene promised. "If she hurries, she'll even manage it before your concert in Blenheim. That's the other place you wanted to wear it, right?"

"If I'm not in prison by then," Elaine sobbed.

Charlene tried to persuade her to have something to eat. But she could not be calmed and did not get ahold of herself until it was time for them to leave. Timothy followed the girls, limping through the salon past his mother, who sat in steely silence. His father did not appear at all. Either he was already at work in the mine, or he was drunk—still drunk from the night before or drunk anew.

William had spent the entire night celebrating the simple fact of being alive. After his daring ride and his subsequent efforts to prove his vitality to Kura in every position he could think of, he shuffled along almost as gingerly as Timothy.

Nor had the constable gotten a good night's sleep. Along with his assistants, he had spent half the night managing the recovery and return of the corpse and corroborating the first testimonies.

After examining John Sideblossom's mortal remains, Dr. Leroy looked haggard as well. Still, he had not found anything to contradict William's representation of what had transpired.

"So we have ascertained," the justice of the peace said, concluding the inquiry into the fatality, "that John Sideblossom, standing on the box of his wagon at a full gallop, attempted, in a sort of tug of war, to wrest the riding crop from the hand of William Martyn, who was riding alongside him. An unexpected jerk to the side caused him to lose his balance. When he fell, his coat remained stuck to the crop's handle, and the man was dragged to death. Does anyone have anything else to add?"

The listeners shook their heads.

"Not a very pleasant way to die," the constable remarked, "but nor was he a very pleasant chap. Which brings us to you, Miss Lainie Keefer. Or Elaine Sideblossom, if I understood you correctly last night. What's all this about a shooting? Why were you living here under a fake name? Why was Greymouth the only 'safe' place for you, and why couldn't Sideblossom have a talk with you instead of kidnapping you like he did?"

Elaine took a deep breath. Then she told her entire story in a quiet, uninflected voice, her eyes fixed on the ground.

"Are you going to arrest me?" she asked once she had finished. The prison was attached to the constable's office. It was empty at the moment but relatively spacious. On weekends, every corner of it was used as a place for men to sober up.

The constable smiled. "I don't think so. If you'd wanted to run off, you'd already be gone. Besides, I need to corroborate all this first. It's all still a little confusing to me. More than anything, I find it strange that I never heard so much as a whisper about any of it. Sure, Lionel Station is remote, but I think that a young woman on a wanted list, and what's more, due to such a spectacular crime, would have caught my attention. But you shouldn't plan on leaving the country just yet, Mrs. Sideblossom."

"Miss Keefer," Elaine whispered.

"So you don't want to continue to be called Sideblossom, no matter what," inferred the justice of the peace. He was a kind and sober-minded man whose civil occupation was running the town's telegraph station. "Wholly understandable if your story proves true. And considering that you've just engaged yourself to someone else. I hope that you are not seriously considering simply going ahead and getting married a second time, Miss Keefer! You should get your divorce proceedings under way right away."

Timothy nodded. "I believe there's a lawyer in Westport. Perhaps we could telegraph him." The constable handed the transcript of their proceedings across the table for Elaine to sign.

"But we still need to talk about Blenheim," William said. "I understand, of course, that you have other concerns at the moment, Lainie—"

"You don't really believe that after all that, she'd still go to Blenheim," Timothy yelled. His left side hurt like hell, and he just wanted to put this turmoil behind him. Elaine laid her hand soothingly on his.

"Of course I'll go to Blenheim," she said, tired. "If I may." She looked at the constable anxiously. Timothy awaited what he hoped would be an answer in the negative.

The lawman looked from one to the other. "What's all this about Blenheim?"

As William enlightened him, he talked up Elaine and Kura's performance so much that it sounded as important as, say, rescuing the South Island from barbarian invaders.

Timothy rolled his eyes. "My God, William, it's just a concert."

"For Kura, it's a great deal more than that," Elaine contradicted. "And I'm not going to run away, constable."

The constable shook his head and chewed on his upper lip, a habit he shared with Elaine. She smiled at him.

"I'm not much afraid of that, Miss Keefer," he said finally. "I'm more worried about your personal safety. Thomas Sideblossom will learn about the death of his father no later than tomorrow. Are you sure he won't plan some act of revenge? Is he capable of that?"

Elaine flushed and turned pale by turns. "Thomas is capable of anything," she whispered.

"He might have been," William objected. "But after the incident with the pistol . . ."

In spite of himself, Timothy was impressed with how carefully William expressed his thoughts. He may have been timid on a horse, but he would have made a fantastic attorney.

"He rarely leaves his house and is entirely dependent on assistance. He's as good as blind, constable."

"But he would not be beyond planning an attack," the constable insisted.

"We just won't let Lainie out of our sight," William said.

The constable gave his visitors a skeptical look. Timothy, exhausted on his crutches, and William, the sight of whom would have made a corpse feel sick—he wouldn't have hired either one as a bodyguard.

"You must already know it, Miss Keefer," he said finally, "but remember that the spirits of the Maori won't protect you if you leave Greymouth." He smiled wearily.

"They weren't all that helpful yesterday either," Elaine replied.

William and Timothy began to argue as soon as they left the constable's office. As they all followed the justice of the peace to the telegraph office, Elaine had a strangely light sensation, as though she were floating above everything. But a new thought brought her down to earth.

"Mr. Farrier, my parents are in Queenstown. Could we telegraph them as well perhaps? If everything is being made known anyway?"

Although she knew that the justice of the peace was answering— she could see his lips moving—for some reason, she could not make out the words. Everything suddenly began to spin, and Elaine lost herself in a cloud. Although not unpleasant, she felt far, far away.

Elaine heard the voices as though from a distance as she slowly came back to herself.

"It was all a little much for her."

"The head injury."

"Nothing can be allowed to happen to her."

The last voice belonged to Timothy. And it sounded very desperate and tired.

Elaine opened her eyes and found herself looking at Dr. Leroy, who was checking her pulse. Berta was fiddling around behind him. Apparently, they had taken her to the little hospital. Timothy and the owners of the other voices she had heard were not in the room.

"Do I . . . Is it something serious?" she asked quietly.

Dr. Leroy smiled. "Something very serious, Miss Keefer. In the coming days, you must be sure to eat properly, not to tie your corset too tight . . ."

At that moment, Elaine noticed that someone had opened her bodice and corset and, predictably, she blushed.

"Above all, put your affairs in order with respect to divorce and marriage. You're pregnant, Miss Keefer. And when I deliver the baby, I'd rather call you Mrs. Lambert."

"By the time the baby is delivered, we'll have long since been in Wales," Timothy said delicately. Berta Leroy had brought him the news and admitted him to see Elaine. She would not allow the young woman to stand up until she had eaten a proper breakfast. Roly was already on the way to the baker—and spreading the news faster than any telegraph could have. "We plan to leave all of this behind. I don't ever want to have to be afraid of this Sideblossom fellow again."

"Maybe I'll be in prison when the baby comes." Elaine murmured. "There's going to be a trial, Tim. You can't just stick your head in the sand, or in the coal dust in Wales. I'm just happy that they're even letting me go to Blenheim."

"You don't really mean to play piano in Blenheim? Now, in your condition?" Timothy looked at her, uncomprehending.

Elaine stroked his cheek.

"I'm not sick, dear," she said softly. "And Kura would probably say, 'The day you can't play the piano anymore is the day you die.'"

Kura was waiting for Elaine and Timothy when they finally left the doctor's office.

"William told me about the baby," she said, looking vaguely uncomfortable. "You . . . you're happy, aren't you?"

Elaine laughed. "Of course I'm happy. It's the most wonderful thing that's ever happened to me in my life. But don't worry, I'm still planning to go to Blenheim. Starting tomorrow, we'll begin practicing again. Is that all right? I'm still a little worn out today. And I wanted to send a telegram today as well."

"William told me that too," Kura said, looking unusually awkward. "Lainie, I know it's asking a lot, but couldn't you wait a bit longer? If you write your parents now, they'll be here in two days."

"Well, two days might be pushing it a bit, but . . ." Elaine looked at her cousin with astonishment. She did not understand why Kura would ask such a thing, but it looked as though it was important to her.

"Elaine, if they find you, then they'll find me too. The next telegram will go to Haldon, and I . . . Understand me, Lainie, I don't want them to find me here as a barroom pianist. If this concert in Blenheim is successful, then I'll be a singer with her own program, on her own tour. I'll be able to point to newspaper articles. I can say we'll be going to London." Kura's eyes lit up at the mere thought of it, but her voice sounded doubtful and almost imploring. "But if your parents hear me singing at the Wild Rover, when they figure out that I've spent a year doing odd jobs without success . . . Please, Lainie."

Elaine hesitated. Then she nodded.

"We'll give it a week," she finally said. "I just hope it will be that successful. I've never really seen myself as an artist."

Kura smiled. "Maybe your boy will be one. Or girl. Either way, I'll give it a beautiful grand piano when it's born."

6

Elaine did not find the journey to Blenheim difficult. On the contrary, she enjoyed the view out of the coach, first of the mountain's often-breathtaking rock formations and later of the vineyards above Blenheim. Kura, however, was oblivious to all of it. She stared ahead blankly, seemingly entranced by melodies that revealed themselves only to her. In the eternity within her head, she lived through the hell of failure and the joy of roaring applause by turn. William only had eyes for Kura and appeared to be as impatient for the performance as she was; naturally, it marked a new beginning for him as well. If Kura found success, he would give up the sewing-machine business and dedicate himself wholly to the task of making his wife a star.

Given that both William and Kura viewed this performance as the decisive turning point of their lives, the burden of the concert weighed rather heavily on Elaine at times. What was more, she worried about Timothy, for whom the three-day journey was undeniably a challenge. Elaine insisted that they not cover too much ground each day, and they moved forward almost as sluggishly as she had on her ill-fated journey from Queenstown to Lionel Station. The roads were uneven and poorly maintained in places, and by the second stage of the trip, Kura was complaining that all of her bones hurt.

Although Timothy did not say anything, he looked as though he felt the same way. He tried to counterfeit a good mood, but Elaine noticed his tense expression and the deep shadows under his eyes. Whenever he actually managed to rest, he moaned in his sleep. When she slipped into his hotel room at night, he was usually awake, reading something in an effort to distract himself from the pain in his hip.

None of which boded well for the plans to emigrate that he continued to talk about.

Elaine dreaded the six-week journey by sea. She imagined the ship as a constantly rocking tub and Timothy having to fight for balance with every step he took on deck. After that, there would be the journey from London to Wales, probably by horse. And, finally, the disappointment if everything did not go as Timothy had hoped.

Elaine was no longer as optimistic as her fiancé. Naturally, she believed him when he told her that he had received loads of job offers before. But would the mine operators hire him now? A mining engineer who would be reliant on the eyes and ears of others underground? Who was even limited in the buildings he could inspect aboveground? In Greymouth, he had Matt Gawain, whose practical experience Timothy complemented with his technical knowledge and who would keep Timothy honestly and competently informed. He also had Roly, who handled myriad small daily tasks for him without being asked and who acted as though it were the most natural thing in the world. Would he be able to manage without Roly? Though his assistance went largely unnoticed these days, the boy was almost always nearby. But if Roly were no longer there? If nobody were there to automatically saddle and lead Timothy's horse away, carry his bags, or fetch any little thing for him? Elaine could take care of many of those things for him at home. But in a strange town?

Of course, Timothy must have considered all that as well, especially with the journey revealing the limits of what he could bear. Perhaps that was the reason he had become increasingly quiet, almost sullen, the closer they got to Blenheim. It could not really have to do with Thomas Sideblossom. The justice of the peace had informed them shortly before their departure that they had not yet succeeded in informing the Sideblossoms of John's demise. Although a messenger had been sent to Lionel Station, Zoé and Thomas Sideblossom had not been there.

"They're supposed to be up north seeing some doctor," they had been told. "He claims he can remove the bullet from Mr. Sideblossom's head, or at least that's what the Maori on the farm understood. They didn't have any contact address, so we'll have to wait for them to return, which hopefully won't be long. We'd like to send the body to them in Otago, but if we don't receive any confirmation soon, we'll have to bury him here."

Elaine was sure that the Maori on Lionel Station had understood the reason for Thomas Sideblossom's trip perfectly well. Thanks to John Sideblossom's special "personnel policy," there were perfectly schooled servants like Arama and Pai, not to mention Emere. Did she mourn him? And did it seem strange to her that young Zoé Sideblossom would bury him after she, Emere, had shared her bed and borne his children for so many years?

Zoé Sideblossom still did not have any children herself. William knew that her first child had died at birth and that she had suffered a miscarriage after that. He had told Elaine that much. So there were no legitimate heirs aside from Thomas. It was strange that Zoé was taking such good care of Thomas, but she might have simply been happy to have an excuse to leave the farm, whatever the reason.

In any case, almost no one believed that anyone was hatching evil schemes aimed at Elaine. As a result, the men did not strictly follow their resolution not to let Elaine out of their sight. When they finally reached Blenheim, Timothy retired immediately to his hotel room—a sign of the weakness that was so hard for him to acknowledge. Elaine sent Roly after him.

"Make sure he relaxes a bit. The reception tonight at Mrs. Redcliff's is bound to be taxing."

Roly had not really needed any encouragement. The excuse of bringing Timothy's bags up to him would have been sufficient for him to check on his patient.

William took his leave under the flimsiest of pretexts—which Kura would undoubtedly have seen through if she'd had even minimal interest in anything other than the concert that would be taking place the following evening. William knew what he owed Heather Redcliff, née Witherspoon. Indeed, he found her in the middle of preparations for the reception that evening. Her "William, that is really very inappropriate!" sounded so inviting that he put on a hangdog face but made no move to leave the house right away.

The opportunity to let the maids putter about on their own for a short time did eventually present itself. The cook was relieved not to have anyone peeking into her pots, and the children had already been sent to stay at friends' houses in anticipation of the reception.

"I can hardly wait to see Kura again," Heather declared finally, straightening her hair as she accompanied William outside.

"And I look forward to finally meeting this Mr. Redcliff I've heard so much about," William said with a smile. "We'll arrive at eight."

Kura and Elaine spent the afternoon looking over the concert hall in the hotel and going through their program once more. At first, Elaine was shaken by the size and elegance of the room. In fact, she was generally impressed with the hotel, which was far more distinguished than the White Hart in Christchurch and could not be compared in any way to her grandmother's hotel.

"The acoustics are exceptional," Kura declared. She had already performed in Blenheim once before with Roderick's ensemble. "And this time we'll have the stage ourselves, all to ourselves. No other singers or dancers. The audience will only be listening to us. Isn't that a wonderful feeling? It's like champagne." She spun around on the stage.

Elaine found it more alarming than wonderful. Her heart was already pounding in anticipation, but she was still much less anxious than Caleb would have been. Her stage fright would motivate her, and the resplendence all around her would lend its radiance to her playing. Kura had no concerns about Elaine. She had known dancers in the ensemble who trembled with excitement every evening, only to improve with each performance. Elaine was like that—she would be sure to do her job well.

Elaine was already playing better in their rehearsal than she had in Greymouth. Though that may have had something to do with the impeccably tuned and very expensive grand piano the hotel had made available to them. Elaine was intimidated by the instrument at first, but she played with visible joy.

Both of the girls were in high spirits when they finally went to their rooms and dressed for the evening. Mrs. O'Brien had indeed managed the feat of tailoring a new dress for Elaine in only a week. This one was made of a darker velvet, as the azure-blue fabric had been impossible to get ahold of again on such short notice. But it looked equally beautiful. The night-blue tone brought out the shine in Elaine's hair and emphasized her pale skin. It made her look more serious and less like a girl.

Kura did not have a new dress. She and William had spent all their savings on the trip and the concert announcements, and William had to decline when she asked him to sew her a dress himself.

"Sweetheart, I only have an imperfect mastery of this miracle machine. Only a small number of the women who buy them will ever sew as well as Mrs. O'Brien. To be honest, I didn't even think it was possible before that woman laid her hand on her first Singer. She's a natural-born talent. I've already wondered whether she could be persuaded to study to be a saleswoman. But if we meet success in Blenheim, I'll be done with Singers, and you'll be buying your wardrobe in London."

So Kura planned to perform in her wine-red dress. Even in an old dress, she cast a shadow over all the women around her. At the Redcliffs' reception, admiring looks followed her around the room before she had even been introduced as the evening's guest of honor. Heather Redcliff greeted her effusively, and Kura even let Heather embrace her.

"You look as ravishing as ever, Kura," Heather said enthusiastically. "You've become an adult, and it suits you marvelously. I can hardly wait to hear you sing."

Kura could only return her compliments. Heather looked better herself. She looked softer—and that night, she was beaming from the inside out, the reason for which William Martyn was not wholly innocent.

Julian Redcliff proved to be a ponderous, somewhat heavyset man of middle age. Though he could be described as red-faced, exposure to wind and weather, rather than an overly intensive enjoyment of whiskey, was the primary cause of it. He had thinning hair, attentive brown eyes, and a firm handshake. While William felt that the man was appraising him, Timothy thought him likable from the start. The two were soon involved in a conversation about railroad construction and the various difficulties of laying tracks over mountains.

"We must have a drink together in my study afterward," Julian said almost conspiratorially when he noticed that Timothy was beginning to have difficulty standing. "I have some fantastic whiskey. But first I need to put these greetings behind me. My wife seems to have invited everybody in Blenheim I know but don't like. Find yourself a seat and have something to eat. After what this squadron of cooks cost—who spent all day getting on our nerves—the buffet must be a wonder to behold."

Heather spent the better part of the evening introducing Kura and Elaine around. Elaine hardly managed to eat a thing. Kura charmed everyone to whom she was introduced. Though most of them admired her for her appearance alone, a few of the guests appeared to be genuinely interested in music and admired the richly decorated *putorino* flute that she had brought along at William's insistence. For many guests, it was an experience to see and even touch the Maori instruments up close.

"Can you really conjure the spirits with it?" one woman asked Kura with interest. "I read something about that. The flute is supposed to be able to sing with three different voices, but they say that only a few have the talent to wake the spirits with it."

Kura was just about to explain that the spirit voice of the *putorino* was more a question of breathing technique than spirituality when William interrupted her, giving his talent at *whaikorero* free rein once again.

"Only the chosen—they're known as the *tohunga*—can draw this very unusual sound from the flute. And when you hear those sounds, you'll no longer think of it as mere superstition. It may only be a breathing technique, but these voices touch a person deep inside. They ask questions, and they give answers. Sometimes they even fulfill sensual desires." He winked at Kura.

"Well, go ahead and show us how it's done," said an already slightly drunk young man accompanying the young woman. "Conjure up a few spirits."

Kura looked embarrassed, or at least pretended to be.

"It doesn't work that way," she mumbled. "I'm not a magician, and besides, the spirits are not circus ponies that one summons to trot about."

"Oh, what a shame, I would have liked just once to see a real spirit," the man quipped. "But perhaps it will happen tomorrow at the concert."

"The spirits touch a man when he least expects it," William explained seriously. Then he laughed unashamedly in front of Kura when the couple had left. "That's how you do it, sweetheart. You need to present yourself with more of an aura of mystery. Many people can sing the "Habanera," but conjuring spirits is something special. Your ancestors won't hold it against you."

"If things go on like this, you'll soon be telling fortunes," Elaine teased her cousin.

Kura rolled her eyes. "He's also reconsidering whether I shouldn't appear in traditional Maori attire after all."

Elaine giggled. "You're supposed to get tattooed and take the stage with bare breasts?"

"Not the former, but there's no question he's thought about the latter. What he actually mentioned was a 'bast skirt.' I don't even know what that is," Kura said, smiling. She had long since stopped taking William too seriously.

"Kura? Miss Keefer? There you are. Come here, there's someone else I'd like you to meet," Heather Redcliff said, fussing over them once more. She had a corpulent man and his no-less-rotund wife in tow. Following them was a rather strange-looking couple who required more time to cross the room. The man leaned heavily on the woman and a walking stick. He was tall but looked somehow crooked. His face was all but hidden behind a pair of dark glasses.

"Dr. Mattershine and Louisa Mattershine. The doctor is a surgeon at our new hospital. A real expert in the field. And his wife . . ."

Elaine didn't hear another word. She stared as though hypnotized at the woman behind the Mattershines, who was slowly inching closer. A narrow, symmetrical, and classically beautiful face. Soft golden-colored hair set in a heavy bun at the nape of the neck. Beautiful brown eyes that made a striking contrast to her light skin color.

Zoé Sideblossom.

Elaine's mouth went dry. She stared at the dark-haired man at her side. Though he had no doubt once been slim and muscular, he now looked deformed and twisted. Body and face alike were spongy and bloated. Yet the hard line around the mouth was still there, as was the crease between his eyes that betrayed his concentration when he would . . .

Elaine felt a cold sensation surge through her. She wanted to run, but she could not. Just as she had not been able to do so often on Lionel Station.

"These are our guests, Zoé and Thomas Sideblossom." The doctor's wife took over the introductions. Though friendly and considerate, she also liked to spread gossip. So she continued quickly before Zoé and Thomas reached the group and could hear what she said.

"We brought them to cheer them up a bit. They've had a hard time of it. The young man was severely injured in an accident with a gun and is now a shadow of his former self. And she is his . . . hmm . . . stepmother, a love his father found late in life. Well, and yesterday she learned that her husband . . . Like I said, a hard time. Come here, Zoé, dear, these are the artists."

Zoé and Elaine stared at one another. Zoé was wearing black, so she had to know. Naturally, Elaine had not believed for a minute that the Sideblossoms' staff had no way to reach them.

"You." Zoé's voice sounded expressionless. She seemed to push Thomas away from her a bit. It was almost as if she hoped that he would concentrate on Mrs. Mattershine, to allow her a few personal words with Elaine. "I was amazed at you back then, you know? But you . . . we . . . Oh God, we should leave."

Zoé seemed as seized by panic as Elaine. Yet neither of them saw any possibility of escaping the situation.

"Mrs. Kura-maro . . . How does one pronounce that, my dear? And Miss Elaine Keefer."

Perhaps Thomas would not have noticed if his hostess had not accidentally given Elaine's real name. They had agreed that she would appear one last time as Lainie Keefer, but "Lainie" seemed to be just too unusual for Louisa Mattershine. Or was it something in Elaine's aura that betrayed her—an aura of fear that Thomas knew only too well?

"Elaine?" It was the same voice. It touched Elaine in her innermost recesses, seeming to compress her heart. "My Elaine?"

The man balled his left fist on his stick.

Elaine's eyes widened in fear, unable to look away.

"Thomas, I . . ."

"Thomas, we should go now," Zoé Sideblossom said calmly. "We agreed to leave the past alone. We all regret what happened."

"*You* wanted to leave the past alone, Zoé darling." The last word sounded threatening. Thomas Sideblossom straightened up, to the extent that he still could. For most people, it may not have been a particularly terrifying sight, but Elaine stepped back, her hands grasping the air. It was as though Timothy and her time in Greymouth had never happened. Here was Thomas, and she belonged to him.

"And you!" He spoke in Elaine's direction as though he could see her before him as clearly as he had back then. "*I* don't want to leave anything alone, my beloved Elaine. My father is looking for you, you know . . . or *was* looking for you. Now he's supposedly dead. Maybe you had something to do with that too, you witch?"

The guests around Elaine, Zoé, and Thomas who had been following his outburst watched the deathly pale girl in front of him and the young woman desperately trying to pull him away.

"Thomas, come now."

"But in the end, he found you, Elaine."

The words rolled off his tongue as though he were hungry to say more. He made an unsteady step in Elaine's direction.

"I'll take you back. Not today, not tomorrow, Elaine, but when it suits me. You should be expecting me, Elaine . . . just like back then. Do you still remember? Your white dress—so sweet, so innocent—but even back then, you talked back. You always talked back."

Elaine's whole body shook. She was utterly paralyzed by fear. If he had wanted to take her then, she would have gone with him—or fired a gun once more. But she did not have a gun. Elaine raised her hands helplessly.

But then a muffled sound, an arduously produced melody from another world, broke through the tense silence between Elaine and Thomas. A voice, somewhere between a whisper and a moan, arose. Loud, hoarse, threatening.

Elaine had never heard this sound before. But of course, she recognized the instrument. It was the spirit voice of the *putorino*.

Kura played with concentration, starting with long, plaintive notes that gradually became faster, eerier. Logically, the notes should have begun to sound shriller, but instead they became hollower, scarier. And they wrapped around Kura like a ghostly aura. Kura stepped over to Elaine, then between her and Thomas Sideblossom.

The man had been frozen in his aggressive stance since he had heard the first notes. Then his body visibly lost its tension, and his threatening expression changed to one of panicked fear. His glasses tumbled off, and his destroyed face became visible to all—a twisted, contorted face that seemed to lose all its hardness with the music. Behind the features of the malignant man appeared the face of a distraught child.

"No . . . please . . . not . . ." The man stepped back, lost his balance, fell. Then he screamed, tried to shield his face with his arms, and rolled onto the floor.

Elaine did not know what she was seeing and hearing any more than the other observers. But she noticed everyone around Kura and Thomas drawing back. She might even have believed in the magic of the flute if Kura herself had not looked just as mystified by the crumpled man in front of her.

Thomas was still whimpering when Kura finally stopped. She did not seem to know what she was supposed to do, but she hurled a few words at him in Maori that appeared to complete derange him. Elaine felt she had to add something. Quickly and hoarsely, she uttered the first sentence in Maori that occurred to her.

Then she backed up, retreating just as timidly as the other people in the room. Kura, however, maintained her poise. She turned her back to Thomas and left the room, head held high, every inch the victor.

"A doctor, we need a doctor," Elaine heard Zoé Sideblossom's voice and then Heather Redcliff's as though through a fog. As she walked out of the room, she wondered in passing where Dr. Mattershine had run off to, but she didn't care. When she found Timothy in the study having a relaxed conversation with Julian Redcliff, she fell to her knees in front of him, and buried her head in his lap.

"Lainie? What's wrong? Lainie?"

One of the guests rushing past the entrance to the room answered for her. "That Maori witch killed a man."

"Nonsense, he's not dead," William Martyn said, supporting Kura, who was completely disoriented. She could have kept herself on her feet without him, but he felt he should be prepared to assist her when the magic—or whatever it was—had drained from her unnaturally rigid body. "He's just had a shock. But how that happened . . ."

"Find an explanation among yourselves," said Julian Redcliff, who was rapidly gaining esteem in Timothy's eyes. He had brought Elaine, who had come completely unraveled, and Kura, in her agitated state, into the safety of his bedroom. He scored points with William as well by producing a bottle of whiskey right away. With an awestruck look at the flute in Kura's hands, he took another deep drink himself before taking his leave. "I'm going to sally out and calm the hysterical. My wife chief among them. Perhaps afterward, you can explain to me how you knock a grown man to the floor with a flute. To be honest, this is the first time that art has really impressed me."

"I don't know either," Kura said, reaching for the bottle. "I have no idea. When the man began to threaten Lainie, and she looked like she was about to fall down dead with terror, I just started playing. Hoping to draw William over, really. He can't resist the spirit voice. I thought if I played a bit of it that he would come, thinking he needed to feed the guests a line." Kura laughed nervously. "But then the man reacted so strangely. The flute clearly terrified him. So, naturally, I kept playing."

"What sort of song was that anyway?" William asked. "Some kind of conjuration?"

"Now you're being absurd, William." Kura shook her head. "It was a lamentation for the dead. From a *haka* Caleb wrote down. But we thought it too sad for the program, and it's quite difficult to play. The volume works for a room, but it would not fill a hall."

"So Sideblossom became completely hysterical because he heard a sort of . . . er . . . keen?" Timothy asked incredulously.

Kura nodded. "You could put it that way. The equivalent would be if a Maori man were to collapse because a *pakeha* played "Amazing Grace.""

"And the curse?" Timothy continued. "I hear that you said something afterward."

Kura blushed. "I can't translate that. But it's . . . well, a *makutu*, an insult. I can assure you that something along those lines gets said every day among jealous men or brats without any consequences—other than maybe causing one of them to punch the other in the nose."

"And what did *you* say?" Timothy said, turning to Lainie. "Didn't you also add something at the end?"

"Me?" Lainie started as though woken from a gloomy dream. "I hardly know any Maori. I said what came to mind just then. Something that roughly means, 'Thank you, you also have a very good-looking dog.'"

"That explains everything, of course," remarked William.

"But the Maori woman who manages the Sideblossom household also has a *putorino*," Elaine said. She spoke without inflection, as she always did when she recalled her time on Lionel Station. "And I hated her, because whenever she would play, Thomas seemed to fly into a rage, and then he would be even crueler than usual. But I don't know if it was the spirit voice. I never listened that closely."

"She probably couldn't," said Kura. "It's not easy. My mother taught me to do it. And I didn't find it scary. Marama would play the spirit voice for me when I couldn't sleep. Then she would say the spirits sang me to sleep."

"Emere was Thomas's nanny. Maybe she did it the other way around?" Elaine reflected. "Perhaps she scared him with it?"

Timothy shrugged. "Whatever the case, we'll probably never know. Maybe he was just scared that Elaine would sic Callie on him. He deserved it. Though he may be terrified now, I'll nonetheless feel better when we put a few thousand miles between us and these crazy people. I'm just sorry about your concert, Kura. After this evening, no one is going to come."

William grinned. "I wouldn't count on that."

7

Around ten the next morning, the hotel's business manager appeared with an urgent request to be allowed to bring fifty more seats into the concert hall.

"It might affect the acoustics, and the crowd cannot be good for their concentration, but people keep rushing in. This morning there were a few remaining tickets, but they were gone by five after nine. Now they've lined up downstairs, and we don't have any more seats."

Kura graciously gave permission for the new seats. Elaine did not care one way or the other. William beamed, and Timothy realized he did not understand the world anymore.

Around noon, the man returned with a bottle of sparkling wine and the offer to let them spend another night in the hotel free of charge as long as the artists would give a second concert on Monday.

"All of our rooms have been booked as well. People are hoping to catch something from their rooms. People keep outbidding each other for the rooms near the hall. I don't know what happened yesterday at your reception, but everyone seems to have gone mad about your concert."

William promised to consider the matter as he set out with Kura, who was in high spirits, to explore the city and investigate the situation. Kura showed no sign of stage fright; she was wholly in her element.

Elaine was preoccupied by matters of a completely different nature. She had learned that the Sideblossoms were staying in the same hotel, a circumstance that nearly paralyzed her. Elaine could not be convinced to even step out of her room until it could no longer be avoided. She entrenched herself in Timothy's bed and started at every noise. Though she would have liked to post Roly in front of the door to stand guard,

Timothy waved off that suggestion. Roly had already spent the entire previous afternoon in the room with his boss. He was now eager to see the city, the famous bay, and some whales, if possible.

Timothy put a few dollars in his hand for a boat ride, explaining, "You can't see anything from the shore." Roly thanked him profusely and left with the promise to be back in time for the concert.

"Weren't the Sideblossoms supposed to leave today?" Timothy asked hesitantly as Elaine crawled under the blanket. "God knows they must have better things to do with the death in their family than linger around here scaring you."

"Thomas can't travel; you heard it yourself." Elaine had gleaned this information from the business manager, who had carried on at length about how he could have rented the Sideblossoms' suite three times over that day. But the invalid had suffered a breakdown, so Zoé Sideblossom had been forced to extend their stay. "And you cannot simply toss the people out of their room, you understand," the business manager had said.

"I don't understand why he still scares you," Kura said impatiently. The Martyns had returned late that afternoon and were perishing to relay the news they had heard. Both of them rolled their eyes when Elaine instead delivered her report on the Sideblossoms in a trembling voice.

"If it comes to it, I'll give you the flute. You can blow into it once and pay him another compliment about his nice dog, and he'll fall right over again. Though the man is clearly crazy, he's completely harmless. You said yourself that he's too sick to even leave his room. But you should hear what they're saying in town. The way they look at me! Even Mrs. Redcliff seems a little . . . superstitious."

"Some people are saying Kura's music has the power to curse, while others are going on about its miraculous healing qualities," William said, reveling in his wife's sudden fame. "Either way, everyone wants to catch a glimpse of her—but then, when she appears, they make an awestruck circle around her. It's unbelievable! Shall we change now, dear? The first people will probably be arriving soon, and we need to think of our strategy for the reception after the concert."

The Martyns floated out of the room. The spirits were undoubtedly on their side.

Timothy gave Elaine a pained look. "Lainie, is it very important to you that I be present for the concert tonight? I know you'll play beautifully and look ravishing. But after these stories of miraculous healings, people are going to stare at me like a calf with two heads."

For the first time that day, Elaine forgot her own panic and noticed the tense, narrow face of her beloved. Timothy had lost more weight in the last few days. The excitement, the renewed injuries, and the arduous journey had exhausted his strength. He looked as though he could not stand to suffer another shock or any further indignities.

Elaine kissed him. "I don't mind if you stay here. I'll be right back up afterward anyway. I'm not going to subject myself to that reception. Kura will manage it just fine on her own. And as far as stage fright goes, I'm well aware that it doesn't even matter whether someone plays the piano next to Kura tonight or a seal balances a ball. People are only coming hoping to see a wonder."

Timothy smiled. "In that respect, a seal might even be better. She could control it with the flute like a snake charmer. I can hear you two from here anyway. Roly and I were able to enjoy the rehearsal yesterday. So remember, you won't be alone!"

The business manager had pulled off the remarkable feat of packing two hundred fifty paying guests into the concert hall. Before Kura and Elaine took the stage, William had feared the rumbling in the audience would drown out the music. But once the girls had appeared and Kura had said a few words of introduction, one could have heard a pin drop.

Likewise, the fear that people would quickly lose interest if a miracle did not occur by the end of the first piece proved unfounded. On the contrary, Kura took her audience captive. She gave the performance of her life, and by halfway through the concert, no one was thinking of curses and miracles anymore; they had simply given themselves over to Kura's magic. She swept Elaine right along with her. Seeming to truly comprehend the meaning of their music for the first time, Elaine finally put her heart into her playing and was hardly outshone by Kura.

Even Timothy, who now knew the program down to its last note, noticed the difference. He was standing on his room's balcony, letting the hypnotic summons wash over him and enjoying the breathtaking view of the bay and the lights of Blenheim. The melancholy of the *haka* Kura had selected for the concert's midpoint touched him. Timothy was tired and dejected. Though he yearned to be far away, he keenly felt the fear of failure. He would rise to the challenge—but what would he do if they wanted him as little in Europe as they did here? In Greymouth, he could follow Caleb's example and crawl back to his parents' house if all else failed, keeping himself occupied in one way or another in an effort to give his life some meaning. But in Wales—with a young family and no income?

Roly followed him onto the balcony and picked up on his gloomy state of mind.

"What is it, Mr. Lambert?" he asked shyly. "Are you in pain?"

"Just fretting, Roly," Timothy said quietly. "How was your day? Did you see any whales?"

Roly nodded energetically. "It was unbelievable, Mr. Lambert! They're so gigantic! But so peaceful. I was scared to death at first when one of them swam toward our tiny boat."

Timothy smiled. "They're supposed to be very similar to people. They say the whales sing."

"Hopefully not by caterwauling like Mrs. Martyn . . . Oh, forgive me, sir." Roly was no admirer of opera. "Will we see whales when we go to England too, Mr. Lambert? The man who drove the boat said there are smaller ones too, dolphins, and they swim alongside the big steamers."

"So you want to come along to England?" Timothy asked, astonished. "What does your mother say to that?"

Roly laughed. "Oh, she doesn't need me anymore. She's making real money with her sewing workshop. But you, you need me. Don't you, Mr. Lambert?"

The boy looked up at him almost anxiously. Timothy bit his lip.

"I might not be able to pay you anymore."

Roly frowned and mulled that over while in the hall below them the spirit voice of the *putorino* evoked the return of someone's love. But then his face brightened.

"But you don't need me all day anymore, of course. So I can find another job, and I won't be a burden to you. I just don't have money for the passage." Roly's countenance darkened again.

Timothy, deeply touched, forced himself to smile.

"We'll manage, Roly."

Roly beamed. "We will."

As the two of them were basking in the comforting feeling of security that the song of the spirit inspired, a muffled commotion and screams suddenly ripped them from their reverie. There seemed to be a fight taking place in the apartment above theirs or at the other end of the hallway. It sounded as though furniture was being toppled. A man roared something incomprehensible; then his voice died out. A woman screamed hysterically. Something seemed to tumble down the stairs.

"Go out there and see what's going on," he instructed Roly. "Where is it even coming from?" He followed Roly out into the corridor in front of his room, but this was apparently not the center of the action. Chambermaids and other hotel staff hurried past them in the direction of the commotion. Curious, Roly wanted to set after them, but Timothy held him back.

"Wait, I've changed my mind. Whatever just happened, there will already be more than enough people standing around who can't help as it is. Rather, help me change. Quickly, I'd like to go find Lainie. We'll go fetch her. I have a bad feeling."

Timothy and Roly reached the hall just as the concert was about to end; meanwhile, ambulance carts were pulling up to the hotel, and the hallways filling with commotion. Timothy took the lift, which was apparently forbidden to the hotel staff. Only the excited lift boy could give them any information.

"Someone went on the rampage—that funny fellow from suite three, I think. He always scared me. Madeleine says there's blood everywhere, and the woman looks frightful."

Roly clearly would have liked to see all of that for himself, but Timothy pushed him to hurry. "That sounds a lot like Sideblossom. Oh God, and what did Lainie say earlier about his room? The manager could have rented it three times over because it lies directly over the hall. And even in our room, we heard every note. The chap must have flown into a rage while Kura was playing the *putorino*."

Kura and Elaine, still beaming, bowed to their audience. As William stood at the edge of the first row and applauded, trouble was erupting in the back of the hall. The business manager was speaking with Heather, and Dr. Mattershine was called out of the room.

Timothy and Roly met Elaine as soon as she left the stage.

"You did come!" she said, smiling radiantly at Timothy. "Wasn't that wonderful? I could almost get used to it. In any case, now I understand what Kura sees in it. So many people."

Elaine embraced him, but then she realized from his serious expression that something was amiss.

Heather Redcliff was trying to clear up something with the manager.

Julian Redcliff joined Timothy and Elaine.

"They're trying to find other rooms for the reception. It can no longer take place in the foyer, because all hell's broken loose in there. That chap from yesterday, Thomas Sideblossom, just tried to kill himself and that young woman."

"He suddenly went mad," Heather reported breathlessly, "and attacked her. His stepmother, right? That's a strange relationship. Though she managed to escape, she fell down the stairs in the process.

Then he tried to slit his wrists. The manager is beside himself. The room looks like a battlefield."

"Is he dead?" Elaine asked tonelessly.

"No, both of them are alive," Julian answered. "But he did not go mad so suddenly. Only once—"

"His room was right above the hall," Elaine said quietly. "He heard the spirit's voice."

Elaine refused to give a second concert under any circumstances. She wanted to go home as quickly as possible—to Queenstown. Timothy could only convince her with great effort that she had to return directly to Greymouth to avoid risking arrest. He, too, felt an urgent desire to get away from Blenheim, the Sideblossoms, and whatever spirits there might be as soon as possible. William and Kura, however, wanted to remain for the time being. It would be easier for them to find a new pianist in Blenheim than on the West Coast, and Kura wanted to give a few smaller concerts in the meantime.

William summed it up succinctly. "At the moment, it doesn't matter whether she plays the piano, sings, dances, or trains seals; the people want Kura. I told you the concert was going to be a success. And it would have been even without this . . . well, incident. But now it's a sensation!!" He looked as though he wanted to kiss Elaine for having married and shot Thomas Sideblossom.

Timothy had arranged for their departure the next morning, but he delayed when Julian Redcliff appeared along with a massive breakfast that he'd had brought to Timothy's room, and informed Timothy of the latest news over tea and toast.

"I thought you might like to know what ended up happening yesterday," he said, stretching and looking relaxed.

Timothy still lay in bed looking as though he had not slept at all, and Elaine emerged from the bathroom looking pale. She felt sick almost every morning these days, but Kura assured her that was normal. "I can tell you how to avoid it, however," she had declared happily. Elaine waved her offer away wearily. She never wanted to hear about counting days or vinegar douches ever again.

Julian pushed the table with all the breakfast dishes on it over to Timothy's bed, serving him quite naturally before launching into his story.

"The Sideblossoms are both still in the hospital, but in the end it was not half so bad as everyone initially thought. The young woman has some bruises and a black eye. And got quite a shock, of course. But she was responsive this morning, Dr. Mattershine said. And they could have released the man as soon as they admitted him. He didn't lose enough blood to even be worth mentioning. But he's mentally deranged. They've sedated him. As soon as the medicine's effects wear off, he lashes out again. He's going to an asylum today that special- izes in such cases. The woman will be driven home—there are still some unpleasant matters that she must see to there if I understood Dr. Mattershine correctly. But I'm dying of curiosity. What do those people have to do with you, Miss Keefer?"

Elaine remained quiet as Timothy gave a general account of her past. "We never thought we'd run into the Sideblossoms here. But I guess that's what people call a twist of fate."

Julian laughed. "It's what the spirits wanted. And they've avenged you, Miss Keefer, if I may say so. You won't ever need to fear that man again. Anyone who's admitted to such an asylum doesn't come out again easily. And when they do release a person, he's just an empty shell. We had such a case in our family. If you fall into the hands of those doctors, you can say good-bye to your life. It's worse than a prison."

We'll see, thought Elaine. She loved Timothy, but at the moment, she wanted only to return to Queenstown, to the arms of her mother, to the order and cleanliness of her grandmother Helen's hotel, and to the happy chaos of Nugget Manor. If nothing else, the nightmare of separation from her family was at an end. She planned to telegraph her parents as soon as they were back in Greymouth.

8

Elaine bent over the sewing machine with a furrowed brow and tried to guide the thread along the complicated path between the spool and the needle. When the thread broke for the third time, she came to the conclusion that she possessed no skills whatsoever as a seamstress. But that was true of the majority of Madame Clarisse's girls. Over the last few days, they had all given their easygoing boss's new acquisition a try.

Relinquishing his demonstration model to Madame Clarisse on especially good terms had been among William's last tasks in Greymouth. "This could smooth the girls' path back to an honorable life," he had claimed smoothly. Madame Clarisse gave the thing a thorough try after that and came to the conclusion that nothing was surer to keep her girls in the den of iniquity than the prospect of life with a Singer.

Elaine ripped another thread and cursed.

"Can't you show me how it works?" she said, turning to Timothy. "You are an engineer, after all, aren't you?"

Timothy was leaning on the piano in the pub's barroom practicing darts. It was not easy to maintain his balance without crutches, but he didn't seem to care. Most of his darts missed the board.

"Dearest, I've already given it a try," he said good-naturedly, "but I can't figure the thing out either. Though I could maybe build you another."

Timothy would have given a great deal to be able to build anything at that point. He longed for a task that demanded more of him mentally than the daily training of his legs, which was a great source of frustration because he had made so little progress recently. He still hoped to be able to walk without splints someday, but it would never be without crutches and never more than a few hundred yards. The realization that he had almost reached his limits sapped his will during his exercise regimen.

"Then we'd just have two of these machines," she said. "Nothing more. I think I'd rather *buy* clothes for the baby." Elaine appeared to be in the midst of one of her periodically recurring phases when she feverishly embraced domesticity. She, too, was looking desperately for any activity that would distract her from her fears and broodings.

Timothy left his game of darts and wrapped his arms around her.

"I wish something would finally happen," he sighed. "This waiting is driving me crazy. They must have come to a ruling in Otago by now. If only this trial would start. And nothing's moving forward with the mine either. There are evidently a few people interested in having a part in it, Matt says, but it's all dragging on endlessly."

"While other people have nothing more to be worried about than getting married," Elaine remarked, pulling an invitation out from under the sewing machine. "Look, Florence Weber brought it by personally. She's marrying Caleb Biller on the twenty-fifth of October. That's exactly how she put it. *She* is marrying him. She's going to swallow him whole."

While Timothy was still searching for a reply, the door to the street opened, and Roly stuck his head inside.

"A few people from Otago just arrived at the constable's office. And they want to talk with you right away, Miss Keefer. Everything looks real official; there's another constable, and a gentleman in a suit there too. I thought I'd let you know before the constable himself—"

"That's fine, Roly," Elaine said quietly. "Thank you." She reached for her shawl. "Are you coming, Tim?"

Elaine had been dreading this moment, but now that it had come, she was astoundingly composed. However it ended—at least she would know where she stood.

Timothy put his arm around her. "What kind of question is that? We're going to see this through together, Lainie. We've made it through worse."

For the first time, Elaine felt impatient at Timothy's disability. It seemed to take forever for him to put on his jacket and take the few steps out onto the street. The new arrivals' horses were tied up in front of the constable's office. A bony gray horse and a stocky black one that struck Elaine as familiar for some reason.

She would have liked to run away, and Timothy, for his part, would have happily delayed the moment of truth. Though he had been impatient and ready to face anything just a few minutes before, he now felt that he couldn't take another blow. A trial, perhaps jail . . .

Elaine entered the building with her head lowered. Suddenly, she heard Callie howling. The little dog pushed past Timothy and raced into the room. Elaine looked up, confused—and saw Callie leaping up on someone, barking excitedly and wagging her tail. She was greeting none other than Ruben O'Keefe.

"Daddy." Elaine whispered the word once before shouting it and flying into her father's arms.

"Your mother and I played poker to see who would accompany the constable, and I won!" Ruben explained with a smile. "I'll admit to having cheated though. Oh, Lainie, we were so overjoyed to hear from you. We'd begun to think you were dead!"

"Were you looking for me?" Elaine asked quietly. "I didn't know. I thought you'd be angry with me."

Ruben drew her close once more. "You silly girl, of course we looked for you. Very carefully. We knew that John Sideblossom was after you too, after all. But not even Uncle George could find anything out."

"Which is no surprise," the constable added. "Can we perhaps come to the business at hand? Although this is a particularly interesting matter, I do have other more mundane tasks to attend to."

No one believed this latter point, and even his colleague only nodded with some effort. He was a younger, enthusiastic-looking man whose uniform still looked freshly ironed despite the ride.

"Jefferson Allbridge," he introduced himself. "And you are Elaine Sideblossom?"

Elaine swallowed. She had not heard that name in so long. Nervously, she felt for Timothy's hand, but since no one had asked him to come in, he had remained standing by the door.

The constable finally took notice of him.

"Come in, Mr. Lambert, sit down. Jeff—this is Mr. Timothy Lambert, Miss Keefer's fiancé."

Ruben O'Keefe gave his daughter a confused look, then turned his gaze on Timothy. He had calm green eyes, curly brown hair, and a mustache that made him look older than he was. Timothy laid his crutches aside and took a seat in one of the chairs in the office with some effort. Under Ruben O'Keefe's eyes, he felt like he was like running the gauntlet. Timothy was afraid of rejection, but Elaine's father pushed the chair in for him.

"Sit down, Elaine," Ruben said kindly. Elaine was the only one still standing at that point, as though she wanted to face her judgment on her feet.

"All right then, Mrs. Sideblossom," the constable began. Though his face looked serious, Timothy saw the waggishness in his eyes. "First things first, I must request that you withdraw this nonsensical self-indictment that you recently presented me with. I do not hold it against you. You were in a mentally compromised condition after your abduction, and the doctor has assured me that you also . . . But perhaps you should tell your father about that yourself. In any event, we do not plan to pursue any further action against you because of your false testimony."

Elaine turned flush and pale by turns. "False testimony? But why?"

"Naturally, you never shot your husband, Thomas Sideblossom," Jefferson Allbridge explained. "Of course there were rumors to that effect, but my . . . er . . . predecessor looked into the matter, and Mr. John Sideblossom, as well as Mr. Thomas Sideblossom, once he was fit to be questioned, both testified that it was an accident. Mr. Sideblossom had been cleaning his gun. Well, these things happen."

"I . . ."

"No one ever pressed charges, Elaine," Ruben O'Keefe said. "We didn't know that either, or we would have looked even harder for you. From the very start, it seems that Sideblossom intended to settle the matter privately, so to speak."

"But everyone knew—William, Kura . . ."

"Where did you see William Martyn?" Ruben asked, taken aback. "And Kura? But, no matter, we can talk about that later. In any case, naturally everyone knew, constables included. Please cover your ears, Mr. Allbridge! Things like that can't be kept secret in a house full of servants, especially not when twenty sheepshearers can serve as witnesses. One of them found Thomas—and a midwife was also present. He owes his life to that woman. She acted very bravely. But of course everyone could put two and two together and figure out what happened. The constable could have held the Sideblossoms too, for what they did to you, but then again, there were relations and dependents."

"The case was dropped last summer," added Jefferson. He sounded almost apologetic.

"Looking back, it was a fortunate stroke of fate," remarked Ruben.

"I've looked into the matter seriously," Jefferson continued weightily. "Particularly this story about the abduction. Although John Sideblossom never pressed formal charges over the shooting, he had launched a very aggressive search for you, Mrs. . . . . Miss . . ."

"Just Lainie O'Keefe," whispered Elaine.

"From what I've been able to find in the records, he had informants in practically every large town on the South Island. Some fellow out of Westport gave him the decisive clue. But his man here in Greymouth covered for you, Miss O'Keefe."

"He covered . . . But why?" Everything was spinning around Elaine again. Timothy took her hand.

"His contact in Greymouth was a miner down in the Blackburn Mine," said the constable. "The man is Maori."

"And a son of Emere, Sideblossom's housekeeper," Jefferson added. "That's why Sideblossom thought he was loyal. In addition, he was in a relationship with a girl who served as your lady's maid, Miss O'Keefe."

Pai? Or Rahera? But Pai had been in love with Pita. Elaine was having difficulty keeping everything straight.

"And the girl belonged to a tribe that was having difficulties with Mr. Sideblossom, to put it mildly."

"Rahera!" Elaine cried. "John had caught their tribe stealing and kept Rahera like a slave as punishment. She was terribly afraid of the police. Yet I always told her it would be better to testify."

"You could have listened to that advice yourself," the constable grumbled.

Jefferson gave him a cross look, as he was anxious to conclude his speech. "In any case, the young man was torn between his loyalty to his relations and his love for his sweetheart. Then, during your escape, you stumbled upon his own tribe, Miss O'Keefe, which received you very kindly, and the matter was decided."

"That's why the chief's wife said I would be safe in Greymouth," Elaine mumbled.

The constable nodded. "Which cleared up the most burning question for me. I've spent hours chewing over why my town of all places is such an ideal destination for more or less fallen women."

"Your engagement announcement was what did you in," Jefferson continued ungraciously. He clearly took umbrage at interruptions.

Elaine reddened. Her father once again looked from her to Timothy by turn.

"My parents insisted on the engagement party," Timothy said, feeling he needed to justify himself. I wanted to scrap the entire thing after I found out Sideblossom was still alive."

"And I planned to turn myself in right afterward," Elaine said.

"If you'd done it earlier, John Sideblossom might still be alive," the constable said sternly.

"And he would have continued to pursue you," Ruben added. "He never would have let it go. If you had contacted us, Lainie, we would have sent you overseas. No one could have protected you from him here."

Timothy nodded. "We had the same idea," he said quietly.

"The death of John Sideblossom does not appear to have caused anyone much grief," Jefferson remarked. "In his household either. The employees appeared to be rather relieved. This Emere woman above all, whom I would have thought quite loyal. But she was talking about spirits that had taken their revenge. In the meantime, the son has become completely deranged. According to the information they provided, he's in an asylum in Blenheim. Apparently unresponsive at the moment. Well, that's the gist of it. Are there any questions?"

"I . . . I'm free to go?" Elaine asked.

Jefferson shrugged. "That depends on what you mean. There were never any legal charges against you. However, you remain married."

Elaine scooted her chair closer to Timothy. "Would you hold me anyway?" Elaine whispered to him.

Timothy pulled her closer.

Ruben formally took his leave of both constables, thanking Jefferson Allbridge in particular.

"On behalf of my currently otherwise-engaged daughter as well," he said. "We'll clarify this matter of the marriage and the engagement. So, where can I rent a room for a few nights?"

"And this time it's definitely the right one?" Ruben asked his daughter sternly. He had spoken at length with Timothy and was now taking Elaine to task.

Timothy had ridden home. His family's cook always produced enough food for a whole regiment, but he wanted to inform his parents that he had invited the father of his future wife to dinner. Well, Timothy thought, at least the poised, distinguished, and prosperous-looking Mr. O'Keefe would please Nellie. With Marvin, it would depend on what time he had started drinking.

"This time it's the right one," Elaine confirmed radiantly. "It took me a long time to figure it out. But I'm absolutely certain!"

Ruben raised his eyebrows. "We'll see what your mother has to say. Based on past experience, I would not particularly trust your instincts or mine."

Elaine laughed. "William would probably direct you to Callie on that point," she said, giggling lightheartedly and scratching her dog.

Ruben made a face. He was still bewildered by this business with William and Kura, who all of sudden seemed to be good friends of Elaine's. Other questions took precedence, however. One of which he hardly dare ask.

"And what about his . . . er . . . condition? I mean, I think he's a nice sort and seems to know his stuff. But he's . . . an invalid. Can he even . . ."

Ruben turned away.

Laughing, Elaine rubbed her still rather flat stomach.

"Oh yes, Father! He can."

Kura and William went to Caleb's wedding if only to prove that they did not hold a grudge. To Kura, that was important for personal reasons; to William, it just made good business sense. Caleb's music arrangements had struck a chord with the public. They were the ideal mix of art and entertainment, contemporary composition and folk music. If there was ever going to be a sequel to "Ghost Whispers," a renewed collaboration would be desirable. In order to secure that, William also buttered up Florence Weber, as it was clear to him who would be pulling the strings.

Nevertheless, on their wedding day Florence used a light touch. She serenely ignored Caleb's animated conversation with the young female pianist William and Kura had brought with them from Blenheim. White-skinned, light blonde, and almost ethereally beautiful, she seemed to experience reality only in harmonies and notes. In daily life, she proved to be even less conversational than Kura—Marisa Clerk did not merely answer only with yes or no but often ignored the question altogether. Elaine found her dull, but she drew downright unearthly notes from the Billers' piano. Her piano dialogue with Kura's *putorino* gave new dimension to the piece. The music even appeared to captivate Florence herself, at whose patronizing request the artists gave a small taste of their skills.

Florence, however, was not disposed to criticize anyone on her wedding day. She floated through the festivities, her radiant felicity almost rendering her beautiful. Not that her far-too-elaborate and overly laden wedding dress—bedecked with flounces and little bows, pearls and lace—did much to emphasize what few advantages she had. Florence had ordered the dress in Christchurch, and it reflected the tastes of the Weber and Biller ladies. Caleb appeared to shudder briefly at his first glimpse of the church but then composed himself commendably. Both participants presented the picture of harmony—at least during the official portion of the event.

Caleb kissed the bride according to custom in the church and then once more after the ceremony in front of the assembled workers of his mine. Later, he opened the dancing with Florence, who tried very hard not to lead. Afterward, however, each of them retreated to his or her realm of interest. While Caleb chatted with Marisa about music, Florence spoke with the business manager of the Blackburn mine about extraction techniques. She no longer spoke to Timothy Lambert. Now that they no longer ignored her, she assumed the attitude of the other mining bosses, treating Timothy with the same kind indulgence she would treat a child who simply will not understand why he cannot play too.

Timothy ended up alone with a glass of whiskey at the edge of the festivities. He observed the lively goings-on from the winter garden of the Webers' town house. Elaine danced giddily with her brother Stephen, who had shown up unannounced two days earlier to surprise his long-lost sister. Though she waved to Timothy occasionally, she was wholly absorbed in seeing her family again, and Timothy could not hold that against her. He liked the O'Keefes and enjoyed talking with them. But Ruben was deep in conversation with Greymouth's justice of the peace just then, and Timothy did not want to disturb them. Maybe it was nonsense, and the men would have been happy to include him, but he hardly dared join any group anymore—too often he only provoked embarrassed looks at his crutches when he did so. The women were even worse than the men. Their pity came across as condescension, and they treated him like a sick child.

Timothy had tried to move past the bitter realization that, as far as the people who counted in Greymouth were concerned, the Lamberts' heir had died that December twentieth in his mine. The miners might still venerate the shadow of him as they would a saint, and the better society might, in certain respects, grant him the status of a martyr, but no one had work for saints or martyrs.

Kura and William ended up joining him, both overheated from dancing and, in truth, in search of a quiet corner to exchange caresses. After Blenheim, the two of them were more in love than ever before. Not even Ruben O'Keefe, who could never entirely forgive William and who still treated Kura rather coolly, could resist their glow of marital bliss.

"What are you doing here?" Kura asked, tapping Timothy on the shoulder. "Sitting around and moping?"

Timothy smiled at her. She was wearing a new dress—a silk affair in various shades of blue from the workshop of the superbly talented Mrs. O'Brien—and flowers in her hair like a South Seas beauty. Now that she had been recognized as an artist, she wanted to dress in a suitably sophisticated manner, and given her good taste, she knew precisely how to fully emphasize her looks.

"I'm sitting here trying not to envy Florence Biller too much." Timothy tried to make it sound like a joke, but his voice sounded bitter. "Starting tomorrow, she's going to take over the Biller Mine, probably not in one blow, but she'll have an office there in no more than a month. Meanwhile, I have to watch strangers, investors, take over Lambert Mines and parade other engineers in front of me who have no advantages over me other than that they could beat me in a race."

"Has your father found buyers then?" William inquired. "I haven't heard anything yet."

Timothy shrugged. "I'll probably be the last to know. At the very least, I'll know after Florence."

Kura smiled. "You're speaking up a little late," she teased. "If you'd announced your interest in her position a little earlier, Caleb would doubtless have preferred you to his dear Florence."

9

A re you going to town? If so, I can take you."
Matt Gawain, who had become close friends with Timothy by now, observed Timothy struggling onto Fellow while one of the Lamberts' stableboys hitched an elegant coach horse to Nellie Lambert's private chaise. It was a cold, wet spring morning, and Matt thought the covered coach would be greatly preferable to a ride through the rain.

Timothy, however, shook his head grimly. "I'm not riding for my own amusement but to build up my muscles. Did you know that the simple act of sitting on a horse exercises fifty-six muscles?"

Matt shrugged. "And how many does the horse use?" he asked.

Timothy didn't answer but looked with astonishment at the fine vehicle Matt was just then climbing into.

"How did you earn the honor of being able to drive my mother's own caroche? An excursion with Charlene? On an ordinary Wednesday?"

"You don't really believe that your mother would lend me the coach for Charlene, do you? No, it's for a meeting with an investor. I'm supposed to pick the gentleman up from the train station and drive him here before the Webers get their mitts on him. Old man Weber arranged the meeting somehow, but your father wants to handle the negotiations on his own. So far he's even sober." Matt took the reins, and Timothy began riding alongside the coach.

"Typical that he didn't breathe a word to me about it. I'm fed up with the whole business and can't leave soon enough. There's a ship leaving for London next week. But once again without us."

Though Timothy was in pain due to Fellow's fast pace, he slackened the reins when he saw that his horse was trying to keep time with the coach. Matt saw Timothy's contorted face and slowed his bay's step.

"Looking ahead, you should buy a horse with gentler movements," he commented. "You'll need to buy a new one in Europe anyway."

Timothy shrugged. "Explain that to Lainie. She insists we take our horses. She's like her grandmother Gwyneira in that way, she says. A new country, fine, but only with her horse and dog. I have no idea how I'm supposed to afford that."

"It sounds like her family has money," Matt said, letting his horse amble. He was in no hurry and was dry where he was sitting. Timothy, however, looked as freezing and uncomfortable.

"But will they spend that money to send the daughter they've finally found again overseas?" Timothy had his doubts. "Before we go, she still wants to go to Queenstown and the Canterbury Plains to say her good-byes to her whole family."

"I don't think that Lainie of yours wants to leave New Zealand at all," Matt said. In fact, he was sure of it, but thought that maybe Timothy needed to hear it more gently.

Timothy sighed. "I know," he muttered. "But what am I supposed to do? I don't have any future in my profession here. And what else can I do? Ruben O'Keefe offered to have me go into business with him. They're opening a new branch in Westport soon. That's where they all are today, looking at space to lease. But I'm not a salesman, Matt. I have no gift for it, and, to be honest, not the least interest."

"But Lainie . . ." Matt had heard about the offer through Charlene and was trying to raise a delicate issue cautiously.

Timothy waved it away. "Yes, yes, I know. Lainie's helped out in her father's store since she was little. She could manage the business while I build birdhouses—if I'm lucky."

"Which reminds me of Florence and Caleb Biller," Matt remarked.

Timothy nodded. "With the slight difference being that Caleb enjoys that sort of life. He actually prefers researching Maori culture to busying himself with rocks. And he'll end up making money from it too. In fact, he is already. William and Kura have been rather generously splitting the profits from their concerts with him. I, how-ever . . ." Timothy shrugged. "Besides, I'm not the kind that would adjust easily to living off his wife's inheritance or his father-in-law's largesse."

"What about something else? Outside of mining or being a sales-man?" Matt goaded his horse as it was getting late.

"I've thought about rail construction," Timothy said. In fact, he had been doing nothing but mulling over possible occupations for weeks. "Julian Redcliff in Blenheim dropped a few hints. But, I can't delude myself, Matt. There aren't even any fixed offices in the railroad business. When you're inspecting sites, you travel around, sleeping in tents or whatever shelter you can find. It's wet and cold. I wouldn't make it."

Timothy lowered his head, defeated. He had never said it out loud, nor would he ever complain about how much the first winter after the accident had afflicted him. But, as Dr. Leroy had brutally made clear to him, he would not get any better. Only worse.

"Wales isn't exactly known for its warm, dry climate either," noted Matt.

Timothy bit his lip. "It doesn't have to be Wales or England. There are mines in Southern Europe too . . ."

Mines just waiting for someone who got around on crutches and didn't speak the local language. Though neither one said it aloud, the men shared the same bitter thought.

They had reached town by this time, and Matt stopped his team in front of the train station. The train had already arrived, and Timothy saw a tall, somewhat older but slender and exquisitely dressed gentle-man descend the steps. The investor, presumably.

"I guess I'll invite the man to come with me," sighed Matt. "And in doing so, likely usher in my own fall. I have no doubt he'll put a university student in my place, and I'll soon be back to swallowing coal dust as a foreman again."

Matt had effectively been running the mine for the last few months. Although Marvin Lambert was in the office almost every day, he impeded decisions more than he made them.

"Will I see you at the pub later?" he asked.

Timothy shook his head. "Probably not. I'll be at dinner in town, but it's a family dinner at one of the nicest hotels on the quay. Ruben O'Keefe is paying. They're expecting some uncle out of Canterbury, so probably a sheep baron of some kind." Timothy sounded indifferent. He couldn't help but dread the prospect of more family arriving to try to keep Elaine on the South Island.

Matt waved at him. "Then enjoy yourself! And wish me luck. I'll let you know tomorrow how it went."

Timothy watched his friend go, casually jumping over a barrier to reach the platform more quickly. Matt spoke to the older gentleman politely and then took his bag with a smile. At least the young foreman would have the chance to convince Marvin's new investor of his expertise during the tour of the mine. Timothy really did wish him luck. But he envied him even more.

Elaine looked lovely as she greeted Timothy in front of the hotel. She was wearing her dark-blue dress and stroking the horse that her father had ridden over and that now stood next to Banshee. It was a family reunion for the animals, too. It turned out that the black horse was Banshee's foal that Elaine had left behind in Queenstown after she had gotten married. Timothy hoped she did not want to take him overseas now too.

Timothy had asked Roly drive him that evening. His ride that morning had been as much as he could handle. In order to work off his impotent rage, he had stretched it out more than two hours. Besides, he was wearing his evening clothes. This uncle of hers was some sort of important personality, and Elaine had hinted that there was something to celebrate. "They didn't tell me what it was, but Uncle George telegraphed my father yesterday and he was very happy after that and spoke to the hotel about this dinner. There'll be champagne!"

Although Elaine was clearly excited about the evening, Timothy's enthusiasm was limited. He was beginning to fear meeting new people rather than looking forward to it. Too often they seemed embarrassed just by the fact of being introducing to him. They desperately sought topics of conversation that didn't touch on any taboo subjects and were visibly uncomfortable standing or walking around in Timothy's presence. If things kept up like this, he would become a hermit.

Timothy put a determined smile on his face and took Elaine in his arms. She was joyful and frolicsome and greeted him at once with a detailed description of the new store in Westport. Apparently, the location was ideal, right in the middle of town. And the town itself was lively and attractive and at least as big as Greymouth. Elaine could obviously imagine living there and running the store, and Timothy was all but ready to resign himself to it. Selling housewares and clothes couldn't be all that bad.

The two crossed the hotel foyer, Timothy forcing himself with some effort to remain polite when a porter scurried around him as though he would happily have carried him to a room for a tip. He could not let himself be so sensitive as to think of every walk in public as some kind of gauntlet. Nevertheless, Timothy was relieved to discover that the table for Ruben O'Keefe and his guests was not located in the hotel's luxurious main dining room but in a no less elegantly decorated side room. Elaine's father, her brother Stephen, and the heralded Uncle George were already standing with drinks in their hands at the window, which boasted a view of the quay and a choppy sea.

All three of the men were looking outside and only turned to Timothy and Elaine when they came closer. Timothy greeted Ruben and Stephen before looking with surprise into the inquisitive brown eyes of the man Matt had picked up from the train station that morning. Elaine greeted him before Timothy, however, and the man she called her uncle embraced her. The older gentleman hugged her firmly before she pulled away, laughing.

"So we finally have you back, Lainie," he said. "My compliments, child. I never would have thought someone could hide from me on this island."

Lainie smiled, embarrassed, and took the glass of champagne that her father offered her.

Timothy used the break to finally reach out his hand to "Uncle George," who introduced himself with a firm handshake and self-assured gaze. "George Greenwood," he said. He didn't even seem to notice Timothy's crutches and leg splints.

"Didn't I see you at the train station this morning?" he asked before Timothy could even give his name. "You were there with that Mr. Gawain who showed me around the Lambert Mine."

"And? Did you like it?" Timothy blurted out. He became aware of his faux pas at once. "Forgive me. I should introduce myself first. Timothy Lambert."

"Elaine's fiancé," Ruben noted, smiling. "Supposedly the right one, finally. Mr. Greenwood has news about the divorce, Tim. Good news!"

Elaine looked as though she were perishing to hear the news, whereas Timothy could think about nothing except the mine. How had Matt presented himself? And his father? How were the negotiations going, and might they already have come to some agreement?

"Lambert?" asked George, sizing up Timothy with a probing look. "Any relation to the mining Lamberts?"

Timothy nodded. "The son," he said with resignation.

George furrowed his brow. "But that can't be."

Timothy flared up at him. Suddenly all his pent-up anger and frustration surged inside him, and he could not restrain himself.

"Mr. Greenwood, I have my problems, but I can provide accurate information regarding my parentage."

George did not look angry. He smiled.

"No one is questioning that, Mr. Lambert. I'm only a bit surprised. Here . . ." He reached for a few papers that he had carelessly thrown on the table earlier, "It's the information in the prospectus, but read for yourself."

Timothy reached for the files and skimmed the section on the subject of "heirs."

Marvin Lambert's only son is sickly and in all likelihood will never be able to manage the company. The desire of the family to quickly liquidate at least a portion of the mine can be understood by the need to ensure the invalid's income in perpetuity . . .

Timothy went pale.

"I'm sorry, Mr. Lambert," George said. "But after this report, I would have thought that the son in question was more likely in a sanitarium in Switzerland than on a horse at the train station in Greymouth."

Timothy took a deep breath. He would need to calm down if he was going to make it through this evening.

"Forgive me, Mr. Greenwood, but I had no idea. To whom do I owe this depiction of my health? My father or Mr. Weber?"

"You know of Mr. Weber's involvement?" George Greenwood asked.

"Word is all over town," Timothy replied. "And Florence Biller, Mr. Weber's daughter, would no doubt be thrilled to consolidate the management of the Biller and Lambert mines. That would give her two mines." He turned away. "Perhaps I should have taken Kura's advice."

"Kura's advice?" Elaine asked jealously.

"A bad joke," Timothy said wearily.

"And why is it exactly that you don't want to manage the mine?" George asked. "Interested in something else altogether? Ruben said you might take over the business in Westport."

Timothy bristled. "Sir, I'm a mining engineer. I have diplomas from two European universities and practical experience in mines in six countries. It's not a question of not wanting to. But my father and I are of differing opinions on a few important matters concerning the management of the mine."

George's alert gaze wandered over Timothy's body.

"Is your condition a result of these . . . differing opinions? You can speak frankly; I know about the explosion in the mine and its largely obscured causes. And also about two men, including one from management, who went into the mine immediately following the accident. One of them is dead."

"As far as my father is concerned, the other one is too," Timothy said hoarsely.

Elaine interrupted. "Will you finally tell us something about the divorce, Uncle George?" She had been horsing around with her brother and was entirely unaware of the serious turn that the conversation between Timothy and her uncle had just taken. "You two can talk about the mine afterward. Besides, I'm hungry."

Timothy was not hungry. He looked George Greenwood in the eye.

"We'll talk about it at greater length tomorrow," George said. "Tête-à-tête. Come to my suite at nine and bring along your diplomas. Though I think we'll come to an agreement very quickly. After all, I just bought sixty percent of your mine's shares, Mr. Lambert. I get to decide who's dead."

George Greenwood took his time with the news of the divorce. Only when the first course had been placed in front of him did he finally begin answering Elaine's persistent questions.

"Thomas Sideblossom will agree to the divorce," he finally declared. "One of our attorneys spoke with John's widow. She's staying at Lionel Station at the moment but will return to Blenheim and speak with him as soon as she has settled matters in Otago."

"She can talk all she wants," Elaine said doubtfully, "but what makes her think Thomas will listen to her?"

"Oh, according to Mrs. Sideblossom, the divorce is in his own interest," George said, smiling benignly. "As soon as it's finalized, he plans to marry his former stepmother."

"What?" Elaine exclaimed with such force that she choked on her crayfish cocktail and began to cough. When she finally regained her composure, there was panic in her eyes.

"She can't do that," she whispered. "Zoé, I mean. She . . ."

"I asked her twice myself if she was sure," George confessed, "before the connections made sense to me."

"Oh?" asked Stephen, surprised, playing with the food in his glass. He did not like seafood and was trying to remove the crayfish tails inconspicuously from the other components of the appetizer. "But it's obvious. The lady really doesn't have any choice." Stephen made a crayfish tail disappear under the table, where Callie greedily seized it.

"But Thomas is . . . He's awful. I have to warn her," stammered Elaine, laying her silverware down as though she intended to leap up and leave right then to contact Zoé Sideblossom.

"Thomas is in an asylum for the mentally deranged," Timothy reminded her gently, laying his hand on hers. "He can't hurt anyone anymore."

"Precisely," Stephen continued calmly, "but he remains the heir of Lionel Station. And the way I figure it, this John Sideblossom fellow never made a detailed testament stating that his wife was to be provided with a certain bequest in the event of his death. In which case, she's more or less penniless right now. She could perhaps continue to live on Lionel Station, but even in that regard, Elaine could make things difficult for her."

"Me?" Elaine asked, taken aback. She seemed to have regained some of her strength.

"Of course you," her father said. "As his wife, you still constitute Thomas's next of kin. You have the power of disposal over his goods, and if he should die, you'd be the sole heiress."

Elaine turned pale again.

"It gets better," Stephen went on, savoring his words. "If, for example, these doctors in the insane asylum succeed in driving out what's left of good old Thomas's reason—they won't need more than a year or two for that—you could have him legally incapacitated. And from then on, you'd be the mistress of a handsome farm and twelve thousand sheep. Isn't that what you've always wanted?" Stephen grinned.

Elaine ran her trembling hands over the tablecloth.

"You should also think about Callie's needs," Stephen added with a serious face. The little dog wagged her tail when she heard her name and looked up at Stephen adoringly, hungering for another treat. "She's a sheepdog after all. She needs a few sheep."

Only then did Elaine realize that her brother was joking, and she attempted a feeble smile.

"In all seriousness, Elaine, from a financial perspective, you might want to reconsider the divorce in light of all this," said George Greenwood. "We're in an excellent negotiating position. Perhaps Mrs. Sideblossom would be amenable to arranging an alimony agreement."

Elaine shook her head violently. "I don't want any money from them," she whispered. "Let Zoé have it. I just never want to see him again."

"We should be able to arrange that without any trouble," George said. "According to my attorney, Zoé is planning to relocate to London. As soon as her future husband is capable of travel and their marriage is finalized. She's already found a suitable and pleasant sanatorium in Lancashire where she can safely lock him up. Apparently, the asylums in England are more modern and offer greater chances of recovery."

Stephen smiled. "Even more importantly, however, London is much more attractive for young widows than a remote corner of Lake Pukaki."

"I hope she'll be happy," Elaine said seriously. "She was not very nice to me, but I believe she's been through quite a bit. If she finds what she's looking for in England, that would be all right with me. How long does your lawyer think it will take, Uncle George?"

"You can start working on your dancing again," Elaine said tenderly. It was much later that evening, and she was a little tipsy from the champagne and the prospect of finally being free. Timothy kissed her in front of the hotel stables while Roly hitched Fellow to the chaise.

"And if I understood Uncle George correctly, we won't even have to go to Wales."

Timothy nodded and stroked her hair.

"And if *I* understood Uncle George correctly, I'll be calling the tune soon enough," he said fiercely. "Florence Biller will be amazed at how much life is still left in the Lambert Mine." He smiled. "I just feel sorry for Callie on account of all those little sheep she'll be missing out on." Callie heard her name and leaped up on him. "Of course, we could get ahold of a couple and let them pasture in the mining compound."

Elaine laughed and petted her dog. "Nonsense, she'll be herding children soon!"

10

Timothy Lambert took possession of his new office. It was somewhat smaller than his father's—just to keep up appearances. Officially Marvin Lambert was still in charge of his mine. Still, Timothy commanded more space than Matt Gawain, whose office adjoined his own. Both rooms were located on the ground floor, brightly lit, and offered a wide view of the most important mining structures. Timothy had the headframe tower in view, so he could watch the men arrive for their shift. Soon he would also be looking out over the tracks on which they would be conveying the coal they had extracted directly to the train line. But even now there was brisk activity out front. New mining lamps, modern helmets, and trolleys for moving the coal underground were being delivered, and Matt was out speaking to a group of new miners, some of whom had come directly from coal-mining regions in England and Wales. George Greenwood had advertised for new immigrants with mining knowledge in the immigration ports of Lyttelton and Dunedin.

Timothy took a deep breath but had little time to take a closer look around his new domain, because Lester Harding, his father's secretary, materialized to welcome him. The disingenuous servility of the man immediately robbed Timothy of his good mood.

"Shall I bring you an armchair, Mr. Lambert? It would be a little more comfortable for you. Would you like a glass of water?"

Timothy did not want to get angry, but if he did not put this man in his place at once, he would get on his nerves every day. So he merely cast an appraising look at the no-doubt-comfortable-but-low leather armchair that had been placed next to a small table and a tiny house bar in a corner of his office.

"I don't know about you, but I generally prefer to work at my desk rather than down there," he explained frostily. "And since I am of a normal height, the chair at my desk suits me just fine. After"—he looked at the clock—"less than a minute in this office, I don't need any refreshments either. If Mr. Gawain comes in later, however, you are perfectly welcome to serve us some tea." Timothy smiled to take the edge off his words. "Until then, just bring me the balances for the last two months, and the catalogs for our most important construction-material suppliers."

Lester Harding exited the room with an indignant expression.

Timothy forgot him immediately. Time would tell whether he could work with the man. If not, he could find another secretary. There was no rush. He would run this office and this mine according to what he thought best.

Florence Biller stepped into her new office. It was a little smaller than her husband's—just to keep up appearances. And a good deal smaller than Caleb's father's, but he had already announced his intention to gradually withdraw from the business. After all, his son was now working there diligently.

Just that day, Caleb had sat at his desk for almost two hours. Florence had not even noticed when he had left the house. As she passed by, she glanced almost tenderly at his blond head, bent low over his books and papers—none of which had even the slightest thing to do with mining or coal. Caleb was working on a treatise on the geological link between Maori greenstone—or *pounamu*—and Chinese and South American jade, as well as its mythological significance for the Maori and Aztec cultures. The subject positively enthralled him. The previous evening, he had given Florence a lengthy presentation on the relationship between the various occurrences of jadeite and nephrite. As a good wife, she had listened to him respectfully, but during business hours, he did not bother her with it. Florence quietly closed the door between their rooms.

Her office! It was not only brightly lit and inviting, but, most importantly, it offered a view of the mine's buildings. The Biller Mine offices were on the second floor of a warehouse, and from Florence's window, she could see the headframe tower, the entrances to the mine, and the tracks that ensured the rapid transport of the extracted coal to the rail depot. It was the most modern facility in the region. Florence could not get enough of the view, but then she was interrupted by the entrance of a secretary.

Bill Holland, she remembered. Still a rather young man but one who had been employed by the Billers for a considerable time.

"Is everything to your satisfaction, madam?" he inquired in a servile manner.

Florence took a look at the furnishings in her office. Bookshelves, a desk, a small sitting area in a corner—and a tea set. She frowned.

"It's very nice, Mr. Holland. But could you please store the tea-kettle and the china in your office? It will disturb my concentration to have you tinkering with those in here. You can see to that during your lunch break—or no, rather do it now."

The man had to be put in his place. Florence thought of Caleb, who had no doubt forgotten to have breakfast that morning. She smiled. "Following that, take a cup of tea in to my husband along with a few sandwiches. And please bring me the balances for the last two months, along with the catalogs for our most important construction-material suppliers."

Holland withdrew with an indignant expression. Florence watched him go. Time would tell whether she could work with him. It would be a shame to have to let him go. He did not seem to be stupid, and he was exceptionally handsome. If he also proved discreet, he might go straight to the short list. After all, she would eventually have to decide which of their loyal employees was worthy of siring Caleb Biller's heir.

Florence smoothed her sharply cut dark skirt and rearranged the neckline of her flouncy white blouse. She would need a mirror! Though there would certainly be people who would wonder at the management of the Biller Mine over the next few years, she had no reason to be ashamed of her femininity. Florence had time. She would run this office and this mine according to what she thought best.

Emere strode through the rooms of Lionel Station. The old Maori woman walked slowly, holding her *putorino* flute clenched in her hand, as though she needed it for support. Lionel Station. Her home and that of her children. The house to which John had brought her so long ago, when she had still been a princess, a chieftain's daughter and ward of a sorceress. She had loved John Sideblossom then—enough to leave her tribe after he had lain with her in her family's sleeping lodge. Emere had thought that she was his wife until he came home with that girl, that blonde *pakeha*. When Emere had asserted her claims, he had laughed at her. Their connection did not count. Nor did the child she was carrying below her heart. John Sideblossom wanted white heirs.

Emere let her fingers wander over the new furniture decorated with intarsia that Zoé had brought with her as a new bride. The second blonde girl. More than twenty years after the first had died. Not entirely through no fault of Emere's—she was a skilled midwife and could have saved John's first wife. But back then, she had still hoped that everything could be like it was before.

And now Zoé was the heiress—or would manage to become it. Emere felt a certain esteem for Zoé. She seemed so fragile and delicate, and yet she had survived everything—what John called "making love" and even the births with which Emere had "assisted" her.

The old Maori had long since made her peace with Zoé. Let her keep the farm's profits. Arama would see to that, down to the last penny. Emere did not want any money. But she wanted the house and the land, and Zoé was not interested in that.

Emere entered the next room and tore open the curtains. No one was to shut the sun out of here any longer. She took a deep breath after she had opened the window. Her children were free. No more John Sideblossom, who had first sent them away and then enslaved them.

Emere waited impatiently for Pai to return with the last child. She had sent the girl to Dunedin to retrieve her youngest son from the orphanage. The child she had borne a few months after the flame-haired girl had gone away. The girl through whom the curse she had placed on John Sideblossom's heir so long ago had finally fulfilled itself.

Only once had she ever demanded something for one of their children: a little land signed over to their firstborn. But once again, John had only laughed—that was when Emere had learned to hate his laugh. Emere should be happy, John had said, that he let their bastards live. They would never inherit anything from him.

That night was the first time he had forced Emere into his bed—and he seemed to enjoy it. Ever since then, she had hated everything about him, and to this day, she did not know why she had stayed. She had cursed herself a thousand times for it, for this fascination that he had exercised on her until the last, for her worthless existence lived between longing and hate. More than anything she cursed herself for having let his son by that white woman live. But back then, Emere had still had scruples about killing a defenseless baby. By the time Zoé's children were born, no more.

She had then taken her firstborn son to her tribe. Tamati, the only one of her children who did not look like John. He had now fulfilled his destiny by protecting the flame-haired girl.

Emere raised her *putorino* flute and paid homage to the spirits. She had time. Zoé Sideblossom was young. As long as she lived and Lionel Station generated money, Emere was secure. No one would lay a hand on the house or the land. And later? Rewi, her thirdborn, was smart. John had recently brought him back to the farm, but Emere was thinking of sending him back to Dunedin. He could continue his schooling, perhaps attain the profession of that man who had recently spoken with Zoé. Attorney. Emere let the word roll around on her tongue. Someone who helped others attain their rights. Perhaps Rewi would someday want to fight for his heir. Emere smiled. The spirits would see to it.

11

Timothy Lambert danced at his wedding. Though it was only a short waltz and he leaned heavily on his bride, the guests applauded wildly. The mine workers tossed their caps in the air and cheered for him just as they had at the race, and Berta Leroy had tears in her eyes.

Timothy and Elaine married on Saint Barbara's Day, exactly two years after the legendary Lambert Derby. There was once again a happy celebration on the mining compound. George Greenwood presented himself as the new controlling partner and introduced himself and his business manager, Timothy Lambert, by supplying all their employees and half of Greymouth with free beer, barbecue, games, and dancing. The only thing missing this time around was a horse race.

"We didn't want to take the chance of my bride riding off," Timothy said to loud acclaim in his toast before he kissed Elaine in front of the entire workforce. Everyone roared again. Only Elaine blushed. After all, her mother and grandmother Helen were among the spectators. Fleurette and Helen waved to her supportively, though. Both of them liked Timothy. Even Fleurette's famous intuition had raised no objections.

The reverend did not need to wage a battle with his conscience over his flock's passion for gambling this time. He was faced instead with the quandary of a divorced bride. However, Elaine did not present herself in white but wore a pale-blue dress trimmed with dark lace—from Mrs. O'Brien's workshop, of course. She had even foregone a veil, opting to wear a crown of fresh flowers instead.

"It has to have seven different flowers," she insisted, causing her friends to scratch their heads. "Then I can lay it under my pillow on the wedding night."

"But beware you don't dream of someone else," Timothy teased her, recalling her story about that long-past Saint John's eve.

In the end, the reverend sidestepped altogether the question of how to address the unconventional marriage and Saint Barbara—whom he, as a Methodist, had never venerated—by performing the service out in the open and supplying the town and those gathered with an all-encompassing blessing afterward. He had reserved Timothy and Elaine places in the first row, and Elaine's brother Stephen played "Amazing Grace."

Kura-maro-tini would certainly have enriched the festivities with more complex rhythms, but she was not present. Timothy and Elaine would see her on their honeymoon, however. Elaine not only wanted to see Queenstown again but Kiward Station too, and Helen was keenly interested in Kura's music program. Thus, everyone with the exception of Ruben—who had to return to tend his business— planned to travel to Christchurch after the wedding to attend Kura and Marisa's highly anticipated farewell concert. The artists, with William by their side, would leave for England afterward. Concert dates in London and several other English cities had already been set. William had initiated contact with a well-known concert agency that was planning their tour.

"So in the end, Kura's getting exactly what she always wanted," Fleurette said disapprovingly. She had not seen Kura again in Greymouth and was still upset. Granted, she would have cared much less for William as a son-in-law than Timothy, for whom she had quickly developed a heartfelt affection. But Kura and William had hurt her daughter, and as a mother, she was slow to forgive that.

"What are they doing about their little girl?" Fleurette asked, remembering Gloria. "Is she going with them to Europe?"

"Not as far as I know," answered Helen. The ill will caused by Kura's marriage to William had not lasted long. The women's friendship was too strong to let anything come between them. They had resumed their correspondence soon after Kura's wedding and shared their concern over Elaine's disappearance during the last few years. "The little girl will stay on Kiward Station, for the time being anyway. No one knows what Kura will want to do next. But thus far, neither father nor mother has shown the least interest in Gloria. Why should that change now? And dragging a three-year-old across half of Europe would be nonsense."

"And so Mother's getting exactly what she wanted too!" Fleurette smiled. "A second chance to raise the heiress of Kiward Station, in a way that aligns with her values. Tonga must already be sharpening his knives."

Helen laughed. "It won't be all that bad. With Kura, he tried using love after all. How could he have guessed that there would be someone else who was even better at *whaikorero*?"

The rail line between the West Coast and the Canterbury Plains was now running, and Elaine had been looking forward to her first train ride with great anticipation. Timothy had just been hoping for a less arduous trip than the ride to Blenheim. They were not disappointed. Their honeymoon trip was a truly luxurious affair, given that George Greenwood had a private parlor car at his disposal. He generously made it available to the married couple, and so Timothy and Elaine made love on its rattling bed and poured champagne, laughing as they did so.

"I could get used to this!" Elaine declared enthusiastically.

Timothy smiled. "Then you should have remained Kura's pianist. She's still raving about her idol's private train car. What is that woman's name again?"

"I don't know, some opera diva . . . Adelina Patti! Doesn't she actually travel with her own train? Maybe you should have started working with Julian Redcliff. As a railroad man, you probably get a discount on trains." Elaine leaned happily against Timothy's arm.

The McKenzies were awaiting the travelers at the train station in Christchurch, and Gwyneira wrapped her arms around Elaine with great emotion. Unlike Helen, whose features had grown more haggard and severe over the last few years, Gwyneira seemed to have hardly aged.

"How could I have aged gracefully with a house full of children?" Gwyneira remarked happily when Helen paid her a compliment. "Jack and Gloria, and Jennifer is still quite young too, and such a sweet girl. Look!"

Jennifer Greenwood, who was still teaching the Maori children on Kiward Station, blushed as she greeted Stephen O'Keefe. The two of them were discussing—employing impeccable legal-argumentation language—whether one was permitted to kiss in public or not. They ended up doing so behind Jennifer's parasol.

"That will be the next wedding. After he completes his studies, Stephen's going to start working as a corporate attorney for Greenwood."

Helen nodded. "Much to the dismay of his father. Ruben would have liked to see him as a judge. But c'est la vie. Now, someone's grown up!" Smiling, she pointed at Jack and little Gloria. Jack was now eighteen, a tall young man with wild auburn locks who reminded Helen greatly of a young James. Despite his lankiness, he moved with astounding dexterity as he steered his tiny companion through the muddle of the train station.

"Railroad," parroted Gloria as she pointed like Jack at the steely monster.

"Dog, come!" she said next, with considerably more enthusiasm, reaching for Callie. Elaine whistled for her dog and indicated that she should give her paw to the little girl. Callie was distracted by other things though, Jack's own dog most of all.

Elaine took Gloria by the hand. "She's certainly pretty," she said. "But she doesn't look a bit like Kura."

That was true. Gloria did not resemble either Kura or William. Her hair shone neither black nor golden blonde, but rather, brown with a hint of red. Her porcelain-blue eyes were a little too close together to lend distinction to her face. And although Gloria's features still contained their baby roundness, they might later be a little too square to be beautiful.

"Thank God," Jack remarked. "By the way, Lainie, your dog must have gotten some pretty slipshod training. It doesn't look good to have a Kiward collie running all over the platform, letting strangers pet her. The dog needs sheep!"

"We'll be here for a couple of days, you know," said Elaine, smiling.

Kura's concert in Christchurch was a triumph. She had expected nothing less. Indeed, she had floated from one sensational success to the next. Kura and Marisa attributed this to their talents as musicians; William, to Kura's reputation as a spirit conjurer. In every interview, he lapsed into obscure innuendo, and Kura feared he had already supplied the agency in England with similar stories. She did not bring it up with him, however. She did not really care why the people came. The main thing was that they talked about her and paid for their tickets. Kura enjoyed being rich again. And she had done it all on her own.

Marama and her tribe had not only attended the concert but enriched it with two of their own *haka,* performed at William's express request. Marama took it as an apology for the affront at his wedding when he had not allowed the tribe to perform, and happily agreed. She was a conciliatory soul and quick to forgive. And when her singing voice, as high as though it were soaring among the clouds, mixed with Kura's dark, powerful organ playing, William would have loved to sign her on for the entire tour right away.

The White Hart's hall was quite a bit more diverse than usual that day. Tonga had come to Christchurch with half his tribe to pay homage to the heiress of Kiward Station and to say his adieus, likely forever. However, most of the Maori did not stand out. Almost all of them wore Western clothing, though they sometimes combined the various articles rather inexpertly. Tonga appeared in traditional clothing, and his tattoos—he was practically the only one of his generation who wore them—lent him a martial air. Most people initially took him for a dancer. When he joined them in the audience, they edged away from him uncomfortably.

Tonga was also the only one who frowned over Kura's performance. He would have preferred to retain the purity of the Maori songs than have them arranged for Western instruments.

"Kura will remain in England," he told Rongo Rongo, their tribe's witch doctor. "She sings our words but does not speak our language. She never has."

Rongo Rongo shrugged. "Nor has she ever spoken the language of the *pakeha*. She belongs to neither of our worlds. It is right that she seeks her own world."

Tonga cast a meaningful look at little Gloria. "But she's leaving her child with the McKenzies."

"She's leaving the child to *us*," Rongo Rongo said. "The child belongs to the land of the Nghai Tahu. To which tribe, she will decide for herself.

Jack sat with Gloria in the second row. He was making a big sacrifice for her, as he would never have set foot anywhere near a Kura-maro-tini concert of his own accord.

"I can certainly understand why that fellow in Blenheim was out of sorts," he had told his mother. "I'd probably end up in an asylum after spending that much time with her too."

Neither promises nor threats from Gwyneira had been able to convince him to go the concert. Then, however, Kura had insisted on the presence of her daughter, and Jack changed his mind at once.

"Gloria's only going to scream again. Or worse, she won't scream, and Kura will suddenly have the idea that she has talent and have to go with her to England. Under the circumstances, I'd rather go and keep an eye on her."

Gloria did not scream but merely played with a wooden horse Jack had brought along, clearly bored most of the time. When Kura conjured the spirits on the stage, though, the little girl scampered out of their row and ran down the aisle to the back of the room, where the Maori were seated and Tonga was leaning against the wall with a threatening expression on his face. Jack did not follow the girl, but he watched her out of the corner of his eye. It was no surprise to him that Gloria had fled all the caterwauling and preferred to play with other children. He, too, was happy when the concert was finally over. He left the hall with his parents—James winked at him, likewise relieved—picking Gloria up on his way out.

The little girl was with a somewhat older Maori boy who was wearing, to Gwyneira's amazement, a traditional loincloth. Moreover, the boy was not only decorated with the typical amulets and bands of a Maori child of good family but he was also already sporting his first tattoos. Though many *pakeha* were disgusted by them, Gloria did not appear to be bothered by them.

The children were playing with wooden blocks. "Village," the boy said, pointing to the fenced-in complex in which Gloria had just set another house.

"*Marae!*" Gloria declared, pointing at the biggest of the houses. Next to the meeting hall, she had also marked out storehouses and cooking lodges: "Here *pataka*, here *hanga*, and I live here."

Her dream house stood next to a lake drawn on the ground in chalk.

"And me!" the boy exclaimed, self-assured. "Me chief." Tonga appeared behind Gwyneira, who was listening to the children with a smile.

"Mrs. McKenzie," Tonga said as he gave his customary bow. He owed his comprehensive *pakeha* education to Helen O'Keefe.

"Kura-maro-tini impressed us greatly. It is a shame that she is leaving us. But you still have an heiress," he said, indicating Gloria. "This, as it happens, is my heir. Wiremu, my son."

Helen stepped behind the two of them. "A handsome boy, Tonga," she said, flattering him.

Tonga nodded and gazed, lost in thought, at the children at play. "A handsome couple. Don't you think, Mrs. McKenzie?"

Wiremu was handing Gloria a seashell. Gloria gave him her wooden horse in return.

Gwyneira beamed at the chieftain. But then she restrained herself and met his gaze with a mischievous gleam in her eye.

"Children will be children," she said.

Tonga smiled.

Afterword

D aily life in a New Zealand coal-mining settlement at the end of the nineteenth century is described in as much detail as possible in this novel. The descriptions of the work in the mine and the miners' all-but-unbearable living conditions, the miners need to seek comfort in alcohol in the evening, and the representation of the local brothel as a "second home" are all historically documented, as is the often inhuman greed of the mine operators.

Nevertheless, *Song of the Spirits* is a historical novel only in a limited sense. The social history is meticulously researched, but many settings and historically important events were changed or are purely fictional. For example, though there existed in the area around Greymouth roughly one hundred thirty coal mines from 1864 until modern times—operated privately, jointly, or by the state—none of them belonged to a Lambert or Biller family, and no former mine operator had a comparable family history.

The mine accident depicted in the novel is based on that of the Brunner Mine in the year 1896 with respect to the number of dead, the first rescue attempts, and the cause of the accident. Sixty-four pitmen and both of the first rescue workers perished; all of that is recorded. Recordings of the witnesses' memories of the event exist as well. With the necessary research, I could have used the names of the victims and those they left behind. However, it is precisely this sort of painstaking documentation of New Zealand's history that makes it difficult for me—and ethically questionable—to set a truly *historical* novel in New Zealand. And by "historical novel," I mean a story in which several somewhat fictional characters act in original settings in front of a real, researched backdrop. The plot should not seem tacked on but clearly and strongly influenced by factual occurrences.

New Zealand was first discovered in 1642 by Dutch seafarer Abel Janszoon Tasman and mapped in sections in 1769 by Captain Cook. The North Island only first started being settled by whites in 1790, and the first forty years can be considered narrative material only if one is enthusiastic about whale and seal hunting. True settlement did not take place until circa 1830. Although New Zealand's history is relatively short, it has been all the more precisely recorded as a result. Practically every town has an archive that contains the names of the settlers, their farms, and often, details of their lives.

Theoretically, as an author, one could "pick and choose" at his or her discretion and endeavor to breathe new life into real history. In practice, however, we are not dealing with people of the Middle Ages, whose traces have been lost over the course of centuries, but rather with people whose descendants may still live in New Zealand. Naturally, they might take offense if a stranger took their great-grandparents and furnished them with a fictional personality—particularly if it is one as unsympathetic as that of the Sideblossoms.

Since New Zealand is not as large as Australia, for example, one cannot plant completely fictitious farms and towns in real-life settings without some problems. For that reason, I have denied myself the pleasure of letting my readers follow in the footsteps of my novel's characters. Landscapes and settings—the surroundings and architecture of farms like Kiward and Lionel Stations, for example—were altered, and historical personages supplied with new names.

Nevertheless, some information can be easily verified. For example, the name of the sheep breeder who caught the historical James McKenzie can be researched with a few mouse clicks. I can assure the reader, however, that he had as little to do with my John Sideblossom as the real McKenzie with his counterpart in this novel. James McKenzie, it should be noted, is the only one whose name is not fictional, as his fate has been lost to history. Two years after his trial, he was given a reprieve, disappeared somewhere in Australia, and was never seen or heard from again.

If there are any other similarities to real farms or personages, they are purely the product of chance.

Acknowledgments

I would like once again to thank everyone who helped make this novel happen, above all, my editors Melanie Blank-Schröder, Sabine Cramer, and Margi von Cossart, who really pored over every detail to make sure it was correct. My miracle-working agent Bastian Schlück also deserves mention. And as always, Klara Decker, who helped with the Internet research and test reading—I'm filled with awe every single time someone can retrieve the name of the chief secretary for Ireland in 1896 from the Internet with three mouse clicks. I'd also like to thank the cobs—and the other horses too—for not throwing me off when, on their backs, I lapsed into daydreams of love and sorrow in New Zealand, and my friends, who remained patient when I withdrew for entire weeks after leaving nothing more than the note "I'll be in New Zealand."

My border collie, Cleo, was both an inspiration and a model, this time for Callie. In appearing in this novel, she will have superseded her namesake in *In the Land of the Long White Cloud* in age. The breed does indeed live a long time. Nevertheless, thank you to everyone who kept track and wrote to ask whether a dog can really live to be twenty years old. You can't get anything past discerning readers!

About the Author

Sarah Lark's series of "landscape novels" have made her a best-selling author in Germany, her native country, as well as Spain and the United States. She was born in Germany's Ruhr region, where she discovered a love of animals—especially horses—early in life. She has worked as an elementary-school teacher, travel guide, and commercial writer. She has also written numerous award-winning books about horses for adults and children, one of which was nominated for the Deutsche Jugendbuchpreis, Germany's distinguished prize for best children's book. Sarah currently lives with four dogs and a cat on her farm in Almería, Spain, where she cares for retired horses, plays guitar, and sings in her spare time.

About the Translator

D. W. Lovett is a graduate of the University of Illinois at Urbana–Champaign from which he received a degree in comparative literature and German as well as a certificate from the university's Center for Translation Studies. He has spent the last few years living in Europe.